The Forever Street

Frederic Morton

Simon & Schuster Paperbacks
New York   London   Toronto   Sydney

Simon & Schuster Paperbacks
Rockefeller Center
1230 Avenue of the Americas
New York, NY 10020

With thanks to G. Schirmer, Inc., for permission to quote lines from *Die Fledermaus*, translated by Ruth & Thomas Martin, published by G. Schirmer, Inc.

First Simon & Schuster paperback edition 2005

SIMON & SCHUSTER PAPERBACKS and colophon are registered trademarks of Simon & Schuster, Inc.

For information about special discounts for bulk purchases, please contact Simon & Schuster Special Sales at 1-800-456-6798 or business@simonandschuster.com.

Manufactured in the United States of America

10 9 8 7 6 5 4 3 2 1

Library of Congress Cataloging-in-Publication Data

Morton, Frederic.
    The forever street : a novel / Frederic Morton— 1st Simon & Schuster pbk. ed.
        p. cm.
        1. Jews—Austria—Fiction. 2. Jewish families—Fiction. 3. Vienna (Austria)—Fiction. I. Title.

PS3525.O825F6 2005
813'.54—dc22

                                                                    2005042619

ISBN 0-7432-5220-9

TO MY FATHER'S FATHER
BERNHARD MANDELBAUM
AND MY MOTHER'S MOTHER
REGINA UNGVARY
IN LOVING MEMORY

Prologue

DIFFERENT MEMBERS of the Spiegelglass family had different opinions of the Brick. Some considered it a sacrament. Others suspected—without ever saying so—that it was a millstone handed down from parent to child. For a sacrament it looked scruffy; it resembled a bathing sponge, ocher and creviced, rectangular and fossil-dry; stuck into its crevices were yellowed slips of paper which did not make it look prettier.

For a millstone, on the other hand, the Brick was rather light. It weighed a shade under three pounds. The day would come when swastikas would bloom like daisies in Austria; a day on which Leon Spiegelglass would carry the Brick easily in a box under his arm, running.

That was how the Brick left Vienna. It had gotten there a quarter of a millennium earlier with the Turkish armies of siege. In the summer of 1683 the Grand Vizier Kara Mustafa encamped before the Austrian capital, retinued not only by an assault force of three hundred thousand scimitars but also by a pet ostrich, a troop of caparisoned camels and a gang of captured Hungarian stonemasons.

The masons, forced to build Mustafa's headquarters, had no idea that they were erecting an abode for the Brick; that these walls would enshrine the Spiegelglasses' access to God; that here the family would cultivate an instrument transmuting into His eternal order all the perverse shocks of tomorrow down to the propeller roar of the Messerschmitts. Back in 1683 the masons only knew that they must ply their trowels for the glory of the grand vizier.

Embroidered tents, like those which served his sub-pashas, would not do for the Turkish commander. He decreed that his personal residence, his stables, and the barracks of his janissary guards be raised in stone. Each of the half-dozen buildings had a flat roof. Each roof wore a slim, comely little minaret. Through the shape of his lodging the grand vizier announced Muslim grace and Muslim power to Habsburg's battlements.

For spiritual invigoration Kara Mustafa equipped himself with three items from Jerusalem: a sliver from Mahomet's Rock at Mount Moriah; a marble egg carved from a pillar of the Church of the Holy Sepulcher; and a brick-shaped fragment taken from the last remnant of the Jews' last temple, the Wailing Wall. When the grand vizier's quarters stood finished, the triad of talismans was placed under the great pillow of his divan.

This was on July 20, 1683, at the beginning of a blood-drenched siege. On September 13 the Vienna militia flooded forth from the city gates, swords pointed, gonfalons flying. At the same time, the cavalry of the emperor's Polish allies galloped down from the Vienna Woods. Together they overran the Turks. Kara Mustafa barely managed to snatch up the sliver of Mahomet's Rock. Three months afterward, on December 25, the sultan had the grand vizier strangled with a cord of braided blue silk. The aga of the Janissaries burned his belongings. And the sliver from the Prophet's Rock disintegrated among charred debris.

As for the egg carved from the Church of the Holy Sepulcher, it was claimed as trophy by Rüdiger von Starhemberg, the Habsburg generalissimo. He entrusted it to his chaplain, who in turn cut up the egg with an ax dipped in holy water. His Reverence then distributed (some say sold) the pieces as blessed amulets against the plague.

Only the Wailing Wall Brick remained. The court apothecary received permission to stab it one hundred times with a long needle he had anointed in fat rendered from the carcass of a two-headed calf. (This created the fissures in the Brick through which the Spiegelglasses would, in time, address the Almighty.) But then the needle, having done its work, failed to phosphoresce under the new moon. Gone was the hope of turning that piece of Jewish stone to gold. The Brick became one of alchemy's final failures.

The Brick was returned to one of the grand vizier's six houses, all of which had been declared Crown property. For decades they threw their minareted shadows into a void. Empty, protected by the double eagle seal from all intruders except mice and swallows, the buildings moldered in a minor wilderness west of Vienna's ramparts, east of the first gabled villages of the Vienna Woods. In between, no construction was permitted; nothing that might obscure the lines of fire from the cannons of the capital. For the sake of any new war, only the dregs of old war were permitted here: rusted caissons, spokeless wheels, a dusty tangle of highways and, in the middle of the vacuum, those six stone houses. They were His Majesty's forgotten booty, yet the shadow of Kara Mustafa still stained them. In popular lore the cluster of roofs became *die Antichristkuchl*. The Kitchen of the Antichrist. That was what many a father would call that spot, crossing himself, telling his children to walk faster.

In 1761 the Brick changed proprietors. Empress Maria Theresia had run out of money; her minister of the exchequer improvised elegant ways of extorting it. The head of Vienna's Jewish Community Council was summoned. His Excellency announced that through an act of All Highest benevolence on the part of His Gracious Sovereign, the law preventing Jews from owning real estate would be suspended in one particular instance. He was empowered to sell to the Israelites the Brick of the Wailing Wall buried in the cellar of one of the houses of the Antichrist's Kitchen, plus the house, plus the other five houses, for the sum of fifteen thousand talers, subject to a yearly real estate tax of twenty-five hundred talers.

The Jew was only vaguely familiar with the history of the Brick. He did appreciate, however, that the moment marked an advance for his people. What might have been a confiscatory pogrom was now a negotiation. And so the Jewish community of Vienna took title to the Kitchen of the Antichrist for twelve thousand talers, adding two thousand talers as yearly levy payable in advance.

Most of the city's Jews had scant information about the Brick. Those community officials who knew made sure to leave the new acquisition untouched. No display was made of the object. No plaque was raised. It would not have been politic to flaunt Jewish ownership of the Antichrist's Kitchen. The site was treated like a secret embarrassment. A custodian—usually recruited from the ghetto's poor—kept the walls of the six houses mended, their roofs caulked, their doors locked, and the Brick from the Great Temple safely buried in a tin box under an upended wheelbarrow in the cellar of the easternmost of the six houses.

It wasn't until one hundred and ten years later that the Brick and the Spiegelglasses began to converge, slowly. Shacks and vegetable patches had sprung up around the six houses. The Antichrist's Kitchen was now known simply as Türkenplatzl—Turk Place—for by that time the fiendishness of the grand vizier's specter had faded. By that time, too, Tziganer Nassig had appeared.

This personage had been born in a Jewish village in Slovakia, close to the hamlet of Varungy, where the Spiegelglasses lived. But soon he styled himself into a quite Western gentleman named Dr. Jacob M. Nassig. He carried a valise with a gilt lock guarding his law diploma from Graz University. Furthermore, he had acquired accomplished red mustaches, a neurasthenic Pekingese lapdog and a courtly way with opportunities—of which the razing of Vienna's fortifications was one.

After the year 1870 most of the bastions had been leveled. Gone were not only the walls but the restrictions of the Middle Ages. From all over the empire poured thousands of peasants anxious to join the advancement of industry and progress. In the capital the demand tripled for horsemeat, for stale bread at half price, for tuberculosis remedies and for potions against Secret Diseases, for charms, soothsayings and necromantic healings.

To supply such needs Gypsies trooped in from Hungary. But at the city gates shakoed municipal guards turned them back. This was where Tziganer Nassig offered his service and where he got his name. He explained a certain wrinkle of the law to the Gypsy king. Yes, a Vienna ordinance forbade his people from living in the capital. But nobody could prevent them from trading there as long as they could prove "a domicile in a permanent structure outside the city."

The six Kara Mustafa houses fit the requirement perfectly. Of course, the Jewish community still owned them, together with the Temple Brick. No matter. Tziganer Nassig installed himself as tenant, paying the community some one hundred gulden above its monthly tax expenses. He also made himself responsible for the wages of the current custodian of the Brick, a pious widower afflicted by a stutter.

Here at Turk Place, as the site was now officially identified in the Lower Austrian fiscal rolls, Tziganer Nassig subleased much of the space to the Gypsies and thus endowed them with a suitable legal address. Here he stabled their horses, manufactured and stored their good-fortune devices and realized to his gradual amazement that they were cheating him of a much larger part of their earnings than he had anticipated. More sudden was his discovery one morning that the custodian of the Brick had vanished. The man left behind a note in jaggedly calligraphed Yiddish saying that his daughter Tamarah would assume his duties but that he himself was "traveling to Jerusalem to report to the Grand Rabbi the pollution of the Holy Brick by Gypsy horses stabled under the same roof."

The message did not disturb Dr. Nassig. A whole new tide of events generated in his mind an idea; a rather handsome idea; a Gypsy-less idea; a very up-to-date idea; indeed an idea so modern that its consequences were unforeseen. It would anchor the name Spiegelglass to the Brick.

I

On a gusty April day in 1873 Dr. Nassig pulled up his trouser cuffs against some mud. This mud was unmitigatedly rural, though only a morning's ride away from Vienna by an old horse. With some fastidiousness the doctor stepped from a covered wagon down into the village of Varungy. His Pekingese protested. It could not follow its master because the Gypsy driver held its silk collar. The kiss Dr. Nassig blew the dog stopped the barking and confused three women by the well.

Dr. Nassig walked straight to the door of the synagogue where Rabbi Asher Kohn gripped the brim of his hat with both hands. The wind wanted the hat. It billowed the blacksmith's apron of young Berek Spiegelglass, who was nailing a lock onto the synagogue's door.

Dr. Nassig gave a French bow before the rabbi. "My learned master," he said. And then, after blowing the Pekingese one more kiss (which silenced its growls at passing geese), he informed the rabbi that he, Nassig, was pleased to offer work, housing and prosperity for everyone in Varungy in a location very close by the imperial capital itself.

Any man saying such words five years earlier, or indeed during any of the three hundred years preceding, would have been considered mad. For centuries the village had been dedicated to the worship of God and to the raising of geese, two stable pursuits expected to last forever. But nowadays nothing lasted forever. A strangeness had fallen upon the land. No longer did the huge four-horse vans from the slaughterhouses to the north stop by the village. They no longer bought Varungy's famous geese, fat and sleek and snow-white. Now the vans went to the district town of Szatmar, where a giant new goose factory force-fed the birds (using Tasmanian slaves, it was rumored) and supplied the pâté maker at Strasbourg with fatter goose livers at a cheaper price.

The men of Varungy could no longer support themselves by tending their fowl or by growing maize for bird fodder. Most had to stoop the day away, gathering flax in the fields of the Gentiles. Once the village geese had been placid and plump. Now they were scrawny, ravenous, dirty, ragged, furious—a web-footed mob in Varungy's one street. They rampaged through kitchen larders. They snatched sandwiches from children's hands. They even pecked at the Torahs in the synagogue. Indeed, the day of Dr. Nassig's visit marked the first time in village history that a lock had to be put on the prayer house (some desperate birds had been known to nudge the door-knob open), young Berek Spiegelglass officiating as locksmith.

But at least the geese stayed in the village. It was the people who were moving out. The teacher no longer received his salary, nor funds for ink, quills and grammar texts; he had become a court clerk in Bratislava. Soon a wildly bearded goat was circling the blackboard and dining on old test papers in the schoolhouse. The innkeeper had abandoned his inn for a tinker's cart; starlings whistled from nests built into the tavern's bottle shelves; tails of field mice whisked in and out of taps of wine barrels gone dry. Varungy's blacksmith shut up shop. He'd also been the village circumciser as well as railroad mechanic at the freight-line stop. But babies were no longer being born at Varungy; the station depot was about to be shut down. The blacksmith left for Budapest to serve as farrier for the equerry-in-chief to Prince Esterhazy. Before his departure he girded the waist of his journeyman, Berek Spiegelglass, with the guild belt that made the young man smithy-master of the village. But what horses were there to shoe? The rabbi himself had to travel to the district town twice weekly. Here he earned his bread by teaching chess openings to a flax jobber—a rabbi who must push pawns under a gorgeous silver crucifix.

All of which explained why Berek Spiegelglass was attaching a lock to the synagogue door during Dr. Nassig's visit and why Rabbi Kohn did not frown at the idea of moving what was left of the village. The rabbi lifted his hat to wave its sail-like brim in the wind. For some reason this was the only gesture that would stop the perpetual riot of two hundred mangy geese in the street.

"Move all of us?" the rabbi asked in the temporary silence. "To Vienna? But how can one accomplish that?"

"Learned master," Dr. Nassig said. "There is nothing modern man cannot accomplish with a good lawyer at his side. In our capital the emperor is building a boulevard with birdhouses the size of this synagogue. In May he will open the Vienna World's Fair—and that's where you people have your chance."

"*We?*" the rabbi said.

"*You,*" Dr. Nassig answered. And went on to pronounce words the rabbi thought couldn't be right because he heard them through Berek's hammering of the lock, through the renewed natterings of the geese and the yaps of the Pekingese. Dr. Nassig appeared to say, under all these noises, that he himself had opened an exhibit at the great fair, showing the Seven Wonders of the World; and that he would sell there, to thousands of visitors, medallions containing not only a grain of salt from the Sea of Galilee on which the Savior of the Gentiles had walked, but also a grain of the Brick from the Wailing Wall sacred to the Jews; that he, Nassig, would manufacture the medallions himself and that these enterprises would provide prosperous employment to Varungyers once they removed to Vienna.

"Ah," the rabbi said. He recalled Dr. Nassig's sorties through the village. The doctor hawked, through an earringed associate, horoscopes printed in serpentine letters on purple paper. "Jews don't shoot about like Gypsies."

"Nobody will shoot about," Dr. Nassig said. "You will reside in very excellent premises I have leased, just outside the capital. You just need a residential permit from the emperor, that's all, based on your people's employment in my medallion factory."

The rabbi took a bitter breath. "From the emperor. Yes, I will ask him in my spare time."

"You can wait till month after next," Dr. Nassig said easily. "Till Whitsuntide. When you bring him the goose."

"*Bring* the goose!" the rabbi said.

Of course, the Whitsuntide goose was never *brought*. It was an annual tribute sent at a great worshipful distance. For generations Varungyers had presented their most ermine goose to the Crown— a formality reaffirming the emperor's direct overlordship that protected the village from the anti-Semitic whims of local magnates. But the goose was simply given to the imperial mail coach when it passed through on the way to the capital. In Vienna the bird was handed on to a charity designated by the Court. No Varungyer would dare bring his own person along with the goose.

"No, no," the rabbi said.

"I'm just a humble lawyer," Dr. Nassig said. In fact, he let the wind humiliate his mustaches into disorder. "But I have researched the law. The right of presentation of the Whitsuntide goose is joined to the right of petition in personal audience. Absolutely. If you petition for a Viennese residence permit for your people, His Majesty will grant it. He likes to encourage factories like mine. He wants more industry. You will see when you ask him."

"Ask—*him*?" the rabbi said.

"You just take the Whitsuntide goose to him and make a reasonable request," Dr. Nassig said. "I will arrange the paperwork beforehand. It's easy. I have friends in the Chancellery."

"You see, I am an old man," the rabbi said. "Last year I had a kidney affliction."

"How sad," Dr. Nassig said. "In that case, I will have to help another village."

Dr. Nassig was on the point of walking back to the wagon. The history of the Brick might have taken an entirely different turn if, at that moment, Berek Spiegelglass had not raised his voice. Having just driven home the final nail, he straightened up to say, "That medallion, sir? For the World's Fair? What did you have in mind, bronze or brass?"

"Oh?" Dr. Nassig said.

"Because brass is a lot cheaper," Berek said.

"Who is our young man?" Dr. Nassig said.

"Him, he's the son of Meyer Spiegelglass, the goosedown maker, the pillow man," Rabbi Kohn said with much more energy now that the topic was shifting. "The widower Spiegelglass, may he rest in peace, did you know him? This is his son Berek."

"I see, we have an orphan here," Dr. Nassig said.

"Meyer died of an evil kidney," the rabbi said, touching himself above the hip. "One must be careful in the later years."

"Very careful," Dr. Nassig said, his eye steady on Berek. "Alas, in the end, most of us are orphans. And an orphan might be even better for a personal petition than a rabbi."

"Thank you, Berek, for the lock," the rabbi said.

The wind blew, it set shuddering the canvas of the wagon, it deranged the Pekingese's combed fur, it flooded with dust the plumage of hordes of geese, it whined down Varungy's half-dozen roofs, their chimneys lonely and smokeless in the plain. And Dr. Nassig in his flapping, belted greatcoat slowly retwirled his mustaches.

Berek Spiegelglass departed Varungy for the Imperial Palace in Vienna on May 3, 1873, seven days after his eighteenth birthday. It had been a nervous week for the remnants of the village.

First came the problem of the right goose. A worthy specimen had to be searched for amid the rabble of stringy creatures—a stately bird, fit to be the Whitsuntide tribute to Franz Joseph I. The one Berek picked was not only bulkier but stronger than the others. Three men had to help him hold it down in the waters of Varungy Brook until the grime was washed from its feathers. After that they dried it in the whitest cotton left in the village: it was wrapped in one of the snowy burial garments which would not be used because not enough people lived and therefore died in the village. The procedure infuriated the animal into honking guttural German-sounding curses. Not until Berek had the idea of feeding it brandy-soaked corn did it subside into grunts. At last it settled down on the floor of the wicker cage to await transport to His Majesty.

Then there was the matter of Berek's clothes. His smeared

blacksmith's apron would never do for an imperial audience; nor would his old holiday suit, which exposed his ankles. Here the rabbi—by way of penance for not making the Vienna trip himself—helped. He gave Berek the frock coat and trousers for which he had grown too chubby. Berek's cousin Riddah found him a bowler of her late father's.

More difficult was the money question. Two weeks before the crucial day Dr. Nassig appeared again. He handed Berek an audience-admission card featuring the two-headed Habsburg eagle in gilt bas-relief. Dr. Nassig also brought the precise wording of the petition drafted beforehand in Vienna—as well as some unexpected news. He'd been in touch with the Palace Chancellery, and while the emperor in his graciousness was likely to grant the petition in audience, there was a certain requirement to be met *a priori*. Dr. Nassig explained the Latin phrase in courteous detail. It meant "first," or "before the fact." In other words, "in advance." A residency bond of twenty gulden had to be posted in advance—six hundred gulden *in toto* (meaning "in total sum," Dr. Nassig smiled)—since thirty Varungyers had requested the privilege of living and working in the imperial capital.

There was not—there never had been—such a thing as 600 gulden in Varungy. On the other hand, there was something else, the rabbi recollected: namely that chew-mouthed antiques dealer from Eisenstadt who prowled all the emptying villages in western Slovakia. This man had offered 410 gulden for the six ancient mezuzoth, the six decorative tubes containing holy parchments, nailed to the doorposts of Varungy's six main houses.

Some settlements in the area could boast of mezuzoth even older. None were as exquisite as Varungy's: slim and conchlike, crafted of delicately twisted iron inside which the scrolls with the sacred phrases were curled. Because of the beauty of these mezuzoth, the dealer came again after getting the rabbi's letter. Again he squinted at the doorpost treasures. His mouth chomped on a celery stalk to help the brain calculate. He sighed. He raised his bid to 480 gulden, shivered at the rabbi's demand for 600, shook hands on a compromise of 560. Now only 40 gulden were missing: a raisable amount.

Berek had earned his journeyman's credentials at the smithy by repairing the oldest mezuzah. And that was only one of the reasons why he wanted to ram that celery stalk down the dealer's throat. Berek could not accept the loss of the mezuzoth. He would not tolerate the death of Varungy nor people like the dealer who traded on that death and thus helped assassinate the universe.

These were an orphan's emotions. The village was his father and mother. And what was the village? A few farms, barns, middens scattered about a center that consisted of two huddles of three houses each; low mended roofs leaning toward one another across an uncobbled alley. But when Berek came home from a day's work he saw them leaning toward *him,* the very drainpipes reaching out with a welcoming and parental sweetness. They were his parents; parents who had never frowned, glowered, threatened, spanked or in any other way betrayed him; parents whom he'd never seen stumble, wrinkle, wince, go bald or fail. Never, that is, until the blight of the last few years. Until then the puszta heaven floating above—that entire cloud-streaked vastness—had been divinely rooted in the six tin chimneys of Varungy.

And now, looking up at the sky, the only young man left in the village, Berek felt that he was the agent of God's permanence here. In fact, it was the idea of permanence which had attracted him to his trade. Iron might rust. Dust and soot might cover it. But those were changing masks under which the same metal endured. You could melt iron into disorder, make it boil and sting until only tongs but no human hands could touch it—all this in order to reshape it into a new form that retained its old substance. Inside it always remained itself.

Now Varungy boiled with the disorder of its geese. Shingles were melting from its roofs. Perhaps no human life would touch it while—the emperor willing—its inhabitants went to Vienna. But in the end it would reattain itself.

Only the week before, this faith of his had been confirmed by an odd source: a Gentile girl. The decline of Varungy had led him to do horseshoeing in nearby Christian villages—and, incidentally, to encounters with baptized flesh. Berek did well in forgotten attics, in high grass and locked sheds. He had a delicately hooked nose combined with eyes so blue and deep and steady, you never expected them to blink. His beard was coal-black, the kind of black that made the dimples all the more surprising. He was as deft with soft skin as with hard metal. Soon he'd learned how to stroke women into incandescence.

This one, daughter of the district surveyor, had told him of an "official" rumor. To celebrate the twenty-fifth anniversary of the reign of the emperor of Austria, who was also the king of Hungary, a highway paved in silver would be built from Vienna, the imperial capital, to Budapest, the royal capital—and the glitter of that thread would run right through the Varungy region.

The district surveyor's daughter was the only Christian girl Berek ever kissed *after* he had once more put on his apron. He kissed her because she had impregnated him with an idea. Next week, when he and the Whitsuntide goose stood face-to-face with the emperor, he would add an item to his petition. He would tell Franz Joseph that all the Varungyers, engaged in medallion making in Vienna, would soon master all the metal arts. He, Berek Spiegelglass, would see to that. And he would ask the emperor to then let the villagers return to Varungy on the imperial payroll. They would build and maintain and repair forever the Slovakian part of the silver ribbon linking the sovereign's two residences.

Of this he said nothing at home. He just told the others that he'd be very busy, preparing for the task ahead. During the day he learned the words of the petition he was to recite in the palace and which the rabbi repeated for him, over and over again. The night's work he did alone, in secret. It was still more important.

After there had fallen the first of the last four dusks Berek was to see in Varungy, his furnace began to glow. In the darkness of that first night he went to the abandoned inn. He chopped from its wall an iron hook on which horses had once been tethered. In his smithy he cut the hook into six pieces, heated them to softness and wrought them into the shape of six slim, conchlike mezuzoth. The second night he spent firing and hammering, perfecting the fine rills and twists. The third night he put the six in the cage of a canary, long dead, that once had belonged to the teacher now court clerking in Bratislava. In the creamy mist of a three-quarter moon he lowered the cage into Varungy Brook. On the bottom of the waters pebbles gusted over the "mezuzoth" and performed excellent feats of corrosion. The fourth night he pulled the cage up by its rope; he let its wet contents weather in a breeze carrying owl hoots and lilac scents. While the village slept and his six creations rusted, he unscrewed the real mezuzoth from Varungy's six doorposts and carried them to the cemetery. He buried them next to his father and mother. He said Kaddish over his parents' crinkled little tomb. He smiled at the freshly turned earth beside it. There was no death here. After his village was whole again, he would raise those six from the ground once more.

The next morning was the morning of the day. Berek Spiegelglass pulled on the rabbi's frock coat. Its sleeves were so long they tickled his knuckles. Its black was too solemn for a face with young dimples. What mattered, though, was that the antiques dealer drove up, just in time. In a tobacco pouch he carried the 560 gulden complementing the 40 which the rabbi had ready. The dealer was nibbling on a carrot, lips moistening with each nibble. Berek tried not to look as he handed over the six counterfeits he'd rendered so finely ancient.

This happened at noon. Not too long afterward, the barks of a Pekingese were heard in the distance. Dr. Nassig's greatcoat loomed up in the Gypsy wagon. Six hundred gulden changed hands. Berek pushed the bowler down on his forehead. Faces filled those village windows which were still alive. The rabbi waved a newly laundered handkerchief. Berek lifted up to the Gypsy driver a cage shrouded in cotton; from within sounded the thick honks of a rum-drugged goose destined for the emperor. Berek climbed aboard with a small satchel. He only expected to stay away one night. One never knows when one will be overtaken by the journey of his life. Away the wagon rolled, away toward Kara Mustafa's brick.

During the trip to Vienna Berek stayed under the wagon's canvas with the goose. Outside, it would have been exposed to dust; the whiteness of its plumage might have suffered. He remained inside to guard it and therefore never saw the landscape stream away. He found himself in a lantern-lit tent that was bouncing to some hooves' tattoo. He felt that he was not really leaving home. Somehow it seemed that Varungy was expanding faster than the tent was moving, that in fact they were heading for some secret nocturnal center of the village he had never known before.

Meanwhile, there was company: a corpulent rosy-cheeked person in a blue smock and a cossack cap. At Dr. Nassig's introduction the man jumped up from a straw pad, boot heels clicking.

This, Dr. Nassig said, was Herr Alois Schall, his valued associate and most accomplished designer. And *this* was Herr Berek Spiegelglass, the finest blacksmith-mechanic in Slovakia, two personalities whose handshake—bravo!—he was so happy to have brought about. Such a partnership, it just had to be successful in the capital. And *here* (Dr. Nassig gave a bow down to a sack on the wagon floor), here was material for the medallion. Very special stuff, specially shipped from the Holy Land to Prague, where Herr Schall had collected it— nothing less than salt distilled from the Sea of Galilee, on which Jesus Christ had walked!

Berek had been about to sit down on the sack. He sat down on the straw pad instead. Herr Schall joined him, crossing himself. Barking began at the front of the vehicle. The Pekingese had been chained to the driver's seat to keep it off the goose.

"Gentlemen, I'm being paged," Dr. Nassig said. "Pardon me."

Now Berek was alone with his first authentic stranger from the big city. The man turned out to be friendly and unintelligible. Like most Slovakian Jews, Berek knew some German—German was, after all, a comprehensible garbling of Yiddish. But Herr Schall's language sounded quite like the rattling of the wagon wheels. Berek had to keep shrugging his shoulders. Whereupon Herr Schall lifted a forefinger to indicate a remedy. From his smock pocket he produced a stack of little rectangular newspaper clippings, selected one, rolled himself a cigarette. Suddenly the exhalation of smoke enabled his mouth to transform its mysterious stream of Viennese dialect into a semi–High German Berek could unravel into a series of questions.

It was all right to indulge? . . . The goose tolerated smoke? . . .

The straw pad was comfortable? . . . Had Herr Spiegelglass gotten permission from his rabbi?

Berek, having nodded yes all along, now said, "What? What permission?"

"Permission for a Jew to work on something Christian," Herr Schall said. "A medal with a crystal from the lake touched by the Savior's feet."

"Oh, that's all right," Berek said.

"Oh, that's good," Herr Schall said. "Me, on my side, I have dispensation from Father Smylk. I can work with pieces from the Jewish Wailing Wall. In fact . . ." Herr Schall pulled out of his pocket a wafer-thin cardboard disk from which he blew some dust motes as if it were a freshly cut diamond.

"In case you are interested," Herr Schall continued, holding it out with curved pinkie. "It's my model for the medallion."

Drawings covered both sides of the disk. One was a rather beautiful miniature landscape of a lake with a figure, bearded, robed, haloed, strolling across waves. The other side showed the Wailing Wall lined with prayer-shawled figures on their knees. Just as Berek held up these details to his eye, the wagon stopped suddenly. The lantern hanging from the canvas top, never steady, took flight. It swung away, dimming the light; it swung back and hurled such brightness at the cardboard disk as to make it transparent. Jewish scene and Christian panorama ignited into a single image. Berek saw Jesus wandering across the backs of Jews before the Wall. Wanderer and kneelers burned together in an underwater conflagration.

For a moment Berek became dizzy—not so much with what flashed at him as with the weight of his journey. He used his hand to steady himself against the canvas wall. He fastened on a practicality.

"That hole there," he said, pointing to the center of the cardboard disk. "What's that?"

Oh, that was for the glass bead, Herr Schall said. Inside the bead would be visible a salt crystal from the Sea of Galilee as well as a grain from the brick of the Wailing Wall.

"And the item is going to sell in the hundreds of thousands!" Dr. Nassig's voice said.

Up front the Gypsy driver had parted the canvas curtain for the doctor, who reentered the covered part of the wagon. So buoyantly did he twirl his red mustaches even while being jarred by wagon jolts that Berek was encouraged to ask him a question: how could one put a salt crystal and a stone grain into a bead of glass?

"Ah." Dr. Nassig smiled. Apparently, the squeak of the wheels caused him to mishear the question. Yes, he said, it was the bead of glass which made the design perfect. A typical Schall touch! But Herr Spiegelglass would soon see the Nassig Seven Modern Wonders Show in Vienna. *There* was an example of Herr Schall's designing talent! Visitors from all continents, eager to see the great exposition at the capital—they were bound to patronize the Nassig-Schall exhibit right by the fairgrounds. It would put them in just the mood to purchase a medallion commemorating Judeo-Christian prodigies.

And then Dr. Nassig began to enumerate the miracles of modernity displayed at his show: a perfect small-scale model of the famous balloon that had crossed the Indian Ocean, rising from an accurate replica of the Taj Mahal; a steam engine of very advanced American manufacture traversing Niagara Falls on a tightropelike trestle, with a red Indian in full feathered headdress as the locomotive engineer; a parachutist descending from the Leaning Tower of Pisa; a New York City elevator rising to the top of a translucent skyscraper with President Lincoln, might he rest in peace, as passenger; the British battleship *Marlborough* steaming through the incredible Suez Canal, steered by Queen Victoria herself. Not to speak of other wizardries of progress.

"How were the ticket sales while I was away?" Herr Schall asked.

"Promising," Dr. Nassig said. "Wait till the shock of the crash wears away. It's just a scare. They'll be trooping in."

"Crash?" Berek asked.

"The stock market crash," Dr. Nassig said. "It's just panic mongering. The government won't stand for it."

Berek had never heard of a stock market crash before. He felt that if he admitted that, Dr. Nassig would never call him "Herr Spiegelglass" again and Varungy would shrink instantly into a square inch of goose excrement.

"Maybe," he said. "Maybe I'll find out the truth about the crash from the emperor tomorrow."

"Capital idea!" Dr. Nassig said. "Wonderful. You bring up the point before His Majesty."

"Is there a special way of talking at the audience?" Berek said, thinking about that extra, silver-road item he would add to the petition.

"Indeed, and it's time to rehearse protocol," Dr. Nassig said. "Now. Over there. Let's assume that object is our monarch."

Lying at the back end of the wagon, "that object" was a pouch containing goose fodder—rum-soaked corn. Even in the lantern's dithering light there was something elegant about it; Berek's cousin Riddah had wrapped the sack in white linen and tied it with a crimson ribbon. After all, the pouch would travel to the palace.

"Now, Herr Spiegelglass, if you'll watch me and follow my motions," Dr. Nassig said. "On entering the audience room, you will look down. You never look up to where our sovereign awaits you standing. You'll approach him with your face down, your hat pressed against your heart—very good, you press it very well—and you'll know what direction to take by just following the frayed part of the carpet—"

"Frayed?" Berek said.

"Of course," Dr. Nassig said. "Thousands of petitioners have walked there before, and the path is left frayed on purpose so that you find the direction without looking up. It's a beacon leading to the All Highest Lord. You walk along the frayed line in small humble steps like this."

The frayed line reassured Berek. It was a bridge between Varungy's threadbareness and the splendor of the capital. He followed Dr. Nassig, imitating his gait. Behind him Herr Schall did the same. The three swayed along in the rocky wagon, passed the goose cage from which came inebriated snorts, swayed on toward the feed pouch.

"Now, when you catch sight of the emperor's shoes," Dr. Nassig said, "you will stop. You will stand there, head bowed—yes, that's good, that's very sincere bowing—you will stand, head bowed, for a full seven seconds. Remember, the lectern at the emperor's side has a sheet with facts of your life you yourself may not even know. He must be given a chance to look them over. After seven seconds you raise your eyes for that one moment's direct glance at him while you say, 'Your Apostolic Majesty, my Most Gracious Emperor and King!' Then you lower your eyes again to pronounce your petition. You have learned your petition by heart?"

"Yes," Berek said, looking down on the bobbing floor of the wagon.

"Very good," Dr. Nassig said. "Except you don't look at the floor at this point. You don't look at the emperor's face either, but you look at his hand resting on the lectern. It always rests on his lectern. You look specifically at his ring finger—will you remember that?— because there will be on it a diamond so powerful they say its side facet reflects the dream you dreamed the night before. But the main facet, facing you, that's the important one for your guidance. That one gives you back your mirror image in miniature. It's your chance to see any flaws in your posture which you can then correct on the instant. Any questions, please?"

The Pekingese had begun to bark. Dr. Nassig turned and screamed something passionate. Silence.

"Now," Dr. Nassig said. "After the monarch has responded favorably and perhaps explained about the stock market, you will begin your retreat. Now, this is interesting. The signal that tells you the audience is over will be a gentle pull of the wire—"

"What wire?" Berek asked.

"How silly of me," Dr. Nassig said. "I have not mentioned the wire. This is a very fine wire, just a thread. Before you enter the audience chamber, the adjutant will hook it into the back of your collar. They're trained in that. He'll pay it out as you advance toward the emperor. When the audience is over, the signal will be a polite little wire tug at your collar. You commence walking backward toward the door, facing the emperor. But have no fear, you'll walk backward in the right direction, straight toward the door, by just yielding to the pull of that wire. Those adjutants are brilliant in hauling petitioners back out. That's all. Easy. You see?"

"What if the wire hook doesn't catch?" Berek felt the tight fit at the back of his collar.

"If it doesn't catch," Dr. Nassig said, "if there's any little mix-up of any kind, there's still no cause to worry. I have a perfect thing for you to do. Herr Schall, do we have a Leo horoscope of the police-chief kind?"

Herr Schall took from his trouser pocket a stack of what looked like golden playing cards wrapped in tissue paper. He spread the cards into a fan and gave Dr. Nassig one.

"Here," Dr. Nassig said. "Our emperor was born on August eighteenth, under the sign of the lion. This is the Leo horoscope for this year—look at it, printed in blue velvet on golden silk, costing us twenty gulden apiece but not for sale. Literally priceless. We present it to police chiefs, burgomasters, etcetera, wherever there is prejudice against Gypsies doing business in a town. It won't fail you tomorrow."

"Uh, thank you," Berek said.

"It should set your mind at ease," Dr. Nassig said. "Any little mishap—this card will cure it. You just present it to the adjutant on your way out. You tell him that this modest golden gift is an extra token of respect to His Imperial and Royal Majesty, an emblem of apology, presented with humblest compliments by you and by Dr. Jacob M. Nassig. And that will make everything smooth again."

"Also compliments from Alois Schall," Herr Schall said.

"Of course, Herr Schall's, too, as designer of the horoscope, that is understood," Dr. Nassig said. "But are we clear about tomorrow now? All clear and serene? I want you to sleep well."

"Well, I wanted to ask you," Berek said. "About the glass bead. How can you get a salt crystal and a stone grain into a bead?"

"Exactly," Dr. Nassig said. "I will address that problem. At my hotel tonight—that's when I meet the gentlemen cofinancing our venture—exactly that item will be at the top of our agenda. We will engage a glazier-artist of the first water to handle that."

"Another thing," Berek said. "To make the glass bead stick to the metal, we'll need a special glue—"

"We'll get *the* most special one, because you are a most special young man," Dr. Nassig said. "I see you crafting an extraordinary medallion. You'll cross that bridge beautifully when you come to it. You don't even know yet what a wonderful bridge crosser you are!

Meanwhile I trust you'll be comfortable sharing Herr Schall's quarters tonight."

The Pekingese had started barking again—but barking into a silence altogether new. There was no creaking or shaking of wheels. The wagon had come to a halt gently this time, but with a finality that ran cold down Berek's back.

"I'd better hurry and get my end of the business organized for our big day," Dr. Nassig said. And he did a funny thing. He gave Berek a long, lingering pat on the young beard. Then he shook hands briskly with both Berek and Herr Schall.

"Breakfast at eight, gentlemen. Rest well."

He tipped his hat, parted the canvas, collected the Pekingese, stopped the barking and became footsteps tapering away.

Outside, Berek thought, my God, right outside must be Vienna.

II

IN LATER YEARS Berek Spiegelglass would try to recall what it had been like to climb down from the Gypsy wagon into the center of his future life. Whatever he could recover from the moment was always touched with childhood and fatigue, with singsong and wood smoke.

The daydream he'd nursed during the journey appeared to have spilled into the very real evening breeze brushing his face as he stepped out. After hours of travel he arrived in Varungy, where he had started—Varungy a bit transformed, to be sure, and moved close to the emperor's residence.

He found this other Varungy lit up erratically by oil lamps and flames from an open fire. There was the same group of six two-story houses, somewhat bigger perhaps, and with the mezuzoth elevated from doorposts to roof corners. The Imperial Palace gleamed with the most fantastic glow less than half a mile away.

It turned out that Herr Schall had never heard of mezuzoth. He said that those things up on the roofs, those slim, twisted, conchlike turrets, were minarets. That's why this place was called Turk Place. And those strong lights over there were not the Imperial Palace. Those were gas lamps, the first Berek had seen, which illuminated the huge army drill grounds separating Turk Place from the city gate.

And still Berek felt eerily at home. It wasn't just the six houses. It was the black-haired men sitting cross-legged and chanting around a bonfire between the two short rows of roofs. The songs struck him as a very old, shut-away memory now awakened. His tiredness, beginning just then, seemed to have collapsed a fence inside him and readmitted the scene into his brain. When he'd been very little, toddling through a Varungy still healthy—hadn't he heard just such singing in its one street?

Herr Schall shouldered the salt sack. He led Berek over the cracked tiles of a house entrance into a ground-floor apartment. On its door a sign said (Herr Schall held up the lantern to read it to him) DR. NASSIG & CO. LTD.—OFFICE. The office consisted of a big desk with a little castle made of glass. This was an inkstand next to which Herr Schall dropped the sack of Galilee salt. Berek followed suit with the goose cage and with the feed pouch, jarring the inkstand. The ink did not stir. It had dried inside the castle with flaring black patches.

But something moved in the adjoining room. A girl was putting bedclothes on two cots. Herr Schall made his shoulders square, his neck very erect and official. He introduced. This was Fräulein Tamarah Liftitz.

Before long the *Fräulein* would become much more than a wife to Berek. Yet their first encounter wavered in the blue fog of his exhaustion. Perhaps Tamarah Liftitz—coming on top of everything else—was just too much to absorb. At the sight of the pillow in her hands, the full weight of four sleepless working nights tumbled down on him. What he noticed that evening was only the little red lilies printed on her babushka and the fact that her pinkie was so much smaller than the other fingers of an already small hand smoothing linen.

His limbs ached for bed. But he could not lie down until the girl had finished her work. Meanwhile, Herr Schall took him to the adjoining house on Turk Place. Once upon a time, Herr Schall said, this building had been a Turkish stable. Now it was the Gypsies'. The smell of axle grease, the acridity of horseflesh, the stamping of hooves and the snorts of nostrils inside feed bags . . . these impressions remained fragments of a broken picture. They all whirled, still separate, into a dream Berek dreamed minutes later when he fell onto a cot at last and was swept into a procession of hundreds of carriages, all drawn by striped stallions along an arc gleaming toward Varungy—a pageant headed by Rabbi Kohn turned into an emperor in flame-tinted robes, his head glowing with a crown of feathers, of rubies and of flowers.

In Varungy Berek's cousin Riddah had a music box whose key had been broken off. It could no longer be wound up. Yet now and then, unpredictably, it would stammer a bit of music, a phrase from a melody that would remain forever unknown.

The next morning for a moment Berek thought that this was the sound that had awakened him. But it wasn't Riddah in Varungy. It was a girl elsewhere, with sewing scissors she pinged against the lid of a metal box.

The girl, Tamarah, sat by a window full of sun. When not pinging, she embroidered a long gown of gorgeous black silk. It was studded with golden numbers, each wreathed in green laurel leaves. Berek had taught himself simple mathematics in Varungy; he recognized that all the numbers were 25's. What he didn't understand was why the girl was suddenly so pretty. And what there was about the room that wasn't right.

The girl no longer wore the babushka of the night before. Her black hair was drawn back into a severely braided bun from which only tips stuck out—tips the size of her little nose. Under her dark blond brows her eyes were blue and softly shaped, softened still further by the tired mauve under her lower lids. She pinged her sewing scissors against the lid again. Berek yawned, and she smiled about a quarter of a smile. The ping was a gentle gong with which to waken him.

"What's the matter?" he said. Something was.

"I want to . . . to show you something." She touched a brownish brick encased in a tin box lying on his night table. At the same time he saw the sun light up the other cot's emptiness.

"Herr Schall is gone," he said.

"Before he . . . he comes back, I want to show you," she said. "This is the Brick from our Wailing Wall, from our . . . temple in Jerusalem."

"Oh yes, for the medallion. Where is Herr Schall?"

"He was in . . . a hurry. But you see, one mustn't make . . . make money out of the Brick. One mustn't take pieces out of it for medallions. It would be against God."

She had a slight stutter. Each time her tongue slowed, her hand with the too short pinkie covered her mouth. He had to harden his lips against a smile. Very factually, he said, "We'll just take one grain from the brick for each medallion."

"Not even one grain," she said. "The Brick is really . . . really from the Great Temple. Truly."

"What?" he said.

"You write something to . . . to God," she said. "You put your writing into the Brick. Like the pilgrims in Jerusalem, when they come to the Wailing Wall. They put their messages into the . . . the Wall cracks."

He looked at her hand before her lips. It had tiny bolsters for knuckles.

"You write something to God," she said. "You put it into the Brick. It will be answered."

He was too sleepy still to discover the exact wrongness in the room. Certainly, the girl's crazy words were no help.

"I'm sorry," he said. "Did Herr Schall leave a message for me?"

She shook her head. "Before he comes, you write God something." From under the Brick box she pulled a notepad and an ink pencil whose tip she wet with her tongue.

He wanted to get out of bed to look for Herr Schall. But he had no trousers on. And he didn't know how to write.

"Our teacher went away from our village," he said. "There was no longer a school when I was a child."

"Oh. Then I will write for you. You dictate. Any . . . anything you want to ask God?"

He heard the beating of big bird wings from the next room. The goose was still there. "All right," he said. "I ask that the emperor should grant our petition today."

"*P-l-e-a-s-e G-o-d t-h-e E-t-e-r-n-a-l,*" she wrote. Her brows, slightly curved and surprisingly blond against the darkness of her hair, moved up and down in rhythm with her pencil. "*M-a-k-e t-h-e E-m-p-*

e-r-o-r g-r-a-n-t o-u-r p-e-t-i-t-i-o-n." She took another break. "And how shall I sign? Your name?"

"Berek Spiegelglass. I have to get ready for the audience."

"*B-e-r-e-k S-p-i-e-g-e-l-g-l-a-s-s.*" She tore off the sheet right below the signature and furled the scrap into a little scroll. "Here is your prayer. You put it in the Brick."

He sat up with the sheet wrapped around him and began to pull on his socks.

"Put it in the Brick," she said. "That's the test. I know from my father. If the Brick takes your prayer, there will be an . . . an answer. You put it in."

He took it. And he put it in. It found a fissure instantly—one of the alchemist's holes. A moment later it looked as if it had been there for a long time, like the half-dozen other little curls. The Brick seemed to have grown the scroll as a porcupine grows a quill.

"You see!" she said. She was smiling fully for the first time, her eyes half closed as if she were basking in the sun. And that moment he knew at least half of what was wrong. The sun was much too strong.

"What time is it?" he said.

"When I heard the Christian bells it was eight."

He was a country boy. He could tell from the angle with which the light struck the window. It must be closer to nine.

"It's so late!" he said, now fully awake. "We're supposed to meet Dr. Nassig here right now! My audience at the palace is at ten."

"At the palace you tell the emperor to put the . . . the Brick under his protection," she said. "It can't be touched."

"We need a grain for each medallion—"

"It can't be touched."

"But there'll be a factory for the medallions," he said. "My village already spent money—"

"*I will pay back the money!*"

She shook away her stutter with a headshake so fierce it loosened her bun into tossing braids. "Princess Wallers!" she said. "She'll pay me fifty gulden for this gown! It's for the ball, the twenty-fifth anniversary of the reign! You tell the emperor! And I'll get more! Another twenty gulden when I embroider the laurels in two colors!" Footsteps sounded outside. "It's just the crash," she said, speaking lower, faster. "Otherwise, there'd be more embroidery work. But I'll get more. I'll give you the money. Just save the Brick!"

She had closed the Brick box, whisked it under an extra piece of gown cloth. "I'll put it in with your stuff. You take it to the emperor for protection!"

He was astounded by the force coming from her soft face. But he had no time for astonishment. Herr Schall's breathlessness filled the room.

Herr Schall, who would escort him to the palace, had rented a swallowtail frock coat, bought a white carnation for his buttonhole and borrowed his brother-in-law's fiacre.

Berek's first fiacre ride was also the most turbulent of his life. Mud sprayed up. It threatened his audience clothes as well as the goose cage on his lap. Luckily, he came upon a blanket under the seat. Berek did some tight tucking, narrowed his eyes against the rush of streets and made his mind rehearse the words of his petition. But the image of the embroidering girl interfered. So did Herr Schall on the driver's seat next to him.

Berek was surprised that a man in a top hat could be so distraught. Herr Schall kept muttering into the wind what he'd already muttered at Turk Place. He couldn't locate Dr. Nassig. He kept trying to remember the name of Dr. Nassig's new hotel; the doctor had mentioned it before he, Schall, had left for Prague to pick up the Galilee salt. What in the name of the Virgin was it? Because just now, trying to learn what kept Dr. Nassig, he'd found the old Nassig hotel shut down for renovations. The new one—Herr Schall cursed at a vegetable cart they almost overturned—the new hotel had to be the fancy Inner City kind, right for business meetings. That was it, for God's sake—a hotel breakfast meeting! That's why Dr. Nassig had not shown up at Turk Place! He had been waiting at his hotel!

"Is this the Inner City?" Berek asked.

Of course not, Herr Schall said, not at all, no point going to the Inner City now, no going crazy, running from place to place guessing which hotel, no, no—no, the surest place was the Seven Modern Wonders exhibit, the doctor always checked the ticket sales there every morning. And Herr Schall's whip snapped over the two white horses' manes, which floated like twin little snowstorms through the scudding air.

It was a comfort to know that this was not Vienna's fancy Inner City through which they were passing: long files of low housefronts, all as shabby gray as the clouds which now hid the sun and therefore the time from Berek. Out of an endless succession of windows hung damp bedding or old heads astonished at the fiacre's speed.

At last, they left the cobbles for a wide, crunching gravel path. Ahead loomed something like a tremendous square, filled with buildings and fronted by a tall portal. Berek had once seen a picture of it in a newspaper. It was the entrance to Vienna's World's Fair.

But the fiacre never reached it. The horses had slowed, not because of a specific signal but in response to the curious fact that Herr Schall seemed to be turning, openmouthed, into stone. When the carriage stopped, only Herr Schall's right hand could move. With mechanical slowness the hand reached into a pocket in order to roll a cigarette. Before it got to a match it failed altogether. Tobacco and cigarette paper dropped from the driver's seat to the ground. Herr Schall himself did too, but he fell on his feet.

On tiptoe, as though stalking a monster, he began to approach something about a hundred yards away. It consisted of splintered, discolored, disordered ash-strewn heaps. Nearby stood a policeman with a metal-trimmed helmet. Herr Schall began to talk to him. As he spoke, his hands rose up, in stages, toward his top hat. When he returned to the fiacre, both of his pink cheeks were being squashed by his fists. Berek realized that Herr Schall could be only a little older than himself. He looked so boyish in his dressed-up suffering.

"Fiend," Herr Schall choked out at the wheel spokes. "That—is—why—the—fiend—made—me—go—to—Prague. Get—me—out—of—the—way . . . while—he—collects—the—insurance."

Berek barely managed to keep the goose cage from crashing

down. Suddenly, Herr Schall had pulled him off the fiacre, dragged him close to the debris.

"Look!" Herr Schall said. "Look!" It was as if a second pair of eyes would lessen the pain of the sight. "Our Seven Modern Wonders Show!" Herr Schall's finger gored the air with such vehemence that the white carnation in his buttonhole wobbled. *Here!* That had been the long-distance balloon rising from the Taj Mahal—that blackened rag among the embers! And this singed hulk in the middle, ah, half the Union Jack was still left on it, that had been the British battleship steered by the Queen! And where was President Lincoln? Where was Mister Abraham Lincoln going up a New York skyscraper in an elevator? Buried under those ashes? And where was Dr. Nassig himself? Off and gone with the insurance money! That police officer over there, he had cosigned the damage statement over a week ago! Where was justice?

"That's terrible," Berek said. "But if Dr. Nassig is gone, do we need him to manufacture the medallions?"

"Five hundred gulden invested in that fiend! On my side we invested five hundred gulden in the Modern Wonders. And who designed them? Me! He must hang!"

"Perhaps we should calm down and think," Berek said.

"And he wanted even more! It's every penny I could raise. I'm finished! Fiend!"

"In Varungy we gave him all our money for the bonds," Berek said. "But we should think this out."

"What bonds?" Herr Schall said.

"The residency bonds," Berek said. "So that my village can move to Vienna."

"All fake and cheat!" Herr Schall said. "All you need is the petition. No bonds! And that's no salt from the Sea of Galilee. That's just a sack of fake. Sweet Jesus in heaven, please let him hang!"

"Is my audience card real?" Berek pulled it out together with the horoscope of the police-chief kind.

"Of course." Herr Schall snatched it, threw it down. "I arranged that, through the Wallers office. What *I* do is real! I work hard! For what? For nothing!"

"The audience could still be good for something," Berek said.

The trouble he had taken with the goose, his work on the mezuzoth, the money for the bonds, the girl pinging on the metal lid—it could not possibly be all in vain.

"Ah." Herr Schall stared at Berek. He pushed back his top hat. "Your audience. Right! Absolutely right." He picked up the card, blew on it, handed it to Berek. "You can still go to the emperor! You tell him about this fiend. Turn the imperial police on him! There is a God in heaven. Let's go!"

Berek turned to climb up to the driver's bench, but Herr Schall raised his arm. "No, no. You get in back. You sit in the dignity seat. We must make the right impression to hang the fiend!"

Off they drove, even faster than before. So fast did they start that the blanket dropped from the fiacre without their noticing. Again mud splashed from the road and threatened Berek's trousers. To keep them clean for the emperor, he took off his jacket and laid it inside out over his knees. That way stains would not show when he put it on again. He didn't want to think too far ahead; neither about making the medallion, nor about saving Varungy. He mustn't be eaten up by worry. He concentrated on the words of his petition, on protecting his clothes and dealing with the goose. Till now the bird had been quiet, but now it honked wildly. With each bounce of the carriage it took flying leaps against the cage walls.

Berek thought of the rum-soaked corn which had calmed the animal before. He opened the feed pouch tied to a bar of the cage. From inside, wreathed in laurel leaves, the number "25" stared at him. This was a piece of the gown material in which the girl had swaddled the box with the Wailing Wall Brick. It took him unawares. Her sweet stammer pulsed in the "25." Berek lifted the Brick in its wrappings, scooped up a handful of the corn that was below, fed the goose, let his finger brush over the "25"—and heard the rumble of the cobbles melt into smoothness beneath the fiacre wheels. They were rolling along on nobler pavement.

To the left and to the right there carouseled the Ringstrasse, the famous circular boulevard the emperor had already pulled partly out of the ground. Where the city walls used to be, the imperial government was now constructing theaters, ministries, hotels and mansions. Around Berek curved endless scaffoldings surrounding endless emptiness—metal skeletons and mounds of masonry and huge raw-edged fragments of stone. It looked like a panorama not half built but half demolished.

Perhaps it was the girl's stammer about the remnant of the Great Temple. Perhaps, the shambles of the Seven Modern Wonders. The dust of destruction whipped into Berek's nostrils. The fiacre zoomed past ferocious blasting, along upheavals of earth and spatterings of mortar. He saw the Temple being laid waste several times over in different grandiose styles of havoc on successive segments of the boulevard. And he saw not only the Temple ravaged. He saw the silver highway crumpling even before it was finished, an arc of rubble dripping down from the horizon. He saw his own poor little Varungy reduced to broken walls and plaster dust. All that survived of multiple ruination was the Brick the girl had put into the feed pouch.

Herr Schall yanked at the reins. The fiacre halted. Before them towered a cast-iron gate, overwhelming as a cathedral's shadow. Berek pulled on his jacket. Yet even here, at the emperor's own palace, the volleys of disintegration would not stop. Sounds like artillery broadsides ricocheted against massive walls. The guards who came forward ignored the noise. They frowned at Berek, squinted at his audience card, waved on the fiacre. In an inner courtyard a man in silver and green livery acted bored by the commotion. He pointed at the shaking, honking goose but didn't look at it.

"Would this be an offering to His Majesty?"

"Yes, sir," Berek said.

Letting his silver-green arm hang down, the man snapped his finger. A second man in silver and green lifted the cage away. A third silver-green man wanted to take the feed pouch. But Berek had untied it from the cage and gripped it with both hands. Inside was the Brick, to be placed under All Highest protection. Another boom reverberated.

"He must be *hanged!*" Herr Schall whispered from the driver's seat. "Beg His Majesty! No clemency!"

Booms caromed off fretted balconies. "This way to the audience chambers," said the first silver-green man. "Let's not linger. And let's take off our little hat."

With his head bare, with Herr Schall left behind, Berek walked alone among giants consisting entirely of scabbards, epaulets and boots. They pointed and kept him walking on the gleam of the parquet.

At an oil painting bigger than a village fair, he was stopped. A man under a white-plumed helmet checked Berek's name against a list and told him he was three minutes late. A man with a cocked hat and brilliant gloves announced, not particularly in Berek's direction, that foundations were being blasted for the Imperial and Royal Museums on the other side of the Ringstrasse and that if any explosion interrupted the petitioner, said petitioner was to stop and to begin the interrupted sentence anew for His Majesty's understanding. Another man in another cocked hat kept his gloved right hand on the golden hilt of his sword and, with his left, picked a goose feather off Berek's shoulder. Then, with a languidly commanding finger, he indicated that he wanted the feed pouch opened. Berek gripped it. But the gold hilt was too daunting. Berek opened. The man saw the laureled Imperial anniversary number, gave an absent grin and motioned permission to close. At that moment a paramount creaking overrode the rumble of another detonation. Two lackeys had grasped two doorknobs as high as their necks. The wings of an enormous gold-and-white door were parting. In the next room, Berek knew, stood his sovereign.

A crimson carpet led him forward. There was no frayed path in it. Still Berek advanced bowing, his bowler pressed against his heart. No wire hook had been fastened to the back of his collar as Dr. Nassig had predicted, yet Berek kept following Dr. Nassig's instructions. His feet clumped along the exalted carpet. He had nothing to hold on to except the doctor's advice and the feed pouch with the girl's Brick.

Four legs of a high desk made of rosewood told him to halt.

"Your Apostolic Majesty," he said. *"My Most Gracious Emperor and King!"*

He lifted up his eyes. He was astonished. The ruination would not even stop before the emperor's face. Berek had seen that face often before, on coins and on postage stamps. But the booms sounding that moment shook the young monarch halfway into old age. They blasted his forehead into baldness; they weakened the skin around his eyes and even burst some tiny veins on his left cheek.

"Your Apostolic Majesty," he said. *"My Most Gracious Emperor and King!"* But this second start, too, failed to give him the momentum to go on. By now he ought to be saying what the girl had asked of him. He should be pleading for the survival of the Brick and of the Turkish Place that was the Brick's dwelling and that looked like Varungy and might be Varungy's continuation . . . But its preservation against the world's wild booming blows . . . how could he entrust it to a coin face which had grown old before his eyes?

"Your Apostolic Majesty, my Most Gracious Emperor and King!"

The imperial forefinger tapped against the desk. Twice, impatiently. The sound jarred Berek's tongue into continued motion. "Would it be allowed?" he said, pressing the bowler so hard against his jacket that dried bits of mud began to flake from the lining down to the carpet. "Would it be allowed to settle thirty people from the village of Varungy to Turkish Place near Vienna for . . . for the purpose of"—here he began to stammer, perhaps to fortify himself with the girl's passion—"for the purpose of manufacturing in a new factory a . . . medallion . . . a medallion . . . ."

"Yes?" the emperor said. He had a hoarse, unnervingly ordinary voice.

". . . a medallion celebrating the twenty-fifth anniversary of the emperor's reign? . . . Please?"

Thunder of three closely spaced explosions. They sent aftertremors through a baroque clock standing some nine feet tall in the corner of the room.

"An anniversary medallion?" the emperor said. "What do you mean?"

"It would look like this." Berek opened the feed pouch. He was beckoned to step closer. He obeyed. In his blue general's coat Franz Joseph I bent down and saw the laureled number "25," crowned by the initials "FJ," the gown material in which the Brick was wrapped. The emperor's nose sniffed slightly. His supreme sensitivity toward the improper registered what had eluded his court officials. He smelled a strange smell. It was the odor of rum-soaked maize below the Brick.

Franz Joseph I straightened up. He glanced at the audience memorandum on his desk. His head performed a headshake of surprising ease considering its constraint by so tight a silver collar.

This petition, Franz Joseph said, was for an employment and residency permit involving the manufacture of a religious medal. The anniversary of the reign was not a religious occasion. Therefore the petitioner's request did not conform to the written petition. In such cases petitioners had to apply for another audience at another time to present their revised requests.

Silence. Then two things happened almost at once. Another blast exploded at the building site of the Imperial and Royal Museums. And drops came slowly from Berek's eyes. They rolled down into his young black whiskers. It was the first time he had cried in ten years. All good timing is instinct. Berek's tears were superbly timed.

The emperor saw them and connected them and the peculiar smell to his misgivings throughout that morning. Lately, an appalling incorrectness—of which the stock market crash was just one example—had been afflicting his lands. It had affected his own judgment. For reasons of efficiency and economy in troubled times, he had yielded to his architects: he had allowed blasting across the street during audience hours. It had been an incorrect decision. The consequent disorder must have pushed this young man into deviations like the alcoholic smell or the tears which otherwise were appropriate only in the case of clemency-seeking mothers. He, Franz Joseph, might be responsible for the incorrectness unfolding before him. Therefore, some lenience might be exercised.

"However, in this case . . ." Franz Joseph said. It now came to him that the young man, by his very agitation, proved a finer barometer of the proprieties than those who had preceded him in audience. They had been deaf and dumb to the improperly sanctioned explosions. "However, in your case," Franz Joseph said, looking for the young man's name on the audience memorandum, for personal recognition was an important part of royal correctness. "In your specific instance, Herr Spiegelglass, we will consider your request, though it involves manufacture of a medallion whose nature is not . . . not exactly religious." Franz Joseph scratched himself momentarily on his ear. The gesture expressed the energy of a slight smile which would have been uncalled for at this juncture. "We want to encourage industry in difficult times. Request is granted on receipt of a written emendation of the petition."

To a blast not half as powerful as the hammer inside his chest, Berek retreated with his back toward the titanic door. He did not require a hook in his collar to tug him in the right direction. There was no need to give an adjutant the horoscope of the police-chief kind. He floated past scabbards, plumes, spurred boots, sword hilts. He bounded down a gargoyled ramp. He hugged the feed pouch because it contained the girl's Brick and, hugging it, ran toward Herr Schall, who sat in the fiacre in the courtyard and who slowly lifted his top-hatted face from between his fists.

III

BEREK SPIEGELGLASS had become the creature of a speed that could not be resisted. With the feed pouch on his back he lunged up to the fiacre driver's seat next to Herr Schall, snatched the reins and thundered the horses from the palace courtyard out into the Ringstrasse. More explosions sounded from the building site. But Herr Schall, excited, heard them as cymbals of vengeance. To him they announced, along with Berek's glowing face, that Dr. Nassig had already been handcuffed by the emperor's bailiffs. But then it became clear that they were driving the wrong way.

"Wait," Herr Schall said. "The Palace of Criminal Justice is over there!"

"We are going to our street," Berek said.

"What street?"

"The Turkish Place," Berek said.

To Herr Schall it didn't matter that this country blacksmith called Turk Place "our street." What mattered was Dr. Nassig.

"You mean he hasn't been caught? He has our money!"

"Something more important!" Berek called out into a brightening noon, over the sun-filled clatter of his speed. "We have permission!" he shouted. "The emperor said we can make another medallion! Is this the right way to our street?"

But he would have known even without Herr Schall's nod. He was steering the horses by the sun, westward beyond the great cannonading smithereening scaffolds, beyond city limits, where a sweet cluster of small houses, his new Varungy, awaited him.

"What other medallion?" Herr Schall called.

With his left hand Berek opened the feed pouch to show the piece of gown material with the Imperial anniversary number. "We'll manufacture a medallion like that!" he called. "Sell it to the fair visitors! You just have to change the petition!"

They had left the smooth paving of the Ringstrasse for cobbles that clanged against the fiacre wheels. Again and again, Herr Schall shouted that rewording the petition was very hard, that it took special care and skill and would take a long time. Finally, he screamed that it hadn't been him—it had been an acquaintance of his on Prince Wallers's business staff who'd written the petition in the first place. The horses scrambled to a halt. Berek had stopped them with a rein pull and the *whoa* whistle once used by the Varungy teamster.

"Your *acquaintance* did the petition," Berek said. "Where is your acquaintance?"

"At Prince Wallers's *palais*, but—"

"Where is this *palais*?"

"We passed it five minutes ago."

Berek handed Herr Schall the reins and jumped off.

"You drive there and ask the acquaintance to change the petition."

"But the point is," Herr Schall said, "Dr. Nassig, this Antichrist—"

"That's finished," Berek said. "Now we move on to the new medallion with a new petition."

"It's a good idea, the anniversary medallion," Herr Schall said, staring desperately at the "25" number, dropping the reins.

"Then drive back to the acquaintance with the good idea!"

"But you see, the money lost with Dr. Nassig," Herr Schall had to say now. "Most of it belonged to my acquaintance."

"You didn't tell me!" Berek said. But he didn't care. He had gotten past the emperor himself. He couldn't let the acquaintance stand in his way. Not with the Brick in his lap.

"All right," he said. "You tell the acquaintance he has to write a new petition. Otherwise, there's no medallion, no income, nothing. He'll never get back his money."

"You think so?" Herr Schall said.

Berek closed Herr Schall's fingers round the reins. "No question," he said. "Tell him. Right now."

"Actually, it makes sense," Herr Schall said.

"I need a pawnbroker for smithy tools," Berek said. "I must make a sample medallion."

Herr Schall watched the cobbles rotating under the fiacre. In the course of two quick rides the future had melted into vertigo. It would be a relief to turn it over to this demon of a Hebrew bumpkin—at least until the cobbles settled down again.

"All right," he said.

"Is there a pawnbroker on the way to our street?"

"All right," Herr Schall said. "Yes. There's a pawnbroker around the corner to the left."

"See you at the Turkish Place," Berek said. "Bring back the new writing from the acquaintance."

By the time Herr Schall's hand began to roll the cigarette paper, Berek had turned the corner.

Everything served Berek Spiegelglass that day, including the stock market crash weeks earlier. Ripples from the crash had caused an endless variety of destitution. Even an out-of-the-way pawnbroker on Vienna's edge offered a rich assortment of objects unredeemed. Berek found a bellows damaged by only a moderate tear; coal tongs that would do for smithy work; a usably big hammer; and a steel tart mold, more or less of medallion size, that was not fatally dented.

All these he took. In exchange he left behind the frock coat and vest given him by Varungy's last rabbi. Both featured mother-of-pearl buttons to whose resale value the pawnbroker had taken a fancy.

Five minutes later Berek spied the little minarets of Turkish Place. Their silhouettes inscribed upon the sky the shape of the mezuzoth he had buried in Varungy's earth. Again it was like the re-birth of a view in which his childhood had been steeped. So much that had been lost, abandoned, betrayed, fragmented . . . here it seemed to grow whole again, in that small vista ahead. There it was in an alley standing alone beyond an empty drill ground. Elsewhere the world roared and shattered. Here was a haven cozy against the grandiose chaos.

And then, coming closer, he picked out the girl sitting on a bench before one of the six houses. He recognized her by her dark braids, her blond eyebrows and soft bodice. His soul rose together with his flesh. He had known Tamarah for less than a day. Never be-fore had his desire for a new girl merged with longing to embrace something remembered, something somehow redemptive. Maybe that was why the sight of her released such need in him. He must weld himself into her no less than into the pavement touching her black, bright-buttoned shoes. Girl and street joined into the same marvelous flesh he yearned to make his bride. He could not wait to lay claim on Turkish Place with every member of his body. He began to run.

A few hours earlier Tamarah had watched the young blacksmith board the fiacre in his fine frock coat. Now he returned on foot, without carriage, without any outer garment. He was loping across the drill ground in his shirtsleeves, holding on to his bowler. On his back bounced, like rucksacks, the feed pouch and a bellows. Tama-rah sat on a bench in the sun, leaning against the wall of Turk Place No. 5, and looked down again at the gown she was embroidering for Princess Wallers.

Arrived before her, he opened the bellows and took out the tools he'd just bartered for his clothes.

"Fräulein Tamarah," he said. "Do you have a ladder?"

There was one in the Gypsy stable. She pointed and stood up; the simplest way to cover her confusion was to walk away and get what he'd asked for. He restrained her, cupping her wrist with both his hands.

"I will fetch it myself," he said. "Now, please. Could you mend the tear in these bellows? And after that, will you put on your High Holiday dress?"

"What?"

"Your High Holiday dress."

His breath high from running, his steady glance, his solemn smile—they all bore down on her. She looked away from the black of his beard, the light blue of his eyes.

"Will the emperor . . . protect the Brick?" she said, shielding her little stammer with four fingers.

"The emperor worked out all right," he said. "We'll make a different medallion that won't use up the Brick."

"Good," she said.

"You and me," he said. "We'll be the protectors of the Brick."

"We?"

He had taken the Brick box out of the pouch. Now he extracted the Brick itself, kissed it, and laid the kissed Brick before her feet.

Pleasure and embarrassment rushed into her head, but not the right words with which to ask about the High Holiday clothes.

"That's a leather rip," she said, tapping on the bellows. "I don't know if I have a needle that's strong enough."

She hated blushing in bright daylight. Quickly, she replaced the Brick in the box and retreated into her house with box, bellows and embroidery clutched in her arms.

On Turk Place it was the beginning of the Spiegelglass principality. Berek walked into the stable. Horses and wagons were gone, off with the Gypsy men for the day's forays. Berek kicked out of the way the fodder bags stored in the fireplace. He cleaned the flue with a broomstick and began to carry in logs from the campfire site in the street. Gypsy women watched, tightening the babushkas around their heads. The very idea of flames under a roof narrowed their eyes.

Berek ignored everything except his purpose. Humming that craft-absorbed rapt working hum later to become famous on Turk Place, still sporting the bowler, striding about like a possessed, half-dressed fop, he kept carrying logs to the fireplace, lit them, grinned, found the ladder and hauled it outside.

Hammer stuck into his belt, he climbed the lowest of the six houses, swung the hammer and lopped a minaret piece so cleverly off the roof that it dropped into his open palm. He climbed down to the Gypsy stares, returned to the stable and searched it till he found a small stove with a flat top. With one heave he upended it. With two hammer blows he tested its solid cast-iron bottom, facing upward now. "All right," he said to himself aloud. "That'll do. That's an anvil."

Tamarah came in and put the bellows down by the fireplace. "It's mended," she said.

"Thank you." He stared at her. She was wearing a cloak of rough homespun. "We have an important matter together," he said. "That's why I said holiday clothes."

She turned slightly to let the flames light up the long skirt under the cloak.

"I used to go with Papa to the synagogue in this," she said.

"Good," he said. "We also need the Brick. The matter involves the Brick."

"It's in the other house," she said. She didn't ask what matter. It was a question to which she didn't want to provoke an answer.

"We should go to the other house anyhow," he said. "This is not something for the stable." He fanned the fire with the bellows, threw on another log. Past Gypsy eyes they walked together to the house where he had slept the night before. They parted, briefly, while she went up the wooden stairs to the mystery of her rooms to fetch the Brick. He opened the door that still said DR. NASSIG & CO. LTD.—OFFICE. His shirt had become smudged, and he needed a garment to cover it. His appearance would have to do justice to what was coming now. Maybe he could borrow something of Herr Schall's. There was a locker next to the cot; inside hung nothing except a cape. It was only a rain cape. But it was black with the blackness of a judge's robe. He stood arrayed in it when she entered in her long dark dress, the Brick box in her hand.

"You still have the writing pencil?" he asked.

"There," she said. She sat down at the desk on which the goose had slept the night before. Against the glass castle with the dried ink leaned a notepad next to a pencil. Actually, he had seen the pencil. But he needed a little more time; some more introductory words. He waited while she put down the Brick and took the pencil in her hand.

"Please write a request to God for me," he said. "To be put into the Brick."

To brace himself he gathered the cape firmly about his shoulders. "Please tell me when you are ready," he said.

She lifted up the pencil a bit, to indicate that she was.

"All right, then." He began to dictate. *"I pray to God."* He reached up to adjust his bowler to a straight, undashing angle. He wanted his head to be reverently covered. He listened to her pencil make only the faintest whispering sound across the paper. From the window came a beating of sparrow wings and the crying of a Gypsy baby. All these sounds seemed to form a tune, as if pencil, sparrow and baby were members of one orchestra. Suddenly the light from the window took on spooky rainbow tints. What was happening here? He had to ceremonialize this new anchorage in life since everything old had melted away. This darling girl with the pencil—she was the anchor, and just because of that he suspected her. How could this creature set off such prickling of warmth and hope inside his skin? He felt ambushed by her importance. Yet it was a marvelous ambush, enveloping him in something that would otherwise die on the Slovakian plain. *"I pray to God,"* he said as he stood very straight in the rain cape, *"that Tamarah Liftitz—am I say-*ing the name right?—*that Tamarah Liftitz will marry me and that we will live together on Turkish Place with our family and with people from my village, Varungy."*

He had said it in one valiant breath. She had stopped writing midway in the sentence.

"This is too fast," she said at the glass castle.

"I can say it again, more slowly," he said, though he knew what she meant.

"Yesterday was the first time we met."

He looked at the line and a half she had written.

"It doesn't matter," he said. "This has to be."

"This has to be?"

"Yes."

"If you are sure," she said, "my father . . . my father has to be asked."

She had a lovely, very vertical handwriting, the line bolder than he had expected from so finely sharpened a pencil.

"*You,*" he said. "Are *you* sure?"

She bent her head down to the sheet of paper. The motion amounted to a nod. "My father lives in Palestine. A letter takes long. There is time to . . . to think."

"We will write him," he said. "We will telegraph. Meanwhile you write this."

Her pencil did not move.

"Later you will teach me to write," he said. "But now please write my prayer to God and we will put it into the Brick."

Her pencil moved shakily and wrote out Berek's prayer. She tore off the part of the sheet it covered. He rolled up the paper, thinking suddenly that this was very much like Herr Schall rolling a cigarette. But the frivolousness of the thought did not help him. The moment came when the Brick accepted the little scroll he pushed into it. He touched Tamarah Liftitz's skirt on the waist. She entrusted into his hand her small palm rough from janitor work. But her cheek, offering itself to his kiss, was flawlessly smooth. "Tamarah," he said to the warmth of the cheek. All of a sudden, struck by the irrevocability of his move, staggered by it, he threw off the rain cape. He informed her that he needed another sample from Princess Wallers's gown for the medallion and ran back to the stable to get to work.

In subsequent hours Berek dismayed a variety of people. The first was Tamarah herself.

She met him in the stable with the sample he'd asked for. He pushed logs with the poker and told her that he wanted to see the inside of all the houses on Turkish Place.

"Right now?" she asked.

"I have time while the flames are building."

"It's not 'Turkish,' it's . . . it's 'Turk Place,'" she said.

"'Turk Place,'" he said undeterrably. "I should see what the rooms look like."

"There was no chance for me to sweep today," she said.

"That's all right." He threw down the poker.

Tamarah was charged with keeping the premises clean. But Gypsy braziers, tripods, coal mounds and blankets littered the ground-floor halls of the Turk Place houses. Upstairs, the rooms were storage bins stuffed with the debris of treks long past: saddles that the tribe had worn out in the Balkans; Sicilian earthenware mostly cracked but garishly colored; hundreds of pebbles from some Spanish beach, big as hawk eggs, on which jagged charms had been painted. And sand and pottery splinters everywhere.

This housekeeping disaster was not Tamarah's fault. Yet she hated having to show him sleaziness just after the ceremony with the Brick. Berek looked around, nodded, grunted. He gave in to her refusal to let him enter her own small quarters. But he shook his head as though he failed to understand that this would not—not yet—be seemly. The worst came at the door next to hers. It was a high, arched entranceway, designed originally for the giant eunuch in charge of the grand vizier's camels.

"Look at that," Berek said. In Varungy, Rabbi Kohn's house had been distinguished by a door taller than the others. "This is for our son. After he becomes a rabbi, this will be his study."

Tamarah was not prepared for an embarrassment so intimate— the mention of a child she would have by the man next to her.

"We haven't even asked my father yet!" she said.

Deaf to her discomfiture, he ran his hand up the doorjamb of his future son's room. She walked away abruptly.

"I'm sending off the telegram to my father," she said.

"And send a letter to Varungy," he called over his shoulder. "Care of my cousin Riddah Mainzer, Varungy, Slovakia. Say I'm not coming back. They should come here. I'll let them know when. All right?"

Tamarah was too upset to do anything but nod.

After disturbing her Berek returned to the stable and proceeded to disturb the Gypsies. He hammered into pieces the bronze chunk of minaret he had felled. With the coal tongs he plunged one bit into

the fire and placed it, half melted, into the medallion-sized tart mold
he'd gotten at the pawnbroker. All along, as he goaded the flames
with great pantings from the bellows, Gypsy women gathered at the
door, clutching their children. Campfire creatures, they were terri-
fied by the indoorness of the blaze, by the fury to which Berek had
roused it. And they saw that he had attracted from the distance another volcanic apparition.

As it emerged from the city gate, it looked like a blasting site that
had detached itself from the downtown construction areas and
begun moving westward. It was detonating its way across the
drill ground toward Turk Place. It was surrounded by a livid cloud
from which Herr Schall suddenly catapulted. Smoke-stained and
top-hatted, he brushed past the Gypsies into the stable.

"It's the chief steward!" he said. "Herr Spiegelglass? The chief
business steward is coming! From the Wallers office! You should
prepare yourself!"

At the upended oven serving as anvil, Berek was hammering the
red-hot fragment of the minaret.

"There's trouble!" Herr Schall said. "Please stop!"

"I have to work the metal while it's hot," Berek said. "This is
very old bronze."

"But we have a problem, I ran ahead to warn you!" Herr Schall
said. "My acquaintance, you see, the money my acquaintance advanced, that was from Prince Wallers's funds! He's been dismissed!
And the steward wants the money back and he won't even rewrite
the petition!"

"It's all right, the girl here will do it," Berek said. "She reads and
writes and she will be my wife." He was comparing his handiwork
with the "25" pattern on the gown material.

"The caretaker girl?" Herr Schall said. "Fräulein Liftitz?"

Berek nodded and began hammering again.

"JesusMariaandJoseph," Herr Schall said. "Congratulations. But
now there is this very bad situation—"

"We will live here and work here," said Berek, whose hammering now punctuated an awesome commotion on the street outside. Herr Schall crossed himself and ran to open the other wing of the stable door. An eruption rolled in on huge wheels. It rumbled and spewed and bedeviled the whole stable with black vapors. When the air cleared, Berek became visible, still hammering. Herr Schall stood desperately at attention. Four sobbing Gypsy children rubbed their eyes at the monumental tricycle.

It had a smokestack on top of an open steam engine that looked like a brass octopus. In front sat the driver, in sooty livery, goggled, sharply visored, ramrod straight. He resembled the tamer of a metallic beast, who had himself been turned into mineral. Behind him and above him, lofty on an upholstered rococo bench, an older gentleman was hunched, all in black. His hair and the buckles of his shoes were silver. One hand tapped a riding whip; the other held a handkerchief before his face.

Herr Schall's voice began quavering. "I have the honor to present," it said. "This is the chief business steward of Prince Wallers, and this is Herr Spiegelglass . . ."

Berek's hands were occupied with hammer and tongs. Herr Schall lifted both Berek's bowler and his own top hat in salute. Berek hammered.

"*Spiegel . . . glass,*" the old man said, tasting the name from the height of his tricycle seat. "Busy, busy, Bang-Bang Spiegelglass." He spoke with a falsetto that sounded indolent and yet rang clearly over Berek's blows. All of Herr Schall's vehement headshakes at Berek had not been able to stop the din.

"Well, well, a little inventory." The old man didn't so much look around the stable as droop his handkerchief at the fly-ridden, splintered ceiling beams, at the smeared horse stalls, at the wet straw mixed with mud on the floor.

"So those are the assets," he said. "That is the factory. Excellent security on which my ex-associate loaned out our money. All those wonderful machines here. Very pretty collateral."

"Sir," Herr Schall said. "We are just starting—"

"Of course you are," the old man said. "Nowadays ambitious

young men are always just starting, much loud wonderful excitement, boom-boom, bang-bang, hooray. They finish nice and quiet in
some ditch. Fine smells in this factory."

"If I may repeat," Herr Schall said, "I didn't realize that my acquaintance was using the wrong funds—"

"But he didn't realize either," the steward interrupted. "He
didn't realize he'd be found out; he's the wave of the future and the
future never thinks it will be found out. And our legal friend, with
that lap rat of a dog, what was his name?"

"Dr. Nassig," Herr Schall said. "Dr. Nassig's behavior was a
great shock—"

"Oh, not a shock," the steward said. "He's not interesting
enough for that. He's just traveling a little farther to *his* jail. They
have tedious dungeons in Buenos Aires. And so we come to our
Bang-Bang Spiegelglass here—"

"Please! You must please excuse his noise!" Herr Schall said.
"He is fresh from the country, uneducated. But he has special—"

"Obviously." The steward looked at Berek. "Look at that youth
go. Bang-Bang, off on his own special way into the same ditch. Is he
bang-banging our Wallers copper? Did my ex-associate loan him
that, too?"

"I'm sure, no," said Herr Schall, who hadn't seen Berek lop off
the minaret.

"You think your Bang-Bang here could be a mechanic for this
car?" the steward said. "Work off our damage that way?"

"Oh, wonderful," Herr Schall said. "Yes, he could, and I could
help, too. He's just not—not showing to good advantage now. It has
not been an easy day—"

"On the contrary, much too easy. Look." Not looking anywhere
but at his handkerchief, the steward slapped his riding whip against
the side of the tricycle. There was a plaque with an artfully interser-
pentined monogram of the letters *A*, *F* and *P*. "Young entrepreneur,
AFP, whatever the name. One of our Lord High brass button manufacturers. That's what AFP's problem was: he had it much too easy
until the crash. Metal from us on easy credit. Thirty button machines
on easy credit. This steam car on easy credit. Three more years and he
would have gotten a little knighthood on credit—do we follow so far?"

"Yes, sir," Herr Schall said.

"But Bang-Bang Spiegelglass over there. Does *he* follow? One is trying to educate him."

"I'm sure he follows," Herr Schall said with a tentative smile, for Berek had stopped hammering at last. Berek had bent down to pick up a long nail which had dropped from the underside of the tricycle's chassis. The chauffeur extended his hand for it.

"In a minute." Berek began to tap and stroke the hot metal with the nail, using it as a shaping tool.

"Very good," the steward said, watching him. "Nothing stops the modern bang-bangs. They'll use everything until they get their due. Gentleman AFP must have gotten a very nice straw hat in debtors' prison. And the bailiff has his thirty button machines downtown. And you know what we have at Prince Wallers's office? We have these three wheels."

"It is a fine vehicle," Herr Schall said.

"It's a horror, a punishment," the steward said. "I'm riding it to prove to myself that I'll miss nothing by missing modernity. I can't even clear my sinuses with its smoke, and the motor keeps losing its bowels, and boy Bang-Bang here doesn't even want to be its mechanic, does he?"

"I have to make a medallion," Berek said. "Excuse me, sir." On his way across the stable he stepped around the front wheel of the tricycle. Holding the hot metal with the tongs, he plunged it into the horses' watering trough.

Herr Schall ran over to the trough. He pulled his top hat down to cover the whisper his teeth ground out at Berek: *"Stop! Please be a steam car mechanic, just for a few weeks. Just on the side, in your spare time—"*

"No. But I could use the steam car engine right here." Berek lifted the cooled metal piece out of the water in order to inspect it.

"Insane!" Herr Schall whispered and yanked the tongs out of Berek's hand to hurry over to the tricycle and present the metal piece to the steward on his high seat.

"Sir, look, the craftsmanship," he said. "I mean, don't mind what he says. Look what he can do!"

"He can make me wet." The steward wiped drops from his

black velvet lapel. But all of a sudden his nose grew a pince-nez. A cackle coughed out of his face. "Bless us. It's not only wet, it's wrong. It's even more wrong than it's wet." He brought closer to the pince-nez the fretted laurel leaves of the medallion model, the delicate angles of the emperor's initials rising in bas-relief from the bronze disk that once had been part of the base of a little minaret.

"It still needs polishing and finishing," Berek said.

But the steward waved away the interruption. "It's so wrong it doesn't even manage to be vulgar. So Bang-Bang Spiegelglass did that? Man's not fit to repair our modern steam car. We need a competent vulgarian."

Berek put out his hand for the medallion. "I need it back. I have to take it out of the mold before it sticks."

The steward gave a still more impatient wave. "Bang-Bang Spiegelglass doesn't even know how to make sensible junk. This isn't ten hellers apiece. That's a two-gulden prestige item, absolutely unsalable."

"Oh, but, sir!" Herr Schall said. "Maybe we can find a prestige market! The medallion comes from a pattern on Princess Wallers's ball gown—"

"Devils and saints!"

Another cackle came down from the tricycle. This time it was wholehearted and hoydenish. "That's why the thing is familiar," the steward said.

"Excuse me, sir." Berek took the tongs away. He immersed the medallion in the horse trough again and began to knock it against the side of the trough.

"Tell you what, we'll save the day with a joke," the steward said. He leaned back on his seat, folding his handkerchief vivaciously. "We'll have Spiegelglass bang out—how many?—mm, I think three hundred and forty of these. And when he's done, we'll put Bang-Bang and partner in jail. Illegal exploitation of a private design, complicity in fraudulent loan solicitation, etcetera. No problem. And then we'll confiscate the three hundred and forty medallions. Damages and all that. Now, there'll be three hundred and forty guests at Their Graces' ball. We'll have three hundred and forty ball favors ready. That's how we'll recoup our loan loss. Rather neat."

"Sir!" Herr Schall said, pale. "We didn't exploit a private design! I'll make another design—"

"Why? We'll confiscate Bang-Bang's medallions," the steward said. "Let's not spoil a good thing. Ball favors keyed to Her Grace's gown. It's always so tiresome thinking up favors. This way the work is done."

"But—why confiscate?" Herr Schall said. "We can produce the medal on order for you! I can perfect the design for you! We'll deliver cheap! We'll deduct the money you lost from our bill! Sir? Couldn't we do it that way?"

"Oh, I suppose we could," the steward said. "I suppose we should, to keep Spiegelglass banging. But it'll be less fun."

"Sir, thank you!" Herr Schall said. "Wonderful. Thank you! And maybe we could use that AFP factory downtown, that bankrupt one—"

"No."

The sudden word came from Berek. "Nothing downtown," he said. "Turk Place. I work here and stay here." He had pounded the medal disk loose from the mold and placed it on top of a horse stall to let it dry. Then he nodded at the pistons of the tricycle engine.

"Sir," he said. "If you can't use the vehicle because of the smoke, leave it here."

"I see," the steward said. "So Bang-Bang can put *his* monogram on it. So he can show off with it after he's made his first million. He'll puff-puff down to the Palace with it, where his son will have a mansion—"

"My son will be a rabbi here on Turk Place," Berek said.

"Will he?" the steward said. "How interesting. Bravo. And an adorable rabbi, taking after Papa. What else does Papa have on his mind?"

"Excellency means *you*," Schall said to Berek.

"I think I could use this tricycle motor," Berek said. "I could make a factory machine out of it."

"Nothing nicer than a well-bearded innocent young Jew," the steward said. "All that juicy confidence ready to be corrupted. I should have met him when I was ten years younger."

"Actually, I also need a ribbon of bronze," Berek said, absorbed in the motor. "For a test run for the medallion favors."

"The man is priceless," the steward said. "In the end, his crash will be priceless, too. Shame I won't live to see it. Well, I can launch him toward it, with a ribbon of bronze."

"High-copper bronze would be good," Berek said.

"Very well, high copper for better banging," the steward said. "If it helps him work off the debt, we'll even throw in this abominable tricycle. Let him take it. It is hereby stricken from Prince Wallers's assets—this entire monogrammed obscenity I declare broken down and beyond repair and abandoned and the property of whoever stubs his virile Jewish toe on it." The steward's riding whip touched the driver on his shoulder. "Find me a carriage."

The driver jumped off, saluted, departed. Whereupon the steward rose from his seat. Standing, he turned out to be a small, wispy creature with an askew left shoulder and the legs of an old gazelle. He beckoned to Berek and Herr Schall to help him down the brass steps.

"If a petition needs emending," he said, while his silver-buckled shoe kicked away a clump of soiled stable straw, "it can be done at my office."

"Thank you, sir." Berek didn't quite finish the "sir." The steward cut him off by turning to him directly for the first time.

"Welcome to the future," he said. "All three wheels of it."

IV

WHAT THE FUTURE HAD TO BRING, sooner or later, was a fight.

The Gypsies did not like the change on Turk Place. They resented Berek's indoor fire and his proprietary airs. They were suspicious of Dr. Nassig's disappearance and the sudden steam carriage towering in the stable. Berek seemed to have turned the doctor into a swollen, triangular creature. The Gypsy chief decided to apply some countermagic. He began to make a death's head mask just large enough to fit a huge dog.

It was used before the end of Berek's initial week on Turk Place—a headlong week.

The good bronze promised by Prince Wallers's steward failed to arrive during the first few days. That didn't stop Berek. As miners quarry a mountain, so Berek Spiegelglass quarried the colossal tricycle. First, he separated from the vehicle's side the plaque with the baronial initials. He cut it into six pieces, which he heated and hammered into the shape of bells—a form characteristic of Varungy's house shields. He gave the raw shields to Herr Schall and asked him to design for them pretty numbers from one to six that would go with the words "Turk Place" in pretty letters.

While Herr Schall bent over a pad, Berek, with enormous blows, amputated the tricycle's front wheel. Into its wooden spokes he screwed five of the many kerosene lanterns stacked in back of the stable.

Next came some ladder work. Berek drove holes into the ceiling beams to hang the lanterned wheel as a chandelier. The stable would be his factory. He would need good light during the short days of winter.

These labors took four days. On the fifth, Herr Schall handed him a lacy design for the house shields. "Thank you," Berek said. "Good. Time for you to go to Prince Wallers's office."

"Just me?" Herr Schall asked.

"Yes, for the bronze we need," Berek said. "And the changed petition, they ought to have that ready by now. And some cash in advance for the medallion order, at least fifteen gulden, because my fiancée is paying for our food."

"Perhaps I shouldn't go alone," Herr Schall said.

"I'm too busy here," Berek said. "And they should also draft a money agreement between you and me. I've been thinking about that."

"I've been thinking, too," Herr Schall said.

"You get one gulden out of every three earned here," Berek said. "Is that all right?"

"One out of three," Herr Schall said. "I was thinking one out of three plus room and board."

"Plus room and board." Berek ascended the ladder again.

"That's all right," Herr Schall said. "But maybe I shouldn't go by myself to that office." Herr Schall's ears still shivered from the razor-blade echoes of the steward's voice. "At least I should take with me your Jewish brick."

Berek stopped work for a moment. This was the first time Herr Schall had mentioned the Brick. "You don't need it," he said from the ladder.

"It cast a good spell for you with the steward," Herr Schall said.

"It will cast a spell from here," Berek said. "Go on."

Herr Schall went. He went slowly, tightly wrapped in his black rain cape though the sky was only spotted with clouds.

Four hours later he came jaunting back, carrying a flagon of wine. His free hand waved an envelope. It contained the new petition not only calligraphed in black ink with red capitals but already approved by the emperor's scrawl. Its language now said—Berek called Tamarah in from next door to listen to Herr Schall's vibrant reading—that All Highest permission was asked (and, through the All Highest signature, given) for Berek Spiegelglass's partners and employees to live at Turk Place in order to engage in the production of metal articles of all kinds.

Herr Schall also had other papers to whip out in triumph: a note from the steward's assistant, promising good bronze as soon as it arrived from the smelter; an earnings agreement between the two partners; *and* an envelope with fifteen gulden cash advance.

"Herr Spiegelglass," Herr Schall said. "I think we should have a drink together now."

Berek would have preferred working on the lights. But milestones must be honored. He descended the ladder.

"We'll celebrate there." He pointed up to the driver's bench of the tricycle. It was the most solemn seating space in the stable. Tamarah ran to get two wine glasses. Then she signed the earnings agreement on behalf of Berek while the two partners helped each other, rather ceremoniously, up the steps of the vehicle.

"Here's to us!" Herr Schall said.

Berek lifted his glass as high as Herr Schall's, tasted, and tried to smile past the tartness in his mouth.

"To the punishment of Dr. Nassig!" Herr Schall said, having refilled his glass to the brim.

"He didn't deserve to run Turk Place," Berek said. Herr Schall drank bottoms up again while Berek was capable of only a sip. But he didn't want to insult Herr Schall. While Herr Schall closed his eyes to savor the pleasure on his tongue, Berek poured the rest of his wine down the upturned trumpet of the car horn.

"Good, good stuff," Herr Schall said. "Listen, we're going to be a success they won't forget in Vienna. Here's to no more 'Herr'!" Herr Schall drank up his third glass. "Here's to you, Spiegelglass."

"Here's to you, Schall."

"Here's to prosperity!"

"Here's to the future of Turk Place," Berek said.

"Listen," Schall said. "Since I get a third, I've got a third of the Brick, right?"

"Of the Brick?" Berek said.

"Sure, we're partners now. Come on, drink up!"

"Well, you'll get a third of the good we get out of it," Berek said, "because you'll be with us on Turk Place."

"No, a third of the Brick itself," Schall said. "Come on, partner. Fair's fair."

"The Brick is different," Berek said. "It's Jewish. And it belongs to my fiancée. Do you see?"

Schall said nothing. He stared. Something weird was coming at him. A death's-head with the body of a bull mastiff snarled in the doorway. The Gypsy chief had waited until Berek had extinguished the indoor fire for the weekend. With that deterrent gone, he played out the leash of the apparition against the enemies on the tricycle.

"Spiegelglass!" Schall clawed at Berek's shoulder.

Instinctively Berek's hand reached for the car horn and squeezed it, hard. Sodden with wine, it screeched, burbled, hissed, sprayed. The death's-head mastiff recoiled and ran off.

"Did you see that?" Schall breathed.

"It was just a Gypsy stunt," Berek said.

"But we chased them off with a better stunt," Schall said. "Je-susMariaandJoseph. Did we do that with the Brick?"

"Well, yes, I did," Berek said.

"All right." Schall filled yet another glass. "You work the Brick. Tell you what. It's Friday afternoon. We'll have partners' drinks every Friday afternoon. Done?"

"Done," Berek said.

Schall raised his glass. "Partners forever! Nobody can stop us!"

Berek raised his glass, too.

"We'll show Dr. Nassig!" Schall propped his elbow on something that wasn't there and was caught by Berek, who helped him down. He brushed against the car horn. It made a sound like a submerged sigh from a familiar voice. For a moment Berek thought it was a call from Tamarah drowning.

Tamarah's drowning call haunted his mornings. His late mornings. Berek was something of a slugabed. His heroic energies would not flag even at night, yet he was always the last to rise on Turk Place. At the start of his second week there he woke, as usual, in the former Nassig office. His head rang with an echo of the girl's voice that came, sweet and yet desperate, from the bottom of a glass-green lake. But as the dream drained away before the sunlight, he saw that she was alive and active, and perplexing. Schall had already left to prepare the fire in the stable. On his partner's empty cot lay clothes he didn't recognize. She must have put them there. His own clothes were gone.

The real daylight Tamarah stood in the doorway. He had to yawn himself into understanding what had happened. The night before she'd said abruptly that he needed a change of clothes, having brought none from Varungy, and that her father had left some garments before departing for Palestine.

"There is soap and water in the . . . the stable courtyard," she said now, with her emphatic little stammer. And to indicate that Berek must not put on the new clothes as long as he remained unwashed, she threw him Schall's cape to use as a bathrobe.

Sure enough, behind the stable, next to the well, he found a bucket steaming and seething with suds. A clothesline had been strung from the top of the well to the stable roof. Berek immersed himself in the bucket and rinsed by the well. Then he did the same with his old set of clothes, which she had dropped on the ground with a towel on top. He dried himself, pulled on his new clothes, strung up his old wet ones, and came for warmth to the stable's fireplace. She was waiting for him.

"After the answer comes," she said, "the wash will be taken care of."

She meant, of course, the answer to Berek's telegram to her father asking for her hand in marriage. It had not yet arrived (and neither had a reply from Varungy). Until then they were not engaged and he must scrub his pants himself.

She lived—and made Berek live—by a code that was precise and, for him, unpredictable. "Be-rek Spie-gel-glass," she said slowly while he drank his breakfast coffee the next day. This was puzzling. Until then she'd never called him anything: neither "Berek" nor "Herr Spiegelglass"—just "you" whenever that was necessary. Apparently, any direct form of address had to wait for the Answer, too.

"Yes?" he said.

"So it is just those two names," she said. "Berek and Spiegelglass. The way they are . . . are spelled in the petition. Nothing in the middle."

"No, no middle name."

"I also have just two," she said, walking away. That afternoon he saw a doily peeking from her apron pocket. Sketched out in rough stitching were two pairs of letters. He couldn't read yet. But he could guess: BS and TL. *Berek Spiegelglass* and *Tamarah Liftitz*. She'd begun embroidering a hope chest of linen things.

A few days later, in her low-key but sudden way, she said, "Tomorrow the market has a Hungarian chicken sale."

"Good!" He almost added, "About time!" The fact was that she served him mainly cheese, beans and potatoes. Every other day he got meat. Two exactly cut slices of boiled beef.

"I suppose people brought up in a poultry village like Varungy enjoy chicken," she said.

"Yes!" he said. "Thank you!"

It turned out there was little to thank her for. When he woke up the next morning, she was just passing by with a pail of plucked feathers. When he returned after work, he inhaled the dear childhood fragrance of boiled chicken. What was set before him was boiled beef, exactly sliced. The same thing happened the next "meat day." No chicken. Her kitchen was on the second floor. He'd never been there or in the rest of her quarters; quite pointedly she'd refrained from inviting him upstairs. He could not see the inner workings that produced his deprivation. But he could ask. He took a deep breath.

"Did something go wrong with the chicken?" he asked.

"Some things take . . . take time to learn." Her hand no longer went up to hide the little stammer, and she smiled the half smile that was more firm than demure. He understood. She was practicing his kind of cooking and would eat the rehearsals herself as long as she saw fit. He would see no drumstick on the table before the Answer came.

And until then, apparently, he'd have to eat without her. Her breakfast, of course, was long over by the time he woke to the biscuit and black coffee she left for him at half past eight. At 1 PM her broom handle knocked against the stable door. A signal that cheese, bread, sour milk and butter were waiting for him and Schall in the former Nassig office two doors away. While they ate, she swept the streets, having had lunch an hour before.

Dinner was hard. Schall always went to the tavern by the city gate for his smoked pork. It was impossible for him to go to bed, he said, unless he had his pilsner. His sleep gland needed beer. Berek sat alone before a dish. He could hear her move about upstairs. The faint, sensuous creaks of beams combined with the tang of chicken and, on later evenings, with the aroma of spices she had begun to use. All this touched him with a sort of gentle provocation. It was the promise, the myrrh and frankincense of a still distant bridal chamber. When would he ever be nearer?

Outside, beyond the splotched rays of his kerosene lamp, Gypsy gutturals hissed; beyond them, in the great world's night, villages drowned and boulevards erupted. The beef on his tongue was tender. But he needed the hands, with the tiny pinkie, that had prepared it. He needed her womb and face and voice to truly own Turk Place, to make it a live, warm fortress against gales accelerating across the earth. He tapped his foot against the floor. The sound made him feel less alone.

But dinner had one good thing. Berek knew that he would see Tamarah soon afterward, that in fact he'd sit with her on the same bench. This was the tricycle's rococo passenger seat, upholstered with ocher plush, from whose height Prince Wallers's steward had been so disdainful.

On his second day at Turk Place Berek had unscrewed it. He dragged it out of the stable toward Tamarah's second-floor quarters as his personal offering. Of course, he was not allowed to bring it upstairs. She stopped the gift in the hall of the ground floor. There it was left. Evenings, as soon as he had finished his meal (he never discovered the secret of her timing), she would come downstairs and walk toward that bench in the hall.

She always came with her arms full, carrying the tin box enclosing the Brick, two candleholders with candles, her notepad, and a copy of the newspaper *Wiener Zeitung*. It was typical of her talent for burdens that with so ungainly a load she still walked with a light step. She sat down in one corner of the plush bench, which looked arrogantly ornate against the dim paint blisters along the walls. She placed the candles on a projecting molding, lit them, propped pad and newspaper on top of the Brick box balanced on her lap, took out the pencil from behind her ear, which for a moment, and for a moment only, was revealed, round and white, under the darkness of her hair. School was in session.

She would start by reading aloud to Berek the *Court Gazette* on the second page. This part of the newspaper made the most sense to him. The emperor—Schall and the steward apart—was the only Gentile Viennese with whom Berek had had anything like a genuine conversation. Tamarah would spell out for him S-c-h-ö-n-b-r-u-n-n, the name of the summer palace into which His Apostolic Majesty had just moved, identifying each letter by sound and shape. He repeated after her—repeating sometimes the pauses in her halting speech. He did quite well, considering that he was also breathing in, helplessly, the soft nutmeg scent of her braided hair, the laundered smell of her apron flowing around the modest disposition of her thighs, and hints of those mysterious herbs which were sophisticating the withheld chicken.

The time of her writing, as distinct from reading, lessons depended on the length of Schall's supper. She would start that part of her instruction only after Schall had returned from the tavern. Between nine and nine-thirty he'd walk in, lifting his hat and keeping his spine very straight to display sobriety even at such an advanced hour. With a bishop's stateliness he would flounder toward his cot in the former Nassig office. Invariably, he'd be unable to close the door behind him. She'd placed a spittoon just inside the threshold. The partly open door meant that Schall, however lost in snores and dreams, continued to keep Berek and Tamarah company. In the semipresence of Schall as quasichaperone she could begin the writing lesson even though it involved touching.

"Careful now," she would say. He would take the pencil and, with her hand guiding his, try to repeat the outline of the letter *a* she'd drawn for him. Being an artisan, he was intrigued by the strokes, sidebars and angles out of which one could craft the alphabet. But often he would overshoot the mark on purpose. She'd have to apply some corrective pressure—her callused little palm against his. Sometimes he'd have the nerve to press back. "No," she would say. "Your stroke is . . . is too long." (Many years later, when he was a widower who could write well, he would now and then catch himself leaving gaps in his lines that were an echo of the gaps between her words.) On such occasions her stammer could become quite pronounced. To hide it she would turn her face away from him and from the Brick box that served as their writing desk. He'd be enchanted by the profile of one dark-haired temple and one dark blond eyebrow frowning over the flutter of one blue eye.

But when his pleasure became too palpable, she could cut it off in a manner that was firm and strange.

"We rest now." Her hand would disengage itself from his. She would lean back, take a long breath. Within a second she had fallen asleep.

Whenever that happened, he would at first resent this almost deliberate fainting away, this instant remoteness. But then he'd notice how the pallor of her closed eyelids contrasted with the mauve fatigue spots under her lower lashes. He saw how deeply her breast fell after it rose with each breath. She reminded him of a lovely bell swinging back and forth yet too worn out to toll. She would hug the Brick box to herself even in her sleep, but often the notepad would slip off her lap. He'd bend down to pick it up, quickly kiss her skirted ankle, brush his fingers over the laces of her boots that ended in such dainty bows, replace the notepad on top of the Brick, push the candles flush against the wall so that they would not drip on her, and then tiptoe away into the former Nassig office, to lie down, not far from Schall, on the other cot.

Of course, he'd leave the door open. Before he could settle in his sheets, he'd hear her wake up in the house hall, on the tricycle seat. She'd give a startled little snort. The last sound was her feet shuffling upstairs, heavy with the Brick and the candleholders and the progress of his education.

During the contest for Turk Place Tamarah spent herself even more than Berek did. It wasn't just her needlework for her "married linen" in addition to the ball-gown embroidery she did for Princess Wallers. It wasn't just the hours in her invisible kitchen, training herself in chicken cuisine. It was the Gypsies.

At the end of the second week Berek finished work on the house shields cut out of the tricycle plaque. He had exquisitely incised their numerals after Schall's design. Now he nailed them over building entrances in accordance with the practice at Varungy: odd numerals on one side, even on the other, the lowest numbers starting in the east. He made the stable building No. 1. No. 3 came next, abutting in turn on No. 5, which contained the former Nassig office as well as Tamarah's still taboo quarters upstairs. The houses opposite he numbered 2, 4 and 6.

The morning after he'd put up the shields, he found each one smeared into illegibility. The Gypsies had blotted out the numbers with some charred wood sticks dipped in grease. Furiously, he ran into the stable to look for the ladder and clean up the damage. No ladder. He thought it had been stolen—until he ran out again to discover that Tamarah had already gotten hold of it. She was standing on the top rung, wiping away at the house shield of No. 3.

He argued. She kept wiping. *She* was the caretaker at Turk Place, she said. She could not be stopped, nor could the Gypsies' anger, nor his own resolve.

His next enterprise was the paving of what would be the delivery area before Turk Place No. 1—the stable about to become his factory. The whole street was uncobbled; mud would mire any vehicle delivering heavy metal during unlucky weather. Berek unscrewed the four broad brass steps by which one boarded the tricycle. He also hammered loose the carriage's entire brass floor from its rear to its engine. With Schall he dragged the floor out of the stable, placed it in front of the entrance, and laid the four brass steps alongside it. Of the cannibalized tricycle the engine was still left, resting on the chassis and on the two remaining wheels as on a barrow. The two men wheeled the engine into the street on the "barrow." Through a rearrangement of the pistons Berek converted the mechanism from a locomotive to a riveting machine that used bolts he'd found in the toolbox under the driver's seat. With the machine he riveted the various brass plates into one continuous metal pavement.

Next morning the earth looked chewed up all around the area. The Gypsies had tried to dig up the "pavement" in vain. Berek grinned. He didn't grin the following day, when his new pavement ran and stank with human waste—that is, the part not yet cleaned up by Tamarah. She was already in full tilt with bucket and mop by the time he'd finished breakfast and came upon the mess.

He tried to take the mop out of her hand. She held on with such force that one of her braids came loose. *She* was the caretaker here. "What you can do," she said with a fierce stammer, "for . . . for cleaning up better you can make . . . a water hose."

"I'll do something still better," he said grimly.

Plumbing had been, in any case, next on his agenda for Turk Place. He had his eye on the railing that surrounded the passenger area of the tricycle. It consisted of coils of tin tubing elaborately finished with chrome outside; but inside—as he had determined with a few proving hammer blows—they were entirely hollow. He cut away all turnings except one, which he heated and changed to a ninety-degree angle. Altogether, he produced some sixty pieces of pipe, each about three feet long: the length of Tamarah's hair come loose. Once he'd glimpsed it tossing at the top of her stairs.

Working first at the fire, then over the anvil, he tapered one end of each tube so that it fit tightly into the next. Now he was ready to lay an aboveground main that led from the well behind the stable, through the stable, out the door, to turn right at ninety degrees along Turk Place Nos. 1, 3 and 5.

The Gypsies began to react to the metal snake before it had grown twenty yards. The women no longer carried their refuse to the garbage-cart stop by the city gate. Instead, they made each house entrance into a fountainhead of trash with which Tamarah had to deal. Berek couldn't have helped her now even if she had let him. There was no time. Again and again, he found his pipeline choked with sequined rags, with limbs of half-decomposed vermin, with pebbles big as baby skulls, pitted with eye sockets—all objects viciously hard to dislodge.

One night, after he'd sweated away a day unclogging the pipeline, Tamarah stopped midway in her writing lesson. His hand trembled so much from his chores that he could not manage the loop of the letter *b*.

"We will write something to the Eternal," she said. "That will help."

Usually, they practiced with the pad placed on top of the Brick box. But this time she took out the Brick itself. She put it on the floor before them. It lay there, bare, glinting a deep golden bronze. The candle flames twitched like brilliant marionettes in the draft of the entrance hall; in their light the Brick seemed to breathe through its crevices, to stir like some extraordinary pet, the little scrolls on its back wiggling.

"Come on," she said. As support for the writing pad she'd put the box lid on her lap; then she handed him the pencil. Her hand cupped and steered his. Slowly, she spelled out the words; the message they wrote together required their pencil to thread its way through vast labyrinths of the alphabet yet unknown to him. *"Please, God the Eternal,"* they wrote, *"make the Gypsies go away from Turk Place."*

They rolled up their request into a scroll and pushed it into the Brick.

V

THE GYPSIES did not go away the following morning, but two men came to Turk Place who had never been there before. One had a big mustache dripping off on both sides of his mouth. The other had a small black mustache whose ends stabbed up. Suddenly, they stood before Berek in front of Turk Place No. 3.

"Good day," one of them said while Berek pulled something violet and furry and funny-smelling out of his water main. "Are we addressing Dr. Jacob Nassig?"

"No," Berek said. "Good day."

"Are you in Dr. Nassig's employ?"

"I am in nobody's employ," Berek said. "I am Berek Spiegelglass."

"Spiegelglass," the Small Mustache said. "Oh, you are that Spiegelglass." He pulled some papers from some very deep and capacious inner jacket pocket. "Here we are. 'Berek Spiegelglass.' Yes. We've had a notification involving you from the Secretariat of His Majesty's Chancellery. License for the manufacture of metal articles on a site owned by the Jewish Council, etcetera, etcetera. Are you aware this is a council-owned site, Spiegelglass? This is Turk Place, isn't it?"

Berek nodded at his beautiful new house shield, which answered the question. He was hitting the water pipe with a poker to loosen some other matter wedged inside.

"Very well," the Small Mustache said. He had to compete with the poker and therefore identified himself, very loudly, as the real estate consultant for the Jewish Community Council of Vienna and the Big Mustache as the council's rabbi in charge of outer districts.

"Very well," the Small Mustache said, looking at another of his papers. "Our records here say that Turk Place is a religious site with a custodian—hello, do you hear me?—a site leased by Dr. Jacob M. Nassig, who has not paid rent for the last six months."

"Dr. Nassig hasn't paid the custodian either." Berek pointed at Tamarah, who was busy with her broom at the other end of Turk Place.

"What is she a custodian of?" the big-mustached rabbi said. "Our records aren't clear."

"Of the Brick," Berek said, clanging his poker against the pipe.

"What?" the Small Mustache asked.

"Of the Brick," Berek said. "And because she hasn't been paid, she has to make money with embroidery."

"What brick?" the Small Mustache said.

"From the holy wall of the Temple in Jerusalem." Berek worked the poker.

"From the Wailing Wall?" the Big Mustache said. "Are you sure?"

"Of course."

"Well, such charming hearsay isn't necessarily religious," the Big Mustache said. "Some might treasure it more as folklore."

Berek didn't know what he meant by "folklore." In any case, the Big Mustache looked like a toupee advertisement he had seen in the *Wiener Zeitung*—not like a rabbi.

"The Brick," Berek said, "will be the center of our street when my people come here from Varungy."

"Oh?" the Big Mustache said. "I'm sorry. I can't hear you with that noise."

Berek repeated what he'd said.

"Well, 'your people' right now are Gypsies," the Small Mustache said.

"They'll be gone soon," Berek said.

"You're not going to scare them off by banging against a pipe," the Small Mustache said. "I wish you could, because they're embarrassing us. There's a sanitary complaint against this place, and we at the Jewish Council, we're the owner of record."

"I'm making improvements here for after they're gone," Berek said. His poker was still trying to knock loose the obstruction inside the pipe.

"*If* and *when* they're gone," the Small Mustache said. "Herr Spiegelglass, it might be worthwhile for you to listen to us. *We* will determine any changes here—we at the Jewish Council. Hello?"

"Yes. I can listen while I work," Berek said.

"We determine changes here," the Small Mustache repeated. "Dr. Nassig is no longer a tenant since he's failed to pay rent. His lease is terminated. We control the premises."

"All right, then I can lease it from you," Berek said.

The Mustaches looked at each other.

"Maybe I can even buy part of the Place. Maybe this house here."

The Big Mustache stepped a small step backward. The Small Mustache pulled out a notebook. "Indeed," he said. "Herr, uh, Herr Spiegelglass, for buying this house, what sum would you have in mind?"

"Three hundred and forty gulden." The figure had jumped into Berek's mind because of his deal with Prince Wallers's steward. He was to deliver three hundred and forty ball-favor medallions.

"Hmm, now that's an interesting number," the Small Mustache said.

"I couldn't pay it all at once," Berek said, wielding the poker.

"As owner or lessee you'd be responsible for the property." The Small Mustache nodded at the vista of wet, stained laundry spilling from windows, odorous litter along the housefronts, and three dancing toads a Gypsy boy was pricking with a fork in order to tease them into finer leaps.

"I mean, not just responsible for paying for the property," the Small Mustache said, "but responsible for the condition of the property. Do you know what you'd be taking on?"

"There'll be no problem after the Gypsies are gone," Berek said.

"I'm going to say something that should be clearly understood,"

the Small Mustache said. "Perhaps in fairness to yourself you ought
to stop the noise for a moment."

"Almost finished." Berek clanged the poker and shook the pipe.

"The tenant here defaulted. However . . ." the Small Mustache
consulted another paper. "The Gypsies hold a sublease valid another
three years. They might try to use that. And if that fails, they might
claim squatters' rights—"

"That's all right, they'll leave." Berek smiled, happy, for just
then the thing inside the pipe had become unstuck. It rattled. He
had finally knocked it loose.

"Isn't confidence nice," the Small Mustache said. "If we do rent
or sell the place to you, who'll see to your side of the contract?"

"My side of the contract?" Berek said. "Oh, the Wallers man. In
the business office there."

"*Prince* Wallers?" the Big Mustache asked.

"Yes, the business steward," Berek said. "He was here. He's advanced us money for an order."

"Has he," the Small Mustache mused. "Well, we'll convey your
position and your information to the council. Good day."

"God be with you," the Big Mustache added.

"The same to you," Berek said.

What he was finally able to pull out of the pipe was the
shrunken half of a muskmelon, alive and dappled with golden mag-
gots.

On the morning of that visit Berek entirely cleared the pipe. He
cut three holes into it, spaced evenly along the length of Turk
Place. Then he signaled Schall to start pushing the pump at the
well. With a mighty gurgle three sudden rivulets flushed away
the Gypsy debris before the buildings.

After lunch Berek found fright dolls staring from the pipe openings. Out of each hole bulged a face wrinkling with straw, with a
broken carrot for a sneer and liver spots made of feces.

Berek flushed them away and bolted the holes with hubcaps
from the tricycle wheels. Very soon thereafter both Berek's and

Schall's headgear dissolved into the night. Berek's bowler forever, whereas Schall's top hat reappeared, looming high against the morning sky, perched rakishly on the skeleton of a cow's head, which, in turn, sat impaled on one of the rooftop minarets of Turk Place No. 5.

Schall cursed. Berek had time for only half a frown. The sun above the top hat on the cow skull was the sun that burnished an auburn sheet of metal. The same morning a horse cart had arrived at Turk Place with the first shipment of Prince Wallers's bronze. Now Berek could get started on a sample run of the medallions, the princess's ball favors.

That day he went lunchless. Without letup he drove Schall and himself, wielding screwdriver and monkey wrench, reorchestrating cogwheels and transmission belts, until the tricycle's steam engine had been born again as a stamping press. When he came to his dinner at night, Tamarah awaited him by the table. Her hand held an envelope with a crimson stamp which showed a sickle moon. It was a Turkish stamp, she said. It was her father's answer from Jerusalem.

"My Tamarah," she read aloud to Berek, "may God preserve us in a world where the chief rabbi of Holy Jerusalem says it is just rumor about the Brick at Turk Place. This means that the Eternal does not wish us to have the chief rabbi for guidance. The Eternal means to test our own knowledge of the good and the not good. We know it is not good for you to live with the young man under one roof unless betrothed. And even as betrothed not good, unless the young man removes the polluting Gypsies from the Brick. If he will remove them within a moon, then he can stand with you under a *chuppah* and see your hair upon the pillow. Then the Eternal shall bless you with the shining of His face. Be a good wife but remain my little one, so far away across so many mountains and rivers. I am too weak to come. Your father."

Reading aloud, she didn't stutter. But when she pronounced "see your hair upon the pillow," her voice turned lower and she averted her face.

"*Tamarah,*" he said when she was finished. Her shoulder seemed unaware of the touch of his hand.

"The Gypsies," she said with a very even tone. "Can you remove them in a month?"

"Of course!" he said. "Earlier. We already put a prayer for that in the Brick. In three weeks!"

"All right, then," she said.

Rays from the kerosene lantern spiraled around him. She had just consented to their engagement. He kissed the tips of her braids peeping out of her bun and wondered if he really felt them tremble against his lips.

"Here." She'd turned around and put two sudden ten-gulden notes into his hand. "For your equipment expenses."

"What do you mean?" he asked, twice stunned. Though he needed, come to think of it, expensive screw blocks, hook bolts and cutting chips to make his stamping press perfect. The gulden he'd gotten as advance were all gone. "What do you mean?" he said again with greater heat.

"The lady-in-waiting gave me a down payment," she said. "I've taken on more needlework from Princess Wallers."

"Thank you," he said. It was humiliating to be supported by his fiancée. Instinctively, he understood that she used the humiliation to cool him down. He understood it, but he didn't like it. He wanted to kiss her braid tips again, this time with a passion not altogether sweet.

She stepped away. "In three weeks, then," she said. "Or four. There's much to do. Nobody has come from your village yet."

"My God, Varungy," he said. Now he was really cooled down. She had put into exact words something that had long bothered him but which he'd kept vague by wrapping himself in the blur of daily problems.

"How long have we been waiting to hear from them?" he asked. "When did you write that letter for me to Varungy?"

"Over twenty days," she said.

"You must cable," he said. "Go to the post office and cable my cousin Riddah Mainzer there. They should all come for the wedding, which will be in three weeks—is three weeks all right?"

"A month," she said.

"Which will be in a month at the latest. They should all come and stay here and work here with me. Will you send that today?"

She nodded. "I have a lot of . . . of other work to get things ready," she said. "There'll be no time to study until then."

She put her father's letter in her bodice and went upstairs. And, indeed, there was no school that night nor on a number of nights thereafter.

Suddenly, a linen sheet had been suspended across the bottom steps of the stairs that led to Tamarah's quarters. Since she didn't explain, Berek didn't ask. But it seemed to be there to underline the chastity of their betrothal, and also, perhaps, to counteract the rife sound of hammering and planing which came from above.

She was "getting things ready" up there—reshaping her maiden quarters into living and sleeping accommodations fit for the needs of a married couple. But with Tamarah's new carpentering noises her old cooking scents faded. Except for Friday night's chopped meat, topped with one Sabbath mushroom per serving, she had neither time nor funds now for anything but cheese and eggs and lentils.

Schall shared the frugality. Not much of a diet was served at house No. 5 during this, the climactic week of the conquest of Turk Place. Schall had retrieved his top hat from the cow skull on the roof. But on the last step down from the ladder he tripped and, though unhurt, tore his left trouser leg beyond darning. The new garment he had to buy cost him the last of his tavern money. Evenings, the two men now ate side by side under the girl's nuptial hammering. Schall chewed his dark bread and cheese next to Berek without mitigating Berek's dining solitude. At this point Schall had stopped talking.

He smoked more than ever. As he puffed his cigarettes rolled in newspaper cuttings, Berek would sometimes try to decipher the print dangling from his partner's mouth. It was a sort of substitute for the reading lessons discontinued by Tamarah. But it was hard. The print would vibrate with urgencies imprisoned inside Schall's mouth. Friday came and Schall didn't even talk during their after-work wine. The weekly ritual was already well established; Berek and his partner repaired with a flagon to the driver's seat of the dismembered tricycle, which now stood in a stable corner. That Friday Berek tried to encourage his friend by downing a—for him—heroic two thirds of a glass. Schall emptied one and a half and vibrated, wordlessly, the bisected headline of his cigarette. Silence was broken by a kepied postman at the door.

"Good afternoon! Herr Spiegelglass?"

The letter he was handed constituted Berek's first piece of mail on Turk Place. It contained—he could not doubt it—an answer, long past due, to his Varungy cable.

He tore open the envelope and ran to Schall, who frowned at the one paragraph on the sheet and said it was from the Council of the Jewish Community of Vienna concerning the property known as Turk Place near the city's western gate in Lower Austria.

"Oh, that," Berek said. "Good."

Seven hundred gulden, Schall said, puffing as he read, jiggling the cigarette with mounting fierceness. Four hundred gulden for the purchase by Berek Spiegelglass of Turk Place No. 1 and for the lease by Berek Spiegelglass of Nos. 3 and 5 as well as 2, 4 and 6 for an annual rental of sixty gulden each, said rental including an option to buy at a mutually determined price, an agreement along these lines being forwarded to Prince Wallers's business office for contractual execution, faithfully yours and signature illegible.

"Fine," Berek said. "But this means that Varungy still hasn't answered."

Whereupon Schall slapped the letter into Berek's palm, threw down his cigarette, stamped on it and then said in one enormous sentence that this was it, that did it, seven hundred gulden for a Gypsy-infested hole when there wasn't enough money even for a pork chop or a beer, it was all of one piece, so clear, it all fit together, the thieving Gypsies and everything, with all due respect to his partner, who apparently just didn't want to see what it all meant. It was all too plain and intolerable, for he, Schall, had a fiancée too, though he'd meant to keep that private, but Fräulein Steffi Dengler was a police sergeant's daughter, cultured, a subscriber to three magazines, and now he'd be unable to see her even on rainy days, for the Gypsies had stolen his rain cape, his only decent rendezvous garment. It was so obvious that it was all one conspiracy, the Gypsies and the seven-hundred-gulden connivers from the Hebrew community, all agents of Dr. Nassig, infidel Antichrists, all used by Dr. Nassig to destroy them, Schall and Spiegelglass, before *they* could capture *him,* in fact he'd seen Dr. Nassig's Pekingese run among the Gypsy dogs the night before last, already a dead giveaway, but now after this, this seven-hundred-gulden plot, that was the topper, he would kill the first Gypsy crossing his way and he didn't want to end up on the gallows, it would be a slaying provoked by the Antichrist, it would trigger a riot in Vienna on top of the crash, it would set off Armageddon the year of the emperor's jubilee—no, he had to leave, he was sorry, but it was too much.

He had risen to his feet. He kicked out of his way the fragment of a Gypsy saddle and buttoned his coat conclusively. He was not only Berek's skillful and indispensable ally but a living part of Turk Place. Berek could not let him go.

"Wait, Schall," he said. "We'll be rid of the Gypsies soon."

"Yeah?" Schall said. "How?"

Berek could not tell him that he and Tamarah had asked the Brick for their departure. "The Gypsies will be gone by next week," he said. "I swear."

Schall just shook his head and rolled his eyes.

"I have an idea," Berek said. He took out the small wad Tamarah had given him and peeled off eight gulden. "You go away from the Gypsies here," he said. "You go to Varungy with this money. Find out what's happening with my people and bring them here in time for my wedding. By that time the Gypsies will have blown away."

"How do you know?" Schall asked.

"Not one Gypsy will be left," Berek said.

"You swear by Moses?"

"By Moses," Berek said. "And—and by what is holy to me here."

Schall shook his head at the bills Berek was holding out to him. He rolled himself a cigarette. Berek added another two gulden, almost the very last he had left.

"From my wedding reserve," he said. "Buy yourself a new black rain cape at Bratislava. My cousin Riddah says it's cheapest there. It's on the way to Varungy."

Schall breathed out a heavy cloud of smoke. "If Fräulein Dengler visits here," he said, "if she should inquire, you tell her I'm on a business trip."

It was not Fräulein Dengler who came visiting the next day. At 10 AM Berek sat in the stable that was not yet a factory, at work on the trial batch of ball-favor medallions. He had hand-polished the first three when a voice came curling through the door.

"Mr. Bang-Bang! Hello? Oh, Mr. Bang-Bang, won't you come out?"

Berek finished polishing the fourth and came out. In a four-horse landau Prince Wallers's business steward was lolling next to a turbaned personage with a three-pronged beard.

"Well, here he is," the steward said. "And damn if he isn't holding just what I came for, the little devil. Aren't those our ball favors?"

"They're just hand-polished," Berek said.

"Still warm to the touch," the steward said. "Rolls hot from the oven. Will you hand up two, Mr. Bang-Bang? One for me and one for His Highness the Plenipotentiary Extraordinary?"

"They'll look better machine-polished when I can afford a machine," Berek said.

"A machine?" the steward said. "Just one? A man of your means? Your cheerful commitments?" He raised a folder from his lap. "I have here a contract by which you'll be buying one of these Turk pavilions here and renting the other five. Bravo!"

"That's my intention," Berek said.

"For an easy seven hundred gulden the first year!" the steward said, tossing the folder down to Berek.

The steward made Berek angry. But it was a useful anger which helped him act more firmly in the face of a four-horse landau.

"I'll get the money," Berek said, holding the folder.

"It does my sinuses good to watch you," the steward said.

"Such a precocious entrepreneur. Most others, they dance their way toward bankruptcy. You *start* there. Exquisite. And the work is as exquisite as the man." The steward held Berek's hand-polished medallion up to his turbaned companion. "Look, Sir Plenipotentiary. Did I promise too much? Observe the veining of those bronze laurel leaves. And look at the reverse side. What in the world? What *is* that emblem, Mr. Bang-Bang? A square bullet?"

"It's just a trademark," Berek said. He didn't want to add that it was a tiny representation of the Brick or that it would brand all his future manufacture.

"A square bullet," the steward said. "Original. Quite in key with starting out bankrupt—"

"I'm not bankrupt," Berek interrupted. He remembered the word unpleasantly from his newspaper-reading sessions with Tamarah.

"Well, if you're not, it's because we won't let you be, spoilsports that we are." The steward nudged his companion, cackling. "We're just too jealous of so much young originality—right, Sir Plenipotentiary? Shall we show our friend the matter at hand?"

The turbaned beard nodded to a lackey behind him, who handed him a wooden disk which he handed on to the steward, who in turn reached it down to Berek. Carved in bas-relief, the disk displayed a lion brandishing a sword in its right forepaw as it faced the Habsburg double eagle, both animals bowing at each other with all three of their heads.

"Glory be to the sworded lion, the imperial Persian crest," the steward said. "Our dear Plenipotentiary Extraordinary here is the envoy of His Majesty the Shah Nasr-ed-Din, who will grace the jubilee of our emperor by visiting our World's Fair"—the steward performed a sitting obeisance and focused a pince-nez on a sheet of paper—"but His above-said Majesty the Shah also wishes to mark the occasion by awarding a bronze medal based on that disk—Plenipotentiary dear will correct me if I fuzz these figures—by awarding a first-class, or double-sized, medal to our emperor; fifty second-class, or normal-sized, medals to principal members of the Persian entourage; another fifty normal-sized medals to equivalent notables of the Austrian Court; and four third-class

medals, half-sized, to the four assistants of his chief astrologer.
Very sweet. Mr. Bang-Bang, can you produce these quantities and
sizes by November?"

"Oh," Berek said. "My associate, he's the designer, he's away on
a business trip."

"I should have known from the square bullet," the steward said.
"Mr. Bang-Bang is above an order paying seven hundred gulden in
advance. The man does not want to be solvent. He has too much
character. He won't even look at the contract."

"I think we can do it all right," Berek said, looking at the folder
full of printed clauses. "My fiancée does all the paperwork."

"A paperworking fiancée!" the steward said. "Even *that* is original. You tell your ink-stained peach that all the figures are in that
envelope together with your real estate transaction and our own
contract for the ball favors. And tell her . . ." The steward crooked
his finger at Berek. "Come closer with your rosy ear. This is confidential. Closer. Now. Tell her that it's no mistake that the Persian
contract is dated earlier than ours though you're already bang-
banging away on our favors. There's a special reason for that. I'll tell
you why, if you'll trade secrets with me."

"What?" Berek asked.

"You give away your secret, I'll give away mine."

"I don't know what you mean by secrets," Berek said, determined not to betray that his trademark was the Brick.

"All right, I'll tell you what I mean by mine." The steward bent
out of the coach window down to Berek. A tiny scissors flashed.
There was a click by Berek's ear. The steward had snipped a curl of
Berek's hair. "I've dated your Persian contract earlier," the steward
whispered, "because of the ninnies in our office. They think it's peculiar to award a contract to an unknown like you. They think it's
modern to be suspicious. But if dear Plenipotentiary gives you his
order first, you'll be known in the field, no? You'll be exalted by the
patronage of His Persian Majesty, yes? We'll make wonderful modern sense together, yes? You understand? Say yes."

"Oh," Berek said. "Yes. You cut off some of my hair."

"Apparently," the steward said. "Now your turn. Your secret."

"What secret?" Berek said stubbornly.

"Why do you want to buy this dump? Or even rent it? And what have you done with our darling dinosaur?"

"Dino-huh?" Berek asked.

"Our great big belching tricycle. Where is it?"

"The tricycle is sort of all over the place," Berek said. "I've been making things out of it."

"Ah, creativity," the Steward said. "And this . . ." The satin-sheathed hand flew up and fluttered across a Turk Place strewn with ruptured mattresses which had rained from the windows that morning and over whose spilled gray guts swarthy cherubs ran naked, tossing spiders at each other. "This must be a masked jewel of a place. Is there a gold mine underneath here? Tell."

"There may be something else," Berek said. "You never know."

"Aha," the steward said. "What?"

"What," Berek said. "I'll tell you what. This place is going to be here when the rest of the world has gone to hell!"

He'd said it furiously, not quite knowing why and not to the effect intended. The steward's cackle rose into a high wheeze, into an explosive aria of a guffaw. Heaving and shaking, he put against his lips a snow-white handkerchief which he then waved at Berek with a motion that was derisive and amorous at the same time. He nodded to the driver; floated forward with his black velvet jacket, his silvery shirt, his melodious cough, his snip of Berek's hair, his four ebony horses, his Plenipotentiary Extraordinary with turban and three-pronged beard, and was gone.

During that embattled week Berek never set foot outside Turk Place. But on the day following the steward's delivery of the contracts, Tamarah took them and put on her brown bonnet and went to Prince Wallers's office. She brought back not only the signed and executed documents but, with a wrinkle on her forehead, some information from one of Prince Wallers's lawyers. It would take a week to make the purchase and lease of Turk Place effective, the lawyer had said; but it would take months, if not years, to evict the Gypsies.

As if in confirmation of the news, the Gypsies made the litter of mattresses reappear. The evening before, Tamarah and Berek had dragged them away to the garbage-cart stop by the city gate. Now here they were again, teeming across the gutter, proliferating in death, their open bowels crawling with ants. Berek kicked them into a pyre at which he hurled a lit log from his smithy.

No mattress rematerialized from the ashes. But the next day Tamarah's brooms—the indoor as well as the outdoor one—were broken. Berek stopped hand-polishing the ball favors. He went to the toolbox of the late tricycle, where he kept the sawed-off shaft of the vehicle's steering wheel. He took it to the fire and forged it into a steel pole whose end was a blade, pointed and sharp like a bayonet.

After the Gypsy men had returned in the evening, Berek waited for them to gather in their usual campfire circle. Then he emerged with his weapon held high. He carried it all around them. They looked and began to sing louder those strange songs, those darkly wailed fairy tales in a forgotten tongue which Berek—despite himself—heard echo from the far side of the sunset, from a childhood hidden in an iridescent maze below Varungy. Nevertheless, he marched on, bayonet raised like a flag. The Gypsies looked and frowned and wailed.

They did nothing else that night until he'd retired to house No. 5; until he'd eaten the dinner waiting for him; until he'd lain down next to a cot that remained empty, for Schall was still away on his mission to Varungy; until Tamarah had finished her needlework and her connubial carpentry on the floor above. The Gypsies did nothing until Berek had sunk deeply into a dream about a bearded ant queen waltzing. By the time Tamarah shook him awake, very little was left of the cataclysm except dust and disarray and smoke.

Some time after midnight the Gypsy men had tried to kill the stamping press that had once been the tricycle engine. This machine had begun to devour their campsite by day. They would destroy it at night. It was their sunlight enemy. They were not prepared for its lunar cunning. Nothing warned their horses, which always returned to the stable in the evening when the machine was quiet. The Gypsies had no idea that Berek, tardy riser that he was, always left the machine fully fueled and primed so that he could proceed full blast at once when he finally came to work in the morning. All the Gypsies knew was that the demon must be burned. When they put a match to it and kicked its valves, the counterpounce was devastating.

The vomit of hot vapor, the steamy spew, the thunderstorm of detonations set the whole stable quaking. Within two seconds each horse became a nightmare. Eighteen animals turned into a cauldron of boiling hooves, of manes, tails, and nostrils spuming. They reared up high to the cobwebs of the ceiling, they bumped into Berek's wheel-chandelier, they set it swinging like a manic pendulum, and finally they crashed through the stalls.

Screaming, the Gypsy wives thrashed themselves out of their beds. Infants squalled, hags floundered through the dark; huge Romany hounds bayed, wild shapes collided and stampeded, and throughout, relentlessly, the machine kept steaming, roaring, raging as the Gypsy men, cursing, hung from the amok necks of their horses to yoke them to the wagons. Women, children, dogs all screeched and kaleidoscoped into a sort of systematic panic. Families snatched up blankets, grabbed amulets, horoscopes, saddles, cooking pots, clothes, trivets, talismans, and tossed them all, together with their babies, into the wagons and jumped in themselves. By the time Berek stumbled out of the house glaze-eyed, clutching the bayonet, all he saw was ruts.

New ruts left in the drill-ground earth, wagon-wheel ruts swerving off southward in the kind of headlong curve that never will return.

They were ruts, he realized, lit up by a jerky uneven glow—a fire. He rushed into the stable, shut off the engine's blare, and joined Tamarah in her desperate dance. Together they stamped out the flames twisting up from the floor straw.

Then, choking, they went outside. They found themselves alone among the empty houses of Turk Place. They stood side by side.

They heard each other panting. It took minutes for their eyes to stop tearing, for their breaths to calm.

The air was cool and black. Above the minarets swam moon-made ghosts of tiny clouds. Berek did not look at Tamarah, his fiancée. He knew that she stood next to him. She had on her nightgown. She was wrapped in a blanket down to her slim calves. His arms felt sweet and solemn and incomplete.

"Tamarah," he said. "Now it is really ours."

VI

THE PICTURE taken of Berek and Tamarah's wedding showed the bride wearing a cravat. This strangeness was not Tamarah's but the picture taker's. It was Boas Mainzer who clicked the shutter, thereby making his debut as a photographer in Vienna.

Before changing profession he'd spent years as Varungy's last baker but one. In 1871 he had married Berek's second cousin Riddah. When Boas was a husband of less than five months, a flour sack fell on him. It broke his shoulder, left his right arm weak for the rest of his life, and turned him after a while into a man who made his living hooded in black cloth.

His wife, Riddah, became the village baker in his stead—perhaps the only female baker in the Habsburg realm. Of course, she was illiterate, being, like Berek or her husband, of Varungy's final and teacherless generation. Yet she had her way of learning. She remembered Boas's instructions by singing them to herself. Singing, she worked her way through the hot cellar nights, kneading, mixing, molding; she wove weights and measures and recipe procedures into the lyrics of Hungarian ditties and Yiddish songs.

Berek, who hummed at work, had gotten his habit from her. But his hum was coiled, tense, focused, wordless. Riddah's voice roamed free and full, sweeping helter-skelter through sundry airs and sometimes just lapsing into a rich la-da-dah-dah-dah. . . .

Her body, no less than her voice, had a massive grace. She moved too fast to be stately. She was gusto and bosom and hips. She munched and scratched as she warbled and baked, her body and tongue never losing the beat of her chore. Her buoyancy could be magnetic. Two roosters left from her father's barnyard trailed her wherever she went. They clucked to her chanting and pecked at the bread she cubed and sometimes prechewed for them. These cocks crowed at twilight; their mistress had turned them into night fowl, and, like her, they awoke evenings.

In those years Riddah's hair was like a rude sunburst, dark red and unkempt. Three juicy, heart-shaped moles sat on her right cheek and turned from brown to pink when she laughed—laughter that was never a titter but either a rough deep-bellied chuckle or a breast-shaking guffaw. In June of 1873, the announcement was posted on the shack serving as the railway depot that Varungy would no longer even be a local freight stop. Only Riddah's (and because of her, her husband's) cheek did not turn pale.

The announcement appeared the day after Berek's inexplicable message that he would not return from his audience with the emperor. For the others, two dozen or so, left in Varungy, the last hope was gone; there seemed to be no point waiting for the chance to settle in Vienna. They began to scatter. By cart and by foot they trudged away toward rumors of jobs in Carpathian flax mills. The mob of geese remained together with Boas and Riddah Mainzer.

Riddah kept waiting indomitably. Soon something like a golden coach might be calling, sent by her cousin Berek. Ever since she'd become a baker, the world had overflowed with routine miracles. Each dusk she went down into a basement, a dank, black morgue of flour sacks. She would scratch her belly and sigh a hearty sigh that was the beginning of a tune. Ten owl cries later she had spun, out of pale dust and water, a huge soft corpse of dough into which the sound of her singing, the smell of yeast and the heat of the oven would breathe a transforming breath. She emerged each dawn from underground, her arms full of the astounding fragrance of fresh bread.

She knew that Berek's delay was part of some similar magic he must be brewing at the emperor's palace. Meanwhile, she had a summer's supply of ferment and flour. She had the devotion of two scruffy, angry roosters, which kept off the geese. She had her husband, Boas, who delivered to the countryside the crisp ribbed rolls and the fluffy rye loaves that tasted not only of anise, poppy seed and caraway but of her songs.

Boas was a thin man who liked to slant a black beret over his ear-locks even before his accident turned him from a baker into something of an *artiste*. At first he expressed his artfulness by the way he transported his wife's wares: one breadbasket hanging from each of his bike's handlebars, a third basket piggybacked on his left, good shoulder, and a fourth strapped deftly to his right hip for balance. An extension of Riddah's cheer, he'd whistle on his way to customers and sometimes even on the road back. This was remarkable because in the bankrupt spring of 1873 very few Slovakian peasants could pay cash. Often they bought their bread with used goods. One of Boas's earliest transactions involved the delivery of 170 poppy-seed rolls to the funeral feast of the mayor of Horoczin, a few highway windings away from Varungy. For that batch of rolls Boas received the dead man's hobby, that is, the photographic equipment he had left behind: a huge black accordion camera complete with tripod, an enormous black cloth, many glass negatives and a kitchen drawerful of developing equipment; he was also given an introductory course in photography by the priest, whose teeth were stippled with poppy seeds from Riddah's rolls.

In Varungy, Boas set up his tripod. He aimed the camera at a slightly cracked but flower-painted cupboard which he'd gotten for a week's supply of pumpernickel and which stood in the street, being too huge to pass the Mainzers' house door. Boas groped inside his black tent. The sharp click of the shutter frightened the geese. A few hours later the cupboard's image actually swam into sight in an acid bath in the attic that did nicely as a darkroom. Boas Mainzer had found his métier.

The cupboard on the empty street was soon joined by other objects bartered for Riddah's bread: a weather vane in the form of a stork; a one-armed chair, finely carved; a fretted bedstead; five prayer stools; and a tavern table to which was glued as centerpiece a wooden rabbit dying picturesquely of an arrow.

Boas photographed all these as soon as they were carted in by Riddah's customers, before rain could splotch them or the geese mar them with droppings or with feathers. Only some pieces were too big to be carried inside. The real reason why the Mainzers left them outdoors was that their shapes made Varungy look less deserted.

Eventually—and rather vaguely—Boas planned to collect his pictures into a sort of sales catalog. But there was another, more immediate thing on his mind. Each time he gathered around himself the Egyptian darkness of the camera cloth, in one corner of which an image began to glow, each time he pressed the lens release . . . he sensed the opening of a Higher Eye. Just as the street assembly of silent furniture seemed like a rapt new congregation filling the empty village, so the dark ritual gadgetry of photograph making performed the office of the locked synagogue; and he, Boas, replaced the rabbi, who had gone to Bratislava.

During the day, when Riddah was sleeping, Boas felt that the ceremoniously clicking camera was not only the one other creature awake in the village, it was the only creature capable of preserving life. In a world fast dispersing, running away, rusting—this camera of his could command things to stand still. To survive. To endure magically and neatly, on a firm rectangle of paper.

The first of the two men who visited this last phase of the village's life was Siddo Berger. Sitting on the milk wagon which had given him a ride, he arrived with a small but genuine leather suitcase and a walking stick. His real name was Isidore Berger, and the crash had closed the notary's office in Brno, where he had been clerking. There were no vacant jobs in town or even in the region. The search had used up Berger's savings. With his last pennies he came to Varungy for the silver cuff links which, he remembered, his father had hung on a hook inside the night table. Their sale would bring him enough cash for a celluloid collar and train fare for a job hunt in Vienna. His parents' house, however, offered only an unhinged door, dead leaves instead of furniture, a gashed mattress, and starved goslings whimpering through muddy rooms. Berger did not even have the means to leave the village. For two weeks he roomed with Boas and Riddah. He checked accounts and filled out tax forms for nearby farmers who fed him in exchange. The third week his luck materialized in the form of Herr Schall.

Schall did not wind up in the dead-letter office, like Berek's other missives to Varungy. (The village post office had terminated along with its rail depot; thus all mail or cables directed there became officially dead.) No, a live Schall appeared, complete with cigarette and a new black rain cape cheaply bought at Bratislava. He rumbled in on an oxcart he had hired at the train stop closest to Varungy.

The moment he spoke his first sentence, both Riddah and Boas knew that the great call to the capital had come at last. The stranger's utterance contained, unmistakably, the words "Berek Spiegelglass." They could understand little else of the man's Viennese dialect, yet this just enriched the glamour of the smoke he exhaled and made more admirable the angle of his cap.

Fortunately, Siddo Berger, practiced in handling Viennese customers, could translate. In exchange for transportation to the capital, he also lent a hand. There was much lifting and carrying to be done. In her excitement Riddah decided to take to Vienna not only personal belongings but her bakery implements, a piece of rye sourdough, the furniture weathering before her house and, naturally, her roosters. But even when all that had been loaded, Riddah still felt that too much had been left behind. The oxcart was already in motion when she jumped off. She ran through the village a last time, from empty house to empty shack, snatching the tip of a drainpipe, the corner of an eave, a moldy ember from a fireplace long cold, a sliver, velvet with moss, of a doorjamb, a piece of flooring, a doorknob, a bit of window glass turned iridescent and smooth-edged

with age. All these fragments she thrust into a flour sack and with it
jumped back on the oxcart that meanwhile had gone on, squeaking
and bumping inevitably farther and farther away from the known
world.

The train ride to Vienna, Riddah's first, confounded her with
shapes heaping past the window of the fourth-class compartment. It was the only class Schall could afford—considering extra
freight charges—and the only class accepting the two roosters
Riddah cradled in her lap. What bewildered her was the endless
supply of villages just like her own that veered up and dissolved
away under a sky that, she'd always assumed, had been vaulted
specifically for Varungy.

For consolation she opened her flour sack of souvenirs. In a
flash of panic she saw nothing but nameless debris. How was that
possible when she knew exactly what piece had been taken from
where? Outside, an excess of buildings and fields kept on stampeding, heedless. Riddah feared they would sweep away all her knowledge of the identity of things. Suddenly, she felt that while she still
had such knowledge, it must be preserved in the form of a list of her
Varungy souvenirs properly matched to their former owners. This
list had to be written down, but she could not write. Nor could
Boas, who was busy anyway, shielding his camera against the jolting
of the train. She did not dare approach Schall; he was smoking such
a cosmopolitan cigarette. So she asked Siddo Berger, who shrugged
and jotted, on the back of the long train ticket, that the piece of
wood came from the doorjamb of Mendel Bartik's abandoned
house, and the lump of coal from the widow Timberg's bin, and the
window glass from the house of Baruch the Shohet, may he rest in
peace. . . .

In Vienna the troop debarked into a railroad station as vast,
crowded and hysterical as six county fairs jammed together. It upset
Riddah's roosters. A blast of steam from the locomotive outraged
them. They rushed at the iron wheels. Riddah, followed by Boas, ran
to retrieve her birds. When the couple returned, they discovered

that of all the clutter of their baggage on the platform, just the flour sack with Varungy mementos had been stolen.

This was so bad that at first Riddah would not board the van-coach Schall had hired. But a downpour like a cavalry charge overwhelmed her consternation. Sheets of wetness veiled the streets, shaking like the capes of hussars. Big-city raindrops drummed with imperial dash against hard pavements. Somehow the sound backed Boas's assurance that the emperor's police would ferret out the thief.

By the time they reached Turk Place, the clouds gave way to blinding gaps of brightness. Riddah blinked and hugged her roosters. Sobs broke from her.

The disappointment was simply too drastic. Riddah's visions were as ample as the rest of her ways. What had she not expected of Vienna? Perhaps something like Dr. Nassig's workshop placed right behind the throne room? Or Boas's elevation to court photographer? Or her own appointment as His Majesty's purveyor of poppyseed rolls, mistress of a bakery draped in purple?

Maybe all of that. Certainly nothing like Turk Place. Nothing like this mean version of the universe she had just left: this small heap of houses still rancid with Gypsy smells, still charred with debris from dead campfires. At least the dying of Varungy had been redeemed by meadows all around. Here cold ashen dust came from the vast drill ground to the left. And from the right, the turmoil of a market jangled.

Riddah cried. She sobbed in full-throated tides. As soon as he had paid the coachman, Berek put his arm around her shoulder to soothe her with the two most precious things he knew—the Brick and Tamarah, his bride.

It didn't help. Riddah cried. Tears ran from her eyes to her bosom in generous rivulets—not even under the Nazis, more than sixty years later, would she cry like that. The loss of Varungy came alive beneath her heart. It was a sudden, bruising pang against which Berek's introductions and explanations were of no use. To her the Brick looked like a dirty stone. Tamarah's pale cheeks and tight braids seemed sickly and prissy. Why had they left home for these dry specters? Riddah would have cried still longer if her husband, Boas, had not seized the Brick.

"Wait, Riddah," he said. "Wait. This has been photographed."

They were standing in the entrance hall of No. 5. Boas ran outside, bowed his head down to the Brick that was pressed against his heart, lifted his face to the sky, closed his eyes—and opened them wide with revelation.

"Photographed!" he said. "Not by anyone down here. Look for yourself. Do what I did!"

He thrust the Brick at Riddah, who looked down at it and then up to the sun. When she closed her eyes, there emerged slowly on the inside of her lids an exact photograph of the Brick complete with all its venerable fissures.

"You see?" Berek said. "Photographed for us by *Him*. It's meant to last! It's really from the Temple! Riddah, it's all right."

And everything became better. Riddah's sobs began to taper. Beyond the minarets of Turk Place she saw huge violet flags of smoke rise from the city toward the late light. She saw Tamarah raise a hand with a tiny little finger. Riddah saw that the girl's eyes shone with a rare blue and that her knuckles were small pillows worn raw. Berek's betrothed now looked like a beauty and a worker, perhaps as genuine as the Brick. She scooped up her two roosters, used a tail feather to wipe away her tears.

"When is the wedding?" she asked. Her voice had regained its rough warmth.

"In three weeks," Berek said.

"By then I'll be settled," Riddah said. "I'll bake the feast bread."

Now she no longer needed to hug the roosters. She put them down and let them go. And to their first crowing on Turk Place she opened her arms to Berek, to Tamarah, for an embrace.

Money was the immediate problem preceding Berek's wedding. True, Schall had agreed to defer his earnings percentage until after the second Wallers payment. True, Siddo Berger entered Berek's employ on very painless terms; he accepted cot and board as salary as long as there was still no substantial clerking—only errand running—for him to do. And Riddah pitched in. At the market she had bartered a Gypsy cradle for three flour sacks and the stork weather vane from Varungy for yeast cakes, a cask of sugar and a bag of salt. Now she produced all the bread eaten at Turk Place.

All that helped, but not enough. The fourth day after Riddah's arrival Berek had to have a talk with the others in the former Nassig office. He asked Tamarah to write out the arithmetic of their situation. Her script was small but sharply angled. It made her reckoning look relentless.

They still had on hand the down payment from the Plenipotentiary Extraordinary, plus a small sum the pawnbroker had given Berek for the silver-chased suede pouch in which the Persian payment had come, plus some money left from the advance on Prince Wallers's ball favors and from Tamarah's embroidery money. But Berek would have to pay out the first installment due on his purchase of Turk Place No. 1, plus the monthly rent on the rest of the premises, plus the fees for the marriage license. This left them a total of seventeen gulden. They needed eight gulden a week for food. By the third week not a penny would remain. Yet their next income, namely the final payment for delivery of Prince Wallers's ball favors, was more than a month away. That was how long the hand-polishing and finishing of the medallions would take. Starvation lay ahead.

"How about not buying that house here?" Schall said. "Just rent it like the others. It's a lot cheaper."

"*Renting,*" Berek said. "If I only rented here, it would also mean only renting the Brick."

"We could save a hundred gulden," Schall said.

"There'll be no wedding here," Berek said, "with the Brick just rented."

Tamarah put down her pencil. "I put another message into the Brick," she said, very low, to Berek. "A prayer for money."

Berek stood up. "It'll come out all right. We'll ask the steward for a second advance."

"Who will?" Schall asked. "Me?"

"It doesn't matter." Berek crumpled the paper with the computations. The meeting was over, the issue resolved. "It'll be all right."

But would it? Schall, as he had feared, was dispatched to Prince Wallers's office. He returned empty-handed. The old steward was sick. His deputy had said that he could not disburse further money without goods received.

"It'll be all right," Berek said. Right in front of Schall's eyes he squandered more of the capital they didn't have. He instructed Siddo Berger to go to the office of the *Wiener Zeitung* to find out how much it would cost to print a small advertisement.

"An advertisement?" Schall said. "In the newspaper? My God, even a small one must be expensive. Why an advertisement?"

"It'll be all right," Berek said. "It's to tell the Varungyers, wherever they are, to come to the wedding. It's important." And almost in the same breath he informed Schall that he would need a private coach the night before the ceremony. Would Schall's brother-in-law, the one in the coach business, come up with a good price?

Schall didn't bother to puzzle about the coach. A fast honeymoon on the wedding eve might be one of those exotic Hebrew customs. What he could not stand was the way Berek was steering them all straight to the poorhouse.

"The coach will be four and a half gulden," he said to Berek the next day, over their regular Friday afternoon wine.

"That's not too bad," Berek said.

"It adds up," Schall said. "And the advertisement you want to put in the newspaper, that must be at least two gulden."

"It's two and a half," Berek said. "It'll be all right."

After a pause Schall said, "You'll be completely broke two days before your wedding. I just figured it out."

"It'll be all right," Berek said. "About your earnings share that you let me owe you. You'll get it back."

"That's not what I mean," Schall said. Though it did mean that he could not replace his smoke-seared jacket and therefore could not call on his young lady. He had no money to dine out and therefore had to eat with the gimpy-armed Boas, which was bad luck. It also meant dreams like the one last night where the crimson-caped pope himself, though suffering from a cold, had administered the Eucharist, giving Schall a thin, aromatic biscuit that, to Schall's shock, was carved from the smoked pork he'd gone without for days, ever since sharing the Israelites' table.

"Meanwhile, here's half a gulden for beer," Berek said.

"No," Schall said.

"Take it."

"You'll be out of eating money," Schall said. "I'm warning you."

"*Take it.*"

There were times when Berek's blue eyes took on the cold, taut sheen of a stone aimed at you from a slingshot. Schall took it.

"It'll be all right," Berek said.

Monday morning Berek sent Siddo Berger into the city. Siddo took along his walking stick and most of Berek's funds. At the office of the Jewish Council he paid the eighty gulden due as the first installment of Berek's purchase of Turk Place No. 1. The excise stamp validating the transaction cost only half a gulden in the capital, not a full one as in Brno. Fifty unexpected groschen were left in Siddo's purse; enough to buy wooden cuff links at a secondhand notions store. Therefore, his way back took him past two notaries public. In both offices the receptionists performed the same head shake. Business was still wretched because of the crash. No candidate for a clerking position, no matter how decently accoutred his shirtsleeves, need apply.

And so Siddo Berger returned to Turk Place to help sandpaper ball-favor medallions for which payment would come too late. "It'll be all right," Berek said, pocketing the installment receipt, and they all—Berek, Schall, Siddo—sandpapered on till nightfall.

At dinnertime the three men divided among them six boiled potatoes and two slender strips of beef. Then Siddo and Schall retired to the cot room they now shared, while Berek and Boas took the alphabet lessons Tamarah had resumed now that Boas's presence made respectable the late-hour nearness of her fiancé.

They still studied over the Brick box. But Boas was, of course, a beginner compared even to Berek. And the light was frailer than in earlier sessions, for they economized by burning just one candle.

And the school hour was shorter. In the middle of demonstrating the double loop of the Gothic letter *h*, Tamarah would let her braided head loll against the back of her chair. She'd drop off, not out of chastity but in exhaustion, after eighteen hours of embroidering, sewing, carpentering, cooking and scrimping. She fell asleep and, in contrast to earlier days, could not rouse herself after a while to go upstairs to bed.

But it would be all right. Berek would blow out the candle. With Boas he would walk across to Turk Place No. 6, where he had a bachelor mattress in the attic, while Boas lay down in the bed next to his wife's on the second floor.

And as Boas stretched out, his wife, Riddah, rose like the moon. Riddah was as nocturnal at Turk Place as she had been in Varungy. Followed by her roosters, singing, she groped her way to the well in the backyard of No. 1, splashed her face lavishly, combed her hair by way of running three wet fingers through it, hung a lantern around her neck, and sang her way to No. 5, where she gathered up Tamarah, the Brick box, the writing gear, the candleholder with candle, gathered them all up in the infinite capaciousness of hugely dimpled arms. As always she sang a little apology song for having misjudged the darling, braided, slumbering Tamarah-creature at their first meeting, climbed with her freight upstairs, laid Tamarah down like a doll in the twin bed the girl had carpentered, placed the Brick box under the bed, pinched off and ate a bit of the huge raw cabbage that was to be cooked as the next day's ration, munched the salt beef left for her as she washed the dishes, soaped them in the suds pail, rinsed them with the water pitcher, clattered and sang (she had no real conception of noise versus quiet, but Tamarah was much too worn out to be awakened), left pans and plates to dry in a helterskelter pile, shambled back to No. 2 to mix dough in a Gypsy cradle and then, for the next six hours—between punching down dough and baking it in the oven Berek used, upended, as anvil, between hurling playful Yiddish curses at her roosters for their greed and prechewing for them the heels of stale rye loaves—she buckled down to the night's main work.

She had forced Tamarah to yield the janitoring chores to her. She chanted and broomed away the wilderness of Gypsy debris that still flowed knee-high through the rooms of Turk Place Nos. 2, 4 and 6. Berek had glued together the outdoor as well as the indoor broom broken by the Gypsies, and Riddah liked to wield both at once, kicking the clutter ahead of her in the rhythm of a czardas dance. Small objects she simply tossed out of the window, producing an echoing shower in the night. Sometimes brooming, sometimes dragging, always singing, she spirited the night's harvest to the refuse collection point. Then she pulled pieces of her barter furniture from Varungy into the newly cleaned area. She scratched her left breast, took the freshly baked batch out of the stable oven, tore a steaming loaf in half and, chewing serenely what would have singed any other tongue, lay down at dawn next to her husband, who often talked out of a dream that twitched his disabled hand. *"My fingers. . . ."* Boas would mumble. *"Berek—Berek! Watch my fingers! . . ."* Riddah would stroke his cheek and calm him with a loud, loving buss dotted with crumbs. "It's all right," she'd say. For her it was and would be. Her roosters clucked and dropped their bills into their feathers. The three fell asleep at once.

Of all people, it was Boas who brought it off. He made things all right financially for Turk Place. Boas was something of a nuisance just because of his admiration for Berek as Lord of the Brick. He followed Berek about, positioned and repositioned the camera in the stable so that it tellingly immortalized the young master at work. In his zeal he stumbled over a hammer one morning, fell, and broke the tip of one of the tripod legs. In three minutes Berek restored the limb by riveting the fracture with a pin. Then he thrust the tripod at Boas.

"Now go!" he said. "Don't interrupt me anymore. Make photographs where they make money! Help a little! We could use a little help!"

It was the only time he would ever speak roughly to Boas. But it was a crucial roughness. Boas tried to make money instantly. That morning he began wandering about, looking for someone who would pay him to make pictures. There was nobody on the drill ground to the east of Turk Place. To the west most of the market stood empty because it happened to be Ascension Day. Finally, he spied a small crowd at the far end of the shuttered stands. When he got nearer he discovered a number of dressed-up people grouped around a girl who was at least half snowflake, dazzlingly white in lace and ruffles, standing before the market chapel. She was the daughter of the market president, ready to be confirmed as soon as the bishop arrived.

To the crowd the delay was redeemed by the appearance of a genuine photographer. Boas wore the full panoply of what was still a rather exotic profession in the outer reaches of Vienna. The market president, a maize farmer from the adjoining county, found himself intrigued by the man's beret, the artistic limpness of his arm, the huge black flutter of the camera cloth and the mystery of the accordion box with its three stork legs. The arrival of something like a court magician made the occasion almost royal. True, this photographer turned out to be one of the Israelites new on Turk Place. On the other hand, these Israelites were just the ones who'd gotten rid of the Gypsy plague. And what made Boas conclusively welcome was the market president's watch chain. It was sterling silver, double-linked, brand new and very worthy of posterity. The market president wore it now for his Maria's confirmation. He intended to wear it again the next day for his uncle's funeral. On the spot he engaged Boas to photograph both events.

On that next day Boas found that he had only one glass negative plate left. All the others had either been exposed or broken during the journey from Varungy. The one still intact must be reserved for Berek's wedding next week. Of course, there was no money to buy another. Boas decided to use again, this time for the funeral, the plate with which he had photographed the girl's confirmation. The decision reflected his unlimited confidence in Berek.

"Sir, my cousin Berek Spiegelglass is a technical genius," he said to the market president when he showed him the developed confirmation/funeral picture. "If you want the two exposures disentangled, I'm sure he can do it."

The market president stared at the photograph. His snow-white daughter hovered like an angel above the coffin, the confirming bishop bent down to the graveside priest, and one of the wheels of his daughter's festive, lily-garlanded fiacre was the funeral wreath.

The market president had seen real photographs before. Compared to this vision, they had been puny paintings in dull colors. What rested in his hand astonished him with the miraculousness of the new art. Nobody he knew had anything like it.

"How much is your photograph?" he asked.

Boas tried to gauge the price from the man's expression. "The way it is now?" he asked.

The market president nodded. At the funeral his wife had not let him wear the too bright double-link silver watch chain. Here it was in the picture, its gleam lighting up both ceremonies.

"Nine gulden, including the developing and everything," Boas said. "Per copy."

The market president reached into his pocket. "I need two more copies," he said. "For Maria's godfather and for the reverend. Make it three. The Most Reverend would like one, too."

Turk Place was saved. There was money for food until after Berek's wedding.

AT 11 AM on Monday, July 2, 1873, Berek Spiegelglass was to be married to Tamarah Liftitz. The night before, Berek vanished. When he had not returned by eleven-fifteen of the following morning, the attending rabbi's hands, folded behind his frock coat, began to clench.

This was the rabbi of the big mustache who had first set foot on Turk Place with the real estate consultant to the Vienna Jewish Council. Rabbi Mayer, in charge of outer districts, was young, sturdy, and practiced in maintaining an energetic sympathy for backwater coreligionists who might someday form a congregation in want of his ministry. But long before 11:15 AM his understanding smile had been put through a series of tests at Turk Place.

Days earlier he had yielded to Herr Spiegelglass's request, conveyed by Siddo Berger, that he come to the future bridegroom for a discussion of wedding arrangements. During his chat with the man,

Rabbi Mayer drew on all the pastoral patience at his command. The rabbi had to inform Berek that it wasn't customary to perform the ceremony in a street—in Turk Place here—instead of a synagogue. In fact, it wasn't customary for him, the rabbi, to come visiting here (even for half a gulden for expenses) instead of Berek visiting *him* at the Jewish Council office. Also, it was irregular to have the so-called Great Temple Brick—an uncertified and uncertifiable sacramental object—included in the ritual. The rabbi had to confess that ordinarily he would have hesitated to officiate at such an affair. However, there was a special circumstance. The chief rabbi had received a note from the chief business steward of Prince Wallers—an inquiry about appropriate apparel at a Jewish wedding like Herr Spiegelglass's. In the Austrian House of Lords Prince Wallers had been active in religious legislation. A Wallers executive coming to a Jewish wedding constituted a serious matter. The rabbi hoped that Herr Spiegelglass would be serious about arrangements.

Herr Spiegelglass was busy turning a nail into a ring at the anvil. But he said that he was very serious. It would be all right. And he disappeared on his errand the night before his wedding day.

For the first time since his return from his audience with the emperor, Berek left Turk Place. On the eve of his marriage, at midnight, he was ready to depart, already in the bridegroom clothes which Boas had gotten in exchange for three basketfuls of bread. Berek wore a swallowtail vested suit with silk-edged velvet lapels, and he carried a shovel. Soon Schall's brother-in-law drove up with his coach. Berek climbed in, gave the man precise instructions and, with precision and purpose, fell asleep.

Three hours later the driver shook him awake. In the grainy lantern light Berek saw weeds growing out of Varungy's cemetery wall, two feet from where the coach had stopped. Varungy itself had slipped away down the chute of darkness, just as Berek had intended. He wanted to see nothing of it, not even a mortar crumb from his dear, dead village—not even from the corner of his eye.

Without looking left or right, Berek headed straight for his parents' grave. He said Kaddish, placed a pebble on the headstone, took three steps to the left. That was where he had buried Varungy's true mezuzoth two months before. He began to dig with the shovel. Chestnut trees tossed leaves into the graveyard in gusts he couldn't feel. An owl hooted faraway memories. He used his humming as a shield against them.

A heavy branch had fallen from an oak, anchoring itself in the earth just above the fifth mezuzah. It didn't stop him. He pried it loose with the shovel handle and exhumed all six within the hour. On the way back in the coach he cleaned the mezuzoth and restored their gleam and would have returned in good time for the wedding except for one of the two bay horses. There was no problem while he scraped the earth off the mezuzoth. But when he began to polish, the hiss of the sandpaper upset the horse. Ten miles before Vienna it reared and sprained a knee and slowed them down to a hobble. As they finally limped into Turk Place, church bells tolled noon from the distance. Berek was an hour late. Rabbi Mayer, waiting, waiting, had licked his mustache wet in an effort to refresh his smile.

At Berek's emergence from the coach, the *chuppah*—the wedding canopy—went up. Berek had made it the previous week from the tricycle's canvas top, and its four poles were raised by a hired market hand, by Riddah, who wore her best white babushka, and by Siddo Berger and Schall, looking like twins in their morning coats rented at the same store. Prince Wallers's business steward sat in his carriage, arms akimbo, under a top hat. Boas hissed, twitched and grunted inside the black camera cloth; he had turned into five legs—his and the tripod's—that kept shifting about for an angle that would include all the essential elements in the picture.

During the entire waiting period nobody had bothered to present Rabbi Mayer to Prince Wallers's chief business steward, who stayed in the carriage. Still, regardless of circumstances, the rabbi remained stalwartly civil. He welcomed the tardy groom. He suggested that Berek brush the mud off his trousers. He obeyed when Boas shouted through the black cloth that the rabbi had better move nearer to the bridegroom for the preliminary photograph. He stood close to the groom even though the groom, for reasons best known to himself, exuded the smell of sweat through the swallowtail coat.

The rabbi was careful to say nothing critical even when he discovered that there was no customary marriage contract.

"I suppose we are ready to receive our princess," he said. And Riddah let out a lusty scream. "*Kalleh!*" . . . and then, translating, doubled the volume of her yell: "BRIDE! . . . hey, BRIDE!"

Tamarah came out of the door of No. 5 Turk Place. She wore the long white dress she had made, pieced out here and there with small laces. Her eyes looked down at the white cloth in her hands. Slowly, she walked toward Berek, who stood alone before the canopy. She circled him, slowly, seven times. Then she began to unroll the cloth. It was a long prayer shawl she herself had sewn. Berek and she wrapped themselves in it. Thus bound together, they stepped under the canopy, next to the chair on which the Brick rested. Berek gave his bride the ring he had forged from a nail. Tamarah took from her sleeve a little square of marzipan and gave it to her groom's tongue to sweeten his mouth. The ritual of union was accomplished—except for one thing as far as the rabbi was concerned. It developed that the glass the groom was to stamp into the ground at this point was missing. Riddah slapped herself resoundingly on the cheek. She broke into a guilty chortle that almost brought down the canopy. The glass had been her job and she had forgotten.

"Well, that really matters only in one sense," the rabbi said. "It's unfortunate only because without a broken glass we cannot symbolize our remembrance of the destruction of the Temple."

"That's all right, we have the Brick, so for us it's undestroyed," Berek said, kissing the bride. The rabbi's face had to remain amiable, for just then the five-legged camera-animal called through the black cloth and asked them to hold still and smile, for the main picture this time.

They did. Whereupon Berek said, "Excuse me." Before the rabbi's incredulous eyes he began to hammer something into a doorpost. At first the rabbi attempted to ignore the racket by inspecting the wedding presents, such as they were, displayed on Berek's "water main" along the gutter. Riddah had baked a big rye loaf in the form of a heart; it was not entirely complete, for during the wait for Berek, Riddah had nibbled off the tip of the heart to make sure the taste was right. Schall had laid down a nosegay of violets, which had always struck him as a Jewish sort of flower. Siddo Berger had brought two rolls of confetti for a note of cosmopolitan gaiety, but he had not dared throw them, so they also lay on the water pipe. Boas's contribution would be the wedding photograph twice exposed, the doubleness having been so successful with the market president. It wasn't ready yet; Boas had just run into his house to develop it. Meanwhile, the gift the rabbi found most commendable came from the Christian excellency who was being helped down from his carriage just then.

"Dear Frau Bang-Bang Spiegelglass," he said. "I have read your wedding announcement in the newspaper and I intrude shamelessly without an invitation."

Tamarah blushed and the rabbi took a step forward. "You could not be more welcome, sir," he said. "I take the liberty of saying that even though we have not been introduced. My name is Rabbi Otto Mayer—"

"Yes, yes," the steward said. "I rather prefer to attend weddings where I'm not invited because they're more interesting, like this one."

"Please let me call Berek," Tamarah said, but didn't have a chance to turn toward her hammering bridegroom. The steward pressed a gold coin into her palm.

"A Venetian ducat," he said. "Pawn it. Don't sell it. It'll have gone up in price by the time you get it back. And then you can pawn it for that much more. Help me up, Pepi."

"Bye-bye," the steward said while Pepi, the lackey, helped him back into the carriage. "Bye-bye, paperwork bride. Congratulations. He's loud, your lover, but he's sweet. Bye-bye."

Her mumbled thanks were lost under the clatter of coach wheels rolling away. Moments later Berek finished hammering, and Rabbi Mayer realized what all that noise had meant.

The rabbi would have accepted the absence of a wedding supper, which was, after all, one of the perquisites he had a right to count on. He would have accepted the absence of a marriage contract; the absence of the symbolically broken glass; the absence of elementary courtesies such as an introduction to His Excellency.

All that he was willing to tolerate without a word, for the sake of the occasion. But not what he saw and suspected now. He turned to Berek.

"Those objects you have just attached to the doorposts," he said. "They seem to be mezuzoth."

Berek nodded and handed the rabbi his fee of a gulden note, wrapped in the folded front page of the *Wiener Zeitung*.

"But you can't put up the mezuzoth *now*," the rabbi said.

"Actually, I wanted to do it before the wedding," Berek said. "But the horse limped and I was late."

"Herr Spiegelglass," the rabbi said. "One *never* attaches a mezuzah on the day one establishes a household in a building. One does that *only* in the Holy Land. Nowhere else! Surely you know that!"

"We have the Brick here," Berek said.

"You should take those mezuzoth down. I advise you to wait the obligatory thirty days before putting them up again."

"It's all right, we have the Brick here," Berek said.

Under his top hat the rabbi's hair tingled and stiffened. "You should realize what you are doing. You are saying this is not the diaspora. That's what such an action amounts to. You declare this . . . this place here Zion. Herr Spiegelglass, you have taken it on yourself to do away with Israel's exile. That is acting like God!"

"Look!" Boas was shouting as he ran out of his house. "This picture's even better than the market one!"

"It behooves me to tell you," the rabbi said to Berek, who made no move to unfasten the mezuzoth, "that the legitimacy of this ceremony today has been compromised—"

"Look!" Boas said and thrust the doubly exposed photograph at the two men. "But careful! It's still wet."

Wet and new, there shone in the noon breeze the wedding portrait doubly exposed: minarets sprouting from canopy poles, Tamarah's face mounted on a male cravat, and the rabbi himself with a nosegay for a head.

"You see," Berek said to the rabbi. "*There* is the Brick." And indeed the only detail in the picture that remained unambiguous and unscathed by the wild surrealism was Berek's hand touching the

Brick, fingers resting against its side so that the little scrolls wedged into its top would not be disturbed. "You see it?" Berek said.

The rabbi nodded—but not at Berek; rather at his own inward conclusion. He now recognized what this was: a deep-seated aberration that had overtaken all these Turk Place people. He would not be able to cure them at this point by creating a scene. They might use it to turn against him Prince Wallers's executive, who seemed to have a bizarre weakness for this crew.

"Yes, I do see," the rabbi said. "Good luck to you all. Details I have raised may have to be discussed later. The marriage certificate will be mailed to you in good time."

"I will photograph it, too!" Boas said.

VII

Once, carpentry sounds had come from Tamarah's virgin quarters down to Berek the bachelor. Now the sounds seemed to continue secretly into his life as a husband.

To get her place ready for marriage Tamarah had made simple changes in a simple room. The two single beds that had stood in opposite corners (one for her father, one for herself) she had combined into twin beds sharing a plain chestnut headboard. For Berek she had fashioned an equally plain night table and had given the easy chair a longer back. When Berek laid his hand on any of these things, he seemed to feel the pulse of those prebridal hammer blows, perhaps because her furniture, like live creatures, kept multiplying on the sly.

He still slept late. When he rose from bed, she was long gone, and he would see a new footstool before the easy chair. Or the washstand had suddenly developed a second and bigger basin so that he could do the vigorous splashing he liked. His coat no longer hung on a hook but on a hanger proportioned exactly to its size. All these new objects always felt warm, as though she'd just brought them in on tiptoe, seconds before he'd opened his eyes.

After a while he discovered a pattern, or rather suspected it. She never presented a new item unless he had been with her on her side of the bed the night before. Was that really more than a coincidence? He hesitated to ask. It would have been a violation of her reticence, that reticence of which her stutter was only the outermost ripple and which was fused into the deepest part of their bond, which made every touch of hers—her finger on his cheek for a split second after adjusting his collar—more dear.

So in the end, he never put the question. But he speculated. Sometimes he wondered if her new offering might be a sort of compensation. She could not give him as much ardor as she received on the pillow under that chestnut headboard. Their minutes of intimacy took place in a dark that was absolute and slightly smoky: she always snuffed out the candles a moment before. But through his kisses his lips knew that she kept her eyes steadily closed beneath him and that there was a little vertical wrinkle on her forehead that spoke more of resolute consent than of passion.

One evening in September she began the alphabet lesson by spelling out the word "child." It took him almost a minute to understand. Then she overrode both his kiss and her blush to return sternly to the loops of the letter *h*.

After this news their touching became, occasionally, different and deeper in the slightly smoky dark. During certain breakfasts he turned over on his tongue the memory that he had been able to entice her beyond mere compliance. Just on those mornings he would find yet another little convenience she'd crafted for him. Why? To put a "respectable" distracting surprise between him and that midnight memory?

Waking into a November day in 1873, he came on new lasts in his shoes. With his soles still warm from the made-by-Tamarah warmth, he drank the breakfast tea she had (as usual) ready for him. Since she averted her face from his drowsy thanks, he didn't notice that her cheeks, never ruddy, had turned paper-pale. The air was peculiarly mild for late fall, a mildness that continued the languor of bed even after Berek went to work at Turk Place No. 1.

Schall happened to be away at a machinery-supply house in the Inner City, pricing a toggle-joint press. It was a milestone of an errand. Berek had saved enough for his first "bought" machine. The Wallers's ball favors and the shah's medallions had been delivered and paid for. And despite the depression, Berek even had another order. The shah wanted 587 invitations incised on bronze to be sent to 587 sovereigns and potentates on all continents, requesting the honor of their company at the Teheran World's Fair in the coming year. Schall had already designed wedding-cake lettering afloat on a mist of arabesques.

The workshop in which such high summonses were to be produced was no longer a stable, not yet a factory. On hot days the huge space still exhaled a faint pungency of horse. In addition to the tricycle-wheel chandelier, and the smithy in one corner, it featured something like a heroic meat grinder—an approximation of a press, which Berek had strung together out of the last scraps of the tricycle organs.

Siddo Berger, in bow tie and vested suit, was the only worker in the place. An assistant-notary-public-but-for-the-depression, he refused to wear a mechanic's smock. He also refused to be deft when instructed to do a mechanic's work. For a trial run of the Persian invitations, Berek asked him to grease the makeshift press. Siddo put the oilcan to the wrong valve. This unsuitable touch seemed to recall to the machine its origins as a moving vehicle. Convulsively, it started away from Siddo's hands, hopped a yard and collapsed into a clanking heap.

A little later in the day Berek would have been angry. At 9 AM this was just the sort of thunderclap to wake him fully. No longer yawning but humming, he settled down to refashion the machine out of the shambles. The door flung open and he never even got to raise his hammer.

It was Tamarah, arms crossed over her stomach, one of her braids dangling wildly. A deep red had spread down her apron. Berek caught her just as she dropped.

In the General Hospital one hour later, after a crazed ride in an ambulance drawn by four whinnying horses and driven by a coachman who parted traffic with a trumpet, Berek stood before a Sister of Mercy. Her coif like a helmet, her habit stiff and imperious as white steel, the nurse barred the way to a door which had swallowed—how many minutes ago?—Tamarah on a stretcher. The only live thing about his wife had been the little vertical wrinkle trembling over a face that seemed to have become a gray dinner plate.

The nurse held out the wedding ring he'd made of a nail. She also had a piece of paper.

"This seems to be her only valuable," the nurse said. "Please sign that you received it."

"I want to see her!" Berek said.

"Now, now, the doctor is satisfied," the nurse soothed. "She'll be able to have other children. Sign here for the ring."

"I want to see her! She hasn't finished teaching me the alphabet!"

"She has to be cleaned up," the nurse said. "You may visit in two hours. If you don't at least sign with a mark, we can't give you the ring. We can't be responsible."

"Give it to her! It's hers!" Berek said.

He couldn't tolerate the waiting room, full of spittoons and broken faces. He had better things to do for Tamarah than just wait. Only when he was trying to leave the hospital did he realize that it consisted not just of a corridor but of an endless ambush of buildings, huge courtyards, withered parks crawling with wheelchairs—a whole malevolent universe full of ugly smells, white coats and coughs.

This was a vast trap that had been lying in wait for years. Some blunder had made him step into it, into a place where his baby would be stuffed as just another lump down some bloody trash can, and where his own Tamarah had come so close to a garbage death that she had to be "cleaned up."

The blunder must be undone. He stood in the street, in a breeze that had freshened and chilled since the morning. Urgently, it cut through his thin work smock. He began to run toward the Inner City.

A block before the office of the Jewish Council, he slowed to make his breath less high. In the anteroom he placed both his fists on the receptionist's desk. He had to know right away, he said, at what specific house on Turk Place outside the western city gate, at what specific building there, the Brick from the Wailing Wall had been deposited.

"Sir?" the receptionist said.

"The Turks," Berek said, "two hundred years ago, into what building did they put the Brick? It's essential!"

"Sir, maybe somebody else knows what you mean," the receptionist said.

After overcoming a variety of alarmed stares, upset eyebrows, closed doors and clerks looking very interrupted, Berek arrived before a gentleman who ducked his bald head into a file case, kept it there awhile, ducked it out again to mumble something about missing records and the only available reference to the matter stating that the designation "religious site" covered Turk Place period, no specific indication of a specific house.

"All right," Berek said. "So all of Turk Place is involved with the Brick."

"Brick," the baldhead said. "There is no specific indication of a brick—"

"I only own Number One Turk Place," Berek said. "I just rent the rest. That means I just rent most of the Brick. That's the trouble. I have to buy all of Turk Place when I can. Right now I must buy Number Five, where my wife just miscarried. How much is it?"

"Ah," the baldhead said, stunned by the mixture of obstetrics and real estate. Berek's fingernails were raking furrows into the blotter on his desk. "Calm yourself," the baldhead said. "You mean the amount necessary to purchase the premises?"

"Yes, how much? This is urgent. A family isn't possible for me until I own more of Turk Place. How much is Number Five?"

"I see, how much," the baldhead said. "One moment."

He immersed his face in another file. "It happens there is some current correspondence on the matter. It is under discussion."

Berek put both his fists on the man's desk. "Listen! I have to go see now how my wife is. But you better discuss it with *me*. You better write me about it, plain, to Turk Place. Remember, Turk Place by the western gate!"

"You have impressed it on my memory," said the man.

Three mornings later Berek found Tamarah sitting up in her bed in the General Hospital ward, asking for her embroidery kit. The nurse nodded. Berek said no—not because he meant it but because he loved the animation revived in the precious face, the force with which her still pale lips could argue. The next morning he brought her the kit. That afternoon, returning home, a letter for him lay on his anvil. He handed it to Schall to explain its meaning.

The letter was from the Jewish Council, and Schall summarized its message: The cooperative board of the market next to Turk Place wanted to buy Turk Place No. 5, intending to use the house eventually as administrative and weighing office. They had bid 500 gulden. The Jewish Council was willing to sell the house to Berek for 520 gulden. The offer would remain good for three days, and the signature was illegible.

"I can buy Number Five," Berek said. "We'll cancel the toggle-joint press."

"Wait a minute," Schall said. "They're delivering the press next week. They promised."

"With the refund I'll have just enough for Number Five."

"But we need the press," Schall said. "For the Persian invitations."

"There'll be other orders."

"But we have no other order," Schall said. "The crash! We'll lose the shah!"

"It'll be all right," Berek said. "Cancel the press."

"*Cancel*," Schall said. "I am sorry. No, no. This is too much now. I am very sorry. No more."

Schall marched off to his room at No. 5. A half hour later he came out with rain cape and satchel, his round cheeks flushed with a vehemence he had gotten from a bottle under his cot. He stopped at No. 1, where Berek was testing the reincarnated little makeshift press, Siddo Berger assisting.

Schall held on to the doorpost and said it was bad enough what Dr. Nassig had done. But this made it worse. It destroyed all prospects. It was the last straw. He didn't give a damn the last straw had to happen just when Frau Spiegelglass was unwell. Nobody around here gave a damn about *him*. About his, Schall's, domestic prospects. There was a wonderful young lady. She came from a family with a harpsichord, she could play Schubert without sheet music. She drank only beverages that could be sipped with a straw. He wanted to offer her the kind of home someone like her deserved. And he would never be able to do that here. He was sick of fighting the craziness here. Nobody believed him, nobody ever listened to him, and it didn't matter anymore; the greatest mistake of his life was over.

"Turk Place is no mistake," Berek said. "Have some coffee, Schall."

Schall didn't want coffee. He had given up trying to light a cigarette with one hand only. His other hand, with which he'd steadied himself against the door, let go. He gave a stiff, enormous bow and wandered off across the empty drill ground, following an erratic but solemnly turned path visible to himself alone.

"It'll be all right. He'll come back," Berek said to Siddo Berger, who less than one hour later gave notice, too. There was no point staying with a "factory" that had no funds for wages or equipment.

Berek went on humming. Nothing mattered, for next morning he brought home his Tamarah. He carried her upstairs against her slightly stammering protest, gentled her down into the easy chair on whose flat arm stood a bunch of welcoming violets in a vase so overwatered that—against *his* protests now—she rose instantly to pour off the excess even as she smiled her thanks.

After a couple of days Schall did come back. He appeared in front of No. 1 with the same satchel, a very sober face, a letter and a strained clearing of his throat.

"Good day," he said. "This is just to deliver something."

"Good day," Berek said. "Come in, Schall."

"I have been asked to hand this over," Schall said. "From Prince Wallers's business steward."

The envelope was of such weighty paper it felt like a linen napkin in Berek's hand. He broke open the scarlet seal and gave the sheet inside to Tamarah. Since he refused to let her out of his sight for fear she would return too soon to her heavier chores, she had to do her embroidery next to him in his workshop.

"*Dear Mr. Bang-Bang,*" Tamarah read aloud. "*A last word on my last day in office, which is just as well because my liver is now impossible and my liege lord Wallers, whose family used to crenellate three castles every generation, will now smear across God's good earth six hundred and thirty new tenements from the city gate to your anointed Turk Place and possibly beyond. The crash has done away with most of the tenement smearers we supplied, and so we will do the smearing ourselves, which kills a dainty saint like me. But to the point—*"

"What?" Berek said.

"Please, now comes the important part," Schall said.

"*But to the point,*" Tamarah read on. "*Your Schall has come to me about his Dr. Massive, whose name I no doubt misspell but the cleverness of whose evil almost exhilarates me past my pain—*"

"He means Dr. Nassig," Schall said. "You see? He believes me!"

"*—past my pain,*" Tamarah read on. "*Now, in my present torment any man with a genuine hellish villain is a man I like to encourage. Therefore, dear Bang-Bang, let us help your Schall. Give my successor in office a statement confirming that your Schall has indeed designed the ball favors you produced. This will procure your Schall the job of designing the ornamentations that are to wreathe the blueprint sheets for our tenements, pretty plans for ugly smearing being nobe . . . noblesse oblige.*"

Tamarah's stammer, which never bothered her while reading aloud, returned with the foreign words of whose pronunciation she was unsure.

"I did not ask for his request," Schall said.

"There is more," Tamarah said. "*As for you, Bang-Bang, I've made a mistake in not taking advantage of you. I should have tried, you would have kicked, I would have let go, satisfied that you're a provincial little prig not worth the trouble. Now I am unsatisfied and you are deluded. Why are you deluded? Because I have handed you favors without asking for any in return. This is no way to instruct you in the way of the world, and a gravely misleading example. There is nothing blinder than the uncorrupted. Start to see. If you ever have some extra cash, my successor's mind is as open as his palm. If you ever have some extra zinc, my successor's wife has loved zinc roses ever since she saw a silver one in milady Wallers's anteroom, which is as far into heaven as she ever got. God help me, I'll soon get much farther into another direction. Much too far even to hear your bang-banging, you stubborn, blue-eyed Jew-slob, or to remember that little black lock of yours I snipped. It's the only Bang-Bang piece that won't go stale. The rest of you will wrinkle and bloat and crumple, thank God, for that makes it easier to say good-bye. Good-bye. F. von L."*

"He even gets sick in a funny way," Berek said. "I don't like him."

"I didn't ask him for it," Schall said, "but he means, please write me a letter of reference."

"Tamarah will write it," Berek said. "Let's go to Number Five, Schall. Look at your apartment."

"My apartment?" Schall said.

"I'll show you," Berek said.

He showed him. During Schall's absence Berek had converted the former Nassig office into a parlor-kitchenette similar to his own upstairs—a sociable chamber with furniture Boas had bartered for baked goods: a walnut table, scratched but shining and aromatic with lemon oil; three chairs that almost matched; and a stately cast-iron stove that had a stack of tiles for its fourth leg.

"Of course, your bride can make changes," Berek said.

"My bride," Schall said. "Well. In point of fact." He recleared his throat and shook his head because the tobacco pouch in which his fingers groped was empty. "Her father said, only someone with a steady future in these times. Only a municipal employee, nobody from beyond city limits. Now she's got some lamplighter hanging about."

"There'll be a steady future here," Berek said. "The blueprint job at Wallers isn't steady?"

"A lamplighter!" Schall said. "No, the damn blueprints are just piecework. Ninety heller apiece. They said maybe twelve pieces a month."

"All right, you do those on the side," Berek said. "You live here rent-free and you work with us again."

"Thank you," Schall said. "What work? Did you really cancel the big press?"

"Of course," Berek said.

"And the Persian shah order? It's canceled?"

"Of course," Berek said and told Schall that his wife was now embroidering petit point handbags for some of Princess Wallers's ladies-in-waiting and that he was making embossed brass frames for the bags.

"How many bags?" Schall said.

"Eleven," Berek said. "It's nice smithy work."

"But you can't live on eleven. You can never buy machines with that. And you still owe installments on Number Five! If at least there'd be rent coming in. You ought to look for tenants!"

"That'll come too," Berek said.

"But it's too far away from town! They won't run a tramway until it's all built up around here. You see?"

"It'll be all right," Berek said.

"You don't see?" Schall said.

"Don't worry," Berek said. "Put down your satchel."

Schall put down his satchel and worried for years. The others on Turk Place were busy with other things. Boas began exchanging photographs for food; he never failed to return from the market with a basket full of lettuce, carrots and goat cheese. By night Riddah sang and baked more rye loaves now than they could eat. The proceeds from the surplus, together with Tamarah's embroidery, paid for the rest of their vegetable stew. Berek smithied his handbag frames; while that lasted there was beef on Friday nights. Schall designed tendriled vines around the blueprints; his ninety hellers apiece sufficed for smoked pork, cabbage and pilsner once a week at the tavern. But most of the day Schall and Berek worked at making furniture to fill the rooms of the houses at Turk Place, planing, nailing, riveting briskly but without profit or tangible sense. Often it seemed to Schall that those six buildings were wavering in the breeze as Dr. Nassig's mirage and that he wasted his best years on the polishing of a void. Schall worried.

Schall worried while Berek continued to prettify the emptiness. From his only two "factory" orders so far—the ball favors and the Persian medals—a good deal of scrap metal was left. Berek melted and hammered various pieces into ornamental grillwork. Then he affixed it to ground-floor windows: handsome protection for residents who did not exist. Schall worried.

Schall worried because no pipeline linked Turk Place to the gas mains of the capital. Yet Berek asked Schall to sketch out for him some gas lanterns "in Turk Place style." Schall shook his head and wet his pencil. The sketches before him, Berek hummed at the anvil, incandescing metal shreds, fusing and sculpting the debris. After some weeks of that Berek installed three lantern posts on Turk Place. Fluted and fretted, each of their joisted glass heads was topped by a slender minaret. He didn't mind that their flames were as phantom as the tenants whose way they lit. Every time he passed one of his lantern posts, he stroked it as one might stroke a sacred tree. "It'll give good light," he said to Schall.

"To whom?" Schall asked, because he worried.

"People," Berek said.

"What people?" Schall said.

But there was no point even asking such questions. Shortly after that conversation Tamarah Spiegelglass began to put flower boxes on all the windows of Turk Place, including those that looked out of uninhabited rooms. The boxes grew hanging carnations whose shoots she watered daily and trained down the walls. They were green dust catchers. For just then a dust cloud imposing as a mountain had risen up to the east of Turk Place. On the site of the drill ground, construction of the Wallers tenement had begun. It did not stop day or night and was soon compounded by a rival project (financed, Schall read, by an Anglo-American trust) to the north and west of the market. A constant distant echo of shouts and thuds surrounded Turk Place. Even on windless days an ash-colored powder appeared like a fine glaze of frost on walls, panes, roofs and particularly on the window-box flowers.

People came from the cloud. The first time Berek saw them he was on a ladder fixing a molding on No. 2. The people came closer. They removed oil-stained caps and waited for Berek to come down. They stood there, trousers tied with cord, cigarettes burned down to a desperate edge from which smoke veered sharply as if these men traveled, even while immobile, at a helpless speed. One of them had a leaflet. He gave it to Berek with a little bow.

Berek could not really read it. Tamarah had not resumed alphabet lessons after the hospital. He did recognize the design of the lettering. He looked at the door to the workshop where Schall stood, but at that moment Schall retreated. Berek turned back to the men and said in angry High German, *"What do you want?"*

They tried to answer him in German, though they were obviously Balkan peasants. They attempted the consonants of the boss language, looking down hard at the ground as if afraid it would abandon them. Because of the very harshness of Berek's question they did not dare come to the point. They began with explanations, they mumbled digressions. Their farms had been yanked away, from right under their boots, by banks whose names they couldn't pronounce, because of arrears they didn't understand. They'd come to Vienna to earn food, to find a foothold, but the earth would not stay in place. Everything kept shifting. Sometimes they hauled stones for the Wallers project by the western gate. Sometimes they carried bricks in the east of town, where textile mills were being built, or in the south, where shoe factories were going up. The labor contractors piled them onto horsecarts that took off in unpredictable directions. Their families camped along the Danube under canvas shelters that would no longer be there when the horsecarts brought them back. The tent alleys always regrouped during the day to make room for new arrivals. The evening was full of screeching women, wives screaming their husbands' names to guide them "home."

And now they wanted a real home. They pointed at the leaflet.

"I'm sorry," Berek said. "We have nothing for you now."

He folded the leaflet in two, then tore it in two along the folded line, letting one fragment drop.

They looked down to where it fell. They looked up at Turk Place: the solid grillwork guards of its ground-floor windows, the minarets, the shiny new lanterns with their flutings. They lowered their eyes to the earth that had started stampeding again. A rush of wind killed the glow of their stubs. As they put on their caps, they were blown away.

Berek went into the workshop. Schall stood just behind the door, hands shoved into his pockets, ready.

"You made this leaflet," Berek said.

"It's a favor from the father of a very nice young lady," Schall said. "He has a first-class print shop."

"You didn't tell me you had this printed."

"You told me there'd be tenants. They don't come by themselves."

"The right ones will," Berek said.

"These could be right!" Schall said. "For now, they could. They could double up, triple up, three, four families in one flat. We could fill up every room! They could pay something! We could pay for the machines we need—"

"The machines will come."

"Without money?" Schall said. "Without money I can't even say 'good day' to the new Wallers steward! We have no orders—"

"No more such leaflets."

"Don't you want tenants?"

"They'll lose their jobs," Berek said. "There'll be no rent. It'll cost us more than it brings in. It'll just mess up Turk Place."

"But you won't get any better kind out here," Schall said. "What are you waiting for? Some millionaire from Varungy?"

"The first new tenant here will be my son."

Schall took his hands out of his pockets. *"Your son?"*

"Yes," Berek said.

"You mean to say? I didn't know! Congratulations!"

"Not yet," Berek said. He crumpled the rest of the leaflet. "When she is pregnant again, then you congratulate. Then we can see about other tenants."

"Only then?"

"Only then," Berek said. "Because they'll come with children. Before then I don't want to see children here. Not other people's."

"But listen, Spiegelglass," Schall said. "Are you really going to wait on the chance—"

"It's not just chance."

"But how do you know . . ." Schall said. "I mean, the joyful event, how can you be sure it will happen?"

"You can make sure," Berek said. And he let the crumpled paper drop.

The day the two made sure, they put on their good dark clothes. It was a Christian holiday and they decided to take time out, though work continued at the tenement site even on Corpus Christi Day. They walked a good stretch south of that toil cloud, toward the tram that would take them to the Prater fairgrounds. Berek went arm in arm with Tamarah; his right hand held the Brick.

It was June, yet so gusty it could have been March. The wind seemed to have scooped up a whole throng of bell-ringing echoes, bells from all the city's churches. A mass of spectators spilled across the tram stop, the men waving their boaters, the women tossing flowers at the Corpus Christi procession, whose heart seemed to be passing just then. Berek caught whispers about the poor cardinal having to hold the heavy monstrance in the wind, and how the field marshal needed a cane this year, and why the archdukes followed the Knights Hospitalers instead of preceding them as usual.

The Spiegelglasses, standing too far back, heard more than they saw. They glimpsed only saluting hands, brocaded church flags thudding in the gusts like heavy sails, and, between flags and hands, a succession of plumed hats floating like birds against a backdrop of old palace walls.

It was the festival of a God other than Berek's. Yet the hundred bells heaving heaved for him, too. Their heavy music tolled a glory, a continuity, a purpose that must end with the shout of a child on Turk Place.

Suddenly, the sidewalks emptied. Of the procession only horse droppings and petals were left in the gutter. Tamarah picked up a geranium shoot she put in her pocketbook to plant later in one of the window boxes. The tram came, and when they got off at the fairgrounds, half the sky was encircled by the giant new Ferris wheel.

The wheel was impossible to miss, but it also seemed impossible to reach in the chaos, the brass-band blare, the shouts and sizzles of hot-sausage stands. Tamarah took a newspaper clipping out of her pocketbook. The advertisement said that the Ferris wheel, erected on the site of an exhibit of the Seven Modern Wonders, was a wonder itself since it was Europe's biggest, from whose top you could view the glaciers of the Alps as well as the plains of Slovakia for two hellers per seat. You could get to the admission booth from the tram stop by heading for the cannibals' kraal, walking past the balloon-borne midgets at Aeronautica, before turning left at the frigate of Grimmo the Pirate.

Dozens of people clogged the entrance. But Berek managed to attract the attendant's attention by raising a twenty-heller coin. He told the man's ear that he wanted to take all eight seats in a car and did not expect change. Minutes later he and Tamarah curved toward the sky in a small railroad carriage all their own.

The wild air made their car creak and tremble. After a while their ascent became more quiet. When they were high enough to look for Turk Place, they couldn't find it. They strained their eyes westward beyond spires, beyond cupolas and domes, beyond the enormous gray courtyards of the General Hospital, but they did not see a trace of their street. The horizon had sucked it away. Where it should have been was an oval of brown mist, next to something like a titans' cemetery that had been vandalized and from which giant skeletons now rose in revenge.

Tamarah clung to her husband. He told her what it must be: Those huge bones were scaffoldings from the Wallers tenement project; the brown mist was construction dust that had been driven by the wind across Turk Place. As he talked, their carriage traveled yet higher. Through its eastern window they could glimpse the Danube arcing away into the green horizon of Slovakia, under a sky whose fierce blue was uncompromising except for a single cloud.

By that time the car was mounting the wheel's highest point. For the sake of that point they had come: From here they could see both Turk Place and Varungy at once. Tamarah removed the lid from the Brick box. Berek kept staring at the cloud, which remained anchored exactly above the spot where Varungy had once been. It was a small cloud, but it looked rosy-warm, solid, touchable, and had features as distinct as a familiar face. A massive little sky-borne village, turrets spiking huddled roofs, it kept floating in place. It was Turk Place, chiseled of pink weightless marble, suspended like Varungy's soul over dead Varungy.

Berek pointed out the resemblance, and Tamarah nodded as if she'd already noticed. She pulled pencil and notepad from her pocketbook and now placed his index finger on the wrist of her writing hand so that he could participate in the shaping of the sentence. *"Please God the Eternal,"* they wrote in the railroad car, 280 feet up in the air, *"let us have a healthy child."*

The message was in the Brick, and the Brick rested in the box, by the time they descended. Down on earth the crowds seemed much more convivial now. Tamarah pointed out a sign saying PROHASKA'S ICES, and Berek remembered Schall raving about Prohaska's raspberry sherbet. He bought one for Tamarah, one for himself, and loved the faint blush on her cheeks during the unwonted frivolity of licking an ice. Suddenly, he felt they were stumbling into the honeymoon they'd never had. He took her into the beer garden next door. Only by looking at each other very hard could they keep back a smile at the bartender's grimace when they ordered only seltzer. They danced the polka with the Brick box between them as if it were a third member of the family. They went into another beer garden, and this time they had to turn away chuckling when another bartender made exactly the same "seltzer" face. They danced again and decided to have a supper consisting of nothing but every ice flavor Prohaska offered. When they'd finished with apricot, it was late. A tremendous line had formed for the tramway, for which there was no more money in Berek's pocket anyway.

And so they walked home, clear across town, striding from twilight into night, past the city's fantastic changes, from medieval grottoes to bravura plazas to flat, low masonry, to the dust cloud over the Wallers construction site, to the minarets of Turk Place; and the marvel, though not the day's final one, was that they felt barely tired.

They went to their apartment upstairs. A gleam new to Berek came from Tamarah's eyes. With a forthrightness still more unfamiliar she gave a little head shake when he wanted to light the candle on his night table. She lit only the one on hers and turned away as she undid her hair. From the way she blew out the flame he knew that this time she would not just lie there waiting to be clasped.

Afterward, they didn't go to sleep. He heard her pull on her clothes in the dark. She then went to the *Kabinett,* the small chamber next door. He'd always stayed away from it, ever since she had returned from the hospital, because of the cradle stored there. For so long it had stood in that room in vain. Yet, having dressed, too, there was no way not to follow her.

She sat close to it—the Lower Austrian painted peasant cradle Boas had bartered for a name-day photograph after she had become pregnant. Now Tamarah was measuring a finely textured white blanket against its length.

"You can take care of *that,*" she said. She pointed to a cross daubed in pink on the cradle's side.

"Tamarah!" he said, hoping to be amazed.

"No, not yet," she said. "But you can take care of that meanwhile." As he took out his jackknife to scratch away the Christian sign, she began to cut the blanket to the cradle's size.

From then on it became a habit lasting for years. After Berek and Tamarah had been together on her pillow, they would dress and go to the "son's room" next door. Tamarah had stopped giving him alphabet lessons after the miscarriage. But in this room they had other work. The Brick box lay in the cradle there, tucked under the blanket. They sat to the left and right of it. Tamarah knitted tiny wool jumpers and hemmed a coverlet of white cotton. Berek whittled a rattle, sized for a six-month-old's fist. Together the couple kept pace with the growing up of whoever would be their child. Tamarah sewed a burlap pattern and stuffed it with straw until it became a snub-nosed teddy bear ready to delight a tot past his first year. Still later Berek dragged a huge wooden block upstairs. In the son's room his knife began to shave the block into a rocking horse. As soon as the boy was man enough to mount it a little gong in its mouth would sound.

The son's room was locked; their nocturnal work was inside, a secret. By the son's-room hour Schall had long retired to his flat downstairs. Boas was in bed across the street. Only Riddah knew, after she'd knocked on the door one night.

Riddah's capacious hips were designed to bear many babies. Still, it seemed natural to her that her womb slept through the years, as if in sympathy with Tamarah's. Meanwhile, her baking had expanded. She had an assistant now: Susi, daughter of one of the market's potato vendors, a bulky white-blond albino whose skin blistered after ten minutes in the sun. Destined for night work, she became Riddah's moonlight assistant. Riddah taught her the arts of mixing and kneading dough, of molding and baking and of the cordial cursing of fowl. She sang out instructions, encouraging Susi to memorize recipes through chants. The girl, with her alto voice, learned as melodiously as her mistress once had under Boas.

Sweating and singing with Susi, Riddah had developed a new braided poppy-seed roll she wanted to sell to the construction gangs. "Taste," she said to Tamarah that night when she entered what she didn't know yet as the son's room. She stuck a bit of roll into Tamarah's mouth—and only then noticed the couple's work by the cradle.

"Ha! Wonderful!" she said, throwing her arms around Tamarah. "Why didn't you tell me?"

Tamarah couldn't answer, for the force of the hug had knocked the roll down her throat. "There's nothing yet," Berek said. "We're just preparing."

"Say, I'll prepare with you," Riddah said. And sure enough, the next week when she saw candles flickering in that certain window at No. 5, she promptly tramped into the son's room. Out of her apron pocket she pulled a hollow slice of beef bone and a flour-caked metal file. She flopped down on the floor next to Tamarah and clacked the file against her teeth. "Big ones, huh?" she said. "Mine's going to have fangs like a wolf." She began to shape the bone into a teething ring, but very soon savage cackling broke out in the dark street. "My damn little idiots!" she said, running to the door. Her cooks were squabbling.

She could never join the Spiegelglasses for more than a few minutes, either because she had to slap some peace into the roosters, who had a tendency to fight in her absence, or because she had to bawl out the albino for overbaking the crescents. There was never enough time. Each night at 3 AM two wicker baskets full of fresh, hot rye loaves and crisply ridged rolls had to be ready for sale to the construction gangs coming off the night shift. The two young women would heft the baskets onto their shoulders and march off into the wee hours, singing.

The press of nighttime business left Riddah little margin for work on the teething ring. When she finished at last, the two roosters following her were the grandsons of those she'd brought from Varungy, hatched by hens kept in back of No. 6.

It never occurred to Berek that he and Tamarah were patient in their hope. Not even when Schall finally cleared his throat during one of their Friday afternoon drinks.

"Spiegelglass," he said. "You see, I don't remember anymore. But what was the exact date of your marriage?"

"July 2 in 1873," Berek said. "Why?"

"This unusual young lady," Schall said. "She's the niece of the cathedral apothecary. She only drinks jasmine tea and her brother is a Dominican friar. Next week the brother is going to make the pilgrimage to Mariazell, and she's going to ask him to include you among his supplications."

"What do you mean?" Berek said.

"He's going to include your fulfillment," Schall said.

"My fulfillment?"

"He's going to pray for your family fulfillment," Schall said. "But he needs particulars like the marriage date."

"Thank you," Berek said. "That's very nice. But we've already made sure about fulfillment. We don't need anything in addition."

VIII

B y the summer of 1879 Tamarah was sewing leather and Berek fashioning the buckle for a valise. They were making a schoolbag for the child to come. Work continued apace in the son's room—not in the rest of Turk Place.

A long time had passed since the last order for handbag frames or, for that matter, for Tamarah's embroideries. Neither Prince Wallers's new steward nor the princess's ladies-in-waiting provided any business. The factory remained machineless. Schall went back to designing and hawking horoscopes. Boas had lost most of his customers: with the market cut off from its trade by the building site, the vendors could no longer afford a luxury like photographs. Too little income dribbled in from Riddah's roll peddling. The money stopped and the rats arrived.

Turk Place was now surrounded by labyrinth after labyrinth of baroque barracks, raw exteriors completed, still empty and yet alive with scrabbling and scurrying. It had started—so Schall heard—with a mass of mummified flesh dug up by a pile driver just south of the former drill ground. A heap of Janissary corpses from the Turkish siege had no sooner been found than devoured. And now the rats, sated and multiplied, poured upward from fundaments and ditches. To each tenement one small ornamental balcony had been allotted, held up by an undraped Juno. Now rats climbed the cement breasts, wandered through warrens of narrow two-room flats, scuttled out the still paneless windows and down gargoyled drainpipes. Rat droppings dappled the giant concrete lilies flanking many a house entrance.

Actually, the rats were part of a buoyant ferment running through Vienna. The whole city resonated to the triumph in Bosnia-Herzegovina. This was a region so deep in the Balkans, so far beyond Varungy, that Berek had never heard of it. But Schall—who had also become much more animated lately—knew all about it from the *Wiener Zeitung*. He explained it frequently to Berek: Bosnia et cetera was this rotting Turkish province under the infidel sultan, full of chaos and corruption. Habsburg troops had fought gloriously to bring some Christian order into the murk down there. They had proved to the world that Austria was as vital as ever, that the bad aftereffects of the crash had long passed, that the time had come for a new spirit and bold moves. Sure, factory business was so-so, but that had never fazed Spiegelglass before—certainly it shouldn't now, with good news definitely ahead. So what was the matter with Spiegelglass?

Schall had reason to ask. A reversal appeared to have taken place between the partners. Just when Schall grew confident, why did Berek grow wary? What *was* the matter with Spiegelglass?

Two mornings before Schall repeated this question with special insistence, an envelope had arrived from the Jewish Council: "'*Because of the brightening real estate climate*'"—Tamarah read the letter aloud to Berek before their dinner together—"'*and because of the urbanization of the area outside the former western gate, there has been an increasing interest in the premises of Turk Place. Therefore, in accordance with the first-refusal courtesy extended to Herr Berek Spiegelglass in the past, the council hereby makes known that a bid has been entered for two of the four buildings remaining in the Jewish Council's possession. The bid is in the amount of 1,300 gulden for houses No. 2 and No. 4 at Turk Place and will be accepted unless Herr Spiegelglass decides to top it within five days. Faithfully,*' signature illegible."

After years of sweating over his anvil; after overcoming the Gypsies along with other troubles; after hundreds of weeks of scrimping and meatless dinners—after all that, Berek had accumulated a chunk of banknotes wrapped in one of Riddah's small sugar bags and kept by the Brick box in the cradle. The bills added up to 1,252 gulden. Forty-eight too few.

That was what was the matter with Berek Spiegelglass. Berek had to confess it to his partner. But Schall was in much too good a mood.

"Forty-eight gulden?" he said. "That's nothing."

It was the week Schall had bought, from a pawnbroker, a star-shaped glass ashtray on which had been incised the blazons of the imperial capital. Whenever he smoked a store-rolled cigarette—he now indulged in those on select occasions—out came the little glass star from his breast pocket.

"Less than nothing by 10 AM tomorrow morning," Schall said. "I'm not at liberty to tell details before then. Actually, yes, I'll tell one thing. Certain arrangements have been made. This street will be the first to have gaslight around here. The first street outside the big projects—how do you like that?"

"That's nice," Berek said. "Arrangements? With who?"

"It's what I'm not at liberty to tell." Schall writhed deliriously under the constraint. "Arrangements arrived at the day before yesterday, which will be made definite tomorrow." Schall tapped a fine smidgeon of ash into the glass star. "This young lady I know," he said. "Her uncle is opening a winehouse tonight. A glass of Kremser and a puszta sausage free to anyone invited. You and your wife, would you care to join us? Sort of in precelebration?"

"Thank you, but I have a headache," Berek said.

He wanted to be with Tamarah that night. Afterward, he and she finished making the school valise for their future son. And he really did develop a headache. He still had forty-eight gulden too few to save Turk Place Nos. 2 and 4. Despite the herb tea Tamarah made for him, he could not fall asleep until long after midnight. Next morning, walking into the workshop after nine, he found Schall waiting with another man.

The man was massively cravatted and bellied and stood with one arm akimbo. Schall introduced him as Herr Scherschny of the

Municipal Gas Works. Herr Scherschny said he wanted to acquaint Herr Spiegelglass with the embedment schedule in the Western Region.

"Which schedule?" asked Berek. And heard that the schedule called for the evacuation of Turk Place for two days starting Wednesday. During this period the gas main was to be laid and the new metropolitan gas lanterns would be put up.

"But we already have our own Turkish-style lanterns," Berek said, "and we never evacuate Turk Place."

"You see?" Schall said to the gas personage. "I knew he'd want to keep his lanterns."

"We can accommodate only so far," the gas personage said. "My men are equipped to handle only standard lanterns."

"Your men won't work here anyway," Berek said. "We'll embed the gas main ourselves."

The gas personage put his other arm akimbo, too.

"This is a special place," Berek said. "It had special fundaments built during the Turkish siege. They might collapse on you if you don't know them."

The gas personage said in that case Berek would have to assume all responsibility.

"In addition, we want to lay underground traps against vermin, to protect Turk Place," Berek said. "We'll do it ourselves."

The gas personage said he would have the pipe and other material delivered there Monday. By Thursday next, at the latest, the main had to be embedded, ready for inspection, for connection to the next segment, this was a modern utility and not a matter of whim, good day.

"It's not at all a whim, good day," Berek said.

"Don't worry," Schall said when they were alone. "Herr Misch can handle him if he makes more problems."

"Herr Misch? The new Wallers business steward?"

"All right." Schall glistened. "The cat is out of the bag." With meaningful slowness, with a ceremonial smile, he pulled a folded

piece of paper from his trouser pocket. "I might as well show you
before Misch comes. That way the meeting will go faster."

"Meeting?"

"Look at this." Schall had unfolded the paper. It was a typical
Schall design, made of fine feathery pencil strokes. "Recognize it?"

"It looks like the emperor's eagle," Berek said.

"Of course, but what's in that claw? An owl! The Bosnian crest!
Our eagle is carrying the Bosnian owl in its claw. You see? A victory
badge. Everybody will want it! Our soldiers triumphant in Bosnia-
Herzegovina. A surefire seller. First run of at least ten thousand, on
sale at every tobacconist! What do you say?"

"Someone could do all right with it."

"Someone?" Schall said. "Us! We'll use cheap ten-millimeter
brass, stamped in bas-relief—"

"I can't buy a stamping machine," Berek said. "I've got to use
my capital to fight that Turk Place bid. I'm still forty-eight gulden
short—"

"You'll get an interest-free loan," Schall said. "Plus half a ton of
brass on credit, all from Herr Misch—"

"Why from Herr Misch?"

"Remember yesterday?" Schall danced around him gloriously.
"Didn't I say something was in the works? Misch's going to tell you
himself any minute! He'll be here at ten."

"When did this happen?"

"Three days ago! That's when we laid the groundwork, him and
me! All you have to do, on your side, is not drive up the price of
Nos. 2 and 4—"

"You're talking about Turk Place," Berek said.

"Yes," Schall said. "You see, it would only be to our advantage if
he personally bought into local property. For a man in his position
to acquire an interest here—"

"*He's* the one?" Berek said. "*He* put in that bid at the Jewish
Council?"

"Well, you see, he wants to be in business for himself. You can't
blame him, something on the side, not just killing himself for the
Wallers lordships day and night. And it makes such solid sense to
establish an inn at No. 2 and No. 4 combined. An ideal location

when all the construction is finished and the workers move in. The proletariat likes to drink. And in exchange for your not driving up the price—"

Berek was shaking his head with a precision that stopped Schall in mid-sentence.

"No outside owners at Turk Place," Berek said. "No taverns and no drunks."

"Wait," Schall said. "That'll be all right. I told him you have special feelings about that, like with the gas lanterns. So he'll take half ownership as long as you don't counterbid to drive up the price—"

"I will drive it up," Berek said. "I'll take out a loan."

"But this is unreasonable," Schall said. "Let me explain—"

"No split ownership. Otherwise, I can't have a family here."

"Spiegelglass! This is such a chance!"

Through the open door Berek saw Tamarah on the other side of the street. She had begun to paint the window guards of Turk Place No. 2.

"Herr Misch will fix it so we get metal on credit from the Wallers mines. The lordships won't even know—"

"I'm sorry," Berek said.

"Wait," Schall said. "This is no good. We're getting too excited. Let's sit down, nice and cool. Look at the facts before he comes."

Berek began to bend the wires around the opening of a small cage. It was a trap to protect the Brick room against rats.

"There's time to talk it out," Schall said, listening to the quarter-after-ten bells. "He'll be late. He's already late. He might be quite a while yet. You know, he's busy, pulling everything together for such an undertaking. Come on. Sit down, Spiegelglass."

Berek bent wires.

"You see, it wasn't really a secret from you," Schall said. "Because he's such a hard man to reach there was nothing definite. It was all vague, just hints, till I nailed him down Wednesday. I didn't want to bother you till then. You've been so funny lately. But now it's sure. That's him coming now."

The white paint Tamarah brushed on the window guards of No. 2 was exactly the color she had painted on the guards less than a year ago, color barely faded. She inclined her head sideward in concentration. Her hand moved with such steady, graceful purpose that Berek, forty feet away, sensed the sharp fragrance of the paint as well as the nutmeg tang of her hair under the pale blue headcloth. He breathed in that double scent. It strengthened his fingers as he bent the wire.

"You'll find out Herr Misch is really a nice man," Schall said. "So easy to talk to, once you're in a deal with him. We had two beers together. He's not like that old high-falutin' count before him. This is a man like us—"

"I'm sorry," Berek said, eyes fastened on his wife.

"Very well." Schall began to fold, in very sharp creases, the paper with his sketch of the Bosnian victory badge. "Something should be understood before Herr Misch arrives. He needs a designer with my experience. Any inn he opens will be quality. He will need specially designed dishes and napkins. I might be forced to make my own arrangements."

Berek watched Tamarah.

"Wonderful opportunities are waiting in the world," Schall said. "Bigger than any dinky six houses. Bigger than waiting forever for a baby—"

"*Schall? Spiegelglass?*"

A lackey's voice called down from a gig which had stopped before the workshop.

"Ah, Misch is so busy, arrangements have to be consummated in his office," Schall said, walking away. "I'll inform him of your decision. Good luck."

But Berek, rat trap in hand, strode forward, too. "I'll inform him myself, to stay away from Turk Place." He let Schall get into the carriage first. Meanwhile, he walked over to Tamarah and gently took her hand, the one that held the brush. He had her stroke a bit of paint onto the wire of the cage, to take the scent along.

The carriage drove into the tenement project and stopped.

"But this isn't the steward's office," Schall said.

The lackey pointed to a hole in the unpaved gutter. A ladder stuck out of it like the nose of a mole.

"You mean, he's down there?" Schall said.

Three minutes later they stood in a burrow whose vastness

touched Berek through the breeze on his cheek, whose darkness was split and cracked by lantern beams.

"JesusMariaandJoseph!" Schall whispered. "Prince Bertram Wallers! . . . His picture was in the *Salon Journal*! He gave the hunt ball for the diplomats!"

A man in blue livery parted the black, carrying a lantern and a rifle; then came another with two lanterns, and then a thin bespectacled young man under a green hat, with a green cape and gray-green breeches. The lackey who had brought Berek and Schall gave them a slight push forward.

"Serenity," the lackey said among echoing footfalls. "These are Schall and Spiegelglass."

"Who? Yes, the Bosnian hooray people," the green man said. "The Bosnian hooray badges. That order is canceled."

"Serenity!" said Schall with a bow that was lost in the dark, for the green man had walked on, with all the lanterns following him. Schall had to run to catch up. "Serenity," he said, holding on to Berek's arm. "Canceled? Herr Misch—"

"Canceled," the green man said. "It never existed, isn't to be talked about, never ever, I can't be embarrassed by it when I start ambassadoring in St. Petersburg."

"But, Serenity," Schall said. "Your business steward, Herr Misch—"

"Misch's canceled as of yesterday, good-bye when we found him out," the green man said. "No more middle-class finagling. My brothers are taking over management, might as well do the messing up ourselves." The voice was rapid, heedless, doleful, soft, but the echoes of the long cavern through which they were marching amplified it into authority. "Let's see that," the voice said.

"That" turned out to be the trap which a lackey took from Berek. The green man had extended his arm for it.

"For foxes?" the green man asked, leading it close to his face.

"It's for rats," Berek replied.

Even the sniffing from the green man's nose reverberated with a sort of sad power in the concrete corridor.

"Paint?" the green man asked. "House paint?"

"Yes," Berek said. "I need the trap back."

"Good idea, paint, blocks out man smell, we ought to use it for bear traps, deer blinds, so on," the green man said. "You shoot?"

"What?" Berek said.

"No, not often, we don't often hunt," Schall said. "Serenity, if we may—"

"Who made the pretty trap?" the green man asked.

"Me," Berek answered. "It's not finished."

"All those workers' houses we built, *they're* not finished, but they're not pretty, think they're pretty?" the green man said.

"They started the rats," Berek said.

"Ratty, awful, ugly, rotten, if we didn't build it ugly somebody else'd build it uglier, first man I can talk to about it," the green man said. "Ugly, ugly everywhere, everything that's going up, gives you a headache in the middle of the night. Except maybe down here, this sewer. That might be all right one day."

"Oh, this will be the *sewer*!" Schall said. "Serenity, it will make an impressive sewer."

"Not now," the green man said. "Not in a couple of years, when the shit starts rippling, not for the next few centuries. But maybe in six hundred years." He sighed. He had come to a stop. So did the lackeys with the lanterns, the lackey with the rifle, and so did Berek and Schall. "About the year 2300, that'll be about the right time." The green man adjusted his glasses pensively. "Everything nice 'n' collapsed and wrecked by then, all the uglies, the palaces, the tenements all gone, nothing but young fresh Mongols stomping on the ruins. And then the Mongols will have this thing here dug up. Oh, come on, please, do light up the ceiling."

The lackeys lifted their lanterns.

"See the vaulting, the groined vaulting? Imagine, half a thousand years from now? Five hundred years of shit weathered on groined vaulting, about the best thing you can leave behind. The *cloaca maxima*? Most beautiful thing the Caesars left in Italy, ever seen it in Rome?"

The lackeys didn't answer. Berek didn't understand. "I'm sorry, Serenity," Schall said. "I've never been in Rome. I've been in Prague."

"Say around the year 2300," the green man said. "The young

fresh Mongols, they'll spit and stomp on everything, but our sewer they'll dig up and they'll say, 'Hmm, good!'" The green man gave the trap back to Berek and walked on. "Cheers me up. When I shoot badly, I take a walk down here for cheering up. Meanwhile, I'll need ten traps for St. Petersburg. *Rifle.*" With a motion that was swift and sure he took the gun handed to him. Sorrowfully, he laid his thin cheek against it as if about to cry against its butt.

The long cavern crashed and leaped with the explosion. Ahead, a small tailed shadow twitched and lay still. The green man handed back the rifle to his gun bearer. "I can't shoot St. Petersburg rats when I'm ambassador. I've got to trap them. I can't make Bosnian hooray badges either, not with my family metal, never, when the czar hates our Bosnian victory right in his own backyard."

"Serenity!" Schall said as a lackey kicked the rat away. "Serenity, now we comprehend! High diplomacy. We had no idea! But we will be so glad to make you traps! We've had the privilege before. We made ball favors for Serenity's mother during the World's Fair."

"Ah?" the green man said. "The ball the czar missed. He complained about it during accreditation last month. He came two days late for Mama's ball back then. You have one of those favors left?"

"Oh, delighted!" Schall said. "If not, we'll make Serenity one!"

"One favor, ten traps," the green man said sadly. "Ready for pickup Thursday before I leave."

Berek thought about the amount he lacked so badly to buy Turk Place No. 2 and No. 4. "The price will be fifty gulden," he said.

"Ah, there goes another," the green man said. "*Rifle.*" And then, with another tailed shadow scuttling away ahead, he laid his melancholy face against the gun.

On their return Berek and Schall found that the utility crew had left a pile of thick pipe tubing and shovels before No. 1 Turk Place. What they did not find—though they looked everywhere in the workshop—was one of the ball favors they'd made years ago for Princess Wallers. By Thursday they had to produce the favor;

also to make ten rat traps; also to embed the gas main under the street. All in little more than forty-eight hours.

Berek said two extra days could be gained by doing away with the nights. And then they started working away toward the crucial fifty gulden.

Luckily, Schall kept a file of his designs, including the one for the favor. While the light was good, Berek worked out the details on a piece of bronze. At twilight he joined Schall in digging the gas-main ditch his partner had started at No. 6. Boas had stayed up that night, holding the kerosene lamp to help them see if the lumps that resisted their shovels were stone or just compacted earth. Tamarah didn't sleep either. She kept her kitchen stove going from dusk to dawn with hot tea, hot soup, and boiled sausages. Schall repeatedly mentioned the construction workers' canteen serving cold beer all night, but Tamarah insisted that only warm meals could keep the blood going in times of stress. Before dawn Riddah and her albino assistant, Susi, came by for the third time, wanting to pitch in. The diggers still felt strong and sent the women back to their bakery chores.

After sunrise, when the light was good again, Berek smithied the fine details of the ball favor. But the scrap bronze he worked on was coarse. It needed tempering and polishing that exhausted the morning. Berek finally finished at 2 PM and placed the favor in the gray velvet box of the silver earrings he had given Tamarah for her last birthday. She had brought the box along with beef stew. After that Berek and Schall rolled the gas pipe into the ditch, which now extended halfway along Turk Place. That evening they began digging the second half, feeling not so much fatigue as a peculiar interpersonal twitch that jumped from Berek's left knee to Schall's right shoulder. It was as if the two men and the six houses of Turk Place were wired to the same rogue nerve. They laughed about it over the coffee Tamarah made.

Sometime after midnight their shovels clanged against brass plates. Years ago they themselves had taken these plates from the steam tricycle to pave the gutter in front of No. 1. The brass had become the fundament of hard-packed mud and took four hours to dislodge, each hour another spiral into a new and differently vi-

brating layer of exhaustion. Just when Schall said he would try to
stand on his head to fight off dizziness, Berek let out a yell. He had
fallen, softly, into an underground hollow. Schall found him in what
turned out to be a half-clogged tunnel, next to a blond mane twisted
around a giant sickle. The sickle, they decided, was a scimitar. The
blond mane remained a mystery. They had happened on a subterranean passageway the Turks had constructed to connect house No.
1 with No. 2 opposite.

For a while the tunnel made the shovel work less grueling. Soon
a second dawn came up over their nonstop labor. They tried to re-
vive themselves with the hot goulash Tamarah had ready. Schall said
he had to go to the privy and staggered back with a stein of beer. It
was high time for Berek to turn to the ten rat traps for the embassy
in St. Petersburg. When he had finished the first three he took them
into the workshop and placed them along the wall next to the boxed
ball favor. When he returned to the ditch, Schall, still digging, had
begun to draft aloud, with shovel hisses and panting breath, the
note to Prince Wallers that he wanted to place in the ball favor's
box. The note went through many feverish variations. Over and over
again it beseeched His Serene Highness, the ambassador, to con-
clude an extradition treaty with the czar that would make the Rus-
sians deliver Dr. Nassig to the Vienna prosecutor, since the villain
might well be hiding across the border, creating trouble between
empires and confusing managers like Herr Misch.

By then it was late afternoon and the light was wearing out once
again. Berek's fingers seemed to hang in stinging rags. The fingers
bent wires endlessly, creating trap after trap. It would have been easier to endure the pain indoors, under the kerosene chandelier of the
workshop. But Berek continued laboring in the ditch to keep Schall
company. Schall could keep up his strength better if he had an audience for his note drafting. Berek himself had acquired spectators.
They looked down from the tops of No. 2 and No. 4. Those were the
houses for which the endless effort went on and on; somewhere beyond the unrisen moon all that sweat would bring the fifty gulden
that would complete their purchase. The minarets on their roofs
had turned into masks. Hidden eyes watched Berek work. They
watched sometimes with the gloomy black irises of the rabbi of

Varungy, sometimes with the hard blue of the emperor's. But they watched.

And then Tamarah appeared. She brought lentil soup. Berek did not touch it. If he stopped, the masks would snigger and he would not be able to move again. Tamarah began to help Berek. She carried the finished traps into the workshop; she bent wires that multiplied into infinity. Berek saw her cheeks erode together with the daylight. He told her to stop and rest. She shook her head. But then Riddah's arms came around his wife and pushed her away. Riddah took over and helped Berek bend wires and in between spooned the cold lentil soup. That night the roosters were cooped up in the bakery basement, and that night the albino managed the bread alone. Riddah had done many baking chores in advance during the day. This meant that she had also gone without sleep, but she seemed unbothered except for the hiccups that came clucking and laughing out of her mouth after she had finished the soup. She combined the hiccups into a rollicksome Slovakian lullaby. To its strains Berek jumped into the ditch to carry on for Schall, who had crumpled by the beer stein, still whispering new drafts of his note. The whispers stopped after a while; Riddah's song-tossed hiccups still rang like a recurrent bell in Berek's ear. Berek floundered on some great giddy crest, but his hands lived a life apart. They still knew exactly what they must do. They must couple the joints of the gas main to the feeder pipes of the gas lamps and the houses. They must and they did. And just when Berek thought he was finished, there leaped out of the night a blue-white sunburst.

Over a hundred lamps in the tenement project had been lit to test gas pressure. Their simultaneous brightness shook the clouds above the capital into an enormous billowing, smoldering flag. It flashed out and furled in one instant, and curled itself around Berek.

He woke up in the ditch. The sun blinded him from a late-morning angle. Schall was snoring at his side. Boas was asleep on his feet, leaning against a house wall. Riddah slept sitting on the curb.

"Tamarah!" Berek called.

A sound came from the workshop. He ran inside. The boxed ball favor and the traps were gone. Then he saw his wife stretched out on the floor.

"Tamarah!"

"They took it away an hour ago," she said with lips so pale he could hardly see her smile. Her fingers were a frail white lattice bent around a wedge of red bank notes.

IX

A WEEK LATER the Wallers Metal Company delivered half a ton of brass to Turk Place. The metal had been promised on credit by the fired steward, and Berek had no way of paying cash for it now. Schall went to the Wallers office, but the clerks did not find the item anywhere on any ledger. Their records would be embarrassed by the return of a shipment that could not possibly exist. Brusque shoulder shrugs told Schall not to bother hardworking people about specters.

The change in Wallers management led to confusion all around. Work on tenement interiors came to a halt. After a while it resumed at a much tardier pace. For Berek the delay was useful. Because things had slowed, local real estate was heating up less rapidly. When Berek went to the Jewish Council to buy No. 2 and No. 4 (the extra fifty gulden rounding out the twenty-three hundred required), he could negotiate a tolerable new rent for the two buildings he did not yet own—No. 3 and No. 6. The council leased them for three hundred gulden annually.

Still, six hundred gulden a year was not an easy figure, especially if Berek added to it the money he needed to feed his crew and the sum he laid away—never less than five gulden weekly—toward the purchase of the two houses that would make him full owner of the street of the Brick.

He'd never have managed if the market next door had not gotten into trouble. First it had been disrupted by the installation of underground utilities. Later the construction site west of Turk Place (even bigger than Wallers's) had commandeered much of the market area. There was a scramble for space. And so, for daytime use only, Berek leased some upper-floor apartments at Turk Place to the market's licensing office and to its bureau of weights and measures. Ground-floor flats he rented—also for daytime only—to vendors of pots and pans, of country linens and farm-made soaps. Food sellers were excluded. Tamarah was strong on that point because of the refuse and the rats.

Soon the dry-goods man at No. 4 offered more than homespun cloth. He also sold ornaments Schall designed and Berek hammered, humming, across the street in the workshop: costume jewelry made of the Wallers "spectral" brass; well-wrought birthday bracelets for the ladies, with their own sign of the zodiac in bas-relief; name-day cravat pins for men, with their initials incised at a small extra charge; half-moon earrings suspended on cobweb chains for girls before their engagement and heart-shaped brooches for those after.

As customers, Berek had many of the craftsmen who now worked on tenement interiors: glaziers, carpenters, plumbers, masons, locksmiths, whose wives and daughters brought them their midday goulash and whom they often bought gifts. Boas stood by to immortalize the buyer's generosity with profound flourishes of black cloth and camera. He photographed the gifted one so that the new trinket showed to advantage on a daguerreotype costing only forty hellers.

The earnings from all this were sometimes fair, sometimes not. What was always wonderful, day after day, was six o'clock in the evening. It was the hour when the market clerks put on their gray coats and black derbies and left their upper-floor offices; when the vendors locked up downstairs; when Tamarah's broom swept away every scrap of extraneous presence; when the gas lanterns began to gleam alive and to define the fluted shadows of their posts across a silence that renewed itself every night in young expectation. That was when Berek and Tamarah would dream of the first new soul to spend the night sleeping here—their son.

Friday nights, following the blessing, the candles and the meal, Berek lay with Tamarah on her pillow. Afterward, they still went to the son's room but only to dust it, smiling, for a few minutes. It was now a landscape studded with equipment for childhood years, from a playpen to a small desk awaiting the schoolboy's homework. A long time ago, when they had finished the desk, Tamarah had suddenly stopped polishing it with lemon oil; she had sunk to her knees and laid her head on the desktop, tears dribbling onto the half-oiled wood. Berek had lifted her up. He had taken her to the chamber next door, which was still empty, and then pushed the cradle with the Brick box after her.

In that chamber they now spent the Sabbath day, for it was the chamber of their unborn child's unborn child, the grandson's room. On Sabbath morning Berek would enter it with Tamarah. He would remove the coverlet from the cradle so that the Brick box was revealed. He would remove the lid from the box to show the Brick itself. He would wrap himself in the tallith Tamarah had made and in which they had been wed. He would chant the first of the eighteen benedictions that turned the room into a temple. As Torah he had the Brick, masonry that had once sheltered the most precious of all law scrolls. As minyan—the quorum of ten men required for Sabbath prayer—he had his own person plus Tamarah plus eight slips of paper in the Brick addressing God together with him. And since it was the Brick, it didn't matter that neither Tamarah nor the slips were male. As Sabbath reading from the Torah, Berek, who had never been taught letters as a boy, had his memory.

"Hear, Israel," Rabbi Kohn had called out in Varungy, as though summoning an urchin gone fishing too long by the brook. "Hear, Israel, the Lord is our God, the Lord is One!" And that was what Berek called out after the eighteenth benediction. His call overrode the workaday noises of the market outside and summoned the generations that must come.

That done, Berek and Tamarah would take up hammer and needle for the next phase of their Sabbath in the grandson's room. They repeated the making of the props of growing up, from toys to inkwells, as in the son's room, but they made them in a different setting. Berek had nailed hooks on all four walls and strung cords from these to a small circle of more hooks on the ceiling. Next to the mezuzah Tamarah had glued handgrips on the doorjamb for holding on. The room simulated a gondola suspended on ropes from a giant

balloon like the one exhibited at the Prater fair. After all, their grandson would do his playing and his studying in the aeronautical age;
that age had to be honored in his room.

So the couple was busy from morning to sunset, with the Brick
uncovered and Berek hooded in his tallith. They did not violate the
Sabbath, for their actions were the hallowed opposite of work. This
was not labor but a celebration of the future. Tamarah did not cry
again, even as the decade unwound toward 1890 and no fruit of her
body broke the cycles of the moon. One day she did feel her nostrils
stiffen with the danger of tears. It was a hot Saturday morning, and
swiftly she left Berek's side. She returned with two saucers filled
with crystal shavings from the market's iceman. Over one she had
poured strawberry syrup, over the other apricot jam.

"Remember Prohaska's?" she said. She pointed to the window.
Through the open casements came, on cue, the "Vienna Bonbons"
waltz she'd paid the organ-grinder five hellers to play.

"That time by the Ferris wheel!" Berek said. Because of their
pallor her cheeks enchanted him when they did blush even slightly.
He seized her as he was, in his prayer shawl, and whirled her around
to the three-quarter beat until, parched, they fell on their "Prohaska" ices, spooning them up, mixing them up, exchanging apricot
and strawberry, mingling the flavors into funny colors, laughing,
licking, dancing again, soaring, in memory and anticipation, under
their grandchild's great balloon.

They did the same thing the following Sabbath. It became their
weekly festival of births to come, year after year.

But while the couple's Sabbath purpose remained steady, the
everyday churn of events threatened to overrun it. Both vast tenement projects, to the east as well as the west, finally approached
completion. Turk Place had become the heart of an enormous
body of cobble and concrete. And there were people grabbing for
the heart.

An odd sound made Berek look out of the workshop one afternoon, a sound like that of a hornet buzzing against a window. It

turned out to be a man scratching his ring across the house wall of No. 3. Another man stood close by. Both wore bulky blue woolen overcoats, too warm for the weather and too fancy for the neighborhood. A third man, in a short frock coat, Berek recognized all too well. He was an agent from the Excelsior International Water Company.

"Pleasure to see you again, sir," he said. "Privilege to introduce you to the brothers Schiener. Have you seen the rails they're laying to where the city gate used to be? The horse-tramway rails, very exciting? Messieurs Schiener are major stockholders there and they have a very creative idea for you."

"Please don't scratch the wall," Berek said.

"Oh, no harm came to it," the scratching brother said. "They are such good solid walls. I also want to compliment you on the spaciousness of the rooms."

"Who let you in to see them?" Berek said.

"We have the blueprints from your Israelite Council," the other brother said. "They still own Number Three and Number Six. In those rooms you can sleep four Vienna-born proletarians each. Maybe six from Moravia, where they're not yet so particular."

"Big ground-floor apartments," the first brother said. "Why waste them on market people? The ground floors will be great for, say, a brandy shop. Or a pawnbroker. A lottery seller would do well. There'll be lots of numbers players."

"Not to speak of a hardware store," the first brother said. "For repairing vandalism and so on. The problem is no plumbing."

"That's where the creative idea comes in," the agent said.

"All those new tenements have plumbing," the first brother said. "A toilet and a sink on every floor. No getting around that. That's the sanitary code of the City of Vienna for you, and pretty soon this place is going to be part of the city. There's just no point buying the houses here from your Israelite Council if we don't put in plumbing. You can sweeten those housing inspectors only so far."

"But now, Herr Spiegelglass," the agent said, "now we have a very creative idea for a solution all around."

"Have we," Berek said.

"The brothers Schiener have made such a fine offer to the Israelite Council," the Excelsior agent said. "A fine sum for houses Number Three and Number Six if the council puts in plumbing. But, you see, Excelsior is not in a position to go to the expense of laying water mains and plumbing pipes just to supply two houses in this street. It would pay for us only if you agreed to do the same with your fine buildings. As I explained to the brothers Schiener, it is not that Excelsior is greedy—"

"You have already explained it to me at other times," Berek said.

"But now there is a new marvelous idea—"

"We are comfortable here as is."

"With *this*?" the first brother Schiener said, giving a mild kick in the direction of Berek's water system—the old steam-tricycle tubing that linked the backyard well to the outdoor sinks he had recently embossed in copper, next to the house entrances.

"Here is the marvelous idea," the agent said. "The brothers Schiener will generously contribute one quarter of the cost of indoor plumbing for your houses here. I'm most happy to tell you that the council will contribute another quarter—so you'll get your plumbing at half cost! And Excelsior can go ahead!"

"No, thank you," Berek said.

He didn't have a penny to waste on new investments. He was saving too strenuously for the very houses the brothers were pawing with their fat, damp hands. The bank-note roll wrapped in the sugar bag under the Brick was far too thin to match serious bidders with such ringed fingers and such powerful overcoats. Meanwhile, Berek had to keep bidders from being serious by keeping plumbing out of Turk Place. Only no-plumbing stopped them from reaching deeply and obscenely into his street.

"I'm sorry," Berek said.

"Herr Spiegelglass, you'll want to consider this further before saying no," the agent said.

"If it's a question of cash," the other brother Schiener said, "there's such a thing as a mortgage. We can arrange that, too."

"No, thank you," Berek said.

"Don't you realize the potential here?" the first brother said. "This way all you got here is just—just an annex to a farmers' market. What is that nasty chicken?"

Schall, witnessing the scene helplessly, had been unable to restrain one of Riddah's roosters, which had waked up early in a particularly unpleasant mood.

"What have I done to that chicken?" the first brother said.
"What's the matter with it? . . . Get away from me!"

"Perhaps—perhaps another time," the agent said, lifting his hat
and driving off with the brothers, leaving behind a scratched wall,
visiting cards (in case Berek changed his mind), a nettled rooster, financial quicksands and Schall's bafflement.

As the eighties had unrolled, Schall had become fatter but not
more resigned. He saw that Vienna was shaking off at last the
long pall of the stock market crash. Great things smoldered on
the horizon; it was a crying shame not to participate in the greatness. A month before the monumental Parliament Building
opened in 1883 Schall sketched its Grecian facade inside an oval
frame. He showed the drawing to Berek during one of their Friday afternoon drinks together. Tens of thousands of people, Schall
said, would stream to the capital to see the building and to watch
the Parliament in session. There was a fortune in selling them a
souvenir medallion. Berek already had the raw material, since a
good deal of brass was left from the "spectral" shipment. All he
needed was to buy a power lathe and a big stamping press. He
could generate the cash by taking advantage of the renting or
sales opportunities of his Turk Place real estate. Didn't Berek see?

Since it had become too delicate over the years, Schall no longer
mentioned directly Berek's notion that a son of his had to precede
other full-time tenants at Turk Place. The issue remained unspoken
on both sides. But it lived in Schall's urgency as well as in Berek's
stubbornness.

"We'll do better than cheap tourist medallions," Berek said.
"Meanwhile, we're getting along on our quality brass jewelry. We
can wait."

Schall waited till 1885, when the mountainous silhouette of
City Hall was finished, next to Parliament on the Ringstrasse boule-

vard. He showed Berek his souvenir idea, and Berek said it would be best to wait. He said it once more in 1888, looking at Schall's souvenir rendition of the Renaissance magnificence of the Imperial and Royal Court Theater, about to have its premiere performance.

What was Schall to do? He told Berek that he must go see to a sudden toothache. And he went to consult not a dentist but the manufacturers' directory in the city's main post office. That day he called on four makers of costume jewelry. Four times he unfolded his designs. The one boss who was interested put on, put off, a shifty pince-nez and talked about ten gulden a week to start, but shook his head at an earnings percentage like the kind Schall had with Berek, the kind that entitled Schall to think of himself as a partner and to introduce himself as such. Schall folded his designs again.

When he returned to the oriental lampposts of Turk Place, he was surprised by a not very logical pang of relief. Why should he feel at home here? After all, his ambition remained ungratified. So did other emotions. In 1889 his Sunday afternoon excitement was Fräulein Deller, daughter of the market's leading cookware vendor. For the last three years the Deller nickel-plated merchandise had gleamed on several big stands inside and outside of Turk Place No. 4. Fräulein Deller outgleamed it all. Dark-eyed, faintly freckled, with emphatically flounced sleeves poised over her father's accounts, she was the kind of young lady you didn't ask to an Italian coffee with cream roll unless the café terrace had a concert band with a sashed conductor. And unless you were capable of long-range intentions.

In February of that year Fräulein Deller told Schall that in three weeks her father would move out of Turk Place with his colleagues, back to the restored market area. The chores of relocation would make her too busy to see "casual acquaintances" after that, even on weekends. With a dainty exactitude that infatuated Schall almost to the degree that it frightened him, Fräulein Deller's lips shaped the ultimatum.

"Oh," Schall finally said. "Your father, and especially you, you will be truly missed."

The point was, he could not afford to surrender to marriage.

And once more Berek had supplied that point. Again Schall could not blame himself for falling short of a desirable match. The problem was Berek's eternal waiting. Because of Berek he still did not have the means to be more than "casual." He could relax awhile longer. It was not his fault that his private life had not yet turned forever serious—as eternally and unmercifully serious as Berek's.

X

O N A SABBATH MORNING in July 1889 Berek and Tamarah had planned to make a chessboard together for their future grandson. But when he entered the balloon room, Berek stopped dead at the threshold. Tamarah sat by the Brick box, a newspaper in her left hand. In her right, with the lovely, too tiny pinkie, she held something he had not seen for sixteen years. Suddenly, his wife had produced what she had kept out of sight for so long: the notepad on which he had once practiced the alphabet on the basis of newspaper stories.

"I think we . . . reached the letter *l*," she said.

He stood there, staring, rubbing the half-painted chessboard.

"Then the hos . . . pital interrupted," she said.

Her small, deep smile rode on a small nod. It made her meaning unmistakable and therefore overwhelming. That day Berek was thirty-four years and three months old. He had the face of a stern youth in his twenties, except for the gray that dusted the upper part of his black beard. Tamarah's braids, still drawn tightly around her shapely head, were the same lustrous black; the blue of her glance still shone under her high-curved brows. Only the weariness under her eyes had gradually darkened from mauve to violet, and sometimes Berek wanted to light a candle close to her face to drive the dusk away from her cheeks. But now—now the little smile she smiled lit her with a morning light.

His chessboard dropped to the floor. She let go of newspaper, pad, pencil, put them down on the Brick box. Their arms rose toward each other. He felt a bit of wet from her eyes on his shoulder. He didn't brush away his own tears. They must not be touched. The reason why they were being wept was too important.

Then the two sat down together. He bent forward until his lips pressed gently against her apron where the new child was growing at last. She unfolded the paper to the Court Gazette page, just as she had sixteen years ago when she had been pregnant. His thumb and forefinger closed around the pencil for the first time in so long. Together they spelled out a paragraph saying that His Apostolic Majesty had received Rainer Bertram Prince Wallers on the occasion of the prince's home leave from his embassy in St. Petersburg.

"We'll brush up quickly on all the letters . . . up to *l*," she said.

He kissed the little stammer on her lips.

Almost as a natural part of the after-amazement, a man appeared the next morning in livery under a cocked hat. He said he was to lead "Spiegelglass and wife and partner" to where His Serene Highness expected them.

Tamarah happened to be in the workshop. The man began to move ahead with such speed that Berek held his wife back. She must walk slowly and with proper caution. But even at that careful pace, Berek soon saw the carriage. Gold and white, with rosy wheels and a snow-white horse, it stood against the raw cement of the first row of tenements, under windows still smeared with the chalk marks of glaziers. The phaeton looked the way a chime sounds, ringing silver against a tedious drone.

"Wait!" Schall whispered. And stopped. "We should think."

"It's all right," Berek said. "We read it in the paper yesterday that the prince is back."

"But, you see, the money we owe him for the brass," Schall said. "I just remembered—that half ton! We never paid for it."

"It's all right," Berek said.

"What if he says it's an overdue debt?" Schall asked. "What if he charges interest? We should think of something."

"My wife is expecting again," Berek said.

"Expecting?" Schall said. Tamarah turned away her face. "Now? After all—you mean, really *expecting*?"

"Yes," Berek said.

"You really mean it? A baby?"

"Of course. Let's go," Berek said. "Everything's all right."

"JesusMariaandJoseph! Congratulations! Congratulations to you both."

"Thank you," Berek said. "Now come on."

In the phaeton sat Prince Wallers, dressed in gray rather than in the green of years ago. He had grown blond-gray mustaches that curled upward across thin cheeks toward his spectacles.

"Serenity, the people you wanted," said the man under the cocked hat.

The prince didn't answer. He was busy adjusting the blanket on the lap of a woman seated next to him. To Berek she looked like the figurine on top of Riddah's broken music box. Above the blanket she was wrapped in a coat of pearly porcelain. She wore a huge brown ceramic-looking hat. There was a veil instead of a face. The only human things visible were three fingers, two of which had rings and all of which looked like polished, mottled bone, holding the hat brim down over the hidden forehead.

"Serenity," the lackey said again. "The people you wanted. Spiegelglass and wife and partner."

"Yes, rat traps and so on," the prince said. "Good. With Wife, how do you do. This is Wife's work, is it?"

He still spoke in the same doleful tone, and lifted up a footstool covered by exquisite black and yellow embroidery: the two digits of "60" twined intricately into "FJ"—Franz Joseph's initials. It was the year the emperor would turn sixty.

"Yes, sir," Tamarah said. "That was commissioned by the princess's lady-in-waiting."

"When did you do that?" Berek asked, amazed. Tamarah squeezed "Shush!" into his hand, and Berek remembered that recently there had been an unexpected extra in their small cash reserve.

"Pretty footstool," the prince said. He was talking to where the ear of the figurine next to him might be, under the veil. "See, Mama? Nice footstool." He turned to Tamarah. "Now, we also need a ball gown with that pattern for Mama here. You know, a '60-FJ' pattern. I'm told Wife did a nice ball gown for Mama years ago. Am I told right, yes or no?"

"Yes," Tamarah said.

"My wife is expecting," Berek said. "She can't be overworked."

"We'll need it by December," the prince said. Next to him the veil of the figurine had begun to tremble. It was stirred by small air puffs from a voice that cracked and split into feeble soprano fragments which the prince had no trouble understanding.

"Oh, Mama!" he said. "By December we'll be so fit, we'll be sorry we didn't give the ball in November!" He tightened the blanket around the figurine. "The czar couldn't come here anyway before December. But he gave me his word at the bear hunt, in December he'll definitely come. Wife will have the gown ready by December?"

"Yes," Tamarah said. With another hand squeeze she shushed Berek.

"Look, up there," the prince said. A lackey was handing the footstool to another lackey, who was standing on a ladder. "An order for friend Spiegelglass," the prince said, pointing up to the "60-FJ" design of the rising footstool. "We need five hundred and fifty ball favors with that pattern by December, yes?"

"In bronze?" Schall said, and immediately took a step backward, aghast at his own forwardness. "Forgive me, Serenity. I'm Schall, the partner."

"Of course, bronze," the prince said to the figurine's presumable ear. "And even better bronze, the best bronze, for the house-number shields, they're important, they'll have the same pattern, see it up there now?"

The lackey on the ladder held the footstool above the tenement entrance. The black-yellow design hovered near the concrete armpit of a Juno supporting a half-painted balcony. "All the six hundred houses we built here," the prince said to Berek, "you'll make their house-number shields with Mama's ball favor as motif, yes? We'll put the shields above the entrances like that, little number in foreground, big ball motif in background, plus street signs to match, you can do that?"

"Oh, Serenity, yes," Schall said. "The challenge!"

"In the very best bronze," the prince said to the figurine's ear, "to commemorate Mama's ball 'cause that'll make Mama really be there to give her ball. She can't make six hundred house shields lie, can she now? Course she can't, she'll have no excuse. She'll *have* to be well by then."

The figurine's head gave a nod and a dim chuckle, and the prince raised the gloved bones of the hand to kiss it.

"*Bravissima!*" he said. "And even much later, the year two thousand plus, all the ugly stuff here will be long stomped under, even *then* Mama's ball motifs will still be here intact among the debris, hundreds of them, unscathed, not a wrinkle, 'cause they're the very best bronze, clear?"

"Yes, very much," Schall said. "Thank you, Serenity."

"House shields and street signs take much more work than ball favors," Berek said. "That's not a uniform lot. They're individual pieces. I'll have to calculate the price."

"The Mongols'll find no prettier things than that above the sewers," the prince said. The figurine's veil began to dimple to delicate and tiny coughs.

Soon Tamarah's pregnancy blew up to a size that made it hard to remember the slightness of her real figure. Berek was not alarmed. Certainly not at first. Tamarah reflected a great burgeoning that had spread beyond her belly into the street. It was as if the ferment on Turk Place tried to keep pace with the one in his wife's flesh, as if both were fed by the same sharp need—as if, indeed, they were both part of the same force, which was tremendous, long pent up, already visible, still impending.

Within a week Berek received fifty-five hundred gulden from the Wallers office as advance for the three huge orders: ball favors, house-number shields and street signs. Within a month he had bought houses No. 3 and No. 6, gaining possession of the whole of

Turk Place. At the same time he purchased two stamping machines and three toggle-joint presses. The former Gypsy stable at No. 1 bloomed into a factory at last.

But the surge at Turk Place went beyond that. Berek would require at least eight workers; the Duchy of Lower Austria mandated that any shop employing more than six must meet certain sanitary standards. Therefore, Berek loosed the Excelsior International Water Company not only on No. 1 but on all his houses. Dozens of workmen dug trenches, laid feeder lines, embedded drainage systems, carried sinks and screwed in toilets, basins and faucets.

Dozens of other men lined the wall of the former stable, waiting to be interviewed by Berek for jobs. In the middle of the hall, pits were being scooped out of the ground to anchor the presses that had already been delivered. Meanwhile, they hulked in a backyard shed.

Siddo Berger, located by Schall in a notary's office in the city, had been reclaimed as clerk for the factory by the offer of a higher salary. He shepherded the apartment seekers whom Berek admitted now because they had already been preceded by his son; this son, currently residing inside Tamarah, occupied the most desirable space of all on Turk Place. The apartment seekers stepped off the just completed horse-tramway line that led up to the site of the former city gate. They were no longer day laborers staggering out of a dust cloud but men in three-piece suits and very white shirts. Now that Turk Place was to be blessed by a full complement of utilities, it had become a convenient residence for tradesmen catering to the neighborhood's working-class population. At Siddo Berger's side, Boas played assistant rental manager. He pointed out the unusual architecture of the houses, together with photographic close-ups of the minarets, while Siddo Berger explained clauses of the lease he had prepared with Berek.

Turk Place had turned into a busyness, a buzzing, clanking and hammering, a yelling, whirring and thudding. In Berek's ear it all formed a concord tuned precisely to that other new vigor working inside Tamarah's body. For this reason he always had an anxious moment when, at day's end, the orchestra of tools and voices faded. Again and again he could taste the silence like something suspicious on his tongue. He couldn't help fearing that during the long pause of darkness he would lose the special pitch that continued the on-going energy under Tamarah's heart.

But then he would hear Riddah rising in the night. He would hear Riddah singing, flanked by the two roosters and the albino, singing and baking, holding in her single husky voice all the diverse chords of the day, carrying on the beat as she kneaded and molded, preserving it safely through the black hours until the choir of sledgehammers and monkey wrenches materialized again after breakfast and took over the burden of a crucial harmony.

In December of 1889 each corridor of each house at Turk Place had acquired an oaken toilet as well as a zinc basin with running water from a swan-necked spout. At No. 1 the presses were in place, thumping with the first batch of the house-number shields Schall had designed. By that time—as the first tenant faces appeared in windows—Tamarah's pregnancy had begun to overwhelm her.

The delicate curves of her eyebrows, her dainty braids, her schoolgirl arms were like parts of a small doll protruding at random from a huge round swell. Though these parts seemed fragile, their fragility glowed. Her cheeks kindled into a rose color so increasingly vivid, she looked ruddy if not febrile when the first snow fell. Her hair shone; her hands with their toy pinkies never rested for a moment.

To help his wife, Berek had hired Resi, the albino's sister, a red-head forever sucking on a candy. But Tamarah joined her on all fours scrubbing the two ground-floor apartments at No. 2. They had been combined into a single hall that was to be the synagogue where Berek's son would be rabbi. With the maid Tamarah painted its interior blue; whitewashed the niche destined for the Torah scrolls; affixed sconcelike lanterns to the walls. Distended though she was, Tamarah also finished the old princess's ball gown and kept as well to all her regular chores, cooking and cleaning as before. She did yield to Riddah's muscular insistence to let the albino wash the dishes during the night. In the day Tamarah never stopped laboring with arms that had become Kewpie appendages to a heroic womb.

During the alphabet lessons with Berek she was expeditious, even urgent. She virtually drove Berek's hand as it progressed from the sharp elbow of the capital *L* to the Gothic windows of *M*. One evening, while he practiced the comma intersecting the oval of *Q,* her fingers let go of his. She pitched forward onto the box of the Brick.

Dr. Xavier Huber, who'd only recently moved into an apartment nearby, met any professional challenge with the constant important blinking of his eyes. He blinked his eyes with such stolid portentousness that Berek noticed it even as they ran in the gaslight. Berek also noticed that Dr. Huber raised his legs very high to keep his boots as free as possible from the dust of Turk Place in the throes of renovation.

All this was fortunate. Berek could concentrate on his dislike of the doctor and thus remove himself a little from the pounding of his heart. Dr. Huber ordered Berek out of the bedroom into which he'd carried Tamarah. But at least this left Berek alone with the Brick and the two black hairs of his wife's he found on top of its box. He kissed them both and said the eighteen benedictions.

A quarter of an hour later Dr. Huber opened the door.

"Is everything all right?" Berek whispered.

Blinking, the doctor pulled on gray gloves.

"Are my wife and the baby all right?" Berek said.

"It would not be accurate to speak of 'the baby.'" The doctor exhibited a smile and smoothed his gloves' wrinkles. "Frau Spiegelglass is carrying twins."

Berek seized the Brick box and pen, brushed past the eye blinker, shut the bedroom door behind him, kissed a Tamarah who was perspiring but already sitting up. No words were spoken while he lifted out the Brick and pulled a slip from one of its fissures, the one saying *"Please, God the Eternal, let me own all of Turk Place and have a healthy child."* He crossed out *"a"* and *"child,"* and then, with her hand so thin but warmly steering his, wrote *"children"* instead.

For one more month Tamarah swelled on and worked on and, evenings, escorted Berek past *q* to *r* to *s*. Then, one dawn, a sound followed by a shadow pierced Berek's sleep.

Tamarah stood by her twin bed, stooping like a bloated ghost in the gaslight that swam in from the window. She was changing her pillowcase to a specially embroidered linen one he'd seen her work on weeks before.

"It's time for the bed . . . to look right," she said when she noticed that he was awake. The moan that followed flung him into his clothes.

The only further cries heard on that Turk Place dawn were those of the two boys being born. No sob or sound came from Tamarah's locked mouth. The delivery, though successful, left in Berek a sense of incompletion so odd that he tried to keep it secret from himself.

After the birth Tamarah's cheeks retained their heated color. She fell asleep with her still doll-like arms at attention by her sides, her eyes closed tautly, somehow vigilantly, turned away from Dr. Huber. The physician said—eyes blinking authoritatively—that Frau Spiegelglass's fatigue was to be expected. After all, the lady was over thirty. Besides, the two little premature gentlemen had arrived in mint condition but in a healthy hurry from which the mother would need a few days to recover.

One of the "premature gentlemen" had dark brown hair, the other, black; both had jaws remarkably square even in miniature. But until the abrupt glare of the eighth day of the twins' lives, Berek wasn't even sure of the color of their eyes. Curled into the twilight of closed window shades, they lay on Berek's twin bed—Berek himself having moved to a cot. Tamarah would not let them be taken from her side. A second cradle—in the son's room next door—had long been added to the first. Both remained empty. Tamarah wanted her babies next to her, arm-close.

She left them only at the usual alphabet-studying hour of 10 PM, and then only for a distance of three yards, where, by the light of a single candle delicate enough not to disturb two tiny slumbering pairs of eyes, she would guide Berek's hand along the angularities of the upper- as well as the lower-case letter *t*. Lesson finished, she would sigh and smile. She'd let herself be helped back to a bed whose character had changed since it had received her sons.

The bed seemed to have become secretly mobile. Berek began to feel that it moved with a motion he couldn't see, heading for a destination he could not imagine. Three times during the day, at least twice at night, Tamarah would sit up as though awakened by a change of landscape. She would take the twins, nestle them both against her body and stroke their cheeks while their minute lips stroked her nipples. When she was done, she would gentle them back to their side of the bed and fall asleep, and, sleeping, become a sort of sentinel. She always slept turned toward the twins. Her curved eyebrows flattened into the most finely tuned expectancy; a still-pregnant mother's expectancy poised, primed for a culmination waiting on the far slope of the horizon, waiting at a point toward which the bed was rolling.

Her babies hardly ever waked her. They cried so seldom. And when they did, they barely mewed, like sleepy kittens. Sometimes Berek felt that they, too, were waiting to arrive at some spot that would allow the full, safe untwining from their mother—where, fully born, they could burst into lusty yelps.

Even the Jewish Council contributed to that impression. It appeared that as far as the Jewish Council was concerned, the Spiegelglass children were not yet residents of this world. Siddo Berger had filled out their birth certificates, Tamarah had signed them and the albino's sister had taken them to the council within hours after the birth. Almost a week passed; the mail still did not bring the validated certificates. It looked as though the council refused to acknowledge the presence of the babies or to honor Berek's request—relayed along with the certificates—for a *mohel* to perform the circumcision. On the sixth day Berek stormed the council building.

The administrator's office was on the floor above the real estate department. It had an anteroom with an imposing rug and an upset secretary. Berek barged past her.

"Now, who's this?" the administrator said. "Spiegelglass? Oh, yes—never mind, Fräulein Lazar, no need to call the porter, we are all intelligent adults. Do be seated, Herr Spiegelglass."

"I need birth certificates for my two sons and a *mohel* for the circumcision," Berek said, standing on his feet.

"Interesting to meet you, Herr Spiegelglass," the administrator said. His beard, his pipe and the tweed of his jacket were all the same russet color. "Your case was discussed just this morning."

"This morning is very late," Berek said.

"Oh, we haven't been idle here," the administrator replied. "Your birth certificates have been processed. I mean, processed up to the point where we couldn't locate you in the necessary registers—"

"*Locate* me?" Berek said. "I've bought all the houses on Turk Place from you!"

"Turk Place," the administrator said, puffing at papers on his desk. "That's right. That's the real estate department. In fact, the information there, that's what puzzled our people. We thought that a gentleman with your—your real estate interests—you'd be in the congregational rolls of the Inner City, where our more substantial fellow worshipers—"

"I have nothing to do with the Inner City," Berek said. "I live on Turk Place."

"It's not a simple case," the administrator said. "You see—here, we do have a record of your marriage. But the reverend who performed it, Rabbi Mayer, he no longer serves here in the capital. He now has pastoral charge of our coreligionists in the Tyrol, and the wedding itself did not take place in any of our houses of worship as far as we can tell—"

"It took place in my street," Berek said.

"In any case we also looked for you in the congregational rolls of outer-district synagogues, including the old ghetto synagogue in the Leopoldstadt, and you are nowhere in—"

"Nowhere?" Berek said. "I live in a house that has the Brick from the Wailing Wall!" He had not really raised his voice. But his not quite clean boot tapped hard enough against the thickness of the rug to produce the pulse of a distant drum.

The administrator looked down at the tapping, then looked up at the ceiling.

"Won't you take a chair," he said.

Berek stood and tapped.

"Herr Spiegelglass." The administrator leaned back. "If I may ask. Where do you observe our sacred holidays?"

"At home. By the Brick."

"A synagogue has no importance for you?"

"We will have a Brick synagogue on Turk Place," Berek said. "I have cleared space for a synagogue rent-free at No. 2. One of my sons will be rabbi there."

"How very nice," the administrator said. "Very commendable. But right now—"

"Right now I want my sons' birth certificates and a *mohel* for the circumcision."

The administrator looked away from the tapping foot. "Well, here we have the problem," he said. "To validate the birth certificate it must be countersigned by the rabbi of your particular congregation. You have no particular congregation."

"I have Turk Place with the Brick," Berek said.

"We understand, we have taken note of that." The administrator shot another glance up at the ceiling. "Alas, that doesn't make much difference in this situation—"

"It has already made everything different," Berek said. "After seventeen years it has given my wife two sons at once!"

"Congratulations," the administrator said. "Very nice. And we appreciate your providing a synagogue rent-free. Now, we are men of reason, you and I—"

"I want the birth certificates and the *mohel*."

"Wait, give us the chance to develop a solution together," the administrator said. "Your rent-free synagogue. We will inspect the site and authenticate it as consecrated premises and then—it is still outside the city limits, isn't it?"

"It's been consecrated ever since the Brick," Berek said.

"Of course, but this will make it official," the administrator said. "And since it is outside the city limits, we will assign our good Dr. Ackermann, our rabbi handling matters of provincial worship, we'll put him in charge of the synagogue site—and *he* can sign the birth certificates. There you are."

The administrator gave a happy little pipe puff.

"How long will that take?" Berek asked.

"Oh, we don't dawdle. Even with the inspection and authenti-

cation procedures and so on, you ought to have your birth certificates within a week—"

"Too late."

"Oh, now, please," the administrator said. "I have already
squeezed the rules—"

"My sons must be circumcised on the eighth day, in accordance
with tradition," Berek said. "That's the day after tomorrow."

"Well, until a birth is officially registered, we can't assign a
mohel—"

"It must be done on the eighth day," Berek repeated. "One of
my sons is going to be the Turk Place rabbi."

"My esteemed Herr Spiegelglass," the administrator said. "It
won't hurt our tiny rabbi a bit if we wait just a few days longer."

"I'll do it myself the day after tomorrow," Berek said.

The administrator stopped puffing. "Yourself? Circumcise?"

"I was the blacksmith in my village, Varungy," Berek said. "In
Varungy the blacksmith was also the *mohel*."

"This is Vienna," the administrator said.

"I live at Turk Place," Berek said. "Good-bye."

The day after next, the indelible day, was uncommonly bright for
February. As long as he lived, the day would burn in Berek's
mind, an image made of silence and of winter sun.

Everything was very bright, very still. In the morning Berek
kissed Tamarah and took the two babies from her bed to put them
into their cradles. Schall helped carry the cradles downstairs and
then gave Berek a silent wave. He had volunteered to stay by the
mother's bedside.

Both twins were slumbering quietly. The wheels Berek had put
under the cradles neither creaked nor wheezed as Berek pushed
them toward the factory. Even the heavier cradle in which the Brick
was hidden betrayed not so much as a squeak. It was Sunday; street
and market lay mute, sunny, empty. Berek pushed on into the factory—a workerless hushed array of shanks and chains, pistons and

levers. He pushed on into the office, which was a cubicle behind a partition. It seemed to be waiting for him like a brilliant shrine floating in the sunlight of the backyard window.

On the desk glittered knife and bowl, the utensils of circumcision. Of the three chairs, one was unoccupied, reserved for the prophet Elijah. Riddah, the godmother, sat in the second chair, having bound her usually carefree hair with a red ribbon for the occasion. Godfather Boas, who was also the holder, sat in the third chair.

Riddah lifted one of the infants out of its cradle and gave it to Boas to hold. She unswaddled it. And just then, as Berek tested the knife with his thumb, he felt rather than heard the cry. For a moment he thought he had already cut into the baby's flesh, and yet the cry was more than distant. It was a phantasmal baritone, as though it came from far off, not only in place but in time, from the man the baby would become. Perhaps for that reason the cry further reinforced the silence.

Berek proceeded. He placed the Brick box on Elijah's chair. He whispered the benediction: *"Praised be Thou, oh Lord, Who hast hallowed us by Thy commandments and commanded us to make our sons enter into the covenant of Abraham our father."* Berek took the naked, black-haired infant from Boas and put it on Elijah's chair with the Brick. For one minute he let it become a pink, wrinkled little prophet. He returned the child to Boas's right knee. *"In memory of thy paternal grandfather, Feitel,"* he whispered, *"I name thee Ferdinand Feitel Spiegelglass."*

Berek took the other, brown-haired baby whom Riddah had unswaddled and had given to Boas to hold. For one minute Berek changed him to the prophet Elijah on the Brick box. He placed him on Boas's left knee, whispering, *"In memory of thy maternal grandfather, Chaim, I name thee Conrad Chaim Spiegelglass."*

He kissed his little Ferdinand, kissed his little Conrad. He positioned the bowl beneath them and took the knife. He made the incision on Ferdinand, then tore rather than cut off the foreskin, remembering from his *mohel* days in Varungy that the wound healed faster after a warm hand than after a cold edge. As in Varungy, he dropped quickly to his knees to suck up most of the blood. He repeated the procedure with Conrad. And only now, with the wail of both babies rising into the sun's rays, with their voices vibrating into the red taste on his tongue—only now did the silence all around collapse.

Suddenly that other cry, heard minutes earlier, expanded to its true shape in his ear. It had been Schall shouting. And then, right afterward, there had been a click with which, very quietly, the partition door had opened. He shook the sounds away, as he dabbed with disinfectant. He looked around. Riddah was gone.

It took him half a minute to absorb that. Then, in one moment, he was gone, too. He was out on the street, in Turk Place, which was still sunny, still quiet, yet shaken by a secret earthquake whose center was a single small object he saw lying before the entrance of No. 5. It was a gray leather glove. Dr. Huber's.

"Tamarah," he cried. He cried again, doubly loud, to make up for his delay in answering Schall's shout. *"Tamarah!"*

Schall had a rectangular mirror at the entrance to his apartment on the ground floor of No. 5. There, at the bottom of the stairs, Berek met Riddah coming down from his own apartment just as he was about to rush up. The mirror threw its reflections into his eyes and shocked him still more with flecks of bright crimson. His mouth was bloody, so were his hands, but Riddah's hands were also smeared with red. The mirror flashed all that at him as they collided.

But it was a collision on purpose. She blocked his way.

"Tamarah!" he cried. "She's bleeding! She's sick!"

"First finish with the boys," Riddah said in a voice he didn't recognize.

"Let me go up!"

"Have you finished with the boys?"

"Yes, let me go up to her!"

"You still have the boys," she said. "Your boys will—" Then, released into her sudden, enormous sob, he fell against her and, embracing, their bloodinesses mingling, they walked up the stairs together, toward his dying wife.

XI

FOR THE REST of this world's centuries no breath would come from Tamarah's lips. And the world brawled on without losing one beat. On a tree in the backyard, sparrows bickered while Tamarah's pinkie, spotted with blood, curled for the last time. Her pregnancy had swelled to plumbers' hammers and to the boom of presses in the factory. On the Monday after the Sunday of her death the hammering and the booming noised on exactly as before.

Stunned by the continuity, Berek washed his wife's flesh on the kitchen table. Her form had resumed its usual, fragile sweetness. She seemed almost more normal and familiar than during the recent months, when she had been alive and distended.

After the tradition he remembered from Varungy, he placed her face downward inside the shroud: her eyes must not be blinded by the shining of the Lord at the moment of resurrection. For the sake of that moment he folded into her shroud her nightgown, her sheets, pillow and handkerchief, all stiff and dark with her dried blood, so that it would liquify and return to her fast as her vital fluid. In her right hand he put a wooden fork to help her burrow upward from the grave. By her left he placed a covered dish of water with a linen strip, for the bathing and drying of her soul. This done, he sewed the shroud together.

That night Riddah did not bake. She lit the candles by which Berek dug in the large backyard garden of the factory at No. 1. His shovel hissed in the midst of winter-shriveled shrubbery. Then Riddah helped Berek move his wife from the kitchen table to the grave.

Perhaps Tamarah had lost yet more weight. Perhaps Berek's shovel-stunned muscles were too numb to feel. Whatever the reason, it seemed to him that the shroud glided by itself, winging like a long bird through the gaslit dark. He needed only one hand to guide it. The other held the Brick.

Behind him walked Boas, cradling the two babies in his good arm. Siddo Berger followed; so did a tall woman obscured by a sail-like large hat. Her father was the brother of Tamarah's father, she said. She'd read her cousin's burial announcement, which Schall, on his own, had placed in the *Wiener Zeitung*. Schall himself followed the thin procession with his cap against his heart. He watched the ceremonies from the factory's back door at a Christian distance.

By the grave they all—except the tall woman—tore off bits of their clothing. All, including the tall woman, helped Berek lower the shroud. They all cast bits of earth into the grave. But only Berek took the circumcising knife and shaved off one grain from the Brick and let it flutter down to his Tamarah. Berek alone grasped the shovel to fill the grave with earth.

After he had prayed the Kaddish, the tall woman stepped up. She said another Kaddish should be said, for Tamarah's father. He, too, was dead. She said that her own father, who had lived with him in Palestine, had sent her the news a year ago, after it had happened. Tamarah's father had not wanted word of his illness to reach his daughter lest it lead her to desert the Brick.

Berek prayed the Kaddish again. Then the tall woman said her name was Hester. She would not be able to make a mourning visit tomorrow; she had her tobacconist's shop to run behind the cathedral in the Inner City. Without another word, with a sound more like a low gasp than a rip, she tore off a piece of her blouse and gave it to Berek. While the silk was still warm in his hand, she was gone. Suddenly, wildly, like wolf cubs in the night, the twins began to cry.

If there had been mourning visitors to the Spiegelglass apartment, they would not have found Berek there. He did not eat in the room where he used to have his meal with Tamarah. He hardly ate at all. Between baking stints at night Riddah boiled some beef for him which he left untouched. Mornings he nibbled at some rolls while Boas cooed over the cradles in the next room. When the moon was up, Riddah saw to the bottle feedings; after the sun rose, the albino's sister took over the task. Berek did not come near the twins. He tossed on the cot he'd used many years ago, sharing bachelor digs downstairs with Schall. The vital details of his life—the twin beds, the evening dinner, the babies: all must be kept at a distance. Touch them and they would shatter. Sharp mirror fragments might slash him.

He did not even work in the factory. He worked under it. His day was spent in the half-collapsed Turkish tunnel discovered during the digging for the gas main. He cleared the passage that led from the hall of No. 2, down to the cellar across the street, under the factory, where it became a stopped-up tube. With the shovel that had dug Tamarah's grave he kept scooping away in the blackness like a blind, infallible mole. He did not rest until he had created a compartment directly beneath the faint pulse of the presses. Up there Schall had taken charge. Down here Berek placed the Brick box in the compartment. He put a bolt on the compartment door. On the gate that opened onto the tunnel at No. 2 he hung a lock.

Underground or above, Berek moved with an unshaven, unstopping, unhumming, somnambulistic slowness. Nobody dared inquire about the nature of his work below. But above, on the surface of the earth, practicalities were waiting.

One was a smooth-shaven, melodious-voiced young man who introduced himself as Rabbi Dr. Wilhelm Ackermann. He had had the sad duty of signing Frau Spiegelglass's death certificate, heaven be her resting place, and he had come to pay his respects to Herr Spiegelglass and to say that he looked forward to organizing the Turk Place synagogue in the future and that, as for the present, he applauded the sentiments which had led Herr Spiegelglass to an interim interment of the remains on his own property—a perfectly understandable act, since next month at the new Jewish section of the Vienna Central Cemetery a more progressive and meaningful funeral liturgy—

"What do you mean, 'interim'?" Berek said.

"Temporary," the rabbi said. "A temporary burial."

"It is not a temporary burial," Berek said. "It is permanent."

Oh, Dr. Ackermann said. Well, this was the wrong time to raise such a matter. Important as it was, it could wait, it was too soon after the bereavement. First Herr Spiegelglass must get some rest and perhaps a better perspective, and second . . . second, Schall came along, carrying a plate of roast-beef sandwiches, saying that the house-number order was almost finished. They ought to discuss the street signs after Berek had eaten something and gotten some rest.

"Later," Berek said. He said nothing else. He turned away from the sandwiches. That day he did get some rest, though not at home.

Without a word to anyone Berek left Turk Place and took the slow train meandering from Vienna to Bratislava. He carried nothing with him except some gulden bills and the piece torn from the silk blouse of the tall woman. He always kept the piece in his hip pocket. He slept on the wooden bench of the fourth-class compartment until he was waked up by the conductor. Then he slept again, stretched out on the oxcart he hired to take him from Bratislava to Varungy. A hand shook him out of some river dream. He sat up—nowhere.

Varungy had become a silo, a vast tombstone, as massive and stolid as the sky. The silo cast a shadow that broke the line of the railroad tracks, fell on the charred skeleton of what had once been the train depot, and darkened the weed-choked wall of the cemetery.

It was some man from Budapest, the peasant with the oxcart said. It was all the Budapester's doing. He had bought the land and broken up the houses into masonry pieces and built the silo out of the pieces. The geese were dead or scattered. But you could still see the doors.

Berek saw them. The doors of Varungy lay snow-flecked among last summer's stinging nettles. One door had become the base of a dead anthill. Others were half decayed, looking like huge, rectangular warts of earth. Finally, he recognized the synagogue's gate. It was the biggest and best-preserved door, having been carved of oakwood. It still had the heart-shaped lock, now rusted cinnamon, which Berek had made as a young blacksmith.

He pulled this door along the underbrush. While the peasant, head shaking, lashed it to his cart, Berek went to the cemetery, which had entirely drowned in furze and heather. He said Kaddish by the wave of brambles most likely to conceal his parents' grave.

He went back to the cart and lay down again. The sun had come out. From his pocket he took the silk shred of the woman's blouse. He tied it around his head, across his eyes. It was faintly perfumed and full of sleep. To cart bumpings he slept his way back to Bratislava; to train bumpings, back to Vienna. Another cart brought him and his cargo to Turk Place. At the sight of him Boas came shouting with relief. Riddah, just up, offered him her hot-sausage breakfast. He went past them to that corner of the factory which was still a smithy.

Nobody dared interrupt him while, for the next three days, he forged a trellised wrought-iron frame for the door, the door of the synagogue of Varungy; while he fused Tamarah's embroidery needles into the door's heart-shaped lock; while he dug a hole at the head of the grave in the backyard of No. 1; while he wedged the lower third of the door into that hole, then tamped down the earth around it. Tamarah had a tombstone.

Next morning he found that it had begun to lean. He dug it out again, reset it more deeply, closer to Tamarah, strengthening its anchorage with stones.

"Spiegelglass?" Schall's voice said.

"I don't need help," Berek said.

"There is someone here." Schall had come through the back door of the factory, followed by a man wearing an overcoat with black fur lapels and by a lackey carrying a cardboard box.

Berek shook the door-tombstone. It remained firm. It maintained its ninety-degree angle against the earth.

"At His Serene Highness's command," the man said. The lackey opened the box for a moment to show the long ball gown, gorgeously black and yellow, that Tamarah had embroidered for the princess.

"Your wife is to take in four centimeters at the waist without damaging the embroidery pattern," the man said. "Serenity's mother has lost further weight."

Berek had shed his coat for the digging. Now the heat of exertion was gone and a breeze colder than October stiffened the leafless shrubs around him. In his pocket his fingers tightened around the silk shred, the one from Tamarah's cousin. His lips were too numb to explain about "your wife."

The man screwed a monocle into his left eye. The monocle surveyed the silence. "This alteration is to be done by next week because of the state of the princess's health," the man said. "Is that understood?"

The lackey put the box into Berek's hands. The fur-lapeled man unscrewed his monocle, which kept staring from his hand. The two men left together with Schall, who shook his head, openmouthed.

For minutes Berek stood in the breeze, the box in his hands. He dropped it on the ground, walked through the factory noise. "Where is the man?" he asked Schall at the front door. Schall could only point at a cloud of dust.

Coatless as he was, Berek walked to a fiacre standing at the new tramway terminal. "To the Wallers *palais*," he said.

All he wanted was to be near the Wallers man awhile longer, near such astounding certainty that "your wife" would yet be able to take in four centimeters of a gown. He didn't believe in that certainty. He could not hope for it. He just wanted to be warmed by it a bit longer. But the breeze had grown to a wind, and the wind blew through the fiacre door and spread the chill beyond Berek's lips. The wind drove shivers across scudding house walls and into Berek's bowels. He knew now where it came from. The wind blew in through the door that stood upright on Turk Place earth.

When he had washed Tamarah's body, had prepared the shroud, had filled it and buried it; when he had traveled to Varungy and brought back the door that was to serve as her stone—when he had done all that, he had still done it with Tamarah. But the moment he had placed the door on her grave in perfect upright position, that had been the moment severing her from him.

It was impossible that the wind should blow without her. But the wind blew. It blew on a transgression against the Brick, against its command to endure. It blew, very cold, at Berek on the speeding seat. It blew at his sudden stump. It blew at an amputation which had not fully seared him until now.

He rose up against the pain. The fiacre was passing through the center of the city. Wheels rattled across the huge shadow of the cathedral spire. Berek, on his feet, shouted that the wind blew too cold, he had forgotten his coat, he must get off. The driver mumbled and began to slow. Berek found a gulden bill in his back pocket, put it on the seat and jumped.

Probably he had fallen. His left knee stung. But he could walk. He walked and he felt warmer. He followed the warmth to its source behind the cathedral. He stood before the tobacconist's shop. It had a sign saying CLOSED FOR LUNCH. By then he knew enough of the alphabet to make out the words. He ignored their meaning just as he ignored his knee. He knocked. He knocked again. After that the cathedral knocked for him. The great bell of St. Stephen's rang, ancient, formidable, cast of the metal of 180 Turkish cannons captured after the siege. It struck twelve-thirty. It tolled twice.

The clangor loosened the door. Berek merely had to touch the knob. Before him opened a small room at whose other end was a counter filled with pipe racks and a row of newspapers neatly stacked. Behind it, next to a midget potted palm, nibbling from a box of chocolates, sat Tamarah.

Berek had seen his wife's cousin just once before: during the funeral, her head covered by a hat, at night. Now in the daylight, with her face bared, she had Tamarah's curved blond eyebrows set against the dark, braided hair. She had the same pale blue eyes and even the same faint vertical wrinkle dividing the smooth white of the same forehead.

"Oh my God," he said amid the after-echoes of the bells.

The woman got up. She was much taller. Tamarah's face rose on a much higher, more voluptuously fleshed pedestal. Calmly, the fringes of her bodice swayed.

"Don't stand out there on the threshold," she said. "It's freezing without a coat."

He stepped closer. Her chocolate breath came at him. So did the tang of pipe tobacco. The mingled scents awakened his stomach. Much more amazing, they seemed to cure not only his amputation but the transgression against the Brick.

"I want you to be at Turk Place," he said without even thinking.

She took a small step back. A small, light step close to dancing, then took the same step forward again. Her heels gave off clicks that told him that despite her body's opulence, her feet were little, as little as Tamarah's.

No words came from her in reply. She took up the box of candy and held it out. He took a chocolate-coated almond. He realized that he had been starving himself for a week. He was ravenous. For a moment their lips moved in the same rhythm, munching. A late bell tolled the half hour in the distance, and she smiled.

XII

SHORTLY after Berek Spiegelglass's second wedding he built a double door for his bedchamber. The bedchamber itself had traveled. It was now downstairs, in the flat Schall had left for more spacious quarters across the street. Berek constructed a private staircase between the two floors of his enlarged apartment, the lower serving as hall, dining room, and the bedchamber double-doored to stop all sound.

Nobody much noticed any of this because it merged into the general flux and flowering of Turk Place. The wedding itself proceeded almost on tiptoe. It took place in the still pewless synagogue at No. 2, to the sniffling intonations of a junior rabbi whose nose suffered from the smell of fresh paint. The rabbi was junior for a reason. Someone at the Jewish Council, in charge of such matters, had become aware that Herr Spiegelglass was re-entering wedlock less than four months after his first wife's decease. The council did not want to sanction such haste with the presence of the synagogue's future minister, Dr. Wilhelm Ackermann.

The junior rabbi finished his chore on Turk Place in time to witness a much more prominent occasion happening nearby, a little later in the day: the lord mayor of the imperial capital cutting a scarlet ribbon that hung where the city gate had once been. He declared all that lay before him—the tenement regions, Turk Place, the market, everything up to the Vienna Woods—an integral part of the capital, to be known henceforward as its 17th District, called Hernals.

Of course, this act of municipal union attracted much more attention than Berek's nuptials. But even if many eyes had stared at Berek's second wife, few would have noticed her resemblance to the first. For one thing, she was distinctly taller. For another, her face remained something of a secret; she favored lavishly brimmed hats that disclosed little beyond a curved lower lip. Even hatless she managed to be not much more revealing. In the evening she liked the light dim. With one very soft breath she could extinguish three offending candles. After moving into Turk Place, she'd begin the day by combing her hair forward, whistling faintly. This produced bangs which not only hid her upper features but which were tousled in a way that disarrayed, subtly and interestingly, the line of her chin and cheeks.

She did not, of course, stutter like Tamarah. But then her laconic hoarse voice was not often heard. She talked little. However, she rustled. When she walked, even when she sat, a resonance surrounded her. Her body seemed to stream audibly along the inside of her tiny-waisted long-swelling dress. It was the sound of a natural force delicately diminished—like the surge of a magnificent rapids filtered through distance to a whisper.

Rabbi Ackermann could not escape the whisper. He first heard it during his pastoral visit following the marriage of the synagogue's landlord. The new couple's hall and dining room were still largely unfurnished, but the emptiness only amplified the female rustle. Somehow the rustle moistened the air as Berek, still in his work smock at 9 PM, led the rabbi toward his wife.

Rabbi Ackermann went into the preliminaries of a hand kiss that was really quite proper at Turk Place now that the street had become integrated with Vienna. But the rustle from the immobile woman together with her hatted height disoriented him. His hand kiss was aborted into a bow. He let himself be ushered to the room's one armchair, a yard away from the double doors of the bedroom. Silent for longer than was his wont, the rabbi decided to dispense with the usual pleasant conversational preludes. He would call himself—and the situation—to order by proceeding to the matter at hand.

Frau Spiegelglass breathed at three candles along the wall; three

flames swooned and died. Then she poured kümmel. The splash of
liquid against glass counterpointed the undervoice from her clothes.
It stiffened the rabbi's resolve. As soon as he had toasted his hosts'
health, he confessed that he had come to face, together with them,
a certain problem: the beloved grave in the backyard of No. 1 Turk
Place. Unfortunately, any new cemetery, large or small, could be established only in those areas of the capital that still had a rural or
garden character. Such was the law.

In response to this the door snapped open. A woman in a white
baker's apron strode through the room, followed by two helter-
skelter roosters. Berek Spiegelglass introduced her as his cousin
Riddah, shooed the roosters out the door, and said that the grave
was permanent and the area was rural in the sense of the presence
of chickens.

Rabbi Ackermann gave a smile as polite as it was firm. Nobody
appeared to notice that it was negative. The aproned lady scrambled
up the staircase to the second floor of the apartment "to look after
the babies." The second Frau Spiegelglass went up after her, leaving
behind, somehow, the aroma of her rustle.

Rabbi Ackermann took another sip of kümmel. He felt its lush
sting only now but hardened his nostrils against it. It was a pity, he
said; the matter of the grave could prevent the proper and fitting in-
auguration of the synagogue. Lately, the Vienna city government
had jumped to exploit every opportunity for anti-Semitism. Therefore, the Jewish Council might hesitate to petition the Imperial
Chancellery for His Majesty's customary personal attendance at the
consecration of a new house of worship in the capital. The council
might not want the All Highest presence to call attention to the un-
licensed grave at Turk Place.

Herr Spiegelglass absorbed this by getting up and adjusting,
with vigorous blows, the askew leg of the stool on which he had
been seated. The chicken lady in the baker's apron blurred down the
staircase and out the door. A moment later Frau Spiegelglass flowed
down, bearing a shallow silver bowl. In it rolled nuggets, rich and
brown and enigmatic, which she offered to the rabbi.

They were, his tongue discovered, chocolate-dipped fig balls.
Their two-toned sweetness harmonized quite cunningly with the

kümmel Frau Spiegelglass poured him anew. She was going to grow violets in the graveyard garden, she said from under her hat; she planned to make candied violets for the opening of the synagogue.

"You see, a garden," Herr Spiegelglass said. "Not only chickens, but a garden. Rural. Legal for a permanent grave."

Not he but his wife carried the day, however. Her rustle, her lofty twilit face, and those excellently manipulated fig balls framed the birth of a new approach in Rabbi Ackermann's mind. It was an approach based on a fresh insight. He realized that his future parishioners here possessed a potential that was eccentric, perhaps, yet for that very reason unusual and vital—it deserved encouragement. Aloud he admitted (savoring another fig ball) that the Jewish Council could only benefit from strengthening and supporting the congregation-to-be in the new 17th District. Actually, it might be his duty to say so to the council. After all, he did not consider his service at the synagogue as a mere marginal assignment. The future synagogue here should be a forward-looking center of the Jewish heritage, capable of all ceremonials of life and death. Therefore, he would be glad to support a license for a cemetery based on the rural elements still enriching the area. And he would take it upon himself to apply for the emperor's presence at the consecration.

Ushered out, the rabbi completed the hand kiss he'd begun half an hour earlier at his entrance. Only then, when his lips touched the second Frau Spiegelglass's knuckles, did the rustle stop.

Hester Spiegelglass not only saved the rabbi's visit, she also saved the synagogue's consecration. The event would bring the emperor himself to Turk Place. As a consequence, it began by confounding most of the important congregants.

These gentlemen lived in a middle-class archipelago strung out into the tenement sea. There was Herr Pellmann of the Café Pellmann, which featured, besides much wooden furniture and lager beer for workers, a few upholstered banquettes and marble tables at which factory assistant managers sipped coffee *mélange* topped with cinnamon-sprinkled whipped-cream dollops. There was Herr Stelnitz, the pawnbroker, who introduced modernity into the 17th District by making pawned electric lanterns the centerpiece of his window display. There was the florist Herr Schönfeld, who sold funeral wreaths on long-term credit as well as boutonniere carnations at a special courtesy discount available to every unmarried police lieutenant in the precinct.

All these men had been mere worshipers at an Inner City synagogue they could reach only after a long trip in the fiacre. At Turk Place they debarked in greater dignity after a much shorter and cheaper ride. Here they came into their own as members of the synagogue board.

They had not expected to be dismayed at their inaugural visit to what was after all their own house of God. True, they were satisfied to find, to the left of the pulpit, the board members' pew set apart from the rest according to custom. On the right side lay the small but thick Persian rug under the armchair reserved for His Majesty. But in between had been placed not only the new Torahs in their velvet vestments but also a double cradle and a tin box on a sort of tripod.

Rabbi Ackermann smiled and explained: the cradles held the infant sons of Herr Spiegelglass, who provided the space rent-free and who was therefore board president. In the tin box Herr Spiegelglass kept a brick reputed to date back to the Great Temple.

All of which was very well but did not keep box and cradles from obstructing vital sightlines. Those items would not let the emperor see the board; nor the board, the emperor. Board members would not be able to make a definitive report to their dinner tables tonight on how far into salt the salt-and-pepper sideburns of His Majesty had progressed. It wasn't fair: the Jewish Community Council levied a sizable religious tax on all the faithful in the board-member bracket. Their money had paid for the synagogue's interior. And they in turn had a right to be repaid by, among other things, an imperial anecdote. They did not appreciate being deprived.

Matters became even less satisfactory with the appearance of Herr Spiegelglass. Though he wore a morning coat, he also wore brown boots and a cap instead of a top hat. He did not say "It pleases me very much to have the honor," as was usual at the introduction between personages at a flattering occasion in the capital. He just crushed fingers with a callused hand that had never known a manicurist. The man was still very much a Balkan Jew who had little compunction about letting his origins obtrude. Slovak consonants grated in the accent with which he called out briskly—in fact, brusquely—that everybody had better stand together closer— still closer!—his cousin Boas wanted to take a photograph in the vestibule.

Cousin Boas fussed with his camera for quite a while. When he was finished, the board needed a few more minutes to spread out into a thin, reverent line suitable for welcoming the emperor. By that time it was a quarter past eleven. Franz Joseph, whose punctuality the newspapers praised and recorded daily, was late. Board members began to raise eyebrows at one another. Perhaps, Herr Pellmann breathed to Herr Schönfeld, some Crown official had gotten wind of that brick-and-babies business. But his and all other whisperings suddenly stopped. Or rather they were superseded by a very low but magnetic sound.

Hester Spiegelglass had entered. She carried the mirror that had once hung in the hall of No. 5, in front of Schall's old apartment. It had become her gleaming serving tray. Petits fours topped by candied violets lay arranged there in bright rows glitteringly reflected. She walked along the receiving line, offering her dainties. So casual but at the same time commanding was the song of her skirts; so rosy the color of the parasol dangling from her wrist; so sumptuous her height yet so fastidious her waist, that some board members thought she must be a sort of female herald of the Court.

With bows, with fingers painstakingly arched, they grasped a petit four each. The rabbi, who had retreated to the lavatory to clear his throat in private as he always did before officiating at a public event, had missed her entrance. Returned, he was about to introduce her. But at that moment a giant clanged into the foyer. Much taller than Frau Spiegelglass, thigh-high boots at attention, plumed hat against medaled breast, he quietly pronounced two words. They shivered along the walls.

"His Majesty."

Franz Joseph I lit up the room. His uniform of sky blue froze the board's munching cheeks. There was no way to hide the fact that their mouths were full. They could only mask the embarrassment a bit by bending even more deeply from the waist, and by holding their lifted top hats as screens before their faces. They stayed that way until the emperor and king, with the simplicity that was legend, said, "Good day."

Whereupon they were released into uprightness. Hester Spiegelglass stepped forward. Her little curtsy presented the monarch with the petits fours on the mirror. Surprised but not displeased by what must be a quaint Israelite custom, the emperor accepted one and led it to his mouth.

"Scented, very nice," he said.

To the thrill of everyone present, he began to chew. Hester Spiegelglass stepped up to the giant and he, too, partook. During the next five seconds Apostolic Majesty, adjutant and board members all chewed in almost the same rhythm.

The magic of that unison transfigured the entire morning. It sweetly narcotized the babies so that they slumbered in peace through the solemnities which followed. It suffused Rabbi Ackermann. Having delivered his benedictions over Torahs, infants and Brick, he said that he as well as all of his coreligionists here would remember until their dying day what had happened this hour beneath this roof: that on the opening day of the 17th District synagogue a great ruler and his devoted subjects had shared some sweetness together under their common Lord.

And Hester Spiegelglass, watching from the women's balcony—standing there alone, for the upstairs pews had not yet been delivered—took another petit four from the mirror reposing on the balustrade and softly rustled and softly munched.

Perhaps Berek Spiegelglass was the only man not surprised by Hester's performance at the consecration. He had come to expect peculiarities. Months earlier she had ambushed him during their bridal night.

In all matters leading up to the wedding she had been downright complaisant. For example, she seemed to understand that Berek wanted his wife in Turk Place full-time. Willingly, she sold her tobacconist's shop in the Inner City. The proceeds—320 gulden for the franchise, 80 gulden for furnishings—she handed over to Berek, who could well use extra money just then: due to the princess's "lingering indisposition" (as a note from the steward's office phrased it) the Wallers imperial birthday ball had been canceled together with the order for ball favors. Hester's "dowry" helped fill the income gap. Half of her 400 gulden paid for the last installment of the factory's third toggle-joint press. The rest of the sum Berek returned to her. After all, she needed a fit wardrobe as bride and principal lady of Turk Place. Hester spent the money warily. She did not buy an overweening wedding dress—no train, no ambitious cape. She chose a petaled hat, a bodice modestly brocaded, and a skirt that, though it made the wearer's body speak, contained no hint of a bustle. An ensemble so sensible that it would make any shock more shocking.

For the wedding supper Berek had reserved a table at the Café Pellmann, in the upholstered first-class section. It was protected from the proletarian part by a screen on which had been painted a copy of Michelangelo's account of the Creation. Berek noticed that his new wife ate the fried chicken in an interesting way. She kept shifting the fork to her right hand while her left lay languid and pink-gloved on the tablecloth. She nodded when Riddah, after a bare-handed attack on four drumsticks, left abruptly: there were the babies to be tended, the albino having assumed cradle duty in her absence, and there was the night's baking to be done.

Boas stayed on, transfixed by the delicious traffic between the bride's plate and her lips. Hester remained amenable even when he became effusive toward the end of the second bottle of Kremser. He almost pushed over Michelangelo's *Creation* in his attempt to position his tripod and camera for the perfect angle that would do justice to such an exciting couple. Hester let him put the bridegroom's hand on her upper arm in various possessive poses. Finally, Boas became altogether rapt over the manner in which he'd draped Berek's palm over Hester's shoulder. He ran for the shutter under his black cloth, shouting, *"Don't you dare! Don't you dare move a millimeter!*" Until that evening Berek had never touched her above the elbow.

Schall had been a quiet member of the party, defending himself with—unrolled—cigarette smoke against the second Mrs. Spiegelglass's faint perfume. The Café Pellmann did not serve beer to wedding parties in the upholstered section. But even if it had, he would have refused. Somehow he felt that this was a night in which to stay alert. When Boas, swinging yet another bottle of Kremser, began to sing, "Shine for me, oh moon of love," Schall took him and his camera home in a fiacre.

And so Berek was alone with Hester. Alone, they walked the gaslit half mile to Turk Place.

Rain had begun to fall. A rain so light that the moist glitter all around looked like the street's natural secretion. It rose from the cobbles on which the couple walked arm in arm. It seemed to be the perspiration of every stucco goddess that held up a tenement balcony as she watched the couple pass. A fleshly juice gleamed even from the laundry left out by wives who'd gone to sleep before the weather changed; dim silhouettes of blouses and trousers twitched under clothespins, and ogled and oozed.

The pair strode past it all. Hester lifted her face to the wet as though she disdained the protection of her hat. She did not open the parasol. She swung it with an easy sportiveness, as if it were the cane of a man on the town.

They arrived at Turk Place. Berek's key unlocked the door of the almost finished synagogue at No. 2. Another key opened another door inside, not easily visible for it was part of the vestibule's wallpaper pattern; it led from the vestibule down into the Turkish tunnel. With a kerosene lamp he ushered Hester along the passage leading to the factory. He showed her the compartment, under the presses, where the Brick was kept. He took it out and, Brick box under his arm, led her back. Just then he heard something—music echoing oddly against the tunnel walls. He turned around. His lantern lit up a mouth organ between her lips; a very small instrument exquisitely finished in tortoiseshell. It was, she said, stopping the music for a minute, a gift from a dear acquaintance. He locked the tunnel and the synagogue doors and asked if by any chance he knew the giver. She must have misunderstood; instead of answering, she said that it might be nice to have music at one's wedding, especially music that one could make oneself. She opened her lips for the instrument again.

She was playing slowly, with a slowness that was almost teasing, Johann Strauss's "Voices of Spring" waltz. The tune accompanied the rustle of her clothes and their footfalls as they climbed the stairs together to what was now their apartment at No. 5.

In the bedroom Berek saw that the Venetian blinds had been left open. He closed them. Yet this made curiously little difference. The drizzle had been succeeded by fog. It diffused yet enlivened the gaslight, transforming it into billows of glow that appeared to be traveling with ease through house walls. Just as the mouth-organ waltz persisted into the bedroom, so the mist entered, too. It lapped at the couple's feet, washed along the floor and seemed to set adrift chairs, beds and furniture legs.

Berek ignored it firmly. Firmly, he placed the Brick box on the night table. He lifted the lid to display the slips wedged in the Brick's fissures. Hester watched him. She'd sat down in a chair without removing her hat, without stopping "Voices of Spring." The waltz still dripped slowly from her lips. Perhaps she was floating, too. Perhaps the room was dissolving slowly, musically, into a lake.

But Berek ignored that. He told Hester about the Brick's place in the family tradition. As his wife, she was now entitled to insert her prayers and requests into the ancient stone. She kept playing the mouth organ, barely nodding. But the nod loosened her hat. It fell to the floor. Her lips kept brushing the waltz out of the harmonica. An irritation began to heat Berek. He didn't pick up her hat. He let it lie there looking like a perverse water lily. Instead of touching her tenderly, as had been his intention for this moment, he tugged hard at the drawer of his night table. He scraped it open. In it lay pencil, notepad and newspaper—all the paraphernalia of his alphabet study that had come to a stop when Tamarah had stopped. He scooped them out and plunked them down next to the Brick box.

"With Tamarah I've learned up to the letter *t*," he said. "We'd better continue from there."

There was no reply. She made no move except to recline a little deeper into the chair, her mouth against the organ, teasing out the waltz, making the room and the mist ripple around her slowly in the rhythm of her beat.

"Let's go," he said.

He sharpened the pencil. He was about to thrust it at her—when she put her left leg up on the night table. This was so amazing, he let go of the pencil. She had raised her leg fluidly and naturally as if abandoning herself into a lazy backstroke in a pool. Not only that, but then she put her other leg on the table, very close to the Brick, almost touching it, almost treading on it.

"I wouldn't do that," he said.

She kept playing the mouth organ, stretched out on her back. Her shoes were scant black patent-leather pumps that showed her well-fleshed ankles, her narrow instep, even the roots of her toes.

"Watch out for the Brick!" he said.

She kept playing. He felt that she controlled, demonically, the drizzle, the fog, the liquification of the room. He grasped her ankles. The dark silk stocking was smooth, stretched tautly around much warmth—and strength. Strong as he was, Berek could barely budge her.

"Watch out!" he said.

Her answer was more waltz, with a refrain like a snicker, very close to a taunt.

"All right!" he said.

For better leverage he dropped to his knees. One heave separated her from chair and night table. He catapulted the whole conspiratorial body into the air. Her waltz slurred into wild chords. The mouth organ dropped to the floor yet continued playing, mouthless, on the floor. Her heat and her weight in his arms, he half staggered, half danced for a moment. She screamed as they fell together. She screamed fiercely, but with a fierceness that frictioned and fit into his own, which he felt spilling through her arms and thighs and tongue, surging in the very pores of the fog that still surfed around them, a fierceness pulsing in the waltz, buried as it was with the harmonica under the warm heap of her dress, a fierceness that melted silk into nipples, that ran through gaslight and rain, through Turk Place and Varungy, running through moons and shadows, running with a speed no night had known before.

The real surprise came a little later.

She was the first to rise from the floor. With small, barefoot steps she walked toward the night table. He had, of course, just sated himself with her body. Yet now that he saw her erect, unfolded, her nakedness was a costume so powerful that it erased the clothed woman, the Hester who had met his eye until today. Their struggle had thrown her bangs back over her head. The kohl she'd used so subtly on her lids that he'd never even noticed it—now it had smudged into little patches under her eyes. Her braids had come undone at the tips. And the resemblance which had played hide-and-seek with him for months now sprang into her face fullblown. There was—without hat, without bangs—the fine forehead divided by the single little wrinkle; the lovely, tired cheeks; the severe braids loosened by a long day's work. There was Tamarah.

But not only Tamarah's features had been resurrected. His wife pulled the room's one chair closer to the night table and then, with a humility doubly poignant because she was naked, picked up and carried over a stool. She sat down on the stool, took the material for alphabet study out of the drawer, and bent over the notepad which still recorded his last writing attempts so many weeks ago.

"Would you like to . . . to go on?" she said.

What had interrupted her question was a sudden breath, a little after-gasp of ecstasy that would repeat itself quite often. A new, higher and softer voice spoke out of her nudeness costume. Embedded in that voice, her interrupting gasp was Tamarah's stutter.

Berek got to his feet and walked to her.

"We'll start with the letter *t*," he said.

They bent over the notepad together. And that was how he reconsummated, by the Brick, his one and only marriage.

XIII

WITHIN A WEEK of that bridal explosion Berek had their bedroom moved downstairs and double doors installed. But at first the precaution seemed pointless. For the next few days Hester embraced every aspect of matrimony except the one that had given Berek the most incandescent moments of his life.

Mornings, Hester Spiegelglass went into the twins' room and devoted herself to making duplicates of all the toys of which Berek and his first wife had made only one. She let Resi, the albino's sister, see to lunch and to much of dinner. Not that the new mistress of Turk Place avoided the kitchen altogether. She never put on an apron, yet most of her afternoons were spent on the concoction of an astounding variety of unheard-of desserts—a chestnut mousse, a ginger soufflé, carrot slivers marinated in a mysterious syrup—each of which made the end of Berek's dinner a wonderfully irregular treat.

Then, at night, when the couple closed those double doors behind them, the letdown: she'd bought a chinoiserie screen on the far side of which she changed—unrustling—from her dress into a stolid sort of white nightgown in which she promptly burrowed into bed. When he touched her, the response was a drowsy, not too logical mutter, something about her mouth organ having been damaged "last time."

"Then get another damn organ," Berek said.

"I'm replacing it," she mumbled. Immediately came a very deep

and, to him, uselessly female breath. She slept. The covers tumesced
with the rising of her breasts.

Yet what she said was true. She did replace the mouth organ
very soon and rather unforgettably. Coming home for dinner, he
found a horse van and, just unloaded on the sidewalk, an upright
player piano and a carved wooden piano stool in the form of a
baroque mushroom. Hester sat on the mushroom, swiveling under
her hat and saying that she'd kept the instrument in storage until
now; it was the gift of a dear acquaintance, but much too large for
the one-room flat behind the tobacconist's shop in which she had
lived as a single woman. Now it would be perfect for the extra room
upstairs.

"What is *that?*" Berek said, looking up. The moving men had
appeared with hammers at a second-floor window.

"Oh, the piano is too big for the stairs," she said. "So they have
to enlarge the window. They have to get it in through there."

"Put the hammers away," Berek called. "The piano goes into the
anteroom downstairs."

"I'm upstairs a lot," Hester said, swiveling. "It'd be better
there."

"Nobody lays a hammer on Turk Place," Berek said.

"I'd like it upstairs," Hester said. "The acoustics are better."

"*Down!*" Berek said to the men.

Down the men came. Hester swiveled coolly on the stool and
said she wasn't sure yet. Maybe it was all right to have the piano
downstairs. Or maybe she'd send it back to storage. She'd think it
over till tomorrow. She kept sitting and rotating on the piano stool
in the street. She sat there after Berek had sent the men packing
with a small tip. She swiveled on the stool, whistling faintly between her sharp white teeth. As the van drove off she threw a lever.
The keyboard twitched. All by itself the piano began to play the
"Radetzky March" in the street. She swiveled to it under her hat.

Berek turned on his heel and went inside. The table was set. He
washed his hands, waited another minute for her to follow. Then he
shouted for his dinner. Resi brought in braised beef and peas. The
piano played outside while he chewed opposite her empty chair. He
shouted for his dessert. Resi trembled in with a plate of daintily

pyramided sugar-dusted vanilla crescents made by her mistress. Berek ate them. On his tongue lusciousness crumbled into sand. He pushed away the plate and went outside again.

She was swiveling to the third repetition of the "Radetzky March." A small crowd goggled at the sorcerized piano. Smiling for their benefit, as though it were a game, Berek picked her up together with the stool. Smiling, she held on to him, pulling hard, hurtingly, at the hair on the back of his neck.

He carried her into the house, and the strain of the weight affected him less than the pain at his hair roots and the thrust in his loins. At the apartment door he dropped the stool but not her. Inside the bedroom, her legs embraced his waist, thrusting back at his thrust. He let the double doors snap shut behind them, but they were too far gone to reach the bed.

Again they clashed superbly, body raiding body. When that was over, so was the "Radetzky March," which had been playing once more out on the street. During the stillness she rose in her humble opulence of flesh and hair and carried chairs to the night table and pulled the writing material out of the drawer. "We can . . . continue," she said with her shuddering stutter. That evening they reached the letter *v*.

After a while the stage managing of their very special clandestine war became more and more sophisticated. He learned from her how to maneuver commonplace spats into the magnificent offensives they would wage at one another: fantastic campaigns of flesh against flesh, infiltrating, charging, detonating in marvelous hostilities.

On an August day in 1890 he headed for his lunch at No. 5 earlier than usual, just in time to see his wife return from the market. Hester's head supported a mountainous hat. Nearly every passing face turned. After the meal he asked her why she wore such huge things.

"I didn't know you were so interested in fashion," she said. "Of course that hat is too big for shopping. But you see, my dresser is in the bedroom. And not much sun comes in the bedroom. My only light is bad gaslight. And if you're different from the rest of civilization and have no electric light, it's easier to put on a big hat than a small. Do you see?"

She'd mentioned it before: the electric light in her former Inner City flat as opposed to the gaslit provinciality of Turk Place.

"I see," he said. "I should install electricity so that you can put on smaller hats."

Her shoulders conveyed the faint, rustling suggestion of a shrug. With the miniature nail file carried ever ready in her sleeve, she began to make more pointed still her already finely pointed fingernails. He and she were locked into battle position.

"Look," he said. "We've just delivered the last batch of those house-number shields. There are no new orders in the factory. I can't spend money on new lights."

Lips pursed, she blew filed particles off her fingers.

"I think Turk Place is good even in gaslight," he said.

"You think," she said. "Perhaps it would help your thinking if you did it under electric light sometime."

"Tomorrow I'll be under electric lights," he said. "I have an appointment under electric lights. They'll make no difference to my thoughts."

"You? Such a modern appointment?" she said with nasty surprise. "Where?"

"At the Jockey Club," he said. "Prince Wallers wants me to meet him there. I'm sure there'll be electric lights. It won't make any difference to me."

"The Jockey Club?" she said. "Two blocks from my old shop? You at the Jockey Club? That would be interesting to see."

"Maybe you'll see it," he said. "Maybe I'll take you along."

"Maybe I'll have time." She smiled at the perfection of her fingernails, which four minutes later raked just short of laceration delectably across Berek's hips.

The next day Hester wore a pastel-green hat that was relatively small. Berek almost admired her when neither her face nor the quality of her rustling changed as he led her past the columned portals of the Jockey Club, around the corner, down a flight of pockmarked stairs into the club kitchen.

It was a cavern whose enormity was made more abrasive by some twenty naked lightbulbs. They poured a harsh and yellow-grained glare over the cooks, the pots, the scullions, the scurry, the litter, the shouts, the eggshells and the clanking.

"This is where you meet your prince," Hester said.

"It's the Jockey Club with electric lights," Berek said.

On a table nearby lay a heap of plucked pheasants with wild red eyes and slit necks. Hester just puckered her nostrils and wandered off toward the pastry chef in the corner—at the very moment the prince came in. He wore a suit so black it made his cheeks, his glasses, even his mustache look like paper. As he kicked onion peels out of his way he was followed by a lackey with a long cardboard box.

"Wife has done no alterations on the gown, not a millimeter," the prince said. "Now she'll have to do it overnight."

"What?" Berek said.

"Mama's gown is still much too big." The prince's voice sounded as though strained through a sieve. Onion peels, wispy as feathers, flew from his kicking black shoe. "I promised Mama she'd wear it yet, I promised it would fit perfectly. I'm seeing this through myself. Alterations are to be made tonight."

"You mean that ball gown," Berek said.

"Mama so loved the gown," the prince said. "She was too sick for a fitting. But she's not sick anymore, now she'll wear it forever and the chaplain says he's been told . . ." The prince didn't go on. An onion peel had attached itself to the point of his shoe, and he bent down with a groan to brush it off. "The chaplain says the gown has been fitted, it's six centimeters too big at the waist. So Wife will fix that instantly overnight. Mama needs it to repose in the chapel to-morrow."

"Repose?" Berek said.

There was no answer.

"She died?"

The prince said nothing.

"I'm sorry," Berek said.

"Six centimeters to be taken in without harming the embroidery. Mama adored the embroidery," the prince said. He groaned again, for another onion peel had become stuck to his shoe. He tried to kick it off in the direction of Hester, who was chatting with the pastry chef, shaking her head at the glare from the ceiling.

"Better tell Wife to start work at once," said the prince.

"This isn't her," Berek said.

"I don't care, it's to be done overnight in time for the chapel," said the prince. After a nod from him, the lackey with the cardboard box had started toward Hester.

"My wife, the one you mean," Berek said. "She died six months ago."

The lackey stopped.

"That's why I sent the gown back without alterations," Berek said.

"Died." The prince pushed his glasses back on his small nose. "You, too. Died. Why?"

"I don't know."

Berek didn't know. He didn't know why just then Hester had to unfold her parasol against the glare. The raising of her arms molded her and her shirtwaist into a fulsome caricature of Tamarah. The sight was like syrup thrown into Berek's eyes.

"But this, who's this?" the prince asked.

"This is someone else," Berek said.

"Crying helps only so much," the prince said. "I don't have someone else after Mama. I can't even stay at home while Mama reposes in the bedroom, it's too killing for me, I have to do all my town business in the club."

"Nobody is crying," Berek said.

He was not crying, but he could not control the blinking of his eyes. He had expected none of this, and he resented what was coming at him, all at once, from inside and out.

"Busy helps," the prince said. "I have three hunts next week. I'll be heraldic consultant to the minister of war. You're keeping busy? You're doing the house-number shields for us, the street signs?"

"I've finished them," Berek said.

"You're making other street signs or things for someone else?"

"No," Berek said, blinking.

The prince had taken out a handkerchief to flick the stubborn onion peel off his shoe. Then he laid his cheek against the linen, as he had laid his cheek against the gun down in the sewer, aiming. He was aiming at Hester. Through his blinks Berek saw that Hester, twirling her unfolded parasol, now stood at a dingy part of the kitchen wall dotted with six porcelain light switches.

"Switch plates," the prince said. "I'll keep you busy making switch plates. I'm no longer ambassador in St. Petersburg, but I'm decor chairman of the Jockey. We need switch plates upstairs, every-where. Protect the walls here against smudging butlers. I give you an order for fifty switch plates, embossed in bronze with the Jockey crest."

"Excuse me," Berek said.

He had seen that Hester was reaching for a light switch. She was always making rooms dimmer, and she was about to turn off some light here to soften the glare. He ran forward in time to pre-vent her. Somehow the motion of his legs stopped the blinking of his eyes. He took her parasol, folded it and let her have it again. She followed him back to the prince.

"I'm sorry, sir," he said. "This is my new wife."

"Ah," the prince said. He looked at her curtsy. "No, she couldn't make the alteration, she'd harm the embroidery," he said. "We'll find an overnight seamstress. I'll send you the crest for the switch plates. You keep busy, busy helps."

He was gone. A fat-armed apprentice boy in a smeared apron bowed after him and began to hack off the heads of the wild-eyed pheasants.

"I think this Highness once came into my shop," Hester said. She walked toward the stairs, through the metallic roar of the kitchen, acknowledging a salute from the pastry chef, a stately, rosy sweetmeat once more shaded by her parasol.

XIV

THE NEXT DAY a Wallers courier brought Berek the drawing of a coroneted centaur on a piece of cardboard measuring ten by twenty centimeters. That was the crest of the Jockey Club and those were the dimensions of the switch plate on which it was to be engraved.

Schall fell lustily to designing and to informing Berek of gorgeous prospects. He was acquainted with the sister of the Jockey Club's chief butler; once he'd escorted her to an accordion-playing contest. From her he knew that this was not only the most unmercifully aristocratic club but that it had three hundred members with at least two castles or mansions apiece. That made six hundred residences, each with at least twenty rooms, totaling twelve thousand if you figured a minimal one switch plate per room. An order for twelve thousand switch plates when these fifty caught on with the Jockey set!

Schall was wrong. They did not catch on with the Jockey set at all, if only because so many of its members owned country seats still beyond wiring.

And yet Schall was right. The switch plates caught on magnificently on July 30, 1891, when no less than three very quick rain squalls darkened the noon hour. That day the Vienna Industrialists' Association held its first annual benefit luncheon on behalf of the capital's police officers' widows. The Jockey Club contributed to the occasion by providing, gratis, its main dining hall. None—not a single one—of the regular members used the club that day. Just their absence made all the more preciously significant to an industrialist's eye the smallest traces of their being. Every hint of the blue-blood mode became a revelation.

As a result of that luncheon, eighty thousand gulden were raised for police widows, and thenceforward all along the Ringstrasse, salad no longer was served before the main course but after, just as at the Jockey; parquet floors were waxed to a much less aggressive shine; butlers' gloves changed from snowy silk to off-white cotton. And electric light switches soon acquired ornamental bronze switch plates.

The Jockey switch plates had attracted particular attention during the three showers striking the city while luncheon was served. They produced three dimnesses so stark that the staff had to turn on the electric chandeliers three times. When the affair was over, the guests complimented the maître d' on the tenderness of the venison. And questions were asked about the provenance of those most excellent bas-relief switch plates.

Within a week Berek received the first order, and the Turk Place factory made switch plates for many a controlling shareholder's salon. Spiegelglass presses stamped out switch plates emblematic of memberships in small, select middle-class groups like the Styrian Millowners Fellowship (textured with waterwheels) or the Lainz Lawn Tennis Club (embossed with crossed tennis rackets). Other, still better customers were large monarchy-wide associations like the Imperial and Royal Lawyers' Brotherhood (featuring blindfolded Justice asoar on eagle wings) and the Austro-Hungarian Medical Academy (switch plates with a knight wielding an Aesculapian sword).

Berek delivered these items for three to four gulden apiece, in quantities ranging from two hundred to nine thousand. He had tapped a sizable and steady market for a high-finish product. And no matter what diverse heraldry his factory imprinted on the front of switch plates, their back always bore the small trademark of the Brick. The Brick appeared to have brought permanent prosperity to

Turk Place at last. And yet it could not—at least not yet—close a gap in Berek's soul. He was a father numbed to fatherhood.

Success brought Berek a number of things, including an excuse: a man so busy was unable to give much time to children. He kissed the twins good morning after his breakfast and good night before his dinner. Invariably, whenever he touched his mouth to their foreheads, they cried. In fact, they cried very often, as if to make up for their remarkable quiet, months earlier, when their mother had been alive. They cried in low, suddenly interrupted tones which sounded to Berek like an echo of the stammer in Tamarah's voice. The tiny, vibrating pink babies seemed like parts of her remains, unburied and undead.

Berek preferred to conjure up Tamarah whole, in his own way. Furiously, he would churn her out of Hester's body. After their lovemaking, his first wife would emerge from the bed of his second marriage to stay for a while and help him practice the alphabet, whose study he had now completed. She would bend with him over the notepad that was propped on the box holding the Brick.

Clasping tempestuous Hester was a prelude to the raising of his sweet and tranquil Tamarah. It was a reliable sequence. There seemed to be nothing reliable about the twins. They were like midget ghosts, unruly, uncanny, uncontrollable. The sight of them put a pang and a fear in his heart. That was why he saw little of them even on Sunday, when the factory closed. He kissed the little foreheads and fled to the office, where Siddo Berger helped him catch up on paperwork left over from the week.

It was his cousin Riddah who played parent as well as widower in his stead. Riddah had hired a bench hand for her bakery, in addition to the albino. Now she could spare more time for other things. At midnight she got up and walked with roosters, tools and lantern to the yard behind the factory at Turk Place No. 1. She seeded grass around the grave's door-tombstone; she planted yew; she trained ivy up the low wooden fence Berek had erected the week after the funeral—but which he had not had the heart to touch again.

Riddah also mothered the twins. As soon as her bakery work was finished after sunrise, she ran, still aproned, across the street to the nursery at No. 5. No morning passed without her checking on the milk formula the albino's sister had prepared. She herself diced the boiled carrots and mashed the peas for those teething little gums. And only she could bring that soft choir of two child voices to a stop. Just before retiring at 11 AM, she'd go once more to the sons' room. Within two minutes the crying ceased, mysteriously.

"They'll take a nice nap now," Riddah would say when she walked out. And they did, for hours.

This was a feat Berek's new wife could never bring off. Hester's ways, so persuasive elsewhere, failed with the twins. Even the toys she gave them were ineffective. Ferdinand, the elder of the brothers by half an hour, had received the one rattle his parents had made long before he was born. One day Hester made a second rattle for Conrad, whittling it out of soft wood with her manicure scissors. She handed it to little Conrad, who stared at it, sniffed it, gave a peculiar quick cough, dropped it and cried. She then gave it to Ferdinand, who refused even to hold it. Instead, he put his own Berek-and-Tamarah-made rattle into his mouth and crawled away, both twins now crying together.

Hester took the rejected present. Back in her bedroom she smoothed the rattle with her nail file until it was as polished as a jewel. Again she went to the sons' room to present once more the gift she had now improved. She opened the door at 11 AM—that is, the time when Riddah did the impossible and stilled the children's wails.

What Hester found was Riddah kneeling before the two cribs that had been pushed together very closely. Riddah had uncovered herself and offered her breasts, milkless yet marvelously nippled maternal white pacifiers, to both boys at once. The two crying little mouths became sighing little lips. In a moment, even before Hester could turn away, the twins were asleep.

That afternoon Hester rode the horse tram to the Inner City. She returned with a new music roll for her player piano. Next morning, when Riddah had gone into the sons' room at eleven, Hester turned on the piano. The "Voices of Spring" waltz radiated tinkling from the keys and danced up the stairs to the twins. The music was not loud; it was muted by the distance it must travel, the door it must pass. Yet while the melody sounded, Riddah could not quiet the boys. They kept crying—not at the disturbance but with it. Sobbing, they became part of an odd harmony. They sobbed and sobbed until Riddah swept down the stairs, shut off the mechanism and swept upstairs. Almost instantly the crying ceased.

Next morning "Voices of Spring" kept the boys crying once more. On the third day Hester pushed the lever in vain. Inside the instrument the mechanism writhed, but no tone came from the keys. Hester opened the piano. Snow had fallen on its innards. Hammers and strings lay under drifts of bakery flour.

The two women were too strong for petty quarrels. An hour after the blizzard had befallen the piano, Hester made a call from the public telephone booth which had just been installed at the tram terminal. In the afternoon two hairy giants in a horse van picked up the instrument. Next day at breakfast, Hester said that the boys were over a year old now and needed some real greenery to play in. The backyard gardens of Turk Place weren't enough. It was the absence of fresh air that made them cry so much. Berek nodded.

And so Hester Spiegelglass bundled the twins into a horse cab after lunch. When the three returned in the evening, the boys' cheeks were ruddier, they cried less and, for some reason, ate practically nothing for dinner.

Riddah watched and let all this happen, again and again, for more than a week. On the eleventh day she joined the Spiegelglasses for breakfast together with her husband. Boas wore a velvet jacket and was full of introductory remarks that faded into coffee sips and sheepish chuckles. He was happy to tell Berek. . . . It was amazing to be blessed after all. . . . It was such a delayed and long expected joy. . . .

"I'm going to have a baby," Riddah said. "So I need some fresh air, too. When Hester takes the boys out today, I'll come along."

So she did. She simply boarded the cab, climbing in after the twins. The end of the ride, she discovered, was a weathered, crenellated manor which now served as warehouse and maintenance center for the Bösendorfer piano manufacturers. It stood at the edge of the city, between the outermost tenements and a meadow sloping steeply into the Vienna Woods. The caretaker's kitchen opened onto the field, close to a shack in which Hester had stabled her player piano. The kitchen was small, cluttered with kindling wood, pots and the warp-shouldered caretaker's wife; yet Hester strode easily back and forth inside, making ladyfingers and wine-cream, producing batters and aromas with elegance and speed. The tip of her hat feather tickled flies off the low ceiling. Her piano played "Voices of Spring" in the shack.

But the personality of the instrument had changed. Obviously, it had been cleaned and repaired. Still, it was not the way it had been before Riddah had cast flour into its works. Its sound was not only dimmer but emerged strangely angled, seeming to come less from the apparatus itself than from a different source altogether. It was like a ventriloquist who in throwing and veiling his voice could give it a very different, even contrary character. The "Voices of Spring" had changed from exuberant to distantly pensive; it could have been intoned by mourners at Turk Place.

If that was an illusion, the two boys seemed to share it with Riddah. At home they had cried in a tone sadly echoing their mother's. Here the piano produced the tone for them. In assuming their grief, the invisible player released the twins from sorrow. They were allowed to be tumbling children.

It was the first time Riddah heard Conrad's peculiar coughing laugh. Brown-haired Conrad lay in the grass with his legs up. His feet conducted a music much brisker than the "Spring" waltz. Ferdinand, darkly tousled, was more seriously busy even at that age. He toddled from dandelion to marigold, tapping each flower so that it swayed like a pendulum. Systematically, he was trying to make the whole meadow move to the music.

Riddah watched. She began to sing la-la-la in the fast beat to which the boys were moving. But then Hester came from the kitchen bearing a plate of vanilla-scented ladyfingers. Riddah said, "Stop. Not here." Hester looked at her. She bent down and offered the plate to the boys. With the arm that could punch down thirty pounds of yeast dough, Riddah scooped up a whole scythe swing's worth of grass, strode to the shack, yanked open the top of the piano.

"*Stop,*" she said. "It's all right to play and cook here. But eating, we only eat at Turk Place with Berek."

Hester adjusted her hat slightly. She withdrew the plate of sweets. Riddah did not drop grass into the piano. That evening the twins came back not only with glowing cheeks, but with a fierce appetite and ladyfingers saved for a Turk Place feast. For the rest of the week Riddah gave up her afternoon sleep to participate in the outings. After that the boys were trained, with Hester's apparent acquiescence: you played out in the meadow; there you had far-off music, and smells of sweet things to come, and promises of happy savors; but you consumed and consummated only at Turk Place at night.

That was how stepmother and twins spent afternoons through July, August and September. In October the meadow turned brittle. The air stung. And so Berek agreed with Hester: the twins' summer, at least its pastry scents and its three-quarter time, should be brought into the city, into his street.

It was trucked there by three heavy dray horses. The player piano returned to Turk Place—but not to the ground-floor living room of the Spiegelglass apartment at No. 5. Seized by an unheard-of mechanical giraffe—a crane causing much wonder in the neighborhood—the instrument was hoisted onto the flat rooftop of Turk Place No. 6, the largest on the street. Subsequently, there also soared slowly through the air a heating stove, a baking oven, boxes full of pans and dishes, sandbags, a dozen potted ferns and enough glass for a baronial hothouse.

By December work was finished. The roof of No. 6 had become

a glass-covered musical kitchen park, complete with sandbox and guarded by little minarets. Here Riddah put out to pasture Bissy III, the oldest of her third-generation roosters, who was the twins' favorite playmate. Conrad studied Bissy language. Soon the boy could make his cock-a-doodle-doo ring with any number of emotions from triumph to terror and including even boredom. He could speak rooster before he learned to say "please."

His more earnest brother, Ferdinand, loved to comb Bissy's balding tail. And, young as he was, he began his crusade against flies. With grim accuracy and with a matador's formality, he wielded a flyswatter though he was not much taller than its handle. He was sure the flies ate Bissy's feathers and fed on fronds. And so he buried what he had swatted in fern pots, where Bissy liked to peck them up. Bissy gave little doodle-doos in gratitude.

While Ferdinand swatted and rich chocolate gusts of Hester's Sacher torte bounced off the glass roof, Conrad played a game that combined architecture with nihilism. With his watering can he wetted down the sandbox. He'd start piling one moist firm pailful of sand on top of another. Humming like a soprano imitation of Berek's hum during one of his work binges, Conrad would raise up a tower with relentless speed. But then, as the tower began to lean, his face would ease into a grin. Often he managed to time the leaning stage to the approach of the piano waltz's climax. It came. He'd give his creation a tender, lovingly pushing caress. To Johann Strauss, the tower crashed apart. Conrad dropped himself down among the shambles, convulsed with his cough-laugh, wallowing in gritty ruins, ready to start all over again.

The twins were vigorous, quirky, and very dirty at the end of the day. But they hardly ever cried anymore. Berek no longer saw them as continuations of Tamarah's death. All of a sudden, they were strapping little boys. His sons! In that high-up playground romped the future of Turk Place. If Hester stayed with them the whole afternoon, he wanted at least an hour or two later on. There was more time now, evenings. He'd mastered the alphabet so thoroughly, practice was no longer necessary. (When he wrote out factory bills, his letters *a* to *s* were Gothic, in accordance with Tamarah's old-fashioned script; whereas *t* to *z* were in the modern Latin hand, dating from Hester's instruction.) Not only did he have more leisure at night, but the boys could go to bed later, thanks to their long, still Riddah-induced naps. And so began the institution of the Underground Voyage.

After dinner Berek would piggyback his sons, one on each shoulder, across Turk Place, from No. 5 to No. 2. There he'd unlock the wallpaper door that led from the synagogue's vestibule down into the subterranean passage. He'd lift the boys off his neck and put them onto the double seat of a little wagon he had specially built.

"All right, everybody close their eyes!" he would command.

As he pushed the wagon slowly along the tunnel, he would begin to tell a story—always the same one: the tale of his first journey from Varungy to Turk Place. He told it largely through sound effects. As in a dream the boys were set adrift in the blackness of their shut eyelids. They floated through a grotto of amazing noises: the owls and cuckoo cries of the Slovakian fields; the clip-clop of horses' hooves; the honk of a goose; the wail and crackle of Gypsies singing around a campfire; and, in rising volume, the detonations of the building sites around the emperor's palace that led, after an anteroom hush, to the hoarse wizard-voice of the emperor himself and to the thunder of the hammer blows when Berek had used the Gypsies' stable oven as an anvil.

"*Now,*" Berek would say to the twins, "open your eyes."

The boys did. The wagon had arrived at the end of the tunnel. A lantern lit up the compartment in the wall where the Brick was hidden. From the keyhole of its small door hung a little bowlful of chestnut-puree hearts coated in chocolate. The boys would grab for it, and Berek would say, "Something even sweeter is inside the wall." This set the twins yowling and jostling one another, each trying to be the first to lay an eye against the keyhole. But before either could get a look, Berek plunked both back into the wagon. Munching, laughing, they were whooshed back along the tunnel, through the vestibule and out into the street.

*   *   *

The chocolate-coated chestnut hearts were Hester's contribution. Yet it was understood that she herself never came near the tunnel game. By another unwritten law she continued making duplicates of the various toys Berek and his first wife had made years earlier for what they'd thought would be their one oldest son. Hester made a second teddy bear out of canvas and straw; a second wheelbarrow with a hidden music box; a second wooden wild-maned little rocking horse. In contrast to earlier days, the twins fought for the gifts when Hester brought them into the rooftop playground. Invariably, Ferdinand won. But as soon as the prize was in his hand, he would sniff it, smell his stepmother's perfume and drop it as though it had seared him. Conrad would laugh, coughing, on the floor where Ferdinand had pushed him. He'd pick up the present with two fingers and put it before Bissy III. The old rooster's wattles would swell and darken, his wings thrash, his beak open. But he would never peck. He'd run off in a shudder of feathers. The present would remain unclaimed on the floor. In the end, Riddah would place it along with the others behind the glass door of a chest she kept in her apartment. There they lay like exotic trophies from an unknown land.

Of course, Hester herself was an exotic item in the 17th District. Yet just that made up for Berek Spiegelglass's lacks. The more Berek prospered, the less you could escape it: he was plain to a fault. The man ignored a rule honored without exception by the Christian burgher tenants on his street. They always wore some middle-class insignia, small but unmistakable, at work or at home. The sort of thing that distinguished them from the laborer folk all around.

You couldn't miss the napkin sticking out of the business-suit pocket of Herr Skalka of Turk Place No. 3. The single exposed corner of white linen said "innkeeper-boss"; the napkin itself indicated membership in the table-serving trade, but the fact that Herr Skalka carried it in executive mufti meant that he was not a waiter but an employer of waiters who on occasion might help out his staff by way of example. Herr Schedlmayer of No. 4 did not wear a white smock coat like a worker-barber but a white jacket over "good" striped trousers; this identified the owner-barber who shaved select customers in person yet never did any sweeping up that might dirty his lower garment. Herr Milz, also of No. 4, wore overalls like the three carpenter journeymen under his hire; but his overalls were blue, not gray, with an extra breast pocket for the cigar.

Alas, Berek Spiegelglass, who owned a whole factory, was entirely blind to such shadings. He stuck to a brown smock not a whit less dingy than his youngest apprentice's. This was a breach all the more startling because of Herr Spiegelglass's origins. As a Jew, he should have erred in the other direction. It behooved a Jew to be something of a clotheshorse, particularly if he had overcome his garlicky background and was now your resident landlord in the 17th District. A man like that should be relied on to sport a silk cravat with a nicely excessive sheen, to draw on himself the envy of the proletarians, away from his Christian peers.

On such counts Berek Spiegelglass made a very inadequate Jew. Those of his own faith were just as irritated. He disoriented fellow members on the synagogue board. His ways confounded the sense of direction by which they guided their life and that of their children. To them progress meant this: start poor and primitive in the East, far off in Galicia; finish rich and sophisticated in the West, somewhere near the Ringstrasse. What seemed so confusing was that technically Spiegelglass was ahead of them on that path. He had fancier customers and owned more real estate. Yet the man remained serenely uncouth. Take his rustic boots. Take his thank-you letters for donations to the synagogue on behalf of the Hebrew needy; he wrote them in an unashamed scrawl mixing Latin and Gothic characters helter-skelter. True, he did have his Sunday coffee in the marble-table section of the Café Pellmann—a weekly ceremony of the Jewish middle-class summit in the 17th District—but he stirred his coffee with a salt stick and often strayed into the café's wooden-table hinterland where his designer sat because lager was not served on marble.

And then there were those little brass "Elect Novak" badges. Everyone knew that Spiegelglass had made them almost for free in exchange for a questionable favor. When Herr Novak had become city councillor, he had officially attested to the semirural character of the Turk Place neighborhood. This had satisfied the ordinance under which Spiegelglass could keep his own private burial ground in back of No 1. It did not satisfy the board members. The very presence of such a thing—not to speak of the grotesque door-tombstone above the first Frau Spiegelglass—gave the street a throwback character, almost a barbaric cast.

Most annoying was a certain attitude underlying all these crotchets—an attitude close to arrogance. The naïve arrogance of a Balkan chieftain, to be sure, yet arrogance just the same. Spiegelglass was not an easy man to be cordial to in the board members' pew. No wonder Rabbi Ackermann went on sick leave before many a High Holiday.

But if Spiegelglass annoyed, his wife fascinated. To the Christians she was a thrilling sight of a Jewess, as gorgeous as she was suspect. Her glitter lit up what remained so stubbornly obscure in Berek Spiegelglass. She made it easy for you to see what you had to watch out for, what to resent, in Jews. No Christian lady in or near Turk Place matched Frau Spiegelglass's splendorous hats or arresting air; which meant, of course, that there had to be more here than met the decent eye. Was it true that the woman's former tobacco shop included a back room with perfumed mirrors? It was a relief to be reminded by this Jewess that whatever seemed glamorous turned moldy on inspection.

For members of the synagogue sisterhood, Frau Spiegelglass was a reassuring subject for gossip. She breathed an urban verve that overrode the roosters of Turk Place and even the backwoods disarray of her husband's beard. In that respect the scandal she caused at the bakery opening seemed almost a comfort.

Until the early spring of 1892 Riddah's loaves and rolls—all those not delivered by the albino to regular customers in the neighborhood—were sold informally in the house entrance of No. 6. Meanwhile, a real bakery shop was being built in the space of a ground-floor apartment of the building. The final phases of construction coincided with the eighth month of Riddah's pregnancy. His first wife's tragedy had branded Berek's mind. To remove the burden from Riddah he asked Hester to take charge of fixing the interior of the store. And he told Riddah that baking was hard labor; she had to limit herself to one supervisory visit to the cellar at night. Apart from that she must remain in bed.

As Riddah had once worked, so she now rested: monumentally. She actually caught up on sleep lost for the past five years. During the day the principal sound in her bedroom was the creak of her mattress moving to the force and depth of her breathing. At night, her usual worktime, in her sleep she sang incomprehensible variations of the work songs she would have sung down in the cellar, while her hands kneaded the eiderdown coverlet into hundreds of rolls and dozens of loaves.

Sometime before dawn the baby would knock against the inside of her belly to tell her she was hungry. She rose and climbed down into the cellar, munching sausage into the finest bits in case some should dribble into the baby's mouth. She checked on Herr Feister, the master baker who had been taken on as her substitute and who was the godfather of Schall's nephew. Herr Feister had written down the recipes the albino had sung to him as Riddah had once sung them to her; he did quite well by them except for a tendency to understeam the whole-wheat buns. Riddah checked on that. Then she went upstairs again, poking her lantern light into the nearly finished bakery store. She shrugged her way past the pleated purple curtains Hester had put up. Hester, on her part, showed similar tolerance in the morning. She sighed only a little sigh when she ordered the albino's sister to sweep up the chicken droppings. Riddah's fourth-generation roosters still trailed her on her nightly rounds.

The time came, however, when the truce between the two women urgently needed renewing. Display shelves for the bakery store had been delivered; one night Riddah discovered that Hester had lined them with doilies as pink and lacy as lingerie. Riddah tore them up.

At noon the next day negotiations were conducted at Riddah's bedside. Hester promised to use only doilies of plain white linen for Riddah's solid and earthy baked goods. On the other hand, Riddah nodded at Hester's idea to include confectionery among the store's wares, and agreed to let Hester develop that line and to use lacy pink doilies for such dainties.

Thus, a compromise came about as well as the confrontation that would make the bakery-shop opening notorious. Hester apprenticed a girl named Anna and taught her, in her own kitchen, how to puree chestnuts, grate almonds, melt sugar and sculpt chocolate. Anna blushed more easily than she learned. It was hard work teaching her, much harder than making the twins' toys. Hester, who hated the sheen of sweat on her skin, began to force a request she had made of her husband before. She wanted a private bathroom.

Usually, she brought up the subject at dinner. Berek was long literate by then and would have the evening edition of the *Tagblatt* propped up at his plate. He would dispose of the matter by quoting some bad news from the financial page. The matter did not stay disposed. On the eve of the bakery-store opening he found an astounding wooden booth rigged up around the corridor sink before his apartment door. Inside, a hose connected the tap to a raised shower head.

"Who did this?" he said.

"I asked Herr Milz to send up a carpenter," Hester replied.

"What for?" Berek said.

"It's a shower," Hester said. "I have to be fresh tomorrow for the store opening. We still have no bathroom."

"We use the public showers by the tramway station," Berek said. "The women's section is no longer good enough?"

"The towels are torn and the women stare," Hester said.

"A private bathroom would need new feeder pipes underground," Berek said. "It'd be a problem with the Brick tunnel. It's too complicated."

"Ah, the Brick," Hester said. "Very well, let the Brick keep you clean. I'll use my shower."

"Not this one," Berek said. Five well aimed kicks of his boot smashed down the stall.

Hester watched till he was finished. She walked into her apartment, unbuttoning as she went. She stopped at the dining room table, on which the albino's sister had already placed the pot of beef stew. Hester took off the lid and squashed her blouse into the stew and threw the pot on the floor, blouse, stew and all. Berek walked in after her just as the albino's sister, sobbing, ran out. Berek walked on into the bedroom where Hester stood, damp, naked, nipples falling and rising fiercely.

"Ah, the Brick man," Hester said. "He loves no-wash stink. Want to come smell my stink?"

"I'm coming," Berek said.

Two locks clicked, but the double doors barely sufficed that night.

Next morning Hester left by the back door of No. 5 in an overcoat buttoned over her nightgown. Behind her tottered Resi, the albino's sister. She had to carry not only a tub of hot water but the shower head, hose and a bundled garment. They crossed the backyards of Turk Place until they reached the well near the graveyard behind the factory. Here Hester had seen a huge wooden crate which had housed a recently delivered press. She told Resi how to convert crate into shower stall and to connect it to the well and curtain it.

No one stopped them, though the factory hummed in full gear. Berek was gone. Schall had left too, having been fetched away a few minutes earlier by the night baker desperately out of breath: the baker had made all the special store-opening rolls, he had brought them up to the store, everything was fixed up there, all the guests invited to the opening had arrived, but there wasn't anybody to receive them, not a soul from the boss family, no Herr Spiegelglass, it was terrible, somebody had better come and take over.

So Schall came, but he couldn't take over. In the new bakery store's window stood a beribboned rubber plant. Inside, almost as motionless, waited the neighborhood's burgherdom, Christian and Jewish, from Herr Pellmann with the pince-nez to Herr Milz with his curved Sunday pipe. The men honored the occasion by their silver-handled canes, the women by their solemnly sleeved dresses. And here was Schall in his work smock, helpless.

Luckily, he was smoking factory-made cork-tipped Egyptians by then. To mark time he offered cigarettes until his case was empty. He improvised further by going to the roll bin and presenting poppy-seed crescents as though they were cigars. But then he ran out of stratagems. The guests began to clear throats, shift feet, exchange glances. The embarrassment mounted together with the irritation. Here was another case of nerve typical of the Spiegelglass clan. And just as Schall thought of simply running away, Hester appeared.

To protect her wet hair she wore a high turban fashioned of a striped crimson-and-black towel. She billowed into the store in a golden cloud of a bathrobe. It streamed from her neck down to her ankles, and at the top no less than at the bottom, small faint exhalations of vapor spoke of fresh-washed skin.

Behind her came the cornucopia she had developed in her kitchen. Resi pulled the four-tiered chocolate-studded confectionery cart whose aromas combined with the draped purple of the window curtains into an aura so opulent it suggested not a backwater bakery but a prestigious bordello.

And then, as though to give tongue to it all, a woman's voice rose from beyond the ceiling. Rich screams resounded in a hearty sort of agony, one sumptuous cry after another from a womb in the very ecstasy of procreation.

It stopped. Hester, who had smiled throughout, smiled into the silence of petrified faces all around her. She reached into the cart. She handed out cookies smothered in honey-glazed coconut flakes; she bestowed chocolate-embroidered gingerbread hearts, rum balls impaled on candy toothpicks, miniature oranges made of marzipan.

The guests took them, but the screaming had started again and they let the sweets lie in their mouths. To chew would have been to make a fleshly sound and thus to add to the carnality of the moment, to become its accomplice. Silence once more. Hester ate a marzipan orange. But no other jaws moved. Nothing happened until there was a stomping down steps. Berek burst in through the back entrance of the store.

"Everybody upstairs!" he said. "Come on! You're all invited! We've had an exciting time up there all morning."

They all stared at him.

"What are you waiting for? Say hello to the new boy. Follow me!"

Hester laughed. Schall threw down his cigarette. Some of the guests swallowed their candy whole, and then they all followed Berek upstairs into the Mainzer apartment. Only a few of the crowd could get a clear view of the bedroom, yet for weeks the spectacle would animate street-corner chats in the neighborhood.

On the night table stood a tin box holding some brick-shaped stone. Riddah Mainzer lay in the double bed, one arm around a sizable bald baby. Her free hand held a cheese sandwich she wolfed down so exuberantly that Dr. Huber (blinking slowly as always) averted his face as crumbs sprayed into the childbed pillows. Boas swept them to the floor, where the roosters pecked them up.

"We'll name him Markus!" Riddah said to the crowd. "Isn't he a monster? How do you like that? Two openings the same day! Berek, I want more cheese!"

XV

THREE YEARS after their cousin Markus was born, not long before the twins reached school age, Berek Spiegelglass bought a piece of chalk. Then he went to the Brick tunnel to draw a line through its entire length, marking it with X's at twenty-six evenly spaced intervals.

Next he crafted two school desks with not only wheels but wheel-works under each seat. These desks he rolled into the tunnel, replacing the wagon on which the boys had once traveled nightly from "Varungy" to "Vienna." One evening after dinner Berek did what he had often done before. He marched his boys down into the passage that began behind the wallpapered door in the vestibule of the synagogue. This time he raised his hand. "All right, sons," he said. "You're ready for a different sort of ride."

At first it didn't seem to be any kind of ride at all. There were just the two desks with two inkwells and two notepads. And there was Papa bending down to teach the brothers the Gothic lowercase *a*. He showed them hair strokes and bold strokes. He insisted on exact angles and correct pen grips. Ferdinand's forceful little fist had a tendency to blot. Conrad was overly ambitious with extra loops and curls. But after a week both boys had mastered the first piece of the alphabet. That's when the ride began.

On the night of the fully achieved *a*, Papa Berek stooped very deeply twice, first with one match, then another. He lit the fuel box beneath the boys' wheeled desks. The tunnel filled with a fiery fog.

"Throw down the lever in front of you!" Berek shouted. "Keep it down till I say 'up'!"

Thunder rumbled, the tunnel tilted, walls shook, the desks trembled and moved. The boys rode through miles of savage hisses, of sparks both heavenly and hellish—and along about three yards of chalk line.

"Up the lever!" Berek shouted.

The twins obeyed. The two steam tricycles—for the desks were mounted on small replicas of the vehicle that had become the factory's first machine—the two tricycles stopped.

"You are now one mark closer to the Brick," Berek said. "We have arrived at the letter *b*."

It didn't take the twins too long to reach *c*. They needed only a few days to progress from one chalk mark to another toward their destination. After *p* Berek introduced another element of schooling. "Now, sons," he said. His voice ricocheted along the long, narrow, kerosene-lit cavern. "Sons, when I learned the alphabet with your mother, I practiced on newspaper events. You know something? Most of the people in the events are gone. The events, nobody remembers them. My sons should practice on things that keep. Listen." And he told them of the Great Temple in Jerusalem and the Romans trying to destroy it all; and the survival of one wall; and the stone taken from the wall by the Grand Vizier Kara Mustafa—the stone that was the Brick that was now the core and heart of Turk Place, and which received messages from Spiegelglasses to God.

"In Hebrew school they'll never teach you about the Brick," Berek said. "That's why I don't send you there. Now try to spell the story with the letters you know."

The boys tried, with half an alphabet. And the gaps they left in words, the sudden blanks in their lines, reminded Berek of his first wife's darling stutter. He was almost sorry when the gaps began to shrink. By July of that year his boys had attained the letter *t*. Berek, repeating his own pattern, had them switch from Gothic to Latin characters, which were much easier and faster to learn. Within a month the twins had traversed the last part of the alphabet and arrived not quite at the end of the tunnel.

The day after their final practice on *z* Berek led his sons by the hand to the wallpapered door in the synagogue's vestibule. At the entrance to the passage stood the two tricycles, each decorated with a Chinese lantern.

"This is a party journey," Berek said. "Everybody aboard! This time we go all the way!"

With their father striding ahead, the two boys chugged after him amid spouts of glowing steam and striped glitter from their lanterns. They stopped only when they could not continue further: before the compartment in the wall that closed off the passage.

"What's inside there?" Berek asked.

"The Brick!" chorused the boys.

"Once we got candy here," Conrad said.

"Can we write a message to the Brick?" Ferdinand asked.

"Not till your Bar Mitzvah," Berek said. "But you can *tell* me a wish. That's part of the party."

"Let's see," Ferdinand said. "I want a Brick photo from Uncle Boas, so if this Brick gets lost I'll get another just like it from Jerusalem."

"Silly son," Berek said. "This one will never get lost, and there isn't another one like it. Make a good wish."

"Oh," Ferdinand said. "I know. I want to ride this tricycle out on the street, not just in the tunnel."

"Fine," Berek said.

"But with the Brick mark punched on it someplace secret," Ferdinand said. "Like on the back of the badges you make."

"Fine," Berek said. He turned to his other boy. "Now you tell me a wish, Conrad-son."

"I'm dizzy," Conrad said. The Chinese lanterns, swinging from the tips of their flexible sticks, had set his eyeballs rolling.

"The Brick will fix that," Berek said.

He had unlocked the compartment door and flung it open and made things worse for Conrad. The air current not only closed the tunnel door Berek always left ajar for ventilation but made the Chinese lanterns orbit like burning planets. The Brick, displayed on top of the box lid, seemed to be flying into an orange-streaked chaos through wild clouds of light and shadow.

"Go on, tell me your wish," Berek said to Conrad.

"*I want outside!*" Conrad yelled.

He didn't yell like a child, though. In extreme situations he already had the habit of voicing not so much terror as a travesty of terror. "*Outside, I want to go outside!*" Conrad roared with the deep bass tremors of a big bruiser, barrel-chested and mortified.

"Well, that's easy," Berek said.

With force he slammed shut the compartment. The air current so created opened the door at the mouth of the tunnel.

"Hey, look, the Brick brought the light back in," Ferdinand said, and both twins chugged away toward the synagogue's lamp glow.

On their little steam tricycles Ferdinand and Conrad Spiegelglass rode to school for the first time in September of 1896. The ride was short and it almost didn't come to pass.

First their stepmother's objections had to be overcome. Hester wanted the twins to go to a "good" grade school downtown in the Inner City. Other middle-class parents in the Turk Place neighborhood sent their little ones downtown and that included the Jewish Café Pellmann boy as well as the children of Catholic Herr Skalka the innkeeper. But other parents weren't Spiegelglasses.

Berek said that the twins should do their studying as close to Turk Place as possible. Hester said the nearest place was the mangy tenement grade school in the Carlgasse. Berek said he didn't care about that. Hester said she cared very much. The argument came to a head behind the double doors of the Spiegelglass bedroom on a humid August night. Next morning Berek went to work with a bit of dried blood covering a deep little tooth mark on his upper lip. He sent Siddo Berger off to register his sons at the Carlgasse Grade School, five minutes away.

On the first day of school the twins themselves became a problem. Instead of leaving for the Carlgasse, they ran up to the roof garden of No. 6, where they had spent the play years of their childhood. The sandbox was still there, and the many ferns, and the pastry kitchen where Hester still liked to mix chocolate batters in the afternoon, and Bissy the cock who had gone blind and who was, for his own protection, confined to a hay-carpeted cage.

The twins hooked their fingers around the bars of that cage. As soon as Hester dislodged one boy, the other reattached himself. Disgusted, she summoned Resi and departed for an Inner City public bath with pine-scented soaps and special spray showers. Resi could not pry the twins loose either. She didn't dare disturb Herr Spiegelglass in the factory. She shouted at the twins and screamed herself into a sobbing fit, which, in turn, set the twins crying, their hands still firmly glued to the cage.

The boys might never have seen school that morning if Riddah hadn't entered the roof garden with her little Markus and her two fifth-generation roosters. Sleepy as she was, near her morning bedtime, Riddah righted things with a hug and a shout. She enveloped the boys in an embrace which was even warmer and larger than her large warm arms. "That little flat-topped truck!" she called to Resi as she stroked the boys. "See the one over there? The one to move the big ferns? You put Bissy's cage on it. The boys can roll Bissy to school with them—you hear that, silly twins? . . . That's right, no more crying. You can let go. With Bissy you can go to school."

And with Bissy and two moist, slightly hairy and very powerful smacks from Aunt Riddah, the boys went.

Like the tenements around it, the Carlgasse Grade School was only fifteen years old. Like the tenements, it had aged rapidly, gracelessly, into a chipped stucco hulk. The two Doric columns by its entrance were pockmarked, greasy, and before them waited the twenty-seven students of the new Form I. Herr Witsch, the teacher, a man with a lyrical wave to his gray hair and a determined tic in his left eye—Herr Witsch had a philosophy. He felt that the camaraderie among a group of children who would spend the next five years together must be cultivated briskly from the start, on the first day of the first semester. Hence, he never allowed a class to begin its existence in driblets. It must assemble in front of the school in its fresh-born entirety. Only then did he let it troop up—in a body—to the classroom.

And so, since two pupils were still missing, twenty-seven little working-class boys waited on the street in their mended and ironed churchgoing knickers, their boots laced not with laces but with cord (cord was cheaper and lasted longer) and, pinned to their lapels, tin crosses which the priest had blessed at a special start-of-school mass before breakfast. The twenty-seven stood in nine rows of three boys each, making no sound. Soundlessly, Herr Witsch's left eye ticked. Then the silence was broken by the hiss of two small steam engines.

Distraught and disheveled, Resi appeared first. Behind her Ferdinand and Conrad Spiegelglass chugged into view, in sailor suits, astride their motorized tricycles. The second tricycle, Conrad's, towed a wheeled cage whose bouncing had reduced the indignant rooster inside it from a strut to a stagger.

There were titters from the waiting troop. There were accelerated and aggravated compressions of Herr Witsch's eye. There was some disorder. And of course there was an inevitable delay. It took Resi a few minutes to whine explanations. The tricycles and the rooster had to be parked in the janitor's mop room. And the march up to class lacked the precise solidarity Herr Witsch had envisioned. On the stairs some of the boys tripped over each other to get a better look at those sailor-suit crazies.

Yet the very peculiarity of the twins' arrival was a sort of blessing. Its complications masked for a while something which otherwise would have been obvious and instant: the difference between the Spiegelglass boys on the one hand, and all their fellow pupils on the other. The two brothers were the only ones who were not Christian and the only ones not grievously poor.

Berek was aware of the contrast. But until he received a note from Herr Witsch, he had no idea that Bissy the rooster was attending school along with his sons. Once Berek knew, he also understood. His boys wanted a live piece of Turk Place to accompany them during their school day. In his emphatic mixed-script scrawl he composed a reply to Herr Witsch stating that since the boys' mother was dead they needed the comforting presence of a pet. He trusted the teacher would let them bring along the bird in the future.

Herr Witsch had an ancient feud with the school janitor over the man's slobbiness; the mess in the janitorial mop room became at least more interesting with the addition of a chicken coop. Furthermore, Herr Witsch appreciated the local resonance of the Spiegelglass name. The fathers of some of his previous students had worked in the factory at Turk Place. Herr Witsch agreed to Herr Spiegelglass's request. For the next years Bissy the cock became the pivot of much of the twins' typical student day.

In the end, that day tended to collapse into scuffling disorder. Yet through Bissy the morning usually got off to an amicable start. This took place half an hour before instruction started, at 6:30 AM in the mop room, Bissy's residence during school hours. Regardless of the season, the mop room was always an icy chapel where mop strings froze together into rigid clumps like the marble beards of saints. But the twins had found a way of keeping their darling from dying of cold. Next to the school lay a pile of building stones destined for an additional wing of the school which was never to materialize for lack of funds. The twins dragged ten of the stones inside, piled them around the smoking stove in the school lobby, and then placed them, as a sort of hot-water bottle, against Bissy's cage.

In this they had the help of the whole class. It was less a favor than a game. In his blind old age the rooster had grown a halo of white feathers on his comb. It reminded the other boys of illustrations in their book of Bible miracles. Only half jokingly, they called the bird "St. Bissy." St. Bissy, warmed by the stones, exhilarated by the commotion around him, preened and crowed. To repay his helpers with some fun, Conrad flapped his arms into wings and trilled a roosterish yawp. Boy and bird joined in absurd arias that contained, on Conrad's part, snatches of singsong lectures hilariously characteristic of Herr Witsch.

Every morning Conrad was a tremendous mop room success.

But Ferdinand did his bit, too. He shielded the class from Xavier Zettl, who otherwise might have been its terror. Zettl was repeating the first grade for the third time; as the oldest boy, he towered and scowled above all the others. His footgear was huge even for his size. He wore hobnailed boots still streaked—so he explained—with the blood of their previous owner, namely the corpse of his sergeant uncle, shrapneled to shreds above the waist in the Bosnian campaign. Each of Zettl's monstrously booted steps echoed like the tramping of a whole battalion of desperadoes.

Zettl had no other footwear and, quite often, hardly any hair. For six weeks out of sixteen his head was a bullet, massive, pale, bald to prickly. Every four months his mother sheared him and took the harvest from his scalp to the wigmaker. He had beautiful silken blond hair which paid for a week's bread.

To Zettl the stalwart maintenance of his illiteracy was a form of manliness. It was his way of getting even with life. In his previous two years at school he had punched any fellow pupil who had refused to do his homework for him. Now Ferdinand saved the class from his fists. After all, Ferdinand had learned the alphabet in the tunnel, before entering school. Mornings, in the mop room, when the first class bell rang at 7 AM, Ferdinand had always just finished Zettl's exercises. "Bullet" Zettl would do his famous rocket-to-the-ceiling spit, one of his grim-faced signs of good humor; Bissy's haloed blind head would grope about comfortably in the cage for bread crumbs to peck; the class would still be smirking over Conrad's singsong rendition of you-know-who and the group would march up the stairs into the classroom with just the lockstep unity Herr Witsch expected.

It seldom lasted beyond noon. At midday an invisible chasm would begin to divide the earth. The twins went home for lunch. The others—whose mothers spent the day in factories—had their sandwiches in the schoolyard. After the trash can there filled up, a jinn would rise from the food wrappings and tickle the nostrils of the twins when they came back. It was a dank, sweetish, enigmatic scent that hinted at life on some livid edge, exciting just because it was not readily imaginable.

But lunch had also endowed the twins with an emanation. Hester had no time to wash them thoroughly and therefore rubbed their faces with eau de cologne. The effect of this intrigued and irritated the other boys when the twins returned to school. The faintest whiff of that scent was enough to exclude others from the Spiegelglass world, just as the sandwich odor excluded the twins from the mysteries of the tenement. A front line was drawn; it sharpened during the mathematics test that always afflicted the afternoon.

Conrad Spiegelglass, very quick with figures, finished the quiz fast and just as fast jotted down the answers on a piece of paper he hid under the desk and folded into an artistically winged glider. He would wait until Herr Witsch turned his back to write his daily ethical motto ("Loyalty is Royalty") in the exact middle of the blackboard. At the right moment Conrad launched his missile. Across six rows of school desks the paper creature flew, looking rather like a white, thin, elderly bird; it resembled not so much Bissy as Bissy's liberated soul. Without fail, it landed on Ferdinand's lap. Ferdinand needed at least a minute, working behind his back, to smooth out bird soul into cheat sheet. He had barely enough time to copy out the answers himself and could not pass them on to Zettl. It happened that Zettl sat next to him—the tallest boys being assigned the back row—and Zettl's gory hobnailed boot would stamp on Ferdinand's foot. Zettl resented losing the chance for an undeserved good mark. It was another missed revenge on the world.

The resentment would expand later in the afternoon, when the previous day's homework was returned, graded. Of course, Herr Witsch had long noted that the Spiegelglass brothers and Zettl scrambled their Latin with their Gothic characters. But since both scripts were taught, that kind of patchwork marred the writing of other students as well. The Spiegelglasses and Zettl were at least systematic about their lapse: Gothic from *a* to *s*, Latin from *t* to *z*. This pleased Herr Witsch's sense of order. As for the fact that the handwriting of Spiegelglass, Ferdinand seemed frequently identical with that of Zettl, Xavier . . . it amused Herr Witsch more than it incensed him. Actually, it was also a contribution to orderliness. Herr Witsch was ever at war with an increasingly anarchic world. Zettl had been too long a source of turbulence. Let the Jew boy help get

Zettl through and out of school. It was a step toward restoring harmony.

No, the problem, and the reason for Zettl's resentment, lay not with lettering but with punctuation. Ferdinand made sure to end each of his sentences with a square period, representing the Brick. After all, the Brick shape was branded on the reverse side of all the badges his father made in the factory; it ornamented the hubcaps of the Spiegelglass tricycles. Ferdinand marked his own output of phrases accordingly. When he forged Zettl's homework, he would, out of sheer habit, make some of Zettl's periods square while he left others round. For such dissonance Herr Witsch would visit a demerit on Zettl's paper. But in Ferdinand's work all the periods had right angles; it satisfied Herr Witsch's need for uniformity and always received a higher rating.

This difference at his expense diminished Zettl's sense of tricking fate through counterfeits. Each afternoon he felt that Ferdinand Spiegelglass, supposedly his helper, was also his diminisher. By 3 PM Zettl did nothing but stomp on Ferdinand's foot. By then Ferdinand was ready to stomp back.

Hostilities came to a head during athletics, the school day's final segment, taking place in the hall of the firehouse next door. As a rule, Ferdinand went there without his twin. For at 3:30 sharp, Conrad would come down with one of a select variety of ailments. A colic would strike him and fell him despite all his attempts to contain it by noble contortions. Or a brute toothache would bend his head backward. Or a coughing fit combined with a dizzy spell would make him slump forward, mouthing, not voicing, a groan so that the class should not be disturbed.

Did Herr Witsch believe these indispositions? The point was that he respected them. All of Conrad Spiegelglass's brief illnesses were punctual, disciplined and conscientiously sustained, so reliable in their incidence that they were worth rewarding: Herr Witsch usually excused Conrad from athletics. He was permitted to convalesce in the mop room with Bissy and the tricycles.

Ferdinand, however, was an athlete of high caliber, even threatening Zettl's hegemony in things muscular. Ferdinand matched the fierceness and monkey speed with which Zettl climbed the ropes that hung down from the second story of the firehouse. In the broad jump Ferdinand actually beat his rival, who was handicapped by the rigidity of his hobnailed boots. Only in the so-called dismissal run would Zettl do better. Dozens of rope coils studded the yard connecting firehouse and school, and the boys, schoolbags on their backs, would run in the mazed space between the coils, through the school lobby, out into the freedom of the street.

That was the "school's out" procedure at Carlgasse. Often the conflict between Ferdinand and Zettl made a shambles of it. Zettl, through his expertise as repeater, knew much better than all the others the labyrinth of ropes in the yard. Zettl always led the pack. What helped Ferdinand were his own long legs as well as the goad of a certain suspicion. He tore after Zettl, not too far behind. The moment he had crossed the yard and set foot in the school lobby he'd stop and listen and—without fail—hear Conrad's breathless chuckle. It was an infallible sign that his brother had been plunged into war. The moment Conrad started to fight was the moment Conrad started to laugh.

Ferdinand would rush into the mop room, where he'd find Zettl attempting to smash the tricycles into bits and Conrad resisting with chortles and feeble jabs. Zettl would fling him aside into the mops and would have resumed punishing the tricycles except for Ferdinand's shout.

"Watch out!" Ferdinand would cry.

He would confront Zettl with solemnly raised boxing fists. The very stateliness of this challenge to his supremacy would outrage Zettl. He'd let his arms dangle in contempt for the upstart, only to lash out with abrupt groin-crushing kicks which Ferdinand sidestepped to land fine, formal punches on Zettl's stubbled skull.

It was a duel not only of styles but of smells. The small room and the sweat intensified Zettl's dank sandwich odor as well as the scent of eau de cologne imparted to Ferdinand by his stepmother. This aroma affected the other boys' reaction when the sounds of battle drew them into the mop room.

No matter how often they saw it, the spectacle never lost its eeriness. Zettl—*Zettl!*—the school's long-established traditional scourge, was being defied. It was like witnessing a very brazen breach of a law of nature. And the exotic perfume coming from Ferdinand marked him as a foreign transgressor, wielder of some illicit Jewish magic. The other boys, pressed forward by the momentum of their run, panting rather than thinking, would attack Ferdinand from behind. For allies Ferdinand had only Conrad, who tried to defend him with random slaps and deep guffaws, and Bissy, who gave off wild coloratura cackles.

"Stop!" Herr Witsch would shout.

He would come after the children because he suspected that the esprit de corps he had imposed on them was only a varnish for the more normal state of fratricide. Yet he didn't really mind the brawl: once the savagery faced him in full bloom he could extirpate it that much more effectively.

"*Stop!*" he would repeat with a voice like a wire whip.

They would stop. To everybody's perennial surprise he would let the class off—again—with a mere warning. The fact was that Herr Witsch didn't mind the brawl for another reason. For just as fratricide lurked below the esprit de corps, so the derangement and licentiousness of the janitor's mop room lurked below the orderliness of Herr Witsch's classroom. This was a chance to undo both lurkings at once.

Since everything had been knocked about anyway, Herr Witsch could instruct the boys to sweep up and to arrange mops, brooms, dustpans, shovels and brushes into tidy regiments standing at attention. Then he could dismiss class with a nice sense of anarchy staved off for another day. Zettl would walk away with a grin; he'd been caught in a scrap without being punished, he'd gotten away with something, he was a little closer to getting even with destiny. For Bissy the skirmish had the effect of a massage. During the afternoon he usually drooped, but all the excitement would rouse his sparse tail and sweep the hoarseness out of his voice. For the rest of the day his crowing would be youthful.

As for the twins, they'd arrive home on their tricycles dusty, buttons torn from their sailor suits. Hester would take them to the roof garden. There she'd activate the player piano into "Casey would waltz with the strawberry blonde" and other new American hits. She would sponge the dirt off the brothers' elbows and then start to sew on new buttons while they still wore their suits. (In her mind the mending of empty, peopleless clothes smacked of a seamstress's meniality, whereas sewing buttons "live" was a sort of tickling fun game.) Meanwhile, Conrad would give her a sober, low-key account of the rusty knives of the lynch mob they'd escaped as well as of the berserk dogs besieging the school and the water scorpions crawling from tenement sewers.

"Really?" Hester would say.

With a tap on Ferdinand's cheek she would, smiling, address the question to him. Ferdinand would nod, not at her, not at the question but at his homework, which he punctuated with little square bricks. The boys would be neat once more when Hester led them by the hand to Berek at dinner.

XVI

IN THE SPRING of 1902, the final semester of the twins' years at Carlgasse, the tricycles did nothing but gather dust in the roof garden of Turk Place No. 6. Even Conrad, who was half a head shorter than the husky Ferdinand, had long outgrown those tot-scaled toys.

The brothers still rolled their cooped rooster to school. But the cage, too, had become inappropriate, except as a kind of sedan chair for the blind, precious, immemorial creature. There was no need now to confine St. Bissy. He hardly moved about anymore. Imperceptibly, the colors of his plumage had transfigured themselves from vigorous browns and vivacious reds to a misty black that shaded into translucent gray. He was no longer a bird but a luminously mottled shadow shrunk to the size of a pigeon, a shadow with an ivory beak and a halo of feathers above the pale suggestion of a rooster's comb.

At home or in school St. Bissy sat in an unearthly repose. But every half hour or so he would lift his head; he would spread the silvery filigree that was now his attenuated tail; his bill would open to pronounce a remote yet affecting message, something like the echo of a chant rolling down from a mountaintop distantly glimpsed from Varungy's plain. After which he would give a gentle, haloed nod and subside once more into preternatural tranquillity.

The more ancient he became, the dearer he was to the Spiegelglass boys. Influenza swept Vienna in April 1902, and to protect Bissy the twins covered his cage with gauze before taking him to school. Of all people, it was Herr Witsch who came down with the disease.

The substitute teacher turned out to be Herr Helffmer, a young man whose eyebrows curved upward in perpetual alertness. Three very sharpened pencils pointed like fixed bayonets out of his breast pocket. At the start of his second day he called out:

"Zettl, X., Spiegelglass, F. To my desk."

The two boys came forward from the last row.

"Very nice," Herr Helffmer said. He held up two sheets of paper. "These two pieces of homework are in the same handwriting. And they make the same mistakes, confusing Gothic with Latin scripts. Any comments?"

The two boys stared at their shoes.

"Very well," Herr Helffmer said. "The culprit who made a copy of his homework on the other's behalf will say his name. Then he will make a fist with his right hand. He will beat his fist twice against his chest."

The boys looked at each other. Ferdinand raised his hand. "Spiegelglass," he said.

"Two demerits for Spiegelglass," Herr Helffmer said. "One for copying, one for not making his hand into a fist. Now Zettl. I've looked into the records. Zettl is a past offender. Left back twice in an early grade. Now, this means that all of his past homework may be invalid. Let him prepare himself for some appropriate news. Dismissed."

Early next morning, when the twins left for school, the Turk Place night watchman stepped into their path. In Spiegelglass employ for three years, the man was fat, with cropped white hair and eyes that watered and blinked in the daylight.

"Good morning, young sirs." He touched his hand against his temple. "Zettl says you should say *he* copied out the homework for *you.* Because that's not as bad for him as the other way around. Please."

"What?" Ferdinand said.

"Because if he copied it out for you, it shows he can do the work, he would just get demerits, but he wouldn't be suspended. The teacher said so."

"But me copying for him is true," Ferdinand said.

"But that way he is finished," the night watchman said.

"Are you his father?" Ferdinand said.

"I sleep in his room," the night watchman said. "In his bed while he's in school."

"I will have to think about it," Ferdinand said.

There was much to think about that morning. For the last two days Bissy had left unpecked the maize kernels strewn on the bottom of the cage. His crowing had become fainter but it lasted longer, as long as three drawn-out sighs. In the mop room the brothers pushed the heating stones closer to Bissy's coop.

Zettl didn't come to class. But an additional very sharpened pencil pointed out of Herr Helffmer's pocket. During the mid-morning intermission, the twins rushed down to see Bissy. In the lobby, by the open door of the mop room, they passed a woman with a bandaged ankle. She knelt before the crucifix over the school entrance.

"Oh!" she said. "The young gentlemen twins! I was going to pray to Him to find you. Xavier told me about the twins—which one of you will save my Xavier?"

"You are Zettl's mother?" Ferdinand said.

"See, here you are. He answered my prayer." The woman coughed out a little beer cloud. "You'll help Xavier. You'll say the right things about him copying for you, so he gets the diploma."

"I'm sorry," Ferdinand said.

"He'll get no job, nothing, without a diploma."

Ferdinand had thought about the problem. It was impossible for him to state that Zettl had written the papers with the square-shaped periods. Ferdinand could not disown the little Brick marks he had made. It would dishonor the Brick itself. He was about to say "I'm sorry" again. But at that moment Bissy's halo stirred behind the gauze-veiled cage bars; he rose up in the pearly shroud that was his plumage and uttered his chant.

"*Jesus and Maria!*" the woman said. "The dove! Look! The Holy Ghost. It's the Savior calling." She dropped to her knees. "He'll save my boy! Bless the Redeemer."

"We have to get back to class," Ferdinand said.

The twins rushed upstairs again. Without Zettl the day seemed askew. Just before the last period Ferdinand thought he heard an odd noising and a cry from below. But he couldn't investigate. Herr Helffmer said he would not give out bathroom passes during the final school hour. Conrad, despite an especially persuasive attack of bronchitis, was not excused from athletics and promptly (and actually) sprained an ankle jumping in the firehouse hall. After Herr Helffmer signaled dismissal, Ferdinand was the first to reach the mop room—and the empty cage.

There was no hesitating. Ferdinand knew where to run. On all of Zettl's homework papers he had put not only Zettl's name but Zettl's address—Sautergasse 16. Sautergasse started three blocks from the school, and after stomping over smeared cobbles for a few minutes Ferdinand stood before No. 16.

"Look who's here," Zettl said, leaning against the house entrance under the number shield adorned with the design of Princess Wallers's ball favor.

His scalp was in a nasty phase of unshavenness, and he wore no boots. Ferdinand, who'd never seen those naked feet before, saw that the insteps were plated with calluses.

"Give me back our Bissy," Ferdinand said.

"What you goin' to give *me* back?" Zettl said.

"You don't give me, I'll take him," Ferdinand said.

"What's the matter, Jew?" Zettl said. "Can't stand losing something?"

"Let me pass," Ferdinand said. Zettl was blocking him.

"Try," Zettl said.

Though shoeless, Zettl's kick impacted hard on Ferdinand's hip. They fought according to their custom, one kicking, the other boxing. They fought in the narrow entrance hall of the tenement on a floor uneven and treacherous with missing tiles. They fought between two walls with bas-relief eagles whose plaster heads had been crushed but to whom monstrous genitals had been added with a bloodred crayon. They fought while women in babushkas passed without looking up, women bent down by shopping bags heavy from the "stale sale day" at the market. They fought with an extra verve and agility, perhaps even with a sort of ceremoniousness that might have come from the suspicion that this was the last time.

Suddenly, Zettl, as if in imitation of Conrad, sat down and laughed.

"Go on," he said. He was no longer laughing. "Go up. Second floor. Second door to the left."

Ferdinand had never been in such a tenement before, but he didn't need directions. A punch had jarred his nose into sensitivity to a crucial scent: the smell of the proletarian lunch sandwiches, a smell that was now laced with a whiff of burning. He ran up two staircases of splotched stone. He pursued the scent. He pushed open a door, scrambling to a stop in a musty chamber, a corner of which was taken up by a bed. It was Zettl's bed, at least at night, for his boots stood under it. But now the night watchman slept on it in a stained nightshirt. Even in sleep his eyes were watering and twitching at sun rays from a window that had only dust and fly-specked rain stains for curtains.

But the scent didn't come from there. It came, together with a whisper, from the other side of the room. Ferdinand whirled around. From a ceiling hook hung a huge horse's head, smoked and cured to an even light brown, one nostriled cheek intact, the other skeletal where the meat had been neatly sliced away. It was the source of the sandwich odor. Directly below squatted the woman with the bandaged ankle. She whispered a song to a baby she held with both her hands above a kerosene flame.

"Oh, you're the One," the woman whispered. "Aren't you the flesh and the blood? Sure, you're the food in our mouth, right? You're the Lord. You'll help."

The smell of beer mixed with the smell of something singed and with the schoolyard lunch smell from the horse's head. It took Ferdinand another five seconds. Then he knew that it was Bissy whom the woman held. Bissy dead and plucked and having his last quills burned away by fire. Bissy amazingly fresh and pink without his hoary feathers, reborn into a rosy infant, rocked and warmed in the wrinkled arms—and Ferdinand cried.

He cried though he was almost twelve years old and despite the fact that Zettl stood in the doorway.

"You can have *that*," Zettl said.

Ferdinand cried while Zettl scooped up a heap of feathers from the floor and stuffed them into one of his boots. He held out the boot to Ferdinand as though offering a second Bissy, a Bissy become a bouquet of plumes planted in a leather vase.

Ferdinand took it.

"Bring back the boot or else!" Zettl shouted.

It was a shout with a crack in the voice. Ferdinand ran. He ran away from the horse's head, away from the woman with the plucked God, away from the sobbing crack in Zettl's shout, from the night watchman with his twitching sleep, from the obscene eagle at the house entrance. He ran across litter and clogged gutters back to Turk Place and its sweet minarets. He ran to bury the feathers, to bury them deeply together with his grade-school years in the Spiegelglass graveyard near his mother, not far from the Brick.

XVII

FOR A LONG TIME Turk Place remained the only street in Vienna without a concierge. Until 1900 Berek Spiegelglass himself did whatever basic maintenance work was necessary and delegated janitorial trivia, like sweeping up, to apprentices in his factory. Then he yielded—up to a point—to the way of the world. He hired the three Frau Havliceks.

These were the wives of the three Havlicek brothers, all of them locomotive engineers on the late freight shift of the Imperial and Royal Southern Railway. They would finish work anywhere between 11 PM and 5 AM daily, and this in itself destined their women for their vocation. By municipal ordinance all concierges must be insomniacs, for each house in the capital had to be locked at 9 PM sharp and only the concierge could open it until morning. Any tenant coming home after nine rang the night bell and paid his particular Frau Havlicek ten hellers late money. To press the Havlicek button was to push a finger, by remote control, down some rheumy throat in the basement apartment. You heard not so much a ringing as a clapper wheezing tinnily inside a bell, then, after a due interval, the approach of genuine human coughs from an authentic mucous membrane. The key stuttered in the lock. The door growled open. It didn't matter which Frau Havlicek unlocked it. All three had a half limp—from a pre-arthritic hip joint—a half limp which managed to express itself even when the concierge just stood there, waiting for her tip, holding a kerosene lantern turned down so low that it was no more than some smoldering inflammation of the night, the same color as the Havlicek eyeballs.

The three women were not nocturnal but perennial apparitions, never fully asleep nor brightly awake. Even in daytime they were wrapped in dressing gowns whose floral patterns had been laundered away. Even at night they wore over those gowns a rough work apron. Winter or summer, the same gray woolen scarves hid their hair of an unknown nature. They lived mostly in staircases, beyond sunlight and moonshine, hobbling and yet in perpetual motion. Sickness couldn't seem to touch them, for none of the three was ever known to be bedridden. Yet their pallor looked terminal, their words were sluiced through sniffles, their small smiles curved sharply like grins of pain.

Not sisters but sisters-in-law, the three Havliceks had rather similar faces, long and faintly mustached, shaded from white to gray to the exclusion of every vivid tint. Each one was in charge of the house in which she lived as well as the one opposite, and each was known by the house in which her bed stood. Thus the Havlicek No. 1 (with the triangular wart on her chin) janitored as well Turk Place No. 2; the Havlicek No. 3 (with the broom handle always jammed crutchlike into her armpit) also worked in Turk Place No. 4; and the Havlicek No. 5, who swatted flies with her left shoe, unshoed herself as often in Turk Place No. 6.

The Havliceks were more dyspeptic than other concierges. They had reason. At Turk Place they were deprived of an advantage enjoyed by their colleagues. In other streets the concierge was the one stable urban species that made the rest seem vagrant. The landlord wasn't likely to form a living, permanent link with his building. He had taken title to it as an investment. He was a middleman between the developers who sold him the item and the bank to which it was mortgaged. The house itself floated through his precarious ledgers as a temporary entry. For him it had no sheltering roof or maternal walls.

Of course, a tenant might form a longer association with his apartment. But that did not lead to closeness. Especially in the poorer districts like the 17th, dweller lived estranged from dwelling: he could endure his tenement only if he considered its leisurely rats and suppurating ceilings as something quite extraneous to himself.

Even in middle-class oases like Turk Place, a Herr Schedlmayer, master barber that he was, regarded his three-room apartment as a form of provisional island exile, the mainland being a spacious residence in the Inner City with a private staircase leading down to the mirrored splendors of his haircutting establishment. That was where he was headed, though he still lived elsewhere.

Only one race felt truly at home: the concierges. Every small indisposition of any building—a loose tile, a cracked joist—entrenched them in their office the way a patient's catarrh ordained a doctor. A concierge smelled of all the tempers of the house—from a gas leak to a roasting duck. She merged into its intimate humors. She was privy to the discreet avarice of the landlord (painting over a rotted courtyard arch rather than replacing it) and to the furtiveness of the tenants (Herr Skalka Jr. paying double late money at 2 AM, accompanied by a perfumed creature under a blue veil).

On Turk Place the three Havliceks wielded many of the unpredictable privileges of their calling. As concierges, they were menials who could turn instantly into the eyes and ears of an august moral force. They might be laboring on all fours, mired in mops and brown soap, yet their toil was a form of higher investigation from which neither the most inward part of the house nor the privacy of its inhabitants was exempt. Why did Frau Milz, the master carpenter's wife, want to change her turn at the laundry room from Tuesday morning to Wednesday at Turk Place No. 3? Only the Havlicek No. 3 was in a position to know: Frau Skalka, the more lavishly budgeted innkeeper's wife, had recently shifted *her* laundry time to Tuesday afternoon; therefore, Frau Milz wished to avoid an encounter of washing baskets which might reveal that she was about to iron fewer and less fancy petticoats.

Concierges also knew things much darker than this, things that were latent evidence before building inspectors, detectives and bailiffs; things that made a concierge the key figure in a trial that could be prosecuted at any moment against just about anybody. The

Havliceks partook of that knowledge, but it was a knowledge emasculated by the special circumstances at Turk Place.

At Turk Place Berek Spiegelglass came between the three Havliceks and the clandestine powers of their profession. As the highest personage of a house, the landlord usually seemed the most remote. Here he loomed the closest. It wasn't just that Berek Spiegelglass himself had put in most of the utility lines at Turk Place and had laid hand on the history of all six houses aboveground and below, innards and outside walls. It wasn't just the door in the synagogue vestibule at No. 2 which led into an underground passage he kept locked even against the Havlicek No. 1, under whose cleaning jurisdiction it happened to be. It was the manner with which Herr Spiegelglass strode through his short street, humming, touching the lantern posts in recesses not touchable by others. The mystery of his six houses was at his fingertips—and nobody else's. Thus, he stripped the three Frau Havliceks of an important perquisite.

Still, in exchange he gave them something else just because he was neither a "normal" landlord nor a "regular" Jew: his ways offered singular opportunities for gossip—a bonus for any Havlicek. A concierge distilled, controlled and distributed the gossip in her precincts. Its quality reflected on her standing. The Spiegelglass family provided the Havliceks with raw material superior to any available to their colleagues in the district.

Much of the choice talk had to do with a puzzle. Turk Place was the only locality in the district where no bank official ever appeared to inspect rent rolls, shake his head over repair bills, check on vacancies and question the concierge on "problems" regarding a house. For there was no mortgager whose agents needed to verify the continuing value of the collateral. How could Herr Spiegelglass be so grand as to own without borrowing, when he was so unlandlordly in dress, from his village-blacksmith cap down to his farmer's boots? What other man in his position would dirty his own hands putting in a new drainpipe on the roof of No. 4?

And why was Frau Spiegelglass so provocatively his very opposite? Now that she had reached (at last) an interesting condition—what other local lady in her fifth month would shop for tomatoes in a deeply cut green satin blouse?

Possible answers to such questions buzzed each morning around the corridor sinks of Turk Place as wives gathered with their cooking-water jugs. In the center of such huddles a Havlicek would exhale speculations about *him* and *her*. The huddles tightened after Hester Spiegelglass had given birth.

In the summer of 1902 Dr. Huber slapped the baby into its first cry. This arrival had been preceded by another: the very first private bathroom on Turk Place. After she'd been anticipating for three months, Hester Spiegelglass had informed Berek that a woman of her age could go through the remaining half year only with the help of "American ablutions." It turned out that she meant special washings three times a day in three different mixtures of hot and cold, a procedure practical only with faucets of one's very own.

Berek looked at Hester, who resembled Tamarah not only in face but in the size of her swell and in a pregnancy long delayed. He did not want his second wife to bleed the blood of his first. He nodded. And so the adjacent kitchen-and-bedroom flat was annexed to the ground floor of the Spiegelglass duplex at No. 5. The kitchen became a bathroom with cloverleaf tiles, with a tin tub whose scrolled wooden frame matched the sink's, and with a separately chambered toilet whose flush triggered a cologne-water vaporizer.

The second room Hester claimed for her child. Long before it was finished she called it "the salon." She ordered its walls papered in pink fleurs-de-lis. She found a table for it that was petal-shaped and five carved chairs suggesting Bourbon garden furniture. The window curtains could have been cut from the bridal train of an ambitious wedding. When the cradle was delivered, the Havlicek No. 5 caught a glimpse and walked toward her corridor gathering of wives with particularly fraught mien. The cradle, she reported, did not touch the ground; its white wicker floated in a roseate cloud of gauze.

In her eighth month Hester ordered a layette that was all pink lace. Her husky, curt voice announced that the child was going to be a girl. Of course, she turned out to be right, though a bit sooner than she thought. It *was* a girl, a somewhat premature but healthy creature with fine red eyebrows. She was named Ilona after a Hungarian stage actress who long ago had autographed a cigarette pack for Hester during her tobacco-shop days.

Little Ilona arrived on the same day as the invoices for the salon appointments. With one glance Berek Spiegelglass took in the infant's sturdy puling, the mother's robustness and the size of the bills. Tamarah-worry vanished; Hester-reality resumed. He paid for the salon interior. He returned the fancy baby clothes and replaced them with plain flannels. The Bavarian nurse who appeared under a white linen hat and with a formidable suitcase (in answer to Hester's advertisement in the *Wiener Zeitung*) was sent back to Munich with two gulden, two sandwiches and third-class train fare.

One evening a few weeks later Berek found his wife naked from the waist up, cutting up one of her lace blouses. This, Hester said, was for her seamstress, who'd try to make at least one pretty baby dress out of it, so that Ilona wouldn't have to cry her tiny heart out in those proletarian rags. Of course—slash, slash—the seamstress, not used to baby work, might botch the job, and so Hester would have to cut up another blouse, and another gown, and still another until she'd have only a raincoat left to wear at home which might be—slash, slash—very funny.

Berek didn't find it funny. He wrested the scissors out of Hester's hand. She spat at him. Berek turned to shut the double doors between the bedroom and the salon (where the baby slept uncrying) and then closed the double doors to the dining room. He returned to Hester, just barely fast enough: she had scooped up the scissors again and was about to slit her favorite silk shirtwaist. Again he took away the weapon and this time kicked it under the bed. She tried to dive for it, but he deflected the lunge upward and two minutes later, writhing against him on the coverlet, she bit his cheek.

Next morning Hester ordered more infant clothes, of the sensible kind. On the other hand, Berek did hire a nanny, sort of. He limited the job to part time, but the nanny he chose was an interesting little person: the No. 3 Havliceks' daughter Greterl, then eight years old.

Greterl Havlicek had a relentless round face with round blue eyes just as relentless. They not only saw things but saw *through* them right down into the moist underbelly of the world.

Perhaps this was an inevitable gift. Greterl, being a concierge's child, slept with her parents in the same basement room. On the night before her sixth birthday there had risen a moon so bountiful, its rays had even dribbled down cellar windows. Waked by the unwonted light, Greterl had sat up to see two cockroaches on the floor and her two parents on the bed, both pairs coupling almost in unison among the shadows.

But Greterl had more than round blue overexperienced eyes. She had a schedule that was right for Hester Spiegelglass. Like most tenement schools for girls, Greterl's started late, at nine-thirty. This was to let daughters do early chores like marketgoing and potato peeling. But Greterl's mother, the No. 3 Havlicek, required no such help. Her in-law, the No. 1 Havlicek, did all the shopping for all the Turk Place concierge families at a quantity discount, and furthermore, No. 1 had a potato-peeling tot of her own who managed the total Havlicek peeling. Consequently, Greterl remained employable in the morning from seven to nine.

That was when she swabbed baby Ilona; diapered, rinsed and dried the tiny limbs in the fleur-de-lis mist of the salon; clothed the baby and bound its remarkably abundant red hair in a pale pink ribbon—all to faint splashes from the bathroom next door. There Frau Spiegelglass lolled in the pine-scented waters of the sculpted tin tub. As a rule, the bathing, powdering and dressing of both mother and daughter finished at the same time. Their grooming done, the two daintied females took off together, virtually arm in arm. The fragrant daughter rested in the fragrant crook of her mother's elbow:

Frau Spiegelglass departed with her offspring for the roof garden on top of Turk Place No. 6.

Greterl came to the job partly experienced. The previous year she'd practiced on her baby sister, using the dishwater bowl as basin and unmendable underwear as towels. But the reason Greterl handled little Ilona so well was that during those morning hours she was not Greterl, not a janitor's daughter cleaning up after a burgher's wife. Not at all. She was Princess Margrit cosseting her coroneted infanta in the pink elegance of the salon. But like Cinderella, Princess Margrit had a curfew. Instead of midnight it was 9 AM. At nine o'clock each morning the princess lost her baby to the crook of Frau Spiegelglass's arm. At two minutes after nine, the garbage farmer, as the sanitation man was called, grabbed Greterl by the armpits, lifted her up next to his driver's seat, and jolted and bumped her toward school by way of trash pickups at the market.

Each day Greterl hated her expulsion into reality. At one point the exile threatened to become permanent. Her mother said that a better morning job had come along. Frau Spiegelglass paid Greterl ten hellers an hour, but Frau Skalka had just offered fifteen for plucking fowl and washing dishes.

Another little girl would have given in and gone away to hide her tears. Greterl rubbed her round, shockproof eyes. No, she said, no, please, for a difference of five hellers did she really have to give up a king's child?

"A whose child?" said the Havlicek No. 3.

"I'm not supposed to tell," Greterl said. Whereupon she told her mother the great secret Frau Spiegelglass had confided: this baby, Ilona, was not by Herr Spiegelglass; it was an archduke's, who visited Frau Spiegelglass through the tunnel in the Jew church at No. 2 that went all the way to the palace.

Greterl's mother stared. Then—a rare moment—she bent down to kiss her daughter. After that she marched off to convoke many a huddle of heads around corridor sinks. She brought peerless gossip as well as the solution to the local enigma. At last an explanation emerged why Turk Place never needed a mortgage. Herr Spiegelglass had gained possession of it not by ordinary purchase or the usual grubby financing. No doubt it was a bribe from on high—and not just one bribe either, but a nice annual piece of change. For years Herr Spiegelglass had been renting out his wife to some imperial and royal lecher (most probably Archduke Otto, the one who'd once strolled through the Hotel Sacher bar with nothing on except the Order of the Golden Fleece). And right now Herr Spiegelglass legitimized a very *m-m* situation by playing father to little Ilona, who was really a ducal bastard to those in the know. No doubt he collected another nice piece of change. How else would a Jew with so little education and no attempt at manners come into property?

It was an enormously successful tale, permitting Greterl to keep on being Princess Margrit in the salon each morning. After a while she even brought along her rag doll; occasionally, Frau Spiegelglass took away the baby before the usual hour, and then the doll became the infanta—an even truer one because it had pale blue fingernails. It was these fingernails that caused Princess Margrit to lose track of time one day. She tucked the straw-filled infanta in and out of the gauzed cradle too long. When she finally left the building, it was twenty after nine. The garbage farmer's horses were stamping the flies away with mud-caked hooves, and the farmer himself cracked his whip over Greterl's head. He roared at her that she'd be goddamn sonofabitch late for school and he for his beer. He was about to box her ear when she turned her round eyes on him.

"I was kept by Herr Spiegelglass," she said.

"Oh, shut up!" the garbage farmer said, but he stopped cracking his whip.

She was late, Greterl said, because of Herr Spiegelglass, who stayed in bed later than anyone else on the street. He had come into the salon in his nightshirt and put his hand under her skirt.

The garbage farmer had never liked this Jew Spiegelglass. The man's scrap metal from the factory was by far the heaviest, most skin-ripping trash on the route.

"All right, let's go to the police!" the garbage farmer said.

But Greterl, her voice pleading but her eyes a steady blue, said, no, please, that would be no good. Herr Spiegelglass was under the protection of the palace, his wife's baby in the salon, it wasn't his, it had extremely blue blood in its veins, probably the police knew that Herr Spiegelglass had special authority to touch Christian girls, the Herr Garbage Farmer must never tell a soul, not even Greterl's mother, it was a very dangerous thing.

The garbage farmer now remembered that his own wife had once mentioned a peculiar rumor along similar lines. But he wanted to think of Greterl's story as scandalous rather than dangerous, and when he let the girl off at school, he gave her a push which was pretty close to a box on the ear. At lunch he had two beers more than usual and finally decided not to bring up the matter to his buddies, the market porters—just in case it was a dangerous thing after all.

He didn't even say a word to his wife, and somehow his own silence aggravated his unease. Whenever he met Berek Spiegelglass during the next few days, he lifted his hat but held it before his chest as a screen behind which he could cross himself. But that was not enough. Even apart from the malevolent trash there was something too unholy about that Turk Place Jew. The garbage farmer knew he had to do *something* about the information given him. The longer he left that something undone, the angrier it grew inside him.

XVIII

B Y THEN the twins were attending the Municipal Metal Crafts Vocational School, in session from one to five in the afternoon. Mornings they did apprentice work under one of Berek's master tool-and-die makers. One day as the boys were leaving Turk Place No. 5 for the factory at No. 1, through the rumbling of market-bound horsecarts they heard the sound of a window being smashed. Conrad just said, "Crash!" absently. Ferdinand ran around the corner, gasped at the jagged hole in his parents' window, whipped back into the house, unlocked the apartment door, flew past the maid into the bedroom—and saw his father in bed with a piglet.

The animal, rosy, greasy, grinningly dead, had been thrown through the glass pane. It had landed on the pillow abandoned by Hester an hour earlier for her bath. Ferdinand saw his father sigh, stir and sleep on. His father's temple, grayer than Ferdinand had ever noticed before, gleamed only two inches away from the corpse's snout. The piglet lay belly up. A Star of David had been smeared in crimson between its hind legs.

On tiptoe Ferdinand trembled toward the bed to snatch away the abomination. He rushed back into the street with it. The roadway was empty, but a trail of cinders passed near the broken window before veering toward the market—a telltale sign of the garbage farmer's path. Piglet in his arms, Ferdinand ran. The cinders led to the back of the big butcher stand, where the garbage farmer had tethered his wagon. Trash cans crashed near the vegetable booths.

This meant the man was working there. Meanwhile, on the driver's bench up front, Greterl was combing her hair and saw Ferdinand rush up, bearing the piglet. He was not quite thirteen, but he had the height and heaving shoulders of an overwrought lumberjack, and the curls of his hair bounced down his flushed face like springs made of black steel. He stopped before the wagon. Greterl, combing, gave a faint nod. Ferdinand lifted his arms, holding the piglet between them. He ripped the carcass apart. Its entrails spilled across the garbage bins like some gleaming decoration.

Only after Ferdinand had turned on his heel and was gone did Greterl deliver herself of a fine scream.

"It was like—like from the sky," she said to the returning garbage farmer, "it just splashed down here." And not long afterward she resumed combing, another secret richer.

The garbage farmer drove off with her to her school at cobblesparking speed. In the afternoon he went to the Garbage Farmers' Guild to have his route changed to another district. He didn't want to come near Turk Place. He was afraid, but his fear was exalted. He had punished the Jew with a swine and had suffered, in turn, some Jewish demonry. Yet the very fiendishness of the spirits he had roused gave him, from then on, a sense of covert importance, of being something like a plainclothes crusader. From then on he would climax many of his tavern nights by shouting, mysteriously, that any devil taking him to hell would have to be bigger than a house.

The pig became a ghost in Ferdinand's brain. Nobody had seen it sailing through the window. The noise of impact had been blurred by the morning traffic, and it was to traffic vibrations that the breaking of the glass was ascribed. His father never knew what had shared his bed for two minutes.

But for Ferdinand the pig did not fade even after he had avenged it. What had burrowed most deeply into his mind was not the thrown cadaver. He had detoxified that image by throwing the beast back, by rending it limb from limb. No, it was something else: his father's sleeping vulnerability; the gray-bearded, gray-templed head breathing trustfully next to the snout in the bed his wife had deserted. The bestialized bed kept ambushing Ferdinand. And around that bed always pulsed the fairy-tale sounds his father had made when he'd taken his twin sons traveling through the family history in the tunnel—the journey starting in Varungy and ending with the conquest of the street of the Brick in Vienna. Now, along with the hooting of Slovakian owls, with Gypsy wails and the honk of a goose in a palace courtyard, there was a new sound: glass splintering.

Yet the conqueror of the street of the Brick had heard nothing. That was what bothered his son. Ferdinand, who always snapped wide awake at 6 AM, had always admired his father's late-morning sleep—its serenity, its strength. Now he worried over its innocence. He was too young to say such things to himself, but he felt, wordlessly, that the very purity of Berek Spiegelglass's daring had enabled him to seize Turk Place; defending the stronghold was a crisis too grimy for a hero like his father.

His father, he concluded, needed protection during the early, sleeping part of the day. Oddly enough, the chance to provide it came through his brother Conrad's ineptitude. Conrad just couldn't get the hang of hot-iron shaping, while Ferdinand, with his superior strength and reflexes, wielded a journeyman's skill though still an apprentice. Ferdinand told Herr Wenzel, their immediate boss at the factory, that he wanted to tutor his brother in private, someplace where Conrad could concentrate better than in the factory's hubbub.

Each morning, then, Ferdinand picked up a red-hot chunk of iron in a pair of tongs; carried it from the factory to the clothes-drying attic at No. 5, Conrad following with a hammer. Each morning Conrad sang a new ditty he invented as he swung the hammer:

> *Bing, bang, bong!*
> *I'm hitting it all wrong!*

Each morning, from the attic casement, Ferdinand trained a sharp eye on his parents' bedroom window below, scrutinizing every man and vehicle that passed, ready to drop sizzling metal on any assailant. His vigil did not stop until after half past nine, when Berek Spiegelglass would come through the house door, safely awake. The twins would rush down the steps and along the back-yard gardens to arrive at the factory just before their father.

Because of the new routine, the twins' regular workday did not begin until a quarter to ten. Since Herr Wenzel at the factory agreed, that was all right Mondays to Thursdays. Friday morning, however, was devoted to the boys' religious instruction, their Bar Mitzvah being less than three months away. Rabbi Ackermann always had his midrashim and his Haftarah commentaries ready in his synagogue office at 9 AM, when the lesson was to start. The boys, keeping their attic watch, stormed in at least half an hour late, in no frame of mind for the sixth chapter of Isaiah. As a rule, Ferdinand blurted out an excuse that had to do with teaching his brother to shape metal. This happened six Fridays in a row. The seventh Friday, Rabbi Ackermann realized that such tardiness might be an opportunity. Here was a chance to clear the air with Herr Spiegelglass on a whole range of matters. In a note he asked the twins and their father to kindly see him "after evening services on Wednesday."

These words extended a polite invitation to guilt. The Spiegel-glasses appeared seldom enough at weekday services; they never came on Wednesdays. That was the late-mail day at the City Gate Post Office, when a special window opened from seven to nine. On Wednesday evening the two boys and Berek himself expedited factory shipments in order to avoid overtime for the mail room man.

Their procedure always started with a Conrad trick. All day long Conrad had botched things in the factory and at trade school: now he made amends with one of his odd virtuosities. He would bike ahead, not only to the post office but almost into it. He had developed a technique for actually pedaling upstairs, all ten steps of the post office, the big hind wheel of his bike bumping upward, the little front wheel wagging in the air, rider and vehicle resembling an unearthly kangaroo. Everybody standing in the line would grin. But the smiles would stop a few minutes later. That was when Ferdinand appeared with the freight tricycle to unload a dozen huge packages, all of which he piled up at the place in line which Conrad had staked out ahead. People behind him would begin to grumble. Then Berek Spiegelglass would appear. He simply put his booted foot on the biggest parcel. A slow, irrefutable motion, it produced a bow on the part of the postal clerk behind the window. He was a tenant at Turk Place No. 3 and recognized his landlord.

Afterward, on that Wednesday evening of the rabbi's invitation, the Spiegelglasses parked the five wheels of their fleet before the terrace of Herr Skalka's inn. Berek Spiegelglass ordered pilsner for himself, apple juice with spritz for his sons. But only he took a chair facing Turk Place. The twins, sitting with their backs to home, had to guess which of the minarets was in the shade of the evening sun, which still in the light. Ferdinand hit it right. Conrad missed. Then Berek let them turn around. He pointed to the roof corner at Turk Place, which had a minaret piece missing, and pretended to wonder what in the world could have possibly happened to it? Had an eagle carried it off? Or at the Turkish siege, long ago, had some Austrian cannon shot it away? Or what?

Conrad had no idea. Ferdinand knew. "I remember, Papa," he said. "You told us. *You* lopped it off. You needed the minaret metal to make your first medallion."

Berek nodded; as reward he let Ferdinand have two sips of beer. But in the end Conrad also got a sip. Berek, smiling only slightly, said there was a way of telling which of his two sons would be the first to give him a grandson in the years ahead. It would be the twin in whose glass the bubbles of spritz were rising faster. And now it was Conrad's turn to shine. He began to whistle the "Radetzky March," fast, at his glass; unbelievably—yet unmistakably—the bubbles speeded up. Ferdinand put his hand over Conrad's lips. Sure enough, the bubbles slowed.

Berek Spiegelglass, laughing, rubbed his boys' heads together and said, "Hey, time to go. The rabbi's waiting."

* * *

When Rabbi Ackermann received them, he still wore the black vestments of the evening service. But they were parted informally in front, letting the English cut of his gray suit contrast with the dull brown work smocks of the Spiegelglasses.

"We've come from posting late mail," Berek Spiegelglass said.

"Humble chores honor the master." Rabbi Ackermann smiled. "Sir, if you will take a seat. The young gentlemen, too."

They sat down in the rabbi's paneled little office. Behind the rabbi's desk glowed a painting of the tablets of the Ten Commandments, Hebrew lettering with Art Nouveau tendrils.

"If I may, I'd like to get to the point—the first point," the rabbi said. "Your sons' difficulty with arriving on time for Bar Mitzvah instruction. Not that I don't admire the fraternal spirit which I've been told causes their tardiness—"

"I have to teach Conrad metal shaping," Ferdinand said.

"I appreciate that," the rabbi said. "But I'm sure that you will understand—"

"Ferdinand won't have to teach Conrad anymore," Berek Spiegelglass suddenly said.

Both boys looked at their father.

"I've thought about it. Conrad isn't right for metalworking. From now on he'll work in photography with his Uncle Boas."

The twins still stared. This was a change in Conrad's destiny. Their father nodded. He patted Conrad on the shoulder with the same sovereign slowness with which he'd placed his boot on the parcel in the post office. It was a pat expressive of a force of nature to which acquiescence was almost comfortably inevitable. But Conrad's face radiated something far warmer than comfort.

"Papa!" he cried. "Photography! Wonderful! Thank you! I hated that metal stuff!" He kissed Berek's hand and in his exuberance inadvertently slapped the rabbi's robed thigh.

"Very nice," the rabbi said. "Well, to get back to our little agenda, that really takes care of my first point. Because that means our young friends here will not be delayed anymore by metalcraft sessions. Therefore, our Ferdinand should make enough progress not only for the Bar Mitzvah but for Graz."

"Graz?" Ferdinand said.

"Yes, the new rabbinical college in the city of Graz," the rabbi explained. "Some of my colleagues have started it as a reform-minded seminary, and since you, Herr Spiegelglass, wanted one of your sons—I imagine Ferdinand—to prepare for the ministry—"

"But Graz is away from Vienna!" Ferdinand said.

"Blame the powers that be in our capital's Jewish Council." The rabbi sighed wryly. "They'll tolerate reform, but only at a distance. Anyway, Graz is the only place where I have a bit of influence. Ferdinand doesn't have the usual study credits, but with some additional preparation I could guarantee his admission to Graz—"

"I'm not leaving Turk Place!" Ferdinand shouted.

"You're not to shout, either," Berek Spiegelglass said.

"I have to stay here!" Ferdinand shouted helplessly.

The rabbi, interrupted once more, waited with half-closed eyes and a cheerful face until he could resume.

"Please, I have to stay!" Ferdinand cried, unable to tolerate the idea of his father sleeping late, alone, without protection. "I must stay!" he shouted against the image of the dead pig.

His father rose, grabbed his arm, pulled him up and away from his chair, walked him past the door, closed it, slapped Ferdinand's face as soon as they were out of the rabbi's sight—all by way of one motion which was as inexorable as it was, at bottom, gentle. Then he let his son's wracked face fall against his breast.

"You don't shout when I say 'don't shout,'" Berek Spiegelglass said. "But you're staying at Turk Place."

He led Ferdinand back to his chair. "Ferdinand is going to be a master metalworker," he said. "A foreman in my factory."

"Oh," the rabbi said. "Well, he can hardly study in your factory to become a rabbi."

"He and Conrad have the Brick," Berek said. "That's better than study. When I have a grandson, *he'll* be a rabbi here."

"Good. A wise appraisal of your boys," the rabbi said. With much satisfaction he crossed out something on his pad. "A burden less on my mind. I must tell you that. I'm also glad you mentioned the Brick. That's point number two. Now, I understand this souvenir—"

"It's not just a souvenir," Berek said.

"At any rate, you asked that this Brick be part of the Bar Mitzvah ceremony," the rabbi continued, "and as you know, I've been rather understanding of such sentiments in the past—"

"Wait a minute, not just part of the ceremony," Berek said.

"Herr Spiegelglass." The rabbi leaned back with pronounced ease and stroked the open pages of the Bible in front of him. "Do you know what portion of the scripture your boys will be called upon to read at their Bar Mitzvah?"

Berek crossed one of his booted legs over the other.

"It so happens," the rabbi said, "that it will be their turn to read from those amazing early chapters of Isaiah. I was surprised myself at how directly Isaiah's message applies to our problem with the Brick."

"The Brick isn't a problem," Berek Spiegelglass said.

"If I may put it this way," the rabbi said. "The exciting problem is your sons' Bar Mitzvah. In that, I take not only great pride but a certain responsibility. Now, at the climax they are going to read—either Ferdinand or Conrad, we haven't determined that yet—one of them is going to read—if you'll let me quote it to you, I have it right here—he is going to read Isaiah's beautiful outcry, '*Woe is me for I am undone—*'"

The rabbi stopped because Conrad had gotten up quietly and quietly thrown his work smock over his head. The rabbi looked at him. Berek said nothing to restrain his son. The rabbi went on. "'*Woe is me for I am undone. I am a man of unclean lips . . . but then flew one of the seraphim unto me, a live coal in his hand, and laid it upon my mouth and said, 'Lo, this has touched thy lips and thine iniquity is taken away, thy sin is purged.'* Isn't that haunting?"

There was no answer. Hooded in his smock, Conrad had stepped back and was now slowly advancing on his brother.

"The young gentlemen may be a little bored," the rabbi said. "Not that I blame them. So far we've just been studying the surface of this passage. The obvious meaning. But bear with me now. Let's delve a little deeper. Isaiah—our greatest prophet—*unclean?* The answer to which is: yes. Precisely. Isaiah was indeed unclean because he was talking about himself as a member of an unclean generation, encrusted with old prejudices, pagan superstitions, stale practices and so forth—everything that opposed his great prophetic hope, do you see?"

Berek crossed his booted legs the other way. From inside his smock-tent, Conrad's hidden face made low clicking noises.

The rabbi averted his face from the clicks. "Now," he said, "that same prophetic hope lives in the next passage your sons will be reading from the Haftarah—I think Ferdinand might be the right reader for it—and if you'll indulge me in another quotation and I can find the page . . . yes, here it is; it's quite famous, though not often understood: '*Unto us a child is born; unto us a son is given; and government shall be on his shoulder, and his name shall be Wonderful, Counselor, the mighty God, the Prince of Peace . . .*'"

Conrad, clicking, had now reached his twin. The rabbi waited for Berek Spiegelglass to restore order. Berek sat with callused hands folded.

"In other words, 'Unto us the future has been given,'" the rabbi said. "You know, that's the true meaning of that passage for us today, in 1902. Unto us the new twentieth century has been born, with science and the liberal spirit and the most wonderful advances in technics and efficiency and so forth, but also with unknown challenges, you see? Our duty is to be ready for our age, in mind and soul. And my idea"—the rabbi raised his left hand to cover his ear against Conrad's clicks—"my idea is to celebrate this modern duty of ours—to celebrate it electrically at your sons' confirmation."

"Heh?" Berek said.

"Indeed, I did say 'electrically.'" The rabbi savored the word and the surprise. "It's not really such an extraordinary idea. It's logical. You see, that second passage is not only important to our religion, it's the seed of Christianity, our daughter faith. The Christians see it as predicting their Savior. And on your sons' day, well, it's my thought to light candelabra not only in our own synagogue but in the Catholic church of St. Joseph's in the Hollgasse *and* the Lutheran All Angels at the Ulrichplatz, which will all be holding services at the same time—three candelabras in three different tabernacles, lit by three cables all fed by the same voltaic battery. Now, the Reverend Holzla as well as Father Dussler, my New Testament colleagues in their respective churches, they couldn't be more cooperative. In fact, this might amuse you, the *Wiener Zeitung* wants to send a reporter—"

The rabbi stopped. Berek Spiegelglass had shaken his head.

"Understand me right," the rabbi went on. "No, not for pub-licity's sake, but to show that we Jews want the others to share with us this—this fusion of modern technics and religious aspira-tion as implied by Isaiah. You see? And another thing, it will show that in our district, even though we have many disadvantaged per-sons in it, still all diverse religions are united here in progress and in the entrepreneur spirit of which you yourself, Herr Spiegelglass, you are an example, and which is the essence of the future, do you see?"

Berek shook his head. "No reporters with the Brick." Conrad clicked under the hood.

"With all due respect to your Brick," the rabbi said. "It's your sons' entrance into the community—a modern community—that is the center of the Bar Mitzvah."

"The Brick will be in the center, too," Berek said.

"The center?"

"My sons will put their first messages to God into the Brick," Berek said.

"Let me understand you right," the rabbi said. "As center of the Bar Mitzvah ceremony?"

"They'll do it right after the Haftarah."

"Will they?" the rabbi said. "This is fascinating news to me. What messages? Perhaps Conrad is drafting his right now? Is that what he is doing inside his smock?"

"I'm rehearsing to be a photographer," Conrad's voice came muffled from inside his smock-tent. "This is the camera cloth."

The rabbi looked at Herr Spiegelglass, who still did not call his son to order.

"Herr Spiegelglass," the rabbi said. "You don't seem prepared to discuss the Brick-message business with me. Have you talked about it with your sons?"

"Yes," Berek said.

"I know *my* message," Conrad said from inside the cloth.

"I'd be fascinated to hear it," the rabbi said.

"Can I tell, Papa?" Conrad's voice asked.

"Yes," Berek Spiegelglass said.

"God, please, what is the point of the world?" said Conrad's cloth-concealed mouth.

"What?" the rabbi said.

"God, please, what is the point of the world?"

"I see," the rabbi said. "This is getting more and more remarkable. And you, Ferdinand? How will you interrogate the Eternal? Are you ready to question Him even though you haven't wrapped your face?"

"Well, it's not so much a question," Ferdinand said.

"Don't tell me it's a command," the rabbi said.

"No, not either," Ferdinand said.

"That's a mercy," the rabbi said. "What is it then?"

Ferdinand looked at his father. Berek Spiegelglass nodded.

"Please let me continue in his way."

"Would you repeat that?" the rabbi said.

"That's my message," Ferdinand said. *"Please let me continue in his way."*

Arms emerged from the hood that covered Conrad's upper parts and reached out and smoothed back Ferdinand's hair, as if to groom him for a photograph.

"If I may ask," the rabbi said. "Who is the 'he' of your message? God Himself?"

"My father," Ferdinand said, being primped by the hood's arms. "I want to ask God to let me continue in my father's way."

"I see," the rabbi said. "And an electric candelabra is supposed to light up these blasphemies."

"What's 'blasphemies'?" Ferdinand said.

"Insults against God," the rabbi said. "But wait a moment. I am not angry at you. I have no right. We all insult God at one time or another. We're all thoughtless. But when that happens, we should try to be thought*ful* afterwards. What I mean is, let's think your 'messages' through. Both are parts of the same fundamental blasphemy. Say we always continue in the same way as our forefathers, forever. Why, then, did God bother to create the world for us? He made it so that we can develop and perfect it, so that it is worthy of Him! If we just repeat as before, the twentieth century as backward as the nineteenth, there's really no point! Think about it!"

"Well, those are their messages," Berek Spiegelglass said. "It's up to them."

The boys said nothing. Conrad's fingers kept arranging Ferdinand's hair until Ferdinand said, "Stop, you're tickling me."

"But you must see." The rabbi's face remained cheerful, but his eyes were now quite closed. "I'm sure you see that those 'messages' really mock the spirit of Isaiah—his whole point about the future. They mock the entire idea of progress!"

Conrad's hands, reaching out from his smock-tent, were now adjusting his brother's collar for the "photo."

"And, Herr Spiegelglass, if I may be so frank," the rabbi said, "the same thing goes for your preoccupation with your Brick and your private grave, all of which stimulate those decadent rumors— *young man, we're discussing something very serious!*"

The hooded Conrad, at whom the last words were hurled, let go of his brother's collar. His hands retreated into his tent.

"What I mean"—the rabbi shrugged himself deeper into his vestments—"if Isaiah could submit to the live coal on his lips, if he burned away his old prejudices and superstitions, then for heaven's sake, we should follow his example, high or low, landlord or factory worker, without exception."

"The Brick won't burn away," Berek said.

"Perhaps it won't." The rabbi closed the Bible with a thud. "But if your Brick is going to distort your sons' ceremony, I doubt that I'd want it lit electrically. I doubt it very much. And I don't want my Christian fellow clergymen to be linked with it by electric cable—no, sir, not in any way! Never. In that case, I don't want to be mentioned in the press. In fact, I'm afraid I'll have to excuse myself from the whole occasion. I'm sure you'll find someone more understanding— perhaps some miracle rabbi from Slovakia!"

Rabbi Ackermann rose and bowed. With a rich swish of vestments he strode out.

Berek nodded good-bye. Ferdinand brushed his hand over his hair, which his brother's fingers had given a wrong parting. And Conrad's head emerged from the smock-hood at last, disheveled and bright-eyed and grinning. He gave one more click.

XIX

THE RABBI no longer instructed the twins on Friday mornings. Instead, he sent a spindly, earlocked student from the Vienna Jewish Seminary. Soon it was all over the Turk Place synagogue: the neighborhood's paramount family event, the Spiegelglass double Bar Mitzvah, would come to pass without Rabbi Ackermann unless the boys' father agreed to a "regular" ceremony. Nobody knew which of Berek Spiegelglass's sundry irregularities applied here. But many felt that Berek's pigheadedness just might have met its match in the forceful suavity of Rabbi Ackermann.

Eight weeks before the twins' Bar Mitzvah, now intriguingly jeopardized, Conrad began his new career as an apprentice picture taker under his Uncle Boas. He turned out to be as awkward behind a camera as he had been over a lathe. And there was so little business for him to spoil. A new fashion for fantasy photographs had made it impossible to practice portrait photography for profit under the low ceiling of the ground-floor "atelier" at No. 6—or, for that matter, anywhere on Turk Place. Elsewhere, photographers now had two-story studios where their sitters could mount garlanded elephants made of wood and paint, or dinosaurs with handlebar mustaches, or at least a Chinese dragon spreading a fan in a paw. Most people in the 17th District could not afford a "camera painting." But even the master butchers and pawnbrokers of the neighborhood would pay two and a half gulden for a daguerreotype only if they could pose for a "fantasy picture." Boas, who had no space for dream-sized props, came closer and closer to having no customers at all.

So his nephew Conrad, the apprentice, had little to do in the morning but sweep out a lifeless studio. Afternoons, he ran errands for just about anybody on Turk Place—and one of these brought him an inspiration.

He was delivering ten specially embossed bronze telephone receivers from his father's factory to the Jockey Club. He handed them over to Pepi-Schani, the club's assistant doorkeeper, whose duties included the penning of official club mail even though he had difficulty with ornate capital letters in general and with the upper hair strokes of the capital *H* in particular. The *H* disability was excruciating, since each of the hundred-odd weekly invitations contained the word "*Highness*" several times over. Months ago he'd struck a deal with Conrad. Conrad calligraphed pyrotechnical *H*'s for Pepi-Schani and in return received frog legs sautéed *aux fines herbes* from the club's kitchen. But now that he was a photographer's apprentice, he thought of a different kind of fee.

"How about slipping me an invitation for two?" he said.

"For *you*?" Pepi-Schani said.

"Me and my uncle, to come to some nice fancy party."

"You're crazy," Pepi-Schani said. "The head clerk always checks them out."

"The frog legs aren't what they used to be," Conrad said.

"But, you know, an *invitation*. You're not even a baron's bastard."

"I'm a Spiegelglass, a photographer from Turk Place," Conrad said. "My father's embossing your bronze telephones. Why can't we photograph your parties?"

"Jesus," Pepi-Schani said.

On the back of the invoice for the telephones Conrad had penciled a positively voluptuous *H*. Now he crossed it out.

"I'll tell you something," Pepi-Schani said. "Maybe I can let you in by the service door."

* * *

That November, Jockey invitations had gone out for a "Comanche Supper on the Frozen Hudson River." On the appointed night campfires flickered on the rink of the Vienna Skating Club. There was Johannes, grand duke of Toscana, magnificently tribal in chieftain's feathers, borne along on a sedan chair by four skating lackeys. There were princely clans, the Lobkowitzes, the Palffys, the Esterhazys, their Persian-lamb capes hung with wampum. There was Lady Heth-Botters, a visitor from Buckinghamshire, smothered in ermine and bound to a stake comfortably close to a fire, waiting to be roasted. There was Grigor Alexandrovitch, the Serbian crown prince, feeding truffled eggs into the lady's mouth. And there was Uncle Boas with his camera and wool coat, and Conrad with tripod and negative case and thick mittens.

The picture taking went quite well until Pepi-Schani came up suddenly, trembling with more than just cold. "We're in trouble with the *artiste*," he said.

"Who?" Conrad asked.

"*Him.*" Pepi-Schani pointed at a fat man standing with a sketch pad by the locker-room door. "He paints our parties on big screens and sells them to our Highnesses."

"Big screens," Conrad said. "Hey, that's a great idea for our photos."

"But the *artiste* says he's got the concession and you're horning in on it and he's a friend of our head clerk and he'll make trouble—"

"All right, if he makes trouble, tell him we're under the protection of my father's friend Prince Wallers."

"Really?" Pepi-Schani said. "The prince who's our ambassador? Isn't he back in St. Petersburg?"

"Yes, with a stomach cold," Conrad said as if he knew. "You tell the *artiste* that because of our friend the prince we're here as secret investigators."

"But you're not."

"How do you know?" Conrad said. "Private detectives hired at the very strictly confidential suggestion of Prince Wallers before he left for Russia."

"Detectives," Pepi-Schani said. "Why?"

"Why," Conrad said. "I'll tell you why. Because we have to photograph all the faces at the parties to identify thieves and intruders and so on. It's the modern detective technique."

"Jesus," Pepi-Schani said. He'd been beating his arms against the cold, but now he stopped. "You're right about one thing. We had Countess Hoyos's emerald brooch stolen last year at the Lippizaner dinner. That's a fact."

"There you are," Conrad said. "Awful. This sort of thing can't go on. We have to prevent that. When is this year's Lippizaner dinner? We'll keep the date open."

"Actually, next month," Pepi-Schani said. He ran after Conrad, who had been summoned by Boas. "Listen," he said, "you still can't sell any pictures to our Highnesses, all that goes through our head clerk—"

"Who needs *your* Highnesses?" Conrad said. "We've got our own around Turk Place."

At Turk Place it took Boas a few days to carry out Conrad's advice. He shopped for a big screen and bought photographic magnification devices as well as glue. Four days after the Jockey party he and his apprentice pasted the screen with his best photograph—panoramically blown up—of the Comanche ice supper.

In front of this setting stepped Herr Skalka's son, recently become cashier at the Skalka market tavern. The younger Skalka wore newly grown sideburns as well as a coat with muskrat lapels. He sweated under the studio lights, yet the fur harmonized with the fabulously savage winter scene around him. To augment the extravagant background with a serious note, he carried under his arm the first volume of Goethe's collected works.

The resulting fantasy picture circulated through much of the 17th District's younger set. Before Boas fully realized its success, the evening of the Lippizaner dinner arrived. As usual, the Jockey Club held it in the ballroom of the Palais Esterhazy, whose great staircase was covered with a special rug to protect it from the hooves of Thoroughbreds ascending or descending. On this night the lords and ladies rode the white stallions, reins in one gloved hand, champagne goblet in the other. Occasionally, they exchanged the goblets for morsels of roasted partridge impaled on silver forks that were proffered by lackeys on donkeys. Boas aimed his camera through the half-open kitchen door. Conrad, routinely clumsy, broke a glass negative. Nonetheless, they brought home an excellent shot.

The Lippizaner dinner became another famous backdrop at the Turk Place atelier. Many of young Herr Skalka's crowd had themselves photographed against it. They posed in rented riding breeches and lifted rented whips. Quite a few also carried the Goethe volume, to which Conrad had added a touch they didn't notice. On the book's spine he had painted a rectangle. Compared with the dimensions of the screen, it was infinitesimal. But it distinguished the fantasy with a heraldic echo of the Spiegelglass Brick.

On January 29, 1903, the twins' Bar Mitzvah was only three days away and the standoff between Berek Spiegelglass and Rabbi Ackermann continued. The twenty-ninth was the traditional date for the Jockey's *Gschnasfest,* the club's "crazy ball." A highlight of the carnival season, it also promised to be Boas's greatest photographic coup. For the *Gschnasfest* the Jockey took over the Art Students Academy and commandeered its talents. Pepi-Schani did his usual guard duty at the service entrance, only this time he didn't stand aside for Boas and Conrad.

"Sorry, but I'm to tell you something," he said. "The head clerk wants the same arrangement as with the *artiste.*"

"What arrangement?" Conrad said.

"Actually, you might come out better," Pepi-Schani said. "The Jockey has brother clubs in Budapest and Prague, and you can go there and make photographs of all the galas in those places. The head clerk will pass the word along to his colleagues."

"That's wonderful!" Boas said.

"And then you can stick Czech or Hungarian commoners in front of those Highness pictures, the head clerk doesn't care. But from now on he wants forty percent of the money you get."

"Forty percent," Boas said. "On the other hand, that's exciting, the atelier expanding to Prague and Budapest."

"It means working away from Turk Place," Conrad said.

"Oh, Berek would let us," Boas said. "With the extra money I could pay him my rent arrears. We could even help get him bronze-telephone orders in Hungary and Bohemia."

"Better make up your mind," Pepi-Schani said. "Without the deal I can't let you in."

A few feet away was the main entrance to the *Gschnasfest*. Upright crocodiles and witches on stilts tripped past barricades studded with goggling faces.

"All right," Boas said. "The deal is on."

And Pepi-Schani stood aside to let them pass.

All around Conrad swirled perfumes, incense, shadows, crimson lantern rays, quick stabs of adventure, debauch and liberation. He felt as though he'd already been catapulted away from home into a metropolis magically unshackled of workaday bounds, where the streets of Budapest and Capetown, Prague and Katmandu, intersected with abandon. It was hard to carry the big camera and the negative case through this jostling worldwide dream. Boas, who held only the tripod in his good right arm, could concentrate better on the technical factors.

In the first room they reached, they walked on carps and water lilies; the floor was the top of a huge, flat aquarium. Above, from the ceiling, the petals of a rose garden grew toward the fish, blooming opulently upside down. The problem here, Boas said, was camera position. You needed a vertical angle impossible to achieve.

In the next room King Arthur drank from a giant tankard, with bird-filled knights from his Round Table sitting on every other chair, their armor rigid, gleaming, hollow and chirping. Around them writhed a live white nakedness of women in negligees who tried to feed little beaks thrusting out between helmet chinks. Here, Boas said, the flickering of candles would not give enough photographic light.

The next room was the main hall. At first they could see nothing of it, so clogged was the door with ladies in domino masks, with cavemen, gauchos, bandoliered cossacks and plumed musketeers. Then they pushed through. A banner on the wall became visible, inscribed with Greek-styled lettering: TROJANS DEFEND THE DANUBE! What lay before them was the Turkish siege of Vienna translated into a Homeric fable. From the middle of the hall rose the silhouette of a medieval capital in miniature, papier-mâché oriels and gingerbread mansards surmounted by the spire of St. Stephen's gleaming in spun-sugar Gothic. Above this vista, held by wires, floated a cigar-chewing Zeus in marble body makeup. On the ground before the city ramparts growled and stamped a pack of centaurs. Their heads were those of a dozen Pygmies (borrowed from the Prater's African sideshow) in Greek-bearded masks, sitting astride a dozen Siberian wolfhounds—the bodies.

The spectacle, glaring and vanishing to the pulse of magnesium flares, dizzied Conrad. It exhilarated Boas.

"Get out the negatives, fast!" he said.

They were the last words Conrad heard from his mouth. It could have been the screeching of the tripod tips against the marble floor, or the suddenness with which Boas unfolded the black camera cloth; whatever, it enraged the wolfhounds that were the lower halves of the centaurs nearby. They snorted, reared, snapped, foamed through their muzzles—and tore loose from the leashes held by the crest-helmeted phalanx along the wall. After the first ones broke away, the rest erupted. A riptide of beasts crushed forward, a bellowing horde, paws threshing, with Pygmies falling, moaning.

Conrad was mowed down. When he got up, stunned, the flares had died. Then they glared again, and he saw Uncle Boas lying twisted under the camera. Huge, heavy and black, the cube rested on his thin neck like some playfully thrown pillow.

"Uncle Boas!" he cried. "Uncle Boas! Where's a doctor?"

At first he was the only one who cried for help. Masked ladies gave blithe shrieks. It was all part of a most accomplished phantasmagoria. Cavemen, gauchos, cossacks ran after the centaurs, who were fragmenting marvelously into two-legs and four-legs under the upside-down rose garden next door.

"A doctor! Please!" Conrad cried.

He tried to help Uncle Boas up. But Boas would do nothing but sag in his arms and finally drop down to the marble floor again and bleed thinly from his ear onto the black camera cloth. The blood could not keep the flares from going on and off.

"A doctor!" Conrad screamed. He screamed without stopping. When white-coated men from the ambulance finally elbowed their way into the *Gschnasfest,* they were applauded for their costume.

The carnival clung to Boas's end. In the emergency ward the young doctors attending the case thought at first that Riddah was wearing Mardi Gras disguise when she arrived. Actually, she'd come by taxi straight from her nocturnal work, with no time to take off her baker's apron. The long apron flapped as she ran around Boas's bed. She ran and ran but stopped to stare at various points in her circle; for a long time she tried to find a viewing angle from which her husband's boyishly fragile face could be seen in motion once more. None of the angles worked. Boas's shut eyelids kept staring at a fly on the ceiling. Riddah kept running around him, no longer stopping after a while, not even slowing down, not answering anyone who approached her—not even Berek Spiegelglass, who'd followed her in another taxi a few minutes later. In the end, Berek signed the papers that released the body in his care.

In the van, on the way back to Turk Place, Riddah sat by Boas's stretcher and began to snort. Sobs uncoiled in some child-depths of her body. By the time they reached her adult throat, they had been transmuted into sounds like wracked snores. She snored almost the way Boas had snored in the morning when she'd lain down in bed beside him after her night's work.

Now she snored like that when she washed Boas's helpless pale limbs and prepared his corpse and sewed his shroud on the same table in the Spiegelglass apartment in No. 5 where Berek had done these things for Tamarah thirteen years earlier. Meanwhile, the twins had dug a hole in the backyard of No. 1, next to their mother's grave.

Riddah still snored when she followed Boas's coffin borne by Berek and his sons. She herself was followed by her little son, Markus, and Markus in turn by Hester Spiegelglass in a black satin shirtwaist. No one knew how she'd produced so well fitting a mourning dress so fast, nor where she'd gotten the dark baby clothes for her daughter, whom she carried in her arms.

Riddah snored while the prayers were said, without a rabbi as with Tamarah. She threw down into the grave the first clump of soil; and then, as if that weren't enough to close that ulcer in the earth, she unfolded the apron she'd carried under her arm and let it float down onto the coffin. Then she ran off.

Berek said Kaddish. Together with his boys he manned the shovels. Just as the backyard was smooth again, Riddah returned, still snoring, with a burden. When Berek saw her, he beckoned his boys to help him dig again. They dug a hole at the head of the grave. Into it they thrust the hind wheel of the bicycle Riddah had brought. This was the bicycle on which Boas had once delivered bread in Varungy. It had long lain in the attic of No. 6; yet whiffs of their young married years still came from the blackened wood of its basket. The basket and the front wheel rose from Boas's earth and, like a weather vane, moved to the January gusts and pointed to the door, the ancient, weathered but still whole door that was Tamarah's tombstone ten feet away.

Riddah covered her face before the grave of her husband, then covered it once more before the other resting place. She let herself be hugged by Berek. She left the embrace, went across the street to Turk Place No. 6 and began to struggle with the camera in the studio. Not the one that had crushed Boas's skull but the old-fashioned, even heavier one he had gotten at the priest's funeral in Slovakia long ago. Strong as Riddah was, she could barely get it off the stand. She staggered, snoring and panting, at the studio door, when Berek came in.

Together they carried the camera upstairs, to Boas's side of the double bed. They placed it on the pillow, its lens looking upward like an indomitable eye. That was the face. For the body Riddah ransacked Boas's wardrobe. She pulled out his artistic velvet jacket, his spare berets, his darkroom smock, his striped shirts and his best trousers with the twice-stitched cuffs. All of these she bundled into the bed below the camera and covered them with the black camera cloth, which had since been laundered of his blood. That done, she pulled the eiderdown over the shape.

"I can go to work now," she said, between snores. It was 7 PM and her assistant had already started mixing dough in the cellar. "Boas always goes to bed when I go to work. I can't go away with his bed empty."

"You need rest," Berek said.

"I'm going to work. I better start now. I have to finish in time for the Bar Mitzvah tomorrow."

"We'll postpone the Bar Mitzvah," Berek said.

"No. Tomorrow!"

"Riddah, we'll postpone it—"

"I told you—tomorrow!" she said. *"Tomorrow!"*

For once, Berek let himself be overruled. The twins' Bar Mitzvah did take place the next day, on schedule, though not before the congregation in the synagogue but as a private ritual in the Spiegelglass apartment, with mirrors hooded in linen sheets and window shades pulled, with faces bleached and hollow and all clothes dark. The most vivid colors in the dining room were the white parchment of the Torah spread on the table and, next to it, the ocher of the exposed Brick. Berek had fetched it from the tunnel compartment. He'd placed it in the peasant cradle in which once a baby twin had slept.

Ferdinand stammered his way through the opening of Chapter 18 of Exodus and through his verses of Chapter 6 of Isaiah, and put into the Brick the slip on which he had scrawled, *"God, please let me continue in his way."* Then Conrad read. His rhetorical inflections embellished his part of Chapter 19 of Exodus and of Chapter 9 of Isaiah (though midway his big toe had begun to itch terribly inside his right shoe), and he pushed into a Brick fissure the slip on which he had calligraphed—as if it were a Jockey Club invitation—the question *"God, please, what is the point of the world?"*

Under such circumstances the controversy between Berek Spiegelglass and Rabbi Ackermann became moot. The Reverend Ackermann had no opportunity to express his disapproval of the un-ordained burial the day before or to censure the twins' Bar Mitzvah proceedings with his absence. At so private, so muted and recessed an occasion, his nonattendance was that of an irrelevant outsider's. There was no festivity, no celebration. There were no gifts—except, perhaps, one from Riddah.

When the twins had finished reading and the tin box lid had been placed over the Brick, she walked over to the boys. Her arms opened. She crushed both brothers against her with what was not just the old Riddah heartiness but something fiercer. She was chunky, powerful as ever, but by then Conrad had grown to her height, Ferdinand three inches taller. She pushed the heads of both boys down against her bosom that was always scented with flour. Then she grabbed a hand from each boy and laid their palms against her belly.

"Feel it!" she said. "Boas never had a chance to—it started today. Feel!"

The boys stood with their hands against her belly.

"Feel it for him!"

"Something's moving," Ferdinand said.

"His baby," Riddah said.

It wasn't that she cried but that suddenly her cheeks, her chin, her neck, her black blouse were all awash in the snoring rush of tears.

"I've got to sleep!" she said and ran off to the Slovakian camera that lay, lens staring upward, on her bed.

XX

A T THE AGE of fifty-four Alois Schall committed himself to a permanent bond at last. By then many bachelor decades had passed. A number of quite eligible ladies had loomed up and vanished. With each such disappearance the very word "wife" gained in bedeviling importance. "Wife" brooded over him with a finality that was desirable and irreparable at once. The older he grew, hesitating at the threshold, the more he felt that he was still too young for a decision increasingly awesome. And when he found himself making the crucial move, it didn't seem like a forward motion at all, but like a drop through some fireworks-tinted fog.

On a summer afternoon in 1909 Schall tried to uncloud himself with Berek Spiegelglass's help. He wanted Spiegelglass to rationalize this rashness—to validate it somehow. After all, his partner had also made such a decision abruptly, not just once but twice, and with the most interesting success. Over the years the man had come to radiate a certain superb quiet aplomb; it must have something to do, Schall suspected, with his skill in matrimony.

"Spiegelglass, you're experienced in—in, let's say, being serious with women," Schall said. It was the hour of their Friday afternoon drinks. Both men sat at Berek's plain desk in the factory office. Berek's nod encouraged him to go on.

"I've been meaning to tell you," he said. "Sometimes things happen before you know it. It's difficult to sum up. But to make a long story short—" A cracker crumb (Schall always had crackers with his wine) stuck in his throat and numbed his vocal cords.

"Congratulations," Berek said.

"Three weeks from today," Schall whispered, still toneless. "At the Belvedere Chapel."

As a rule, Berek filled his own wine glass only half full. This time he poured to the top and lifted the glass higher than usual.

"I never thought it'd come like this," Schall said. And, having drunk up, grasping the bottle but not yet pouring, approaching but not yet touching the heart of the matter, he told how that day—actually only two months ago!—had seemed just like an ordinary day. He'd supervised delivery of those ladies' favors for the Locksmiths' Guild Festival, those little lock-shaped candy boxes made of brass. He'd brought them to the master of the Locksmiths' Guild, Herr Spaatz at Belvedere Palace, where Herr Spaatz was mechanic in chief for the crown prince's household.

"I remember, we had to make little keys for those candy boxes," Berek said, nodding again to show that it all did make sense.

Exactly, Schall said, and he'd shown Herr Spaatz how to work the little keys, and nothing further would have developed, everything would have continued the same as before if the time of delivery had been in the morning or the afternoon, any hour at all except lunch. But he, Schall, had explained the little keys just before lunch and that—that had been it. Herr Spaatz had invited him to sit down to some veal goulash with him and his sister.

During the last sentence Schall not only poured but slightly overpoured. Berek wiped up the drops with a freshly ironed handkerchief. The gesture honored the arrival of the sister in the story.

"The sister is twenty-nine," Schall said. "The sister is—well, you'll see—she's deputy chief cook in the palace. Her husband's rope broke, climbing in the Tyrol. A widow seven years, but—but she's just not like any other widow. It's astounding. Her name is Anna."

"Nice name," Berek said.

To tell the truth, Schall himself had never thought "Anna" particularly nice until the moment the veal goulash had been set before him, gently, by the sister, who was, in this astounding way, ungen-

tle. She was short, but with a concentrated, electric shortness. You
didn't even need to look at her very directly to feel how much fem-
ininity she packed into five feet one. Anna's face, rather round and
simple, was lit from the inside by her eyes. Those fiery brown irises
had brushed Schall and made him feel as if he'd been stroked by the
smooth flat side of a burnished blade whose edge had cut something
without hurting him. With one stroke Schall's past had been severed from his future. Even after the eyes had turned away again,
they still kept shining on the solitude and confusion his life had
been so far. But no longer. He had become part of a purpose which
had embraced him at the locking of their glances.

There was no way to describe all that to his partner; Spiegelglass had to see Anna in person.

"The—the hour," Schall said (he'd really meant to say "The
wedding," but his tongue could not yet cope with the starkness of
the word). "The hour has been fixed for one PM, three weeks from
today, as I said, at the Belvedere Palace Chapel. By the crown
prince's permission. You'll get an invitation. When you meet her,
you'll understand."

Schall meant that then his partner would not only understand
but, through his understanding, confirm and perhaps define the
logic of an upheaval. But, apparently, Berek Spiegelglass didn't have
to wait until he had made a visual inspection.

"Good for you," he said. "It's about time."

The entire Turk Place clan attended the ceremony in the
Belvedere Palace Chapel. Berek Spiegelglass lined up his people
behind the last pew so that their Jewish abstentions would be
less conspicuous. They were silent while the others sang hymns.
They stood while the congregation kneeled.

All went well until little Lily began to sniff the funny smells.
Lily was no longer the bump in Riddah's belly which the twins had
been commanded to feel at their Bar Mitzvah. She was a curly five-
year-old in a ruffled pinafore, who forgot what her mother had told
her beforehand, that this was a Christian temple in which one had

to keep just as quiet as in a Jewish one. Actually, it was natural for her to forget. The chapel here was so much bigger than the Turk Place synagogue. There were many more people—not only relatives of the bride and groom but the crown prince's whole lower staff, from gardeners to stable boys, to valets, maids, footmen, grooms, kitchen personnel, maintenance crew and couriers. The massed expectancy of the crowd reminded her of something; so did the incense, which tickled her nostrils much like the pungent steam of a locomotive. Only the week before, Berek had taken her to Vienna's East Railroad Terminal to show her the tracks on which her mother had arrived from Varungy a long time ago.

"*Is a train coming?*" Lily asked into the chapel silence, just after the exchange of nuptial vows. Her brother, Markus, was playing finger soccer with a miniature ball inside his pocket and couldn't get his hand out in time to cover his sister's mouth. Hester's daughter, Ilona, only a year older than Lily but already in a sleek silk skirt, giggled. Conrad was theoretically in charge of the small children; he made a dragon face meaning "Shut up!" But he didn't keep Lily from opening her mouth again. Just then, however, Berek Spiegelglass stamped his foot, very slightly. On the instant, Lily closed her lips and the organ flooded the nave with sonorousness.

Afterward, a reception line formed in the palace courtyard. Schall, dazed, thought it was the drizzle that made his Anna hurry. She pulled him toward their coach before he had a chance to present all his Turk Place friends. Eight hours later the drizzle had become a rain which danced on the roof of the Schalls' honeymoon inn in Alpine Mariazell, danced and throbbed through the couple's closer but still preliminary physical acquaintance under a floral quilt. Schall, by way of mitigating the boldness of his hand, whispered how exciting everything had been, the ceremony and everything.

"Yes," Anna whispered back, "despite your Spiegelglass lady."

"Frau Spiegelglass?" Schall said.

"You saw what she wore? . . . When I was wearing blue?"

Anna's whisper, though a digression, was breathy and exitingly
urgent. Schall didn't know what to say and kissed her.

"*I* wore blue as a widow . . . *She* had on this huge white shawl!"

Clothes weren't on Schall's mind. To encourage his male
strength he had concentrated on the opposite, on the dissolution of
Anna's negligee under the quilt, which was proceeding without his
help somehow, as if melting away before the heat of her anger. He
kept kissing her.

"Wearing white at *my* wedding! . . ."

"Oh," Schall said into their kiss. Was that why Anna hadn't
greeted Frau Spiegelglass on the receiving line? Happily there was
no time to wonder. The negligee had vaporized. All of a sudden
Anna's movements were no longer a bit preliminary. They were
amazingly direct, provoking Schall's own virile directness. Within
seconds his bride uttered a shout not only of desire but of will, a cry
whose mysterious assertion stayed with him long after their lips and
their limbs and even the rain had subsided.

For a while Schall remained amazed at his married estate. But
then he discovered that husbandhood in general was really less
remarkable than his wife in particular. It wasn't just that he could
never be sure what Anna would do next; it was the fact that most
of her seemingly strange actions turned out to be, in the end, part
of an inevitable pattern.

He was surprised at first when Anna brought to their apartment
at Turk Place only a couple of knockabout housecleaning dresses
and just one ensemble fit for church on Sunday. The rest of her
clothes remained at the flat she had shared with her brother in the
service wing of Belvedere Palace. She explained to Schall that her
brother was having a special wardrobe chest made in the carpentry
shops of Belvedere. Once that was finished and transported to Turk
Place, she would move all her other garments.

On the Sunday following their honeymoon week Anna went to
Belvedere to check on how the chest was coming along. She didn't
return until almost 5 PM, an hour later than promised. Ordinarily,

this would not have bothered her new husband. But the Spiegel-glasses expected the Schalls for tea at 4 PM—the first meal to be shared by the two couples. It was rather an important date, Schall felt, because of the problem at the reception line after the wedding. Furthermore, the tea was a date that hadn't been easy to arrange. Anna continued to be sauce specialist and deputy chief cook in the crown prince's kitchen and as such had an imposing schedule which often claimed even her weekends.

So it was lucky that Anna was free that Sunday. However, when she arrived not just late but vivaciously late, Schall began to grasp that her vivacity could be the ripple of a very serious emotion.

A few minutes before five Anna took Schall's arm and strode with him from Turk Place No. 6 toward the Spiegelglass apartment. But on the ground floor of No. 5 she quite unexpectedly stopped at the corridor sink. Here the concierge, the No. 5 Havlicek, was filling a jug with her dinner-cooking water.

"And how are we today, Frau Havlicek," Anna said. "I imagine our little attic problem has been straightened out by now."

The No. 5 Havlicek, most dour and difficult of all the Havliceks, went into her greeting stance. She inclined her head and tied her moist apron a little tighter over her faded dressing gown.

"Mrs. has the B-apartment space in the attic," she said ("Mrs." being whatever lady tenant she happened to be talking to).

"No, no," Anna said with a little laugh while lightly holding Schall's arm. "If there's anything I don't have, it's the B space. I gave that back to you when we first discussed it last week. You know that it won't do."

"B apartment gets the B space in the attic," the No. 5 Havlicek said with a stoic cough.

"I didn't know there was a problem," Schall said.

Without looking at him, Anna touched her husband's elbow with two little pats that instructed him not to bother and to leave this footling affair to her.

"Frau Havlicek," Anna said with a bright edge to her conso-nants, "since I'll require attic space primarily for clothes airing, we can't even begin to discuss the subject unless the area involved is at least twice as big as the one you showed me."

"Everybody gets her proper attic space," the No. 5 Havlicek said, nodding at the water streaming into her jug.

"How nice, I'm so glad to hear that," Anna said. "In that case, I'll tell you what my proper space is and why." She reached out and stopped the water noise by turning off the faucet, ostensibly because the Havlicek jug was just about full. "This involves His Imperial Highness, the crown prince, whom I'm serving."

The abrupt introduction of this topic was dramatic, resonating as it did against the sudden silence of the faucet. The No. 5 Havlicek pulled a rag out of her apron pocket and began to wipe away at a stain in a tile above the sink.

"People know that His Imperial Highness's wife was not born of equal rank, just a countess," Anna said. "You may know that after the marriage she was made a Princess Hohenberg but with no special precedence, without a single blessed archducal privilege. But it's not generally known that last month—" Anna stopped for a moment to give the No. 5 Havlicek an opportunity to stop wiping the smudge and to devote full attention. The No. 5 Havlicek continued wiping. All three Havliceks had an iron policy of sealing themselves off with "work" while complaints from tenants were going on. It was a virtuous way of being inaccessible.

"Last month the crown prince's wife was made *duchess* of Hohenberg with very considerable precedence—and all this in the face of pretty sorry intrigues."

Anna spoke the last sentence in a whisper of icy casualness. Such information was the stuff of the most sterling gossip, but Anna's tone intimated that to her it was routine—an incidental part of a picayune argument. Frau Havlicek continued wiping.

Anna's chuckle was as frigid as her whisper. "Those intrigues didn't get anywhere against my mistress. She's a duchess now. You can't stop people from getting what they deserve."

The No. 5 Havlicek had discovered another stain, to the right of the one she had erased.

"Now my mistress will be able to entertain archdukes," Anna said, more softly and icily still. "There'll be a series of dinners at her own castle in Bohemia. My master, the crown prince, he's making a special point of that. He's sending his own chief cook to work there.

Which means that the deputy chief cook, that's myself, I'll run the kitchen at Belvedere. Therefore I'd better have reception dresses ready. Do you know what that means?"

The shaking of the No. 5 Havlicek's head could have been either an answer to the question or irritation over the second stain, which seemed harder to erase than the first.

"A reception dress," Anna said, "is what I'll have to wear when I'm called out to receive kind words about dinner from Their Highnesses. I'll have a big wardrobe to keep fresh. For me that little airing space in the attic is a joke."

"B apartment gets B space in the attic," the No. 5 Havlicek said, "unless it's special permission from the landlord." She spat on the stain to make it less resistant to her wiping.

"'*Special permission*'?" Anna mimicked the No. 5 Havlicek's tired intonation. "Oh, I don't think we'll need to bother about that!"

With a fine, invincible laugh she gathered up her husband on her arm and swept him away so fast, they hardly heard the faucet the No. 5 Havlicek had turned on again to remoisten her rag.

Since the Schalls arrived an hour late, their hostess had to order the maid to warm the coffee again. Yet Hester Spiegelglass didn't seem at all put out. She rustled about smiling in what was for her an undécolleté dress. Things went quite well while Resi served Linzer torte. The two ladies talked about how impossible those new elbow-length kid gloves were (it took minutes for Frau Schall to pull them off) while the men joked about the mysteries of female fashion. It was not until the reheated coffee was brought in that Anna leaned back and explained, apologetically, the reason why it had gone cold in the first place.

"It's my fault," she said. "I stayed too long at Belvedere Palace. But my brother had such exciting news. The emperor is finally acting his age." She paused to contemplate her coffee cup, whose arabesque pattern was a shade too fancy for ironstone china. "I suppose you feel it when you're crowding eighty, even if you are a

Majesty," she said. "Anyway he's letting the crown prince do *something* at last."

"*Mmm!*" Schall said since nobody else reacted audibly.

"From now on," Frau Schall continued slowly, "the crown prince will be conferring all medals and decorations awarded in the name of the Kingdom of Bohemia within the empire. And that's just the beginning."

Again, no special response from the Spiegelglasses. Schall knew that a certain amount of public ribbing between spouses constituted one of the marital arts (he'd often noticed a certain dashing tension between the Spiegelglasses), and so he said, "Why, you never told me about this, Anna. You're beginning to keep secrets."

"I had no idea until this afternoon," Anna said. "My brother heard about it only yesterday—from His Imperial Highness himself. Now, with the right to award medals goes the right to select their maker, and my brother feels very proud. The crown prince has selected him. My brother will manufacture the medals."

"But that's tremendous!" Schall said.

"Now, my brother is already chief mechanic of the household, but for the medals he'll need machinery and staff and certainly a designer—" Anna placed her forefinger on the draftsman's hand of her husband.

"My God, we have all that right here in the factory," said Schall.

"Well, it'd have to be done at the metal shops in Belvedere," Anna said. "But if Herr Spiegelglass is interested in a real partnership with my brother—"

"Very nice," Berek Spiegelglass said. "Except you say it has to be done away from here."

"Of course, at Belvedere," Anna said, "because it's under the crown prince's auspices and the supervision of his first lord chamberlain. It's a pretty unique chance."

"Everything I produce is done at Turk Place," Berek said quietly.

There was a pause. To fill it, Schall reached for the sugar tongs and placed three cubes in his still empty cup.

"I suppose I haven't made clear what this really means," Anna said. Her words now came with the same hard brightness she had leveled at the No. 5 Havlicek. "This means that once this arrangement has been made, it will continue when the crown prince succeeds to the throne. And then he'll order every medal in the empire from us. We'll make them *all*."

"Jesus, that's fantastic!" Schall said.

There was another pause. Anna took the sugar tongs Schall had left by his cup and pinged them back in the bowl. "Of course, it's your decision, Herr Spiegelglass," she said. "We just wanted you to have the choice."

"Some coffee?" Hester said, pointing toward the pot.

"I'm not very good at pouring when I'm the guest," Anna said pleasantly.

The lesson in etiquette seemed lost on Hester Spiegelglass's smile. She motioned to the maid to do the honors. Anna watched their cups being filled and then left hers so pointedly untouched that Schall refrained as well. And yet he felt that *something* had to be said, for heaven's sake.

"Perhaps we should talk it over again," he said.

"But, dear, it's already been talked over," Anna said to her husband. "I know from what you've told me, you've been talking it over, one way or another, for how long? Twenty years? Thirty years? All this time nothing could have been done here without your designs, right? And what have you got for it? A percentage? What is that? Is that a reward for such—such a contribution? Is that *dignity*? Were you offered a true partnership? All right, now you'll be a true partner with my brother—on His Imperial Highness's business! Important business!"

Berek emptied his cup and gave a slight, peaceable shoulder shrug. "We have something important here at Turk Place," he said. "It's been good for Schall, too."

"Has it?" Anna said. "Really. How? Has it made *him* the cock of the walk around here? And what exactly is 'it'?" She turned to her husband. "Can you tell me, Alois?"

"I don't know," Schall said. "I don't know what started all this—"

"Oh, I'll tell you *when* it started," Anna said. "The moment you started working here. You never got the dignity you deserved. That's been the problem, way back, long before me. But you'll get dignity now at the Belvedere. You'll come into your own, just like the crown prince."

"Good," Berek said, retucking a trouser leg into a boot. "Good luck."

The maid had not followed the drastic turn in conversation. She came around again with the cake tray, offering Linzer torte. Anna smiled her away with immaculate courtesy. Then she got up. "Well, thank you very much," she said. "That makes everything very clear."

And Schall, rising to his feet a moment later, felt an abrupt youthfulness thrill its way down his spine. He had accumulated a sizable bank account, but suddenly he saw that it was only the middle-aged fruit of flounderings and gropings. Now, to the smell of the Spiegelglasses' warmed-over coffee, he tingled with a resentment that was marvelously young. He vibrated with a sense of injustice; a long-standing, clever, corroding injustice whose removal would return him to that fresh point in time before the start of the corrosion. The injustice had begun with Dr. Nassig, to continue even more cleverly after Nassig's disappearance. But he, Schall, had not been its patsy forever. He had just let the evil ripen and wrinkle until it was ready for exposure—until he'd gotten himself a wife who was nobody's fool. He loved the way she strode away from the Spiegelglass table, smoothing her long gloves right up to her elbow. Walking behind her with a springy, grim, steady step, with the step of a marine lieutenant, he knew without a doubt that he had done the right thing: the murderous risk of wedlock had paid off.

"Good luck to *you*," he said to the Spiegelglasses, bowing at the threshold. "You might need it more than us."

XXI

By 1913 THE TWINS, now past twenty, had long since moved to the flat at No. 6 Turk Place left empty by the Schalls' departure. But Conrad still had his morning coffee in the dining room of the parental apartment at No. 5. At 7:30 AM sharp Resi would bring in a tray with two cups of coffee, four rolls and a copy of *Wiener Tagblatt*, which Conrad would read backward. He would start, chortling, with the classifieds on the final page that advertised "Sequestered Waiting Rooms of Doctors for Secret Diseases." After a few minutes Resi would poke her head in from the kitchen door, to nod at the second cup of coffee getting cold. Where was Herr Ferdinand? Skipping breakfast again?

"Oh, you know him," Conrad would say. "Up at dawn to blast the swineherds." And he'd drink the second coffee himself.

By "swineherds" he meant Serbia, that unruly chieftancy of hog raisers which racketed against the southeastern border of the Habsburg realm. Compared to the Empire, the hog-raisers' kingdom was puny and primitive; but that didn't keep them from coveting the imperial province of Bosnia-Herzegovina next door. They tried to rouse the Bosnians against Austria with whoops and roars about the Slav heritage they both shared. As countermove, Austria fortified Bosnia's allegiance by literally electrifying it: wiring its cities and linking Bosnian progress to Habsburg heraldry. The covers of all utility manholes, for example, featured a central bronze panel with the imperial seal. And the panels were forged in bas-relief at the Turk Place factory.

Just before his retirement Councilman Novak had planted Schall's adaptation of the seal on the right desk of the Public Works Ministry. Whereupon Berek Spiegelglass had received an order for thirty-seven hundred quadrangles of imperial blazonry to grace every access to sewage or electric lines throughout Bosnia-Herzegovina.

None of the machines at Turk Place could stamp out so intricate a design. On the other hand, few workers were able to hand-punch an engraving thick enough to withstand road usage, as was necessary for the Bosnian item; and those few workers who could tired fast. Ferdinand didn't tire. A massive six feet three, he "blasted the swineherds" all day long by clanging metal onto metal. He began at 6 AM, long before anyone else, and as he worked through the morning, he never lost track of a whisper flowing beneath the clangor, namely the river of his father's breath.

He knew that Berek stayed in bed late and that toward 9 AM he was likely to be sleeping in an empty apartment, unprotected. That was when Hester always sipped tea with her daughter in the roof garden of No. 6. Cook Resi was out shopping. As for Conrad, he had a habit of being shocked by his watch at eight-thirty; he'd throw his paper down and run off to the factory office, often leaving the parental apartment wide open. At that point anyone could get at Berek.

Ferdinand still had not rid himself of the image of the dead piglet on the pillow, next to his father's dreaming face. To shield Berek during his morning vulnerability he hired Zettl—Zettl, his former enemy at school and now the new night watchman of Turk Place. Ferdinand paid Zettl two gulden extra out of his own sixteen gulden weekly wages. In return, Zettl hung around an extra hour in the morning, leaning against the wall of Turk Place No. 5, slicing into his breakfast bacon with a barbarously huge knife, while inside, in the Spiegelglass bedroom, Berek slept on alone with long, steady, firm sighs.

To Zettl only the breakfast bacon made that extra hour of work tolerable. That was why he often decided to come down with a morning colic on Friday, when bacon was impossible for a good Catholic.

Early on Friday, when Berek's sleep serenity was left unguarded, Ferdinand's nerves were wired to his father's breath. One morning he suddenly felt his windpipe warping. He ran from the factory into the street. Before Turk Place No. 5 a carriage waited to take Ilona to her private school in the Inner City—not the usual fiacre, though, but a substitute whose driver was obviously careless about regulations. His coach wheels had no rubber rims; his horses were about to swivel into an illegal U-turn that would have thundered wheels and hooves onto the sidewalk, so close against Berek Spiegelglass's window as to shake him awake.

Ferdinand leaped instantly. His two hundred pounds hung against the reins. He stopped the turn. The driver, cursing, raised his whip. Ferdinand hauled out and slapped both animal rumps so powerfully, they scrambled off to little Ilona's thrilled scream.

His father's sleep was safe. But an alarm kept going off in Ferdinand that day. The fiacre incident had opened a small cut in his left hand. He went to clean it in his father's office, and there, next to the washstand, the incoming-orders book lay open at the current page. He saw the entry for the manhole-cover panels in Bosnia—a big order but now more than half completed. He saw another order, much smaller, for forty fancy switch plates for the apartment house under construction opposite the Opera. Ferdinand had leafed through the incoming-orders book before, but he'd never been so struck by the emptiness of that current page. The two orders on it were recorded in Conrad's Gothic script, whose ornamental acrobatics suddenly looked like a dance in a lost desert. Except for those two items at the top, both dated months ago, there was nothing but a void, lined in blue, down to the bottom of the long sheet.

The void dogged Ferdinand. It surrounded his work at the lathe. It closed in. After more than an hour, when he knew his father would be up, he went back to the office.

"Papa," he said. "Good morning, Papa. This Bosnian order, was this the last design Schall did for us?"

Berek nodded, sipping from the breakfast cup he usually took at his desk.

"I see we have nothing else coming in."

"Oh, Schall will come back in the end," Berek said. "It's happened before."

"Good," Ferdinand said.

But he couldn't leave it like that. He kept standing at his father's desk. The longer he stood there, the more his "good" curdled into a lie. He knew that the market in fancy switch plates had been saturated and that the market for manhole panels would vanish with delivery of the present order. And the blue lines of the empty ledger page cascaded down into an evil darker than bankruptcy. Ferdinand found his tongue shaping words he'd never dreamed of saying to his father, for they questioned Berek Spiegelglass's handling of affairs.

"Papa," he said, "until Schall comes back, what are you going to do until then?"

"Oh, we'll think of something," Berek said.

He clapped Ferdinand on the shoulder, a touch that lingered just a bit, and walked into the factory itself, where he lit the soldering flame, humming.

Ferdinand returned to his lathe. His ears, which had heard the astonishing "we" of "we'll think of something," felt tender; his shoulder tingled where it had been tapped. Had his father ever tapped him like that before? It had been a man-to-man tap, offhand yet warm with meaning. The tap had dealt with the problem by turning it over to him. He, Ferdinand, had to think of something.

This obligation, a gift from his father, turned quickly into bafflement. How could he "think of something" for the factory? The survival of Turk Place was an old game for his father. Could Ferdinand be apprenticed in it? He remembered his father's stories about Varungy, the journey to Vienna, and the Brick. Apparently his father had played the game with a marble calm against which Gypsies and bureaucrats had dashed themselves to pieces. Ferdinand had to learn that calm before he could even try to "think of something."

Each morning he still listened for his father's sleep beyond the double doors. But now he searched the sound for clues. The secret might be in the leisureliness of the exhale-inhale alternation. More than once he tried to assume that rhythm himself. But he found it hard to smooth his lungs into a refrain so long and low and firm.

Sometimes he came close on Saturday evenings. That was when Berek had his "downtown night" with Hester and Ilona. Saturday Ferdinand did all the closing chores in the factory. After the last worker left, he went back to his lathe to finish up some odds and ends, but at a pace no longer driven by the customary turmoil around him. Then he'd make sure that all the motors were turned off, the ventilators shut down and no metal ribbons hanging loose from the presses. Gradually, he'd feel his sweat dry. His breath subsided across the silence into a beat not too different from the sleep pulse of his father.

On such an evening, already on his way out, a pale blue shaft struck his eye. It came from the office, where the gaslight had not been switched off. A moment later his father's face rose from the desk in shades of blue and white. Next to it, yet weirder, a huge ladybug sat on a matchbox. Ferdinand recoiled, rushed forward.

It was all Conrad's doing. His father's face, it turned out, was only a drawing on the desk blotter, propped up on the thick volume of the Vienna address directory. Below the drawing a pair of steel-framed spectacles had been stuck into the blotter—and Ferdinand now remembered that an hour earlier, when Conrad had gone off (as usual, before all the other workers), he had shouted that their father had forgotten his spectacles in the office. Conrad had left the office light on so Ferdinand wouldn't forget them himself, and he had drawn Berek's face as an additional reminder. It wasn't a disrespectful drawing: Conrad's light calligraphic strokes had rejuvenated their father and taken most of the gray out of his beard. And—perhaps to make sure of arresting Ferdinand's attention—Conrad had also crayoned the giant bug onto the matchbox Berek used as a spectacle case. That was all.

Yet he didn't want to see the monster insect by his father's face—a sight that belonged to the same universe gone wrong as the barren blue lines of the empty orders book. He turned off the gas lamp to make the scene vanish. And, suddenly, he "thought of something" for the factory.

For one second he turned on the lamp again, just long enough to grab the spectacles and the matchbox. Two minutes later he was outside the locked gate of the factory, running, running to find his father.

The Crystal Bottle, the restaurant which Hester chose for her "downtown night" with her husband and daughter, lay on the edge of the Inner City. It featured a presumable Arab in fez and caftan limping about with a swan-spouted coffeepot from which he filled cups. Even the establishment's busboys wore vests as gold-buttoned and shoes as squeaky as the maître d's. Its Persian rug, while somewhat worn, had new long white fringes. A waiter was just tiptoeing to the Spiegelglass table in the corner. He carried a napkin in both hands, as if it were something hot and delicate. Tucked deeply into its fold, like a shameful genital, lay the bill.

At the table Berek was running his finger along the tines of the dessert fork and found the metal too grainy to justify the hallmark, indicating silver, on the fork handle. On his plate the fruit stollen ordered for his dessert was untouched. Hester and Ilona, on the other hand, had spooned every smidgen of whipped cream out of their conch-shaped meringues. The leaf green of the mother's huge hat complemented the mustard gold of the daughter's pert bonnet. Their fingers interlaced, the two surrendered themselves to the "Voices of Spring" waltz. Poignantly, the violinist's paunch sagged as he strolled toward them.

All this Ferdinand took in from the door—this, plus the hatcheck girl's missing molar, so wide had her mouth opened at the sight of his sooty work smock. Dressed the way he was, he hesitated to barge in on such ambitious, wine-scented, violin-dripping cutlery tinkle. But that moment the kitchen door opened to release a dead pig. It was small and smiled as it came floating out on a waiter's tray. A cluster of grapes parted its jaws. Otherwise, it was the same pig that had once been thrown at his sleeping father, and indeed it was toward his father that it traveled.

Ferdinand shot forward. "Excuse me," he said to Hester. "Papa, your glasses," he said to his father. "They were left at your desk."

"Thanks, just in time," Berek said, and put them on to frown at the bill.

"You haven't even started your dessert, Berek," Hester said. She turned away and immersed herself once more in the pinings of the violin, which, however, had changed its course away from the Spiegelglasses. With their table now stained by the dingy, intrusive, gigantic Ferdinand, "The Voices of Spring" serenaded the other end of the room instead.

"I'll have the stollen wrapped to take home," Berek said to the waiter.

"Berek, if you *have* finished," Hester said, "Ferdinand can go out again and call a cab for us."

"The tramway is still running," Berek said, paying.

"Public vehicles," Hester said, "will not be used by my daughter at this hour."

Just then the pig was no more than three feet away. Smoke from flaming cherries jubilee nearby scratched Ferdinand's throat. It produced a fit of the kind that would punctuate his whole life: a staccato of sneezes entirely dry but as percussive as a kettledrum. The captain held out his hands protectively against these volleys of germs. He signaled the tray bearer; back the pig traveled into the kitchen for disinfection. It passed Ferdinand—and it turned out to be marzipan.

Somehow this encouraged Ferdinand. He whipped the matchbox from his pocket. "Papa," he said. "Look! Ornamental eyeglass cases! More and more people are wearing glasses—it could get us big new orders!"

Berek put his spectacles into the box and nodded at the ladybug design. "Looks like your brother's doing."

"He was just fooling around," Ferdinand said. "But it could be a good line for us!"

"Maybe," Berek said. "Maybe Conrad will work out as a designer. Come on, we'll call a cab."

He got up, patted Ilona's bonnet out of place (Hester instantly adjusted it), gave Ferdinand a "Let's go" tap and accepted from the waiter the stollen wrapped in the same napkin which earlier had made decent the restaurant bill.

"That stollen is the one thing they do right here," Berek said. "We'll eat it at Turk Place."

Ferdinand walked out by his side. He was inhaling, at least for a glorious little while, his father's calm.

As an idea man for Boas's photo atelier, Conrad had done well. He'd also proved an entertaining companion for Turk Place children. Riddah's boy, Markus, loved the way Conrad could bounce a ball on his forehead while standing on one leg. Markus's little sister, Lily, thought Conrad was great fun. Half her school class followed the sociable Lily home to Turk Place, whose entire roadway she'd chalk with a vast hopscotch maze of her own invention. Traffic would stop before a streetful of little skirts hopping, but Conrad could clear the roadway fast, to laughter: he'd impersonate a princely four-in-hand complete with neighing, whip cracks and even horse apples.

But in 1913 Riddah's children were no longer babies. Markus was a journeyman of twenty-two in his mother's bakery. At ten Lily still had the right to giggle with friends over homework—for an hour or two after school. But before dinner she helped at the bakery counter selling the day's final batch of rolls.

Riddah's children were already doing some of the world's work. Conrad—now twenty-three—still had to find himself. He was too old to play errand boy, too calligraphic for office work. Siddo Berger—still Berek's clerk—could dictate the toughest, tersest dunning note to a delinquent account; Conrad would turn the ultimatum into an absurdly beauteous ink pattern whose execution took two hours.

It made better sense to use his graphic talents for the creation of ornamental eyeglass cases. Spectacles were edging out monocles in Vienna. The spectacles case had begun to outrank the snuffbox as *objet.* Unfortunately, the ladybug case died in the sample stage. Berek's commission salesman reported strong resistance to vermin even if made of bronze. So Conrad tried other design ideas. He came up with winged pretzels or roosters with rose-petaled crests, dream shapes which somehow failed to intrigue the nearsighted.

Berek then sent Conrad downtown to the Pfeilgasse, a street graced by a number of the capital's best opticians. Conrad was to look at their displays for inspiration. Nothing practical came of that either. In the end, Conrad returned home not with designs but with nannies.

The Pfeilgasse rimmed Modena Park, where French or Scottish nursemaids wheeled fashionable prams. One wriggle of Conrad's nose could make any baby laugh. Invariably, that wriggle would be aimed at an infant attended by a well-bloused girl. Conrad himself was a slim, blue-eyed, curly-haired faun; minutes after he produced a happy gurgle in a baby carriage, the nanny behind the carriage would be sipping and tittering at the lemonade stand, next to Conrad. Language problems didn't slow Conrad down at all. Wielding a felicitous pidgin German, he was well on his way to a rendezvous.

Time after time, Ferdinand would come home to their shared bachelor quarters at Turk Place No. 6 to find the blue lampshade in the living room replaced by the pink. Conrad had tailored the pink one from the step-ins of a conquered lady. It was a warning signal: "Please buy yourself a mocha at the Café Pellmann. Heavy stuff in the bedroom."

After this happened often enough, Ferdinand asked his brother why he didn't escort his heavy stuff elsewhere, say, to a hotel.

"Well," Conrad said. "It's like this. Doesn't Papa always bring home the best dishes from the restaurants?"

Conrad didn't seem to understand that the two things were not exactly the same. Conrad also failed to sketch designs which might ease the emptiness of the incoming-orders book. That emptiness was aggravated by the 1913 Christmas greetings the Schalls sent the Spiegelglasses. The card showed a gold-framed photograph of the Heir Apparent to the throne awarding the Order of St. Wenceslaus to Oswald Count Chotek. Opposite the picture an inscription said: *"Coming to you with best wishes from Alois Schall,*

*by appointment medal-maker to His Imperial and Royal Highness, the
Crown Prince. Peace on Earth and Good Will Toward Men."*

Often Ferdinand felt that it was up to him to make Conrad see
sense. Saturday evening should have provided an opportunity for
a frank talk, with the rest of the family away on the "downtown
night." But Saturday evening had a tendency to go awry. Instead
of Ferdinand setting his brother right, it was sometimes almost
the other way around.

Conrad always left the office early, of course, in a great hurry to
start the weekend at the coffeehouse. After closing up, Ferdinand
went to the Café Pellmann himself. It was his one and only—once a
week—recreation. When he arrived, his brother would be long em-
broiled in the billiard room Herr Pellmann had recently added to the
first-class section of the café. A notoriously brilliant player, Conrad
liked the game only if there was a bet involved, no matter how
small. To attract partners he volunteered to assume bizarre handi-
caps: tied a pirate's eye patch around his head to deprive himself of
depth vision or used a mummified orange for his cue ball.

While Conrad kept winning, Ferdinand tried to stay out of the
international crisis, which, along with billiards, had become the
newest rage at the café. With each brandy Herr Skalka, Jr., informed
one and all more loudly that it was Russia which stirred up the
Serbs against Austria; only full mobilization would make the czar
pull in his horns. Otto Schönfeld, on the other hand (he'd just become a partner in his father's florist business), brushed a pastry
flake off the sky-blue trouser leg of the reservist's uniform he'd
lately taken to wearing and said, mobilization, hogwash: Serbia
meant zero to the Russkies; one raid on Belgrade by one regiment of
Austrian dragoons, one Belgrade government building nicely pul-
verized, and the Serbs would become peaceful swineherds again.

To the clicking of billiard balls the argument blazed. Both sides
tried to enlist Ferdinand. He said he must read the papers first to
inform himself. Actually, he leafed only through the financial pages.
He always hoped he'd come upon opportunities for medal or

medallion manufacturers that might fill up the incoming-orders book.

Very seldom could he finish his Turkish coffee without being drawn into a fight after all. He'd have to shove his muscled bulk between Conrad and somebody's fist. Usually, Conrad's billiard partners became furious not just because they lost but because they felt themselves somehow mocked.

The real mockery, however, took place on the twins' way home, after midnight. Walking along, Conrad farcically restaged the evening's games. He'd mime his opponents' habits—their pompous cue-stick chalking, grotesque aim takings, even their table-buggering postures. Ferdinand would laugh and push his brother away to stop this meanness. The push only sent Conrad into a still more hilarious contortion. Ferdinand had to surrender to the guffaw inside him. Laughter rolled from his hips to his throat. It filled his body with waves of a rare freedom, a freedom he never knew in the factory, at home or at the Pellmann; an effervescing surprise each time, a release into childlikeness which swamped his resolve to have a serious talk with Conrad and swept him into playing tag with his brother as if they were twelve again. Like wild kids, they tore through their house hall, past the rheumy, stolid gaze of the No. 5 Havlicek, chasing each other up the stairs to their apartment that seemed, all of a sudden, so preposterously adult.

Again and again, Ferdinand found himself seduced by Conrad, if only for brief minutes, into a sort of abandonment. He didn't realize just how much he held that against his brother until one Sunday night.

It happened to be an unlikely hour for friction between the twins. If Saturday marked Berek's night out with Hester, Sunday meant Berek's night with his sons. Electricity, of all things, had produced this custom.

Volts were to flow through the 17th District, no less than through Bosnia-Herzegovina; soon they were to shine from the minareted lampposts of Turk Place. But Berek refused to let municipal electricians install the central fuse box underneath the street. The box was to be in the tunnel, only a few feet away from the Brick compartment. Berek told the city engineer that his sons would take responsibility for those fuses. Actually, Ferdinand, the family's electrical specialist, performed just about all the work. But since the current would not be turned on for months, Berek directed him to divide the task into many small segments. These he had Ferdinand distribute across a number of sociable Sunday nights during which he kept his son company with a chore of his own.

The two sat cross-legged on the tunnel floor, Ferdinand splicing wires, his father whittling. Much of the Brick's tin box had rusted, and now Berek Spiegelglass was carving a new box out of uncorrodable cedarwood. As for Conrad, he was master of the refreshments; they made the work session a family party. The cramped tunnel space could not hamper Conrad's juggling of cups, plates, saucers and a hot mocha pot. Turned into a waiter with tomcat reflexes, he slithered ceremoniously through the constrictions of this long lantern-lit cocoon of a secret coffeehouse.

Mostly he served desserts Berek had saved from the restaurant of the previous night. In fact, it was a crumbly Café Pellmann chocolate marble cake that started the trouble one Sunday. Conrad stood behind Berek as he sliced the cake. Ferdinand was about to point out that a small piece had dropped on their father's shoulder. Conrad, however, raised a finger to his lips and deftly blew the piece away. That seemed like putting one over on their father, and Ferdinand felt a twinge of anger. Then he noticed that the piece had been blown directly onto the Brick.

Ferdinand didn't want to glance in that direction. The Brick lay exposed so that Berek Spiegelglass could measure it for the new box; somehow Ferdinand felt it should not be looked at, except during rituals calling for its nakedness. Now his brother had made him break the taboo. And he could not take his eyes away. He saw where the bit of cake had fallen on the Brick: between his own tightly furled message (he still remembered twisting the slip of paper years ago at his Bar Mitzvah) and Conrad's. And Conrad's slip—he became aware of that only now—was oddly folded and angled, like a kite. *"What is the point of the world?"* Conrad had asked God, and flown a kite into the Brick. And topped it all off tonight by blowing a crumb on it, behind their father's back.

Ferdinand spun around at his brother.

"You got the Brick dirty!" he said.

"Dirty?" Conrad said. "No. Where?"

"Look!" Ferdinand said.

"That was me? That's just a crumb."

"You think we're all fools here!" Ferdinand said. "You don't care if we starve to death or the world goes to hell or to war or anything!"

"Ferdinand," his father said quietly.

"I swear, Papa!" Ferdinand said. "He contributes zero, he's not designing anything, it doesn't matter if we're going broke—"

Ferdinand stopped. The echoed roar his own voice had produced in the tunnel was shocking. Conrad just stood there, holding the cake plate with one hand, pulling down one twirled end of his new handlebar mustache with the other. The lopsided mustache looked like a deliberate absurdity ridiculing all those accusations. Ferdinand jumped to his feet. His great height forced him to stoop under the ceiling of the tunnel, and the pressure on his neck increased his anger. He shouted yet more loudly to vindicate his previous loudness.

"You think it's all just nonsense!" he shouted at his brother. *"You're just out to jump girls, you think the Brick is nothing and God is nothing—"*

A small crash interrupted him. Berek Spiegelglass, still cross-legged on the floor, had lifted a saucer ten inches off the ground before throwing it down.

"Ferdinand," he said quietly. "Clean that up."

Ferdinand gripped his own throat. It kept him from shouting more.

"Clean that up," Berek Spiegelglass said. "Pick up the pieces."

Ferdinand bent down to pick up the pieces. Trembling, he gathered them into a little heap. Conrad had put his free arm against the wall, his head lolling inside the elbow, his shoulders shaking. Berek Spiegelglass watched his sons in the lantern light. He breathed calmly as if he were asleep.

"The question Conrad asked about what is the point of the world," he said. "That's a good question. Because here at Turk Place is the right spot for him to find out. You missed a piece of saucer over there, Ferdinand."

"I'm sorry," Ferdinand said, picking it up.

"Now sit down," Berek said.

Ferdinand sat.

"You brought up something good, too," Berek said to him. "About no orders coming in. Me, I had no orders when I started here. Remember what happened then?"

There was silence in the tunnel.

"Nobody knows?" Berek continued. "Nobody remembers what I told you two about that when you were little? The things that happened those days I came here from Varungy?"

From Conrad's mouth, buried in the crook of his elbow, a noise issued, wavering and weak at first, akin to crying. It became a little stronger and resembled the honking of geese. It grew in volume and acquired rhythm: the clacking of wagon wheels and the thud of hooves. Conrad was repeating the sounds of the voyage from Varungy to Vienna, the voyage through which Berek had often taken his twins in the tunnel, years ago when they had been tots.

"Right," Berek said to Conrad. "You remember."

"I remember, too," Ferdinand said. "I just can't turn it into tricks."

Conrad was still at it. Face turned to the wall, he sounded the whip cracks of the drive to the Palace; Gypsies wailed; there was the clangor of the blacksmith's anvil; then, in the middle of a choked sob, a falsetto rose high in exasperation: *Bang-Bang Spiegelglass!*

"That's it," Berek said. "Prince Wallers's business steward. I got my first order from the Wallers people. That's the idea. They'll come through for us again. Sit down, Conrad."

Conrad drew his sleeve across his face and sat down.

"Brothers, shake hands," Berek said.

Conrad put out his hand. Ferdinand felt his brother's fingers tremble and resented once more being seduced by him again—not into frivolity this time but into love of him.

"Papa," Ferdinand said, trying to keep to the sobriety of facts.

"Last Monday I was at the Jockey Club about the switch plates. I heard the service people talk about Prince Wallers. He hasn't been in Vienna for months—"

"It'll be all right," Berek said. "We'll write him and they'll forward."

"You dictate to me," Conrad said. He pulled out the long, sheathed calligraphic pen from his jacket.

"First have some marble cake," Berek said. "Remember the chestnut hearts your second mother used to make?"

"Why doesn't she make them anymore?" Conrad asked. His voice was still shaky, but at least he was retwirling the end of his mustache.

"She's still too busy with Ilona," Berek said. "Pour your brother some mocha, Conrad."

Conrad poured. "Thank you," Ferdinand said.

Berek Spiegelglass, cross-legged on the floor, reached forward, his thumb and index finger closing like fine pincers. He caressed the bit of cake off the Brick, put it on his plate. With a spoon edge he divided the big crumb into three. One morsel he placed on his own tongue; the two others he led to his twins' mouths, first Ferdinand's, then Conrad's.

"All right, sons," he said.

And all three men, sitting on the floor of the half-lit tunnel, leaned against the wall at the same time, as if with one motion, at ease.

XXII

T HE WEEK after the dispatch of the letter to Prince Wallers, no answer came. The second week Serbian border guards shot at an Austrian customs patrol. Vienna ordered army exercises in the eastern provinces; to test mobilization procedure young men of conscription age were called briefly to the colors. Berek Spiegelglass procured an exemption for his twins by certifying that they were "managerially indispensable" to the manufacture of the imperial seals. However, many of the factory's unskilled workers had to report to induction centers. This eased the payroll at a time of slow business.

Near the end of the third week, little Lily showed up limping after school. She had a triangular black-and-blue spot where a pebble had hit her on the calf. The tenements had begun to spit gibes and stones. Nobody was sure why. A restlessness, a sullen uncertainty had begun to bulge out of windows everywhere; perhaps proletarian fathers, away in the army, could not control their sons. At any rate Lily wasn't the only middle-class child who came home crying after crossing the slums.

Lily, though, had Riddah for her mother. Riddah grabbed the coal shovel used for stoking the bakery oven. She would have stormed to the very spot in the tenements where her Lily had been hurt—if Ferdinand hadn't pulled the weapon out of her hands.

"Let me take care of this," he said.

He accompanied Lily home from school the next afternoon. The sight of the girl's escort, a giant whose hand calluses were bigger than other men's fists, held back the stones. When she went alone once more, the taunts resumed together with threats of worse to follow.

Again Ferdinand started for school to be her guard—but was stopped by his brother.

"Papa says I can handle it," Conrad said.

"You?" Ferdinand said. Conrad was carrying an oddly shaped chamber pot.

"Well, it's the nastiness of those kids," Conrad said. "The thing is to change their mood."

"Papa said you should do it?"

Conrad nodded. "I'll have them play Still Is the Lake."

"What?" Ferdinand said.

But Conrad had already walked on and away, in the fourth week after the mailing of the letter to Prince Wallers.

Decades before, when Hester had married Berek Spiegelglass, her small trousseau had included a chamber pot in the form of a hollow swan whose curved neck served as handle. After the installation of her American bathroom with adjacent toilet stall, Hester had allowed the Havlicek No. 5 to use the swan as a storage bowl for clothespins in the attic. Now Conrad, having emptied out the pins, carried the dusty porcelain bird into the slums, to the corner of Carlgasse and Veronicagasse.

Here a public water fountain had become a gathering point for the Porcupines, the district's preeminent after-school gang. And here, at the fountain, Conrad filled the chamber pot, floated two rubber balls on its waters and waited until curiosity tickled Porcupines out of the shadows of doorways.

Later, when his brother asked Conrad how in the world he'd ever invented this Still Is the Lake sport, Conrad said it was just a variation of something they'd played a long time ago in grade school. Ferdinand could remember nothing like it. And yet the game

seemed to pour out of the very nerves of the Porcupines, so passionate and instinctive was their involvement.

Of course, the start of each inning always brought commotion
as Conrad dealt out nationalities among the boys. Nobody wanted
to be Serbia, or for that matter Russia, or even France. Austria was
everyone's first choice, with Germany and England (because of its
dreadnought navy) second and third. Conrad settled disputes
among raucous fist wavers on a rotation basis. After this tumult
came a lyric interlude. Conrad conducted it with arms aloft, like the
leader of a choir. The Porcupines were transfigured into harmoniz-
ing nations. Arms linked, the empires, kingdoms, sultanates, com-
monwealths, republics and principalities of the world circled the
chamber pot together, singing with Conrad, "Still is the lake . . .
who'll wake the bird?" The words became more and more melliflu-
ous with the repetition of the mellow and tender tune. "Still is the
lake . . . who'll wake the bird?" Boy sopranos mingled sweetly with
adolescent tenors just broken in. The more ragged the shirts of the
singers, the mangier and tougher their caps, the more touching was
the lilt of their musicianship. "Still is the lake . . . who'll wake the
bird?"

"France!"

Conrad had barked the word suddenly, Gallically.

The concord of countries exploded. Screaming, stampeding,
flailing nations burst away into all directions. France had leaped toward the pot, grabbed the floating rubber balls, flung them, one
after the other, at whatever fleeing land was nearest; and any land
thus hit and wetted was eliminated from the fray, a corpse drying in
limbo. After which the lake resumed its stillness, serenaded and lul-
labyed by a revolving garland of survivor countries—until the bird
woke once again and struck to Conrad's shout:

"Germany!"

Conrad was right. The game soaked up much of the stone-
throwing young energy among the poor. The "starched ninnies," as
the middle-class kids of Turk Place were called, could ford the slums
in greater comfort. Lily never again came home in tears.

Still Is the Lake, in fact, became all too popular. After a while
tenement boys from the entire 17th District converged each after-

noon on the swan-necked chamber pot at the Carlgasse corner. To create extra nationalities, Conrad had to resort to storybook regions like the Congo, Greenland and Nepal; he even awarded extragalactic dominions nobody else had ever heard of, like Nertitootsla. Still, he had no difficulty giving the name of each state its own ethnic accent. And each state, no matter how exotic, was ready and able to bombard all others with European dispatch.

After school the thuds and howls of intercontinental slaughter would punctuate the entire afternoon. The sleep of night-shift workers suffered. Women started up from their piecework at home. Horses at the tramway terminal in City Gate Square would rear. But when a neighborhood delegation finally called on Berek Spiegelglass to complain, he could, in all good conscience, shrug his shoulders. Just two days earlier his son Conrad had turned over the directorship of Still Is the Lake to the nephew of Havlicek No. 3, who charged all participants a fee of two hellers weekly. Conrad himself was now otherwise occupied. The appeal to Prince Wallers had paid off after all. That week the answer had arrived.

At first nobody realized it was an answer. The letter itself carried no hint of any connection to Prince Wallers, though Conrad was impressed by the gilt Gothic imprint:

PRINCIPALITY OF ALBANIA

GOVERNMENT BUREAUS

ARCHDUKE ALBRECHT BARRACKS

VIENNA

That was the top of the sheet. On the bottom a signature jumped from margin to margin with a vehemence that flung each letter beyond recognizability. In between ran three lines of stiff, plain penmanship: *"To Herr Spiegelglass of Turk Place. Request you present yourself here soonest any morning after ten hours."*

Of course, the Spiegelglass men knew about the Archduke Albrecht Barracks. They were being demolished at the other end of town. Berek had bought fifty of their gargoyles for scrap iron out of which to make the last switch-plate order. But—"Principality of Albania"? Conrad identified Albania as one of the least popular Still Is the Lake nations because nobody, himself included, knew where in the Alps it might be. Ferdinand went downstairs into the No. 1 basement to look through recent issues of *Wiener Zeitung*. The No. 1 Havlicek saved them for the purpose of flame-flashing roaches out of cellar crevices. Sure enough, Ferdinand found a foreign-affairs article very happy about the independence Albania had been granted from the Turks, and even happier about the resolve on the part of the imperial and royal government in Vienna to protect the Albanian people against Serbian troops that were occupying and oppressing much of the fledgling state. A map went with the article, but the Havlicek No. 1 had scorched that part of the page. Albania— not in the Alps at all—bordered on a remote, singed blister, far down the Adriatic coastline, somewhere between Serbia, Turkey and Greece.

Ferdinand reported all this to his father and said that perhaps the message from the Albanian Government Bureaus was some sort of mistake. Berek shook his head.

"The letter is all right," he said. "You go to the barracks tomorrow with your brother."

Before a romantic rendezvous Conrad liked to visit Schönfeld Florists. He'd buy a crimson carnation he would then spray with a wine-and-lemon mixture that sophisticated the flower's scent into a sumptuous, unnerving odor. For some reason he armed himself with the same procedure before accompanying his brother to the Archduke Albrecht Barracks next morning. The barracks guard looked at the Albanian letter; inspected the brothers' papers; wrinkled his nose at the overaromatic carnation; coughed, wrinkled his forehead, examined the papers yet again. In the end, he did nod to a sergeant. The gate in the high wall opened.

The brothers stood in a vast, dusty, peculiarly cluttered field at whose far end the shambles of the barracks hulked, windows gouged and roofs shredded.

"And a good day to you, ladies," said Conrad. He raised his hat to a dozen women made of corrugated iron. Their bodices were cleavaged, rusted, perforated. Their necks were chopped-off chimney flues, and they had no heads at all.

"What is that?" Ferdinand asked.

"Stoves saved from the officers' quarters," said the sergeant. "See where you stoke 'em? Right where a woman likes it. Those were the days. That's the kind of stoves they used to make on order for the swanky regiments. Come on, target zone here. Step lively."

He led the brothers forward on the drill ground. They went past large tents painted red and black, past a huge, horseless state coach hung with silver curtains, and came to yet another tent whose side had been pulled open. Inside, a boy on his knees was manicuring a man who was turbaned but otherwise in Western dress. Behind his desk stood a flagstand with a banner—a black double eagle against a red field.

"*Assez.*" Casually, the man kicked the boy away. The man shuffled some papers that lay on his intaglio desk between a champagne glass and a bloody lamb chop.

"Monsieur Spiegelglass?" the man said.

"I'm Ferdinand Spiegelglass," Ferdinand said. "This is my brother, Conrad."

"Oh yes. Prince Wallers is your *patron*?"

"Sir?" Ferdinand asked.

"Oh, I know *patron*." Conrad drew on his nanny French. "*Patron* means chief. He means Prince Wallers is our chief."

"No, our father is our chief," Ferdinand said. "Prince Wallers was our customer. We sent him a letter the other day."

"Prince Wallers is good," the man said. "Your emperor has elevated him ambassador to our Albania. Now he is in Constantinople, making international recognition for Albania against Serbia. He has written us his contentment with you. He says perhaps you can make our moneys."

"What?" Ferdinand said.

"Our Free Albania money pieces. We require it fast."

"I don't understand," Ferdinand said.

"Wait a minute." Conrad scooped from his pocket four copper hellers, which he began to juggle artfully. "Like these, sir? Coins, sir?"

"Ah yes," the man said. "But bigger. More excellent."

"You mean, mint coins?" Ferdinand said. "Coins for a whole country? We are not equipped."

"Not yet for the whole country. We don't have yet the whole country. Meanwhile, just moneys for *them*." He stepped out of the tent and pointed toward footsteps in the distance. Soldiers in shaggy brown uniforms came running from behind the barracks, led by a single horseman with a turban and drawn sword.

"Eighty troops," the man said. "Our officer corps we are training. We shall pay them ten big beautiful Free Albania money pieces a month, maybe for ten months. Then our state shall be ready. Maybe eight thousand moneys in total."

The horseman shouted. At once the uniformed men came to a stop and lifted rifles. The terse thunder of shots rolled against an echoing, sighing, melodious chiming as of many bells rung. Again and again the soldiers shot the stove-women, whose rusted flesh tolled as it was struck.

"You see our warriors?" the man said. "They are very highly passionate. You can make eight thousand money pieces to pay them?"

"What design?" Ferdinand asked.

"One side, this." The man pointed at the banner emblem. "The other side—something also noble."

"We have made medals and medallions," Ferdinand said. "Not exactly coins."

"Good, make it like that. A money like a medal. Like a great reward. Very good, it should feel in the hand like a medal."

"We shall tell our father," Ferdinand said. "He will calculate a price."

"He should also calculate a *plaque* with an executed head."

"A *plaque*?" Ferdinand said.

"I think *plaque* means badge," Conrad said.

This didn't really clear it up for Ferdinand. When puzzled, he usually asked himself what his father would do in such a situation. "The price depends on the quantity. How many of those will you need?"

"Quite many," the man said. "When our officers here are perfect, we will put them in our homeland and they will make a Free Albania Army against Serbia, and a great army requires executers. I think eighty *plaques*, very big, with executed heads, good to see for discipline, hanging on the chest with a silver chain."

"Silver is expensive," Ferdinand said.

"Your government is arranging an alliance loan with ourselves," the man said.

The shooting had stopped. Very softly, Conrad imitated the chiming of stoves being punctured. The man smiled. He extended his hand, touched Conrad's wine-scented carnation, led his hand to his nose, gave something close to a jovial salute. Then he pointed at the turbaned horseman.

"The Excellency needs blond ladies," he said to Conrad.

"I would think so," Conrad said before Ferdinand could stop him.

"He is the Premier and the War," the man said. "I am the Foreign Relations. I have done much study in Paris and a little in Munich. For the patriot morale the riding Excellency requires women not from the street. He requires them fancy, very washed, blond, who are proper for there."

"Where?" Conrad asked.

The man pointed at the huge state coach with the drawn curtains. "His sofa is there."

"Fine place for it," Conrad said.

"And the special ladies," the man continued, "they should go there not too late at night. There should be some light so that the underneath ranks can see them walk to him. It is important for the patriot morale."

"Actually, I know some washed blondes," Conrad said. "And some speak French."

"Ah," the man said. "I will be content with you, just like Prince Wallers." He stood up, clapped his hands, pronounced something guttural. Immediately, the manicuring boy reappeared with champagne glasses into which he poured from a bottle. At the same time, the horseman trotted up, with a smell of tobacco and pomade and the clink of bandoliers.

"This is His Mounted Excellency Eskad Bey," the man said as the manicuring boy handed up a goblet to the rider. "We will toast your great emperor helping our Albania to become a whole country. Please—your glass."

"Thank you," Ferdinand said. He waited until everybody had drunk up. "I will have to ask my father about the price," he said. "Also, we will have to arrange an early payment."

"Your emperor is arranging an alliance loan with ourselves," the man said.

"Yes, I heard," Ferdinand said. "But we'll need something in advance for material and labor."

Another hand clap. The manicuring boy poured champagne again. The man pronounced more gutturals, but softer ones, addressed to the horseman. Goblet held high in his left hand, the horseman reached down with his right, without losing balance or a drop of champagne. He unfastened the spurs from his left boot and threw them. They landed on the desk in the tent, with a heavy yellow clink.

"They're gold!" Conrad said.

"You may give this to your father," the man said. "It is the first payment from Free Albania."

"Up Albania! Down the Serbs!" Conrad said.

They all drank up, on horseback and on the ground. Rifle shots effervesced through the air, and in the distance the stove-women sang their sighs.

For the reverse face of the Free Albania coin, Conrad used one of his misfired eyeglass-case designs—the one with the Bissy-like rooster sporting a crest of roses; it matched the double eagle on the other side. Berek saw to it that on each coin's serrated rim the tiny hallmark of the Brick was stamped. Ferdinand supervised the milling.

Of course, the order was financially welcome. But in February 1914 it turned out to have other advantages as well. Every front page glowered with *"Muscovite Incitements," "Serb Insolence," "Grave Concerns," "Continued Affronts," "Endangered Security Zones"* and *"Appropriate Countermeasures."* The twins were the only young men in the district exempt from the latest semimobilization. "Indispensable for work ordered at the Archduke Albrecht Barracks," wrote Berek Spiegelglass in his capacity as factory owner. Forcefully, he scrawled his half-Roman, half-Gothic script on the conscription forms sent to his sons.

The day they received their exemption, Turk Place had a surprising visitor. Not since the steam tricycle of Prince Wallers's business steward had so haughty an apparatus hissed into the street. A magic fiacre, it moved by a force more powerful than horses, more invisible than steam. It was an autocar, whose golden spokes distinguished it as a vehicle of the Crown. It stopped before the factory to the august sibilance of its exhaust pipe. The chauffeur pushed his goggles up onto his cap that was gold-braided like an admiral's. He barked first at the crowd collecting around him, then at Ferdinand, who had been summoned in Berek's absence.

"You're the owner of the Spiegelglass factory?"

"I'm his son," Ferdinand said.

The admiral-chauffeur pulled out a piece of paper and began to read from it as if it were a proclamation: *"Alois Schall, by appointment medal-maker to His Imperial and Royal Highness the Crown Prince, requests design sketch he made for your factory with border of laurel leaves, as he will use said sketch for medal to be awarded by Imperial Highness to the Bishop of Bosnia at Sarajevo."*

"My father isn't here," Ferdinand said.

The admiral-chauffeur replied by reproclaiming the request at a more impatient speed.

"I can't decide that," Ferdinand said. "I'll see if I can reach my father."

Ferdinand knew that his parents were to meet the director of the Weiss Young Ladies' Academy that afternoon, an interview Hester had arranged on behalf of her daughter. Ferdinand ran to the apartment at No. 5 and found his father still dressing.

"Papa!" he said. "That Schall has nerve!"

Berek Spiegelglass listened to his account while he changed his customary boots for high-button shoes. "Yes, that's the first ball-favor design, the one with the laurel leaves."

"Your brown cravat would suit your jacket better than the blue," Hester said.

"Shall we tell the chauffeur we don't have it?" Ferdinand said. "His autocar is stinking up our street."

"Give it to him," Berek said. "It's right at the start of our design file."

"But, Papa, if Schall designed it here, it's really our property," Ferdinand said.

"Give it to him," Berek said.

"For free? No charge?"

Berek shook one of his leisured, irrefutable headshakes. It overrode not only all objections but Hester's attempt to hand him a brown cravat.

"I just want to ask, Papa," Ferdinand said. "I mean, why do Schall a favor after he left us like that?"

"Nobody leaves Turk Place," Berek said. "He'll be back. No charge."

And so Ferdinand had to return to the factory and riffle through the yellowed designs kept in what was still called "Herr Schall's desk" though Schall hadn't sat there for four years; Berek Spiegelglass allowed no one else to use it. Ferdinand had to find the laurel-leaf sketch and give it to the chauffeur-admiral. Worse yet, he didn't have the presence of mind to retract his hand (like his father's it was embossed with proletarian calluses) when the chauffeur-admiral pressed a fifty-heller piece into its palm.

"Buy yourself a beer," the chauffeur-admiral said and receded in a roar of gilded spokes.

Ferdinand went straight to the income ledger, so full of fury that he broke the pen when he wrote: *"Received fifty hellers as payment for junked design by former employee A. Schall."*

Siddo Berger, the clerk, brought him another pen and smiled at the sum. "What we really need," he said, "is five hundred gulden from what the Albanians owe us."

"Wait a minute," Ferdinand said.

Now that his father wasn't here, Ferdinand asked the question he'd hesitated to ask for weeks. "That money we got for the golden spurs," he said. "That's gone?"

"Well, you saw the twenty sheets of bronze come in yesterday," Siddo Berger said. "That's for making the last run of coins and it's all on credit. We're out of cash."

"I'm going to talk to my father!" Ferdinand said.

But Berek and Hester did not come home for dinner that night. Ferdinand went to the Café Pellmann, where the elder Spiegelglasses occasionally dined weekdays. He found Otto Schönfeld, the florist, in his shiny brass-and-blue reservist's uniform, back from maneuvers, savoring a glass of Gumpoldskirchner.

"Hey, I hear you had a very official autocar in that street of yours," he said. "Are they getting after you for dodging the army?"

Laughter around Schönfeld's table. Ferdinand didn't smile. "Did you see my father?"

"Your father?" Schönfeld said. "Don't tell me the army's after your big chief. They don't want rookies with liver spots."

"He's got no liver spots and he can still stick your mouth into your ass," Ferdinand said. "And if he's too busy, maybe I will."

"Hey, it was just a joke, have some wine," Schönfeld said.

"Maybe I'll stick your mouth in your ass right now," Ferdinand said.

"Come on, don't take it out on me," Schönfeld said, "take it out on the Serbs. Hey, you should've seen those maneuvers. Twenty thousand men along the Serb border, Hussars and tommy guns and everything. We made those Serb mountains shake with our howitzers. And you know? Not a peep out of our Belgrade friends since then. Now they're very quiet. Very nice little swineherds. Even Russia has piped down."

"I asked you a question," Ferdinand said. "Did you see my father?"

"No," Schönfeld said. "But listen, give us the lowdown on the fancy autocar in your street? Just don't get excited."

"That was from the crown prince," Ferdinand said. "About some design for a medal he wants to award in Bosnia. If my father comes here, have the busboy run over and tell me at Turk Place."

"Will do," Schönfeld said. "Award a medal in Bosnia, eh? Ho-ho. You've got to understand what's behind *that*. See, the crown prince is the big Slav lover at court. So now the Serbs are good little Slavs for a change, not working up our Bosnian Slavs against us, so it's nice and safe for Prince Slav-lover to hand out honors down there. But let those Serbs act up again—and watch out. We'll spank 'em with howitzers. And we'll sic the Albanians on them."

"What?" Ferdinand said, already turned to go. He turned back. "What the hell do you mean, 'sic the Albanians'?"

"He's getting excited again," Schönfeld said.

"What do you mean about Albania?"

"Ease up, okay, I'll tell you," Schönfeld said. "You Spiegelglasses are such a funny bunch—you think that street of yours is the whole world, so you don't even care about international power plays—"

Ferdinand had grabbed him by his left epaulette to pull him up out of his chair. *"Albania!"* he said. *"Talk!"*

"You'll tear the uniform, stop!" Schönfeld cried. "I said I'll tell you! I mean, it's obvious. The Albanians are our pawns in that little game. The Serbs make trouble for us on the Bosnian side, we make sure there's trouble for *them* on their Albanian side. The Serbs are quiet, we forget about Albania, okay? Now let go."

"No!" Ferdinand said, letting go. *"We won't forget about Albania!!"*

He grabbed a cue stick and rammed it down on the floor with such force, it became wedged in the carpet. For two seconds it stood like a flagpole before Otto Schönfeld's paling face. By the time it fell, Ferdinand was already running home.

At Turk Place the maid Resi reported that Herr and Frau Spiegelglass had returned meanwhile and retired to their bedroom. Ferdinand could not disturb them. But when he went to the flat he shared with his brother, he found Conrad still up—in fact, changing for some nocturnal foray.

"Listen," Ferdinand said. "Your lady friends you introduced to the Albanians in the barracks, are you in touch with that situation? You know what's going on there? That government owes us money."

Conrad whistled. He took off the cap he'd taken to wearing lately. His upper forehead showed a straight, rather deep scratch line.

"Genevieve's fingernails," he said. "That's what she did to me afterward."

"After what?"

"After being with the premier," Conrad said. "Rough stuff. On the other hand, I got a postcard yesterday. She's now in Paris with him."

"With the premier? The Albanian premier is in Paris?"

"The both of them," Conrad said. "You go figure women!"

Next morning Ferdinand went to the Pellmann to read the current newspapers and then visited the factory basement to catch up on back copies of the *Wiener Zeitung*. What articles he found on Serbia seemed much shorter and blander. Albania was shrinking, as a controversy and as a country. He rushed up to the factory.

"The Albanians haven't paid, Papa," he said.

"I know," Berek Spiegelglass said. "It's all right. We'll send a note."

The note was dictated to Conrad, whose decorative penmanship made do for the politesse his father lacked. Addressing the Albanian Government Bureaus at the Archduke Albrecht Barracks, Berek asked for an immediate interim disbursement of three thousand gulden—out of a total bill of seven thousand—to meet current coin-manufacturing expenses.

No reply came from the Archduke Albrecht Barracks. A week later, however, a letter arrived from the Imperial and Royal Ministry of the Exterior, Department of Balkan Stabilization; the matter of requested subsidies to friendly forces was currently being re-evaluated; all claims dependent on such subsidies would be adjudicated on completion of said re-evaluative process.

It was the first time Ferdinand had ever seen a typewritten paragraph. The sharp, newspaperlike characters in a private letter struck him as wrong, as wrong as the liver spot he saw on his father's hand holding the letter. He hated Schönfeld and the Ministry of the Exterior for almost the same reason.

"Papa," he said. "Let me deliver the coins we have ready. I mean me, personally, together with the interim bill. Just to check on the situation there."

"Go ahead," Berek Spiegelglass said.

Ferdinand had the four thousand coins packed into forty wooden tubes. It took him and the driver more than half an hour to unload the heavy things at the Archduke Albrecht Barracks. The sergeant on guard duty wouldn't let them inside.

"All messages and so on are to be left here with me," he said.

"This is not a message," Ferdinand said. "This is a delivery of official Albanian currency we have been commissioned to mint by the Albanian government."

"We'll store it here for you," the sergeant said.

"But there is a bill, too," Ferdinand said.

"Whatever, you leave it here. We'll give it to them when they're available," the sergeant said.

"You mean they're not there now?" Ferdinand said.

"All I can tell you, we'll give you a receipt."

"In that case," Ferdinand said, "a government receipt for four thousand Albanian coins."

"Accepted for storage," the sergeant said slowly as he wrote out the words, "four thousand coins for whatever purpose on May 11, 1914. Here you are."

"Good day." Ferdinand strode away, leaving behind at the Archduke Albrecht Barracks 3,999 Albanian coins. He had palmed one.

In effect, he had committed theft. Never had he done anything like that before. He told the driver to return to the factory without him; in his state he couldn't bear the passiveness of being crammed into a vehicle. He was walking home. The Albanian coin weighed down his pocket. He rubbed it, thumb against the eagle, forefinger against the rose-crowned rooster modeled after Bissy. If he were still small enough, he could run to his father and cry, "Papa, it's not just our cash problem, it's the unfairness! Do we have to be so helpless? And why is Bissy dead when the weather is so lovely? What does it all mean?"

The weather had been lovely for weeks. But he could not take hold of the sky's perfection nor the blue-gold sweetness of the spring. He was walking home along the Ringstrasse, its huge, triumphant curve. Sanitation men in striped tunics broomed litter from the parade that had honored the German kaiser's visit two hours earlier. They swept apple cores, paper flags, horse manure, all the debris left by cavalry and by applause. Sweeping, the sanitation men stirred the dust from so many marvelously rainless days. Dust rose around Ferdinand. He lifted his eyes and saw statues gesturing by the hundreds on top of the baroque palace, the classic Parliament, the Renaissance university and Gothic city hall. Gods speared heroes down from their chariots, fairy queens stroked unicorns, titans directed acrobatic deaths. A confounding extravagance glittered in the sun; a blinding dance which set whirling his father's liver spots and the singe called Albania on the newspaper map. The universe carouseled through Ferdinand to thunder-music without melody. Away from Turk Place and the Brick there was nothing but grand dizziness and dust. The dust tide thickened. It scratched its way into Ferdinand's nostrils. He sneezed; sneezed again; and yet once more with a vehemence that made him stagger.

One of his great sneezing fits was upon him. To escape the dust that had triggered it, he began to run, away from the Ringstrasse but still in the direction of home. He ran sneezing. Working his handkerchief, his throat abraded and parched, he stopped for a drink at the Turf Café. The cracked red sign was familiar. He'd passed the place before, since it lay midway in the tenement maze between the Inner City and Turk Place. But there had never been any reason to enter. Now when he went inside, the smoky shouting twilight seemed to continue the turbulence of the rooftop figures downtown, but in lowlife caricature. A blackboard was propped up on the bar, and around it dozens of men stepped on each others' spats, soiled gloves waving cigarette butts, stubbled faces yelling. Flies pursued the second hand of the wall clock, a bartender poured burnt-smelling liquid and behind him, on a high stool, sat a woman untouched by the agitation. Her crossed legs revealed slim ankles. Yet she was opulent, handsome under a small tower of black curls. Her black blouse made the white décolletage all the whiter, and whiter still was the sliver of a smile she smiled just then, nodding at some question from a waiter. But she had noticed Ferdinand's entrance. Too tall for the door, he had stooped his way in.

"Good day, the gentleman." Her voice rang with surprising clarity through the din.

"Good day," he said, hoarse from his fit. "I'd like something to drink."

"Brandy or wine for the gentleman?" she said. "Pick your horse before post time."

"I'm sorry," he said. "What time?"

The noise from the other men diminished as they turned to look at him.

"Before the horses start running," she said evenly. "First drink is on the house with the first bet. Does the gentleman want brandy or wine?"

"Soda water," he said.

Her face did not move, and yet he knew that she was amused. But not amused like the others, whose eyes showed a snigger under their askew derbies. The bartender slid a bubbling glass toward him.

"For the gentleman's thirst," the woman said. "What's the gentleman's horse?"

The snigger kept radiating from the men even as they turned back to the blackboard, calling out names and numbers in some code. Ferdinand told himself that these slum gamblers were despicable; sporty scum betting away their children's winter coats. But their shouts were so expert and intent, even their snigger so knowing, that he felt somehow pointless next to them. As on the Ringstrasse, he was besieged by confusion.

"The gentleman's horse?" the woman said again. "Post time in ten seconds."

Everybody crowded around the blackboard. Ferdinand, towering above the derbies, could see the first three names chalked on top.

ALARIC II

JUNG-MERLIN

OTTOMAN

"Ottoman," he said. Something suddenly made some sense. He remembered from school that "Ottoman" meant "Turkish," which related it to Turk Place.

"Ottoman," the woman said slowly. "The tall gentleman likes a long shot."

A bell rang. Silence. All faces turned toward the corner of the bar. There a man with an anchor tattooed on his wrist plugged his earphones into an apparatus. Telegraph keys began to twitch.

"How much on Ottoman?" the woman said.

Ferdinand reached into his pocket and found the Albanian coin. She held out her hand, inspected what he gave her. Her rich shoulders shook with a small laugh.

"Looks like something from the moon," she said.

"That's Albanian currency," Ferdinand said. "It's worth at least a gulden."

Suddenly, she was off the stool. "If the gentleman will come with me," she said.

The back room, whose door shut with soundless promptness, had no windows. An electric bulb hung from the ceiling on a silvered wire and spread a late-afternoon light across the disorder of pillows on the sofa, the rag doll leaning against the wall, the table with telegraph keys next to a vase of geraniums.

She examined the coin under the bulb; let her shoulders shake again; returned it to him.

"Nice-looking if it were real," she said.

"It's real!" he said. "Albania is a real country. This is a very real coin we—"

On the table the telegraph machinery had begun to chatter. It was spitting out a long white paper tongue. His lips were touched by her finger, quite slender for a woman her size.

"Sh . . . ," she said. "The horses are off."

A scent, faint but tingling, came from the finger and its red-painted nail that still leaned against his mouth. The finger kept leaning while she bent over the dashes the telegraph printed on the paper tongue. In the corner of the room a turtle, a clown face painted on its shell, slowly grinned its way across the floor.

The telegraph stopped printing. She straightened up, adjusted her bodice. "Ottoman came in third," she said.

Her finger was gone from his mouth. The withdrawal caused an unexpected deprivation. Yet he felt triumphant for Turk Place. It was a victory for meaning.

"Third place," he said. "That wins something!"

"Sure," she said. "If the gentleman's bet was real."

"I did bet with something real," he said. He held up the coin, thumb pressed against the Brick hallmark on its rim. "You'd better believe me."

"Not good here," she said. She walked away slowly as she fixed a black curl at the back of her neck.

"It's good!" He grasped that curl-fixing hand, spun her around against him. They stared at each other. As if it had suddenly turned into candy, she put the coin into her mouth. She bit its face, looking at him.

"Good bronze," she said. She wiped its moisture off on his palm before she pressed it into his hand. "Maybe it's good on the moon."

Then she turned away as before. This time she didn't get beyond her second step. He brought her even harder against him.

"It means something *here*!" he said. "It's good right here in this room! I won something with it!"

Her eyes, so very close to his, were slightly bloodshot, a brilliant dark green, as steady as the fullness of her mouth. It was a mouth which seemed to hold the touch of a smile.

"We made this coin in our factory!" he said. "It means something and it won something!"

"Let the gentleman try to collect," she said.

"I will," he said. "Right now!"

And indeed all his flesh was rising with the need to do that, to luxuriate not just in her but in the victory of Turk Place over high chaos. That is, all his flesh rose, except his loins. The wet of her mouth still teased the inside of his hand, his thigh burned with hers sliding slightly against it. None of that helped. He would be unable to collect. The thwarting, the humiliation, turned his arms into two fierce cranes. His hands shot under her armpits. She was a tall and plump woman, but he lifted her face to his own yet much taller level so swiftly, so powerfully, that she gasped. A gasp that was also half laughter, and well-aimed laughter at that. Her breath brushed deeply into his nostrils. On the instant, that puff wound up a spring inside him; it uncoiled into a tremendous dry sneeze while he still held her in the air—a catapulting, toppling exclamation which brought them both down as an avalanche of limbs onto the sofa pillows.

Her breasts spilled free, stunning as sudden snow. The coin rolled on the floor and to its sound her legs flashed up, black silk, blue lace, white thigh, and now there was nothing in his body that wasn't rising. He was knotted into a lust that was absolute and helter-skelter, his hesitations blown away together with their clothes. It was as if his whole life had been a drought relieved at last by this mouth, these nipples, that belly, those hollows. He wanted to drench himself in everything at once. One of her hands raked through his hair, the other guided. Only for a moment. Then he collected. He collected what Ottoman had won, collected as her laughing mouth moaned some word. He collected again and again from the marvels of her depth. He collected and he kept collecting the meaning, the spoils, the prize, the certainty, the eternity won by his Turk Place coin.

They lay, flank by flank, in a quiet litter of cushions and legs and arms. Together they listened to noise filtering dimly through the door. On the table the telegraph twitched.

"I think the gentleman was a virgin," she said.

He floated in such uncanny comfort that at first he didn't even mind the lifting of that secret.

"Is that so?" he said.

"Tallest virgin ever," she said.

"How do you think you can tell?" he said.

"After you drank your soda water," she said. "The way you wiped your mouth. Neat. Like a tall virgin."

His shirt was still hanging off his left shoulder. He shrugged himself free.

"Drop in again soon," she said. "Drink some more soda water."

Then he got angry after all, angry and embarrassed and glorious, and turned her around and once more began to collect and to collect and to collect, and on the floor the clown-faced turtle grinned around the Albanian coin.

XXIII

F OR MANY DAYS AFTERWARD Albania continued not to exist. No article in any newspaper mentioned such a country. Nor did its government give signs of life from the Archduke Albrecht Barracks. No payment for the minting of its coins arrived at Turk Place. No substantial new business could be expected in the absence of a designer like Schall. Berek Spiegelglass made no serious effort to replace him, still saying that Schall would sit down before long at the desk still kept empty for his return.

It wasn't Berek's only obstinacy. Siddo Berger told Ferdinand that their credit for metal supplies would run out on July 1 but that his father wouldn't even think of raising a bit of cash by mortgaging a single stone of Turk Place. Most landlords in Vienna had liens on their buildings. Not this one. Herr Spiegelglass just shook his head at the suggestion, and slept late and hummed as smoothly as ever.

Something had to be done. Berek Spiegelglass refused to do it; Conrad was hardly the type; therefore it was up to Ferdinand. And what Ferdinand did was invent excuses to leave work, sometimes as often as three times a week.

That was how frequently he went to the Turf Café. He went, drawn by a double mystery. The first he consummated in the back room. Here Frau Lammer (all he knew was her last name) delivered his flesh from its constraints and goaded it into extravagant jubilation. The second mystery waited, not far from the first, in the front room; waited for him amid the shouts and fumes of the bettors.

Someday before long the chalk on the blackboard there would write out a name that would free the factory from all financial danger. Ferdinand felt the premonition in his bones.

Ottoman had already brought an unlooked-for bounty. During all his visits thereafter Ferdinand bet on any horse whose name carried any overtone of Turk Place. He bet on Henry Pasha. The horse came in second and he was furious at himself for wagering only 60 gulden instead of 500—all his savings—and therefore winning only 380. When Henry Pasha did not reappear on the racing list, he later tried Asian Boy, since part of Turkey lay in Asia. He bet on Anatole, Anatolia being a Turkish province. He even put 40 gulden on Cupid's Bow, for a bow was crescent-shaped and the Turkish flag had a crescent in it. He did not score another win—as yet. Each time it became clear to him, afterward, why: the connection had been much too remote, far less strong than Ottoman or Henry Pasha. Yet he knew that someday the right horse would be led to the starting gate and the right name take shape on the blackboard.

After that bonanza no further visits to the Turf Café would be necessary. But a fantastic speculation began to tease him. At the height of all their intertangling pleasures her lips, smiling, still moaned a word; it seemed to change with each new tryst and he could never understand it. Was it the name of the next winner, conjured by their ritual? A name she masked so that he would return again and again, still keen for a jackpot to come, still in her thrall?

Perhaps it was an absurd idea. Certainly, it was devilish in its stubbornness. He could not prove it, nor find a way of plucking it out of his brain. Far from controlling it, it controlled him. There was no defense against its titillations. When they lay together, he tried to immerse himself deeply in her, to dive down to that electric point which would make her mouth light up into a clearer pronouncing of the secret. In vain. At the crucial moment the mouth laughed and mumbled and baffled. He was not able to gore that mystery through. Instead, he foundered in a mist whose endlessness was irresistible.

In the back room he could not stop his embraces. In the front room he could not stop betting. He disliked the tippling losers there, beer foam drooling from their mustaches down onto their scratch sheets. They seemed to dislike him in turn; in fact, to hate him, perhaps in jealousy over the woman. But she was the boss and he was two heads bigger than any of them. They didn't taunt him openly. Sometimes he heard murmurs behind his back. *"That Gypsy gorilla . . . maybe she likes his nigger hair. . . ."* He had enough self-discipline to ignore them but not enough to stop trysting, betting, losing. The more the factory needed his energy, the more he squandered it, ecstatically, on the Turf Café. The more his father needed money, the more he lost.

It went on and on like that, throughout May and into June of 1914. Ferdinand knew he must stop. He continued. One Sunday he tried to put an end to it by playing a trick on himself. Once more he found himself walking away from Turk Place toward that blackboard, toward the back room with the turtle.

"Ferdy!"

Conrad was calling him, presumably for Sunday billiards at the Pellmann.

"I'm busy," he said. On impulse he added, "Come with me." If Conrad came along, he'd take the woman away from him, and perhaps the obsessions, too.

"Where're you going?" Conrad asked.

"I'll show you," Ferdinand said.

"You've got something crude going on someplace," Conrad said. "Better late than never. Anyway, Papa wants both of us."

"Now?" Ferdinand asked. Berek's Sunday get-togethers with his sons didn't start until evening.

"Papa said *now*," Conrad said.

That moment Berek strode out of the house entrance at No. 5, and Ferdinand knew it was not only *now* but important. Under his arm his father carried the Brick in its new cedarwood box. He looked at his sons, half nodded and strode on toward the tramway station at City Gate Square. His silence and the purposefulness of his steps were a message: "No questions. Follow."

The twins followed. It was yet another seductive June day, mild, lucid, perfect for a weekend outing. Too many passengers jammed into the tram and forced the brothers to form a protective wedge around their father's right arm, the one that held the Brick. They got off, after their father, at the Prater amusement park. It was filled with a huge balloon-happy crowd which became even thicker near the Ferris wheel, where Berek led them. Ferdinand did not mind the absence of explanations. There was safety in being his father's captive. It shielded him from the freedom that would have sucked him straight into the Turf Café.

His brother, however, began to scratch his neck as they stood in the long line before the Ferris-wheel ticket booth.

"Papa," Conrad said, pointing but not looking up at the arc of cars ascending toward the sun, "do we really have to go up there?"

Berek nodded.

"You know me, heights scare me silly," Conrad said. "Could I at least read a paper on the way up?"

"As long as you pay attention when it's important," Berek said.

Conrad ran off. Back he came with a copy of the *Illustrierte Zeitung*, with a mouth smelling of a quick slivovitz and with an Albanian executioner's badge on his lapel. Ferdinand had seen him pin it on as a charm before a particularly tense billiard game at the Pellmann.

Berek Spiegelglass slipped the Ferris-wheel man an extra coin. They had a whole car of eight seats for themselves. Up they went, and as the floor quaked, creaked and groaned under their feet, Ferdinand felt his brother clutch his elbow. For minutes, while they looped through the air at a stately speed, Conrad stared very hard into the *Illustrierte Zeitung*.

"All right," Berek said.

Conrad had to lift his glance from the paper. Whatever it was, now it began.

"Many years ago," Berek said, "I also bought all eight tickets for a car here. I came with your mother. I wanted to have a car alone with her."

"Was she scared?" Conrad said. He had fixed his eyes strictly on his father, so he would not have to see the world drop away.

"We were sad," Berek said. "We were married so long and our

sons were not born. We put a message into the Brick asking for you. Are you listening?"

"Yes, I'm sorry, Papa," Conrad said, for he had to cover his head with the paper.

"It's all right," Berek said. "But when we reach the top, you will look, the two of you. At the top you can see both Turk Place and where Varungy used to be."

"I'll try," Conrad said through the paper.

"That's where we put the message in the Brick, your mother and me, where you can see both places at once. We asked for you and we got you. Now we need income for the factory. We'll ask for that."

He opened the cedar box and took out the Brick, whose little paper rolls and fissured ocher glowed as if a moon were shining out from within. He put the Brick on Ferdinand's lap and used the box as writing desk. From his jacket pocket he pulled a small sheet and a pencil sharpened to an impossible point. The blue breeze took hold of the car. Gently, they rocked toward invisible stars. And Berek Spiegelglass wrote in his mixed script: *"Please, God, continue the factory in business so we can continue Turk Place without mortgaging."*

Berek signed his name, took the Brick from his son, placed the cedar-box desk on Ferdinand's lap.

"Sign," he said.

Ferdinand signed.

"Sign," Berek Spiegelglass said to Conrad.

Conrad scratched his signature fast and clapped the paper back on his face.

"We're not high enough yet," Berek said. "When we're on top, we'll put the message in."

Ferdinand looked to the west. Under the carefree brightness of the sky the smudge of slums spread, vast and sick. But he discovered a fleck of freshly shingled roofs, spiked with sleek pinheads—the minarets.

"I found our street!" he cried.

His father nodded, then turned east where the parachute towers of the amusement park still blocked the view beyond, into Slovakia.

"In a minute you'll see where Varungy was."

They never saw it. The Ferris wheel had come to a halt, though their car had curved not more than two thirds of the way to the top. A moment later the wheel even reversed direction. They began to go down. But Ferdinand did not notice. He was staring at something unbelievable. His brother still had the *Illustrierte* plastered against his head—and there, on the back page facing Ferdinand, up on top, above his brother's index finger, there, as the first entry in the first race at the Freudenau track, was "Mustafa."

"Mustafa!" Ferdinand said. "Papa, my God, wasn't that the Turkish vizier, the one who built Turk Place?"

"Kara Mustafa," Berek said. "I've told you often enough about him. I don't know why we are going down."

"But that means the Brick message is already working!" Ferdinand said. He was sure now that "Mustafa" was the blurred moan he'd heard in the back room the last time. "Papa, if we bet on Mustafa, it's going to be all right! We'll have all the money we need to keep going!"

"We should not be going down," Berek said.

"Papa, I never told you," Ferdinand said. "It sounds crazy, but it's true, I tried it, you bet on any horse with a real Turk Place connection—it wins! At least one of the first three places! We can't miss with Mustafa!"

"Why are we going down?" Conrad asked through the paper. "Are we crashing?"

Ferdinand snatched the *Illustrierte* from his face to show the racing card on the back to his father. "Look! Mustafa! First in the first race!"

"I haven't got my glasses with me," Berek said.

The aging of his father's eyes made the word even more talismanic to Ferdinand. "Mustafa! Here! We should bet everything on it! All the money we have with us!"

"Everybody out," the Ferris-wheel attendant said, for they had reached the ground. "Police orders. It's everybody out everywhere. Don't ask me why. Everybody out, please."

The energy was gone from the amusement park. Nothing moved at the roller coaster, the giant swing, the shooting galleries. Thousands of people milled about, all yanked out of exhilaration and dropped into a daze. Children cried under their balloons. The throng blocked access to the tramway.

"Papa, we'd better get to my betting place before post time," Ferdinand said. "Before the horses run. I know the manager, we can bet on credit—"

A razor of a sound cut off his sentence. His father's Varungy-teamster whistle. It drowned the cry of a newsboy rounding the corner of the Tunnel of Love just then and summoned a fiacre before which the crowd parted.

"Tell the driver where," Berek said, jumping in with his sons.

"Turf Café, Angergasse 16," Ferdinand said. "Quick."

The speed of the coach stirred up Berek Spiegelglass's hair. He smoothed it back, hard. "'*My betting place,*' you said. That's where you've been sneaking off. *You!* It's worse than Conrad. Throwing money away on horses! I want to see that place!"

Berek Spiegelglass's knuckles were white—except for the liver spot—so hard did he grip the leather strap as the fiacre veered. His anger not only shocked Ferdinand, it seemed to petrify the entire city. Faces were welded into windows. Urchins stood in the air, in midleap. When the fiacre skimmed along the Ringstrasse, whole clusters of elegance (ladies in beribboned bonnets, officers in kepis and capes) were frozen, centered around printed sheets. On the roofs heroes, gods and beasts were stunned.

"Papa," Ferdinand said. "Please, I know it doesn't make sense now, but I'll show you, with Mustafa I'll win the money back—"

"Get a paper," his father said. The fiacre had been forced to slow down at an intersection; people obstructed the roadway, transfixed before a newsboy. Ferdinand jumped off, thrust a fifty-heller piece into the boy's hand (he had no smaller change), jumped on again. His father snatched the *Extra!* from his hand and gave it to Conrad.

"Read it to me," he said.

"My God," Conrad said. The fiacre shot forward again, into the tenements.

"Read!" Berek said.

"*Our Crown Prince Assassinated,*" Conrad read over the drumming of hooves. "My God. *In the vilest of deeds, our successor to the throne, His*

Imperial and Royal Highness, was gunned down by Serbian thugs at the Bosnian capital of Sarajevo—you know, that's where—"

"Read!" Berek Spiegelglass said. "Slower and louder."

"—*at the Bosnian capital of Sarajevo,*" Conrad read slower and louder, "*just after His Imperial Highness had awarded Bishop Straszny the Order of the Illyrian Knights. Serbia and all countries implicated in Serbia's crime must now face just retribution—*"

The fiacre had come to a stop. "Those murdering bandits, sir," the driver said. "Serbia, Russia, that whole gang. Here we are, but I think the café is closed. Everything's closed for mourning."

Berek Spiegelglass had already gotten off. "I'll open it," he said quietly, "if I have to smash it open."

Ferdinand did not know how to stop his father. Berek headed for a group of men, the same bunch that was usually inside the café and who now lounged outside, holding bottles. They leaned against the shuttered gate, derbies more awry than ever. Since they could not bet, they drank more, and the sight of the Spiegelglasses raised their mumbles to shouts. They'd never shouted at Ferdinand before, but now the hiss of their consonants was powered with alcohol and with the pent-up breath of the whole city.

"Brought your friends, Gypsy gorilla?"

"Goin' to take 'em all to the back room?"

"Us they lock out, and *you* goin' to get in?"

"Want to celebrate the crown prince's murder?"

"Sure he wants to celebrate, he's not a Gypsy—he's a Serb!"

"His pal looks like a Serb! Looks like a Serb badge on him!"

"Get those Serb goons!"

Somebody spilled beer on Conrad's Albanian executioner's badge. A man lifted his fist at Conrad, but Ferdinand, using his left hand (his right held the Brick), pushed him to the ground. The fiacre driver shouted that he wanted to be paid before any further trouble, and Ferdinand saw two men come down on his father with big bottles. He punched one back, but the other shoved him against the fiacre. He kicked them both into a heap, glass fusilladed against cobbles, and the first thing to vanish was the sky. The shying, rearing horses came between Ferdinand and the sun. Then the hooves fell and squashed all the light that was left.

* * *

He opened his eyes into a bloody, enormous screech coming from his leg. The whole world dissolved into that screech, and in its middle vibrated a policeman and below the policeman knelt Berek Spiegelglass.

"Ferdy," his father said. He had not used that name since Ferdinand had been very small, but the name didn't help.

"Where is the Brick?" Ferdinand screamed back at his screeching, intolerable leg. Perhaps the Brick would stop the leg.

"It's all right," Berek said. "Don't look down. It's going to be all right."

But he looked down and it was terrible and he screamed along with the leg's scream.

"Don't," his father said. "Try to think of something else. They'll need Albania, now there'll be a war. Now they'll pay us for the Albanian coins. Think about that. Don't look down. Help is coming."

"The Brick, Papa!" Ferdinand cried.

"Here," said Berek and took the Brick box from Conrad. "Nothing happened to it. It's all right, Ferdy. The doctor is going to make you all right. You won't even have to go to the army because of the leg—"

"It's not stopping!" Ferdinand cried. "The leg won't stop, Papa, make it stop!"

"It will stop," Berek Spiegelglass said. "Look."

Still kneeling by Ferdinand's side, Berek lifted the Brick box lid and then took out of his jacket pocket the paper the three of them had signed, the message he'd wanted to put into the Brick on the top of the Ferris wheel. Berek now rolled up the paper and stuck it into a fissure of the Brick, and Ferdinand, his leg stopping at last, sank away into that fissure, too.

XXIV

O N TURK PLACE a party marked the beginning of the battle between the world's great powers. That Riddah, of all people, gave it seemed surprising. After all, she kept saying some pretty rash things about the war. She even blamed it for the plaster cast which Ferdinand's leg had become and which he dragged around as if he were attached to a white coffin. It was only the first casualty, Riddah said to anybody who cared to listen. If she had not been a nocturnal, chicken-breeding Jewess of a woman baker and therefore one of the district's prime eccentrics, standing out even against the oddness of Turk Place, people would have thought her a traitor.

She also said she didn't want her son, Markus, to go off to slaughter. In fact, she tore up Markus's conscription notice and ordered him not to come to work with her from that night on. "There's a rumor bakers on one-man shifts will be exempted," she said. "From now on you'll be my one-man shift in the daytime."

And so, in the early, lonely daytime, all by himself, Markus turned out the seven apple strudels and the nine Dobos tortes ordered daily by the Café Pellmann. (An increase over the peacetime quantity of five strudels and six tortes: debates on military operations raised the appetite.) It wasn't easy for Markus. He was used to singing and kneading through the night not only with his mother but with the albino and with two other bakery hands. Now he worked alone in the mute clutter of the cellar.

But Markus did have his soccer ball. He dribbled it from chore to chore, toward the oven and away from it, feinting past flour bins and finessing the ball through a small opening between flour sacks. At 1 PM, his work done, he kicked the ball upstairs, to the backyard of No. 6, which served as practice field for the Young Turk team. Max Stelnitz, the center forward, was already waiting.

Stelnitz, the first dentist in the neighborhood, had his office on the ground floor. It had been militarized into the Temporary Auxiliary Dental Clinic of the 2nd Army Division. He was hardly deluged with patients. At a time of momentous manifestoes, victory avowals, mobilization parades and other flag-proud festivals, few soldiers bothered with something so homely as a cavity. Stelnitz could devote much of his day to Young Turk soccer. Of course, Ferdinand's crushed shinbone did not allow him to play. And Otto Schönfeld, being a reservist, had reported to his regiment immediately. But the other young men of the street were all Young Turk kickers, most of them full-time, too, during this final spell of their civilian youth. Their fathers, for whom they all worked, were treating them to a vacation the way you treat a bridegroom to a prewedding bash. Hans Schedlmayer was given a leave from Herr Schedlmayer's barber shop; as was Ossie Skalka from old Skalka's market inn; as were Rudi and Franzl Pellmann from the café.

Released from workaday constriction, on the edge of tremendous adventure, the Young Turks yelled and stomped and kicked the ball through morning and afternoon. Riddah's bedroom windows looked out on their game. She never complained, because during those weeks she could not find rest anyway. At first she could not close her eyes because she had to wait for Markus's exemption. After his exemption had been denied she could not sleep because she held long discussions with Boas's camera, which still lay on her late husband's side of the double bed. The outcome was a request she made to Herr Stelnitz, the dentist. Would he sign a statement certifying that Markus assisted him in his dental work for the military, if only by supplying "the clinic" with bread, and that therefore exemption should be granted on those grounds?

Stelnitz agreed: the great imperial armies would justly triumph with or without Markus Mainzer. Beyond that, Stelnitz felt that he had, so to speak, a credit of one fib with the emperor. Stelnitz had

already signed a dental-exemption statement—on Conrad's behalf.
Against expectations, it turned out that he had put his signature
under the truth. Conrad actually did do his bit to shore up the
health of the mouths of some Austrian forces. In soccer Conrad handled the ball well only if he scolded it aloud, as if it were a puppy bit-
ing his heels, which reduced the game to farce. But in the dental
office he developed a genuinely valuable faculty. Those soldiers who
did see Stelnitz were usually suffering from toothaches of a very
drastic sort. More often than not extraction was indicated, and Conrad proved to have a marvelous touch with laughing gas.

Most men feared this newfangled anesthesia. Conrad showed
them how easy it was and how funny. He applied an unconnected
narcotic mask to his own face; then pretended to sink away into hal-
lucinations that managed to be hilarious as well as patriotic. Very
popular among his deliriums was a babble between the Little Swineherds (Serbia) and the Big Swine (Russia, France and England)
which these enemy powers carried on as a pandemonium of oink-
oinks with Slavic, Gallic and Anglo-Saxon accents.

It was during the climax of one such pig apocalypse, just prior
to the pulling of an infected molar, that Riddah burst into the dental office in her long white flannel nightgown.

"What shall I do now?" she cried.

She had just gotten up to read her mail. Markus's exemption
had been denied again. The letter, crumpled in her wild hand, instructed her son to report for induction the following Monday, the
same day as most other young men in the neighborhood.

"Something has to be done!" she cried. "We must think of
something! What can I do?"

"You can give us a conscription party," Conrad said through his
narcotic mask. "They just killed my exemption, too. Excuse me.
Oink-oink."

The party didn't get going until nearly midnight. Berek Spiegelglass requested that it start late: Albania, now a prominently esteemed cobelligerent, had not only paid for its coins but placed a

huge, urgent new order requiring after-dark work at the factory. Nobody minded coming at 11 PM. The heroic nature of the gala called for a special hour. But 11 PM passed and Riddah, the hostess, had not appeared at the No. 6 roof garden to attend to preparations.

However, the Havliceks showed up and pitched in. This, of course, was unexpected. Until that evening they had never been seen in anything but a dank, indoor half-light, a light which marked them like a prison uniform. But under the electric lanterns of the roof garden, their aprons almost glittered. Their faces were no longer the same interchangeable drab mask. They developed piquant differences—the saucy small teeth of No. 3, the blond curl peeking from No. 5's babushka, the full, curved lips of No. 1. Stuck into their apron strings were little "mourning pennants"; these displayed the face of the slain crown prince, a black funerary cross above his head, and beside it a red sword to signify the recourse to arms. For all their doleful meaning the pennants fluttered from Havlicek waists like dashing accessories. But the biggest shock about the Havliceks was their speed, after so many years of sour and indomitable torpor. Briskly, they hung streamers with the Habsburg black-and-yellow colors on the wall. They set up tables and arranged cakes baked specially by Markus earlier in the day. From their necks hung silver whistles bought from the same hawker as the pennants—you blew on them and out came the first ten bars of the "Radetzky March." Whenever that prideful cadence sounded, the Havliceks actually smiled. The three were like triple Cinderellas summoned at last from servitude to the challenge of a ball.

The Havliceks conveyed the sense that every stalemate, every injustice, mishap and frustration of the past would be set right now in a flaming denouement. Their confidence seemed to be infectious. That evening Ferdinand switched from two crutches to one and managed to assist with the folding chairs. Conrad was inspired to write out a Mobilization Menu on a parchment scroll he'd gotten many birthdays ago. He calligraphed a list of all the pastries on the tables, from raisin-and-almond buns, to vanilla wreaths, to the Sacher torte on which the imperial war ensign bristled in rum-flavored whipped cream.

Zettl tramped in wearing his hero uncle's Bosnian campaign boots. He brandished a box of Havanas given him by some well-wisher after he'd passed his army physical. Soon valorous cigar smoke filled the roof garden. The Young Turk kickers lit up, and so did the fellow draftees who had arrived with them, namely the Havlicek husbands. Though the Havlicek men were in their forties, baldish and paunchy, they wore, just like their younger comrades, bunches of daisies in their hatbands. The flowers signified that the wearer had been found fit to fight.

Apart from Berek Spiegelglass, only one other man present was too old for the war: Alois Schall. Five days earlier the late crown prince's household at Belvedere Palace had been disbanded. Schall had just resumed his position in the factory, reoccupied his desk and returned with his wife to Turk Place, to a flat at No. 2.

Frau Schall had entered the roof garden, dramatic in a black ruffled dress, black gloves and a black handbag. At first she couldn't help being puzzled by an assembly that included a hobnailed Zettl and unironed babushkas on janitors' heads. But then she noticed the Havliceks' mourning pennants. Since she considered the crown prince's passing a personal bereavement, she decided to be touched by these condolences extended by such simple folk. What really won her over, though, was the sight of Hester Spiegelglass serving gugelhupf slices to one and all. She hadn't seen the woman in years. Frau Spiegelglass had grown heavier, much heavier than she herself. To Frau Schall this was a patriotic moment, and she walked forward with a smile that was unqualified.

By then it was past midnight. Riddah had not appeared. Berek Spiegelglass motioned to Conrad to open the first champagne bottle. Soon there was a staccato of corks against the ceiling, a hurrahing for the emperor, a cutting into the great war-crested chocolate cake. Again Berek signaled Conrad and pointed to the corner. There stood one of Boas's old cameras. Time for the taking of the photograph. As best he could, Conrad tried to do the honors under the black cloth while Ferdinand lined up the men into a properly memorable heroes' portrait. At that point Lily reached under a table and pushed out the surprise. It was a big cardboard box, which she upended into a bobbing of soccer balls. There was one ball not only for each Young Turk kicker but also for the Havlicek husbands and for Zettl. Each man now stood at attention for the camera, one hand holding the ball, the other on his neighbor's shoulder.

Two more photographs were taken, just to be on the safe side. Riddah still did not appear. Conrad ran downstairs to check on her. Meanwhile, the others went on to "bowl." Helmut Milz, the Young Turk goalie, had been busy in his father's carpentry shop. Out of plywood he'd made a small bowling alley as well as small bowling pins on which labels had been glued saying "Belgrade," "St. Petersburg," "Paris" and "London." Using their soccer balls as bowling balls, the men mowed down enemy capitals, again and again, with mirthful clatter, with cheers and with renewed champagne toasts. The general high feeling led Markus to invent an altogether new, triangular soccer game which involved three goals, and he was about to set these up—using bowling pins as goalposts—when his mother Riddah came in.

She walked through the door with Conrad. She wore her working clothes, and her white baker's hat had been pushed down rakishly on one side, toward her flushed cheek. Her left arm came off Conrad's shoulder and flung itself around Markus's neck.

"Come on, Markie-bashi," she said. "Teach me! Teach me soccer!" Hugging him, letting him go, still holding on to him with one hand, she aimed her foot at a ball on the floor, missed, converted the momentum of the missed kick into a sort of dance pirouette, kicked again, missed again, drew her son into a hugging jig, laughed, threw down her cap, and turned to all the others as she jigged, shouting, "What's the matter? Can't you dance?"

And Conrad moved the lever of Hester's old player piano, which still stood in the roof garden. The "Voices of Spring" waltz bounded through the cigar smoke. The men, laughing, joined hands, kicked balls, danced, kicking and roaring—until suddenly they all stopped.

Riddah had fallen to the floor. An odd sound came from her mouth. Her daughter, Lily, ran to her side.

"Mama!" Markus said.

"She'll be all right," said Berek Spiegelglass, who'd been watching her all along.

"Mama! Is something wrong?" Markus cried. He and Lily sat down on the floor next to their mother.

"That's because on top of it she drank champagne," Conrad said. "She kept a bottle down at the bakery."

"On top of what?" Markus said.

"She absolutely insisted," Conrad said. "It wasn't my idea. She said she wouldn't come up here unless I did it."

"Did what?"

"She made me give her a little laughing gas," Conrad said.

"Well," Berek said. "You men have to be at the barracks at five in the morning. It's nearly two now. Time to go."

"But she hasn't really waked up yet," Markus said.

"*Boas!*" Riddah said, prone from the floor. "*Get up! Waltz with me! It's a party!*" Her eyes were closed and she purred at the ceiling.

"Kiss her and go," Berek said to Markus. "Right now. Kiss her good-bye."

Markus kissed her.

"I said, let's go," Berek said to the others and went ahead to the door. Ferdinand limped behind him on his crutch. They all went except for the woman on the floor and her daughter.

"*Boas, you are late,*" Riddah burbled from the floor. "*You should be here. It's my party. Boas? Did you go to war?*"

Lily kneeled by her mother's side. Her dirndl was smudged with cigar ashes from the floor. Lily was eleven years old, but tears much older came down her cheeks. She sobbed and stroked her mother's cheek.

XXV

T HE WORLD RETURNED, closing around him as a chill, enormous room. He sat up on a bed, amid things and noises that did not connect. Near him a giant chandelier lay on the parquet floor; from many gilded arms dangled stethoscopes, bandages and bottles. A cherub rode a fretted silver clock and smelled of carbolic acid. White-coated people walked about, mouths moving soundlessly. Speaking out of a monumental painting on the wall, a field marshal said that the systolic pressure had been brought down to ninety.

This lasted only a few seconds. Then he heard the voice of the nurse who sat on his bed. She looked thin under her big nun's hat of white linen. He would be fine, she said. Everything looked good, now that his coma was over. Soon the aftereffects would be gone, too. The funny way his ears worked, or other confusing sensations—that might come back, but for brief spells only. The best thing was to relax.

But he seemed to be relaxed anyway. "What's going on here?" he asked, sort of curious.

Oh, this was the former imperial palace, she said. This wing was being used as a hospital. Over there, the chandelier had dropped from the ceiling just before the end of the war. Now it was February in 1919 and her own name was Sister Lutz, and this gentleman—a gray-whiskered man stepped forward—was his father, Berek Spiegelglass.

The gray-whiskered man gave him a strong, brief hug, a sighing, prickly kiss, and the nurse kept talking. The memory loss, she said, would be the only thing left from his concussion. It was from some mortar explosion on the Isonzo front the last week of the war. But the best thing was to be relaxed about that, too. Such things could be treated. Very soon he would be able to go home, at least for a few hours at a time.

"Who am I supposed to be?" he said. "I mean, what's my name?"

"You are my Ferdinand," said the gray-whiskered man the nurse called "Herr Spiegelglass."

Ferdinand Spiegelglass. Readily he accepted that as his name. He couldn't remember just what amusement park he'd ever been in, but his emergence into life was a sort of amusement-park ride. Everything was startling, crazy, unserious. It was a "Why not?" world. He knew no past and therefore no regrets. Without specific memories he did not need to face a particular future. As long as he was safe from that confrontation, he had no worries. He was on a vacation from time. The hospital was a daily mirage. People bled and cried beneath golden sconces. He was whole, though still a bit weak. He let himself coast through one long continuous surprise.

When he got his first day pass from the hospital, "Ferdinand" was led "home" by "his father." The old man linked arms and hummed. The old man said it was so good to see that he, "Ferdinand," was walking as well as ever. No problem from that accident which had kept him on crutches—out of the war, in fact, until 1916. They were striding along the curve of a wide boulevard out of which flagstones had been torn by some recent great anger. Over the portals of a mansion three words had been smeared in red paint. KINGS ARE CORRUPTION. All that, "his father" said, was due to the changeover. The monarchy had broken apart into Poland, Hungary, Czechoslovakia and so on. All that was left of Austria was a few Alps and Vienna—a little republic.

"That sounds interesting," said "Ferdinand."

"Our street came through all right," said "his father," as though talking about an ordeal. But to "Ferdinand" the breaking of the old empire was a new fairy tale—knights, dragons and all.

They boarded an electric tram and stood near the motorman, the one place where the car's windows had not been boarded up with wood. "Ferdinand" looked through the glass windshield and saw many children. They were crowded behind chicken wire strung from one classic pillar to another under the roof of a grandiose building. These children, "Berek Spiegelglass" said, were refugees from Bohemia; their parents still had to be found. The children's mouths opened; their cheeks seemed to be moist with sorrow. But it was the rooftop figures on the palace, the naked goddesses and the valiant Titans, from whom the whimpering and the wailing came.

This was one of the last times "Ferdinand's" ears worked funny. They rode on, along sad files of houses, facades dirty and battered as though a muddy army had tramped on the walls vertically all day. After they got out at the tram terminal, "his father" took his arm again. Within a minute they stood before a very short street with minarets. This, "his father" said, was "Turk Place."

Here the masonry was intact and well painted, and people came running out to see "Ferdinand." Quickly, "his father's" introductions created a family and friends. A seventeen-year-old girl, red-haired, with a remarkably short skirt, was his half sister, "Ilona." The scented woman with the big hat was Ilona's mother, "Hester," who was also "Ferdinand's" stepmother. Then there was "Aunt Riddah," a huge, gray-haired woman who smothered "Ferdinand" in her arms and left a little wetness on his chin. The legless man in the wheelchair was "Cousin Markus." And the bright color spot in the bunch, a teenager in a striped skirt and a round flash of a pretty face, that was "Cousin Lily."

But there were more. The chubby older man in the smock was the designer, "Herr Schall," and the woman in the tailored suit, pushing the perambulator, that was "Frau Schall" with her baby. And the two women stepping forward now, both in black, these were the widows "Havlicek," janitors at No. 1 and No. 3 Turk Place, and the one in the dressing gown, that was "Frau Havlicek of No. 5," whose husband had come back from the front alive. And the man who had the hook sticking out of his right sleeve was "Zettl," the night watchman, who not only went up to "Ferdinand" but boxed him happily on the shoulder and said, the hell with sleeping in the daytime when he could welcome back "Ferdinand," and wasn't it lucky that dumb Russky grenade didn't know that he, "Zettl," was a lefty?

Then "Ferdinand" was shown the various houses of "Turk Place"—but not the house at No. 1, which the old man called "the factory." The doctors had said that "Ferdinand" should not be exposed to everything at once. But he was not bothered by any of it. Only at one point was he a bit puzzled. That was when he was led into his parents' dining room. A big wooden folding screen divided the space in half. Behind the partition stood two beds.

"After you no longer spend nights at the hospital," the old man said, "you'll sleep here."

"What's the other bed for?" asked "Ferdinand."

"That's for Conrad," the old man said.

"Conrad?"

"Your brother. He'll come back from the war."

"But the war is over," said "Ferdinand."

"Some are still coming back," the old man said. "Conrad will be back. I've asked for it."

"Who'd you ask?" said "Ferdinand."

"Oh, you'll remember when you remember the rest," the old man said. "You won't have any problems."

But "Ferdinand" had few problems even now. Everything was made easy for him. He was a sort of hero at a synagogue service at No. 2 Turk Place. The rabbi called him up to the pulpit to do the Torah reading—an honor, the rabbi said, given to all war veterans restored by God's mercy to the congregation. Since "Ferdinand" did not recall his Hebrew, the rabbi stood with him before the open scroll, pronouncing softly the words, which "Ferdinand" repeated aloud. He also had the privilege of dressing the Torah in its silver-studded red velvet. It was afterward that the rabbi led him aside for a minute while the cantor sang blessings.

"Perhaps you don't remember Kaddish," the rabbi said in a quick whisper. "It's our prayer for the dead. Please—you would unburden my heart—please, persuade your father to say Kaddish for your dear late brother Conrad."

"He's dead?" said "Ferdinand."

"I have no right to keep this from you," the rabbi said. "The Serbs have returned all the prisoners of war they took at the Battle of Rava. That's where your beloved brother was reported missing. And unfortunately—I had to make a heartbreaking investigation— it was one of those shrapnel massacres with few identifiable remains. I have no choice but to be candid. Apparently no one else will tell you outright. Forgive me for such news."

"'My father' knows all that?" said "Ferdinand."

"He refuses to know it," the rabbi said. "You see, we can't memorialize your sainted brother unless we mourn him. But I can't seem to make Herr Spiegelglass understand. Maybe you can. You see, there is enough misery and starvation. There shouldn't be self-deception, too, or superstition. It makes everything worse. Thank you for trying."

The rabbi took off his gloves to grip "Ferdinand's" hand. Because of the coal shortage, large spaces like the synagogue could not be heated. Everybody prayed in overcoats. Only "Berek Spiegelglass" wore a furry, peasant-looking jacket. He stood very straight and had looked at the rabbi's whispering. Now he gave a slow, definite headshake.

"I don't think I could tell 'my father' such a thing," "Ferdinand" said. "I'm sorry."

Sighing, the rabbi pulled on his gloves.

The rabbi's request was made on a particularly cold spring weekend. But the temperature didn't slow down the soccer at Turk Place. That Sunday, "Ferdinand" came to the home street with hospital buddies for the first scrimmage held under the direction of his "cousin Markus." His cousin, "Ferdinand" had been told, used to do heavy bakery work with his mother before the land mine in Galicia had severed his legs. He was a whirlwind in the wheelchair, though. He assisted Dr. Stelnitz at No. 6 and studied for a dental technician's license that would let him fill cavities or perform simple extractions. But his heart lay in coaching various newly formed veterans' teams. And there had never been a group—you could hear it from his exuberant chair-borne yells—never a group like the one "Ferdinand" brought to the backyard field at No. 6 that Sunday.

Since the men were, like "Ferdinand," still hospital-based, their rations entitled them to real meat three times a week; they were strong, not the usual skeletons pushing the ball. And since they were all amnesia cases, they'd forgotten all their wrong soccer habits. None matched the height or strength of "Ferdinand," but they were quite able-bodied, well nourished, full of a childlike openness. "Markus" loved cajoling, correcting, applauding, even cursing such fine material. He wheeled himself indefatigably after every zigzag of the action, taught the men at the very first session not to use the tip but the side of the foot in guiding the ball and handed out his mother's salt sticks by way of special reward.

Perhaps because "Ferdinand" raised her son's spirits so, the bakery woman took him under her wing. She picked him up at the hospital after her night's work was done at 7 AM. By then he'd already gotten past the one unpleasant part of the day: at dawn he was pulled out of bed for immersions in a cold tub, followed by low-voltage electrodes placed against his temples—treatments which were supposed to jog his memory awake.

Not that he had difficulty retaining things he'd learned since coming out of the coma—like the way "home" from the palace hospital. The reason "Riddah" met him in the morning was simply to provide company and to save him streetcar fare. The ride to Turk Place cost twenty-one hundred kronen the first week and went up to twenty-seven hundred in the second, in headlong inflation. "Riddah" paid no such sums. When the conductor came around for tickets, she handed him a small paper bag, which he held to his face. He inhaled the smell of fresh-baked poppy-seed rolls, touched his cap and moved on. "In my pocketbook I've got another tram ticket," "Riddah" would say to "Ferdinand." "Let's eat it." And they'd smile and munch their way home.

The third week, when the fare they didn't pay went up to

thirty-one hundred kronen, the main doctor said "Ferdinand" could now be "exposed to everything in his previous life." This meant the bakery woman could take him to the factory at No. 1 Turk Place. The old man was waiting for him there. It was a big hall, filled with machines which stood silent and unattended. The workers had not yet arrived. The old man said that usually he slept late but that he had waked early so that he could show his son some things without other people staring. He began pointing to items laid out on a table: beautiful, silver-plated crosses, star-framed medallions, crown-shaped badges and other military decorations. Their manufacture had been assigned to the factory through Prince Wallers, the old man explained. Most of them had been stamped from dies "Ferdinand" had made while his leg injury still exempted him from the war—there on that tool-and-die lathe over there.

"Ferdinand" stared at "his" lathe. Once he had been its master. Now he could not connect it to his hands. He did not even know the function of its wheels and levers—not even their names. The ignorance tightened his scalp. "His father" touched him on the arm, then suddenly turned to the wall.

The bakery woman hugged "Ferdinand" away. Hugging, she led him across the street to Turk Place No. 6, down into the bakery cellar, to two white cupboards. "Listen!" she said. But then she didn't say anything, just shook her head. She scooped a crescent out of a roll basket, thrust it at him. But he couldn't eat, just as she couldn't talk. He just held the crescent in his hand. Finally, she grabbed his other hand and pushed it against one of the white cupboards. It was very cold.

"That's an icebox," she said. "That's where we store the yeast. Now feel the other icebox, the big one. Feel it!"

"It's very cold, too," he said.

"That's where I keep his legs," she said.

"Legs?" he said, though he knew instantly.

"My Markus's legs," she said. Her eyes were swimming. She was munching hard on the crescent she'd taken back. The munching slowed her words, but it kept her voice more steady. "They're from the field hospital," she said. "Where they took them off. I asked for them. Got them for a big donation. I keep 'em fresh. Cold. In formaldehyde. Let people laugh. There's so much research. Someday the doctors will know. They'll put 'em back. Your father asked for it. My Markus knows that."

"'My father' asked for it?"

"This is Turk Place," she said. "Yes. And he asked for Conrad's return. And that you'll get your memory back. You'll work at your lathe. You'll see."

"I wonder how I ever made those medals," he said.

"You'll make better things," she said. "Medals are a joke now. Money is a joke. Here! Eat the rest of the roll! You know how much that roll is? Three thousand five hundred kronen. Tomorrow we'll charge four thousand. You big child, you, so astonished at everything. Come upstairs. Look at them!"

Up on the street a line had formed in front of the bakery. He'd noticed the people with pushcarts before, but now he realized that the pushcarts were sort of purses from which people paid. "Read!" Riddah said and shoved him at a long sheet posted on the bakery doorway. "My daughter writes a new one every week."

It was a price list. The forks—and there were many clattering in the front pushcart—were worth three plain rolls apiece; the bedsprings overflowing another cart were worth five rye-bread loaves; the steel skeleton of an umbrella, two rolls or one sugar bun.

"What are you doing with it all?" he said.

"Big child," she said. "It's scrap iron. Bring it to the factory." She kicked at a huge wheelbarrow filled with scrap payments. "Go on. There's a load right now. You're strong. You'll find out. You'll find out it's true about the legs, too. There's so much research. I have to go to sleep."

He pushed the barrow into the factory. Most of the machines were still unattended, though about a dozen workers had arrived. They were melting down other scrap in a furnace. The old man was wearing glasses now. He stooped over an anvil, hammering a red-hot chunk of iron into a frying pan. Since "Ferdinand" did not really know him, he found it hard to say "Papa."

"Look," he said. It was easier to say than "Papa." "Look," he said. "Hammering, what you do now, is probably much easier than lathe work. Maybe you can teach me that for a start."

The old man didn't look at him. He kept hammering. "Ferdinand" thought he hadn't heard. All of a sudden the old man turned on him.

"You don't have to stand there, dumb!" he said. "You're not dumb! You don't have to be shown! You're a master metal man! You'll remember it all—all at once! I've asked for it!"

"I'm sorry," "Ferdinand" said.

"Meanwhile, stay outside!" the old man said. "Go outside. Right now. Lily's leaving. Go help her sell!"

And that was what "Ferdinand" did, for days and days thereafter.

Actually, he enjoyed those selling rides with "Lily." In its canvas-covered part the wagon carried not only utensils just made at the factory but "Lily's" friends, her fellow students at the Commercial High School, which was open afternoons only—the warmer part of the day—to save fuel.

They were all girls. "Ferdinand" sat up front, reining the horses, and so he seldom had a chance to get a good long look at them. But he was aware of their warm bouncings, swivelings and stretchings on the bench under the canvas, the vivacious shifting of their limbs which made the wagon creak. They were doing homework together in a soprano uproar, constantly questioning each other, and answering, and misunderstanding, contradicting, explaining and calling each other to order, all complicated by the fact that most of the problems they had to solve for the teacher dealt with ledger items at current price levels of millions of kronen.

"Lily" talked faster than any of them—and louder. That was because she sat with "Ferdinand" on the driver's bench and had to shout back over her shoulder through the canvas opening of the wagon. She complained a lot to her friends about how hard it was to write out figures on the bumpy bench and how cold it was in

the open air. Yet she never sat anywhere except next to "Ferdinand"—and seemed largely unaware of him. The only time she
talked to him was to give directions. On such occasions her voice
changed to a much slower, cooler, very adult and correct tone.

"Now, if you please," she would say. "Kindly have the horses
turn right at the next corner. Thank you."

She had light blue oval eyes whose shape was interestingly different from the roundness of her face. Her figure was short but fine,
chastely dressed in a dirndl a size large. A thick, broad, enormous
wool scarf was wound around her neck and jacket. Because of her
rapid turning around to her girlfriends in the back, the ends of her
shawl would fly about and flop against "Ferdinand's" chest.

"Oh, pardon me. I am so sorry," she would say; curtly she'd slap
the shawl ends down for their childish impudence. "Now our course
is straight ahead, if you please."

"Ferdinand" kept his eyes on her pointing white finger. He
didn't like to look left or right anyway. The tenements jolted past,
walls and windows looking as gray, as worn and punished as the
cobbles. He didn't like to see the man squatting on the sidewalk
skinning a white cat; or the house whose construction must have
stopped during the war and on whose roofless, rain-wet staircase a
woman nursed a baby.

But then the street stopped and the Vienna Woods started—a
sudden lavishness that erased everything that had bothered him in
the city. Leaves budded with a princely young green, on trees that
couldn't possibly be rooted in some runty, starving little republic.

They would reach their first village. "Kindly stop in the square,"
"Lily" would say. "Before the church. And make them know we're
here."

He would stop the horses. Thunderously he knocked the whip
handle against the metal hubcap of a front wheel. It took a good deal
of knocking for the peasants to gather around and for the girlfriends
to quiet down. "Lily" would stand up at the driver's bench. In the
formal tone she used with "Ferdinand," she would say, "Good day,
ladies and gentlemen. This is our barter list for today." She read
from the sheet Berek Spiegelglass had given her. When she finished,
the peasants would peer at the goods which the girlfriends had

pushed forward for inspection in the wagon. After peering a good deal they would scratch their ears and put their faces together and peer again. "It might be of help to you to look at the list," "Lily" would say and turn to "Ferdinand." "If you would kindly hand it to them."

She would give "Ferdinand" the list, and he would jump off the wagon with it. Somehow his size always speeded things up. The peasants would pass the list around and begin to make selections by nodding their chins at objects in the wagon. "Ferdinand" would haul down what they wanted—a frying pan newly forged from scrap at the factory; hammer heads; the cutting edge of plowshares or other farm tools whose making Berek Spiegelglass remembered from his blacksmith days at Varungy. "Ferdinand" hauled them down and "Lily's" girlfriends, giggling, whisked their skirts out of his way. "Ferdinand" would also help carry from barns to the wagon the peasants' form of payment: vats of honey; flour sacks for the bakery; cords of firewood; and, for all the Spiegelglasses and their employees, a side of beef, pots of goose fat with crisped cracklings, cranberry preserves, crated apples, lettuces and eggs in wicker baskets he had to promise to return on the next trip.

"If any of you mooches anything at all back there," "Lily" would yell at her girlfriends on the way back, "you'll have to deal with *him*."

It was obvious who *him* was. Yet "Lily" hardly said a word to "Ferdinand" until he had unloaded everything at Turk Place.

"You have been of considerable help again," she would say in her official tone. "Many thanks indeed." And she would run off screaming after her girlfriends, having turned so roundly on her heels that the scarf ends flopped against *him*'s chest.

All that ended early one morning when he walked out of the treatment room at the hospital. A man in fancy green uniform came up to him; he had a beard that was elaborate and curly, smoked a curved pipe and held out his hand.

"Herr Ferdinand Spiegelglass?"

"Yes," said "Ferdinand."

After they'd shaken hands, "Ferdinand" found in his palm a card. *Captain C. C. Cirvic, M.D., Chief Anesthesiologist, Medical Corps, Montenegrin Legion of the Kingdom of the Serbs, Croats and Slovenes. Retired.*

"I've already had my treatment this morning," said "Ferdinand." "And someone will be meeting me here at any moment."

"You mean Frau Riddah Mainzer?" Dr. Cirvic said. "Actually, I've come here instead of her. This is an entirely new approach I'm trying for your problem. Your family gave permission."

"But I don't want more treatments," "Ferdinand" said. "They don't do any good."

"Well, this is very different," Dr. Cirvic said. "Very informal. I just want to chat with you. We can do it on the way home to your family."

"Ferdinand" gave him back his card; against its edge Dr. Cirvic struck a match, which actually ignited. "Ferdinand" had never seen a man get a light like that before, especially since the doctor lifted a leg as he did it, as though that were part of a comic trick. The man seemed more peculiar than suspicious.

"All right," "Ferdinand" said. "I know the way."

"The fact is, I was born in Austria myself," Dr. Cirvic said. "I guess you can hear that from the way I talk."

"But you fought on the other side," "Ferdinand" said.

"Shall I tell you how come?" Dr. Cirvic said. "Do you mind if we walk instead of riding that broken-down tram? I'll tell you a funny story."

The story was as peculiar as his match-lighting method. Cirvic had begun the war as an Austrian army private. But when the Montenegrins captured his regiment, they killed everybody except the doctors. So Cirvic declared himself an anesthesiologist who had graduated summa cum laude from the University of Vienna.

"They believed you?" "Ferdinand" half hoped they hadn't. The man had an engaging, pipe-puffing shamble of a walk. But there was an underhanded glee to his manner. It made "Ferdinand" wonder whether the man was putting one over on him, not just on the Montenegrins. The man got too much joy out of being a fraud.

"Believed me?" Cirvic said. "They *commissioned* me. They made me a sawbones captain, those dumbheads. See, in those days the Montenegrin Legion was just a bunch of bandits with cannons. All they had was a half-ass field hospital they'd wheedled out of the Serbs, with not one blessed medic. They'd never heard of anesthetics. But I helped out a little in that line before the war. I tell you, before it was all over, I had a staff of thirty. You want to try a pipe like mine?"

"I don't smoke," "Ferdinand" said. "How do you know the people at Turk Place?"

"Well, with this sort of pipe I'm not talking about regular smoking," Cirvic said. He took a second pipe out of his jacket pocket. Just like his own, it was made of blond wood, had a small bowl and was already stuffed.

"How do you know about my Turk Place family?" "Ferdinand" asked again. "Did my hospital doctor tell you?"

"Yes, I talked to that clown," Cirvic said. "A yo-yo. Doesn't know his ass from his elbow. Sniff that, please."

Cirvic held the second, unlit pipe bowl under "Ferdinand's" nose. They had stopped in a tenement street; the scent of the tobacco overrode the stench of uncollected garbage. That scent was like nothing he could define—nutmeggy, not quite sweet, somehow secret, like some spicy candy he might have hidden away as a child.

"What kind of tobacco is that?"

"Just puff on it a little," Cirvic said. "Permit me to give you a light."

Cirvic struck the match against the edge of his visiting card and lifted his leg again. "Ferdinand" puffed. The scent went through him. It rid his body of ballast he didn't know he carried. Half his bones seemed to turn into balloons, particularly at the kneecaps. The cobbles on which he walked lazed like fair-weather clouds. Suddenly, a vehement sneeze lifted him off the pavement.

"Oh no," he said. "Not one of my stupid old sneezing fits."

"Hm, you had those before and you remember," Cirvic said. "Isn't that nice tobacco? Though I see I'm out of it for my own next bowl."

"Let me give you mine," "Ferdinand" said, alarmed anyway at the potency of the stuff.

"Wouldn't dream of it," Cirvic said. "I know where to get more a few streets down. Why don't you have coffee here meanwhile?"

He meant a café which was open but deserted and unheated; none of which mattered much to "Ferdinand" when he walked in. The pipe fumes he inhaled now powered his vision amazingly. His eyes had become magnifying glasses. The table at which he sat was made of wood whose grain was an exquisite brown-black mosaic. The ring some beer glass had left on it was like a crown, silvery and dimly glowing.

"Soda for the gentleman?"

The wrist of the woman who stood before him had a tiny sprinkling of gold hair under which he saw the hint of a tracery of sky-blue veins. He didn't know why she was so beautiful. Between her lips, in the half-dark depth of her smile, something gleamed like the moon.

"Yes, please," he said.

She siphoned the soda out of a big bottle. His extrapowered eyes followed the bubbles as they danced from the glass through the curve of her arm . . . until he felt them prickling in his own shoulders. When the glass was full, she didn't give it to him but opened a door.

"I think you'll be warmer drinking it in there," she said.

The back room was indeed less cold. He drew on his pipe and saw an upside-down turtle shell in which two apples lay; red apples inside whose pale flesh seeds were sleeping like succulent black pearls. But then he realized that she stood next to a bed. Instantly, he knew that she had risen from it only minutes ago. The billows of yellow eiderdown still breathed the same warmth as the red sheen of her bodice. The white bedding was an exact landscape of her body in reverse, from the slightly ridged double hollow in the middle, to the pillow faintly tufted with the imprint of her curls.

He had to hide his hands behind his back. His fingers were already spread wide with the need to seize her and to unite her once more with the bed.

"Someone will be looking for me in the front room," he said, not so much to tell her as to remind himself of Cirvic.

"I suppose he can wait," she said. She sat down on the bed, smiling the moon smile that made him do the same. She still held the glass of soda water, and as she raised it to his lips he saw the long dimple on her upper arm. He could no longer leash his hands. His pipe dropped and the glass fell to the floor. His fingers sucked in her whiteness and softness, and she laughed. She laughed her skirts up. His hands rode beyond her stockings into her thighs, and foundered at the destination. The rest of him was also confounded. His body could not remember what must so urgently come next.

"That's okay," her mouth said into his ear. "We've fixed that before." The mouth tingled along his cheek and, softly, blew into his nostrils. He did not exactly sneeze. He uncoiled a moan that was also a convulsion. Recollection began to course through him, to shake and glow and point, from his brain to his sex, even down to his toes. He remembered himself into her. He remembered and remembered, with howitzers tolling and with blazing bells, with flares, command cries and breakneck troops, with blasts, thuds, jolts, that released him and blew him through the war's fireworks—until he caught up with himself at last.

He was no longer "Ferdinand." He was Ferdinand. The explosions were over. He lay with the woman in the back room of the Turf Café.

"The betting people," he said. "Are they still out there?"

"Too early in the day for them." Her finger circled his navel. "Imagine, such a big man, and a virgin twice."

He was at her. Smiling, she pushed him back. "Your friend might be waiting," she said.

"My God! Of course!" He had remembered so much, he'd forgotten that. A button came off his jacket as he yanked on his clothes at top speed. "Excuse me." He ran to the door. In the front room the man sat, smoking, Captain Cirvic who wasn't Captain Cirvic at all.

"Conrad!" Ferdinand cried. The pipe broke in the twins' embrace.

"You're back!" Ferdinand said. "My God! I remember! I can remember! What took you so long?"

"Had to wait until they opened the border," Conrad said. "Hey, you're in fine shape."

"But why didn't you let us know? The rabbi wanted to say Kaddish!"

"That's the goddamn Red Cross for you," Conrad said. "You want them to forward your mail across enemy lines, you'd better be a PW. I was a Montenegrin muckamuck in Montenegro."

"Come on!" Ferdinand said. "I want to go home!"

"I've got a fiacre waiting outside," Conrad said.

One minute after they'd climbed in, Ferdinand realized that he'd left his own pipe. And how blatantly buttonless his jacket looked. And that there was some unfinished business at the Turf Café.

"Wait a minute," he said. "I—I haven't paid for my drink back there."

"Oh, that's taken care of," Conrad said. "I left some of Aunt Riddah's rolls on the bar."

Now there was embarrassment under Ferdinand's joy.

"You knew about me and that café?"

"Listen, I'm my brother's keeper," Conrad said. "Once I tailed you, just before I was drafted. Boy, you must have kept it up pretty good with her, even on crutches."

"Shut up!" Ferdinand said. "What'd you put in that pipe?"

"One learns things abroad," Conrad said. "See, I knew you just needed a fillip or two. That's all it took."

Ferdinand could laugh his shame away. And the short ride was over.

"Turk Place!" Ferdinand said. "Remember our tricycles? Where is he?"

He ran into the factory, and there he was by the anvil, not the man he'd been told was his father, but *Papa*—Papa slightly disguised with new grayness and new folds on his face, yet unmistakably Papa. He embraced Papa. He heard the mortal cadence of the breath inside his arms. He felt the brittle whiskers against his cheek. He trembled as he soared. Shells howled and cymbaled over the foxholes along the Isonzo River. He hugged Papa more strongly. "I remember everything!" he said.

"You know now?" Berek Spiegelglass said, hugging back. "You know how I asked that our Conrad should come back to us? You know where?"

"The Brick!" Ferdinand said. "Let's go and see it! Papa, I want to see the Brick!"

XXVI

AT THE CAFÉ PELLMANN the five o'clock tea dance was held on Sundays. It turned out to be remarkably durable. During the 1920s much more ambitious afternoon *dansants* opened, mostly in downtown Vienna. There gilded saxophones blew, fashionable daughters spooned cantaloupe mousse, eligible sons ordered Manhattan cocktails. Eligibles rose, clicked the soft suave heel click of hussar lieutenants and asked fashionables for the honor of a dance. Waiters lustrous with Rudolph Valentino pomade presented checks to fathers who could afford them: silver brokers, corporation lawyers, university professors, textile vice presidents. Quickly the sums on those checks rose from tens to hundreds of thousands. Affordability went the way of eligibility. A banker's salary barely bought a tailor's meal. Train fare back to Cracow devoured a lifetime of savings. Tonight's fortune turned into the next morning's farce. Such transformations continued until Austria's currency changed from kronen to schillings at the rate of six million to one. By then the music had gone out of many dance cafés.

But the Pellmann five o'clock sailed on. Its clientele was the backwater middle class of the tenement regions where the Spiegelglass family had pioneered. They made do quite steadily with barter. They provided real estate space and craft services for which they accepted in-kind payment. And they survived. Survival in such times was an almost bizarre feat. It warranted flaunting. The place to flaunt was the Pellmann at five o'clock on Sunday.

That was when the billiard tables were wheeled out of the billiard room to make room for the dancing and for the zebra-striped baby grand rolled in by two busboys. Herr Schimko, conductor of the 17th District Fire Brigade Band, sat down on the piano stool in a tuxedo whose lapels were red velvet just like those of jazz Negroes in the fancy downtown establishments. He was under personal instructions from Herr Pellmann to chew gum with dramatic cheek bulgings; it gave his musicalizing more of a Chicago cast. As he struck the first bars of "Doin' the Raccoon," waiters distributed ashtrays even to ladies. In the kitchen "Broadway doughnuts" were being fried in a special deep pan made at the Turk Place factory.

But that was not the only Spiegelglass contribution to the café's five o'clock. Ferdinand dropped by one Sunday afternoon, out of curiosity, to see if perhaps Lily was there. What he found was his brother.

Herr Schimko had just finished "The Gaucho's Lament." Conrad was escorting off the dance floor a woman at least ten years older and twenty pounds heavier than himself. Her makeup cracked under the stress of some extreme amusement. They were walking toward the "brewery widows' table" reserved for the wives of the weekend managers of the huge Jörger Beer Company, which worked seven days a week to reduce overhead. Conrad staged a romantic parting that included a bow, a standard hand kiss and a spontaneous departure from the standard in which he turned the lady's hand over to brush his lips across her open palm. Then he strolled to the bar, lit a cigarette—and received a small envelope from the headwaiter.

"Conrad!" Ferdinand said.

"Hey, welcome," Conrad said. "Want to try a Gauloise?"

"A gigolo!"

"I'd call it a dancing teacher," Conrad said. "I was teaching her some dips, the way they do the Balkan tango in Belgrade."

"But you're a Spiegelglass," Ferdinand said. "A gigolo!"

"Look at it this way," Conrad said. "Gainful employment. Might as well turn a few schillings till I find my civilian legs."

"When were you in Belgrade?" Ferdinand said.

"You know, Belgrade would be good for you," Conrad said.

"That's the south Slav Paris. I had some great weeks there after Montenegro."

"I thought you came home the moment you could!" Ferdinand said, furious.

"So I had a little fun before getting back into harness," Conrad said. "Excuse me." From the piano came "Jeannine, I Dream of Lilac Time," and he was off to the brewery widows again.

The Pellmann had a new Art Deco glass door which Ferdinand almost broke, so hard did he slam it on the way out. He slammed it not only at Conrad but also at himself. His amnesia had not been too different from Conrad's Belgrade. Now it struck him as a sort of Absence Without Leave. You might almost say, a spree. He'd been something close to a deserter from the responsibilities of Turk Place. Perhaps his desertion had injured Berek Spiegelglass.

Ferdinand noticed the injury in the factory, where he now exercised again all his old tool and lathe skills. His father insisted on doing the heavy blacksmith work as before; often flames flaring from the forge lit Berek Spiegelglass's face into a devastation of new hollows, pits, seams—a savagery, Ferdinand couldn't help thinking, given free rein in the course of his amnesiac lapse. For months his brain had refused to recall who Berek Spiegelglass had been before the war. It was as if the failure to preserve the image of his younger father had encouraged the battering of old age.

And then there was another problem, which had also started during his unremembering months. This one ate away at his father by robbing Berek Spiegelglass of some of his essential late-morning sleep. It had to do with the ballet lessons Ferdinand's half sister, Ilona, took at Professor Firlansky's dance studio in the Inner City. Each Sunday the professor held a "breakfast workout" to which his students' parents were invited. The workout started at 9 AM, which meant that Berek, who went with Hester, must get up at seven, over two hours earlier than on weekdays.

One Sunday Berek, returning hours late from the ballet outing, had to be helped out of a taxi by his wife and daughter. His arm was in a cast; when he'd boarded a tram on the way to the studio, he'd fallen and broken his wrist. It was a simple fracture, Hester told Ferdinand. Berek himself said nothing. But the white from the plaster cast seemed to have seeped into much of the black that remained in Berek's hair. His left arm held the broken right one in the sling, an attitude not just of caution but of vulnerability—and to Ferdinand a vulnerable Berek Spiegelglass was an intolerable thing to behold.

"Mother," Ferdinand said to Hester when he finally got hold of her alone. He forced his tongue to shape that difficult word when he had a favor to ask of the woman. "Mother," he said. "About Papa getting up so early on Sundays. Does he really have to watch ballet?"

"Ilona starts practicing at dawn for the workout," Hester said.

"But Papa at his age needs his sleep."

"These days he wakes early anyway," Hester said. "From seven on it's nothing but tossing and turning."

"But that's not like him!" Ferdinand said. "Is he worried about something? Could you find out?"

"From that stubborn man?" Hester said in a tone that was rather irritated, half admiring and quite final. Ferdinand wanted to run down to the bakery to ask Riddah to beat up his stepmother. He couldn't, of course. But he couldn't let the matter rest either. He had to turn to Berek Spiegelglass himself.

While the wrist was healing inside the cast, his father relinquished the blacksmith work to Ferdinand. Often Berek came to watch or rather, Ferdinand felt, to listen to his son's hammering. It was as if the old man searched in the rhythm of the clangor for some Morse-code hint—some answer to a bafflement that was crucial and yet not communicable even to his own child.

"I have a question, Papa," Ferdinand finally said as they stood side by side at the anvil. But then he didn't have the stomach to go on as he'd planned. He just couldn't ask point-blank what bothered his father. "What I want to ask . . . if our factory workers start a soccer team, would you come to the Sunday morning matches?"

"Sunday morning Ilona has ballet," Berek said.

"I'd play on our team myself," Ferdinand said.

No answer. His father stood next to him, holding his broken

arm, head cocked sideward. He seemed to be listening only for the next hammer blow to relieve him of a puzzle.

"*I'd play on the factory team myself,*" Ferdinand repeated, louder.

"Oh yes," his father said, as though awakened. "Soccer. Yes, Markus says you're a great player."

"I'd play at ten-thirty on Sundays," Ferdinand said. "That's when the matches start. Would you come?"

"I guess I've watched Ilona often enough," his father said.

"Good!" Ferdinand said. "That way you'll sleep longer." And let his hammer pound.

Now all Ferdinand had to do was work on Zettl, the old brawler of his school years. The war had changed Zettl's right hand into a hook, yet he was still trying to get even with the world by getting something for nothing. Still night watchman at the Turk Place factory, on Sunday he performed the office of sports steward of the 17th District chapter of the Socialist Metalworkers Union. Mainly, this involved blowing up soccer balls for the Sunday games of the Western Vienna Industrial League. Zettl used the compressed-air hose provided free by the recently opened truck garage near the market. In return for this service he received one schilling per inflated ball plus a free meal after the game, just like regular team members.

Ferdinand's ancient schoolyard enmity with him had become a grin between them, a bit of tacit mutual nostalgia. In class they'd seldom had friendly words. But now, despite the difference in their stations, they addressed each other by the first initials of their last names, like longtime buddies.

"Say, Z," Ferdinand said. "It's time to start our own factory team. We'll provide the balls, and shirts with minarets. Also sneakers if you can arrange a wholesale price with the shoe workers' chapter."

"Hm," Zettl said. "I shall bring it up before the Interchapter Union Council."

"And Markus will be the coach, and me, I'd like to play myself. I was center forward in the veteran team."

"Well, you're S Junior," Zettl said. "We don't go for bosses' sons in our league."

"My father wants to watch me," Ferdinand said. "And I've got to clear the expenses with him."

"Think your old man is going to come up with a good sports canteen?" Zettl said.

"I think I can clear it with him."

"I shall put the matter before the Union Sports Board," Zettl said. "But, hey, S. Not just a soup canteen. Meat. Beef. Okay?"

"I'll clear it with my father," Ferdinand said.

The following week Ferdinand was admitted provisionally to the first scrimmage of the newly formed Turk Place factory team. And four weeks after that the team lost its first match against the Schmelz Zipper Company by a score of 3–2, which Zettl considered an excellent showing for a raw eleven. The same Sunday Ilona couldn't manage her entrechats at Professor Firlansky's "breakfast workout" and thus failed to qualify for Opera Ballet auditions. After Hester returned to Turk Place, she announced this news with a brightness almost resembling Zettl's when he talked about the admirable defeat of the factory team. Hester's smile, though, was made of iron.

"It's all nice and clear now," she said to Berek. "Ilona needed encouragement from us both today. She didn't get it and she lost her chance. Now we know where we stand."

"I had to watch Ferdinand," Berek said. "And it was the first game of our factory team."

"Of course, very important. So now Ilona has a different chance. She can devote her weekends to the Seventeenth District social life." A small, uncanny pause. "It will be wonderful," Hester said.

The following Sunday Hester and Ilona went with Berek to see the factory lose 6–4 against the Obermoser Shoe Buckle Company

(Zettl pronounced it a very exciting score against the runner-up for last year's championship). The Spiegelglass ladies stood out in the sparse male crowd of proletarian caps and jackets with buttons missing. Hester had done some shopping beforehand which had strained, punitively, Berek's cash reserve. Mother and daughter sported ensembles fit for a picnic of higher Austrian gentry: green loden capes, green-embroidered gray loden skirts, gray-green crushed hats. Hester used the occasion to reveal publicly that she had started smoking at the age of sixty-one. Ilona brought along opera glasses quite unnecessary in such a small sports oval; most of the time she focused on a crow circling overhead. When she finally clapped gloved hands, her applause was not only languid but wrong. She mistook a successful Obermoser penalty kick for a Turk Place goal.

After that Hester, smiling her mineral smile at Berek, said, "Let's make a real Seventeenth District Sunday of it. Let's lunch at the Pellmann." And after lunch she said, "Oh, but now we might as well stay for the famous five o'clock tea. From now on we mustn't miss our district gala."

"All right," Berek said evenly. "I've been curious to see it myself."

As the zebra-striped piano was rolled in, Hester took from her huge country-baroness handbag a checkers set over which she and her daughter bent steadily, implacably, throughout all of Herr Schimko's numbers. When Herr Skalka, Jr., marched up to Ilona—her silk legs crossed under the shortest green skirt ever to stun the district—he received a keen smile. It turned out to apply to a brilliant checkers jump and was followed by an absentminded head shake.

From the first, Ferdinand felt the sting in Hester's behavior even though it wasn't directed at him. He excused himself from the postgame canteen and hurried to the Pellmann to sit next to his father, on the side of his broken arm, just as a defensive presence. The family's appearance at the five o'clock had the opposite effect on Conrad. The very sight of Berek Spiegelglass made him stop entertaining the brewery widows. From then on he avoided every Pellmann dance and shifted his Sunday fun, with its incidental earnings, to an establishment in a remote part of town.

The end of Conrad's career as local gigolo impoverished Turk Place gossip. But in some ways the Spiegelglass ladies were a replenishment. Their five o'clock manner was much bruited about at gatherings around corridor sinks in the neighborhood. When Frau Schall heard the No. 3 Havlicek discuss the disdainfulness shown by Frau Spiegelglass in the face of a zebra-striped piano, she knew herself challenged. The following Sunday afternoon Herr Schall joined his partner at the Pellmann not only with his wife but with their three-year-old son, Adelbert.

As soon as the baby grand thumped out "The Gaucho's Lament," Frau Schall pulled a clay-modeling kit out of her pocketbook and proceeded to mold a series of doggies with her little Adelbert. Here, surely, was indifference superior to any leg-showing checkers playing.

It was under such intricate circumstances that Zettl entered that same Sunday's five o'clock. He moved in an air of dignity so heavy, it cost him much of his balance. Using chair backs for support, he worked his way toward the Spiegelglass table.

"Good afternoon," he said. "That wasn't our fault, losing to those Atzger Nail Company punks today, that was the asshole referee bein' blind to all them fucking Atzger fouls, excuse the goddamn expression."

Ferdinand was glad that with the Schalls the table was now so fully occupied he couldn't ask his pal to sit down. "You're right, Z," he said. "There was a lot of fouling."

"I mean, you know old Skalka at the market inn," Zettl continued. "Fucking stingy old Skalka, excuse the goddamn expression, but even him, he says, 'Beer on the house, shit on the referee, this was really a victory!' Blew us to five rounds of pilsner, the whole team."

"Good for old Skalka," Ferdinand said.

"And our goal, man, the goal you shot, S." Zettl directed his lager breath at Ferdinand. "That was a goddamn beauty goal, not like those foul goals from those Atzger farts."

"Well, I got such a good pass from Huber," Ferdinand said.

"Now to business." Zettl drew himself up to an extremely authoritative erectness. "Reason for intruding. A Union Sports Board meeting yesterday. It's not supposed to be official till next week, but I told 'em, shit on next week, after that beauty goal he shot I'll tell him today. Ferdinand Spiegelglass, the hell with being the boss's son. Accepted as a regular member of the Turk Place workers' team as of today."

Losing only a fraction of his equilibrium, Zettl extended his good hand. Ferdinand steadied him by shaking it. "Thank you," he said.

"Same with Markus as coach," Zettl said. "He's still celebrating at Skalka's. You will be in receipt of the official communication next week. Also in that communication it says about our Union Sports badges we want made. Your factory should give us a price."

"That's interesting," Ferdinand said. Only minutes earlier, when Herr Schimko had left his piano for the intermission and the silence had encouraged serious conversation, the men at the table had discussed the need to shift the factory work from blacksmithing back into mass production.

"What do you want on those badges?" Herr Schall said.

"What do you think? Our party flower, the red carnation for victorious socialism," Zettl said. "Plus a soccer ball someplace for sports."

"That's more interesting than that coffeehouse order," Herr Schall said, referring to an order for plain tin ashtrays for a Carinthian coffeehouse chain.

"Also in the official communication," Zettl said, "it'll say about the organizer's honor badge, the carnation plus the number 100, 'cause you don't get it unless you organize a hundred comrades. I'm blabbing ahead of the official communication 'cause you shot such a goddamn beauty goal, and you got to give us a goddamn good capitalist price."

Ferdinand turned to his father. Berek Spiegelglass was not conscious. He had dropped off, his head against the chair back, his left hand holding the right arm in the sling, as if clutching it against a bafflement that pursued him even into a dream, even in the face of the music bouncing once more from the zebra-striped piano.

Never had Ferdinand seen his father fall asleep in a coffeehouse before. The shock, the shame of it was lessened only by the fact that nobody seemed to notice. People were getting up to dance to Herr Schimko's "The Sheik of Araby." Schall's pencil was already sketching a carnation on a napkin. Hester and Ilona were as engrossed in checkers as Frau Schall and her little Adelbert were busy with kneading clay doggies.

But then Zettl's eyes widened. His hook went to his lips. "Sh! . . ." The sight of Berek Spiegelglass asleep collapsed his uprightness abruptly into a sodden fatigue. "Take a nap myself," he mumbled, then reeled and dissolved into the dance-bound crowd.

"Riffraff," Frau Schall said, very softly, to her doggie.

"Here," Herr Schall said, oblivious to everything but the speed of his own pencil. "I'll show you in just a minute. The soccer ball over the carnation could be a simple circle like this. Now for the other badge, for the figure 100 over the carnation, we use two simple circles plus a line. Virtually the same machine die to reduce costs—"

"*Costs?*" Frau Schall said, loudly this time. "It'll cost us our heads if those Bolsheviks take over. Why should we make their badges?"

"Mommy, they're Social Democrats," Herr Schall said.

"It's all from Moscow," Frau Schall said. "They all want to destroy us like they destroyed our monarchy. You know what the crown prince once said to my sainted brother? 'Letting Reds into Parliament is giving Satan the vote.' His very own words, and it's God's own truth." She finally looked up from the clay doggie—not in the direction of Berek Spiegelglass, still lying insensible in his chair, but at Hester. "The rabble molests you everywhere," she said. "You can't even wear fur to bridge dates downtown. I go to my game Wednesday and it's impossible when the tram passes through the slums. They practically spit at ladies with foxes. That's what we've come to!"

At this her husband's sketching pencil stopped. But her prestigious complaint received no sign of solidarity from her peer, Frau

Spiegelglass, at the checkers-playing corner of the table. And Ferdinand now feared his father was in a coma. He lifted his coffee cup and clinked it down on the saucer. His father was not jarred awake. Hester turned to Berek. She stroked the inside of his elbow with a captured checker.

Berek Spiegelglass sat up and shook off his baffled sleep.

"Oh," he said. "I'd better have another cup of coffee."

XXVII

WITHIN A FEW DAYS the Turk Place factory was back in mass production, supplying the Social Democratic Party of the Austrian Republic with (a) 150 sports badges (red carnation with soccer ball); (b) 500 organizers' honor badges (red carnation with the figure 100); (c) 20,000 general membership badges (plain red carnation). As a result, Ferdinand had to escort Frau Schall to her weekly bridge game downtown.

Of course, Ferdinand knew why his father had given him this assignment: the ideological strain on Frau Schall must be eased by some personal gesture. The gesture cost four schillings, including tip. That was the taxi fare from Turk Place to the residence of the Italian ambassador at the Palais Metternich, where Frau Schall's old friend (formerly chambermaid in chief to the crown prince, now head domestic of the ambassador) hosted the card game. Ferdinand disliked the expense even more than Frau Schall's archducal reminiscing, which was melancholy and vigorous throughout the ride.

But her bridge game had something secretly exciting about it for Ferdinand. It took place on Wednesday evenings, not far from the Opera House, where on Wednesday afternoons the dress rehearsals were held. Lily got passes to them, and Ferdinand now had an excuse to take her home. Luckily the bridge started at six, just when the rehearsal finished. Ferdinand delivered Frau Schall by cab to her destination downtown, then hurried to the Opera. When he got there, some vast, vague noise still floated down a hill of white marble stairs. And the attendant at the bottom was in no mood to stop a panting giant who'd run all the way from the Palais Metternich.

Ferdinand climbed steps where the man's thumb pointed. He had never been to the State Opera. Nor had he ever seen *Die Fledermaus,* now being rehearsed for the New Year's Eve performance. In fact, if he hadn't been so tall, he would have seen very little of it even now. The dress rehearsal audience was restricted to the standees' space in the top balcony, and it was packed with friends and relatives of the cast.

Ferdinand's muscles helped him squeeze in. His height gave him a view past silhouettes in front. He looked down on a world of ivory canes, gay monocles, lace-doilied bosoms, gowns of spun silver, goblets, top hats and roguish lips, all gamboling under a pink radiance to marvelous gusts of melody. Some of the tunes he knew from the radio; others Ilona had played on her new gramophone. Yet the music and the luster that now streamed toward him had an unearthly newness and, at the same time, a familiarity that surprised him. Perhaps that was how the world was always meant to be—released from all sweat and stress into one easy, lilting surge. Perhaps his true world before the amnesia had been like that. Perhaps he should have waked up into the bright dance down there on the stage—instead of being stranded in the cares of Turk Place. What if these happy chandeliers had shone on his true childhood? What if he'd grown up in that ballroom, waltzing his young years away amid smiles and uncorked bottles and yielding violins? It was a crazy but irresistible suspicion. For minutes, pressed against a wall in the high darkness, he let himself billow along gorgeous pavilions. Then he recognized Lily and knew who'd started him on this.

Not far in front of him, two heads away, her arms were around the shoulders of girlfriends left and right. She stood swaying, dissolving into the pleasures of the pink-bathed gods below, swaying in easy intimacy with them, the magic ease of old playmates together—the same Lily who was supposed to pick up her mother's unsold rolls tonight, to help Ferdinand take them from Turk Place to the 17th District soup kitchen. She seemed like a double spy knowing the secrets of both an impossible ballroom and a real soup kitchen. Was this why her face lay concealed inside so many of his thoughts lately?

The chandeliers died, the curtain dropped as abruptly as a guillotine. A few houselights glimmered on—very few, for current must be saved at rehearsals. Sparse rays lit up lonely applause. The gods would not take bows. Vainly, a few dozen hands clapped thin echoes into the Opera House, a vault that was immense and empty and cold.

"I'll take you home," he said to Lily. "We've got to do the soup-kitchen rolls."

She nodded without really listening, and she still seemed drenched in pink sunbursts of three-quarter time. Ahead of him, ahead of her girlfriends, she danced humming down the staircase, her long shawl floating, her small pumps tapping on the marble, a wayward fragment of the sorcery that had vanished from the stage.

"You're going the wrong way," he said to her outside. She wasn't heading for the tram station.

"This way first."

He had to follow her to the stage door. Here waited nothing less than a grand duke from the ballroom scene, complete with black fur cape, with sashed tunic and a white feather crowning an astrakhan hat.

"This is Herr Schulbeck," Lily said to Ferdinand. "We've promised to take him to Dornbach."

"Dornbach!" Ferdinand said, for that was a villa quarter in the outer reaches of the city.

"It's just a couple of miles beyond the soup kitchen," Lily said. "See, we owe him transportation in exchange. He gets us the rehearsal passes."

"'Us'?" Ferdinand said.

"My girlfriends and me. We're always together after the show to sing the songs."

Ferdinand counted boyish-bob haircuts. "Us" added up to six, to which Lily, the grand duke and Ferdinand had to be added. Nine trolley fares. Ferdinand hailed a fiacre-bus, a gentrified covered wagon, canvas painted a chinchilla gray for elegance but cheaper than the tram for larger parties. The grand duke climbed up on the high coachman's seat, next to the driver. The girls piled in through the back, all in a heap of laughter and skirts, sliding themselves along benches on either side of the kerosene stove. Lily sat next to Ferdinand. Her shoulder touching his, yet half turned away, she said—between quick asides to her girlfriends— that Herr Schulbeck was the cousin of the No. 3 Havlicek, he had to sit up front, poor man, where his uniform wouldn't get crushed, otherwise the Opera costume department would have a fit, but at that cheapskate champagne manufacturer's birthday party out at Dornbach, imagine, they'd pay Herr Schulbeck ten lousy schillings only if he showed up in his full *Fledermaus* stage outfit, wasn't that chintzy?

"What is he going to do there?" asked Ferdinand.

"Sing the 'Party of the Year' song, what else?" Lily said, and instantly launched into it with her girlfriends. They then followed with another *Fledermaus* favorite, "O Turtle Dove Who Flew Aloft," then "Drink, My Darling, Drink to Me." During the stop at Turk Place, even while Ferdinand loaded the roll baskets onto the vehicle, they choired "Great Eisenstein, You Mastermind," and they kept singing as the horses trotted on once more, into the far side of the tenement district.

At the Friedrich Engels Platz the driver reined the horses to a halt. The girls fell silent. They helped Ferdinand carry the roll baskets to the truck from whose vats goulash soup was about to be ladled. Some of the girls' hands went to their mouths at the sight before them. It didn't look like a soup-kitchen line. Under the rusty street lamps, in light that was a yellow rash blotching the cobbles, there was a cloud in which not angels but the damned were floating—rags and bones clutching empty soup bowls. Ferdinand knew why they were queuing up along this wall in winter: because of the warming steam that came from the exhaust of the Central Laundry. But tonight the shapes that moved through that hissing mist seemed like something from a weird corner of the Opera. And tonight, for the first time, he saw here a Socialist militiaman with visored cap and nightstick. The man stepped out from behind the truck.

"What's that, what kind of a Fascist joke?" the man asked.

The grand duke, Herr Schulbeck, at whom he pointed the stick, shrank back.

"Some joke," the militiaman said. "The czar throwing us rolls! Not bad enough we're starving? You got to have fun with us, too?"

"Kick down the czar!" someone shouted from the line.

"But that's Herr Schulbeck," Lily said. "He's just an extra, he's getting ten schillings for singing in costume—"

"Kick him down!" they shouted from the line. "Stuff a roll up his ass!" The militiaman reached for Herr Schulbeck.

"Leave him alone!" Ferdinand said. He felt his fingers come together into fists. He was about to lunge forward when Lily's hand stopped him.

"Herr Schulbeck, sing!" she said. "Prove it to them!"

The militiaman had already dragged Herr Schulbeck halfway down from the driver's seat. The white feather on his astrakhan hat was shaking, but he began the song he was to sing at the champagne manufacturer's birthday party.

"*What a joy to be here on this wonderful occasion,*" he sang with a baritone whose tremolos mingled with the hissing of laundry steam, "*so unique, so delightful, it's the party of the year . . .*" The militiaman laughed and let go of his neck. Guffaws came from the mists of the line.

"Get out of here!" the militiaman said, and waved the driver on.

Ferdinand and the girls jumped into the fiacre-bus. The girls giggled and then, wheels resuming their forward clatter, Lily's shoulder against his, they all joined Herr Schulbeck's voice, still sounding from up front. To keep proving that he was not the czar he kept singing desperately:

> *. . . nothing could be more intriguing*
> *than this most enchanting atmosphere. . . .*
> *. . . nothing could be more intriguing*
> *than this most enchanting atmosphere.*

XXVIII

ONCE MORE a cash drought fell on the Spiegelglasses. Berek had to buy three truckfuls of brass sheets to produce the badges for the Social Democratic Party—which would pay only on delivery. The coffeehouse chain for which the tin ashtrays had been made paid only forty groschen on the schilling, having declared bankruptcy. Rent control held down income from Turk Place leases. Demand for blacksmithed utensils fell off. To save the expense of an enameler Ferdinand himself painted and fused the red of the red carnation on the badges, giving up many of his evenings, even weekends, for the job.

There was no time to pick up Lily at the Opera or anywhere else. Occasionally, her voice—clear, high and hurried—would sound into his enameling chamber from the street. *"Markus, throw down my gloves from the window!"* She always seemed to forget something or other in her happy rush. But she never rushed his way, and the silence that followed her call was always a deprivation. Sometimes during that silence Ferdinand would do a childish thing. He would put his little fingers into his ears. He would wiggle the fingers. Her voice would appear again, dancing across his eardrums, surrounded by *Fledermaus* violins and trilling out the song of a soprano about to be kissed, passion resonating even the banality with which she masked it: *"Markus, throw down my gloves from the window!"*

Ferdinand also saw much less of his father, which meant he

saw less of his worry. Berek's fractured wrist healed slowly. More alarming was the fact that he dozed off more often in the daytime. Again and again, it would happen during lunch in the Spiegelglass dining room. His body would stiffen to a stop; his hand holding the fork would petrify, his head become glued to the high back of his chair. His eyes remained fixed unmercifully on the oak-leaf pattern of the wallpaper opposite. He did not look like a man who'd simply fallen asleep with his eyes open. He was a Berek Spiegelglass statue, severely molded and painted, crowning some invisible tomb.

At this, all talk at the table would stop. Then resume, very loudly, in a very frightened way. But noise alone could not wake him. Only Hester had an unfailing method. She'd take a toothpick from the toothpick holder. Lightly, she would lead its point along the inner crook of her husband's elbow. A moment later Berek's eyes would start blinking. He would sit up, his left hand clutching the right in its sling, his face rising through that zone of bafflement to which Ferdinand still had no clue. Then he would resume eating his beef. "The meat needs a little help today," he would say in his old voice, and hold out his left hand, the one that was not broken. "Pass the salt."

Outside the factory Ferdinand saw him only at mealtimes now. Berek had begun to avoid the Café Pellmann. The Turk Place soccer eleven was now doing better, but he attended the games so briefly that his son glimpsed him, if at all, only as a momentary ghost. He no longer went to the synagogue on Fridays, not even to Rabbi Ackermann's final sermon before his retirement. The rabbi, however, did pay a revelatory call on Berek Spiegelglass.

The visit came not long after the Friday farewell sermon, rather early on a weekday morning. Though Berek Spiegelglass had lost the ability to sleep late, he was still the last to come to work at Turk Place. So Ferdinand did not miss him at half past nine. But he was surprised to see Rabbi Ackermann enter the factory— running.

"Herr Spiegelglass! . . . Your father! We need a doctor!"

In less than two minutes Ferdinand arrived breathless at his parents' breakfast table, followed by the rabbi.

"Oh, thank God, he's just dozed off," Ferdinand said.

"Are you sure?" the rabbi whispered. "He's still holding that spoon. It was so sudden. We were just discussing the graves problem—"

"The graves?" Ferdinand did not want to prick his father with a toothpick in front of the rabbi.

"Yes, we were discussing the plans that must be made," Rabbi Ackermann said.

"There's no need to make plans for our graves!" Ferdinand said.

"Your father's eyes are open." The rabbi was still whispering.

"That's all right. What is this about the graves?"

"My young friend," the rabbi said. "He must have mentioned his concern to you. There are new municipal regulations. We live in a state-minded age—but perhaps we should go where your father wouldn't be disturbed?"

"No." Ferdinand felt stronger in the presence of his father's sleeping statue. "What regulations? I know nothing. I've been very busy."

"Then I'll tell you." The rabbi took two steps away from the breakfast table and turned his back to it as though that interposed a discreet screen between him and Berek's slumber. "But first I must say: being principled is one thing—being stubborn is another. You see, there was a grace period in which your father could have effected removal to a regular cemetery. That way he would have remained owner of the site here."

"But he *is* the owner!" Ferdinand said.

The rabbi shook his head. "Now the Jewish Community Council has taken title by eminent domain. I informed your father of the options weeks ago."

"Taken title!" Ferdinand said. "My God! So that's what's been upsetting him! Our graves in our own backyard at No. 1! That's impossible!"

"My dear young man," the rabbi said, "no use railing at *me*, I didn't make the law. But there it is. No grave site can remain in private hands within city limits. Your dear father just refuses to accept facts. Perhaps that's why he didn't pass them on to you."

"Then I don't accept them either," Ferdinand said.

"A loyal son," the rabbi said. "Very rare today. Very commendable. But you could serve your father better, believe me, by being realistic. You can't really stop removal of the graves. But it is, as you say, your own backyard, and you can make sure the council doesn't put it to some unworthy use—"

"We'll make sure of other things as well," Ferdinand said.

"Oh, please, let's not be too sure of anything until we hear each other out," the rabbi said. "Now, the International Survey of Jewish Needs—you may not be familiar with it, but it's an organization enjoying eminent support abroad—it happens that I've been asked to spend my emeritus years as director of its Vienna branch. Now, I would rent your backyard from the council to build our branch office in that space—please let me finish—"

"How much rent does the council want?" Ferdinand interrupted.

"I'm not an accountant, young man, I don't have a memory for such figures, something like a hundred schillings monthly. At any rate, I would build a small office to fit its surroundings, say a minaret—"

"No, thank you," Ferdinand said.

"Wait. Furthermore, and this is very much to the point, as leaseholder I'd control better the removal of your graves. I guarantee that your dear departed ones will find a prominent and honorable resting place in the Vienna Central Cemetery, *and* in addition we'll make your father an honorary member of the Austrian advisory board of the International Survey for Jewish Needs. Does that sound reasonable?"

"I'm sorry," Ferdinand said. "Our graves stay right where they are."

The rabbi shot a glance at Berek Spiegelglass—the continued, open-eyed, spoon-holding ossification of that body. He looked away again, with a shiver.

"Very well, I've tried and I've failed," he said. "I shouldn't have expected any better. I've failed all along. I've never been able to drive out the demon here. This whole fetishism of your family's about your little street—"

"I don't know what you mean by 'fetishism,'" Ferdinand said.

"No, you don't know," the rabbi said. "You had no higher schooling, and your brother—let's not mention him at all. You people never even tried to break out of your narrowness. You don't deserve contact with an organization like the International Survey, scholars of rank on the board, trustees like the Montefiores—no sir, benighted remains benighted—"

Clink!

The spoon, whose bowl rested on a saucer and whose handle had been held by Berek Spiegelglass—that spoon now dropped from his fingers onto the table. The sound was laconic and Berek continued to stare unmoved, unmoving, at the Meissen display plate Hester had hung on the wall. But Rabbi Ackermann jumped. He reached for his houndstooth greatcoat on the chair.

"Thirty-four years at Turk Place!" he said. "God knows I've done my best!"

Ferdinand ran past him, out onto the street and into the factory office. Siddo Berger was away pricing a new enamel supply source, and Schall had the grippe. Office personnel consisted of Conrad, who sat with the telephone receiver clamped between ear and shoulder. This left him free to tap the keys of the typewriter—the first one on Turk Place. "To a certain funny, silky, touchy, sulky Mausi," he had started to type while waiting for the connection.

"Billing department?" he said as Ferdinand entered. "Hallelujah, at last. A very good morning to you from Berek Spiegelglass and Sons. To simplify our bookkeeping we would appreciate having our billing changed from monthly to quarterly—"

Ferdinand took the receiver off his brother's neck and hung it up. "Finish that later. Listen. Can we afford to pay a hundred schillings rent?"

"What?" Conrad said. "For what? What's the matter?"

"Can we—a hundred a month? Yes or no?"

"With our cash troubles?" Conrad said. "Why do you think I just called the electric company about billing? The Wallers Metal people want us to cough up by next week."

"Call Prince Wallers in person," Ferdinand said.

"What?"

"You know, the one who helped us through Albania. Papa always told us about him. Call him in person and request longer credit. You're good on the phone."

"You mean now?" Conrad said. "But he may be long dead!"

"Now," Ferdinand said. "We need money for our graves. Tell you about it later. Call!"

Ferdinand ran back to the Spiegelglass apartment, where Berek still sat as before, and he looked for a toothpick with which to stroke his father's arm.

Later that day Ferdinand did not dare ask the awakened Berek Spiegelglass why he had not let his family in on the problem. He did not dare tell his father that Conrad had—vainly—tried to reach Prince Wallers. A narrowing, fiercening of Berek Spiegelglass's eyes informed his sons that the graves crisis was a subject taboo to anyone but himself. Only once did he touch on it, and that was suddenly, in the factory.

"You'd better not mention anything to Riddah," he said.

Ferdinand, who knew instantly what he meant, shook his head.

"That's her Boas lying there," Berek said. "That's my Tamarah. Nobody lays a hand on them. Tomorrow you come with me downtown."

The next day Berek would not allow his son to help him board the tram, even though his hand was still in a sling. At the municipal-relations desk of the new Jewish Council building, Berek did not take a seat as requested. Therefore, neither did Ferdinand. They waited, standing, until the man excavated a file from some deep trough of papers and began to recite "the state of the situation."

"I know all that from the rabbi," Berek cut him off. "All right, if a person can't own a cemetery anymore, all right, then I'll give it to the council on one condition. You lease it right back to me, for keeps."

"On a condition?" the man said. "Sir, all we are obliged to do is to provide reinterment in a regular resting place."

"Leasing it to me means you'll get rent income," Berek said, "and you people are always crying to me for money in your charity letters, how you haven't got enough to feed the poor in hard times. And *this* money from me you turn down?"

"Herr, uh, Spiegelglass," the man said. "If we leased it right back to you, for your family only, that's just cheating regulations. Regulations now say cemetery space has to be in a framework of communal purpose, like the International Survey for Jewish Needs—that's a framework for communal—"

"All right!"

Berek Spiegelglass had stepped forward so firmly that his boot tip thudded against the front of the desk. A moment later the thud of Ferdinand's shoe tip sounded. "In that case, we'll do something communal," Berek said. "Leave it to us!"

"You'll understand, sir," the man said. "This can't be left vague—"

"A soup kitchen," Ferdinand said. "That's communal. There's plenty of room by the graves."

"A soup kitchen?" the man said. "We already have one for our coreligionists. We couldn't afford to staff another—"

"We'll staff it ourselves," Berek said. "We'll foot the other expenses, too."

"That's very nice," the man said. "But even if that's so, your rent would have to be competitive with what we would get from the International Survey—"

"Which is what?" Berek asked.

"I have a notation here, a hundred and ten schillings a month."

"You'll get a hundred and ten from us," Berek said. "Any other questions?"

"Well, I'll put this through channels," the man said.

"Send me the lease form," Berek Spiegelglass said. "Good day."

*   *   *

Ferdinand, of course, did have a question. How were they going to manage a hundred and ten schillings a month plus staffing and expenses for a soup kitchen? He couldn't ask. In the tram on the way back his father surveyed the passing streets with a frown that decreed Ferdinand's silence. Berek, though, did not fall asleep. Toward the end of the ride his hand inside the sling stretched and tensed like a cat awakening. He looked at it, and that was the only time he spoke on the trip.

"I think it's just about healed now," he said. At Turk Place he didn't go to the factory but fished from his pocket something Ferdinand recognized. It was the long key that unlocked the door to the Brick tunnel.

Ferdinand went on alone to the factory, where he found both visitors' chairs in the office occupied. In one sat an elderly fat man enveloped in a loden overcoat. He was talking in a foreign language to his companion in the other chair, who had not taken off his hat even though he was inside a house. The hat shaded a long nose and a cold cigar, and on the man's lap rested a stag's antlers. Behind the visitors Conrad performed a dance, a joyful but entirely soundless jig he converted into a bow as he stepped forward.

"May I be allowed to introduce"—Conrad's hand fluttered toward the floor before the elderly man—"His Highness—Prince Wallers!"

"Spiegelglass? Oh no," the prince said with a rapid asthmatic voice. "Look at him. Witchcraft. Thirty years later, man's not an hour older. Just taller. How come?"

"How do you do," Ferdinand said. "I think you mistake me for my father."

"Not just you, witchcraft all over this place," the prince said. "What a queer little street. Minarets, no cracking walls, no modern rotting. Where's your republican grime? You people alchemists?"

Conrad stepped back behind the prince and pointed his finger at the prince's ear.

"*How do you do,*" Ferdinand repeated very loudly. "*You mistake me for my father.*"

"Well, then you're another son," the prince said. "Then you'll decay like the rest of us, good boy. That's better. Now we can get down to business. The message you left."

"His Highness was told that we had called him!" Conrad cried happily.

"Yes, our message to your office," Ferdinand said loudly. "We hope you can extend credit on your metal—"

"No longer my metal, no longer my credit," said the prince. "All that's left of us at Wallers Metal is the name. Nix can help you there. *Finita la musica.*"

"Oh. I'm sorry," Ferdinand said.

"No wasting time on sorry." The prince pushed his glasses hard against his eyebrows. "An old saying among the emperor's diplomats: regret nothing, trust nothing, hope nothing. Look at this, next to me. Him nix understand German. This is Mr. Highbirn of Pittsburgh, with my antlers."

He gave Mr. Highbirn a slight push with his elbow. Mr. Highbirn took the cigar out of his mouth and put it back in again. The motion seemed to be in the nature of a bow.

"How do you do," Ferdinand said, though the man still kept his hat on.

"He's the reason I'm here," the prince said. "But he's not my point. What was my point? Yes, my point is, trust nothing, not even robbery. Nothing left of us at Wallers Metal, but they robbed us too nicely. Gave me back my office desk set, my office bottles, I always kept the dullest wines there. They even forward all my office calls. Polite. Too polite. You see my mistrusting that? But I'm here on business."

"Well," Ferdinand said, "my father will be here soon."

"Mustn't forget to warn Father," the prince said. "It's all a bit too thin, this current disaster. The war, the wreckage, the wretchedness, awful and all that, but still a bit pinchbeck. A shade too measly still, touch of tin pot about it, you know what I mean? Sometimes just too nicey-nice. *That's* the clue. Not the real thing, not yet. The real disaster will have integrity, it wouldn't have a Mr. Highbirn coming around. If he asks for a match, you nix have—bestial stench from that cigar—you understand?"

"Some of it," Ferdinand said.

"The real thing, don't worry," the prince said. "It'll be absolutely top-drawer, first-class hell. Might be a dignified thing to die of, for an old man."

"Here is my father," Ferdinand said. "Papa, this is Prince Wallers."

"Ah, bravo, the right Spiegelglass," the prince said. "The right wrinkled Spiegelglass, rat-traps and ball-favors Spiegelglass! Remember when the beard was black and wife Spiegelglass made a ball gown for my mother?"

"Yes," Berek said. "Good morning."

Conrad motioned at the prince's ear.

"Yes," Berek said more loudly. "Good morning."

"Remember my mother?" the prince said. "Mama's little front teeth, a tiny gap there, all her life she had a schoolgirl's teeth. This is Mr. Highbirn, given unto us by Pittsburgh."

Mr. Highbirn's cigar saluted.

"Now, Spiegelglass," the prince said. "Of course you've never met my grandniece Isabel-Marie?"

Berek shook his head.

"She has that tiny tooth gap," the prince said. "In the same place, too. Mama all over again. Loves balls, just like Mama. She's going to marry the postal minister of Albania. I'll throw her a wedding fete grand as we ever had at the old Jockey, with my antlers."

"Wait a minute!" Ferdinand said. "Excuse me, but *Albania*, where you were ambassador? We made coins for them before the war! We can do it again, now that they're really a state—"

"No, no, Italian mint is making theirs," the prince said. "And no such thing as 'really a state' in Europe today. Nothing's real. All counterfeit. But the ball's going to be real. One more time, Mama-teeth smiling at a ball, and antlers are going to pay for it."

"Those antlers?" Berek said, nodding at Mr. Highbirn's lap. Apparently, he had not said it loudly enough.

"Because Isabel-Marie's parents were even more robbed than I," the prince said, "and bride's family throws the ball. It's going to be the Wallerses' swan song, my own, too, in Albania. I'm moving into a hut down there, their savagery's more honest."

"Those antlers can't pay for a ball," Berek said loudly.

"Oh yes," the prince said. "Those and four thousand more like them will. What do you think jumped into my mind when I got your message? Why am I here with a Mr. Highbirn?"

"I don't know," Berek said.

"Five generations of shooting trophies in seven hunting lodges which are all something called breakfast pensions now," the prince said. "Four thousand antlers plus, all in the warehouse." He lifted the antlers off Mr. Highbirn's lap and placed a finger on the wooden mounting. "I believe Mr. Highbirn wants our escutcheon here."

Mr. Highbirn nodded.

"That's where he wants one," the prince said. "On all four thousand plus. He has a corner on the antique-antler business in the New World. They sell higher with escutcheons. Moment I got your message I told him, 'Spiegelglass will make 'em for us!'"

"For how much?" Berek asked.

The prince returned the antlers to Mr. Highbirn's lap, speaking English. Though Mr. Highbirn talked back, the cigar barely wobbled.

"Mr. Highbirn says a quarter dollar per escutcheon," the prince said. "Pittsburgh quarter dollars, let's see, that's more than three schillings."

"Times four thousand!" Ferdinand said, turning to his father. "That's more than twelve thousand schillings!"

"When do you need it and when will you pay?" Berek said, evenly and loudly.

"Ah," the prince said. There was more English.

"Mr. Highbirn must depart for his Pittsburgh Sunday week," the prince said. "He must have the lot before he leaves Vienna. The less real things are, the faster they move. But he'll pay cash on delivery."

"What's your escutcheon?" Berek said loudly.

"Very well, clockwise through our quarterings," the prince said. "Upper left, a bear sejant with crossed roses. Incidentally, you may

choose any one quartering, or adapt. Upper right, a serpent redeemed by a cross on its breast. Lower right, a leopard cradling a
babe, some fool Wallers was Count Palatine of Bethlehem. Lower
left, a winged stallion rampant over three fleurs-de-lis."

"A bear and roses would be easiest for the toggle-joint press,"
Berek said.

"But by the end of next week!" Ferdinand said. "Papa, we
haven't paid for the previous metal, and we've got to order more—"

"That part's all right," Berek said. "We'll pay it all with dollar
cash."

"But the work," Ferdinand said. "To make the tool and the die
and to get the presses ready—"

"That's all right," Berek Spiegelglass said.

"And Schall has the grippe just now. I don't see how we can get
it done so fast even with a bear and roses—"

"How about a red carnation and a crown?" Conrad said. He had
suddenly stepped forward.

"A carnation and a crown?" the prince said.

"A very exquisite crimson carnation," Conrad said loudly.
"Finely leafed, with a fretted stem, and a crown symbolized by a circle."

"Good thought," Berek said. "That's already designed and
tooled. Conrad, bring a sample."

"Carnation," the prince said. "Why not? Bastards of the Ho-
henstaufen line had a carnation in their crest."

"We could do four thousand carnation-and-crowns by next
week," Berek said.

"Up to Mr. Highbirn," the prince said. "He knows what kind of
thingamabob makes a knight out of a gangster. Man's going to turn
Pittsburgh into the Holy Roman Empire."

Conrad, who had run out of the room, came back bearing
Zettl's Social Democratic sports badge as though it were a jewel and
his hand a velvet bolster.

"Why, what do we have here?" the prince said. "What is that?
Looks familiar. Isn't that some Vienna political thingamabob?"

"All tooled and designed and ready to go," Conrad said. "Do you
see the lovely fretted stem? Isn't it an elegant carnation?"

Mr. Highbirn seemed to see it. A brief smile had formed around the cigar.

"Well, long as he approves," the prince said. "It is hereby a fifth quartering of the Wallers blazon. Or does he approve? Wait." There was more English. "Indeed he approves. Only he says, the carnation looks too new. Antique it a touch. Make it look older."

"We just won't polish it," Berek said.

"Done!" the prince said.

He got up with Mr. Highbirn and took a sudden step toward Berek Spiegelglass. "Think we did the right thing?" he said. "You and me? I mean, not dying? Hanging on so long? Into all this fakery?"

"Yes," Berek said.

"Well, you're an alchemist," the prince said. "You're strange, even for a Jew."

"Good-bye, Your Highness." Conrad bowed them to the door. "Good-bye, good mister."

Ferdinand stayed behind with his father. "Now we have enough money to keep the graves," he said—and saw his father smile and raise his right hand.

"No sling!" Ferdinand said. He hadn't even noticed before, during the excitement.

"I can write again," Berek said.

"My God," Ferdinand said. "Is that how this happened just now?"

Slowly Berek Spiegelglass nodded. "I put another message in the Brick," he said.

XXIX

ONE SPRING SUNDAY in 1924 a big stone crash-boomed through the window of the Café Pellmann. Like a cymbal blow it ended the zebra-striped piano's rendition of "Me and My Shadow." After that no further five o'clock tea dances were held at the café. Herr Pellmann said it was too risky to continue something so open to misinterpretation, which could be misunderstood as capitalists disporting amid tenements during such hard and increasingly harsh times. The cook who had made the five o'clock gugelhupfs remained on Herr Pellmann's payroll. But now Herr Pellmann had him prepare a different kind of food: the sandwiches consumed at the Spiegelglass soup kitchen each Sunday instead of the weekdays' hot meals.

This Pellmann gesture started a chain reaction, quite an unexpected one, since the soup kitchen at Turk Place had originally been meant for poor Jews only. The chain started with Herr Skalka—not one of Herr Pellmann's coreligionists. But as the owner of the market inn he was also in the restaurant business, and he didn't want to look stingy in comparison with his colleague. So Herr Skalka sent his busboy to put in an hour overtime daily, on Skalka money, at the soup kitchen. Other Gentile liberalities followed. Herr Milz, the carpenter, constructed a rain roof over the soup-kitchen area in the backyard of No. 1. Herr Schedlmayer, being a barber, could not chime in professionally, but he handed a weekly tip to the No. 1 Havlicek for the extra sweeping that had to be done in the backyard every day.

Berek Spiegelglass himself not only footed the main bill for food and for the personnel of three, but his sponsorship of the soup kitchen helped attract the other contributions. The interfaith character of the project struck Dr. Alexander Funclos one night.

He was the new rabbi of the Turk Place Synagogue and some curiosity attended him. According to rumor he had requested the Turk Place post (known for its difficulty at the Jewish Council office) just because of the difficult man who owned the street. After his first Friday night service he accompanied Berek to the backyard of No. 1. Dr. Funclos was a thin, still rather young man of swarthy, delicate features, whose trousers often drooped over his shoes and whose collar was not always buttoned. His casual way with clothes was not quite in keeping with his careful air. As he crossed Turk Place with Berek, he nodded nods which, though faint, appeared to absorb and interpret the entire experience of each new step. Arrived at the backyard, he covered his small mustache by placing the tips of two fingers on it. Above the heads of the people in the slowly moving soup-kitchen line he saw the tops of two fenced grave markers—Tamarah's door from Varungy and Boas's bicycle, both shining with their new annual coats of black varnish. The rabbi also saw, in the soup-kitchen line, an old woman with a cross hanging down what once must have been a nice blouse.

"That's one of Zettl's people," Berek said. "My night watchman. He gives out tickets to union unemployed in the neighborhood."

"Christians," Rabbi Funclos said.

"Christians gave us a hand in this whole thing," Berek said.

"Interesting," Rabbi Funclos said. And though he wasn't walking, though he just kept standing and watching, he nodded faintly.

As soup kitchens went, the one at Turk Place was really interesting. Monday nights Hester Spiegelglass volunteered behind the food-dispensing counter, accoutered in a snow-white cafeteria attendant's uniform and an intricate turban which made the ensemble look like a Tunisian ball gown. Frau Schall pitched in, in a costume as immaculate (with a toque, not a turban) on Wednesday, for Tuesday might have looked too copycat. Other ladies of both faiths served on other days, the Christians manning Sabbath eve on Friday. Sunday was pick-up-your-sandwich day, needing only Zettl's presence to make sure nobody grabbed more than two. Saturday there were hot meals as usual. But since it was also the day off for the paid staff as well as the regular volunteers, that was when the young people came in—the Spiegelglass twins and their generation in the Turk Place neighborhood. For them the soup kitchen was a duty that became a lark.

For everybody, that is, except Ferdinand. As the strongest, he did the most onerous chores. On the roof garden of No. 6 the cooking was done at the oven Hester had installed years before. From there Ferdinand carried the huge heavy kettles of lentil soup, potato-and-beef stew, and sausage broth down three flights of stairs at No. 6, along the street, to the food table in the backyard of No. 1. He didn't mind that. What bothered him was looking at the poor, the women often treading awkwardly in discarded men's shoes, the men wearing singed jackets from fire sales, the children with their thumbs drilled into their mouths as though stopping up a scream, waiting their turn muted, like shrunken adults.

He told himself that he was much luckier than they. The factory was liquid once more and doing well in mass production. Yet when the poor held out their plates to him, he felt misfortune flow from their gaunt fingers into his bones. A chill coiled through him, and he saw that the world's bustle and brightness were a thin mask for calamity. He pictured bodies splintering in the graves a few yards away. He saw Markus's legs twitching like tormented fish in their formaldehyde aquarium. He saw his father's face clamped by the whiteness of his beard as if by a murderous vise. And the poor frowned at him as though resenting that he, on the rich side of the counter, could not give them, along with the stew, even one spoonful of hope.

But they smiled at Lily, by his side, who cut her mother Riddah's rye loaves and distributed the slices. Lily, now past twenty, was a petite, pretty version of her mother young. A silver headband held down an exuberance of dark curls. In the rush of counter work her hair would expand until it overwhelmed the ribbon. Her mane, swelling, made even daintier and sweeter the features of her small round face. And somehow more forceful, too. Lily was the headlong genie of the Saturday night soup kitchen. It was she who took the risk of making Conrad play cook. (Despite Ferdinand's fears, the gamble paid off. Conrad came up with a *Spezial Beuschl*, a strangely spiced but inexpensive and eagerly accepted lung ragout.) Lily also had the idea of assigning Ossie, Herr Skalka's son, to do the paper-work of checking meal tickets and expense arithmetic. Furthermore, Lily had the nerve to enlist Otto Schönfeld. Schönfeld no longer sported the double-eagle tiepin that identified him as an officer of the bygone imperial army; but since his father's death he always wore a tea rose in his buttonhole to signify ownership of the dis-trict's preeminent florist shop. Lily actually got him to act as bou-tonniered orderly, policing the benches and tables set up in the backyard.

Later in the evening, after the poor were gone, Lily's random yells and quick jokes organized the cleanup details: who would spell whom in washing pots, pans, plates, cups. Everybody played along, not necessarily out of obedience or of charity; partly because of the sponsoring authority of the Spiegelglass name, but most of all be-cause of Lily's zest. And when the work was done, the evening be-came, outright, the party it had really been from the start.

At 9 PM or so they adjourned to the roof garden at No. 6, taking with them the case of beer to which Berek Spiegelglass treated the volunteers. Markus cranked up the gramophone. It belonged to Ilona, but Lily had persuaded her to loan it. Ilona would not use it anyway on Saturday nights, stepping out as she did to those fancy weekend dinners downtown which Berek had agreed to resume with his wife and daughter. But Ilona refused to let her records out of her salon—they were a precious collection of imported American tunes from shows like *Kid Boots* or *Smilin' Through*. So Lily appointed herself the music committee. She bought secondhand discs of *Fled-ermaus* songs, some of which turned out to be cracked and thus marred by clicks. The first time she heard the disturbance she shouted, in her impulsive way, *"Koosh!"*—the Viennese "Shut up!" command to a dog. Immediately, this caught on, and dissonance be-came jollity. From then on, everybody preferred cracked records.

The whole crowd would listen for the clicks, to join Lily in a jocular choir:

> *Drink, my darling, drink to me . . . click-Koosh!*
> *drink to all that used to be . . . click-Koosh!*
> *To the days we used to know . . . click-Koosh!*
> *in the rosy long ago. . . . click-Koosh!*

Soon Conrad devised a new dance around the *Koosh* beat. He called it the two-and-a-half-step—two long glides and a quick clicky dip. It became the group's own tribal rite. Altogether, the post-soup-kitchen bash at the rooftop on Saturday nights was a lot more fun than the Pellmann five o'clock. And Lily was its soul.

Just because of that, Ferdinand could not really participate. The blithe rush with which the girl tumbled through the evening increased the distance between her and him. Often he tried to think of something to say to her; a question sharp or intriguing enough to arrest her for a moment, at least to slow her down briefly so that his hand could reach hers—so that then she would pull him along into the tempo of her reality, into that heady waltz-blown universe where she might have been a playmate in his other childhood.

But what words of his could release such magic? He couldn't even dance with her. At secret sessions, late at night at the factory office, Conrad had taught him the fox-trot. But the very thought of asking her poured lead into his kneecaps. Besides, he felt he was much too tall for so sweetly short a girl. Even if he moved forward gingerly, he might step on stockinged little toes; Lily liked to kick off her shoes when the music started.

Her mother complicated Ferdinand's problem. Riddah had a habit of dropping by the party before midnight. New municipal regulations forbade bakery work during the night from Saturday night into Sunday. And so Riddah spent Saturday evening with the young crowd at the roof garden. Her arrival would be preceded by a huge box of ices delivered from the Café Pellmann—their North Pole Special of vanilla, raspberry and chocolate, as well as the sensational new Malaga-grape flavor. Riddah herself would bring a piano roll.

Without further ado she would plunk it into Hester's old player piano.

"Climbing four floors!" she'd say. "Might as well dance while I'm out of breath!"

From the piano rollicked a Varungy merriment, a Hungarian czardas she and her daughter would begin to dance. Riddah turned astoundingly fast for a woman of her age and girth, but Lily became a downright whirligig. Even Markus rotated in his wheelchair—and everything got worse for Ferdinand. As Lily's limbs spun about, her skirt would rise, a canopy ascending to reveal the round, firm pink-stockinged swell above her knees. Ferdinand would turn away with a fierce jerk. The whirligig, noticing, would slow a little; a Lily-arm would emerge from the whizzing Lily-cloud, not only to calm down the skirt but to imply an invitation in Ferdinand's direction. And he would jump up, galvanized, yet still half furious, and begin to turn with her, since with this dance you needn't be particular about steps. The size and whir of his body would set up a wind. At first Riddah, then Markus, then just about everybody else would stop and watch the pair—till the piano roll came to an end and Riddah shouted, "What are you waiting for? The ices are melting!"

Everybody would rush to the food table, except two. Ferdinand and Lily would stand two yards apart, tremendous high-breathing business unfinished between them.

For a long time things remained unfinished, even on Sundays, when there was a more intimate chance for completion. Sunday was picnic day for the Rooftop Club. But Gentile members seldom came along. The young women went to mass, the men to exercises of the Christian Home Defense Corps of the Conservative Party, which most middle-class lads had joined. And the Jewish Rooftop Clubbers climbing into the horse wagon (Lily hired it every week) greeted each other with a now-we're-among-ourselves wink. With special vibrancy they took up the songs Lily intoned as soon as the horses started trotting. Heartiest among the voices was Markus's. He'd been lifted into the wagon; his wheelchair,

attached to the vehicle by a chain, rattled empty across the cobbles like the throne of an invisible emperor.

At the Kahlenberg meadow, on the rim of the Vienna Woods,
they got out, still singing.

> *Always cheerful, never frown*
> *You'll never get a Viennese down*
> *My Mitzi is an angel*
> *My Mimi is one, too*
> *In a town so lovely*
> *I can be true to two . . ..*

Singing crazy new stanzas improvised on the spot by Conrad,
they foraged the forest edge. That was the practical part of the day:
gathering kindling wood for the three big stoves that would have to
keep a backyard soup kitchen warm in winter. They cut branches
and piled them into the little trailer attached to Markus's motorized
wheelchair. He ferried them to the wagon, where the wood was
stacked. Then the horses got their feedbag and Markus his treat.
Never mind that the Turk Place factory team he had supervised was
dissolved because the workers used their Sunday time for Socialist
militia drills. Now he chugged off happily in his chair to the sports
area of the meadow, where boys ran and soccer balls thudded. The
players were expecting their wheelchair coach. He had his pencil
and paper out, ready to note faulty passing patterns.

The others of the Rooftop Club would heave on their rucksacks
for the hike. Ferdinand was the leader, and it was during their summer outings that he became "Jungle Ferdl" to his friends. He would
avoid well-mannered roads and find instead ghosts of paths tumul-
tuously overgrown. Though he carried the heaviest load—the rucksack with the wine bottles—he'd stride ahead very fast. There was a
secret to his speed. Lily always walked right behind him, and he
could hear her breath only if it was high. His swift pace would draw
from her throat a beat of air which not only tingled in his ears but
prickled down his back. He'd weave the sound into his upward
woodland plunge, up along windings mossy and bark-strewn, up between narrow aisles of oak and chestnut, into spiderwebs flecked by

sun and butterflies, past sudden blue jays all aflutter and scamper-
ing hares. Leaves, burrs, brambles were not wilderness to him but
wealth through which her breathing stirred. He never tired of
launching himself through it.

His routes varied, but usually his destination was the same.
He'd steer his flock close to the very top of the Kahlenberg, to the
"starvation meadow." The Rooftop Clubbers called it that because
they'd arrive famished, parched, gloriously exhausted. They'd throw
the rucksacks and themselves into the tufted, clover-scented grass.
Amid Queen Anne's lace and forget-me-nots they'd drop all in a
heap in which Ferdinand and Lily would be neighbors. They'd all
sigh and stretch and curse Jungle Ferdl fondly for his madness.
They'd unwrap the pungent cervelat sausage, uncork the red wine,
slice into the pumpernickel. They'd pass the cup and lean munching
against one another's backs.

"Look!" Lily would say. Like an extra little sunray, her finger
slanted down to the view below. "It's just the most beautiful city in
the world!" And under her pointing, Vienna did array itself in an
unheard-of grace. To the east its spires, its roofs and domes and
towers were cupped with such ordained gentleness inside the
Danube's pastel curve. To the west the green vineyards dipped directly into ripples of streets. Before the picnickers lay a vision of
seamlessly serene charm. It cleansed humanity of all sorrow and
famine, of anger and slaughter. The horizon overflowed with love-
liness that harmonized, that sanctified.

Not only to Ferdinand but to all of them, to these Spiegelglasses, Schönfelds, Finkelbergs, Pellmanns and Levys, it seemed
natural that their grandparents had crawled away from Balkan starvation to just this redemptive bend of a great river; that here their
parents had risen beyond slum screams into a haven of daily meat
and fresh linen; that they themselves had walked away from the
ashes of the Great War alive, to draw into their nostrils the blessed
aromas of the Vienna Woods. These Jewish girls in arch-Austrian
dirndls, these Jewish young men in Alpine leather shorts, with accents as happily native as if their ancestors had sated themselves for
centuries on the mortal beauty of this afternoon—they felt at home,
singing now:

Each year Vienna's spring blooms
once the winter's done,
But for us when May dies
it's forever gone.
From winter's cold the swallows fly
but back they wing in May. . . .
Not us, good friends—when we go
it's good-bye, my dear, good-bye. . . .

And, having eaten, drunk, sung, rested and looked, the Rooftop Clubbers got up again and put on rucksacks and started the hike down. The sun dropped away westward toward the Alps, the light drifted more softly through the leaves, and the group formed into couples. Otto Schönfeld held hands with Fenky, as Julia Finkelberg liked to be called. Franzl Pellmann's beard tickled Wilma Silber's neck. Max Stelnitz had his arm around Hannerl Lazar's shoulder. Only the Spiegelglass twins were not paired off. Conrad was gone. During the end of the picnic he had developed his usual, rather punctual stomachache. Pretending indignation at the usual jokes, he'd excused himself and run off to catch the tram that would take him to some mysterious, enviably unwholesome rendezvous.

Ferdinand, of course, remained. With the others he sang the *Fledermaus* drinking song Lily had begun, but wistfully, without the funny *Koosh!*

Drink, my darling, drink to me
drink to all that used to be
To the days we used to know
in the rosy long ago . . .
Love is but a fleeting dream
like a sweet-remembered theme
From the golden past . . .

Ferdinand and Lily sang the words, descending shoulder to shoulder. But they walked "with" one another only in the sense that neither walked "with" anyone else. They strode side by side but she still moved in a brighter, faster, more effervescent air. Her interruptions kept breaking the common rhythm of their footfalls. Again and again she'd cry, "Hey, wild strawberries!" And sure enough, beyond a tree stump there was a tiny red constellation nobody else would have spied gleaming among the leaves—gleaming up on a steep hill only she could have climbed as fast. A dirndled chamois, she would clamber, pluck and drop the berries into the little basket hanging from her elbow . . . only to give a squeak. She couldn't get down again. Ferdinand would lift her back onto the path. Each time this was a chance for him. Each time he failed. Even the brief, intense touch of his fingers against her warm linen bodice did not help. It couldn't wring from his lips the right words that would pull him and her into some world where they might unite.

And at first it was no different that particular Sunday. The morning haze lasted into the afternoon, and the club lingered on the hilltop until the city had unveiled itself with a freshness that let Ferdinand pick out, in the vast lake of roofs below, the minarets of Turk Place. On the way down, the light was already a sleepy gold, but that didn't keep Lily from spotting and plucking more berries than ever. This made her lag behind; so Ferdinand did, too.

Not far from the lower meadow, she glimpsed yet another red succulence, dotting a difficult high crag. "Ho-ho!" she said. "They think I can't get them up there!"

As she attacked the crag, he stiffened. If Lily could divine berries behind rocks, Ferdinand could hear danger. Through the twilit foliage male voices filtered, intoning the Austrian anthem. But the tune was stained by the wrong words.

"Stay where you are!" he called to Lily.

The other Rooftop Clubbers were already in the lower meadow, and he ran toward them. They were the only holidaymakers left in the meadow, now that evening was coming on. But near them stood three regimental rows of men chorusing the familiar Haydn anthem and yet singing different words. The men sang around a campfire next to the empty wagon—gone were all the branches the Rooftop Club had gathered. The campfire fed on the wood meant for the soup kitchen.

But it was not at the singers that the Clubbers were staring.

"Markus!" Ferdinand shouted.

Disabled as he was, Markus must have put up a struggle for the wood. His hands were bound tightly to the wheelchair, a gag worked in his mouth, his Social Democratic sports badge had been ripped off with such force that his coat lapel hung down, torn. Tucked into his shirt, like a child's bib, was a sheet from his soccer notepad. Two huge words were penciled across it: COMMIE JEW.

"Deutschland, Deutschland, über alles." The men sang the German anthem that also used the lovely Haydn tune. They sang standing motionless, right arms raised, three tiers of brown-shirted, belted, booted statues. *"Über alles in der Welt . . ."*

Ferdinand lunged through them. His blacksmith's kinship with flames let him seize instantly from the campfire a long branch with one end not yet burning. He snatched it up and brandished it at the singers, who stopped, broke ranks, snarled, shrank back from Ferdinand's savagely blazing sally, formed once more into an attack—and suddenly dissipated into shouts of *"Pig Jew!"* and darkness. A troop of policemen had walked into the meadow. Conrad led them.

Conrad, hurrying ahead to his rendezvous, had come on the scene and rushed straight to the precinct station at the tram terminal. But Ferdinand didn't find out about that until later. He was too busy restraining his hand. It wanted so badly to push the firebrand into the face of the police sergeant, who said, "No sir, no use chasing the National Socialists. The complaint must be registered first—anyway, they had a permit for a solstice celebration though they shouldn't have gotten out of hand like that, and do the Jewish gentlemen have a wood-gathering permit?"

Ferdinand threw the burning branch down before those police feet. He made sure that Markus wasn't really hurt and that he was reviving, and then ran back up the path, cursing, because the light was disappearing so fast. He found the strawberry crag. He couldn't see Lily. He called her name against the coming of the night, again and again. No answer. Then he seemed to hear something below. He ran down once more, and found her standing in the meadow.

She had climbed down from the crag by herself, but she must have fallen. There was a scratch on the roundness of her cheek. She had lost her little basket with all the berries. But she knew everything that had happened on the meadow. Her right hand brushed over her eyes, her left reached for Ferdinand's, amazingly. She had never reached for him before. The others had already boarded the wagon. She made no motion to follow them, her fingers tightening around Ferdinand's.

"Go on!" Ferdinand shouted. "Get Markus home! Go on!"

They stood alone, Lily and he. There was a huge, dim glow from the half-moon sky. There were smaller, sharper glows from livid cinders. He felt something shocking: a sense of victory over her. He was no longer staring helplessly at her effervescence. It was gone, at least right now. She had been jolted into his world. They walked under the same hard stars at last.

They walked from meadow to street. A lantern lit up next to a wine garden. *"Wien, Wien, nur du allein,"* a man's voice sang to a zither while a dog barked softly. They sat down on a bench painted wine-bottle green like the lantern. Her hand brushed over her eyes again. He searched his pocket for a handkerchief to give her. Instead, he found Markus's soccer pad and pencil together with the COMMIE JEW sheet. He must have taken them in his furious confusion. He crumpled the COMMIE JEW and tossed it in a high powerful curve over the fence of the wine garden. The top sheet of the pad still showed the imprint of the insult. So he crumpled *that* sheet and the next one and the next, and he threw them all over the wine-garden fence until COMMIE JEW disappeared. With the same élan that could do no wrong, he then put the pad on her lap.

"Write your name on it," he said.

Her small nose sniffed up a sob.

"My name?"

"Yes. Write it." He gave her the pencil.

"Lily Mainzer," she wrote slowly.

He tore off the sheet, crumpled it and threw it over the fence.

"That's not what I meant. Just write your first name."

"Lily," she wrote.

"Now," he said, "write my last name next to it."

She looked at him. He kissed the pink scratch on her cheek.

"Go on," he said.

"*Wien, Wien, nur du allein,*" sang the man in the wine garden, "*sollst stets die Stadt meiner Träume sein. . . .*"

"Write it," he said.

"*Lily Spiegelglass,*" she wrote.

"That's good," he said. "That's how it will be." Their lips met and the zither rang through the lantern light into the darkness.

XXX

Berek Spiegelglass's "grandson's room," the room for the aeronautical rabbi, was on the upper floor of his duplex at Turk Place No. 5. With Hester's surprisingly bland consent he now assigned that floor to Ferdinand as his married apartment. In its stead Berek annexed an adjoining flat below for himself. Meanwhile, Ferdinand had to content himself with whiffs and glimpses of that happy comet who was his wife-to-be.

Mornings, Lily flitted about the masons who were sealing off the duplex stairs; then she jumped onto the tram to go shopping for furniture. Afternoons, her laugh (it always came in short, quick bursts) could be heard from behind the counter of her mother's bakery. Every customer was the occasion for another little party. And evenings, when Ferdinand was finished at the factory, Lily was away at showers and coffee-and-cake socials with which innumerable girlfriends sent her off to matrimony. The only time he really saw his fiancée was at midday. She'd burst in on the Spiegelglass lunch with greetings and apologies for the disturbance. Quickly, she'd pull Ferdinand aside, shove at him a newspaper advertisement for a dining table or a couch. He would nod, trying to hide both his indifference about furniture and his delight at what would happen next.

"You haven't even looked at the ad!" she'd say. He'd nod again. She'd hiss, "Too bad for you if you don't like it once it's here!" And push all of her small body against his for a second, a push that was an impetuous oblique lightning bolt of passion—and would be gone.

He not only loved his Lily's vivacious hurry; he floated, he basked, he wallowed in the knowledge that before long he'd be able to fall on her swiftness, seize it with lips, teeth and limbs and melt it into his flesh and soul forever.

But that sweet imminence was shot through with—with things that kept happening. They didn't exactly threaten his forthcoming marriage, but they disturbed the prospect unexpectedly. Who would have thought Thea Funclos could be a problem?

At first Ferdinand had no more reason to take great notice of her than did the rest of Turk Place. Of course, Fräulein Funclos seemed rather unreligious for a rabbi's sister. Being a music lover, she never missed Friday matinees at the Konzerthaus, which meant that sometimes she reached the Sabbath-eve services at Turk Place only at the end, to walk home with the rabbi "to our bachelor digs," as Dr. Funclos put it.

Like her brother's, Fräulein Funclos's features were Sephardic— they had a deep olive, Mediterranean, almost nocturnal cast, only they were finer, more handsomely arranged. The abstracted rabbi sometimes wore his tie outside the vest of his three-piece suit. In contrast, she angled her small, tight hats perfectly on her black hair. On a rainy night, picking him up at the synagogue, she'd snap her finger at his galoshes. She made sure he kept them at his office, but he always forgot to put them on. When she strolled off with him, her dark-gray stockings (she never wore flesh-colored ones) displayed not only the slimness of her ankles but the length of her stride—longer than the rabbi's.

One evening Ferdinand had a shock. After sending off a business telegram at the main post office, which remained open all night, whom did he see on the terrace of the Café Landtmann downtown? This same Fräulein Funclos—with his brother, Conrad.

"Conrad," he said the next day, "I saw you last night at the Landtmann."

"You should have said hello," Conrad said easily.

"Don't make it a problem," Ferdinand said. "Please."

"A problem?" Conrad asked, with an outrageously perfect imitation of innocence.

"We had enough trouble with the old rabbi," Ferdinand said. "This one will marry Lily and me. So if his sister is going to be one of your fast jobs—"

"Who says fast job?" asked Conrad.

"I'm serious!"

"I'm serious, too," Conrad said. Or rather he sang it with an operatic inflection. It was a recent habit of his, a device that stopped any inconvenient conversation by turning it into absurdity.

Three days later Hester and Ferdinand were inspecting the wallpaper of his future living room when she said suddenly, faintly amused, that the Havlicek No. 3 had told her that Conrad and Fräulein Funclos had been glimpsed in a fiacre together.

"Have you told my father?" Ferdinand asked.

Hester nodded.

"When?"

"A few days ago," Hester said.

But she couldn't have, since Berek Spiegelglass had said nothing on the subject. Ferdinand had never trusted Hester. It would be no surprise if his brother had drawn his stepmother into a conspiracy. His resentment of Conrad burned along his veins.

"I'm going to tell Papa myself," he said.

And he was about to, that afternoon. It happened to be a Thursday afternoon, when Berek Spiegelglass was usually alone, going over Siddo Berger's payroll figures. It was the right time to bring up the matter and to ask his father to put into the Brick a plea to keep his wedding from harm. But when Ferdinand walked into the factory office, he found not only Conrad sitting by his father's desk but Rabbi Funclos.

"Excuse me," he said, and turned back to the door.

"No," Berek said. "You stay."

"We have news," Rabbi Funclos said. Though at most in his mid-thirties, hardly older than Ferdinand himself, the rabbi spoke in a low, raspy voice. This voice, combined with a faint Greek accent (he had been born in Salonika), suggested an ancient Levantine prophet hidden inside his waistcoat.

"Your brother, Conrad," the rabbi said, "has asked for my sister Thea's hand in marriage. I'm very pleased."

Before he could stop himself, Ferdinand took a long step back.

"There's a three-room apartment just become vacant at No. 2," Berek said. "It might be right for them."

"It's very nice," Conrad said, looking like a cheerful virgin.

Rabbi Funclos smiled. "The flat I share with my sister isn't quite as big."

"Conrad, getting married?" Ferdinand said. "That quick? I mean, very good. Congratulations."

"The rabbi will perform a double ceremony," Berek said. "I will make the rings."

And the young, dark rabbi nodded and, smiling still, gave a soft cough.

Ferdinand could not stop suspecting Conrad's conversion to seriousness. The change was bound so closely to his own future. Yet his brother gave every sign of having become a steady and devoted swain. At the Café Pellmann, Otto Schönfeld reported that—guess what!—Conrad had put in a standing order at his florist shop: one rose to be delivered daily to Fräulein Funclos along with a little envelope which Conrad brought each morning and on which he had not only calligraphed her address but inked a design of something like a starry heaven as viewed through something like an exquisite spiderweb.

Conrad himself now stayed away from the Pellmann, probably to escape the ribbing. Nor did he come along to Rooftop Club outings on Sundays. His free time was spent with Thea at the Konzerthaus, at the Musikvereinssaal or at the Opera. When he was alone, he did homework for their dates together. On his office desk lay the libretto for *Fidelio,* its margins crowded with huge-eared stick figures he'd doodled. While typing business correspondence he could be heard humming in an odd falsetto, but with absolute pitch, the finale of the *Eroica*—Conrad, who'd never been known to pronounce the word "Beethoven" before!

For her part, Fräulein Funclos also appeared dedicated in her approach to the matrimonial estate. Since Conrad was no more furniture-minded than Ferdinand, she, like Lily, did the shopping. But unlike Lily's rounded tables and well-padded chairs, the pieces that arrived across the street had severe angles, sparse upholstery, a Bauhaus purity that was laconic and uncompromising. And that wasn't all. One day, not long before the wedding, Fräulein Funclos got out of a taxi at Turk Place in painter's overalls and a bandanna tightly but not uncharmingly knotted about her head. The cabbie unlocked the trunk to hand her a brush, a bucket and a collapsed ladder, all of which she carried up the stairs of No. 2, her long stride taking two steps at a time.

On the second floor, the floor of her future apartment, she unfolded the ladder. Before a quickly assembled, rather thrilled audience of tenants, she climbed the ladder, dipped brush into bucket and began to paint. Her brisk strokes changed the creamy eggshell of the corridor wall into the color of absolutely clean white snow. This, of course, provoked intervention from the Havlicek No. 1.

"Beggin' pardon of the lady," she said. "She got permission from the landlord?"

"It's been discussed with my fiancé's father, yes," Fräulein Funclos said, her soprano clear and hard as a diamond. "Kindly lift the bucket a rung higher."

For a moment the No. 1 Havlicek stood immobile, then dropped the bucket on a higher rung with a thud. That ended the issue with her. Frau Schall was another matter. She stopped Ferdinand on his way to the factory the next day.

"Good morning," she said. "Your future in-law, we have a very active type there, don't we? She changed the color of my corridor."

"Really?" Ferdinand said, though the story had already reached him.

"Just take a look sometime," Frau Schall said. "So white, it makes your eyes ache. You need sunglasses till you get used to it."

"I wasn't aware," Ferdinand said.

"Well, no use fussing," Frau Schall said. "I'm reasonable. I just hope you're going to be reasonable about what I'm going to ask."

"Ask what?"

"Did you know we're going to adopt a little baby daughter?"

"No," Ferdinand said.

"At my age, it's the only way," Frau Schall said. "I've been dying for a little girl to be a sister to my Adelbert. The baptism will be Sunday, June twelfth."

"Congratulations," Ferdinand said, even as the date sank in.

"So the Spiegelglasses won't be the only ones with a big family event," Frau Schall said, smiling. "The auxiliary bishop himself will baptize our little Klara."

"Wait a minute, the twelfth," Ferdinand said. "That's the date of our wedding!"

"Exactly why I'm bringing it up," Frau Schall said. "It's the Most Reverend's only possible day this month. In fact, he cleared it specially for us, he was my crown prince's confessor. Could you change your date?"

"But our wedding invitations have already been sent out!" Ferdinand said.

"All right, just asking," Frau Schall said. "No fuss. I understand."

"Thank you."

"But then," Frau Schall said, slightly louder, peculiarly fierce, her eyes widening slightly, "then *you'll* understand that we won't be able to be there because we have our own celebration—we won't be able to wish you luck, which we can all use more and more in these times, can't we?"

"Of course," Ferdinand said.

"Of course," Frau Schall said. "Good day."

It was the sort of behavior typical of Frau Schall. But in Siddo Berger the prospect of the double wedding produced an unexpected reaction. Over the years Herr Berger, the Spiegelglass bookkeeper, had become thinner, his cuff links smaller, his tie knots more strangled; at the same time, his clothes had turned darker—Sundays excepted. Sunday mornings he called on Riddah in a suit that was pearl gray discreetly striped with midnight blue. The bakery's ledgers were waiting for him on the living room table. Each time Herr Berger would ask permission to remove his jacket; each time Riddah would yell, "Why not?" from another room. Each time Herr Berger would reply, "I am obliged," and then, his hand falling from his jacket button, mutter that actually it wasn't necessary. He'd sigh himself into the chair and assume a strictly professional frown at all the invoice slips that had no business being in the bills-due pile.

Several Sundays before the wedding he appeared at Riddah's apartment in his gray-blue suit as usual, carrying an umbrella. This was odd because the day was cloudless; Riddah, anxious to get back to the bedroom, where she was sewing her daughter's trousseau, paid no particular attention, though she did notice that the umbrella seemed to give off an elegant smell.

The following Sunday Siddo Berger came again with the umbrella, but this time he blocked the door to the bedroom. He cleared his throat and said, last Sunday he wasn't given the opportunity, but this Sunday, well, he felt it wouldn't do to visit a house where there was a bridal event in the offing without—without marking the occasion. He pulled a rose out of the umbrella. Then he stood immobile while Riddah ran for a vase in the kitchen, masking her laughter in coughs.

The Sunday after that Siddo Berger arrived without an umbrella. Instead, he carried a dozen bloodred long-stemmed roses breathing lushly through tissue paper. He had not made himself clear the last time, he said. By "bridal event" he had meant a certain thing. He had meant that now that the daughter was leaving, the mother would be more alone. Therefore, hope could be expressed that the mother would share another person's aloneness in matrimony, which was never too late.

Riddah threw herself at him with a hug so merry he almost lost his grip on the bouquet. Laughing and squeezing, she said, oh, that was nice, that was a good one, that was sweet, no more marriage for her, but Herr Berger could join her tarok round at the Pellmann, and she wasn't even sure she had a vase big enough for those beauties.

She ran off to the kitchen to search for one, in vain; so she went down to the bakery, where she found a glass cylinder sometimes used for the display of giant poppy-seed sticks, and by the time she got back to the living room only the bouquet was left of the proposal. It lay on the table. Siddo Berger was gone, along with the bakery ledgers.

He never returned to Turk Place, neither to Riddah nor to his cubicle in the factory office. Within a day a messenger came with the bakery ledgers, all bookkeeping brought meticulously up to date. The messenger also delivered two bouquets of silk tulips and roses. An accompanying note was directed to Herr Berek Spiegelglass; it expressed regret that the advancing years forced the undersigned S. Berger to leave his place of employment and that he would be unable to attend the wedding because of his cure in Karlsbad. The attached floral greeting was not only his salute to the two brides but his farewell to a family with whom he had had the honor to be associated for so long.

Berek Spiegelglass hired a new bookkeeper who, while thirty years younger than Siddo Berger, had exactly the same Slovakian accent. Berek sent Herr Berger four hundred schillings' severance pay in an envelope that enclosed a little cellophane bag with a tag identifying its contents: a fragment of Turk Place stucco.

At about the same time, Berek gave away another, smaller masonry souvenir from the street. This one went to Resi, his ancient domestic, whom asthma forced to follow her sister—Riddah's bakery assistant—into retirement. As her successor Berek picked, from over a dozen applicants, a woman named Loisi. Hester Spiegelglass ratified the choice with an ironic smile. To other people it wasn't clear why Loisi had been elected. Her previous experience had been as window washer rather than cook. Only after a while did people notice a resemblance. The new Loisi was a stout redhead in her forties. She suggested, to an astounding degree, old Resi's carrot-top corpulence as a young woman.

Under Hester's tutelage Loisi learned quickly how to boil beef, to candy violets, to dust the innards of a player piano. She was vigorous, ready to serve not only the elder Spiegelglasses but Ferdinand's household in the apartment above. Three days before the double wedding she even painted the window frames of

Conrad's future apartment in No. 2—alas, not with exactly
straight edges.

The next day Ferdinand walked out of the factory with his
brother and saw everyone in the street gaping upward. Three
quarters of the body of Thea, his brother's bride, hung out of an
upper window; equipped with her overalls and bandanna but
without benefit of safety belt, she was correcting Loisi's edges
with daredevil brushstrokes.

"My little Picasso," Conrad said.

It shocked Ferdinand. His brother's face showed no concern,
only a smile curving somewhere between appreciation and amusement. How could Conrad be so casual about his Thea's safety after
he had asked her to share his life? It was another unsettling overture
to the wedding.

That very evening Thea pointed to a notice on the music page of
the *Wiener Tagblatt*: Galli-Curci would sing the Queen of the
Night in the Budapest Opera's *Magic Flute*. "How quaint," she
said. "And just during the week of our honeymoon there. Really
bizarre casting. Now that's something to see."

On the instant, Conrad—the mysteriously new Conrad—called
Budapest long distance. He got the box office of the Royal Hungarian Opera Company to agree to hold four orchestra seats, provided
that the tickets were picked up and paid for by noon of the day following. Whereupon Conrad actually took the train to Budapest. But
even the earliest express back to Vienna would be too late for the
stag dinner planned by the Rooftop Club for the wedding eve. The
event was canceled, not with excessive regret. The Clubbers thought
that with Conrad now so nice, pious and regular, the evening would
have been much less fun anyhow. To Ferdinand this reborn twin of
his was uncanny.

With the stag dinner canceled, Ferdinand could work late on the day before the ceremony. The more he got done now, the less of a burden there would be on his father, who'd have to take on extra chores after his sons left for their honeymoons. It was satisfying to Ferdinand to labor on until after 10 PM. It was also exhausting.

Still, it took him over an hour to close his eyes on this final bachelor night. And when he fell asleep at last, he dropped down into a tight, dense dream. He kept on dropping, sinking past the Brick tunnel into a vast subterranean racetrack he hadn't known existed below Turk Place. He'd never been on a racetrack even aboveground, but he was riding a horse made of warm black marble, which galloped and yet barely moved, while hundreds of women laughed and whispered in grandstands that curved all around him and that rotated like a vast carousel. He thought the laughter meant he was heading the wrong way. He turned the horse around. The grandstands came to a halt, then began to revolve in reverse; his horse's legs thrashed, again without moving forward, and the laughter and the whispers continued.

Apparently, they continued until he woke into his wedding day. But he had no real sense of crossing the line between dream and daylight. When he stepped into the street he saw his father as if in some precarious vision, high up in the air, on the roof of Turk Place No. 5, white beard against blue sky, putting a chisel against one of the minarets.

"Papa!" he cried.

Hester, leaving with her maid to pick up the grooms' rented tails, patted him on the shoulder. "He's just circumcising a minaret," she said. "You know how he is."

"What?" Ferdinand said.

"Just lopping off a bit of metal. He'll make your wedding rings out of it. Let him be."

Ferdinand tried to let things be. But it was like riding the horse on the underground track. There was no motion. The hours passed toward what must be his ultimate closeness with Lily. Yet he didn't seem to come any closer. At the synagogue the wedding rehearsal unrolled with the two retired maids, Resi and her sister, like stooped ghosts, standing in for the two brides. Rabbi Funclos, on the other hand, attended in person. In contrast to his predecessor, he made no fuss over Spiegelglass idiosyncrasies. Berek came in his usual boots, holding a giant needle and dragging a big piece of brittle gray cloth. It was a remnant of the legendary steam tricycle, part of the canvas top which fifty years before had served as wedding canopy for Berek and Tamarah. Now its aged cracks had to be sewn before it could be used again. The twins knew all that because they'd helped their father find the canvas in the attic of No. 5. The rabbi had no idea, yet nodded as though he understood.

Central to the rehearsal, of course, was the Brick. It had been brought up from the tunnel in its cedarwood box and lay now before the Holy Ark, in the cradle where Ferdinand had once puled as a baby. The rabbi didn't question its presence; indeed, he took a tape from his pocket, measured the Brick's dimensions, replaced the tape, and nodded at Ferdinand with a nod as infinitely slow, as nonmoving, as if it were a fragment of the immobility-ridden dream.

And then suddenly, with no perceptible warning from watch or clock, the formal white-tie tailcoat had fastened itself around Ferdinand's body, and he strode through pews into the real wedding. It was a reality he could not absorb. Through some fantastic cloud he saw how darling Lily looked in her lacy white satin gown, whose long formal train was eclipsed somehow by the homey wreath of daisies in her hair; her mother had picked them in the Vienna Woods that morning. By contrast, Thea was a monolithic apparition in a snowy ankle-length sheath; its tastefulness did not relent even when she bent over for a moment in the middle of the ceremony (she was just winding the tallith around the bridegroom) to pick up a large crumb that must have dropped out of the heart-shaped loaf on the altar. Riddah had baked the wedding bread for the two couples.

Standing under the ancient canvas canopy, Rabbi Funclos pronounced, as he put it, "a small preface to matrimony." But hardly anyone understood his remarks. Certainly, they didn't make the occasion more real for Ferdinand. As he smiled at the two bridal pairs before him, Rabbi Funclos said that he had been searching the scripture for the right password that would admit these four lovers—one of them his own flesh and blood—to fulfillment of the conjugal mis-

sion. And no line in the Bible seemed more relevant than the exclamation in the 148th Psalm: *"Praise ye the Lord, ye dragons of all
deeps!"* . . . Why just that line? Because by "dragon" the psalmist
meant "serpent," and there was a very good reason why the serpent,
creeping in the nether depths, was called on to exalt God on high.
For in the divine scheme the serpent played sacred roles, not the
least of which was nuptial. It was through the serpent that Adam's
real troth with Eve was plighted. Before the appearance of the serpent the first couple had led a translunar, otherworldly life of phantom bliss, far beyond the compass of humanity. It was only the
serpent's temptation which brought the Creator's encounter with
the created inside the limits of fleshly understanding. Only through
that temptation was love brought down to Earth. Only through that
temptation was the crucial and instructive nature of man's life with
woman shaped—the life after Eden which was to serve as lesson to
humanity for the rest of all premessianic time. Therefore, he, Rabbi
Funclos, had a wish for the two men and the two women who were
about to bestow rings on each other now, he wanted to wish that
the serpentine in their bond be as strong as the angelic, in all the
prodigious, marvelous ways that the Eternal had intended.

For many minutes after the rite was over, Ferdinand still felt the
warmth of the forge-fresh wedding ring (Berek had made it just before the ceremony); felt the coolness and softness of Lily's lips when
he had kissed them; felt the bafflement of the rabbi's speech spoken
with surprising passion by the hitherto so quiet Dr. Funclos.

The entire white-cloth section of the Café Pellmann accommo-
dated the wedding party afterward. Two huge hearts made of
petunias (courtesy of Schönfeld Florists) graced the walls. Yet to
Ferdinand the celebration limped. Part of it was the fact that a
number of chairs remained unoccupied. They were the ones
reserved for Christian guests, and they were empty for a logical
reason: the Schall baptism at St. Joseph's also took place that day,
and so did the celebration afterward at the Schall flat. In addition,
Herr Schimko happened to be a pew neighbor of the Schalls at

St. Joseph's and was thus obliged to entertain the baptismal fest with his accordion. His substitute at the Pellmann zebra-striped piano tapped out sluggish waltzes which Markus tried in vain to pep up by singing their lyrics energetically and pirouetting his wheelchair. Hardly anybody danced. Finally, Ilona asked Zettl— who wore a militantly Socialist red bow tie with his Tyrolean jacket—to fetch her gramophone. Unfortunately, he brought her Stravinsky records, dating back to her ballet days, instead of the Dixieland jazz.

It was not the presence of the rabbi that was inhibiting; he left early, along with Hester and Berek Spiegelglass. Actually, Ferdinand was glad to see his father retire, since the old gentleman had been through a long, arduous day. Yet the slow mood of the party made it subject to the dream which still persisted in a corner of his brain. It seemed to him that time was getting stuck, just like his dream horse. The wedding itself was like a sequel to the dream, performed in the same tempo. The day kept revolving around itself, making no headway toward consummation. He was getting no nearer to his Lily. She sat next to her mother, who stroked and stroked her arm.

Suddenly, the door slapped open. Schall swayed in, bloated in his dark suit, a man in a trench coat at his side.

"Spiegelglass!" he shouted. *"Come on! Let's dig up that gas main!"*

He held a wineglass he now brought close against his eye as if it were a telescope with which to search remote corners of the café.

"Where're you?" he said. "Spiegelglass, come out! 'Member forty years ago? Boy, did we dig a ditch for that gas main, day 'n' night, night 'n' day, Holy Mother of God, young gods we were—Herculeses! Let's show 'em! We can do it again! . . . Spiegelglass!"

"My father has already retired," Ferdinand said.

"Retired, ridiculous!" Schall said. "We got a long way to go before retired! Come out, Spiegelglass, let's show 'em!"

"I can't wake up my father now," Ferdinand said.

"Shut up," Schall said. "Goddamn Jewish son! I'm sick of children! Baptize an adopted daughter! I don't have to adopt! I can still breed! I can breed fifty! I can dig up that gas main with Spiegelglass, good as ever. Where is he?"

Schall looked about so violently, he had to put down the wine glass to prop himself on Ferdinand's table for balance. That was when Ferdinand saw that it wasn't really a wineglass. It was a glass bubble on a stem. Sealed inside the bubble lay a blue-black curl of hair.

"Right, look at that!" Schall said. "Give that to Spiegelglass. It's his. It'll wake him up. Take it!"

Ferdinand took it. On its base a yellowed label said in Gothic script: "*Souvenir of Bang-Bang Berek Spiegelglass, Turk Place, Vienna, 1873.*"

"Where did you get this?" Ferdinand said.

"Who cares, from that sport." Schall's chin jerked at the man in the trench coat. "Who cares if our hair's changed? Who cares, black or white? We still got muscles. Wake up my Spiegelglass! We'll dig up that gas main. We'll—"

He stopped at the sight of two fat young men in dark suits, entering. Ferdinand recognized them as Schall's nephews. Schall took a step back away from them and suddenly passed out in their arms.

"The sport" in the trench coat now took the same step forward that Schall had taken back. "Good evening," he said with a soft voice but a vivid Italian accent. "Allow me, I am Avvocato Deki. It was I who brought this"—he delicately touched the glass bubble—"to Vienna because I am barrister for Prince Wallers. He was already very unwell when your kind invitation comes."

"A wedding invitation?" Ferdinand said. He knew Prince Wallers had not been on the list. Conrad, who had been in charge of mailing invitations, moved quickly behind his bride just then, so that Ferdinand could not even interrogate him with a look.

"Yes, the prince was much surprised," Signor Deki said. "He told me, 'I will be dead for the festivity, but you go there with this, it belongs to Spiegelglass.' And he is dead now in Albania, and we weep, and I bring this to your festivity because it belongs to you, with my congratulation."

"Thank you," Ferdinand said. "What is it?"

"Some very nice little piece of hair," Signor Deki said. "It was with his effects of a long time past."

"Hey, that's right," Conrad said, emerging from behind Thea.

"Remember Papa mentioning it? That queer Wallers business fellow snipped off his hair or something?"

"So it was my duty to deliver this hair," Signor Deki said. "Only I made a mistake. I went to the *strada* Turk Place to the wrong gala there, and I found this"—he pointed to where Schall had just been carried out—"this celebrating gentleman, and this celebrating gentleman led me here. Here is the proper Spiegelglass festivity? The two sons' marriage?"

"Yes," Ferdinand said.

"I am happy," Signor Deki said. "And who is this beautiful lady?"

"That's my sister, Ilona," Ferdinand said as hands clapped for Ilona, who was bringing in the Dixieland jazz records just then. The Schall spectacle and the Signor Deki surprise had given the party just the needed fillip. But it came too late for Ferdinand, and the merriment sounded mocking, like the laughter at the underground racetrack. The dream dawn of his wedding morning still surrounded him, though his watch showed six o'clock at night.

"We have to catch the night train," he said.

"Ah—honeymoon," Signor Deki said. "Bravo. Is that your taxi with much luggage downstairs? Allow me to take your persons to the terminal in my motor. You will be much less crowded."

The nuptial four changed into their going-away clothes. Then they left the Pellmann amid more unreal applause and jolly hooting and a shower of good-luck candy, none of which budged the wedding toward any culmination Ferdinand could sense with mind or body. Nor did he enjoy being "less crowded" in Signor Deki's Mercedes-Benz. *More* crowding would have been better. Some preliminary closeness to Lily was just what he needed. Instead, the spacious, leather-tufted dignity of the backseat enforced a certain distance. Up front sat the other pair with Deki, Conrad offering a variety of baroque condolences on Prince Wallers's passing. Signor Deki answered with a roar of sixty lions—a savage choir that he let loose simply by gunning the motor. Yes, he said, alas, but at least the sadness had permitted him acquaintance with the Spiegelglass family which he hoped to develop more deeply when he motored through Vienna again.

And then time still did not move, it only liquified. The sixty lions, the leather tufting and Signor Deki's trench-coated bow dissolved into the panting face of the train porter, into a baggage mix-up of what valises were to go in which of the two couples' adjacent sleeper compartments, and into the Pullman porter, who kept saying, "Oh, double happiness to the young ladies, double bliss to the young gentlemen," and grinning until he was overtipped.

After that, finally, Ferdinand was alone with Lily. It didn't help. He remained as far away as ever from consummation. Lily sat on the lower bed of the compartment, crying, with one pump fallen off her little foot, the other one still on, her shoulders shaking faster than the clicks of train wheels against tracks, shaking so fast that the gardenia corsage pinned to the shoulder of her going-away ensemble came undone and fell to her lap. She was sniffling that she hadn't really said good-bye to Mama, she hadn't gotten Mama's real blessing, it had all gone too fast, she wanted to go back. Theoretically, Ferdinand realized that she might be presenting him with an invitation. She wanted to be consoled for the absence of her mother by being overwhelmed by her bridegroom. This was the time to seize her, to stop her sobs with kisses. But his lips were like cloth. Useless, his huge arms hung down by his sides. He mumbled to be excused.

Outside, in the train corridor, instead of revving himself up in solitude, he came on Conrad. His brother had pulled out a jump seat next to an open window and had propped a huge black radio set on it. He was fiddling with the knobs, his jacket off, his collar undone.

"Hey, Ferdl," he said casually, as though he had expected the meeting. "Isn't that a nifty gadget? Thea's wedding present from the rabbi. You know, the serpent lover."

Time still wasn't moving. But the train accelerated into a blackness made vast by feeble, distant lights. "We must be passing near Papa's birthplace," Ferdinand said.

"I guess so," Conrad said. "Look, this radio runs on batteries. Thea says you can tune it better on this side of the car by the open window. I'm trying to catch Radio Athens. Thea says they're doing some Wagner opera in Greek tonight and it's hilarious."

"I see," Ferdinand said.

He heard screeches, whistles, whimpers, perhaps from the radio. Darkness blew in from the window; not just any darkness, but the charged darkness of the Slovakian plain out of which Berek Spiegelglass had come. To Ferdinand those noises now sounded like nightingales, chimerical and crazed, from a Varungy which had long ceased to be.

"Don't look so grim," Conrad said. "Honeymooning is fun. You know, like Wagner in Greek. It's easier to get clothes off a woman when she's laughing."

"Leave me alone," Ferdinand said.

"Just find something that tickles Lily."

"None of your business," Ferdinand said.

He couldn't stand his brother's grin. He hated it all the more because he caught himself envying it in some underhanded corner of his mind.

"Why'd you bother to marry anybody?" he said. "Everything is just laughs to you."

"Wait," Conrad said, ear to the radio. "I think I heard a Greek Valkyrie."

"Did you pick Thea because it wouldn't be serious with her?"

"Serious," Conrad said, nodding to the babblings of the radio. "You serious man, you. You better off than me? Try it my way once."

"Shut up!"

"Just thought I'd be helpful."

And that was most infuriating of all, the idea that he had come out to the corridor for help. Ferdinand grabbed his brother by the front of his starched shirt, lifted him bodily, thrust him away. Conrad let go of the radio. To keep himself from falling he held on to Ferdinand's jacket. The two stared at each other until Ferdinand felt a tiny click near his heart. He released Conrad to open his jacket. From the inside pocket he pulled the glass bubble with the blue-black curl—he'd totally forgotten putting it there. It had been cracked, not broken. But that crack was like a tiny mouth. It breathed at him the scent of his young father's hair, an aroma that also spoke of backroom geraniums in the Turf Café, jinns puffed from Dr. Cirvic's pipe, and the smell of a moonlit village dreaming of birds.

Softly and yet quite fast the wedding day changed into his wedding night at last. The change bristled along the very pores of his skin. Each vibration of the train felt like another massage.

"See you tomorrow," Ferdinand said.

He walked down the car and opened the door to his honeymoon.

XXXI

IT WASN'T that little Leon Spiegelglass liked solitude; he just had a talent for it. This became evident in the fine spring of his fourth year. From April to June of 1928 rain chose to fall only at night. The day was made of dew and sun, and Lily Spiegelglass felt that her child should spend his Maytime in the green. Of course, there were no leafy playgrounds anywhere amid the tenements of the 17th District. On the other hand, most Inner City parks had become unsafe because of political demonstrations. So Lily invented a sort of daily tramway party which departed mornings for a nursery school in the Vienna Woods.

With some other middle-class mothers she boarded a non-smoker car of the 43 line and turned it into a rolling picnic. The mothers offered each other miniature sausages for their second breakfast, passed rolls and in merrily coded language gossiped about Greta Garbo's mannish jackets. Their children licked licorice sticks between making frog faces at one another. Leon sat on the lap that had borne him, no different from the other little boys. But he was the only one to sit *facing* his mother. He insisted on that. He shook his head at licorice (too sticky sweet), and he wouldn't have been able to see the frog faces anyway. Though quite nearsighted, he could never tolerate wearing glasses on the streetcar to the nursery school. The fact was that he had inherited a weakness from his father, Ferdinand: a tendency to violent sneezing, which became worse when spectacles were placed on his nose too soon after he woke up. During the early hours of the day he always pushed the glasses off and thus whisked away most of the world. Unspectacled, cozily unfocused, he put his arms around Mommy's sides, his face against her blouse, and drew into his lungs a commingling of coffee smell, of sausage, eau de cologne, softness, warmth and eternity—cruel thing to lose, all of a sudden, when they had to get off the tram.

Moments later, spectacle wings gripped him behind the ears again. The first thing he would see clearly was Mommy going away with the other mothers and the other kids' refusal to cry. He was the only one with glassed-in eyes that watered. This increased his distance from all the other dry and licorice faces. He had no desire to share the sandbox with such people. Nor did he want to run with them on the meadow. He told the teacher his glasses would break in rough outdoor play and got permission to stay in the "rain room" with Frau Greterl.

Frau Greterl, daughter of the No. 3 Havlicek and once nanny to Ilona Spiegelglass, now worked as a waitress in a night café. Mornings, she came along with the tramway mothers to stay at the kindergarten, ready to take any sick or homesick child home at any moment and, in any case, to take all of them home at noon. For this she received five schillings a day plus copies of every newspaper from Communist to Christian Socialist to National Socialist as long as they contained serialized novels. Frau Greterl stooped over them for hours, compared them to clipped-out earlier story episodes she kept in her pocketbook, and all the while sucked on sour drops with wet noises Leon didn't like. He also disliked her for not letting him close the window. (She needed air because reading the novels made her so warm.) Through the open window came the playtime cries of those dry-faced licorice lickers. They taunted Leon with their fun. Just because of that he could never give in and join them after all.

The only thing he liked about the rain room was the newspapers. Not the back parts with the to-be-continueds over which Frau Greterl tongued her candy, but the front parts she discarded, particularly the front pages. A front page always had bold black lettering that looked angry and suited his mood. Leon sensed a veiled nakedness in words—a feeling that print was the trigger of some succulent mystery.

On previous mornings he had already budged a few letter secrets out of Frau Greterl. But on this morning he wanted more.

"What is that one?" He poked Frau Greterl and pointed.

"You're too young to read," Frau Greterl said. "Leave me be."

"That's an *o* and that one is a *t*, right?" Leon said. "What is this one?"

"Such a pest," Frau Greterl said. "It's an *r*. Now leave me be."

"That's an *f*. Isn't that an *f*?"

"That's right," Frau Greterl said. "But that's enough. You want a sour drop?"

"No. Just tell me this one. Just one more. This one here."

"That's an *n*," Frau Greterl said. "Enough! Go out and play."

Leon didn't. He now had the whole word. He possessed its sound. In fact, he had the whole line of giant, angry letters. And he ran to the open window with the front page that was his conquest, and he shouted, he volleyed at the world out there that excluded him from all its fun, bombarded it with the grown-up, magnificent newspaper wrath he now commanded as his own.

"'*Red Front Threatens Stability of Republic!*'" he shouted.

He didn't know what it meant and he didn't care. But he loved the authority exploding from his lips. It made the sandbox kids look up astounded at the window. A little later he had a problem with a headline which started with "Fascist Agitators"—the third word stumped him because of an unknown letter.

"What is that one?" He poked Frau Greterl.

Frau Greterl grabbed and spanked him. Actually, she spanked him at the right time, just before his mommy arrived. Lily Spiegelglass wasn't supposed to arrive, since Frau Greterl had been paid those five schillings to make it unnecessary for any mother to come at noon. Nonetheless, Lily came, worried because in the morning she had left her little Leon in tears once again. Sure enough, she found him, right after being spanked, still crying, a fact which made the rest of Leon's day much easier.

Lily knew what privileges would console her distraught boy. He was the only child who could return home on the tram with his own mother, sitting on her lap. Furthermore—since it was Lily's theory that her son's low spirits had been caused by a skimpy breakfast—

he could have his lunch early, just with her, eating his ground-veal patty sitting perched on her thighs.

But he couldn't manage a nap afterward. As the future aeronaut rabbi, he had the "balloon room" on the second floor of Turk Place No. 5, and that was where he lay in his bed, staring at the ropes leading from the "gondola" to the ceiling, and he just couldn't manage that compulsory nap. The exercise he'd missed in the morning, while the dry-faced ones had run from meadow to sandbox, wouldn't let him rest. It quivered in his limbs. He put on his little leather shorts over his shirt, knotted his shoelaces because he still hadn't learned how to tie a bow, and tiptoed out of the apartment and down the stairs. There he waited until his parents came out of Grandpapa's apartment after lunch.

"Piggyback," he shouted. "Please, Papa, piggyback!"

"Rascal! Back to your nap!" his father, Ferdinand, said.

"The poor child cried again all morning," his mommy said.

"Again?" Ferdinand said. "All right. Come on."

Piggyback they went through the back door of the house. Papa's giant legs could scale the fence between the backyards of No. 5 and No. 3 with one high stride. They were well on their way toward Leon's secret twin brother. Another high stride over another fence, a veering away from the backyard of No. 1 with the bike and the door sticking up from plots in which, Leon knew, his first grandmama and his other grandfather were sleeping. Then Papa cantered past the factory machines still silent with lunch and out into Turk Place itself, where he galloped fast circles around the streetlamps. Leon rode Papa's neck with a cowboy grip. He half closed his eyes against dizziness and pulled his mouth into a steady grin so that Turk Place children, especially Adelbert Schall, would see his smiling horsemanship. On the other side of the street, before the steps leading down, Papa swooped him off his shoulders.

"All right," he said. "Tell Uncle Conrad lunch is just about over. He shouldn't leave all the office work to Grandpapa. Go on."

* * *

Leon went down the stairs into the bakery cellar. During the day nothing went on here. But in the back storeroom Uncle Conrad and Uncle Markus were whacking cards on a little table littered with money.

"Lunch is just about over," he said.

"Oh, go climb your mountain," Uncle Conrad said.

Leon did. He was very thin but very agile. In one minute he clambered to the peak of an alp of flour sacks. It was a good spot from which to peek down on the top of the big icebox next to the regular icebox and to imagine the peephole on the nonregular one. You looked through it and you saw pink things floating, dipping and rising there, in their special fluid, knees and toes darting past. Uncle Markus had told him that his legs slept inside there. But they weren't sleeping forever, like Grandpapa Boas or his other grandmama in the backyard. The legs could be waked up before too long, when the doctors figured out how to connect them back on. And there was something else floating in the tank: the secret that Leon was not an only child. Leon's twin drifted in these waters like a sleeping mystery fish invisible to all but one pair of eyes. Only Leon knew about him. And nobody could wake him up—not even doctors—only Leon could, as soon as he remembered his brother's name. Leon was sure he'd known it at the moment of their birth together. He had only forgotten it. But it would come to him again someday, by some magic clue. Then he would call it out. It would free his brother from his wet sleep, and together they would adventure through the world.

But this wasn't the day for it yet. The card game had finished in the other corner of the cellar. Uncle Markus rolled his wheelchair to the new elevator that would take him to his patients' cavities, and Uncle Conrad yelled, "Hey, alpinist, we can't leave you alone in the cellar. Grandmama's waiting for you."

And she was, three minutes later and four floors higher, on the rooftop garden of Turk Place No. 6. Grandmama Riddah, huge and white-haired, threw her arms around Leon as if she hadn't seen him for months.

"Lennerl-bashi!" she cried. "You thin, thin Lennerl you!" And pushed a raisin crescent into his mouth.

"I'm not hungry, I cried this morning," he said.

"All right." She put the crescent into her apron pocket and took out a tennis ball instead. "I know you. We'll bomb a party first."

Leon wished his twin were there to join the fun of bombing parties with her. The "parties" were huge screens on which photographs had been blown up; pictures of fantastic costume parties which his grandfather Boas (the one who slept under the bike) had taken during the old emperor's Austria. Every day Grandmama propped such a party against the table, today's being a ball on horseback, the men on white steeds and drinking from wine glasses, the ladies nibbling as they sat sideways in their saddles, all looking very snooty. It was like a fancy grown-up playground that kept Leon at a distance and that deserved to be yelled at. But this one he could punish another way. He took the tennis ball from Grandmama and threw it at the horse party. *Boom!*

"That's right," Grandmama said, picking up the ball. "Let's give it to them. Because of them your Grandpapa Boas had his accident." *Boom!* she threw the ball. *Boom!* went Leon, who picked it up next. *Boom!* . . . *Boom!* . . . *Boom!* . . . until an exciting thing happened. Under the force of the shots the party tipped over, and the little red rooster came strutting out. Before Leon had come to the roof garden, Grandmama had wound up the bird and placed it against the back of the picture so that it couldn't move. But now with the picture fallen, the rooster was set free. Forward it marched with paper feathers quivering, with goose-stepping legs and an open beak that screeched cock-a-doodle-doo!

"Now we have *our* party," Grandmama said and went down on all fours. So did Leon, and they raced the rooster for the tennis ball. Now and then everything stopped: Leon rewound first the rooster (behind the tail), then he rewound Grandmama and himself (on their foreheads), giving himself an extra turn of the key which enabled him to win and made him—for the first and last time during the day—hungry. He ate three raisin crescents, for which he got a crushingly happy hug from Grandmama before she went off to her work at the bakery.

* * *

Of course, this meant trouble later, at the big family dinner. Grandmother Hester (she was never Grand*mama*) sat at the head of her big dining table and said, "Well, our little man still doesn't care for the food here."

"I bet your mother fed him between meals again," Leon's father said to Leon's mommy.

"He's just out of sorts, he was crying all morning," Leon's mommy said. "Oh, Lennerl, don't you like your nice mashed potatoes?"

Leon shook his head. He pointed at Aunt Ilona's plate next to him. Aunt Ilona always ate special "slim" dishes, and the only food at the table that attracted Leon was the onion rings around her broiled herring.

"Onion is garnishing," Leon's father said. "That's not nourishment."

"It's all right," Berek Spiegelglass said. "It's like an appetizer."

And since it was Grandpapa himself who said that, Aunt Ilona instantly gave Leon a lot of onion rings and nobody, not even Papa, bothered Leon for a while. But another problem started as the table talk turned to other things. Leon couldn't follow it and felt shut out. Uncle Markus said that Zettl had broken a tooth in one of his Red Militia fights against the Conservative Home Defense Corps; so Zettl had come to Markus's dental office to ask him to write "root canal work" so that the medical insurance would cover the tooth repair. Aunt Thea gave a sharp giggle and said that politics was getting to be a tasteless farce—unbelievable, this German hysteric she'd heard on shortwave, speechmaking from Munich. And she imitated a feverish man-voice screaming *"German honor! . . . German greatness!"* and Uncle Conrad imitated radio static and everybody laughed, and Leon wished his twin in the tank were with him at the table so that they could joke together and not be left out again as during the nursery school morning. He didn't know what "tasteless farce" meant or "hysteric" or "German honor." But "Red Militia" reminded him of the angry newspaper headline whose words he had picked out while Frau Greterl sucked her candy. At least he had something with which to join the conversation.

"'Red Front Threatens Stability of Republic,'" he said.

This caused the greatest laughter of all. Grandpapa reached out and patted him slowly on the face. It was a very special thing to happen and made him feel good and safe—and drowsy. Suddenly he missed the nap he hadn't taken. His head became heavy on one side. He tried chewing onion rings on the other side, for balance. It helped for only a short while. A red rooster seemed to fly around the chandelier with a cock-a-doodle-doo! The Red Front crowed back with a cry that had in it the name of his secret twin, but just before it became a real word in his ears, he fell asleep.

All of Leon's playmates of those days were family grown-ups, and that included Grandpapa himself. One day, late on a Friday afternoon, his father piggybacked him to the factory office and let him down before Grandpapa and Herr Schall. Herr Schall was as white-haired as Grandpapa but much fatter and more dressed up. He had a little dog with a pushed-in face, called Ying-Yang. At the sight of Leon it barked in Chinese, but it stopped the moment Grandpapa raised his hand.

"Here's my aeronaut," he said. "But he's also a big newspaper reader. Schall, excuse me. I have to find out what's going on in the world."

Grandpapa stuck out his great rough palm and Leon put his much smaller hand inside it. Together they walked across the street to the synagogue. Not to where the pews were, but straight through the wall of the entrance hall. With the twist of a key Grandpapa split the wallpaper into a door that opened. Just inside was a kerosene lantern which he lit. Like a giant snake awakening, a tunnel twitched to the lantern's flame. All of a sudden, Grandpapa sat down on two small wagons lashed together by a cord.

"You see these?" he said. "I used to pull your father and your Uncle Conrad in these when they were little. But now I'm old. Think you could pull me?"

The idea of Leon pulling Grandpapa was even more amazing than the tunnel.

"It'll be all right," Grandpapa said. "I put rubber on the wheels. That makes it easier. You're strong."

Leon grasped the handle of the front wagon. He wished he had his twin out of the tank to help. But he managed just the same. With Grandpapa's legs pushing, too, he pulled the wagons through the musky inside of the tunnel snake.

"Bravo," Grandpapa said. "Very good. Now, what's the big news in the papers? That story about your aeronaut colleague, what's his name, Lindshpook?"

"Oh—Lindbergh," Leon said, remembering the name from the big-lettered newspaper banner he had pronounced at the dinner table the night before.

"Tell me about it," Grandpapa said. "Tell me your news bulletins."

In Leon's mind stirred a number of headlines all the easier to remember for being mysterious. Leon pulled his grandfather and called out these mysteries aloud, and the echo of his voice fell into the same rhythm as the thuds of his shoes and the shadows jumping deeper into the tunnel ahead of the lantern's motion.

"'Lindbergh Engaged to Ambassador's Daughter,'" Leon said, pulling. "Oh yes, and 'Unemployment Reaches Record,' 'Austrian Government Curbs Reds and Nazis,' 'Street Battles in Berlin,' 'Is Charlie Chaplin Bigamist?'"

"Good," Grandpapa said, sitting on the double wagon. "But that's just quick news."

"Quick news?" Leon said.

"I mean, here-today-gone-tomorrow news," Grandpapa said. "But now we come to stay-put news. That's more important, because it doesn't go away. Stop now."

Leon stopped. Grandpapa stood up. He took out his key ring. Before, he had split the wallpaper in the entrance hall. Now, with another key, he split the tunnel wall into a little door that swung back in the lantern light. A neat square hole appeared, with a wooden box inside.

"What's in the box?" Leon asked.

Grandpapa pulled out a sheet from under the box and put the lantern next to it. By its shine Leon saw three big headlines, black and moist-looking, freshly printed.

"Oh-oh, my eyes are getting old," Grandpapa said. "Will you read that for me?"

"'*Great Jewish Temple Destroyed in Jerusalem,*'" Leon read. "'*Turk Brings Temple Brick to Austria.*' '*Varungy Boy Comes to Austrian Capital.*' What kind of newspaper is that?"

"Our Turk Place paper," Grandpapa said. "I publish it myself."

"There's no story under the headlines," Leon said.

"That's because we're the story," Grandpapa said. "I told you, this is special stay-put news. Maybe it's given us enough to think about, for today." He took the lantern out of the hole and closed up the wall and locked it.

"What was in that box?" Leon asked again.

Grandpapa sat down again on the double wagon. "Let's go back now," he said. "You know what all that meant?"

"Oh, I know Varungy." Leon pulled and remembered. "Varungy, that's your old place you told me about. With all the crazy geese. You're the Varungy boy."

"Right, but that's not the start of the story." Grandpapa explained about the Temple way back and the siege of Vienna and the Turkish general bringing a Temple brick to Vienna.

"Did the Varungy boy see it?" Leon asked when they were out on the street again.

"I guess we'll find out from the tunnel newspaper next week," Grandpapa said. "Meanwhile, you were such a help, reading for me and pulling and everything, what treat do you want at the Café Pellmann?"

"I don't know," Leon said.

"They've got good apricot cake," Grandpapa said. "Or gugelhupf? Or strawberry tarts?"

Leon wasn't hungry. But he was curious. "Will the tunnel newspaper explain about Uncle Markus's legs? I mean, about how he'll get them back on?"

"You'll be surprised," Grandpapa said. "Now what are you in the mood for at the Pellmann? I saw a very nice chocolate cream puff."

"I'd like onion rings," Leon said.

XXXII

THE HAVLICEK No. 5, peerless economizer among concierges, believed that a lightbulb needed to be replaced only after it dropped from its socket like a rotten pear from its branch. It was due to this dogma that Leon finally discovered that he and Aunt Ilona had something in common.

The older he got, the stranger seemed this lovely, misty creature of an aunt. Her smile was indecipherable; her lips changed color almost every other hour; her left cheek featured an evening beauty spot which vanished in the morning. And on a dark January afternoon in 1934, when he was not quite ten, he and she walked down the stairwell of No. 5 together. It was a dusky stairwell because of the Havlicek's tolerance for nonlighting lightbulbs. Suddenly, Leon felt Aunt Ilona's hand on his shoulder.

"If you don't mind," she said. "So I won't break my neck."

"Sure," he said, surprised, because the steps were easy and there was a bit of sun coming in from the landing window.

"I wish I weren't so vain," she said, her perfumed touch lingering. "If I wore glasses, I wouldn't have to walk around here with that silly grin on my face."

He didn't know what she meant, which, for some reason, made him blush, which in turn made him glad the light was bad so that she was less likely to notice. "It's nice to smile," he said, since he had to say something.

"But around here I've got to smile all the time," she said. "I can't be rude to people I ought to recognize."

"You mean," he said, "you've got bad eyes, too?"

They had reached the ground floor. Her hand traveled from his shoulder to his cheek. "You and me, Leon. We're both nearsighted loners."

Her hand left his cheek, and she herself was gone with a receding dance of high heels. He understood immediately that a beautiful woman couldn't wear glasses. But it took him a while to grasp that she really was something of a loner like him. She was close only to her mother, Leon's grandmother. The two usually had breakfast together and then withdrew for further conversation to her salon. But afterward, she always put her smile between herself and everyone else at Turk Place before vanishing on unexplained trips downtown with no escort other than her perfume. Yet there was a difference between her aloneness and his. In Aunt Ilona's case the absence of company seemed part of an intricate high adventure. With Leon it was a problem beyond his control.

School meant isolation. The boys from "good" Jewish families in the Turk Place area, like Bobby Schönfeld or Hansl Pellmann, went to a "good" downtown grade school; so did the Christian boys whose fathers were bosses, like Fritzl Skalka. Leon hardly saw any of them. He had to follow family tradition and went to Carlgasse Grade School like his father and uncle before him. The pupils there were all workers' kids who spat out—behind the teacher's back— the word *Sch-schpiegel*glass. Leon was the only Rich Boy in his class. The only boy with thick glasses on a thin Jew nose. The only boy forced by his mother to wear checkered knickerbockers. And, worst of all, the only boy who already knew the whole alphabet by the time old Herr Witsch wrote the letter *a* on the cracked blackboard. Instantly, that branded *Schpiegel*glass a teacher's pet. All of Leon's poor marks in math, history and geography could not make up for that. Not even his abominable handwriting redeemed him. He was, however, a ready scrapper, and his bad-boy muscles inside his good-boy clothes along with his street-urchin agility might have impressed the others in gym. It might have made a difference. But he was excused from gym. His teacher, Herr Witsch, recalled that brawls involving Spiegelglass boys decades earlier had marred physical education periods and declared Leon exempt because of his faulty vision.

Another class Leon didn't take was religious instruction. In the school register the phrase "of the Mosaic faith" appeared only next to his and to no other name. Rabbi Funclos chose not to give a course for just one child. Once, after a Friday evening service, the rabbi mentioned to the Spiegelglasses that he had received an inquiry on the subject from the Jewish Community Council.

"I'll make the right bureaucratic noises to fob them off," he said. "If that's all right with the family."

Berek Spiegelglass nodded. "I've been talking to the boy about his Jewish background," he said.

"Of course, what I really should tell the council," the rabbi smiled, "is that we'll all experience God in due time and that meanwhile He needn't be taught in a classroom, especially not to a Spiegelglass."

"What's special about a Spiegelglass?" Leon asked. The question sounded cheeky, with his father and grandfather standing right there. But he asked it just the same because he wished he had less specialness in school.

"We have the Brick," his grandfather said.

At that moment Leon, who had inherited his father's nasal sensitivity and whose membranes had been irritated by the synagogue's mustiness, sneezed.

The fact was that for Leon the Brick was less a privilege than an exclusion. Everyone in the family had seen the Brick itself. All Leon knew was the wooden box lying in the compartment at the tunnel's end. He would not be allowed to open it until his Bar Mitzvah on his thirteenth birthday.

There wasn't even another underage Spiegelglass with whom to wait out the ban. He must bear its brunt alone. On the other hand, he now possessed a high-class secret as good as the Brick, one which was strictly his and excluded everyone else: his twin was no longer confined to the tank holding Uncle Markus's legs. Leon had learned how to summon him from the formaldehyde waters. He had found out his name.

This discovery would never have come about if he'd done his homework at a "normal" time in the afternoon. He didn't because the faintest far-off cry of other children playing would blow away all his efforts at long division. So he got up before sunrise, at five in the morning, long before other boys became audible, even before the maid, Loisi, began to boil milk. He'd take the fresh roll on his night table; his grandmama had left it there, tiptoeing in after midnight from the bakery. He'd scoop up his valise with his school things in it and steal out of his aeronaut room down to the house entrance hall. Sixty years earlier his grandmother Tamarah had taught Berek Spiegelglass the alphabet here during their courtship nights. In 1934 candles had been replaced by electricity, but the light went out every three minutes unless you pushed a button by the door. This button took the boredom even out of arithmetic. Leon let the light go out constantly. Groping his way toward the button in a recurrent end-of-the-world darkness made homework less tedious and more like a game in which none of the other bed-bound, snoring children could participate.

But the best thing about studying downstairs at that hour was something totally unexpected. One dawn he heard the lock of the outer hall click open. A moment later Zettl staggered in with two huge bundles. As night watchman, he had keys to all the house doors at Turk Place, but this was not night-watchman business. He dropped the two bundles, cut their cords, began to fold the sheets of one bundle into the sheets of the other, using his hook with such feverish skill he didn't even notice Leon. When he did, he froze. Quickly, he mumbled that he'd give Leon a copy of "this secret paper" if Leon wouldn't snitch on him and would give him half his breakfast roll.

Leon nodded. He broke his roll in two. In return he received the fully folded-in newspaper and hid it in the inner flap of his valise. He kept it there until school was over, until long after 2 PM, when he knew that his uncles' lunchtime poker had finished in the storage room of the bakery cellar. The cellar was empty. Nobody could watch or hear him at the formaldehyde tank. Here he took Zettl's secret out of the valise. The mystery paper and the underground silence were like Grandpapa's tunnel journal and the Brick.

"*'Parliament Castrated by Fascist Regime.'*" He read the headlines. "*'Socialist Daily Suppressed—Workers Close Ranks in Self-defense.'*"

He read out loud. But just as in the tunnel he could not open the box holding the Brick, so now his words did not bring his twin out of the tank. He repeated the phrases louder. A fly careened about the lightbulb. Nothing else stirred. And then he saw at the very top of the paper a legend saying *The Laborers' Voice* and, above that, the picture of a red carnation.

He had seen it before, but the sight of it at this moment was a message he was meant to recognize. Only a week earlier in school they'd learned the meaning of first names and how his own, Leon, signified "lion." He remembered the teacher saying that each name stood for something strong or beautiful and that everybody must live up to what he was supposed to be, but most of all he remembered, looking at the red carnation, the name that stood for "flower."

"Florian!" he shouted.

The word ran through the cellar. It set trembling the walls of the formaldehyde tank. From the waters his twin brother Florian rose, hardly wet, dressed like Leon in leather shorts and gray-green jacket, but with strong eyes, no glasses, a heavyweight champion's frown, a warrior's scar on his forehead, fair hair, blond fuzz on his forearms, even on his elbows, and tall for his age, so tall that like Papa he was beginning to bald just a little at his temples. Florian's eyes were light blue and he contracted the left one to show that he was invisible to everybody except his brother.

"There you are," Leon whispered. But was he true? Leon had to put him to a test. "Okay," he said, "with you I can take on that bastard."

The bastard, Adelbert, Herr Schall's son, had been asking for it, having long made the most of being five years older and bigger than Leon.

"Come on," Leon said to Florian. "This way."

They left the cellar by the rear door. From the backyard of No. 2 Turk Place came the sound of Klara Schall roller skating. She was eleven, a year older than Leon, and glided about on a square of asphalt that had been put there at her parents' expense. But the No. 2 backyard also contained an oak, the only climbing tree at Turk Place. Adelbert had told Leon to stay the hell off it because it was his "Mata Hari" tree. He claimed that in its branches lived his own beautiful woman spy, whom he had trained like a human pet; she made love to him at night and reconnoitered Reds by day. "She'd spit at a runt like you," Adelbert told Leon.

"I want to climb the tree!" Leon now shouted, crouching with Florian behind the fence dividing the No. 4 backyard from No. 2.

"Off limits to you," Adelbert said, flicking his little riding whip. He wore bootlike breeches and the white-feathered cap of the Youth Brigade of the government's Home Defense Corps.

"I'm going to climb it!" Leon shouted. "We own that tree! My grandfather owns the whole street!"

"Shush, no baby screaming," Adelbert said.

"We'll show you who's a baby," Leon said.

"Shush, Mata's doing intelligence work," Adelbert said. "Funny Red stuff going on at the market. The government's waiting for our report."

"Liar!" Leon shouted. "There's no Mata Hari up there!"

"How would he know?" Adelbert said to his sister, who'd stopped skating. "He can't even see straight. That little clown made himself half blind with all that studying."

It was the worst insult of all, Adelbert's insistence that Leon was a milksop goody-goody bookworm sissy, when, in truth, he was a rotten student and a terrific athlete. "Come on, Florian," he whispered. "Let's show him."

He vaulted the fence to a Geronimo! howl. At his side Florian stormed forward with such a thrust of formaldehyde odor that Klara screamed and toppled in her roller skates. For a moment Adelbert turned toward her. The distraction created an opening through which Leon rushed. Long practiced on his aeronaut room ropes, he slithered along the oak trunk like upward lightning, clambered onto the tree house inhabited by nothing but an opera glass dangling from a branch, punched the glass into a swinging pendulum—and dropped down on the tree's other side just as Adelbert scrambled furiously up the lowest branch.

"Nobody up there!" Leon yelled, running back to the fence with Florian. "Ha-ha! No Mata Hari!"

"Jew runt!" Adelbert screeched. "You can't even see!"

"I saw!" Leon cried. He'd not only jumped back to safety with Florian but received from Florian, acting as Leon's eyes, a quick-whispered delicious report. Leon shouted it: *"I saw everything! Your sister skates without underpants!"*

And then, though Florian had to leave to return to the tank, though Leon's face was burning with his recklessness, though his lungs and heart were tumbling, he had the most glorious, most un-lonely moment of the day.

XXXIII

ONE EVENING in February 1934 a sensation came to pass at Turk Place. Ilona Spiegelglass stepped out of a long car marked "Blue Danube Productions," trailing a poetic white gown, her eyelids painted a scallion green. Overnight she had become the lady harpist of a nineteenth-century orchestra, with whom Giuseppe Verdi had a brief love affair somewhere in the third reel of a film on the composer's life.

For Leon, to whom his aunt had always been a romantic ghost, this came as no great shock. But his father, Ferdinand—Ilona's half brother—was baffled. What had prepared her for an art as exotic as motion-picture acting? Apparently, there had been no audition, no interview or screen test. Just "a call from the studio," as her mother, Hester, put it, with a smile whose faintness shut off further questions.

In 1934 Ilona was still a very slim and rather piquantly pretty redhead at the age of thirty-one. More than a decade before, Hester had begun to groom her daughter for a culmination so rigorously exquisite that most suitors who left their hats at the anteroom of Turk Place No. 5 soon departed again, discouraged if not dismissed outright. As they came and went, Hester kept buying Ilona books on body-firming diets, entered a subscription in her name to *Die schöne Frau*, developed her taste in nail-polish nuances as well as in matching accessories, devoted much marital combat (all unsuccessful) with Berek on behalf of the 570 schillings it would cost to buy her daughter a mink-hemmed "downtown" cloak cut along Parisian lines. For years Turk Place and much of the 17th District had watched Ilona as the minute hand of fashion.

But could this be her fulfillment now? Playing the minor part of a discarded mistress? Breaking into tears before the camera, again and again, during an opera overture in a make-believe orchestra pit? Whenever Ilona described her activities at the film studio, Ferdinand only felt more puzzled. He couldn't say anything out loud because his father, Berek, seemed quite content. So, obviously, was Hester, though she didn't accompany her daughter to the studio. She suffered from an arthritic stiffness in her left knee but preferred immobility to a cane. Her fixity plus her now regal girth and the size of her hats, which, unlike her hair, became whiter as she grew older—whiter, wider and more authoritative—all this kept people from annoying her with frivolous questions about her daughter.

One person was happily intrigued with this turn in Ilona's life: Thea, Conrad's wife and the rabbi's sister. Thea thought it marvelous how Blue Danube Productions reinvented musical history. Throughout Verdi's time, she said, no women had ever been permitted in opera orchestras. The whole thing was an altogether charming fabrication. Indeed, Ilona invited Thea to come along to the set. Thea did so from then on, armed with the sheet music of *I Lombardi*, the opera of Ilona's crying scene.

Usually, Thea returned vastly entertained, in a puckish good mood. One day she gave Leon a megaphone she'd found discarded among broken props. That it didn't work was all the better for Leon. He used its hidden voice to summon Florian out of the formaldehyde tank. But the megaphone also increased his desire to see his aunt in action as a film performer.

Most of the filming was done early in the evening. Therefore, Ferdinand decided to let his son go to the studio the day Berek would be away in Upper Austria to buy presses at the Linz Machine Fair. In the absence of the patriarch, Leon would not miss a true family dinner. Apart from that, his son's film outing concerned Ferdinand little, though his father's journey was troubling. Ferdinand didn't like to see Berek leave home. The notion still haunted him that the old man's breathing would run down beyond earshot of

Turk Place, like some magically fragile watch that could be rewound only in a certain room.

Another anxiety (he had trouble confronting his father with any of them) had to do with the political situation; it had become quite edgy since the Conservative government had suspended Parliament. Just in Linz, where Berek was going, there had been an ugly outbreak between police and the Socialist militia, now underground. And Ferdinand had yet another misgiving, a bread-and-butter worry: why buy new presses now? Was it wise to invest in new equipment in 1934? The idea of getting new machines came from the initial success of the ski bindings the factory had been making. But skiing, like the film business, seemed uncertain ground on which to stake major decisions.

The ski-bindings venture had begun with Signor Deki, the late Prince Wallers's lawyer, whose Mercedes-Benz convertible had been growling into and out of Turk Place at irregular intervals ever since the twins' wedding. The *signore* had arranged for a supply of inexpensive Albanian steel, which made it possible to manufacture competitively priced stainless bindings. At first, while ski resorts hummed at an altitude far above most businesses' during the depression, the factory had done well with bindings. But then bad times overtook even the snow. Sales melted away. The morning of Berek's machine-shopping expedition, Ferdinand soldered a small batch for a Kitzbühel wholesaler. It was also a final batch. The finality made him brood over the new truckload of steel that would arrive before long, to be processed into bindings for which there was no longer any market. In the middle of such worryings, the office door flew open. Someone yelled out a telephone message from Signor Deki. Ferdinand dropped everything to run to his parents' apartment.

The Havlicek No. 5 was already carrying Berek's suitcase to the taxi. This suitcase, leather with civilized brass trimmings, was Hester's victory; her defeat, on the other hand, sat on her husband's head—when traveling he still wore a Varungy felt cap with bent visor.

"Papa," Ferdinand said. "Deki just called from Salzburg. He's coming this afternoon to see you about something."

"You'll handle it well," Berek Spiegelglass said, walking toward the cab.

"I mean," Ferdinand said, "perhaps you should put off buying the presses. Things might be getting pretty rough in Linz anyway."

"They won't be any better here," Berek said.

"But if you stay for Deki, you could get him to stop that last steel shipment. It's past the cancellation date, but you could—"

"It'll be all right," Berek said.

"Because we have no new orders for bindings and—"

"I know," Berek Spiegelglass said. "I'll be back the day after to-morrow." And the cab was gone.

The cab was gone, and Ferdinand was not even sure his father had fully understood him. Sometimes he thought that Berek's odd fits of deafness were, like other symptoms of old age, only stage effects, produced by his father with a tranquil sort of cunning. It was as if his father devised them to stimulate in Ferdinand a tough tranquillity of his own to make him a better, steadier deputy for Berek Spiegelglass.

He went back to the factory and, with a hand obediently steady, managed to solder nonselling ski bindings until a quarter to four in the afternoon, even though Signor Deki had telephoned that he would arrive before three. As usual, the *signore* was quite late. And when he did come, he went not to the factory but to Schall's apartment. Schall explained that the reason for this was that "in a home the atmosphere can be more private."

Of course, Ferdinand knew the real reason. Herr Schall was playing host to the *signore* on superior orders. Frau Schall wanted the prestige of the Deki Mercedes-Benz convertible parked on *her* side of the street. In her flat Ferdinand found his son, Leon, as well as the Schall daughter, Klara. Both children were to take today's trip to the film studio together, under Conrad's supervision; both bobbed silvery yo-yos which Signor Deki must have given them. Signor Deki himself was telephoning exuberantly while Conrad rotated a third yo-yo, with extremely elegant loops, as he sipped brandy. Ferdinand motioned him aside.

"You know what the rule is in Papa's absence," he said. "If one of us has to leave the factory, the other stays. Somebody has to be in charge."

Conrad put down his glass of Courvoisier. It was the most expensive brand in the house, which Frau Schall had broken out for the occasion. "Just wanted to say hello to the *signore*," Conrad said. "By the way, I can't bring the kids back from the film studio tonight. I'd be too late for the club dinner downtown."

"What club dinner?"

"Don't you know?" Conrad said. "The Rooftop crowd. Some of us old soup-kitchen hands, we're having a sort of unofficial reunion."

Conrad's mustache was freshly trimmed. Under his work smock he wore his gray-and-purple on-the-town tie. It was all such a transparent ruse for tomcatting.

"How do you square it with Thea?" Ferdinand asked.

"Oh, she knows I've got the night off," Conrad said easily. "Brother rabbi's picking her up at the film studio anyway. So now he'll take the kids home as well."

"But who'll take the children *to* the studio?" Ferdinand said. "It's too dangerous now for them alone."

"Zettl," Conrad said. "He'll look out for them."

"I'm worried enough about Papa," Ferdinand said. "You hear all these insurrection rumors on the radio."

"Zettl can protect the kids better than I," Conrad said. "If the Reds start something, he's one of them. I gave him four schillings."

"You've got everything figured out," Ferdinand said.

"One tries," Conrad said, giving up the yo-yo after a climactic loop.

"You won't get away with it in the end!" Ferdinand wanted to shout at him, but Signor Deki was approaching and so he just said, "Thank you, Conrad, for going back to the factory, *right now*."

Signor Deki waved Conrad a florid good-bye, then bowed to Ferdinand. "Good day," he said. "I salute the serious brother. The yo-yos are from the Philippines, a small gift to amuse the little ones, an import item of a firm we have the honor to represent. But *this* is for your inspection."

He thrust a folded sheet into Ferdinand's hand and took a long, meaningfully playful step back. His accent seemed to have gotten lighter since Ferdinand had first met him, less specifically Italian. But his extravagantly lapelled jacket, his aftershave lotion and baroque motions brought a faraway air to Turk Place.

"Your opinion, dear sir," Signor Deki said.

Ferdinand unfolded the sheet. It showed a design sketched with one of Schall's thin crayons: a triangular red-white-red badge with a black crusader cross, the emblem of Austria's Conservative government party.

"Perhaps you would care to make one hundred thousand pieces of this, minimum?" Signor Deki said. "For the government of the Austrian Republic?" His voice suggested, and his face barely suppressed, a colossal grin. He snatched the sketch away again as if it were the center of a risqué, sophisticated, wonderfully amusing conspiracy.

"What an order that would make," Herr Schall said, reverently cupping his cognac glass.

"Signor Deki," Ferdinand said. "Before we discuss any new business, I have to tell you the ski bindings have become a dead item. There's no use buying metal to make bindings that don't sell. I'm afraid we'll have to cancel the next shipment."

"Ah, you dear friend, never be afraid," Signor Deki said.

"It's the new Berlin government," Ferdinand said. "They won't let Germans take money into Austria, and only Germans can afford good bindings these days. I'm sorry. It's too bad."

"Wait, please," Signor Deki said. "Too bad? One minute. Maybe it's not so bad that it's too bad. Maybe! Just one minute." Signor Deki folded his arms and, in a sort of choreographed meditation, began to revolve slowly and ruminatively, his chin resting on his thumb. He seemed to adore difficulties; they made an already exciting world even more flavorful. "Aha." He had come to a halt. "This is really very good what you have told me. This is not sorry at all. I should have thought of this earlier. We can use this. With your permission, the telephone?"

Even as Herr and Frau Schall simultaneously nodded, he dialed and began cascading into the receiver a vivacious, whimsical Italian whose wellspring appeared to be the marvelous fact that the Chancellor Hitler government kept Germans from spending money in Austria. During the cascade Ferdinand went to Schall.

"Did you discuss this badge business with my father?"

"No, the *signore* just sprung it on me," Schall said. "I sketched it from what he told me."

"It's the new government emblem against the Reds," Frau Schall said. "I think it's rather elegant. It's about time we made badges for the right side."

"He says they'll pay nine schillings per gross," Schall said.

"Sounds like a loss proposition," Ferdinand said.

"*Loss?*" Signor Deki said. A moment earlier he had finished at the telephone, just in time to hear in that word "loss" a difficulty so adorable it made him seize Ferdinand's arm. "Loss?" he said. "This 'loss' is spelled o-p-p-o-r-t-u-n-i-t-y!" Arm in arm, he walked Ferdinand up and down the Schalls' Persian rug, from one end of carefully combed out fringes to the other, and asked a series of zestful questions: Why did Monsieur Führer not want German money spent in Austria? Was it not to make Austria dead weak with depression? And why that? Maybe because Austria dead weak made it easier for Monsieur Führer to go *zap*? To eat Austria? Hm? And who did *not* want Austria eaten? Hm? Who? Il Duce Mussolini, that was who! And why?

"You tell me why," Ferdinand said.

Oh, but surely Herr Ferdinand could understand why, Signor Deki said. Herr Ferdinand was the ideal person for understanding this. Herr Ferdinand was the big taking-care-of-things brother with Herr Conrad, was he not? Well, Mussolini-Italy, that was the big taking-care-of-things brother with Albania, protecting Albania against internal political madness. So Italy took care of Albanian mines through finance legalities he, Deki, was arranging. Same way now, Italy must take care of little brother Austria, no? Italy already helped Austria in financial and armament ways, *nein*? But why not also in a propaganda way? Which he, Deki, had just thought of? Why not put two and two together? Arrange extra-cheap Albanian metal to make, cheap, Austrian government party badges? Propaganda against Messieurs Soviet Socialists and against Messieurs German Nazis? Wouldn't that be double good for Mussolini? Keep Austria on the Mussolini side?

"You'd better ask Mussolini," Ferdinand said.

"But precisely!" Signor Deki said. Precisely what he had telephoned just now to his Italian embassy friend, and the friend would telephone the precise question to Rome. With extra-cheap Albanian metal, nine schillings per gross would be possible for the factory? One hundred thousand badges? Perhaps much more? Wouldn't it be a nice thing?

"I'll tell my father when he gets back," Ferdinand said.

"You tell Monsieur Father this is going to save Austria better than ski bindings," Deki said.

"Some people have it really figured out," Ferdinand said. "But I don't think my father could pay commission or anything like that."

"Oh, not at all, out of question," Signor Deki said. "But you say 'figured out.' I have not figured out Turk Place, your excellent place. You are very special personalities here."

"You think so?" Ferdinand said.

"Oh yes." Signor Deki turned to his hostess. "Madame Schall," he said. "Your kind brandy." He bowed; he kissed his fingertips and let them blossom like a flower.

"*Merveilleux,*" he said.

XXXIV

SIGNOR DEKI was still at the Schalls' when the children started for the film studio on that amazing day. Up till then, whenever Leon had left the neighborhood of Turk Place, it had been with his parents. The trip to Nussdorf in the northernmost outskirts, where the Blue Danube film studio was located, took place without his father or mother. That alone made it different.

They didn't board a tram. Zettl said they were getting "a free ride" in what turned out to be an open truck filled with crates that smelled of salami and cheese. Klara Schall, gussied up in a blue silk dress, playing with Signor Deki's yo-yo nervously, constantly, had to be helped on. At the last moment her brother, Adelbert, came along, surprisingly enough, since only the day before he'd said that he considered most films "decadent."

It wasn't only that Adelbert's presence was unexpected. His behavior was unnatural: he didn't bait Leon—not even once. He just kept staring at Zettl and at the streets, which, as a matter of fact, began to look odd, too. Leon's parentless outing away from Turk Place seemed to have thrown the whole city out of kilter. By the time the truck reached the Döblinger Hauptstrasse, most pedestrians had been swept off the sidewalks into the houses. Traffic seemed to have sunk below the roadway's asphalt. Only streetcars were left, and they fell sick as Zettl's truck passed them. They slowed down, clanked to a halt between stations; passengers drained away quickly. Soon all the trams became hulks frozen lifeless and hollow into their tracks.

"Well," Adelbert said to Zettl, "looks like your friends turned off the electricity in town."

Zettl didn't answer. Instead, he yelled at the driver up front. The truck went faster.

"Hooray," Adelbert said, still to Zettl. "That means a general strike. So your comrades are playing revolution. You got your little signal from Moscow."

"Maybe we should go back," Klara Schall said, yo-yoing even more nervously. Leon didn't feel really scared, but he was glad she'd suggested it.

"No, I'm gathering intelligence," Adelbert said, staring at Zettl. "What goodies do we have in these crates, Herr Zettl?"

Zettl shrugged his shoulders. He pushed the iron hook in his right sleeve against the palm of his left hand.

"Smells like food," Adelbert said. "From your Red enclave in the market? Stocking up for a nice big siege somewhere? Maybe in one of your Commie housing projects?"

Zettl didn't answer, but the truck was coming to a stop.

"It won't help you," Adelbert said. "We've got the army ready, artillery and everything. We'll defend our Christian freedom."

"This is the moviemaking place," Zettl said to Leon. "Good-bye."

The next thing that happened, after Zettl had rumbled off in the truck, was Adelbert running. He ran to a phone booth in the street, and then around the corner. He was gone with the children's studio passes, which he carried as the oldest. But they got in anyway. Nobody was guarding the door to keep Leon and Klara out of the huge building. Aunt Thea stood at the gate in a perky beret.

"Good, you made it through all this sudden nonsense," she said. She led Leon and Klara (still bobbing her yo-yo) past a number of doors. "Even the security guards walked off the job," she said. "But the actors will finish the overture scene. Too bad for Verdi, if the film really gets done. But such fun for Ilona. Look."

Leon saw a full orchestra, dazzling in black tailcoats and white ties. It malfunctioned curiously, somewhat like the streetcars. It played without sound. A row of violinists sawed their bows in severe silence. In the brass section, faces puffed with blowing-breath and yet just blew stillness out of trumpets, trombones, tubas. Only the cymbals managed a bearable clash; but the clashing was muffled and perversely independent of the cymbalist's movement, detonating vastly in the distance.

In the middle of it all, Aunt Ilona sat at her harp. Her face was screwed up as if she were distressed by such deaf-mute symphonizing. Somewhere in the dim back of the hall, behind a big box Leon recognized only now as a camera, a deep voice shouted, *"Action!"*

Ilona rose in prompt desperation, kicked at harp strings which gave forth only a strangled twang, and staggered away past three clarinetists working their mouths in vain.

"What's the matter with the musicians?" Leon whispered to Aunt Thea.

"Aren't they marvelous?" Aunt Thea whispered back. "They were Huns last week in the Attila film. Look at the Mongol cellist."

"Maybe the strike is off," Leon said. "The electricity is working."

"Oh, they have their own power here," Aunt Thea said. "Real generators but fake music. In the film you'll hear the Philharmonic dubbed in, God help the poor things."

In the distance the cymbal echoes multiplied and began to sound more and more like cannons booming.

"Where's Adelbert?" Klara sobbed out abruptly. "I want my brother! I want to go home!"

This appeared to change everything. The deep voice shouted, "Cut! Good-bye!" releasing the entire orchestra from its seated soundlessness into men rising, muttering, dropping their instruments, running. Aunt Ilona came up with her enormous teardrops still glued to her cheeks, accompanied by a man in a chauffeur's cap.

"Oh, Leon, there's fighting in the city," she said. "We chose such a poor day!"

"I want to go home!" Klara cried.

"Come along, this driver will take us to a safe place," Aunt Ilona said. But the driver never did.

"My responsibility, if you please," Rabbi Funclos said. "I've promised to take the children home."

Nodding slowly, the rabbi materialized out of huge booms all around—a malevolent, systematic, gigantic beat.

"But I'm sure the taxis are striking," Aunt Ilona said. "You can all use my car, which someone sent for me—"

"I have my little auto," Rabbi Funclos said. "Thank you just the same. Come on, my friends."

Outside, the sun was gone, every lamp dead, each window dark. Something much more drastic than night had come upon the streets, down whose depths the rabbi's car steadily plunged. There was a constant lightningless thunder; under it the black city seemed to be boiling.

From the backseat came a jumpy titter. Aunt Thea put the string of Klara's yo-yo against her mouth and used it as a reed on which to blow a Verdi melody, entertaining Klara so she wouldn't cry. In front, Leon sat with Rabbi Funclos, who said, "Well, no point disturbing *those* gentlemen." He veered the car away from an intersection where his headlights had flashed onto a group of soldiers unspooling barbed wire.

"Let's see," the rabbi said. "We might use this time to catch up on your religious lessons."

"All those booms," Leon said. "They sound like a lot of guns going off."

"'Boom! Boom!'" the rabbi said, shifting gears smoothly. "'Boom! Boom!' . . . It sounds pretty terrible. On the other hand, let me tell you something. In fact, it fits right into our lesson. We have secret teachings in our religion which say that there's a lot more in terrible things than—than just plain terror. I suppose no one's ever told you about the cabala?"

"No," Leon said. He was not only very scared; he had begun to resent Klara for not crying; it might put him in the position of being the first to break down, even though he was a boy. But just this resentment gave his eyes a stiff energy that kept them practically dry.

"Actually, 'cabala' means 'that which is received,'" the rabbi said. "Meaning it's secret knowledge you can receive only with special equipment. For example, an hour ago you needed a radio set to receive a proclamation the government was broadcasting. Without that equipment you wouldn't know that they've declared martial law. You understand me so far?"

Leon nodded. He concentrated on keeping his eyes stiff and dry.

"Good," the rabbi said. "Now, the cabala is like an extra-special, very rare sort of radio that lets you know things other people can't even imagine. Without that special radio others can't hear certain special information. Such as that God had to impose martial law, too, ever since that trouble in the Garden of Eden. Stop me anytime you don't follow."

"I follow," Leon said in a loud, firm voice that was to tell Klara in the backseat that she might as well give up and cry first.

"All right," the rabbi said. "Now, under God's martial law, terrible things aren't really terrible. They're just necessary. Which means that 'bad' is really a mask for 'good.' And it will be like that as long as His martial law lasts, until the time of the Messiah."

"I don't think I like martial law," Leon said.

"Well, no," the rabbi said. "Not the way it sounds right now, if you don't have special equipment. You remind me of the time I was assigned to Turk Place. Most of my colleagues don't have that special equipment, so you know what they said? They said, 'Oh, that's a bad spot, that Turk Place Synagogue, putting up with old Spiegelglass and his quirks.' But I had special information through my cabala radio. I knew that spot wasn't bad one bit. You know what the word 'demon'—Well, hello. I suppose that barricade wants us to stop."

"*Your identification,*" said a steel-helmeted face.

The face pushed into the window the rabbi had rolled down. Rabbi Funclos had his wallet ready. "No Socialists here," he said. "Just a cleric, that's myself, as you can see, and my sister and two minors."

A flashlight stunned Leon's eyes. A gun butt rapped against the car's rear. "*Go!*" the voice barked out of the steel helmet and the rabbi restarted the motor.

"Oh yes, demons," he said. "When you learn Greek you'll find out that 'demon' comes from 'divine.' Like 'bad' is really a mask for 'good.' Take the Great Temple at Jerusalem. That should interest a Spiegelglass. From the cabala radio we know that the Great Temple was built by demons under martial law. Does that surprise you?"

"I never thought about it," Leon said.

Terse shots and long screams mingled somewhere in the blackness. The headlights pinned a rush of shadows, and the rabbi kept going. "Maybe we should stop and hide somewhere," Leon said, hanging on to his anger at Klara, who was barely sniffling.

"Yes, except that if we hide from 'bad' we may be hiding from 'good,'" the rabbi said, driving on. "Anyway, the Great Temple. You can read right in the Bible that our forefathers were forbidden to build it with iron tools. That's because we shouldn't use for worship what we use for war—all those bullets flying around here are iron, of course. And so the Temple builders had nothing hard with which to split the marble chunks. They had to go to Asmodeus, King of the Demons. He gave them a magic worm called Shamir. You touched your Shamir to marble and behold!—boom!—the Shamir cleaved it like a hammer. Later I'll spell that for you, 'Asmodeus' and 'Shamir.'"

"I wish they'd stop shooting," Leon whispered.

"Oh, they'll stop when they find other things to do," Rabbi Funclos said. "Here we are."

He'd braked to a halt on the edge of a pit which, as if by some mistake, had opened in front of Turk Place No. 3. Except for that pit, they were back home.

"Well, look at that, I'd better check the synagogue," Rabbi Funclos said. "That hit a little close."

The savage hole in the middle of the familiar home street was like some weird slide-show image thrown onto the cobbles by the headlights. But even after the rabbi switched off the ignition, in the splintering dark Leon could sense the brutality of that crater. Every few seconds great gleams vibrated, whistled, crashed, vanished. Leon saw, with the fierce clarity produced by the very briefness of a flash, that all six houses of Turk Place still stood unscathed, except for the windows, which had become jagged skeletons. He heard a crunching and chinking: Klara was stepping on glass shards as she ran howling to her family's apartment. The rabbi was gone. Leon was scooped out of the car by his father's huge arm. A moment later his father was gone as well. Leon lay in his mother's arms in the candlelit storeroom of the bakery cellar at No. 6.

Everything was all right, his mother said, rocking him into all-rightness. Grandmother Hester, she said, had just been driven off in a car Aunt Ilona had sent, but that wasn't even necessary because everything was all right and safe right here, even the shell hole next to No. 3, that was just a mistake by a cannon before that rebel troop in the market gave up.

"I hate martial law," Leon said to the arms that enfolded him against it.

But everything was getting all right, Mama said. Uncle Conrad (Leon saw him share a pretzel with Aunt Thea), Uncle Conrad had just come back from the Inner City, where even the telephones were working, he'd talked to Linz, to Grandpapa, who was all right, just the workers had walked out of the factory here and they'd walked out of the bakery, but that was all right too because Grandmama Riddah was using the bakery oven for supper, thank God it worked with coal, they were already roasting chickens there because you couldn't use the kitchen ovens in the apartments, all the gas had been turned off by the general strike.

"Where's Papa?" Leon asked the arms.

"He must have gone to the Schalls'," Mama said. "To remind them, because they've been invited, too. We just added some settings."

Leon saw that a tablelike board had been laid on top of a flattened pile of flour bags. Even napkins had been put out, folded neatly. His mother was making a cellar picnic out of martial law.

"You hear?" Mama said. "That's Uncle Markus yelling down the elevator. He's sending down Grandmama's dishes. Bring them to the table like a good boy. I'd better look after the chickens."

The warmth of her arms kept cradling him after her touch was gone. But that warmth, prevailing even against the explosions that trembled from above, didn't make the world less incomprehensible.

Then shadows preceded a group down the cellar stairs: Herr Schall with a kerosene lantern and a big beer bottle, Frau Schall descending gingerly because of her high heels, Klara squeezing a handkerchief and, last, Adelbert, who wore his white-feathered Home Defense Corps cap and worked a yo-yo on a string he dangled from a hook.

"That's Zettl's hand!" Leon said.

"It's my trophy," Adelbert said.

"Where is he?" Leon said.

"I helped them get him," Adelbert said. "As a reward they drove me back here in an armored car."

"But what happened to Zettl?" Leon said.

"Oh, he'll be taken care of," Adelbert said. "You know what the armored car commander told me? Those Reds had machine guns piled up in their housing projects. Hundreds of them, inside double walls. But their fun is over. We've got the howitzers."

"Leon! The dishes!" his mother called.

He went to the elevator, which creaked down from the gun volleys of the upper darkness bearing Grandmama Riddah's flowered dinner service. The sight of Adelbert yo-yoing with Zettl's hook prickled his skin, yet he resented Zettl even as he felt scared for him. It was as if Zettl and Adelbert played the yo-yo in tandem, in a game meant to baffle Leon. He began to distribute Grandmama's dishes on the flour-bag table and wished he had the cabala radio with which to unscramble grown-up secrets. What was the hidden reason for all the explosions and the shooting and the excitement? The grown-ups talked about "politics," but "politics" was the biggest secret of all to Leon. What was it, and why did it shake the streets and make the darkness jump? Leon's only secret was his twin, but tonight he didn't hear Florian moving back there in the tank—usually Florian gave a tiny confidential splash to say hello. Leon wondered if Florian was being standoffish because there were no Leon mysteries to compare with the great grown-up mysteries tiding and roaring everywhere.

"Ferdl!"

The unfamiliar pitch in his mother's voice sent him running to the cellar stairs. "Ferdl" was his mother's name for his father; sure enough, his father stood in the middle of the steps, at the foot of his own gigantic lantern shadow.

"Ferdl, what's the matter?" Mama asked.

Papa pulled Mama and Leon against him.

"Tell me, Ferdl!"

"The shell that hit in the street." Papa seemed not to speak with his mouth. His voice came through his chest as through a tombstone. "The Brick tunnel got blasted open."

"You went down there!" Mama said. "That wasn't safe!"

"I had to look at the compartment," the voice said. "There's no door there anymore. There's nothing. I looked through all the rubble."

"For the Brick?" Mama said.

The voice didn't answer. Papa's long arms pressed Leon and Mama.

"It's gone?" Mama said.

"I can't tell him," the voice said. "When my father comes back from Linz—I can't tell him."

"It'll turn up again," Mama said. "It's our Brick."

"I searched the tunnel," the chest voice said. "I used two lanterns. All the cobbles came loose. . . ."

"We'll find it when the electricity comes back," Mama said.

Papa's arms heaved. They hugged Leon yet harder and saved him from crying. Often Leon resented his parents because he needed them so. Not now. Not while a shell shrilled in the distance like a crazy bird.

XXXV

FERDINAND could tell his father after all, but only by closing his eyes and blurting out the truth the very moment Berek Spiegelglass returned from Linz. He did that right where they met, on the platform of the West Railroad Terminal. The old gentleman, about to follow the porter to the taxi, stood still. For just one moment.

"As soon as we get it back," he said, walking on, "count the number of slips in the Brick. We've put in seventeen so far."

An offhand certainty lived not only in his tone but in the fact that he didn't even mention the subject until days later, when the workmen came with the pile drivers. "Good," he said then, "maybe they'll help us dig it up."

The pile drivers arrived a week after the crushing of the revolt, three days after the reglazing of windows at Turk Place. Most of the damage in the city was limited to recently built Socialist housing projects which had served as insurgent strongholds. None were near the street of the Spiegelglasses. But there had been a Red communications post at the market, and the shell destroying that had also cracked a water main. Water was softening the ground of the whole neighborhood. Wet earth had to be exchanged for dry, underground pipes must be reinforced, fundaments renewed or strengthened— especially those of the factory, because they supported heavy machines. Around the crater in the Turk Place roadway grew a labyrinth of ditches in which men blasted, drilled and hammered all day. Not since the laying of utility lines decades ago had the street worn such an unfinished look. To Berek Spiegelglass the absence of the Brick was merely part of an interim disorder.

Encouraged by him, Ferdinand had launched a new comprehensive search. Evenings, when the street workers had left, he would come out of the factory with shovel, lantern and a blueprint borrowed from the gang foreman. He had devised a program which would probe every nook of every pit. Once he asked Leon to join him.

"The Brick is somewhere in the street," he said. "You've got to look for the brown cedarwood box it's in."

"I know, I saw the box when it was still there," Leon said.

"*Was?*" Ferdinand said. "It's *still* there, it's just been blown into some crevice by the shell!"

"Maybe the Brick was exploded," Leon said.

"It's not exploded!" Ferdinand said. "It's just missing!"

"Missing like Zettl?" Leon said.

An astounding thing happened. His father slapped him as they stood in the trench together. "Off to bed without supper," he said.

Never had Leon been slapped like that before.

He knew one shouldn't discuss very serious things with Uncle Conrad, but that was exactly why he did just that next morning, out of revenge against his father for the still stinging slap.

"Isn't Zettl missing?" he said when he met Uncle Conrad as he was about to leave for school.

Uncle Conrad was licking a three-flavor, seventy-five-groschen ice-cream cone Leon was permitted to buy only once a week on Sunday. "You could say that of Zettl, yes," Uncle Conrad said. "He's ever so extremely missing."

"I got slapped and had to go to bed without supper," Leon said. "Just because I told Papa the Brick is missing like Zettl."

"Oh," Uncle Conrad said. "Well, you see, the Brick isn't extremely missing. Just temporarily, we think."

"Adelbert showed me that newspaper story," Leon said. "It had a 'List of Arrested Insurgents Missing in Escape.' It said 'Xavier Zettl' on that list. So he's missing. And Papa said the Brick was also missing. So that's the same. So I shouldn't have been slapped."

"Okay," Uncle Conrad said. "Well, let me put it this way. It's not

quite the same. Your Papa is looking for the Brick. Nobody is looking for Zettl."

"Why not?"

"I licked the ice only a couple of times," Uncle Conrad said.
"You want it?"

"Maybe somebody *should* look for Zettl," Leon said.

"Hey. Maybe Ilona is doing that." Uncle Conrad began to laugh
in his peculiar way, opening his mouth hilariously but with only
small, slightly amused sounds coming out. "Maybe that's where
she's gone!"

Even if nobody had brought it up, Leon would have noticed after
a while that his Aunt Ilona was gradually becoming sort of missing, too. Once he asked Grandmother Hester about it. "Oh." Hester Spiegelglass's face tightened. "She doesn't have much time for
us anymore. Now she's an international personality."

International meant abroad. It meant summonses by long distance calls and leather suitcases on which the golden, flame-
shaped initials "I.S." had been tooled; it meant sudden, chaotic
departures—Leon being hugged by Aunt Ilona subtly perfumed,
very tense, glamorously scarfed and always so worried over missing the plane connection at Milano that he never found out where
her real destination might lie. Afterward, neither Grandmother
Hester nor anyone else in the family—not even Grandpapa—
seemed to be able to tell him what films, if any, she was making in
which country.

After a long spell as International Personality she returned for
the opening of the Verdi film in April 1935.

The exciting event took place downtown in the Forum Theater.
Never before had Leon found Grandpapa wearing something like a
dinner jacket. (Berek, eyes tightly closed, had allowed Hester to
knot a black bow tie around his neck.) And though Grandpapa wore
boots, they were short and shined. Hester, for her part, had consented to a cane for the occasion and with its help thrust her mon-

umental embroidered figure into a cab. Ilona joined them in the same taxi; Ferdinand's family followed in another.

At the Forum Theater, Leon saw Aunt Ilona jump from the car without waiting for Berek or Hester. Ferdinand, having noticed this, muttered something to an usher uniformed like an imperial dragoon and quickly led Leon down a side aisle of the orchestra.

"I'm not sitting with you?" Leon asked his father.

"This is the children's section," Ferdinand said, and vanished.

It just wasn't true. Adults were finding their seats here. All of a sudden, the evening had changed from glamour to disconcertment. Then Leon saw Aunt Ilona come down the aisle. The vehemence of her stride churned her long blue gown. "Hello, Leon!" She plumped down next to him. "We so seldom get a chance to talk. How are you? Do you enjoy school, how are your teachers?"

It was astounding. She spoke with such vivaciousness, yet her eyes kept blinking. She seemed close to crying. It encouraged him to blurt out, "I don't want to sit alone!"

"They just want to spare you a family fight." Violently, she unsnapped her handbag's silver clasp. "But you won't sit alone. I'm seeing this with you. I'm not going to sit with *them*. I'm not going to have that fight. I'm going to relax with you."

Left and right, dinner jackets and décolletages rustled. Through their sounds came clinks from Aunt Ilona's handbag, so harshly did she rummage through it. "Why don't we chat," she said. "Let's enjoy ourselves. Tell me nice things about school."

"They're letting me take gym now," he said. "I'm doing fine in that. In Latin, too."

"And the other subjects?"

He shook his head.

"Not all right?"

He shook his head.

"Good." She was still rummaging. "Keep it that way. Get them used to a little disappointment."

"What?" he said, flabbergasted.

"Your parents," she said. "I love Ferdinand and Lily. But don't you let them do to you what Mama has done to me."

"What'd she do?" Leon said.

"It's so ridiculous. I'm so sick of it. I shouldn't burden you with it." Aunt Ilona finally found a lacy handkerchief. "I'll never be perfect enough for Mama. I must have the perfect career. The perfect man. Absolutely perfect, like Papa's street is perfect with the Brick. Mama wants me just as perfect, to get even with him. Nothing I do is perfect enough. The company I keep, no good. My—my life situation, no good. Even my belt is too broad. . . ."

She couldn't go on. She dabbed her face. "I shouldn't throw this at you. I'm sorry. Forget it." As the chandelier overhead darkened, her voice became a little calmer. "Mama's right in one thing," she said. "My eyes are no good. I'm too nearsighted to see my own film." Her kid-gloved fingers touched his. "Could I ask you a favor? From one nearsighted Spiegelglass to another? Would you loan me your glasses?"

He took them off and gave them to her.

His cheek stung deliciously with an aromatic kiss, and he never really saw her in the film. Without glasses he could only make out blurs on the screen, blurs that surged about to loud singing or passionate whispering. Here and there he recognized snatches of his aunt's strained voice.

After the film he got another kiss, and then his father appeared to send him home by cab.

Next morning Grandmother Hester's new cane lay broken into many pieces in her dining room. Ilona had left for her international activities again. This time she was gone not only as a physical, perfumed person but also as a subject of conversation, at least within Leon's hearing. Nobody mentioned her, and everybody had something to do in another room when he asked what had happened. Grandmother Hester took to baking chocolate-threaded gingerbread hearts, which, Leon was told, had been her hobby as a young wife. She also bought a brown miniature poodle called Majesty who could shrug his shoulder after eating his mistress's candied violets and to whom she sang the "Voices of Spring" waltz. The player piano accompanied her; earlier she'd had it moved from the roof garden across the street back to her living room.

From that time on, all of Ilona's mail came addressed to Leon. It consisted of postcards showing a Parisian cathedral or an Italian harbor town. On the writing side you had to decipher small outbursts of pink lettering stuttered between pink dots: *"Leon, dear . . . tell family all's well . . . hugs and kisses . . . Ilona."*

Aunt Ilona's postcards tingled with distance at a time when Leon seldom left the district. Before, on Sundays his father had often taken him to the amusement park. Now, instead of the Cannibals' Kraal and the Grotto of the Moon, there was just hot chocolate at the Café Pellmann. Papa was too tired for outings. The nightly search for the Brick had bleached his cheeks. He'd slump the Sunday away on coffeehouse upholstery, next to Berek's tarok game. He leafed through the financial news and yelled at Leon for using chairs as practice race hurdles.

All this changed with the emergence of Lily Spiegelglass's "condition"—some exciting disorder which Leon's parents promised to explain soon. Meanwhile, it required a pillow on her chair, put color back into his father's face, and produced swells of ebullience from Grandmama Riddah.

"Outdoors! Outdoors!" Grandmama said. "Let my girl breathe! Come out with me in the cottagers' bus!"

The cottagers were poor families whom the city had given, free, prefabricated huts on small plots of fertile earth by the Danube so that they could farm their own vegetables. Every Sunday the bus carried a charity safari there, sponsored by the Bakers' Guild and scandalized by Leon's Grandmama. The bus had a green cross painted on its side, and when it rolled into Turk Place that Sunday, Riddah boarded it along with Leon and his parents. Inside sat fourteen master bakers' wives, serious hats on permanent waves, cake-fragrant boxes on their laps, staring. They stared at Leon, who toted a sack of rye loaves, and at Grandmama, who staggered up the bus steps with a big box full of scratchings and cheepings.

Quickly, the other ladies retreated into seats further back to give her more room. Grandmama plumped down in the first row with Leon but she wouldn't let Leon's parents join them. "Never sit above the front wheels!" she said to Lily as the bus bounced forward. "Never ever in your condition! Always between the wheels, for no jolting! Make room for her in the middle!"

The ladies made room. "Want to see my pee-pee-peepers?" Grandmama said to Leon and tapped the box which she'd brought earlier in the day from the 17th District monthly live poultry fair. She opened a flap. A darling chaos of minute beaks and golden feather balls spilled out.

"Oh, please!" said a lady two rows back, with a tray of glazed chestnuts balanced on her knees. "Please, they'll escape!"

"Not from me they wouldn't," Grandmama said. She just chirped softly. The tiny feet stopped, the beaklets fell silent. Then the chicks turned around and scrabbled back to Grandmama's lap. She shooed them all back into the box. All except one, which lolled between her fingers like a tweeting blond tennis ball. "That's him," Grandmama said. "That's Bissy. You know about my Bissy?"

"Sure, a pet you once had," Leon said.

"I still do." Grandmama rubbed her nose against the chick's fluffy belly. "My Bissy wouldn't die on me, not for keeps anyway. See, there he is, a baby all over again."

"But that's not really him," Leon said.

"Who else?" Grandmama said. "See his left little leg? That spot by the toe? That's Bissy. You can't mistake him."

She dropped the squeaky tennis ball into the box. "Now we'll leave him alone, so he can grow up quick this morning. He'll be flying by noon."

"Really *fly*?" Leon asked.

"Listen, we're not talking about just another chicken," Grandmama said. "That's *Bissy*."

"But how can he have real wings by noon?"

"You'll see," Grandmama said. "Whoom. High up and across the Danube. Whoom, zoom!"

A few minutes later they got off the bus and Grandmama nodded at wooded hills by the river shore. "Off with you two," she said to Leon's parents. "Willows and pines and moving water, there's no better air. Walk and breathe! Nothing like it for your condition. Take her, Ferdl."

"I ought to carry the loaves," Ferdinand said.

"Lennerl is doing fine with them," Grandmama said. "And he'll see Bissy fly. Off with you two!"

Off Leon's parents went, while Leon accompanied Grandmama to a cabbage patch where a gray-haired couple had built a shed to shelter the chicks Grandmama gave them. Leon handed them the loaves. To escape their thanks Grandmama simply rushed off—and bumped into the glazed-chestnuts lady.

"Oh, Frau Maiss, good," Grandmama said. "Come along. I'll show you who should get your treats."

She pulled both Leon and Frau Maiss toward an open field. Half a dozen children were working over something on the ground; so was a man, bending down from what Leon at first thought was a camp stool. It turned out to be Uncle Markus on his motorized wheelchair. He had motored out here separately in it.

"Markerl," Grandmama said to him. "This is the nice widow Maiss of the Maiss steam bakery. Frau Maiss, this is my dentist son, Markus. He's been widowed, too, you might say, widowed of his legs, except the time will come when the doctors—"

"Mama, please," Uncle Markus said. "How do you do."

"He's wonderful with children," Grandmama said. "Soccer, checkers, kites, you name it. He could really complete a family. How many little ones you have, Frau Maiss?"

Frau Maiss held the tray of glazed chestnuts away, to protect them against the moist exuberance of Grandmama's mouth. "Mine are not little anymore," she said. "They are over twenty."

"I bet Markus could make them feel like puppies again," Grandmama said. "I just bet! And who knows? Maybe you feel like starting a little one? Markus is—"

"Mama!" Markus said. "If you could give us some room here, Mama. I think our kite is ready."

"Sure," Grandmama said. "Everybody stand back! Look!"

Leon saw the thing on the ground. It was a huge red kite in the form of a rooster whose left leg had a spot. The children had just tied a cord to a hook on its tail.

"I told you," Grandmama said to Leon. "There's Bissy all grown up. See, Frau Maiss? That's what little ones can do with Markus around."

"Here are some sweets for them," Frau Maiss said and put the glazed-chestnuts tray down on the grass. "Good day."

"Where're you going?" Grandmama said. "Markus will show you how that rooster flies."

"There's not enough wind. Good luck," Frau Maiss said and vanished behind the green-cross bus.

"Bissy doesn't need more wind!" Grandmama shouted. "Frau Maiss! . . . Such an impatient woman. Come on, we'll show her, not enough wind!"

"Mama, I do think we should wait for an updraft," Uncle Markus said.

"Wait, nothing." Grandmama tossed the cord spool at Uncle Markus and handed Leon the rooster kite. "Let's go, Lennerl. Run! Everybody run! Make wind! Huff, puff! Here we go!"

She pushed Leon, who started running with the flaring rooster in his hand. Grandmama ran alongside. The other boys stomped with him through the grass.

"Don't hold Bissy back if he wants up," Grandmama said.

Leon nodded, running.

"Let him go when he has no weight," Grandmama panted at his side.

"He still has weight."

"Keep running! Markus, give Bissy enough slack!"

"He still has weight," Leon said.

"Watch. . . ." Grandmama chirped the little chirp she'd given in the bus to make the chicks scurry toward her. The big rooster, as if remembering the sound, promptly fluttered its long red wings and lifted itself off Leon's hand.

"There he goes!" Grandmama cried.

The rooster wavered, dipped, leveled off, rose again at a low angle and then soared so steeply, so lustily into the sky, his sunward leap made Leon's blood jump.

"Terrific!" he shouted.

But Grandmama said nothing. She had stopped running. Leon

glanced back and found her standing transfixed, turned in the wrong direction. Uncle Markus had turned his chair that way, too. The kite's cord spool, fallen from his lap, unwound wildly in the grass, like a berserk animal. In the distance, at the foot of the river-shore hill, stood a man in shirtsleeves, holding something big. Grandmama and Uncle Markus began moving toward him. Leon followed, too, though his nearsightedness still veiled the urgency.

Not until he was closer could he see that the man was huge, as tall as the young trees around him. It was his father, carrying his mother in his arms. Her face was buried against his chest.

"She fell!" Papa said. "She always has to pick strawberries! I told her to be careful!"

"Lily!" Grandmama shouted. "My Lily!"

"She is bleeding," Papa said.

Leon saw no blood. Papa's jacket was wrapped around his mother's middle.

"It's because we still don't have the Brick!" Papa said. "Don't just stare! Call an ambulance!"

But for a long moment Leon could not take his eyes from his father, who stood there, trembling, with his burden. Then Leon turned to Grandmama, who was running off, roaring something he couldn't understand. Uncle Markus sat in the wheelchair with his head thrown back; he blinked up at the sky, as if asking help from the kite. There was no help. There was no kite. The red rooster had vanished. Bissy had fallen into the sun.

Three days later Lily Spiegelglass, back from the hospital, hugged Leon with such force, he felt she'd pressed some of her pallor into his own skin. Soon she looked like herself again. Her chair no longer needed a pillow. In fact, she hardly ever sat down because she busied herself so, organizing the Rooftop Club's reunion outing. Nobody mentioned her condition anymore, but everyone talked about the outing.

It took place on a fine Sunday in August, excluded Leon and the other children and started with nostalgic horseplay. The men patted the size of each others' stomachs. The ladies teased those among them who had violated a rule of their youth by wearing makeup on a hike. But everyone agreed that they were all as fit as ever; it was only their hiking mountain that had seen better days.

The brushland, for example, had developed a nasty picket fence which prevented a reenactment of the club's wild ascent. On the concrete path they now had to follow, Jungle Ferdl could not repeat his trailblazing feats of old. Instead, he walked at Lily's side carrying her raincoat along with his rucksack—the sort of coddling that wouldn't have done at all on the original club hikes and for which he had to take a lot of ribbing.

Conrad, on the other hand, provoked jokes because he was the only husband to arrive wifeless. His Thea had gone to an art opening, he explained. This touched off merry speculations on how he would exploit her absence.

Reaching the "starvation meadow" at the end of their climb, they came up against a shock. Barbed wire. Unremittingly, it bristled around the entire meadow from whose center grew, like some titanic weed, a needle fifty feet high. A Home Defense Corps guard with a bandoliered belly stood by a gate that announced in harsh lettering: SPECIAL TRANSMITTER FOR SECURITY FORCES. EMERGENCY COMMUNICATIONS AREA. OFF LIMITS.

Since the civil war everyone in Vienna had become used to guns and warnings. But this was something like a desecration. It was a rude trespass on a dear memory.

"Oh, really?" Conrad said. "Stay here."

He went straight to the guard. Five minutes later he returned with a face somehow too solemn to be serious. "Let's go," motioned his head. He led the astonished troop through the gate which the guard—smiling—had creaked open.

"Quiet till we get to our spot," Conrad said between his teeth.

Nobody spoke until they reached their old picnic ground, way beyond earshot of the guard. "You see," said Conrad with Balkan gutturals, "we was Montenegro soldiers in World War. We so sorry now we fight Austria that time."

"*What?*" Franzl Pellmann said.

"But we lucky when we captured, we put in PW camp here. Beautiful Vienna city, such good people. I tell guard, we mow grass this meadow, make much hay so cows have milk for Vienna children hungry in war."

"He swallowed all that?" Franzl Pellmann said.

"I show my Montenegro army badge. I tell him, we all fall in big love with Vienna in camp, *ach* charm, *ach* music, everything. When we go back to Montenegro we save up money from hog raising, sixteen years we save, we spend it on this trip with wives we married, we show them view from mowing-for-the-children meadow, we sing beautiful songs we learn here, and this Home Defense butterball thinks we're great, so let's get out the goddamn salami."

Which had them all collapsing into the meadow with laughter as well as with thirst and hunger. And never mind that the men wiped away sweat from hairlines higher than those of a decade ago. Never mind that some women ate their salami sandwiches unbuttered to keep their waistlines from getting still further out of control. Never mind that the exquisite panorama, from vineyards to Danube, was now filigreed with barbed wire. Never mind. The Montenegro prank had pumped youth back into the club's veins and not one of its members forgot one word of the old song as they sang:

> *Each year Vienna's spring blooms*
> *once the winter's done,*
> *But for us when May dies*
> *it's forever gone.*
> *From winter's cold the swallows fly*
> *but back they wing in May . . .*
> *Not us, good friends—when we go*
> *it's good-bye, my dear, good-bye . . .*

On the way down from the hill the reunion hike could not be quite true to the descents of yesteryear. There was no breaking up into couples, bachelors holding hands with girls. Instead, the husbands walked ahead together, arguing about whether to trust the Anglo-French resolve to keep Hitler out of Austria. After them ambled the wives, discussing hair dyes and salad diets. The Spiegelglass twins came last. Conrad stopped often to search for the right kind of grass blade on which to whistle a tune. Ferdinand had joined him. By walking behind the ladies he could keep an eye on his wife.

"Your Lily's all right," Conrad said. "You needn't keep worrying."

"Actually, she got over it very well," Ferdinand said. "I feel better about it, too."

"Good," Conrad said, and plucked another blade of grass.

"It's just as well to wait with another baby until times settle down," Ferdinand said.

Conrad blew on the blade. "That one sounds too fluty," he said. "I'm looking for a sax sound."

"Did you hear me?" Ferdinand said.

"Sure," Conrad said. "Sure you should wait with babies, especially with no Brick. Say, God forbid, it's a boy. What kind of circumcision would it be, Brickless?"

"Is that why *you* are waiting?"

"Huh?" Conrad said. "Me?"

"You and Thea, with having a baby."

"Me and Thea." Suddenly Conrad bent over double, clutching his sides.

"What's the matter?" Ferdinand said—and saw that his brother was contorted with soundless laughter. "It's not funny," he said.

Conrad wheezed helplessly.

"You didn't have a child even before the Brick was lost," Ferdinand said. "I always wondered. But I knew you wouldn't answer straight if I asked."

Conrad was still bent over, choking with hilarity.

"Stop it!" Ferdinand hooked his hands under his brother's armpits and straightened him up with one heave. "I might as well tell you," he said. "I even mentioned it to Papa once, about you and Thea. He said it's all right, but *I* don't think it's all right! I mean, you're married to Thea, but there's no—I've never seen anything real between you two!"

"Real." Conrad wiped tears of amusement from his eyes. "I don't get a kick out of reality. There're better jokes."

Ferdinand pushed his brother against a tree. "Don't play games with me."

"Ow," Conrad said. "My back."

Ferdinand let him go. "You never want to grow up," he said. "For God's sake, you're forty-five years old! Like me! But if you have a child when we get the Brick back and things settle down—you'll see, it'll help you become more responsible."

"Okay," Conrad said. "Here goes a mental note. 'Become more responsible when things settle down.'"

"Stop clowning!"

"Okay, I'm serious," Conrad said. "I swear." He dropped the grass blade and stepped on it. "I swear I'll become truly responsible the moment things truly settle down. Like the moment I see a real green piece of grass that won't go yellow on me in the morning. Okay?"

"You're playing games again," Ferdinand said.

"Hey, here's a juicy one," Conrad said. He plucked another blade and put it between his thumbs. In the timbre of a soprano saxophone he blew the melody they'd all sung earlier on the high meadow with the barbed-wire lacing:

*Each year Vienna's spring blooms
once the winter's done . . .*

The same month Berek Spiegelglass suspended the family's communal evening meal. He said it would resume as soon as Ferdinand had found the Brick. Until then, Hester explained, there was a practical problem: Ferdinand never gave up his search before half past nine at night; Hester's cook, Loisi, could not keep such late hours, they gave her insomnia. Furthermore, both Hester and Lily agreed that such hours would bend Leon's preadolescent system the wrong way. And so, as part of the general interim disorder reflected by the construction work on the street, the Spiegelglass family dinner fragmented.

After his nightly Brick search Ferdinand supped with Lily at the Café Pellmann, at ten. Rabbi Funclos acquired a freckled woman from Lower Austria who cooked an infinite variety of omelettes for the rabbi, for his sister, Thea, and her husband, Conrad. The elder Spiegelglasses ate at home around half past six, before Hester's arthritis began to hurt; Majesty slumped in Ilona's chair while Leon was still busy fighting his way through the graphs of his math homework. Leon himself had supper at seven, his usual time, but in the kitchen with Loisi.

He ate at the butcher block which served as Loisi's table and which stood by the kitchen window. He could look across the backyards of Turk Place to where his two grandparents lay, behind No. 1. No matter how often he turned his back, he turned again to look once more. Until now he had not been too conscious of the graves. In the winter the same snow that covered everything else covered those things, too, and blurred them away. In the summer their grass merged into the greenness of the shrubbery all around. But now the backyard had been partly dug up to check on the water main. Though the plots themselves remained untouched, the foliage around them had been cleared. Now those queer grave markers stuck up into the air all by themselves and seemed to keep rising: the spider-wheeled bike that was Grandpapa Boas; the repainted yet blistering door that was Grandmama Tamarah. They stood out even at night. They changed color as the breeze moved electric bulbs which had been strung above them by the construction gang.

The graves disturbed Loisi, too, but for different reasons. She had bought herself a radio with her Christmas money, and evenings she liked to tune the shortwave to Berlin, where "somebody was finally doing something about the people's troubles." The doings, however, never emerged clearly from the loudspeaker. You heard garbled exhortations, marching bands, male speaking choirs, all overlayed by some metallic blare. No matter how you shifted the dial, the disturbance drowned out every intelligible word. Loisi said it was the fault of the backyard graves. Corpses always fouled up electricity. When Leon, interested, asked how, she began to scream: he had no right to smirk like that as if she was some peasant dumbbell, she knew what she was talking about, she was a Christian Austrian who didn't have to take that, especially not from Leon, who never even finished his first helping, for which Frau Lily would blame her, Loisi, Frau Lily always blamed Loisi for Leon being so thin, Loisi who was doing her best, breaking her back, cooking extra meals at different times, it was typical, Christian people were always taking it on the chin.

Sundays Loisi sang "Stabat Mater Dolorosa" in the ladies' choir at St. Joseph's, and she had to save her voice for that. That was why she never screamed at Leon very long. While she washed dishes, Leon could finish eating undisturbed, composing mock hymns like "Amabat Pater Cupidosa," thereby practicing Latin unnecessarily. It was the only course in which he excelled after entering high school—the *Realgymnasium* of the 17th District. He loved to play with a dead language whose grammar led such an intricately coded life. Each sentence sounded like a melodious cryptogram, perfect for talking to his secret twin, Florian. Only Latin interested him. He couldn't apply himself to other subjects. They had nothing to do with reality. What was the connection between the Battle of Solferino in 1859 and the many beggars who now kneeled on pavements on the way to school? Or between Portugal's three principal rivers and the bike climbing out of Grandpapa Boas's death? Or the isosceles triangle and the sullenness skulking on every other street corner since the Red revolt?

On Leon's report card the coveted mark "1" appeared next to "Latin" as well as "Physical Education." In most other subjects he rated "3," barely short of the failing "4." And he would have been in deep trouble in Religious Instruction had it not been for the teacher.

In grade school Leon had been the only Jew. At the *Realgymnasium* there were five others in his form. Rabbi Funclos, who taught Jewish Studies, required him to take tests in liturgy and Bible knowledge along with the five. But Leon was excused from Hebrew, the tough part of the course. "Spiegelglass has difficult circumstances at home," the rabbi explained to the class. "They're digging up his street, there's noise and so on. He'd just slow down the rest of you. He'll have to catch up later."

Several times the rabbi talked about giving Leon special Hebrew lessons on the side. But nothing like that happened until one afternoon when Leon bumped into Rabbi Funclos as he came out of the faculty room.

Leon took off his cap according to prescribed form. "Good day, Herr Professor."

"Going home, Leon?" Rabbi Funclos said. "I'll walk with you a bit, if you'll stop calling me 'Professor.' I've been meaning to tell you that."

Since Rabbi Funclos was professor of religion at the school, his students—naturally all Jews—always called him "Professor," a much less fraught title than "Rabbi" in a Christian environment.

"Good day, Rabbi," Leon said in a lower tone.

"No, just call me Uncle Alexander," Rabbi Funclos said. "By extension you're my nephew, and furthermore you're my nephew for a purpose—" He stopped to lift his hat to three professors, non-Jewish, of course, who gave him the intimate greeting *"Servus"* obligatory among faculty colleagues; this particular *"Servus,"* however, was qualified by a stiff three-headed bow.

"All right," Rabbi Funclos resumed. "I was saying? Oh yes, you're my nephew for a purpose. Don't think my sister married into your family by accident. There are connections you can't see—certainly not the way you could see that fine bit of anti-Semitic correctness just now. But many important things are not at all obvious. Remember the cabala radio?"

Leon nodded.

"All right," Rabbi Funclos said. "If you know how to tune this radio, you'll learn how to go beyond the obvious. For example, you'll learn that the obvious Hebrew, the one you can read right off the Torah, that's like wrapping paper. It's just the outer skin of Inner Hebrew."

"What Inner Hebrew?" Leon asked. They were walking along at the rabbi's slow, head-nodding pace. He smiled at a man who held on to his carefully pressed fedora so he would not lose it as he bent down for a cigarette butt.

"That which is written in white letters is Inner Hebrew," the rabbi said.

"But there are no white letters," Leon said.

"Oh no?" the rabbi said. "Could you distinguish between the black letters if it weren't for the white space between them? Of course not. Except the whiteness isn't just space. It has a certain shape and it's made up of letters, too. You just have to learn how to read "the white alphabet.""

"Boy, white letters," Leon said. "That's going to be tough to study for tests."

"There won't be any tests," the rabbi said. "I'm not talking about ordinary classwork. The white alphabet is too important for that."

"Important for what?" Leon said.

"Well, think," the rabbi said. "These are bad times, and dangerous times. But they're important. What's important to you?"

Leon didn't know how to answer right away.

"That's right, take your time to think," the rabbi said.

"Will the white letters tell what happened to Zettl?" Leon said.

"Zettl?" the rabbi said. "Oh yes, Zettl. I'm sure they'll tell about that, too. What else would you like to know?"

"Why Grandmama Tamarah is a door," Leon said. "And Grandpapa Boas is a bike."

Slowly, they walked on a few more steps. "Good questions," the rabbi said. "I'll teach you the white letters when you're ready."

They had stopped before the Café Pellmann, where the rabbi always had his four o'clock mocha. "Meanwhile," he said, "you already know more than others."

Leon remained excused from studying what the others in class didn't even realize was Outer Hebrew. Just the same, he received a "1" for excellence in Jewish Studies. Bobby Schönfeld said it was nepotism. Hansl Pellmann said his father wasn't surprised: the Spiegelglasses always thought they could get away with anything. And Bertl Stelnitz did not invite Leon to his chess tournament, where even the losers got apricot-filled doughnuts.

And so Leon did not endear himself to his fellow Jews. For a while it seemed to be different with the Christian majority of the

class. Leon's speed and kicking power in soccer more than made up
for his nearsightedness. Unanimously, he was elected center forward of the freshman team of the 17th District *Realgymnasium*. He
was the only Jew on the team, and for eight days before the first interschool game, everybody called him, jovially, "Spieg." On the afternoon before the match, during their last training session, Fritzl
Skalka came over.

"Where'd you learn to boot like that, with the side of your
heel?" he asked.

"Practice with a friend." Leon didn't like to divulge that he and
his secret twin, Florian, had been cultivating this skill together.

"That's a great trick, Spieg," Skalka said. "I wanted to ask you,
you won't need your cap at the game, will you?"

"My cap?" Leon said. It was a small version of Grandpapa
Berek's Varungy cap; Grandpapa had given it to Leon on his tenth
birthday. "I use it against the sun," Leon said.

"In November we haven't got much sun," Skalka said.

"It comes out now and then," Leon said.

"Well, the point is," Skalka said, "we don't wear caps with our
team uniforms."

"The goalies wear caps," Leon said.

"The goalies, but you're not a goalie," Skalka said. "You're our
center forward."

"It's against the glare," Leon said. "My eyes are sensitive."

"The cap looks Polish," Skalka said.

"My grandpapa bought it for me here," Leon said. "In Austria."

"It looks Polish on you."

"I can't play without it," Leon said, surprised by the heat in his
cheeks.

"Damn it, Spiegelglass," Skalka said. "Don't you see? It's just
too goddamn much!"

"What's too much?"

"Well, we're going to play the St. Casimir freshman team! Don't
you understand?"

St. Casimir was an all-Catholic, therefore all-Gentile parochial
school, and just because Leon understood, he shook his head
fiercely.

"You know damn well!" Skalka said. "Your name is Spiegelglass, you got a thin face and not such a thin nose, and on top of that you'll be wearing that Polish cap and that cap is too much! This is an official interschool game!"

"That's too bad," Leon said.

"I'm the team captain and you better make up your mind."

"Too fucking bad," Leon said.

"It's either no cap or off the team."

Leon heard a small thud. It was the impact of his knuckles on Skalka's cheek. In his anger he hadn't even been aware of throwing his fist.

"I'll get you for this," Skalka said from the ground.

"Go ahead," Leon said.

"Don't worry, I'll wait," Skalka said, still from the ground. "I'm going to get you right, when the time comes. All you Christ killers are going to get it. It won't be long now."

The freshman team of the 17th District *Realgymnasium* won against St. Casimir, even without Leon Spiegelglass. Skalka asked everybody to the soda-and-pretzels celebration at his house. For Leon he used a special invitational formula. "My parents say I have to invite you," he said, "because your grandfather is the landlord."

"I'm not coming anyway," Leon said.

XXXVI

LEON'S POOR GRADES upset his father, already under strain from his long hours of search for the Brick, night after night, after he finished his factory day. But he adopted the rabbi's explanation for Leon's shortcomings as a student: Turk Place was simply too noisy for homework. From then on—and until all the blasting and drilling ended—Leon was to do his studying at the Hernals Metal Company. This was a bankrupt firm, on the outer edge of the district, whose physical plant the Spiegelglasses had leased from the liquidator. The heavy presses of Hernals Metal substituted for the ones at Turk Place that must stand idle while fundaments were being recemented. Hernals Metal also had a quiet top-floor office where Leon could really buckle down to his assignments.

At first Lily argued against his daily trips on foot all the way out through the tenements to Hernals Metal. More than a year had passed since the victory of government troops and still these regions remained dangerous. But Ferdinand said that nowadays a safe or pleasant street was hard to come by anywhere in Vienna, and there was no point in coddling the boy when toughness was one of his good qualities. Lily locked herself in the new bathroom. Its inside bolt had become her resource in their quarrels. No marriage is solid until it feels at home in its particular area of conflict and charts the rules of the joust. The Leon controversy accomplished both things. Ferdinand ended the impasse with a concession hissed through the bathroom door: he would buy Leon that miniature bowling alley.

She came out, sniffling, to embrace her husband. If their child really must brave the badlands daily, alone, to reach the Hernals Metal plant, at least he should attract company when he returned home. After all, miniature bowling had become a very popular game.

It turned out that even miniature bowling could not cure the boy's friendlessness. Week after week the pins lay dusty, untouched under the balloon ropes of the aeronaut room. Leon did make use of the rubber bowling ball. Mornings, it was hidden in his school valise. But in the afternoon, when he started out for his homework "office" at Hernals Metal, he took out the ball after passing the market. The Hernals Metal Company was three kilometers and one secret soccer game away.

"*Veni!*" he summoned Florian. "*Lude!*" And, unable to resist the Latin bidding, Florian came, not only out of the tank but away from Turk Place. They began playing their way through the streets, calling out signals in Latin, outwitting the Skalka team, outdribbling cars at intersections, finessing the ball down the roadway and up curbstones, past trash cans and around corners. They passed a gutted, Socialist-built housing project whose walls were still starred with shrapnel hits. Some nocturnal artist used the ruins as a sort of easel. Every day Leon and Florian saw a pretty new swastika with delicately hooked arms radiating in fresh brown paint from another shrapnel hole. It was at this house that Florian tended to become angry at Leon for missing passes, because Leon let himself become distracted here. Often he thought he saw Zettl come out of the doorway of the building. Actually, it was only a shell-shattered tree in the courtyard which cast the shadow of a man with a hand-hook.

They reached the Hernals Metal Company. Next to its delivery entrance HEIL HITLER! had been smeared in huge letters, a phrase whose height and length had roughly the proportion of a soccer goal cage—perfect for practicing penalty kicks.

"*Hic mane,*" Leon said to Florian. "*Exercere.*"

While Florian practiced his kicking outside, Leon entered. But he didn't climb—not yet—the stairs leading to his top-floor study.

Instead, he went past the thundering presses on the ground floor to a room, way in the back, which had a cot in it. He knew that next morning, at breakfast, his father would ask him the usual question: "Did Grandpapa do some resting on the cot?" But Grandpapa never did. Grandpapa always sat at a huge table full of government badges with their crusader crosses. A workman brought them in, batch by batch, as they were stamped out by the machines. Batch by batch, they had to pass Grandpapa's examination. Leon never even expected him to lie on the cot. It wouldn't be like Grandpapa. All his experience with Berek Spiegelglass fell into a cadence, preordained and uniform, carrying him on a warm, strong current down which he had been borne many times before.

Today found his grandfather bent forward, humming, his Varungy cap so close to a magnifying glass that the visor almost touched the lens. With steady rapidity Berek Spiegelglass scanned one badge after another. Now and then he'd shake his head, reach for a chisel, aim for a certain point on a badge, drop the magnifier, grab a hammer, strike three crisp blows, drop chisel and hammer, push the badge to the "passed" heap on his left, nod, take the magnifier with his right, resume his scanning, all without missing a beat of his hum. He didn't have to look up to know that Leon had entered.

"Ah, my aeronaut rabbi," he said.

"Good day, Grandpapa," Leon said.

"Aeronaut rabbi, sit down," Grandpapa said. "Remember what happened at Sarajevo?"

"Sarajevo in 1914?" Leon was knowledgeable less from school than from similar refrains of previous chats with Grandpapa. "Sarajevo is the place the crown prince gave out the medal we were supposed to make."

"Supposed or not, we didn't make it," Grandpapa said, inspecting badges, "so because we did not make it, what was *not* on the back of the medal?"

"No Brick hallmark," Leon said.

"No Brick hallmark," Grandpapa said, inspecting. "That was no good. But a blurred hallmark isn't any good either. These presses here blur, not like ours at Turk Place. You've got to check out their work. Sometimes—look at this one—the hallmark comes out fuzzy." *Boom! Boom! Boom!* went his hammer to make clear and definite the tiny Brick engraved vaguely on the reverse side of the badge.

"We ever let a fuzzy one go by," Grandpapa said, "we'll have another Sarajevo."

"Like another big war?" Leon said. "It's unfair, I did a long essay on the crown prince assassination, good facts and everything, and Professor Kratz still gave me an 'Unsatisfactory.'"

"Mmmmm," Grandpapa hummed, inspected, nodded.

"If you unfuzz them all, maybe it'll help Papa find the real Brick," Leon said, grateful for Grandpapa's agreement about the injustice of the History grade.

"The Brick will be found regardless," Grandpapa said. "It'll be there for your Bar Mitzvah. And afterward you'll go to rabbi school."

"Rabbi Funclos says I'll have to learn a special kind of Hebrew," Leon said.

"Mmmmm," Grandpapa hummed. "You'll be a Spiegelglass rabbi from Turk Place. That's very special. Aha. Here's another fuzzed one. There. Take the hammer. Hit."

Grandpapa had placed the chisel against another fuzzed hallmark edge. "Go ahead. Hit."

Leon hit with the hammer. *Boom! Boom! Boom!*

"Not bad," Grandpapa said. "Not bad at all for an aeronaut rascal."

He took off his Varungy cap and slapped it across Leon's cheek so sweetly and lightly, it was better than a pat.

"You promised Papa you'd rest on the cot," Leon said.

"And you're supposed to study," Grandpapa said.

"Can I practice a little soccer first?"

"Aeronaut rascal," Grandpapa said. "On one condition."

Next to the "passed" heap of badges lay a plate of chocolate-threaded gingerbread cookies which Grandmother Hester had baked. Grandpapa interrupted his badge inspecting to hand one to Leon. Leon put the cookie in his mouth. It was the condition. He didn't care for gingerbread, but he loved the small smile in the middle of Grandpapa's white beard. It overruled his parents' command. He didn't have to memorize the departmental capitals of France. Not yet. There'd be more soccer first.

"Thank you, Grandpapa!"

He ran out, toward the HEIL HITLER! goal cage.

"*Veni!*" he called out to Florian. "*Lude!*"

That was how Leon's weekday afternoons went until one day late in April of 1937. When he arrived at the Hernals Metal Company, Herr Jansch, Grandpapa's assistant foreman, who was in charge of the factory's temporary branch, stood in Leon's way and told him to go home.

"What do you mean?" Leon said. "I haven't even said hello to Grandpapa."

"Herr Spiegelglass Senior has already returned to Turk Place," Herr Jansch said.

"No! When?"

"Two hours ago, and you should do the same," Herr Jansch said.

"But he is always here!" Leon said. The assistant foreman kept standing in his way with a smile which made the man's square little mustache look askew. The whole thing didn't seem right. Grandpapa's essence was his steadfast rhythm. How could he suddenly abandon it? Now the whole day was pulled out of shape. Leon felt betrayed. Why must he be deprived of Grandpapa, who gave him license for more soccer and less homework? He refused to accept the deprivation and barged past Herr Jansch to Grandpapa's badge-inspection room.

It was locked. Leon knocked. He looked around. Herr Jansch had ducked away. He knocked again. The machines' pounding sounded disorderly. The door opened slightly—to a wedge of twilight. Shades seemed to have been drawn in the room.

"Leon," Uncle Conrad said. "Didn't Herr Jansch give you the message?"

Since the rest of Uncle Conrad was hidden behind the door, his face looked disembodied, like an illusionist's trick, especially since it wore the exact same askew smile as had Herr Jansch.

"Grandpapa is supposed to be here," Leon said.

"I've taken over for him," Uncle Conrad said. "He had to go home. Your Grandmother Hester had a fall."

"What?" Leon said.

"Nothing very serious. The whole thing isn't so serious. Just go home."

"What whole thing?" Leon said.

And then his eyes, adjusting, deciphered the murk in that slice of room. The cot Grandpapa would never lie on—someone lay on it now. Two feet with toenails of crimson wiggled slightly in sheer silk stockings. He couldn't see beyond the ankles.

"The badges have to be inspected," Leon said, "for blurred hallmarks."

"Thanks for reminding me," Uncle Conrad's face said.

"You're supposed to unblur blurred Bricks with a chisel," Leon said. "Otherwise, it'll be like Sarajevo."

"And wouldn't that be fun," Uncle Conrad said. "Well, you run on home now, Leon, and let me go to work with my chisel. Goodbye."

Though Uncle Conrad's mouth straightened, his face, his bare neck and all the twilight around him became saturated with a smile so tremendous and unsettling that Leon didn't ask Herr Jansch for the twenty-groschen tram fare for a quick ride home. He went by foot. He ran, Florian loping by his side.

Back at Turk Place the first thing he noticed was Signor Deki's Mercedes-Benz convertible. It had grown longer and its hood had turned silver since he'd last seen it many months before. The automobile's windows had closed Venetian blinds; you couldn't tell if anyone might be inside. The car enriched the chaos of the afternoon. In the house hall the Havlicek No. 5 motioned Leon toward his grandparents' apartment. There his mother didn't kiss him hello, just told him to go to his room upstairs this instant—only to be contradicted by his father's raised hand.

"Let him stay," Ferdinand said. "He should see the trouble a child can cause."

"Grandmother had a fall?" Leon said.

"She bruised her cheek," Leon's mother said. "She got very upset over a phone call. That's why your grandpapa rushed home."

"That's Signor Deki's car outside," Leon said.

"And they'd better stay in the car, they're not to come up until Hester is ready," Leon's father said. He was in his work smock, and his huge figure paced up and down vehemently enough to make cupboard and credenza groan.

"For once I'm glad my mother still bakes nights," Leon's mother said. "At least she's sleeping through this."

"Who shouldn't come up?" Leon said.

No answer from his parents. But out of his grandparents' bedroom walked a thin woman Leon recognized as Frau Pollak of Pollak's Millinery Shop at City Gate Square.

"Madame Spiegelglass is fine now," Frau Pollak said. "Good day."

"All right," Leon's father said. He walked to the open window and shouted down to the car. *"All right!"*

Again the bedroom door opened. Grandmother Hester appeared, leaning on Berek Spiegelglass's arm. Her little poodle, Majesty, danced alongside her, its tuft of brown head fur ribboned in lavender. Hester herself was a massive billow of lavender, skirts hissing ceremoniously. Of her face she revealed only a faintly reddened mouth, a well-powdered nose and seventy-three-year-old eyes still flashing an unpredictable blue. Chin, cheeks, forehead, jowls were all hidden by a gray silk scarf artfully suspended from her gray hat. Frau Pollak must have created the effect quickly for this occasion.

The elder Spiegelglass couple walked rather slowly, while at the other end of the room another pair, also arm in arm, made their entrance by the apartment door. Signor Deki took off his tweed motoring cap at the threshold. He had grown a Clark Gable mustache finely trimmed for maximum dash. It made up for the fact that he was an inch shorter than his lady. Aunt Ilona—that was his lady—had trained her red bangs down to her tweezed eyebrows. Her fox jacket heaved. In vain her shoulders tried to help her speak. Under the hat veil her finely curved lipstick twitched without a sound.

Meanwhile, Ferdinand had brought two chairs, both held by the angry strength of his right arm, and put them down in confrontation with the younger pair. Here Hester and Berek Spiegelglass took their seats.

"Oh, Mama." Aunt Ilona could speak at last, though hoarsely. "Good day, Papa."

Berek Spiegelglass unbuttoned the bottom button of his work smock.

"Sit, Majesty," Hester Spiegelglass said to the poodle.

"Mama, please," Ilona said.

"You'll be locked away if you don't sit," Hester said to her dog.

"Sir!" Signor Deki said suddenly. He let go of Ilona's arm to take a long step forward.

"Sir and Madam!" he said. "Putting personal matters aside, business first to make it easier, to explain why I telephoned about intruding—"

"We are not interested in films," Hester said, talking down to Majesty, who now sat.

"That is the point!" Signor Deki said. "Not myself either! I am no longer organizing films for the Italian government. No more, no more Verdi movie, no more Italian-theme cinemas for Italian influence in Middle Europe! Finished. Rome is giving up the area to Berlin. *Voilà*. Take it, mein Führer. It is yours. That is my point exactly!"

"Please, listen," Ilona said.

Berek Spiegelglass, unbuttoning another smock button, discovered it was loose.

"Also, the point, please!" Signor Deki said. "I am still assisting Italian-Albanian investments, devising the legal necessities. But now Italy looks in a different direction—Shanghai. Albanian metal processed in factories to be set up in Shanghai, with—"

"Why not Timbuktu?" Ferdinand said.

"—set up in Shanghai with Italian workers and Italian financing, but with management and proprietor participation by optimum elite executives like yourselves. So this would be an enterprise very large scale, major-power protection. With the whole Orient, one must comprehend—China, Indochina, Indonesia—all offering most exciting market potentials, trinkets, gadgets, costume jewelry, do you see? The best possible relocation. Safe, prosperous, very far away from present troubles."

Berek Spiegelglass showed the loose smock button to his wife.

"We have our factory *here*," Ferdinand said.

"Sir," Signor Deki said. "Yes. You still have it at the moment. But you have it in Austria."

"Oh, Papa and Mama, I was hoping you'd listen," Ilona said.

"That is why I have come here," Signor Deki said. "Despite—all the personal difficulties nevertheless. That is why I have taken the liberty—"

"You already took your liberty!"

Ferdinand lifted up and slammed down a chair. The thud released Ilona from her spot on the carpet. She ran toward Hester Spiegelglass, hand outstretched.

"No touching my wife's face." Berek Spiegelglass spoke for the first time. "Her cheek is hurt. She fell after the telephone call."

Ilona stopped a yard away from her mother's side. "Mama!" she said.

Hester's arm reached out and sat Ilona down harshly. Perched on her mother's huge lavender-sheathed lap, she looked like a child dressed up as an adult and in crying trouble.

"Oh, Mama, he does want to marry," she said, "he asked me soon after we were together."

Nobody said anything. Aunt Ilona on the lap tried to undo the clasp of her little satin purse.

"Yes. The very truth," Signor Deki said. "I would even be a Jew. Even today. But Ilona said, *you* would say, 'Marry and live only in this street,' and *I* say, I negotiate well, I have earned my Amalfi villa with negotiation fees, but *this*, this I can never negotiate! This is not compromise, this is surrender!"

"Only marriage in our street is marriage," Berek Spiegelglass said.

In her purse Ilona had found a doilylike handkerchief. Her

mother lifted Ilona's hat veil so that she could dab her eyes with it.

"No, *cher monsieur*," Signor Deki said. "Not for me, not in this street, no life sacraments, no living here for life, I will not be pulled into this madness."

"He doesn't mean it this way!" Ilona sniffled and shook her head. With her handkerchief she caught each tear at the eye corner before it rolled into the face powder.

"What he means is quite plain," Ferdinand said grimly.

"That is right, I do not fear to be plain," Signor Deki said. "For gentlemen of your means, your accomplishment, to see only this little street—"

"It is the street of our Brick," Berek Spiegelglass said.

"Oh, that, yes, she has told me," Signor Deki said. "You have a little piece from a wall. Because of that you will stay here forever? In such times? *Pazzo! Fou!*"

"Shall I throw him out?" Ferdinand asked his father.

"Absolutely, throw me out," Signor Deki said. "Ilona says you call me shyster, seducer, speculator, but I tell you now, a speculator sees better than you—"

He took a step back because Ferdinand had begun to move forward, until Berek Spiegelglass stopped all motion with a shake of his head.

"No, I do not fear. I say a speculator sees better than you!" Signor Deki stabbed his forefinger at his temple so hard, his head bobbed. "You see my little gray hair here? Maybe you see, but you don't *see*. You don't see that it is *change*. Me, I see change, I speculate change, I work with money changing, up and down, politics changing, up this morning, down at night, maybe *poof!*—gone tomorrow, good-bye. I know I myself, I am *poof!*—good-bye. I am humble, I work with that, I don't say, ah, I have a little bit of wall that is forever which makes my little street forever. No, *signore*, I will not marry into that, I will not be pulled in!"

"Just say the word, Papa." Ferdinand looked at Signor Deki, lifting a chair off the ground.

Berek Spiegelglass didn't say the word. He got up, humming, walked to the window, looked down, interrupted his hum briefly with something like a chuckle.

"You are amused by my car, monsieur?" Signor Deki asked. "It is show-off? It is less show-off than you, monsieur. It is new model, and maybe soon I will change it for newer model because then it will be old like I will be old, but *you*, monsieur, *you* don't need a *car*, you don't buy a villa, *you* don't go to opera because you have this street, it doesn't get old. A little patience, monsieur. The Duce Mussolini has a very big friend in Berlin. He has told the big friend, very well, take Austria. I know he has told him, I have my sources. The big friend will take Austria. He will make your street old, monsieur. Very old."

Signor Deki was trembling. Ilona sniffled and dabbed on the lap. Ferdinand tapped the chair against the carpet the way a furious man would drum a pencil against a desk. Lily held her son's arm. Humming, Berek Spiegelglass went from the window to Leon.

"Aeronaut rabbi," he said. "We didn't have our chat today at the other place."

"Maybe tomorrow," Leon said.

"Tomorrow is a date," Berek Spiegelglass said. He tousled Leon's hair and almost as part of the motion reached out to pat Ilona on the cheek.

Hester put her hand into her daughter's purse to pull out a comb carved of ivory. "Comb back your awful bangs," she said. Perhaps she would have said more, but her husband, beard white against his brown work smock, had planted himself next to her chair.

"All right."

The slowness with which Berek Spiegelglass pronounced those words rang with irrevocability. It was the preamble to a verdict.

"Not marrying yet is not so bad," he said. "It doesn't count until we find the Brick. After we have it back, let him convert in the synagogue. Then he can ask for your hand. Good-bye."

Ilona stopped dabbing.

"*Fou!*" Signor Deki said.

Hester crushed her daughter against herself for a moment. "At least shorten the bangs, you little fool," she said.

Ilona put the comb back into her purse together with her handkerchief. "It is the international style, Mama," she said and gave Hester a sniffling peck on the cheek.

For a moment Hester was a hatted, seated statue. Then she stood up fast, amazingly fast for an arthritic. Ilona came close to falling off her lap. Alarmed by the suddenness, Majesty broke into a soprano bark.

"We leave!" Signor Deki said. He had already clapped his motoring cap back on and now led his lady away. Ilona had just enough time to blow kisses to Leon and his parents. Majesty kept barking. From the other side of Turk Place at No. 2, the Schalls' Pekingese barked back, their echoes clashing thinly, as across some moonless plain.

XXXVII

A<small>T THE START</small> of the 1937–38 season of the Vienna State Opera, Thea Spiegelglass made up her mind. Two years of enduring the acoustics of her subscription seat in the orchestra were enough. After testing other locations she determined that only the box in the lowest tier on the extreme right of the horseshoe offered a tolerably undistorted sound.

Buying a box seat fit neither the Turk Place mode nor the salary Conrad drew from the factory. Nevertheless, it was Berek Spiegelglass himself who fulfilled her wish. He handed her a five-hundred-schilling bill. The following month, during Thea's second opera-box evening, she corrected a misprint in the libretto for *Die Frau ohne Schatten* held by the lady in the adjoining loge. Her opera neighbor, Fräulein Ottilie von Schuschnigg, the Chancellor's maiden aunt, quickly became intrigued by Thea's asides, such as the one about tenors whose bel canto mannerisms made a monkey out of Richard Strauss.

Ordinarily, this Spiegelglass-Schuschnigg contact across a red-velvet balustrade might have had no further consequences. But in December 1937 Berek received an express letter from Alba Kleider, Incorporated, which identified itself as principal supplier of uniforms to the Austrian Army. Alba asked if the Turk Place factory could manufacture—on a month's notice—one hundred thousand steel buttons with a bas-relief of the crusader cross, that number being needed for ten thousand tunics for a special-readiness militia the government might decide to organize?

Alba offered eight schillings per gross. It made the query very welcome. After Mussolini had stopped subsidizing the Albanian steel supply, production of the government badge had become unprofitable. The steel militia buttons, on the other hand, could use Austria's own iron ore in Styria and promised to be more lucrative.

"Schall," Berek Spiegelglass said, "let's have a steel-button design."

He said it on Thursday, December 9. On the tenth Schall did not come to work. But the telephone rang and brought Schall's voice, fighting small coughs. That militia-buttons thing, the voice said, he had discussed it with his wife; that might be the wrong article to do right now; the whole militia business might be wrong, it might make Berlin think Austria was mobilizing against Germany, much better for the factory not to get involved, buttons or any other way, things being what they were, so touchy, and at any rate the winter bronchitis had come down on Schall, cough, cough, he wouldn't even be able to make it to their partners' Friday afternoon drinks today, but with the wind letting up, it should be better next week, for the Spiegelglass anniversary, all the best and hand kisses to Frau Hester.

By then Berek Spiegelglass had used the telephone for more than a decade, and still he found it hard to take seriously much of the information or aggravation which came squawking out of that perforated little shell. But this was different. This telephoning Schall consisted of a sort of careful whine he hadn't heard in over half a century of partnership.

"Hold on," he said into the telephone. "The militia buttons would make a big order. You do the design at home. Bring it in Monday."

Monday morning Schall didn't bring it in because he still didn't come to work. "He'll have it for us tonight," Berek said.

"Tonight" meant Berek and Hester's forty-seventh wedding anniversary. Forty-seven was not a round number, yet Lily, who had organized "tonight," thought it a sum large enough to warrant some festiveness, particularly in times whose uncertainty made every chance for cheer all the more inviting. "Tonight" took place at the Café Pellmann, with the Schalls invited and all the family present.

This included Riddah, who had taken the night off from bakery work—her first such extra holiday in memory.

The meal was to start at eight o'clock. At a quarter after, the Schalls had not yet appeared. Lily cared less about missing guests than about the fact that Berek Spiegelglass didn't sit down along with the others. As long as one of the two honorees of the evening wasn't seated, Lily couldn't raise her hand. At this cue Franzl Pellmann himself was to pop the first champagne bottle and the zebra-striped piano would intone the fanfare gorgeously, amplified by the new American loudspeakers to be inaugurated at the occasion.

But Berek Spiegelglass just wouldn't sit down. He kept his watch out, dangling it from its golden chain, circling the gift table. On it lay the heart-shaped rye loaf Riddah had baked, an exact copy of the one she'd made for Berek's first wedding more than six decades before. There were also other presents, brightly wrapped, ribboned, with glued-on little envelopes, and Berek still kept circling the festive heap on the table. Instead of sitting down, he bent over this package and that one, guessing aloud, at uncharacteristic length, what might be inside and who might be the giver.

Finally, at nearly half past eight, Alois Schall heaved himself through the door, corpulent, slow, in a three-piece suit, alone. "Good evening. Congratulations. Isn't this wonderful," he said. He dropped something on the gift table and brushed his white fringe across his pate. "My Anna was just too sick to come," he said. "So weak. I gave her my bronchitis. I'm sorry."

Berek Spiegelglass stared at his watch. He went to his place at the head of the table, next to Hester. He put the watch in his watch pocket but did not sit down. Schall, who had followed him, pulled a sheet out of his jacket pocket, sighed and placed it on top of Berek's cutlery. On the sheet a design had been sketched: inside a circle an anchor shot lightning out of its tips.

"This is not the militia button," Berek said, standing straight.

"Well, I'm catching up, you see," Schall said. "Remember, last month we thought we might propose a military-type button to the raincoat manufacturers, with some unusual design—"

"This is not the design for the militia button," Berek said again. A waiter was distributing cards on which the anniversary menu had been printed, from the liver-dumpling soup down. Berek reached for the card that had just been laid next to Schall's napkin. He tossed it to the floor. All the guests stopped moving. The waiter picked up the card but did not dare put it back on the table. Leon was about to nibble a miniature salt stick, a gala specialty at the Pellmann, but refrained.

"For God's sake, I'm catching up on designs I owe you," Schall said. "That's why I did the raincoat button."

"The raincoat button isn't rush," Berek said. "No need to catch up on that. Damn the raincoat button."

"But the raincoat button could be big, and we discussed it earlier," Schall said. "So I did it first."

"We discussed it could wait till the accessories buyers come to town," Berek said. "This is not the militia button."

"Oh, militia," Thea said brightly just then. "The militia to defend us against Adolf Mustachio? Ottilie says that idea is just about kaput."

"What?" Ferdinand said.

"Ottilie, the chancellor's aunt," Thea said. "Didn't I mention it before? Ottilie Schuschnigg told me yesterday during *Aida*. I guess I forgot because Bruno Walter sprained his wrist. Pitiful what passes for substitute conductors these days."

"The chancellor's aunt told you?" Conrad said, smiling at his wife while leaning away from her as if she were an exquisite though carnivorous orchid.

"Well, then, it's all right, Papa," Ferdinand said to Berek Spiegelglass, who was still standing very straight. "Actually, the story in the paper today, about the chancellor trying to calm down Berlin with a new diplomatic initiative or something, that goes with dropping the militia idea for a while." Ferdinand pushed his father's chair out from under the table so that it was ready to be sat on. "That was just an inquiry to us about militia buttons," he said. "Not an order. Just theoretical, Papa."

Berek Spiegelglass kept standing rigidly for five more seconds. Then he spoke.

"Did you know there'll be no militia," he said into Schall's direction but not looking at Schall himself.

"Well, it was in the air," Schall said.

"All right, sit down," Berek Spiegelglass said. "You and your bronchitis. Sit!"

He put his mottled hand on Schall's stooped shoulder and pushed him down. Both old partners sank into their chairs together. The waiter resumed distributing the menus. Leon bit into the miniature salt stick. And Lily raised her arm. *Pop!* went the cork of the champagne bottle held by Franzl Pellmann. *"Hoch soll'n sie leben!"* Herr Schimko thumped out at the zebra-striped piano, and the new American amplification system gave his chords the brass of a Chicago entertainer. *"Hoch soll'n sie leben, dreimal hoch!"*

Chancellor Schuschnigg never organized a militia but, as though by way of compensation, the winter fashions of 1937 seemed to have been called to arms. In the *Wiener Journal* the women's pages bristled with epauletted blouses, visored cloches, belts like bandoliers. The military-styled raincoat button leaped into vogue. Even Schall seemed surprised that it became the factory's most successful item ever.

Quite as unforeseen was the fact that some of the manufacturing still had to be done in an outside plant. A week before the heavy presses were to be reactivated at Turk Place, a city inspector examined basements and ground floors in the entire neighborhood to make sure fundaments had been fully recemented. He noticed the wallpaper door in the synagogue's vestibule. Berek Spiegelglass was summoned from the factory: the inspector wanted to see him together with the door key. Ten minutes later they stood in the tunnel at the Turk Place fuse box, two yards away from the closed but still empty Brick compartment.

"This is the street's central fuse box?" the inspector said.

Berek nodded.

"And nobody before me noticed the violation?"

"What violation?" Berek said.

"Municipal Utilities Code, Paragraph Eleven," the inspector said. "Underground electric conduits are to be used exclusively for utility purposes. You and your coreligionists, sir, do you conduct rituals in this utility tunnel?"

"This is a storage area," Berek Spiegelglass said.

"It's not my business to inquire what that means, sir," the inspector said. "My business is to inform you that you will stop 'storing' here and keep this conduit clear of your particular religious practices"—he threw his thumb over his shoulder in the direction of the synagogue—"or failing that, you'll provide a new conduit."

"There's never been a problem before," Berek said.

"I believe you, sir," the inspector said. "Before, special segments of the population enjoyed special privileges. But from now on this fuse-box conduit can no longer be connected to your synagogue."

"But this means a lot of reconstruction work all over again," Berek said.

"There might be a lot of reconstruction everywhere," the inspector said. "Times are changing, Herr Spiegelglass."

Berek looked at the Brick compartment. "One thing won't change," he said. "This will continue as a storage area."

"In that case," the inspector said, turning on his heel, whirling his flashlight, "you will build new conduits at your expense."

"That's all right," Berek Spiegelglass said. "But we will continue doing as before."

XXXVIII

THE TRANSFER of the central fuse box to a separate shaft involved a new positioning of the central cable network under Turk Place, which in turn required a relaying of water and gas pipes. Once more hammers smashed curbstones, crowbars gouged sidewalks, trenches were gashed into the gutter. A pearly blanket of the finest grime rose like a canopy above the street. With almost supernatural tenderness it covered the half-naked workers' battalions that stomped their way steadily underground.

"This is good," Berek Spiegelglass said. "Now we can look for the Brick even deeper down."

Ferdinand pursued his nightly search in the newly dug pits, armed with shovel and lantern. He did it willingly, for his father was astoundingly rejuvenated by the upheaval. To Berek it suggested his conquest of the street long ago in his springtime years—vital throes that would now lead to the recapture of the street's heart. In 1938, aged eighty-three, he no longer dozed off at lunch. His hum cut through jackhammers. The Varungy cap sat at a young angle above the white beard.

On the first morning of the new excavation he met old Skalka, who was wincing his way past a pneumatic drill. Berek put his hand on one of his minareted street lamps as if to keep the lamppost from trembling and shouted above the noise that once all this was finished he'd have Turk Place asphalted at his expense.

By noon it was all over the neighborhood: Turk Place would be the first street in the district to have progressed beyond cobbles to smooth pavements. From then on many of Berek's tenants minded the construction noise much less. Jobless families in nearby slums already benefited from the work gangs. Mothers would put pails along the trenches, marked with their names and a scrawled plea to the laborers: *"Please put your lunch discards here."* Every evening the women would scavenge the pails for food scraps and cigarette butts.

The Schalls, however, disliked the commotion of the street work. The first week of January 1938 Alois Schall began a month's cure at Bad Reichenhall, a spa for respiratory diseases in southern Germany. He did not come back when the four weeks were over. His doctors feared (so he wrote Berek on a picture postcard which was plausibly medical, showing throat sprays administered in a sanatorium) that continued exposure to excavation dust might bring on emphysema; therefore, he was forced to take a leave of absence until all such work was finished. Within the month Frau Schall announced that her son, Adelbert, had transferred from the University of Vienna to the University of Munich—not only to keep an eye on his father but because studying had become impossible with the unending street noise.

This hardly sounded unreasonable. After all, Leon Spiegelglass's parents, too, had sent their son elsewhere, though not so far away, for homework. But after a while Leon no longer took soccer trips to the quiet, empty office of the Hernals Metal Company. The Spiegelglasses still used it—heavy machinery couldn't operate at Turk Place while underground cable construction continued. At Hernals Metal, Berek Spiegelglass continued to check the Brick hallmark on thousands of military raincoat buttons. But for Leon's homework another haven had been found right in the home street, namely Rabbi Funclos's study.

The rabbi lived in a small bachelor apartment on the top floor of No. 2. His study faced the backyard, and to ensure extra privacy he'd installed double doors, padded with pitch-black bolsters. In this soundproofed den Leon was allowed to do his school assignments. The rabbi had made the offer shortly after the New Year, as the boy started to take Torah instructions for his Bar Mitzvah in March 1938.

The study at No. 2 was much less fun than the Hernals Metal Company—and a lot odder. When Leon began his visits, the rabbi

said that he wanted to give Leon more than the standard preparation for the Bar Mitzvah; Leon wasn't just any man-child but his sister's nephew. The rabbi leaned back in the study's dark mist of
mahogany, which the window, though large, never really managed
to brighten. In his hand glowed a long ruler. It had been carved of a
wood so white that it seemed to absorb all the daylight failing to
reach the furniture. Meditatively, the rabbi reached forward; he
touched the ruler's tip between Leon's legs, leaned back again with
a thoughtful nod, barely smiling, before Leon could even flinch.

"The changes taking place *there*," the rabbi said, "they're the
main reason for your Bar Mitzvah. Are you aware of that, my boy?"

It was all the more unsettling to be asked such a question during a staccato of high heels. The rabbi's sister, Leon's Aunt Thea,
had come in. She brought her brother's afternoon coffee.

"You see, my task is to relate your new manhood to the law,"
the rabbi said. He rested the ruler on the tray Aunt Thea had set
down on his desk. Like the ruler, Aunt Thea attracted the light
which somehow couldn't fasten on the rest of the room. It made her
look different: it tightened around the waist the pink triangle-
patterned dress she wore and molded her into softer contours than
Leon had ever noticed before. Actually, he didn't *want* to notice; that
only aggravated his embarrassment.

"You know what I'm saying?" the rabbi asked.

The only way was to brazen it out. "You mean that man-woman
stuff," Leon said. "Zettl told me all about that long ago."

"All?" the rabbi said. "So you know 'all' now?"

"I guess most of it," Leon said. Thank God Aunt Thea had
walked out again, with a heedless clicking of heels.

"Now you've just raised a question in my mind," the rabbi said.
"Why did a Zettl have to tell you? Why not your father? Why not,
for that matter, a rabbi, and believe me, I'd never bring up anything
like that if I were your usual rabbi—why is it always a Zettl that tells
a boy?"

Leon didn't know what to say. The rabbi nibbled on one of the
delicately scrolled crescents on his plate.

"Because we are ashamed," the rabbi said. "There is your answer. We all live under the Shame Law written in the Torah's black

letters. Remember the black letters and the white? Black for Outer Hebrew and white for Inner?"

"You said you'd teach me the white letters," Leon said.

"More important is to teach you *why* God wrote them in white," the rabbi said. "Why and how. The white letters were the ones God himself wrote on the first pair of tablets on Mount Sinai—look it up in our Bible: Exodus, Chapter Thirty-two, Verse Sixteen. Make a note, so you remember."

Leon was glad to take pencil and pad out of his valise. It was more like regular instruction.

"That was the unashamed Free Law," Rabbi Funclos said, "inscribed by the Lord's own hand in white letters on the first pair of tablets. But we weren't ready for it at Mount Sinai, just as we hadn't been ready for it earlier, in the Garden of Eden. That's why Moses had to smash the first two tablets. It was our second fall. But the second pair of tablets God did *not* write on, because God's hand will not write the Shame Law. Moses had to do it—look it up in Exodus, Chapter Thirty-four, Verse Twenty-seven. Make a note."

Leon made a note.

"Good," the rabbi said. "Now, on the second pair of tablets Moses wrote the Shame Law in black letters, and it's this same Shame Law that we're still under, until we smash the Shame Law tablets ourselves." The rabbi picked up a sugar lump from the bowl. Very briefly, a grimace fiercened his face as he broke the lump in two. He dropped the fragments into his coffee. "You've got to smash the black letters," he said, "to let the white letters that are hidden all around them, to let those come forward. They're waiting to be released. There's so much freedom pent up under our shame. Why, thank you, Thea."

Aunt Thea had come in again, her hand cupped around a cream pitcher.

"Would you like a crescent, young man?" Aunt Thea said. She'd never called Leon "young man" before.

Leon shook his head.

"Yes, he would, he's just ashamed," the rabbi said with a smile that stopped abruptly. "But now we come to the question: how can we break those black-letter tablets? Well, the point is, they're ripe for it. They already have cracks. It won't be that hard." The rabbi poured cream, lifted his cup and drank down the coffee with a swift, avid slurp quite different from his usual deportment. He put down the cup and nodded slowly.

"A great breaking is going to come," he said. "Much greater than in the past, when our Temple was only nearly destroyed. Do you know why I say 'nearly'?"

At this point Aunt Thea crouched down. She squatted, steadying herself with her hand on her brother's knee. Leon saw under her skirt. He didn't wish to, but he could see under it, as if into some wild midnight field with slivers of pale-moon thigh beyond clouds of black stocking. Meanwhile, Aunt Thea slid her hand slowly along the floor and displayed a pinkie powdered with dust. "And *that* calls herself a cleaning woman," she said. "We ought to fire Sophie."

Supporting herself on her brother's shoulder, she straightened up again. The rabbi took her dusty finger in his hand and blew the dust away. "Come on, Leon," he said. "You must know why I said the Temple was only 'nearly' destroyed. You are a Spiegelglass. You know the answer."

"We've got this Brick from the Temple," Leon said.

"There you are," the rabbi said. "Exactly. The one true fragment left from the Shame Law Temple, and the Great Temple was nothing else because there we prayed to the Shame Law as our Holy Writ, we even sacrificed to it. And your Brick is the one true fragment left from this black-letter Temple—the rest of the Wailing Wall that's supposed to survive, that's just fake. Now: are you familiar with the Encyclopedia of World Religions in your gymnasium library?"

"No," Leon said, glad that Aunt Thea's heels were clicking out the door again.

"It's a ten-volume encyclopedia," the rabbi said. "Just take out the last one. Look up Sabbatai Zevi. Make a note. Last name spelled Z-e-v-i. First name, S-a-b-b-a-t-a-i. Sabbatai Zevi, born in Smyrna in 1626 on the ninth of Ab, the day on which we commemorate the destruction of the Temple and therefore the day on which the true Messiah is born. We know that from white-letter tradition. Make a

note. You'll find Sabbatai Zevi also under the heading of 'False Messiah.' He was slandered as that because he declared the day of the
destruction of the Temple a feast day for rejoicing."

"On purpose?" Leon asked.

"On purpose," the rabbi said. "He knew about the white letters.
He was the first knower. Therefore, he knew that the black-letter
Temple must be smashed. Now make another note. Look up what
Z-e-v-i did on the twenty-eighth of Shevat in the year 5426, that's
February eleventh, 1666, in Christian reckoning. You have that?
February eleventh, 1666. Look it up and you'll learn something new
about Turk Place. Now have a crescent."

Leon did, after he put down his pencil. The crescent was flaky
and sweet, but it was the sweetness of an overripe plum.

"Did Grandmama Riddah bake that?" he asked.

The rabbi shook his head. "My sister, Thea, likes quaint pastry
shops," he said, smiling.

Several times Leon wanted to ask his father about the things he
had heard that afternoon. Each time he was on the verge, his
tongue felt slimy. Rabbi Funclos's study with its pungent
morsels, its nocturnal furniture, its ruler's glow, its forbidden
gleams inside Aunt Thea's skirt—all that was like a conspiracy of
shadow, light and flesh implicating his own body at the spot between his legs to which the ruler had pointed. He told no one except Florian, in Latin. Yet he did not want to conspire too far with
the rabbi, or too fast. Something kept him from searching the Encyclopedia of World Religions for the false Messiah S-a-b-b-a-t-a-i
Z-e-v-i. For two weeks he kept his distance from the entire reference shelf of the gymnasium library. On the Tuesdays of those
weeks—Tuesday afternoon was his "instruction time" with Rabbi
Funclos—he staged stomachaches successful enough to keep him
in bed with a hot-water bottle. At the onset of the third Tuesday's
stomachache, his mother became suspicious. At breakfast she
slapped away the hands he kept against his belly. She called him a
little malingerer, though he was almost as tall as she. That morn-

ing he spent the school break in the library. And that afternoon he returned to the half-lit study at No. 2.

"Welcome back," the rabbi said. "Well, what have we got for February eleventh, 1666?"

"I looked it up," Leon said. "That was right after he was arrested by the grand vizier."

"Who was?" the rabbi said as his sister came in with the afternoon coffee. To Leon's relief she did not squat down to test for floor dust. By this time—late in January 1938—Thea Spiegelglass had begun to attend the midweek open rehearsal of the Baroque Society's chamber-music quintet. She was smartly dressed in a pert brown beret and fawn tailored suit with gloves to match.

"Who was arrested?" the rabbi said and reached for his cup.

"Zevi, this wrong Messiah," Leon said.

"Not 'wrong'—'false,' slandered as 'false' by his own Jews," the rabbi said. "But really true because he uncovered the white letters. All right. He was arrested. And what happened afterward?"

"He was supposed to be garroted," Leon said, reading the last word slowly from his notes. "Whatever that means."

"Strangled with an iron collar." The rabbi smiled. "If we don't know the meaning of a word, we look it up. Anyway, go on. You've got more notes there."

"So right after he was arrested," Leon reported from his notes, "the grand vizier summoned him to his office. That was on February eleventh, 1666. And they talked, and he wasn't garroted. They let him live. That's all I have."

"They let him live," the rabbi said. "One wonders why." He gave a small sigh in aftertaste of his coffee and touched the tip of the long white ruler against his sister's shoulder. She stood next to him, trying to fit a black lock into her beret.

"The encyclopedia doesn't say why," Leon said.

"Of course not," the rabbi said. "It wouldn't dare with its Shame Law black letters. But does it say the name of the grand vizier? That might give us a clue."

Leon looked at his notes. "Oh yes. Kara Mustafa."

"Hmm," the rabbi said. The tip of his ruler mused along the slender shoulder pads of his sister's jacket. "Grand Vizier Kara Mustafa. Does that remind us of something your grandfather may have told you? Or your father?"

"Oh, that's right," Leon said. "Kara Mustafa was the leader of the Turkish siege of Vienna—"

"—the grand vizier who brought a brick to Turk Place," Rabbi Funclos said, "namely the one brick left from the Great Shame Law Temple. Now what does that tell us in turn? About the link between us and our Messiah?"

Aunt Thea had moved away from the ruler's range, though her shoulders remained slightly raised as if still tickled by its tip. Now she stood before a small silver-framed mirror that hung on the wall, reflecting the grainy dusk of the room. She was still trying to cope with the hair curl which had escaped from her beret.

"No idea?" the rabbi said to Leon.

Leon shook his head.

"Well, then, you'll have to be told," the rabbi said. "You'd better be told what no book has been brave enough to print—not yet."

"I can't get my hair right," Aunt Thea murmured in a tone much darker than her usual high, crisp voice.

"You see, our Messiah Z-e-v-i did something very important on February eleventh, 1666," the rabbi said. "He gave the Brick to the Grand Vizier Kara Mustafa so that a man like him, a potentate, would break the Brick with all his power and, by breaking it, break everything built by black-letter rules, every temple and tower that rose up under the Shame Law—do you begin to see?"

"But the grand vizier didn't break the Brick," Leon said.

"*Exactly.*"

The anger of that word had catapulted the rabbi out of his chair.

"He did *not*. He was too small, too soft for his mission, too feeble. He couldn't manage to be the Great Breaker." Rabbi Funclos walked with long, hard steps toward Aunt Thea. "He failed. That's why his siege of Vienna failed. That's why he was killed. And that's why the Shame Law continued, the Martial Law, the Foul Law. All this Shame Morality. On and on it goes, to poison the world. Look around you, beyond Turk Place. On every street corner, children eating bones. Life lived in rags. You show me a face without uncertainty. Or fear, or doubt. Who is happy? It can't go on. That's why the Brick is so important."

"Papa still can't find it," Leon said.

Rabbi Funclos had stopped close to Aunt Thea.

"But Grandpapa says the Brick is still there," Leon said.

"Oh, it's there," the rabbi said. "It'll be there for the right man at the right time. The moment the true Great Breaking is at hand."

Though the rabbi spoke rather softly now, his words uncoiled from his mouth like steel wire. But his touch was gentle with Aunt Thea. Gently, he pushed her hair under the beret while she, as if to help him, arched back her neck.

"Does Grandpapa know all this?" Leon said.

The rabbi, perhaps too absorbed in helping his sister, did not answer.

"I don't think my parents know."

"Let's say they are important instruments," Rabbi Funclos said. "They're not ready for knowledge. We are ready. Aren't we?"

He had tucked Aunt Thea's hair under and was now smoothing the beret over it. His sister's face floated in the mirror as if borne along by his fingers. Her nostrils were fluid, her lips opened and closed so that it seemed she was mouthing, with a secret ardor, a vow of silence which encompassed all three figures in the room. Her hand grasped her brother's. She lifted it toward her face. Slowly, her teeth closed around his index finger. Langorously, she slid it into and out of her mouth.

The rabbi stepped back to his desk. Aunt Thea regained the firmness of her face. "Those rehearsals always begin with some stale, workhorse Bach," she said. "But sometimes they surprise you. I'd better get going."

"I'd better leave, too," the rabbi said. "Leon, next Tuesday we'll buckle down to your Bar Mitzvah reading proper. Now do your homework." And his ruler, which phosphoresced like some snake gorged on the window's daylight, gave Leon a farewell tap.

It was hard to concentrate in the Funclos study even when Leon's homework was not preceded by instruction from the rabbi. Sounds from downstairs filtered into the adverbial clauses of Cicero's First Philippic. The double doors kept out most of the street workers' noise, but there was no such effective insulation between the floors of the house. At No. 2 Turk Place the rabbi's den lay directly above Klara Schall's bedroom. In the early afternoon a German jazz ballad would often flutter up through the polished floorboards, a tenor crooning insinuatingly,

> *Es war einmal ein Musikus*
> *der spielte im Café . . .*
> *und alle schönen Mädchen*
> *die sassen in der Näh' . . .*

Klara Schall would be playing her gramophone. (Frau Schall had bought a fancier, later model of the same brand Ilona Spiegelglass owned.) Usually, at 3 PM the music stopped. The floorboards became mute. A minute later a door would thud from below. Leon knew that Klara would be leaving for her hot chocolate and patisserie at the Pellmann. On this afternoon, the vision of Fräulein Schall's full upper lip coming down on a rum ball made his own mouth tingle. He ran out and overtook her on the stairs.

At fourteen Klara Schall was almost a year older than Leon. These days she favored a dirndl with an innocently abundant bodice and a vivid red skirt whose white flowers matched her stockings. In her blond hair sat a fillet of edelweiss her brother, Adelbert, had sent from the Bavarian Alps. When Leon passed her, she held her skirt against her legs, away from him, as though she were a lady whose daintiness might be splashed by some heedless ragamuffin.

"Well, how do you do, Fräulein Schall." Leon made his changing voice as suavely deep as possible. "With your permission I'll run ahead. I must tell the street workers to stop messing the moment you come out."

"Ha. Ha." She said it slowly to make clear her contempt for the joke. The street workers, of course, stopped anyway at three o'clock for their midafternoon break. It was to take advantage of the easier passage at this hour that Klara was tripping ever so exquisitely down the stairs just now. For the same reason, Uncle Conrad—the only adult Spiegelglass to observe a coffee pause—came out of the factory now, too. When they met on the boarded-over sidewalk, he put his arm around his nephew's shoulder. Leon liked how that must look to Klara: man-to-man. Man-to-man, uncle and nephew walked to No. 5 and climbed the stairs to Leon's apartment.

"Good day, Herr Conrad, I've got your coffee perking," Loisi the cook said at the door. "Frau Lily says today she's really got to take her nap. She shouldn't be disturbed."

Uncle Conrad appeared not to hear Loisi but gave her a pleasant pinch on her cheek. "We've got the afternoon paper for you in the dining room," Loisi said. "Leon, in the kitchen there's doughnuts for you."

In vain, Loisi's offerings; in vain, her briskness. Leon didn't go into the kitchen. Uncle Conrad didn't go into the dining room. They stayed together, man-to-man. Uncle Conrad kept his arm around Leon's shoulder as they both stalked on tiptoe toward the bedroom of Leon's parents.

"Herr Conrad!" Loisi hissed. "I got strict instructions! I'll get blamed! Frau Lily said today she's *got* to have her whole nap!"

"Sh . . . ," Uncle Conrad said. He stroked his hand across the bedroom door until he found a sensitive spot. Here he began to scratch with his fingernails, slowly at first, very softly, but then a bit faster and more urgently.

"It's a little kitten," he purred. "A little hungry Conrad-kitten, but he can't eat alone. . . . He wants to eat with his nephew, and they both want to eat with his Lily-in-law. . . ."

"Conrad?"

It was Leon's mother's voice, drowsy, from the inside.

Uncle Conrad kept scratching softly against the door.

"Conrad?" the voice said again.

"Poor little Conrad-kitten." Uncle Conrad scratched. "Can't eat without his Lily-in-law . . . he's going to starve if he can't eat with her . . ."

"Conrad!"

Leon's mother, laughing, hair disheveled sumptuously, holding her negligee together at the top, leaned out of the half-opened door.

"Conrad, you're impossible!" she said.

"We're just hungry and lonely," Uncle Conrad said.

"All right, might as well now I'm awake."

"Oh, we kiss your hand!" Uncle Conrad said.

"You'll have to give me a couple of minutes to fix up. . . . Nerve of the man."

Uncle Conrad led Leon to the dining room table. Behind the door Leon heard his mother singing softly as she brushed her hair.

"You see?" Uncle Conrad said. "No problem." He lit himself a Gauloise. He gave Leon an "Aztec cigarette," a long chocolate stick wrapped on one end in paper which you could light with a cigarette lighter and which would burn away as you licked the chocolate.

"Learn from your elders," Uncle Conrad said, appraising his excellent smoke rings. "When it comes to women, patience. Never too direct. Just hang in there with good humor. That's the whole secret, Mr. Accomplice."

On and off, at unpredictable intervals, Uncle Conrad liked to call Leon "Mr. Accomplice." A smile, not of the mouth but of his uncle's eyes, spiced the phrase. It was still saturated with that incident at the locked room of the Hernals Metal Company—that moment when Uncle Conrad had peeked around the door he'd opened, behind him a pair of slim feet on the cot, wiggling toes whose nails were painted crimson.

Of course, the door had blocked Leon's view beyond the ankles. The mystery of this hiddenness made the scene persist. Leon became impatient with it, now that hair was beginning to prickle on his chin. Now the vacuum above those ankles rankled. It provoked his whole body the way another vacuum, the vacuum in space

where the Brick had been, provoked and rankled Turk Place into the
street workers' turmoil.

But at night Leon could flesh out the void. He would lie belly
down on his bed. With the weight of his limbs he'd knead into existence the body beyond the crimson-nailed, sheer-stockinged feet:
the slight wrinkling of silk at the knees, the swelling out higher up
near the garters, the hips' cumulating whiteness that crested
around the incredible, outrageous patch of hair, then an interval of
modesty at the waist (seasoned with a little beauty mark) which
flowered shamelessly again into nippled abandon—all topped by
what was sometimes the permanent-waved head of a certain nude
in *Mocha* magazine (available at a special rack in the Café Pellmann), sometimes an olive-skinned mask with Aunt Thea's beret,
and more and more often blond tresses bound with Klara Schall's
edelweiss fillet.

No sooner had this mattress-female been molded by Leon than
she began taunting her creator unbearably, slithering and teasing beneath him, eluding all his attempts at satisfaction. *"Florian!"* Leon
would then have to call. *"Florian, veni!"* And Florian, who had always
known the most insidious soccer tricks, such as ramming your op-
ponent out of the referee's sight; Florian, who must have many of
Uncle Conrad's genes (Leon was just learning about genetics in
school), Florian insinuated himself into the sheets on Leon's behalf
and caught his tormentress in the right spot; Florian thrashed and
pumped and heaved the siren into obliteration—erased her ecstatically from crimson toenail to the last blond wisp on top. *"Gratia te,"*
Leon said to him. And Florian would nod and vanish himself, leaving only a sticky bit of formaldehyde.

Right after Christmas of 1937 Klara Schall had entered the inter-
mediate figure-skating class at the Vienna Skating Club. Every
other week Frau Schall gave a jasmine-tea-and-mint-chocolates
party for her daughter's fellow pupils, the young men arriving in
stitched blazers, the young ladies in pastel skirts and cardigans.
They gave Lily Spiegelglass an idea for Leon.

Her son had still not made any real friends. Leon was a brooder, secretive and sudden. Often he still had a little boy's shyness. But then he'd mumble a mockery that could have come from the mouth of some bitter old worldling. One moment the boy lay on his bed, twisted around some book on the French Revolution that you couldn't find on the school list and which would never improve his poor grades . . . and then before you knew it he'd be scrambling up the ropes of his aeronaut room like a monkey possessed. But *what* possessed him, what bothered, tickled or moved her son, Lily couldn't fathom.

She wanted to discuss it with her husband, but Ferdinand, like his father, Berek, was still too preoccupied with finding the vanished Brick. Lily tried to think Leon's problem through all by herself. Perhaps she could change the boy through the one thing he openly liked: any kind of keen exercise. Lily bought him a season pass to the Vienna Skating Club. The young people there, particularly the figure skaters who were Klara Schall's crowd, had such well bred vivacity. Lily hoped they would smooth her boy into gregariousness better than the rough types around Turk Place.

And, indeed, Leon took to the ice with demonic verve. Homework and Bar Mitzvah preparation left him with only two open afternoons a week. But he seemed to be born for the sport. Within a month he could throw away his low training skates and lace on the "real" ones with braking teeth up front. By February 1938 he was ready for the figure class.

At this point a problem developed. Frau Schall, who had volunteered to find out for Lily, said that at the moment the course had no opening. The news disappointed Lily, not her son. He preferred to stay away from those prissy figure classes; all of Klara's friends there had such nicey-nice, well-behaved fair hair, whereas Leon's black mop was every which way and he had to clamp on his Varungy cap to conceal a fright-wig chaos. Besides, it was better not to be limited to the roped-off section reserved for figure instruction. Leon preferred the main area of the ice, where all the others glided, except that Leon liked to glide in reverse, skating not clock- but counterclockwise around the rink. Often people complained about it. The rink guard growled warnings. To Leon, however, counterclockwise was not just fun but almost a necessity. He had to skate that way to outsmart Broom Toni.

Of course, nobody knew about that. Nobody thought of old Broom Toni as a force you had to outsmart. Broom Toni got his name from his job—cleaning up the kitchen after the Ice Restaurant closed at midnight. Yet the old man arrived as early as Leon, promptly at 3 PM, when the rink opened. Leon watched him take up his position outside the bandshell, which was heated inside but had no room for an extra person. He stood there hour after hour, chewing tobacco, waiting, waiting until the drummer signaled him for a beer or the tuba player for a soda. Each errand set Toni running to the kitchen, and for each he got half a schilling. Leon never saw him collect more than three coins an hour, sometimes none at all. For the most part, Toni just stood there and froze.

But his freezing was a performance which had become positively brilliant in the course of many winters. Toni shivered inside a worn cape. Its loose threads shone like silk fringes under the rink's arc lights, and on its moth-eaten collar survived patches of the gray-green of the Styrian Guard Regiment of the bygone empire, in whose uniforms the band was playing. Toni had learned to tune the chewing of his mouth and the shivering of his limbs to whatever waltz the conductor had chosen. As though he were a tobacco-chewing coconductor, Toni maintained a munchy, shuddery public smile; he turned his quaking shoulders melodiously this way and that; his whole stance claimed that his feet were stamping the ground not to keep his blood from congealing into ice but to celebrate the surging of three-quarter time. Quite possibly, the applause which ended some of the more exuberant band numbers was in part for him.

Leon never clapped. He could not enjoy Broom Toni. Whenever he skated near the creature, he could not escape the impression that the true source of the waltz was Toni's ancient, raddled body, whereas the band was fake, like Aunt Ilona's film orchestra miming the Verdi overture. It was from the St. Vitus's dance of a slovenly skeleton that all the lovely music flowered, and all those well-dressed gentlemen skaters with velvet-collared chesterfields and astrakhan hats, all those ladies in muffs and fur jackets were under

Toni's spell: a carousel of dolls rotated by Toni into a vortex, a merry-go-round waltzing away into damnation.

That was why Leon skated the other way, counterclockwise. He zigzagged against the maelstrom, whisked, pivoted, juggled himself by a hairbreadth past sure collisions, slalomed, veered—until the rink guard's hand came down on his shoulder. Once more he was ordered off the ice for fifteen minutes.

So he let the others billow on toward the brink and went into the restaurant. Through the waltz-muting window he watched the figure skaters on their section of the ice. Here Klara Schall glided, resurrected from the voluptuous death into which Florian had pounded her the night before. She tried a pirouette in front of her instructor. Her blond hair flew as she turned; her little striped skirt lifted above her cleft tights, which made her liable to Florian's renewed vehemence later, at night. But when Klara did her simple "school figures," she changed. Attempting a figure eight, she'd scratch her nose, apparently to enhance her concentration. Her lips compressed and plumped her cheeks—an expression which suddenly summoned the little girl she'd been years ago, roller-skating in the backyard of No. 2. Leon couldn't remember caring much for that little girl, but in the haze of time long gone the child struck him as adorable and safe. That so sweet an apple face could reappear above those rankly female tights astounded him.

"*Next number for couples only*," droned the loudspeaker. "*You may skate the whole rink.*" The rope setting apart the figure classes dropped. The arc lights changed from white to blue to give *Couples Only* a different, more exotic aura. For the same reason the loudspeaker instructed skaters to reverse direction. Not only was it all right now to skate counterclockwise, but Leon's penalty period was up. Here was his chance to do something which would let him tell Florian later that he hadn't been afraid to tackle the daytime Klara.

He stormed onto the ice, braked very close to her on one leg. "Fräulein Schall," he said. "May I have the privilege?"

This was the obligatory formula, which he detested. He intoned it in ironic singsong but couldn't tell if that registered with Klara. The roller-skating little girl had vanished from her face. She didn't even look at Leon or answer him in words. She gave a vague nod, then shrugged at a tall young woman with an incredibly straight parting in her ash-blond hair. "Sigrid, you'll have to pardon me," she sighed as Leon took her arm. "I'll be back in a minute."

Off they glided in rhythmic strokes. Leon pulled her onto the rink's outer track, where the fastest couples whizzed. "One round only, if you please." Klara enunciated an edged adult High German suitable for a downtown sports establishment as fashionable as this.

"I don't count too good," Leon said with an extra-thick 17th District accent.

"Very funny. Ha. Ha," Klara said. "All this immature fooling. You're a bit young for me, apart from anything else."

"What's 'else'?" Leon said. He was glad Broom Toni had left with the band. From the loudspeaker streamed a tango record; a baritone crooned "Oh meine Donna," a ballad that enhanced the ambiance of *Couples Only.*

"Let's not be naïve," Klara said. "You know what 'else' means. You must know who Sigrid is."

"Nope," Leon said and took the curve so sharply, her shoulder had to lean deeply into his. She was such a good skater, though, that his speeding couldn't scare her. Nevertheless, he swore to himself that he would crack this young-lady veneer of hers. He'd make the little girl come back.

"Well, if you don't know who Sigrid is," Klara said, "I must tell you that she is the German ambassador's daughter."

"What do you know?" Leon said. "But that makes sense. She doesn't look like an ambassador's son."

"People like you should be the last to make such jokes about her," Klara said. "Sigrid happens to be the reason why you can't be in our figure class. That's why my mother had to tell yours it's all full up."

They zoomed and Leon hummed his grandfather Berek's hum. Grandpapa always did that with a tough job. The hum toned up Leon's lips.

"The German ambassador's daughter," he said. "She might as well get used to Jews. She's going to be with one."

"'Be with'?" Klara said. "Really. What are you implying?"

"I'm not just implying," Leon said.

Despite the dim blue lights, he could see the change of color in Klara's cheeks. It only lasted for a moment. "Oh, you're just prattling," she said. "You're prattling like a child. What Jew would ever be with her?"

"My twin brother," Leon said.

"Very funny. You haven't got a brother!"

"Just because you haven't seen him?"

She smiled with a tolerant-adult expression. On the other hand, she kept skating with Leon, though it was now more than one round.

"My parents are right," she said. "You Spiegelglasses are crazy. Where are you hiding this famous brother?"

"Underground, at Turk Place," Leon said, and zoomed with her, and hummed the "Oh Donna" tune.

"You don't mean in that tunnel?" Klara said with a superior laugh. "The one that's supposed to lead to the palace? All that Havlicek nonsense? You think I believe concierges' gossip? I really have to go back to Sigrid."

"The Havliceks know nothing about my brother," Leon said. "He makes himself known only to very special young women. He's irresistible."

Her arm, about to pull out, remained inside Leon's elbow. "Let him try Sigrid," she said, repeating her superior laugh.

"My brother doesn't even have to try," Leon said.

"*That's not even funny anymore.*" Klara was so angry, she almost bumped into the couple they were passing. "You know what the German Führer would do if a Jew touched Sigrid? That's his own ambassador's daughter! He'd only destroy this whole city—that's all!"

Leon found himself nodding Rabbi Funclos's slow nod. "Let him."

"This is utterly ridiculous," Klara said. "A brother that doesn't even exist."

"Most people don't know that white writing exists," Leon said.

"Absurd!" Klara said. "So childish! I must get back to Sigrid."

"See, it's in the white space between letters that all the important messages are written."

"Oh sure, and that's where I'll read how handsome your brother is! Tell me another."

"He and I have the same fair hair," Leon said.

"In that case, what's that?" Klara sneered triumphantly at the dark frizz sticking out under Leon's cap.

"That's my outer hair," Leon said. "It's a wig. I keep my real inner hair under the black."

"Ha, prove it! Let's see that other hair."

"Watch," Leon said.

With his teeth he pulled his mitten off his free right hand. On his knuckles were red-blond bristles he'd grown only very recently. "You see?"

"See what?" Klara said.

True, his hand hair wasn't easy to make out in the dim tango illumination. But there was enough light for Leon to notice that the pull of their tightly linked curve taking had displaced the top of her long woolen glove: between the glove and her short sleeve a gap of white skin had appeared on her upper arm. He waited until they'd rounded still another curve. Then he reached out with his free hand and scratched his knuckle hair lightly against the naked spot, just as Uncle Conrad had scratched the bedroom door.

"*Stop!*" Klara yowled. That moment the little-girl mouth was shocked back onto her face while, at the same time, the womanly tights under the skirt fluttered.

"*Crazy, all you Spiegelglasses!*"

She tore away, skated back to Sigrid. Meanwhile, the band was coming back from the restaurant. Broom Toni followed with his shuddering hobble, ready to send the rink into some damnation waltz. The loudspeakers still broadcast the last refrain of the baritone's tango:

> *Oh meine Donna,*
> *Ich hab' dich tanzen gesehen,*
> *Oh meine Donna,*
> *Du tanzest wunderschön . . .*

XXXIX

ONE HOUR BEFORE THE DAWN of March 7, 1938—two weeks before Leon Spiegelglass's Bar Mitzvah—his father sat up in bed. Of the sound that had waked him only an echo was left. By the time he reached full alertness, he retained only the memory of something like a distant firecracker, but a firecracker which had slowed the breeze outside.

Even with heavy-lidded eyes Ferdinand noticed that the quality of darkness in the room had changed. He rose from the side of his sleeping wife, tiptoed to the window. The streetlights were dead. He groped into his clothes, felt his way out of the bedroom to the foyer. He found the switch, but turning it produced no light. His hand kept groping until it touched the shovel handle. Ferdinand kept the shovel and the kerosene lamp near the apartment door—indeed displayed them there for his father's benefit; he wanted to assure Berek Spiegelglass that even though the underground cable work had been asphalted over, his search for the Brick continued in the cellars and basements of Turk Place.

Ferdinand lit the lamp and armed himself with the shovel. In the street's empty dimness he followed the progress of a siren not far away. Five minutes later he stood next to a police van. Its headlamps lifted the shattered facade of the Café Pellmann out of the blackness. In the light a whole snowfall of glass splinters glittered up from the sidewalk; amid them lay a black-and-white chunk—a fragment of the zebra-striped piano which had once played a flourish as Ferdinand and Lily had cut their wedding cake. Now it wouldn't play at Leon's Bar Mitzvah reception.

Instinctively, Ferdinand picked up the chunk. He stuffed it into his pocket as a policeman stepped through the hole where plate glass had been. A second policeman scribbled on a notepad. A third, a very young one, did a bored sort of hopscotch jump across huge letters chalked on the sidewalk before the Pellmann. JEW-OWNED CAFÉ, the letters said.

"A bomb?" Ferdinand asked.

The policeman nodded and balanced his rubber truncheon on the tip of his forefinger. "Yes sir, a big baby," he said. "It knocked out an area fuse. Don't worry, we'll have the lights back on any second."

For the first time the Nazi underground had struck in the district. "I hope there won't be more of that around here," Ferdinand said.

The policeman shrugged, barely moving his shoulders so as not to disturb his balancing act. "Everything's fine, sir," he said. "Nobody got hurt. Nobody was there that time of night. Everybody go sleepy-sleep."

The streetlights lit up at that moment. Ferdinand walked home, forcing himself to concentrate on cool practicalities. Lily and he would have to find another place for the Bar Mitzvah reception on short notice. As he was trying to think where, he spotted a figure standing sentinel-straight on the deserted asphalt, in front of the house door of Turk Place No. 5.

"Papa!" Ferdinand said.

"What happened?" Berek Spiegelglass had his winter coat on over his nightshirt.

"Everything is fine," Ferdinand said, not wanting his father to catch cold or lose more sleep.

Suddenly Berek Spiegelglass pointed.

"You found it!" he said.

His father kept pointing at the lump in Ferdinand's pocket.

"I knew we would get it back!" he said.

By time that they were inside the house. Ferdinand realized what he meant. His father, seeing him with the search tools of shovel and lantern, thought the lump in the pocket was the recovered Brick.

"You keep it safe until the Bar Mitzvah," Berek said. "Keep it secret, as a surprise for Leon."

Ferdinand couldn't say anything.

"At the Bar Mitzvah," Berek Spiegelglass said, "Leon will write his first Brick message and he himself will put the Brick back in the compartment in the tunnel." Ferdinand felt a prickly, white-bearded touch on his cheek—one of his father's rare kisses. He felt the frail, triumphant body press against him. Then Berek Spiegelglass turned to his apartment.

"Now we can sleep well," he said.

"Good night, Papa," Ferdinand said.

Next day Ferdinand was careful not to view the ruins of the Pellmann at the same time as his father. He went after lunch, and nobody noticed that he slipped into his valise an exposed brick. Not just any brick, but one aged and fissured by the explosion. Its color couldn't have been closer to the real thing if his father had guided him in picking it. In fact, the old man's casual certitude throughout the day almost made Ferdinand believe that the sham paper slips which would have to be stuck into the counterfeit would convince his father.

At the dining room table that night nothing could dent Berek Spiegelglass's cheer. Thea complained that Radio Strasbourg had cut short its Poulenc piano program in favor of extra news bulletins about German troop movements along the Austrian border. Berek said announcers always sounded as if they had a toothache and then praised the leeks in the beef soup. He smiled at Lily's failure so far to find another local restaurant for Leon's Bar Mitzvah reception.

"We can still use the Pellmann," he said. "There's the covered terrace they have in their backyard. No problem."

"The terrace itself is usable, but the explosion tore up the canvas roof," Ferdinand said.

"Actually, we considered that," Lily said. "Franzl Pellmann said the canvas can be fixed very fast, only the terrace isn't available. He's got a Hungarian travel group booked for lunch there the same day. Just on that date! It's awful!"

"Oh, Hungarians can be unbooked," Berek Spiegelglass said jovially. "I'll take care of it."

He didn't need to. On the next day—Wednesday—Franzl Pellmann received a telegram from Budapest: the Hungarians had canceled the whole tour "due to unsettled conditions in Austria." That day those conditions blew up into tremendous headlines.

GOVERNMENT ANNOUNCES PLEBISCITE
FOR THIS SUNDAY
AUSTRIANS TO VOTE DETERMINATION
TO REMAIN INDEPENDENT REPUBLIC
NATION TO TAKE A STAND AGAINST
EXTERNAL AND INTERNAL THREATS

Along with the morning papers an official from the Interior Ministry arrived at the factory. His glasses needed constant wiping. He placed a "top-imperative, life-and-death order" of three hundred thousand government party badges to be ready within two days—as a symbol, he said, of the populace's support for the survival of the republic. The badge would help unite the people against German saber rattling.

Luckily, the badge in question was still in continuous production, though at much lower quantities. Furthermore, the presses at Turk Place had been restored to working order and could be used together with those of the auxiliary plant at Hernals Metal. Berek Spiegelglass put his entire personnel on double shift.

But the sudden plebiscite complicated Leon's Bar Mitzvah. In every Austrian hamlet poll booths, often in the form of tents, must be set up. Overnight, the country was out of canvas and canvas craftsmen. Franzl Pellmann telephoned to say that meant the terrace roof could not be repaired in time. The Bar Mitzvah reception would have to be held elsewhere after all.

But where? The Skalka inn in the market was too rowdy and dangerous these days for a Jewish affair. Where else in the Turk

Place neighborhood on which Berek Spiegelglass insisted? Thursday lunch saw Lily very troubled. Ferdinand and Berek had their meals at the factory, of course, being nonstop busy with the government order. Leon had to undergo a midday fitting for what the downtown tailor called his "confirmation suit." Hester was shopping for a silk après-skating ascot which would make a smart Bar Mitzvah present. Only Conrad appeared for lunch, but he wasn't at the table either. He was on the telephone. When he hung up, he threw his arms around Lily.

"Lily-in-law!" he said. "I deserve a kiss!"

"Oh, Conrad," she said. "No funny stuff. I'm not in the mood."

Nonetheless, Conrad waltzed Lily about. "Long live the circus people!" he sang.

"Please, Conrad—"

"But their tip really worked! I called that Bratislava outfit. They rent canvas tops, any shape, any size—"

"Circus people?" Lily said. "You're crazy—"

"Secret of my success. You're not crazy these days, you're dead. Anyway, all we've got to do is go to Bratislava right now, select the right canvas top for the Pellmann—"

"Right now?"

"This afternoon, they put the struts in overnight, collapsible, they truck it to Vienna tomorrow and put it up over the Pellmann terrace—*voilà.* Reception saved."

"Did you say 'Bratislava'? Go to Bratislava?"

"It's a lot nearer than Salzburg."

"Just like that?"

"Why not? Franzl Pellmann will pay half the rental. Come on, we don't need a plebiscite for *this.* Get ready, Lily-in-law."

"But Bratislava is in Czechoslovakia."

"So? It's just overnight back and forth. You don't even need a passport. They just stamp your ID. Someone pretty like you, they give a candy."

"Oh, cut it out," Lily said. "Give me a chance to think. Loisi has the pot roast ready for the oven. I guess the family wouldn't starve without me for one night. But it's insane, going to another country—"

"Bratislava, right over the border! It's not even a couple of hours in the dining car. A picnic. And they've got canvas in every color there, all patterns, much better than the Pellmann had."

"Jolly stripes would be nice," Lily said.

"Great! There's a good train leaving at three this afternoon."

"A bright design on the canvas," Lily said. "That would make up for the way that Pellmann shambles looks. How do you know circus people?"

"Hey, we mustn't forget!" Conrad said. "Bratislava smoked meats! Famous! Sugar-cured duck. And it's cheaper there, too. Perfect spread for a party."

"Yes, I was going to get my thoughts together on the buffet for the reception," Lily said.

"There you are," Conrad said. "Do your buffet shopping in Bratislava. We can make the three o'clock."

"Cured duck, cold cuts and cheeses to go with them," Lily said. "That means I have to make a list now. Oh my God, I have to do some packing. When you go to the factory, tell Ferdinand."

"Wait a minute," Conrad said. "First thing for me now is to telegraph Bratislava for hotel reservations. And I'd better run over to the Pellmann for their terrace measurements. *You* tell Ferdinand."

That afternoon loudspeaker trucks began to pump an exclamation into the air—always the same one, over and over again. Ferdinand could not quite make out what it was; the phrase diffused as it filtered through the machines' clatter in the factory. Though the words wouldn't define themselves, they gained force through sheer accumulation. After a while those spates of sound were like a metallic blizzard swirling right through the factory walls. It disoriented Ferdinand on a hectic day.

This same blizzard seemed to have given his father a cold. Berek Spiegelglass had come to work with eyes and nose running. He hummed hoarsely, rechecking the Friday payroll, having been talked out of more demanding work. In addition to his regular chores, Ferdinand took on his father's task of monitoring the Brick hallmark on finished badges brought in from their "outside" plant. When Lily rushed in with news of her Bratislava trip, the idea seemed like another befuddlement produced by the loudspeaker snowstorm. Ferdinand was far too busy to take time out for clarifications. He nodded and let her go.

A few minutes later a messenger arrived at the office bearing a long paper tube. Berek Spiegelglass unrolled it into a thin stack of plebiscite posters. Across the Austrian colors of red-white-red ran the slogan DEFEND YOUR COUNTRY WITH YOUR YES THIS SUNDAY! Ferdinand realized that this was the very sentence repeated convulsively by the loudspeakers roaming the streets outside. The package came with a note from the Jewish Community Council. *"Building owners of our faith,"* it said. *"Affix these posters to house walls under your control. For our own sake and for the sake of our children, we must do everything we can to ensure a successful outcome of the vote. There is no other way to preserve us from Nazism."*

"I'll take care of the posters," Berek said. He left the payroll schedule and returned half an hour later to say that the rough stucco facade of the Turk Place houses prevented the posters from sticking. They would have to be glued to something firm on which to hang them from the building walls. Behind Berek trooped the Havliceks—all three of them—whom he must have summarily rounded up. The trio not only carried the posters, scissors, paste pots and cardboard; they also contributed to the abnormalities of the day. As if to protect themselves against the loudspeaker gusts outside, they wore a garment over their aprons—the first time in over thirty years that Ferdinand had seen this. They had on brown wool overcoats that looked new yet already smelled of mothballs.

Still wrapped in their coats, the Havliceks sat down in the mail room next to the office. Slowly, they started to cut cardboard and to paste posters, stopping often to mumble, to swat invisible flies, to pick lint off each other's sleeves. They finished at close to 9 PM, just before the end of the factory's overtime shift. They stood up snuffling, sighing: this was the lockup hour for the house doors; they had to see to their keys; there was no time to hang these things right now.

"We'll do it ourselves," Berek Spiegelglass said.

After locking up the factory, father and son drove nine nails into nine selected spots on Turk Place walls. Ferdinand hardly heard his own hammer. The sound was buried instantly by loudspeaker brays echoing down empty blocks.

Their posters hung, father and son turned in at No. 5. But instead of going to his own door, Berek climbed another flight of stairs with Ferdinand. He followed his son into his apartment.

"I'd like to see the Brick," he said.

The question came out of nowhere. Ferdinand stood stunned. It was too much on top of a hard day.

"The Brick?"

His father nodded. And so Ferdinand had to walk, his father right behind him, to his bedroom, to the night table whose drawer he must open to show the brick stolen from the broken wall of the Café Pellmann.

"You have a yardstick? I want to measure it." Berek stared at the thing in the drawer.

"Now?" Ferdinand said.

"I'm going to make a new box for it, for Leon's Bar Mitzvah."

"Defend your country with your vote this Sunday," the loudspeakers bawled through the window, vibrating the glass, blurring everything out of its natural shape: the bedroom which was a caricature without Lily sleeping in it tonight; the brick which wasn't the Brick; and Ferdinand's father, who had turned into a slipshod imitation of the true Berek Spiegelglass. This was just a fretful, sniffling old man who deserved to be deceived.

"No, I don't keep a yardstick in my bedroom," Ferdinand said. "I'll find one tomorrow."

"Where are the messages in the Brick?" the old man said.

"Well, Papa"—Ferdinand was amazed at how fast resentment and fatigue could invent a lie—"until the Bar Mitzvah, when Leon has put the Brick safe in the tunnel vault, till then I thought I'd keep the messages separate. It's safer that way."

The old man said nothing.

"Those paper slips are fragile," Ferdinand said. "They're very old, some of them. They could just blow away."

The old man didn't ask where they were kept. He just kept staring at the thing in the drawer of the night table.

"The color looks a little different," he said.

"When your cold is better," Ferdinand said, "you'll see it more clearly."

The old man took out his handkerchief and dabbed his eyes with it.

"*Berek!*" Hester's voice came from below. "*Supper! Cook must go to sleep!*"

As he turned to go, the old man moved his handkerchief to his mouth. In Ferdinand's arms burned an abrupt ache to embrace the bent figure. Berek Spiegelglass was gone, but for a moment it seemed as though he had blown his son a kiss.

Next morning, on Friday, March 11, Berek Spiegelglass slept late, as usual. But in the apartment above, in his son's living room, a bell sounded vehemently at 6:30 AM. Ferdinand was already up, having risen with the dawn as he sometimes did on busy days. The shrilling of the telephone did not surprise him. Lily had warned that she might call very early, but only to give Loisi her shopping instructions before taking the train home from Bratislava. Ferdinand went on shaving. Then the knocks came against the bathroom door.

"Herr Ferdinand!" Loisi shouted. "Long distance for you! Bratislava! Your sister-in-law calling!"

"My sister-in-law!" Ferdinand said.

Sure enough, when Ferdinand took the receiver, the crisp little voice of Conrad's wife emerged. "Good morning. Just a quick message before I run to the cathedral here—"

"Thea!" Ferdinand said. "You went to Bratislava, too?"

"Didn't you know?" Thea said. "No other place in the world like it for catching Smetana's 'Matin Songs.' The only city where they perform them in a church setting, the way it should be, except they do it at this unearthly hour—"

"Are Lily and Conrad with you?"

"Sure. Right here. Anyway, this is just a message for Lexo. Tell him his passport is in the right-hand top drawer of his study desk. The man always mixes up his papers."

Ferdinand needed a moment to realize that "Lexo" must be Rabbi Alexander Funclos. Thea had so many nicknames for her brother, it was hard to keep up.

"His passport?" Ferdinand said.

"It's Greek, protection as a foreign citizen," Thea said. "Many thanks. I must run."

"Does he need protection?" Ferdinand asked, but she was gone and Lily's voice was on the line.

"Ferdinand? Listen. We think you should all come to Bratislava."

"What's going on?" Ferdinand said. "What's your problem there?"

"Ferdinand," Lily said. She sounded peculiar. "There's no problem *here*. That's why we think it would be a good idea to hold the Bar Mitzvah in Czechoslovakia."

"In *Czechoslovakia?*"

"Well, say in Varungy. That's where we all come from, so it would make a good spot for the celebration."

"Varungy doesn't even exist anymore!" Ferdinand said, astounded. At the same time he heard a "Hello? . . . hello? . . ." which seemed to be coming from a second extension on the other end of the line.

"Hello?" Ilona's voice said. "Ferdinand? Please, don't be mad at me anymore! Don't hang up! It's too important, because it's true there's only sort of a meadow where Varungy was, but we could put up canvas tents and have the Bar Mitzvah, you know, on ancestral ground, you could put it that way to Papa, he should look the place over now, and come quick—"

"Give me back my wife!" Ferdinand said. "This instant, or I *will* hang up! Lily? Lily!"

"Here I am," Lily's voice said. "You have to stay calm—"

"Just what are you up to?" Ferdinand said. "What is *she* doing there? Is Conrad behind this?"

"It's not Conrad," Lily's voice said.

"I bet he's behind it. He can be so irresponsible, and you're always taken in by him—"

"He's not behind this—"

"Put him on!" Ferdinand said. "I should have never let you go off with him. Put him on! . . . Hello?"

There was a vacuum. The next voice Ferdinand heard was one with an all too familiar Italian accent.

"Sir, I am behind this," Signor Deki said. "I have been behind this for days, contacting connections, thinking up ways, telling my Ilona not to go into so many pieces—are you listening, sir?"

Ferdinand was so taken aback, he really just listened, the shaving cream drying on his jaw.

"I telephoned Herr Conrad first," Signor Deki said. "I make the first step with him, because he understands and he is clever about the next step—"

"This is a conspiracy!" Ferdinand said.

"Herr Conrad is out and safe," Signor Deki said. "Your esteemed wife, she is out and safe, and your sister-in-law, and now it is up to you to come and to have good sense with your honored father with whom it will be the most difficult—"

"What is most difficult?" Ferdinand said. "Why don't you talk straight?"

"You must come away," Signor Deki said. "And you must tell your honored father he should leave right now for the village Varungy, this former village of your patriarchs, to look at it as site for your son's religious celebration. You must tell it to him that way, for he will not see the danger—"

"You mean the German danger?" Ferdinand said. "Everybody is using that for his own ends. We've been hearing about the German danger for years—"

"No more years," Signor Deki said. "It is *hours* now. I have information. You must take your family passports and your photos for the visas, Herr Conrad has them in a cigar box on his office desk—"

"I know," Ferdinand said. "He said he was going to get our travel documents early for our summer vacations—"

"Very early summer vacations," Signor Deki said.

"It's a whole plot!" Ferdinand said.

"Please, go to the cigar box," Signor Deki said. "You take what is in there to the Albanian consulate this morning for your visas—"

"We're not going to any Albania!"

"Herr Ferdinand," Signor Deki said. "Since six hours ago, since midnight, the Czechoslovak border will not admit Austrian citizens except in transit, that means only with a passport showing a visa to elsewhere, so kindly please, for your own good! Take the cigar-box contents to the Albanian consulate—"

"You expect me to wake up my father?"

"No, no, you would lose time, take the contents to consulate, Hollstrasse side entrance, they will let you in even before office hours, I have arranged by telephone, they will expedite, then you wake your esteemed father about the religious event in the patriarch village, then with expedited documents you will board the train to Bratislava, where we shall meet you—please! Don't kill my own nerves!"

"You actually expect me to do that?" Ferdinand said. "Go on this wild goose chase—"

"Oh, how I pray it will be a wild-goose chase!" said Signor Deki while there was a moan from either Lily or Ilona on the other extension. "I pray it should all be for nothing, I pray you will never speak to me again because it was all so idiot, but meanwhile go to the cigar box!"

"You don't seem to understand," Ferdinand said. "Just drop everything and run? From our own home? My father has a cold. We finish the government badge order this morning. Also, the invitations to the Bar Mitzvah are already mailed—"

"Go to the cigar box!" Signor Deki said.

"Why?" Ferdinand said. "Once the plebiscite is successful, Germany won't be able—"

"*What—plebiscite?*" Signor Deki said slowly. "You understand me? *What—plebiscite?* Finished. Kaput. Boots are marching. I have my information, I have been talking many hundreds words to you and you still do not understand? *What—plebiscite?*"

There was a silence. Not only on the line, but everywhere. Ferdinand became aware of that now. The loudspeaker trucks were hushed. They had vanished with the night. Stretching the telephone wire, holding on to the receiver, Ferdinand went to the window. Rain, intermittent but heavy drops, had begun to slice across the dawn. Next to a ground-floor window of Turk Place No. 6 hung a plebiscite poster, but someone, probably a Havlicek, had turned its face against the wall. Wet streaks ran down the poster back, tears down a gray cardboard cheek. The shaving cream froze against Ferdinand's stubble.

Yet the next moment he felt not fear but anger. Anger at the Havliceks. Fury at this know-it-all scheming Deki who had cornered him into accepting something utterly intolerable.

"All right!" he said. "But your responsibility! Yours and Conrad's! And don't you make my wife worry!"

He threw away the receiver and wiped the useless cold foam off his face. Loisi came forward to hang up the telephone properly.

"Excuse me, but it's state property," she said.

That was when he noticed that she had listened, not behind the door as usual but, quite shamelessly, in front.

XL

URING THE NIGHT before that day, the government radio had proclaimed all students of all secondary schools in Austria to be "plebiscite volunteers." Leon's gymnasium, like most others, closed early so that pupils might distribute VOTE YES! leaflets.

At noon, after dismissal, students milled about the school entrance between huge stacks of red-white-red handbills. The rain, which had stopped, began again. The trucks that were to take the boys and the leaflets to distribution points throughout the district failed to come. Gradually, the tops of the red-white-red piles became soggy. Fritzl Skalka was whispering prostitute jokes to friends in a protected corner of a portal. After a while he came up to Leon. The twist in his smile suggested a hot laugh. But instead of telling a blue story, he grabbed Leon's cap.

"*Spiegeljew, we got your cap!*" he shouted.

At the same time, Schedlmayer had tiptoed around Leon's other side and pulled the miniature bowling ball out of his schoolbag.

"*Spiegeljew, got your ball!*" he cried.

They passed cap and ball to each other, tossing and catching them to general laughter, yelling and sneering the same words again and again, organizing a whole hilarious Indian war dance around their booty.

And Leon let it happen—happen to *him*, the boy with the most respected fists in class. His hands hung down, not just wetted but disabled by the rain. This squall was numbingly new. Nothing like it had ever come down on the city before. Insidiously angled, it slapped across the streets and emptied them. This rain dissolved not only traffic but the energy of Leon's rage. It dribbled down the gutter. All he had left was the impulse to get away.

"Don't worry, I'll get you later," he said and ran.

He ran home. As his shoes hit the ground, he felt the cobbles turn hollow. He felt they would never become solid or dry again. He saw only one vehicle, a truck bristling and garish with men wearing bright armbands. It didn't just roll, that truck; it hurtled with the malevolent speed of those raindrops falling.

Leon ran, suddenly breathless with nostalgia for the streets as they used to be only an hour ago, before the latest downpour. Everything seemed changed by small but crucial and irremediable degrees. He yearned for some familiar, steadfast fixture. And so he made a detour to go past the beggar near the Pellmann, a blind, white-maned fiddler, the one who had an indomitably placid Seeing Eye dog always at his feet, who played the same Mozart tunes in the same doorway, day in, day out, regardless of season or weather. The man was there today, too; but as protection against the rain he had placed over his head the opened violin case, which looked like a monstrous hat. He didn't play. The dog reared; hackles black, erect, wet, it bellowed at Leon. Leon ran on, still faster. He turned the corner at Turk Place. For a moment, seeing what he saw, he wanted to run right back to school again to start for home once more, this time by a better route that would really take him to his family street.

Pews lay helter-skelter along the sidewalk. Leon thought the synagogue had vomited its insides. Workers from the factory packed the roadway. Though it was lunchtime, none was at the market inn and none looked at the rained-on pews. They all blinked upward, against the weather, looking at the roof of Turk Place No. 2. Rabbi Funclos was strolling there, from minaret to minaret, his black vestments bellying in the soggy breeze, his white prayer shawl fluttering. He walked slowly as usual, with faint, slow nods, and he carried a sort of flag—a tablecloth on which a swastika had been inked inside the double triangle of the Star of David. Under this emblem there was a message, also inked, in large block letters, except for the Hebrew characters of the last word.

HITLER & COMPANY: FULFILL
YOUR MISSION FOR [HEBREW]

Rabbi Funclos waved his flag and smiled at the other men on the housetop. They had real swastikas on their armbands and they were coming at him from both sides of the roof. There were no sounds except for the rustling of the rain and a series of thuds below the chaos of pews on the street.

"My young friend!"

Rabbi Funclos had lowered his flag to point it at Leon.

"My young friend!" he called down. "I'm testing them! To see if they can rise to the occasion! But they haven't smashed the black letters yet! You understand? The black—"

His voice warped into a groan. An armbanded man had seized his prayer shawl, twisted it into a noose around his neck. Another man hammered fists against the rabbi's face, ripped the flag and dragged him to a ladder which stuck up from the backyard side of the roof.

"*Veni!*" Leon tried to summon his twin Florian, to help him absorb this; but even as he whispered, Adelbert Schall strode from the door of No. 2. Adelbert had grown taller and more angular, thanks either to the rain or to his year in Germany, and he wore the same armband as the men on the roof.

"Well, look who's here," Adelbert said to Leon. "Haven't seen you for a while. But right off I'll do you a favor." He ripped the red-white-red badge off Leon's lapel. "I wouldn't wear that anymore, especially if I were a Jew." He threw the badge on the ground. "The Führer's patience finally gave out, you know. Those red-white-red clowns resigned this morning." Adelbert stepped on the dropped badge, crushed it as if it were a cigarette butt. "I did your father a favor, too."

"Where is he?" Leon said. "Where's my father?"

"Oh, just doing some spring cleaning for us," Adelbert said. "We're just keeping him busy and out of trouble for a couple of hours." Adelbert put his booted leg on an upended pew and shook his head. "Typical of you Turk Place Jews. You ought to be creeping into some hole now, with the rest of your kind. But not you Spiegelglasses. No, *you've* got to start with a provocation from your crazy rabbi." More thuds came from below the pavement and Adelbert smiled at them. "You'll thank me for confiscating the synagogue," he said. "I'm having that space cleared in the name of the Reich. If you're lucky, it'll house liberation troops. Troops on the spot will make it nice and orderly around here. Wait till you see how things are elsewhere for your kind. You'll thank me on your knees."

The Havlicek No. 3 came shuffling past and shook her head at a Torah lying half unrolled in the gutter. With an absent sigh she bent down to a silver tassel torn from the Torah's blue velvet cover. She palmed the tassel in her tired way. "Your stuff is messing up our street," she said.

"The street belongs to my grandfather," Leon said.

"That's a joke now," Adelbert said. "Try to find the old geezer. Make him claim the street. That should be fun."

"I'll find him," Leon said.

Leon turned and walked. He walked through rows of workers parting for him, to Turk Place No. 5. He walked through the house hall; through his grandparents' door, which, peculiarly, was open; into the foyer, where he saw nobody; through the dining room, which was empty; to the bedroom, where cook Loisi stood behind Grandmother Hester, who sat at her dressing table in her tailored downtown clothes, combing her dyed hair back. Frau Schall had planted herself next to her. In her hand she held Hester's gold-leaf brooch; her foot tapped with a kind of rapturous impatience.

"Good, just in time!" Frau Schall said at the sight of Leon. "Perhaps *you'd* better tell dear Frau Spiegelglass Senior here—she always played the hoity-toity landlord lady with me, so she doesn't want to listen now when the shoe's on the other foot—so you'd better tell her, tell her my husband came back from Munich yesterday, where he designed a very tasteful National Socialist badge in Viennese style, he's even made a die for it, we could start production right now, except we can't start the machines after lunch, your grandfather has the number combination for the motor switches, and Herr Ferdinand says—you see I still call your father *Herr* Ferdinand, I try to keep things civil even with Jews—"

"You have my grandmother's brooch," Leon said.

"I should say I have!" Frau Schall said. "Compensation owed my husband, damages for years of exploitation, an exploitative profits agreement, we're also attaching the furniture and the apartment. Anyway, Herr Ferdinand says *he* doesn't know the combination to the motor switches—"

"Where's my father?" Leon said.

"He's been asked to sweep the synagogue dirt into your tunnel down there," Frau Schall said. "We'll let him go when he's done, nothing rough, not from us, noblesse oblige, just our rights in what's coming to us. But your grandfather is the one who knows the combination to start the motors, and he's been gone all morning, and somebody better find him to tell us the combination! We can't let another factory get the jump on us with the first National Socialist badge in Vienna! So if we have to smash the motor switch boxes, in all fairness we'll have to hold you responsible for additional damages—*I told you, no valuables!*"

Frau Schall's middle-aged legs leaped. She pulled at a fox fur Hester had just put around her neck, pulled so hard that Hester's blouse tore and Hester herself fell off her chair. Majesty, her poodle, locked into the bathroom next door, began to bark.

"*Quiet.*" Hester said it magisterially, sitting on the floor.

The poodle stopped. Hester grasped the cane leaning against the dressing table. Before Leon could help, she hoisted herself onto the chair again and continued combing her hair, her lifted arm wrinkling the white skin exposed by the tear in her blouse.

Frau Schall slung the fox fur over her own shoulders. "Security against our damages," she said.

"Leon," Grandmother Hester said with a severe voice, combing.

"Your grandfather is at Police Reserve Headquarters, Flohrerplatz. He must return and stop this nonsense."

Leon went before he could hear what Frau Schall would say next. In fact, he ran so he would not hear it. He ran back into the street, again through the staring crowd of workers, toward the taxi stand at City Gate Square. But he stopped for a minute when he saw a group of men with swastika armbands. They were carrying Bobby Schönfeld's father almost as one does a hero. And indeed, Herr Schönfeld wore his officer's uniform, the imperial blue with decorations from the Great War, the regimentals he'd promised to put on the day Germany took over (Leon had often heard him say that at the Café Pellmann), to show the Nazis how well Jews had fought shoulder to shoulder with the German Empire. Now the armbanded men bore him along in his finery. Suddenly, they dropped him to the ground, but without letting go. They pulled his head back, his sobbing, contorted face flashing up at Leon; they dipped his gray beard into a bucket smelling of turpentine. "Alley-*oop!*" they said and lifted him again and brushed him back and forth against a red-white-red plebiscite slogan painted on a house wall. They began to wipe off part of a letter with his turpentined beard. Herr Schönfeld's eyes were wet and twisted; his mouth was open but he said nothing. All you heard was the clanking of the medals on his chest and the chuckles of the men and the strains of the blind beggar violinist who stood nearby. He led the bow feelingly across the strings, nodding, smiling under his black-lensed glasses. Glad of a temporary letup in the rain, he responded to sounds of jollity nearby and played a theme from *The Marriage of Figaro*.

Leon fled from the melody. He ran to the taxi stand, jumped into the first cab and said, "Police Reserve Headquarters, Flohrerplatz."

The moment after he pronounced the words, he realized that never before had he done an adult thing like taking a taxi on his own—or seen so deeply into the adult abyss. Perhaps he had grown up too fast, too rashly, he had not held on to his childhood fondly enough, he should have cupped it between his hands, he should have twined its preciousness more gently around his parents, even around school. Again he called out secretly to Florian, his twin and only friend—"*Veni!*" he called, but the only one who spoke to him was the cabbie, as he drove the taxi through the empty streets.

"You have money for the fare, young fellow?"

Leon had spent his last penny on a Swiss-cheese sandwich in the school cafeteria two hours ago, during his last childhood moments when the world was still the world. He had totally forgotten about paying for the ride. This would have mortified him ordinarily, but nothing ordinary mattered now.

"My grandfather has money," he said. "I'm meeting him."

"At the police?" the driver said. "Bet they all ran away."

"My grandfather doesn't run away," Leon said.

"Everything's turned around this morning," the driver said. "Did you hear it on the radio? I bet all the cops cleared out."

"My grandfather doesn't clear out," Leon said. "Stop!" That moment he'd seen the factory's delivery van parked in front of the stolid police building. The taxi stopped and Leon scuttled over to the van. Grandpapa sat alone in it, next to the empty chauffeur's seat.

"Leon," Grandpapa said calmly, though his voice was hoarse with a cold. "Aeronaut rascal. Smart of you to come. Did you see Arthur around here?"

Arthur was the factory's deliveryman, who drove the van. Leon shook his head.

"We're delivering the plebiscite badges," Grandpapa said. "Arthur's supposed to find someone at the rear entrance because nobody is up front."

"Maybe Arthur got lost," Leon said.

"Maybe he panicked over some stupid rumor," Grandpapa said. "Did you come by that taxi waiting over there?"

"I haven't got the fare," Leon said.

"That's all right. In fact, that's good, because I can use a taxi," Grandpapa said, patting Leon, patting him almost back to grandchildhood again. "We'll take it back to Turk Place and clear up the situation from there."

"Things have been happening at home," Leon said when they both got into the taxi.

"Close the partition," Grandpapa said to the driver, who had turned on the car radio to a drone of urgent announcements.

"I suppose it's going to be like this until the plebiscite," Grandpapa said. "I couldn't even find your father, and Arthur's taking forever, but it really doesn't matter, because I've got my aeronaut rascal here."

"Did Papa tell you where he was going?" Leon said.

"Today nobody knows where they're going, except you and me," Grandpapa said. "Guess what I'm going to do when we're back in Turk Place?"

"What?" Leon said.

"Write a message to the Brick, asking for something that'll knock some sense back into people," Grandpapa said.

"Herr Schall has come back from Germany," Leon said. "His son, too."

"I knew they would," Grandpapa said. "You see? Things are settling down. Say, wait a minute. What happened to your cap, aeronaut rascal?"

"I guess I lost it," Leon said.

"So I'll make you a temporary one," Grandpapa said.

He pulled a plebiscite leaflet out of his pocket. With his swift, mottled hands he unfolded, then refolded it until it resembled Leon's Varungy-style cap. The moment he put the cap back on Leon, the streets outside the taxi window looked more the way they had, earlier in the morning, before Vienna had been rained away.

And when the cab stopped at Turk Place, just about all of the synagogue contents were gone from the sidewalk. No water came down from the clouds. Grandpapa had restored normality to the world—until Leon got out of the cab. That was the instant he saw Fritzl Skalka. Skalka was turning the corner at the head of a bunch which included Schedlmayer and Milz, all wearing swastika armbands now.

"Hey, Spiegeljew!" Fritzl Skalka shouted. "Got yourself a new cap? Off with it!"

Leon shook his head.

"Take off the cap or I'll take off your face!"

Leon shook his head.

Fritzl Skalka hauled off with the rubber bowling ball. Leon ducked. Behind him Grandpapa was paying the cabby. Abruptly, the rain had started once more, and the ball merged into the wet thrust. It was like a bigger black drop. Grandpapa jerked forward. The next moment he disappeared. A marionette lay on the sidewalk, dropped where its strings had been let go, a white-bearded puppet, face down, motionless, its arms spread-eagled in an embrace of Turk Place asphalt.

Everything came to a halt. The rain braked in midair. Skalka stood suspended with the other boys. At the other end of the street three statues were bolted to the sidewalk: Ferdinand dwarfed the two men who, grinning, held him by the elbows. Pistols distended their pockets; on their armbands the swastikas squatted like spiders, crooked-legged, waiting.

Leon's lips were stone. He wanted to cry the redemptive cry he remembered; his baby cry that once had commanded his parents to come running and hug away the dark. But it was too late; he was too old; he could not cry it anymore. Yet his father had heard it. His father shook the men who held him. Still grinning, they let him go. Papa rushed forward and took the marionette under its arms. "You take the feet," he said to Leon.

Together they carried the marionette into Turk Place No. 5, to the senior Spiegelglass apartment. They carried it past Loisi, who watched them, standing at attention in the foyer, wearing the flowered hat she usually hauled out only on Easter Sunday. They carried the marionette into Grandpapa's bedroom and laid it down on the sofa. The marionette, limp as it was, slowed the motions of the three people in the room—Uncle Markus in his wheelchair and Leon's two grandmothers in their chairs. Grandmama Riddah should have been asleep in her flat across the street, as she always was at this hour. Instead, she was sewing Grandmother Hester's blouse, the one torn by Frau Schall. Grandmother Hester sat in her slip. Wrinkles scored the white skin of her shoulders; they made yet more nude her half nakedness. She stroked a comb through her poodle's fur. Both women stopped moving at the same time. Turned to the sofa, they stared at the marionette's stillness.

Ferdinand's long arms swooped forward, lifted Markus from the wheelchair, made him hover like a bird above the sofa, holding him so that his ear was close to the marionette's chest.

"Is he alive?" Ferdinand said.

"What happened?" Markus said, floating.

"He was hit! *Is he alive?* You're a dentist—you're medical!"

"Wait," Markus said, listening now. "I think, yes, the heartbeat isn't bad. It may be just a concussion."

"*All right,*" Ferdinand said. He put Markus back into the wheelchair. His hands vibrated inside his pockets. "That's what he always told us, '*It'll be all right.*' It's *all right* for him to be like that now. If he were awake, God knows what he'd do. It's safer for him this way till we have the passports—"

A sharp laugh from Hester. It shook the creases of her nakedness. "I thought you had the passports," she said.

"Forget Austrian passports," Ferdinand said. "I haven't had a chance to tell you, for God's sake, they grabbed me when I got back from the consulate! Those vermin made me hack up pews, stuff them into the tunnel, even Torahs! I didn't fight them, it would have made it worse for Papa, but I shouldn't have touched Papa with hands that did such things—"

"*Finish your sentence,*" Hester said. "Why forget Austrian passports?"

"Because Czechoslovakia won't let in any Austrians now," Ferdinand said, "even in transit, with visas for elsewhere, that's as of noon today. Deki phoned that to the consulate here just as I got there—"

"Well, that makes everything simple," Hester said.

"Wait," Ferdinand said. "Just an Albanian visa on an Austrian passport won't be enough. So Deki will have Albanian passports prepared for us by the Albanian consulate in Bratislava."

"You and Ilona," Hester said. "Falling for Deki."

"No, he's worked this out," Ferdinand said. "They'll have the passports ready in Bratislava when my train gets there, they'll just paste in the photos I bring, and I'll have the passports back here tonight—"

"Shut up," Hester said to the poodle, who had begun to bark at the excitement. "Daydreams," she said. "You can't get out as Austrians. But you'll get out *and* back to bring the passports. All daydreams."

"I'm going as a train mechanic. Deki arranged it!" Ferdinand said. "For God's sake! Markus, how long will my father stay like that?"

"The heartbeat is good," Markus said. "He should be up in a few minutes."

"Then get the laughing gas," Ferdinand said.

"What do you mean?" Markus said.

"To make him unconscious again when he wakes. So he won't act up and get them angry. Keep him safe till I get back."

"Put him under laughing gas?" Markus said.

"Yes, get it now!" Ferdinand said with a whispered shout whose force sent Markus's chair wheeling out the door.

"It'll be *all right*," Ferdinand said. "Leon will go as my mechanic's apprentice. Riddah, you go as train cleaner."

Riddah bit off the thread on the mended blouse. Hester gave an acrid chuckle and combed the poodle.

"Riddah, it's set up for you. Deki arranged it through the Pullman porter—"

"I have my son, Markus," Riddah said.

"You see, Markus couldn't be a train mechanic in a wheelchair—"

"I'm not leaving him behind alone," Riddah said.

"We hope to get a passport for him later—"

"I stay with Markus," Riddah said.

"Riddah, right now Deki can fix passports only for metal experts, my father and me and our wives, you understand? We're metal experts needed to stimulate Albanian industry—they'll grant citizenship for that fast. But for Markus, a dentist, it'll take a little longer, and for you, too—"

Riddah threw the darned blouse across the marionette to Hester. She shook her head.

"Riddah, your only chance to get out right now is as cleaner on the Bucharest Express."

"I'm no cleaner," Riddah said. "I'm a baker."

"We're losing time, for God's sake!" Fiercely, Ferdinand turned away, to his son. "Leon, you go to Rabbi Funclos's flat while I bring her to her senses. Remember: Funclos's study, the right top drawer of his desk, he keeps his Greek passport there. It shows he's a foreign citizen. They'll have to let him go. Get it!"

"This happened to you in the tunnel?" Riddah said, calm, measuring her mending needle against a gash in Ferdinand's sleeve.

"Leon—go!" Ferdinand shouted. "The express leaves at five!"

Leon went.

To reach the rabbi's flat at No. 2, Leon had to cross a landscape that looked treacherously everyday. The street made believe it was just another rainy afternoon. All the pews were gone, except for a few splinters. The workers had returned to the factory as they always did after lunch. Through the walls came the customary thudding of machines—the Schalls must have started them somehow. It was a businesslike noise at whose heart lay a withered marionette.

At Turk Place No. 2 the stairwell and the third-floor corridor had masked themselves in normality. But the mask bulged with greedy eyes and ears. Doors were open to the width of a grin. Fissures crawled with whispers. For a moment Leon shrank back before Rabbi Funclos's apartment. Here a typhoon had broken through the mask. The entrance door hung sideways, blown off its upper hinges. Inside, the storm had upended chairs, blasted a bedspread against a dresser, crushed a cupboard, dishes leaning broken from its mangled front. The men in armbands had worked with vigor.

In the rabbi's study bookshelves had been devastated into askew boards and ripped pages. The wall mirror was an empty frame—mirror shards glimmered on the carpet. Even the white ruler was in pieces. Leon had never felt very cozy in the rabbi's place, but now it was a violated, mutilated dearness that would never come again. He walked on. He held on to his father's order: get the rabbi's passport.

He stepped across ruins. The rabbi's desk still stood; its inkwell consisted of glass fragments dotting black ooze. He tried to open the top desk drawer on the right. It wouldn't give. With all his strength he tried again. It still didn't open.

"Guess who'll have to clean up *this* mess," the Havlicek No. 1 said, shuffling in through the blasted doorway, listless as ever, draped in her new brown overcoat, carrying a monkey wrench. She shuffled right on to the bathroom, and came shuffling out again a few seconds later. "Nothing in them faucets here neither," she said. "How come?"

"May I borrow the wrench?" Leon said.

The Havlicek dropped it on the floor. "How come no water?" she said. "All the tenants bawling at me. No water, no water. A person can't even stay by the radio."

Leon picked up the wrench, wedged it between drawer and desk, and pried the drawer loose.

"Not my fault somebody hexed our plumbing," the Havlicek said. "Maybe Herr Spiegelglass did. Maybe he put a Jewish hex on it. Out of spite."

"It's not *your* plumbing," Leon said, and handed back the wrench.

Shrugging, the Havlicek shuffled out of sight. Except for three sharpened pencils, the front of the pried-open drawer was empty. But Leon's hand groped into an object further back. He pulled it forward. It didn't look like a Greek passport at all. It was box-shaped, wrapped in black paper on which somebody had written with white crayon. Leon recognized the rabbi's sharp, slanted script.

This object has been placed by divine providence in the hands of Alexander Funclos. It is the Brick from the Holy Temple discovered by Alexander Funclos in the Turk Place shell hole on the Civil War night of February 13, 1934. Since then it has been kept safe by Alexander Funclos to be preserved for

*this ordained day of the Anschluss, March 11, 1938, to test
the new master. Two hundred and fifty-five years ago the
Grand Vizier Kara Mustafa failed to destroy the Brick and
therefore failed to terminate the black-letter world. Will
Adolf Hitler succeed?*

The parcel looked so unscathed, amid the shambles of the
room. The corners of the black paper wrapping were taped together
neatly with cellophane strips. Leon unpeeled them, then pulled off
the wrapping. Underneath, he found the cedarwood box—he remembered Grandpapa showing it to him in the compartment in the
tunnel. He lifted the lid of the box. And here it really was. The
brownish Brick, with little paper slips stuck into its ancient fissures.

Who cared that his father wasn't in the room with him? "Papa!"
he shouted. *"Papa!"*

Two minutes later he was once more in his grandparents' apartment across the street at No. 5. Loisi had turned on the radio as
well as the kitchen light, but he charged past the drone and the
brightness into the bedroom's rain-dim gray.

"I found the Brick!" he shouted.

Grandmother Hester had just put on her mended blouse. At
Leon's entrance her fingers remained curled around the top button.
Uncle Markus, who had brought the laughing-gas gear from his of-
fice, looked up from the dial of the oxygen tank.

"It's really the Brick!" Leon shouted.

One leap brought Ferdinand to his son. He snatched the package away, unwrapped it, opened the box, stared, closed it,
rewrapped it, pressed it against his forehead.

"Where?" he said. "Where did you dig it up?"

"Rabbi Funclos's desk," Leon said. "I didn't see any Greek
passport. But that's where it was."

"My God," Ferdinand said.

He read the message crayoned white on the black wrapping.

"My God," he said again, just as the marionette stirred on the sofa. "Put him under!" he said to Markus. "Quick! Because awake he'll keep the Brick here, he won't let us take it away—is he under?"

"Just about," Markus said, putting the mask on the white-bearded face of the marionette, which became inert once more.

"We'd better take the Brick with us right away," Ferdinand said. He placed it on the bed and blew on it, as though blowing away grime left on the wrapping after contact with his hands. "We'll take it across the border," he said. "Then Papa *has* to leave here when I bring the passports. The Brick he'll follow after. Leon, go to your Grandmama Riddah."

"Come here," Riddah said.

"Kiss her good-bye for now," Leon's father said. "She won't come with us."

Leon went to her. Grandmama's arms came around him in a tight, harsh embrace. "Don't you grow up thin like that." Callused hands cupped his cheeks. Her rough lips touched him softly. "You too big for me to send you a windup chicken?" He shook his head. As if both happy and furious at this, she hugged him fiercely—then almost pushed him away.

Meanwhile, Ferdinand had ripped off his jacket. He pulled on his work smock, punching his arms into its sleeves. "Do I look like a train mechanic?" he said. "Leon, go to your Uncle Markus."

Leon went to Uncle Markus. "I have to keep my right hand on the oxygen dial," Uncle Markus said. He shook hands with Leon with his left. "You know, if you have a chance," he said. "Judging from international matches here, they play soccer much more as an offensive game abroad—write me about it, if you have a chance."

Leon nodded. They shook hands again, then quickly, before their fingers parted, kissed each other on the cheek.

"Now take the Brick," Ferdinand said to Leon.

"Me?" Leon said.

"My hands hacked Torahs," Ferdinand said. "You take the Brick."

Leon took it. He looked at Grandmother Hester.

"Grandmother Hester will come to Bratislava together with Grandpapa," Ferdinand said. "As soon as I bring them their pass-ports tonight."

"Good-bye till then, Grandmother Hester," Leon said.

The poodle yowled. "Majesty, what kind of a good-bye is that?" Hester gave the dog a motherly slap. "Good-bye, Leon. You may give this to your Aunt Ilona." She pulled off the pink ribbon that tied to-gether the little dog's head fur, and gave the ribbon to Leon. For a moment he had to put down the Brick again, to stuff the ribbon into his pocket.

"We'll need a taxi to catch that train," Ferdinand said. And he rushed his son out of the house in which he had been born.

They ran through the closed market, though that was a detour from the route to the taxi stand.

"Shouldn't we go through Turk Place?" Leon panted.

"So they can watch us?" Ferdinand said. "Spiegelglasses run-ning off like thieves? Come on!"

The Brick weighed down Leon's arms as he ran with his father. He dearly wanted to go through Turk Place once more. Until now the street had been just something over which his family made a funny fuss. Now that he was running away from it for keeps, he had to force each step because it felt so unnatural. To leave Turk Place forever while pigeons pecked at puddles—as if they were routine puddles left by some random rain—the heedlessness of that seemed intolerable. "*Veni!*" he whispered, but his twin, Florian, did not ap-pear for a farewell. Not even one trumpet blew taps to dignify the moment. Instead, he heard only mindless repetition: they had passed the market now and were running past ground-floor win-dows, all of which droned with the same frantic radio voice. He wished he could have put his hand against the grained stucco of a Turk Place house. The imprint of it on his fingers might have stead-ied him. Without it he felt his body blown along anchorless, a mote in the moist wind.

"East Railroad Terminal," his father said to the cabbie.

The cab did not move. There was a clatter of heels, Klara Schall threw open the car door Ferdinand had just closed.

"One taxi left and Jews are going to grab it away?" she said. "Klenngasse 12, driver. It's very urgent."

"We have to catch a train at the East Terminal," Ferdinand said.

"These are not Aryans, driver," Klara said. She pulled down her head scarf and let the blondness swell out. "Klenngasse 12. It's in connection with the Führer's reception in Linz."

"Klenngasse 12," the driver said. "First we'll go there."

The car shot forward. Ferdinand said nothing. In fact, he made room in the backseat, his mighty legs retreating before Klara's little dirndl skirt. The rain had done more than change Vienna; it had left only a shell of Leon's father. With a flat, offhand finality, the world had turned upside down. Leon witnessed it, but in a haze, as if surrounded by a mottled dream. As in a dream, Klara's thin voice took on the power of a teacher's—a teacher dressing down a dirty little boy.

"Typical of you kike landlords," she said to Leon's father. "Cheap plumbing, so the water gives out. Not a drop anywhere in Turk Place. You have any idea what this has done to me? I have been invited by the German ambassador's daughter. I'm to go with her to Linz tomorrow. I might be part of the reception when the Führer enters Austria there—with my hair looking like *this!*"

She pulled at one of her blond curls and almost threw it into Ferdinand's face.

"And no way to wash it! Nowhere on your kike street! If it weren't for my Klenngasse girlfriend who put her bathroom—*Tell your son to stop staring at my shoes!*"

"I'm not staring," Leon said.

The fact was that he had looked down. Klara's gillies were drooping laceless from her ankles.

"You are *so* staring," Klara said. "And that's your Jew stuff infecting my mother that made her pull out my laces. On a day like this I'm supposed to slave at the factory! Pack the party badges they're making. But they don't think of the party! They just think, get the stupid machines going, sell, moneygrub! Serves them right they weren't invited to Linz. She's jealous, that's why she pulled out the laces—out of all my shoes, like a maniac. 'You don't go to the factory, you can't leave the house!' Well, I *left* the house. I'm going to wash my hair for Linz—Tell your Jew-boy to stop grinning!"

"I'm not," Leon said. He was closer to crying: his father was suffering all this in silence. "I'm not grinning," he said.

"I saw you, Jew-boy! Just for that, take off the laces from *your* shoes. Put them in mine!"

"Why?" Leon said.

"All right, don't," Klara said. "I'll just tell the cab to drive to the German embassy. That's where Adelbert is working with squads to preserve order, and he'll show you why! Take off your laces!"

Leon looked at his father. Ferdinand made a quick gesture saying don't-move-just-hold-on-to-the-Brick. Ferdinand bent over to undo the laces of his own left shoe.

"Poppa Yid instead of son," Klara said. "It's a known fact, Jews spoil their brats. But your laces are too long for my small shoes, Herr Spiegelglass!"

Ferdinand had pulled out his lace. With one yank he tore the long string into two halves. The very power of that pull flashed as humiliation before Leon's eyes. All his father's strength was obediently serving a Klara Schall. Then a yet worse obedience happened. It made Leon look away. Ferdinand knelt down on the car floor. Tottering on one knee as the cab veered, he laced Klara's shoes.

"Klenngasse 12, Fräulein," the driver said. "Here we are."

Klara reached into her bag and threw some bills on the floor. "My share of the meter," she said. "I'm not a moneygrubber. I just hope my girlfriend doesn't look at my laces. They're Jew-looking."

The driver had jumped out to open the door for her. "Thank you," she said and vanished elegantly.

The driver said, "You want me to take you to the East Terminal?"

"Please," Ferdinand said.

"Then the money she left is separate. No splitting of fares between Aryans and your kind. You give me that money now."

"Yes," Ferdinand said. "But let's go while we get it together."

The taxi sped on. Leon bent over to gather the bills. Again his father's gesture said, stay-as-you-are-and-hold-on-to-the-Brick. His father stooped down, doubled over his huge frame and picked up the bills, one by one, for the driver.

In the immense teeming cavern of the terminal, the hands of a clock high up verged on 5 PM. They had only a few minutes to make the Bucharest Express. Running, Ferdinand pitched forward oddly. But it wasn't only his unlaced left shoe; it was something much weirder. Some invisible knout lashed him into a flight without grace or dignity. Leon felt that with Turk Place left irremediably behind, nothing protected his father or himself from a malevolence which whipped both of them on, beyond all known orbits. Helpless, awkward, they tumbled down the universe, past luggage carts and embracing couples, through locomotive steam and kisses blown from train windows. Finally, they came to rest. They stopped before a kepied attendant leaning against a Pullman car.

"Signor Deki's friends," Leon's father said, breathless. "Train mechanics."

A huge swastika unfurled that moment from a strut in the terminal's ceiling. The attendant glanced up, then at Leon and his father. He nodded at this sudden, wheezing, luggageless pair—the man in the work smock, half shaved and with one shoe loose, the boy clutching a package—as if those two were part of the logic of the day.

"*Ah, oui*, just in time," he said, though with an accent that was less French than extraterrestrial. "I show you the compartment. It must be serviced en route."

They followed him up three steps into the sleeping car, down a carpeted aisle into a compartment that struck Leon as a sort of Victorian spaceship. Its upper and lower berths had rosewood headboards carved with cupids. The marble of the sink was veined. And it was not part of the earth. Though everything in it was solid, nothing was stable. It shuddered. It moved. Its window accelerated first along other train windows on the next track, then against fugitive roofs, finally against clouds falling away before the lavender of an early evening sky.

Ferdinand did not sit down. He kept standing. Therefore, Leon also stayed away from the plush upholstery. His father stood very erect on the tremors of the floor, rigid, as if in expectation. And sure enough, a voice spoke from the wall. "*. . . Yes, everywhere the barriers are falling,*" chanted a baritone that Leon recognized as the radio announcer he'd heard earlier from street-level apartments. "*This very moment barriers are falling along every border separating Austrian provinces from the German motherland, barriers are falling for once and for all in the historic twilight of this evening, barriers are falling along the Tyrolean border with the Reich, along the border of Salzburg, of Vorarlberg, of Upper Austria . . . Yes, my fellow citizens who are also my fellow celebrants, all those barriers are falling together with everything that's mean and ugly, everything that has bedeviled us for too long—barriers that can no longer divide this nation because tonight—tonight the Führer is forging our people into one vast family that is whole and harmonious, that is ardent and joyous—and grateful, too, so very, very grateful. . . .*"

The voice, Leon realized, came from an oval loudspeaker above the door. The voice stopped for a few moments, succeeded by tremendous applauselike static that swirled around his father's head. His father closed his eyes. "This has to be shut off," he said.

Leon could not find an on-off knob. He did discover a button that said "Conductor."

"I could call the conductor," he said. "Maybe he can shut it off." His father stood rigid, eyes closed, vibrating with the train, hands deep in his pockets. Leon pressed the button.

"*Oh, I wish you could see them as I see them now,*" the chant continued from the loudspeaker. "*How I wish you could see them with me at this frontier crossing in Salzburg, young men in field-gray tunics marching across a border that was once a scar and an agony, a line of shame they are now burying with their very boots. And you should see the people jubilating, our farmers, our peasants, our workers and tradesmen come together in a crowd to cheer the young soldiers on—but not just to cheer them, but to love them and to bless them. Can you hear their joy? Can my microphone bring it to you? Oh, and can you hear THIS? Yes, many of you should be able to hear it, just by directing your ears upward, for here they are, almost directly above us, flying in triangular formation, three squadrons of HIS eagles, of the German Air Force which is now our air force, too, the triumphant cloud-borne vanguard of our Führer himself. And to welcome those sky riders of his, let's turn on our lights! Yes, right now, this very moment as you are listening, let's make all our windows shine for them, shine from the Swiss border to Hungary, windows shining through the length and breadth of our land, shining with a shine that calls out to them up there, 'Welcome! We greet you! We want you! We love you! Welcome! Welcome! Welcome! . . .'"*

Two knocks. Ferdinand Spiegelglass stood with his eyes closed, his head bowed now. Leon opened the door.

"There is a mechanic repair problem?" the Pullman attendant said with his not quite French accent. "You have called me."

Leon pointed at the loudspeaker above the door. "We'd like it shut off."

The attendant stepped into the compartment and closed the door. "It is orders," he said. "It must be put on all the speakers from the radio in the mail car. Until the frontier. Afterward . . ." His hand drew a line across his throat.

Leon's father seemed not to have heard. No response came from his bent head.

"It is important to look like a mechanic apprentice," the attendant said. His finger wagged at Leon's necktie. "Please. Just in case."

Ferdinand Spiegelglass said nothing. Leon nodded.

"Also, just in case," the attendant said. "Please, the lights. Everybody turns on the lights. Good evening."

When they were alone again, Leon put the Brick on the lower berth. He pulled off his tie and stuffed it into his pocket, next to the ribbon of Hester's poodle. Ferdinand Spiegelglass kept standing there, head bent, trembling with the trembling, speeding floor. Leon went to the window. It was true. Austria was turning on the lights. Everywhere, lights were springing on. They multiplied against the deepening orange of the horizon: distant lights igniting but not moving, like fixed stars; near lights flicking on, arcing away; big lights like comets, small ones like meteors; massed tiers of store-window lights that burst forth like newborn firmaments; fainter clusters of chalet lights mushrooming with an unearthly momentum, as if the train had barreled not only beyond the outskirts of Vienna but through some tumescing Milky Way, into a festive galaxy.

"Let us signal his legions of the air," the loudspeaker chanted on.

"Let us switch on our hearts for them, let us show them, let us show the whole world how we glow from border to border, on our mountains no less than in our plains, in plazas and in alleyways, in mansions, castles and the humblest hut—let our common pride shine forth from all of them, our pride and, even more, our gratitude. How we glow with gratitude to the man who has made it come to pass at last: the moment when we can leave behind us forever all misery, all divisiveness, all strife, starvation and frustration. The moment when we can turn on every light for him, when millions of us burn with one single wish, the ancient wish of our race for unity and purpose, a wish only HE has sounded in its true depth and force, a wish only HE can grant, a sacred wish on whose fulfillment the moon shall rise tonight! . . ."

Military music followed, drums and fifes, trumpets and trombones, in thrusting and cadenced triumph. Leon's father let it cascade down on his bent head, endured it together with the headlong shivers of the train. Leon put his hands over his ears. He was trying to remember. He searched for shelter in some supporting remembrance. He needed a solid image of Turk Place to shore himself up, to serve him as firm base, as foothold from which to withstand the evil of this plunge—into where?

But his memory had warped. In his brain bobbed fragments of his home street, all fiendishly skewed. The aeronaut ropes of his room at No. 5 hung twisted around a minaret on top of No. 2. A Havlicek crawled down a vertical sidewalk. From the formaldehyde tank in the bakery cellar flashed a porthole; inside swam not only Uncle Markus's legs but also a mouth, grinning: Florian's mouth, the mouth of Leon's twin. Florian had lit the porthole with his Anschluss joy.

Leon had to wipe out the sight. He had to erase it by seeing Turk Place just once again, whole and straight.

"Papa," he said. "When you come back here tonight with the passports, can I come back with you?"

"'Come back here.'" Papa's voice was a toneless echo. "What's 'here'?"

"Back to Vienna," Leon said. "To our street. Because—"

"'Here,'" Ferdinand said. "I don't know what that is. 'Here' they wouldn't do this to my father. Me lacing that little bitch's shoes. I wouldn't do that 'here.'"

Ferdinand Spiegelglass still stood on the trembling compartment floor. His eyes were closed so hard, his lids were ridges. His hands lay buried deeply, like stones, in his pockets.

"The synagogue smashing," he said. "No. There's no more 'here.' It's gone. It's drowning anyway. They'll find out. They must be finding out right now."

"Find out what?" Leon said.

"They gave me a good ax," Ferdinand said, toneless. "Hack up the pews with it. Stuff them into the tunnel. Good ax for other things, too. They'll find out. Good for hacking right through the tunnel wall. Right to the water main. And cracking the main. And breaking the pump. *We* put the water supply into that street. We Spiegelglasses. We're not going to leave it behind."

"Is that why Klara had no—"

"She doesn't even know why," Ferdinand said. "None of them will know. They know nothing about underground connections. They don't even know the street. They'll never know it inside out, like Papa or me. They never took care of it. Papa made Turk Place a street. He nursed it like a baby. And they took it away. They smashed him down. But I did some smashing, too. I want nothing left of 'here.'"

The tonelessness of Ferdinand's voice had narrowed into a hiss. It cut like a saw through the military march. To that hiss Ferdinand grew. Tall as he was, Ferdinand's father grew taller still. He grew tree-tall in the shaking, wheel-mad dusk of the train compartment. The tree and the hiss made Leon less scared. This was a demon countering the demonry all around. He needed to goad his father into more growing and more hissing.

"Papa," he said. "We are supposed to turn on the lights, to greet the Germans."

"The lights," his father said with that powerfully toneless voice. "Yes. All the lights will be turned on in Turk Place. In our 'here.' You know? If we'd left the Brick in Turk Place, the lights would be shining on it now. The lights would kill it."

"We're supposed to turn them on in this compartment," Leon said.

"Are we now," his father said, his hiss sharpening, his body ex-

panding further still. His eyes opened. Uncannily bright, they swept
the rattling compartment. "Let's see. How many lights? Let's not
leave out a single one."

The huge man was still growing. But now Leon didn't like the
way his father's eyes looked around, left and right, up and down.

"The lights, the lights," his father said. "An interesting number
of lights. You count them with me, Leon. Go on."

"The lights in this compartment?"

"I said, count them. Let's start with the berths."

"Two—two lights," Leon said. His teeth felt cold and stuttery.
"One for each berth."

"And overhead?"

"Overhead, there's one—"

"*Three,*" Leon's father said. "Three bulbs to that ceiling fixture.
And one light over the sink. Two and three and one. How many altogether? Add it up."

"Six," Leon said, fearful.

"Six," Leon's father said. "Six, like what?"

"I don't know."

"Six houses at Turk Place," Ferdinand Spiegelglass said. "One
light here for each house. And we're supposed to make them shine
on the Brick. So it wouldn't be the Brick anymore. So the Brick
couldn't help get my father out. Should we turn the lights on in this
compartment?"

"I don't think so," Leon said. "No."

"We'll turn them off for good," Ferdinand Spiegelglass said.

"Papa," Leon said, frightened. His father's fists had broken out
of his pockets like boulders hurled. "But the lights here haven't been
turned on, Papa," he said. "I mean, they're turned off already."

Ferdinand Spiegelglass laughed something like a sob. "Not
turned off enough. Not anywhere near enough. Not turned off
enough to snuff out Turk Place." His fist soared beyond the height
of his head and swooped at the electric sconce over the upper berth
and knocked it off to a spray of shards.

"Papa!" Leon said.

"*No more Turk Place No. 1,*" Ferdinand Spiegelglass said. He
stooped, drove his fist against the sconce of the lower berth. "*No*

more Turk Place No. 2." Upward his fist flew at the triple-bulbed chandelier on the ceiling. *"No more Turk Place No. 3, no more No. 4, no more No. 5,"* he said under a red-stained rain of glass. *"No more No. 6."* He had smashed the last light, the one above the sink. *"No more 'here,'"* and he pushed his knuckles into the loudspeaker over the door. Instantly, the military music choked. The drums died.

"No more lights from out there either," Ferdinand Spiegelglass said. "Pull down the shade."

Leon pulled it down. The compartment quaked in dizzy blackness. The locomotive rushed and hooted. "You hurt your hand!" Leon shouted. He shouted so he wouldn't cry.

"That hand has hurt Torahs," Ferdinand Spiegelglass said. "It's cleaner now. It's being washed. Take the Brick."

"It's too dark!" Leon said. "I can't see!"

"Walk forward to the lower berth. You'll find it."

Leon walked forward. He found it.

"Come to me."

Ferdinand Spiegelglass's voice was softer. It was the voice of the man who was Leon's father again. "Hold it against me," said his father's voice. "Hold it so both of us can feel it."

His father's arm had come around him. The Brick was wedged between their bodies. It touched Leon's face and his father's chest. They stood together in the rushing, churning darkness of the room. Leon felt the warmth of the drops shed by his father's hand as his father stroked his cheek.

XLI

THE SENIOR SPIEGELGLASSES' BEDROOM was one room that remained unlit as the great lustrous night of the Anschluss wore on. But it was not a silent room. Loisi's radio was fevering in the kitchen. To shut out the sound, Hester had put one of her ancient music rolls into the player piano. The hoarse lilt of the "Voices of Spring" waltz ground its way past dim furniture; past Hester herself, who was crocheting a lambswool coat for her poodle; past Markus's flashlight, monitoring the dials of the two tanks, oxygen and nitrous oxide, that fed into the laughing-gas hose; past the Berek Spiegelglass marionette, inert on the sofa, against whose face Markus pressed the anesthetic mask; past the poodle, Majesty, curled at the marionette's feet, true to his habit of dozing near any family member taking a nap; past Riddah, who paced up and down, barefoot, her baker's body still primed for nocturnal action.

When the "Voices of Spring" had labored through the murk for the seventh time, Hester grasped her cane. She rose, shut off the piano and walked to Markus with the strutting limp that marked her old age.

"How long can you keep this up with Berek?"

"How long?" Markus said. "For a while yet. Till your passports come."

"The gas won't kill him?"

"No, you just have to mix it right."

"Mix it wrong."

"What?" Markus said.

"I said, mix it wrong."

Riddah stopped pacing. Into a lull from the kitchen radio splashed a soft, peculiarly lovely sound, like that of a brook running through a dale. Markus trained his flashlight on Hester. Unblinking, her carefully powdered old face gave a nod.

"Mix it wrong," Hester said. "And after you're finished with Berek, you mix it wrong with me. And after me, my dog."

"No!" Markus said from his wheelchair.

"The passports won't come," Hester said. "We'll never leave."

Markus shook his head wildly.

"I'm not going to let them have their fun with Berek," Hester said. She reached for the laughing-gas tanks. That moment Riddah pushed her away.

"Your passports will come!" Riddah said.

Hester gave a small, unmoved laugh. With the tip of her cane she turned right side up the slippers Riddah had abandoned, sloppily, for her barefoot pacing.

Riddah kicked them upside down again. "You'll go to Bratislava!" she said. "You and Berek, and you'll take my letter with you! Nobody's going to mix anything wrong!"

"What letter?" Hester said.

"I'll write it now," Riddah said.

"You?" Hester said. "'Write'?"

Like Berek Riddah had grown up unschooled in Varungy; but unlike Berek she'd never been taught in Vienna. Everybody in the family knew that.

"Yes, write," Riddah said. "We'll write my letter together."

Hester laughed a laugh that rattled like pebbles.

"Laugh," Riddah said. "You know fancy crocheting, but you don't know darning your blouse. I'll learn writing from you tonight."

Barefoot, she marched to the sideboard where Hester kept a notepad and pencil for jotting down shopping instructions to Loisi. Riddah grabbed the pencil as if it were a kitchen knife. She thrust the notepad into Hester's hand. Hester let it drop to the carpet.

"Play all the games you want," Hester said. "The end is the end."

Riddah picked up the notepad from the carpet and slapped it into Hester's hand, much harder this time. This time the pad did not drop.

"When it's over, you have to let go," Hester said.

"Come here," Riddah said from the window. "Here there's enough light to write." And indeed, at the window there was enough light from the conflagration in the other windows on Turk Place, saluting the Luftwaffe, and from the streetlamps, which seemed to burn with special zeal tonight.

"You teach me writing," Riddah said, "or I'll rip your blouse I fixed!"

Hester did not move. "You think you're too good to let go," she said. "I let Ilona go."

"You get over here," Riddah said.

"Ilona married Deki in Florence," Hester said.

"In Florence? She should have married in Turk Place," Riddah said.

"That's why I couldn't even be there," Hester said. "I couldn't even tell Berek. I couldn't tell anybody. You should have seen my pillow at night. But it's fine now. I let go."

"You teach me to write that letter now," Riddah said.

"Berek can't ever let go," Hester said. "You got it from him. You think you're too good."

"Come over for the letter or your blouse is kaput!"

"I tell you what," Hester said. "I'll come over. You can write all the letters you want, and you'll have to let go anyway. That's what I want to teach you. You're not too good."

And so the reason why she strut-limped to the window was just her dislike of Riddah, which was bracing, which took on a keen mintlike flavor against the bitter of this darkness. The old antagonism tasted almost sweet to Hester because it spoke of older, more tolerable times. And while it spoke, the new times clawed at her less deeply from the radio in the kitchen.

Hester sat down next to Riddah on the window sill. Riddah's hand with the pencil in it, that callused baker's paw, tucked itself into the creamed palm of Hester's.

"Now!" Riddah said. "We write what I say. "'*Es-tee-med Sig-nor*

De-ki . . .' Go on, write!" Her elbow jabbed at Hester, and the two hands really began to write. "*'Es-tee-med Sig-nor De-ki, Please get a pass-port al-so for my son Mar-kus's legs. . . .'*" Riddah watched the sounds she spoke become curls, lines, loops on the lined sheet. She was no longer a distraught old woman but a child marveling: from her fingers issued letters that fought like soldiers; the powers of the alphabet sallied forth against the evils of the night. *"My son Mar-kus,"* she wrote, *"he will leave Vi-enna on-ly to-ge-ther with his legs. . . ."* She spoke slowly, very softly, so that her son would not hear her at the other end of the room, concentrating as he did on the laughing-gas dials. *". . . And since my son Mar-kus will leave on-ly if the tank that has his legs can come with him—and me, I will leave on-ly if he can come with me, that is why, Sig-nor De-ki, you must please al-so get a pass-port for his legs. . . ."*

The beef Loisi had roasted remained uneaten that night. Hester Spiegelglass had, of course, canceled dinner. Loisi herself was too excited to eat meat. Her niece had sent her a bag of cross-shaped chocolate marshmallows, which she'd intended to keep for her birthday treat next week; but she chewed on them now—the extravagance of candy as the main dish of her evening meal helped her absorb and celebrate the importance of the hour. Now and then, she ran into the dining room, first always retying her apron strings. It was an old habit, triggered each time she left the kitchen for master's territory; it still lived in her, even on this revolutionary night when she had switched on the dining room chandelier without asking Frau Spiegelglass's permission.

Through the dining room window she could look at a Turk Place that had been sorcered into a lake. From the factory at No. 1, undulations ran along the street. They rippled the reflections of the many lit windows, of the minareted streetlamps and of the tiny stitching of gleams in the sky—Luftwaffe planes moving in triangular wedges past the three-quarter moon. Leaflets dropped by the planes swam like water lilies amid the lapping glitter. Outside Turk

Place the pavements were dry, drably normal, ordinary; from all around people had come out of their homes to draw near, right up to the point on the sidewalk where the water would start to wet their ankles. They stared at the Venetian spectacle as if it were the heart of the sea change come upon the city. Loisi, staring along with them but from a superior angle, felt she was at the heart of the heart. She stood next to the Spiegelglass bedroom: at the very gate of the room which held the wounded Jew commander of Turk Place. It would not have surprised her if a general of the liberators, one of the higher lieutenants of the Leader himself, would arrive to effect a surrender. Loisi went back to the kitchen for the white glacé gloves she'd once thought (while such thinking still made sense) would be right for her wedding. As she put them on, the doorbell rang.

It was old Herr Schall, sagging sideways as if pulled down by the bottle peeking from his left coat pocket. His trouser cuffs drooped, wet, over his soaked shoes.

"Tell Spiegelglass it's just a Skalka plot!" Herr Schall said.

"Who?" Loisi said. "I beg your pardon?"

"Tell Spiegelglass he better turn off the machines!" Herr Schall said. "That's number one! Number two, he better stop this flood he started!"

"*He* started the flood?" Loisi said. "Old Herr Spiegelglass? But he's laid up. The Skalka boy—"

"The Skalka brat hit him, provoked him so he'd start this flood!" Herr Schall said. "Because the Skalkas want the flood! They're all jealous! On a day like today—jealous!"

Loisi pulled off her white glacé gloves. "Would you like some candy?" she said, to sober up Herr Schall into being more understandable.

"Forget candy!" Herr Schall said. "My wife figured out those Skalkas! The Skalkas hit Spiegelglass so he'd flood the street so we'd have no Spiegelglass property to take over. Turk Place damaged, factory finished, the Skalkas don't want the Schalls to be number one around here! Jealousy! My wife has them nailed!"

"But Herr Spiegelglass is wounded," Loisi said. "Herr Markus brought in some medical gadgets—"

"Gadgets?" Herr Schall said. "I bet gadgets to kill the plumbing!

Start the flood! You know, Spiegelglass has special ways with this street. Good you noticed."

"I try to keep my eyes open," Loisi said.

"And the flood makes the factory mess worse," Herr Schall said. "Tell Spiegelglass he's got to turn them off."

"What off?" Loisi said.

"The machines, the machines!" Herr Schall said. "We had to smash the switch boxes to get the motors going on swastika production, but now the switches are all funny and the machines won't stop, and they've got to stop, they mustn't keep pounding with the undergirding all softened by all the goddamn water. Tell Spiegelglass!"

"Well, he's in there," Loisi said, pointing in the direction of the bedroom.

"So go in," Herr Schall said. "Tell him to stop all that with his gadgets. Because then he can stay in Turk Place. I mean, we'll need his apartment, we're giving Adelbert ours, but Spiegelglass can stay in his tunnel down there. For old times' sake. Tell him."

"I should tell him that?" Loisi said.

"Absolutely." Herr Schall pulled himself upright by propping his hand on the doorknob. "Tell Spiegelglass. With his gadgets, all his special Turk Place ways, he can stop the machines in a second. Tell him. It's your duty. We must have swastika production. German emblems must not be destroyed on such a day. So tell him he can live in the tunnel and I'll come visit and talk old times, but he must stop the machines. Go tell him. Do your German duty."

"I can try," Loisi said. She pulled on the white glacé gloves again. Then she retied her apron strings more tightly and went to knock on the bedroom door. She opened it, stared, closed it again. She returned to Herr Schall.

"Herr Spiegelglass is on the telephone right now," she said. "When he's done, maybe you should tell him yourself."

Loisi's eyes had been misled by the darkness in her master's bedroom. The arm holding the receiver was not Berek Spiegelglass's—not yet. When the telephone had rung, moments earlier, it was Markus who had picked it up.

"Markus?" Ferdinand's voice came on after the Bratislava operator's. "Is my father still safe and quiet?"

"Yes, so far," Markus said. "But I can't keep him under anesthetic forever—"

"Pull him out right now," Ferdinand said. "This very moment. How long will it take him to come to?"

"Only a minute," Markus said, turning knobs. "He should stir right away. Did the passports work out—"

"We'll work on yours next, but my father's is ready, and Hester's. Only I can't bring them. I can't use my hand—"

"They hurt you?"

"It's just my hand. But I couldn't trust myself anyway if I went back, I'd get too angry. So we gave the passports—Are you there?"

"I'm listening," Markus said.

"Deki gave them to a sleeping car conductor. Now, you tell Hester to get ready to go with my father—this minute, no poodle, not even a toothbrush, no delay of any kind, you understand? At the terminal they're to board the 10:20 PM Balkan Special—the sleeping car conductor has their Albanian passports. We got them to him through a colleague going to Austria. Clear?"

"Yes," Markus said. "But you know Berek. He won't—"

"Yes, he will, after he talks to Leon, who's standing right next to me. He'd better. *He has to.* Leon is ready to talk. Is Berek ready?"

"I think he is," Markus said.

"Then give him the phone," Ferdinand said. "Here's Leon."

"Grandpapa Berek?" Leon's voice said in the receiver. "Grandpapa?"

"What?" Berek Spiegelglass said, sitting up, yawning, taking hold of the receiver Markus pressed against his ear, confusing it for a moment with his earmuffs of seventy years ago during a happy snowball fight in Varungy.

"Grandpapa?" Leon's voice said. "Hello? Do you hear me? I'm calling from Bratislava. The Brick is here."

"Of course the Brick is here," Berek Spiegelglass said.

"It's in *Bratislava,* Grandpapa. We all are, Papa and Mama, and

Uncle Conrad and Aunt Thea and Aunt Ilona, and my Bar Mitzvah will—"

"They're all in Bratislava still, for shopping?" Berek Spiegelglass said. "They'd better get back to Vienna quick for that Bar Mitzvah of yours."

"But it's now all on this side of the border, Grandpapa! The Brick, too, and I can prove it to you—"

"The Brick's been found again in Turk Place," Berek said.

"Grandpapa, I swear to you, it's here—"

"Why is it so dark?" Berek said, more alert now. "Is that the radio so loud in the kitchen?"

"You see, Grandpapa, we'll have my Bar Mitzvah over here," Leon's voice said. "It'll be in Varungy, where you come from, in a tent, and we already have the Brick here, so you should come with Grandmother—"

"Aeronaut rascal, talk sense," Berek Spiegelglass said. "There's no more Varungy. There's only Turk Place. You calling from the synagogue?"

"No, from Bratislava," Leon said. "That's where the Brick is, Grandpapa. I'll prove it to you. I have the Brick right here, with the messages in it. I'll read the messages to you, so you know it's true!"

"What is he talking about?" Berek Spiegelglass said. "Have that radio turned down."

"Papa says I should read the messages in the Brick to you, so you know it's here," Leon said. "Starting on the left, here's a message, it says *'I pray to God that Tamarah Liftitz will marry me and that we will live together in Turkish Place with our family—'*"

"'Turkish Place'!" Berek laughed. "That's when I didn't even get the name right yet. That was my message when I proposed to Tamarah. She had to write it out for me. Did I ever tell you, aeronaut rascal?"

"I think so," Leon said. "But you believe now that the Brick is here and that you should come—"

"Read more," Berek Spiegelglass said. "It's good Bar Mitzvah preparation. Go on!"

"All right," Leon said, "then there's a message saying—it's a little crinkled—it says *'Please, God the Eternal, make the Gypsies go away—'*"

"And He made them!" Berek said. "A week later they went away. I told you all the Brick was somewhere here on Turk Place!"

"Really, Grandpapa, it's on this side of the border now—"

"*Shut off that radio!*" Berek Spiegelglass shouted.

The radio fell silent in the kitchen.

"Read more," Berek Spiegelglass said.

"All right, to prove to you, here's a message saying, '*Please, God the Eternal, let me own all of Turk Place and have healthy children—*'"

"We did, too, after seventeen years of nothing," Berek Spiegelglass said. "Not just one son, but *two* sons He let us have, your father and your Uncle Conrad. After seventeen years of nothing. Aeronaut rascal, you might even put that in your Bar Mitzvah speech."

"Well, but the Bar Mitzvah is going to be over here—"

"Read more!" Berek Spiegelglass said.

"More?" Leon's voice said. "Papa says, it should be enough to convince you—"

"*Read more,*" Berek repeated.

"All right, there's another one, it says, '*Please, God the Eternal, give the factory orders in our miserable depression—*'"

"In the end we always got orders," Berek said. "We never had to lay off more than a couple of workers. Say, aeronaut rascal, what are *you* going to write to the Brick? Time to start thinking about that. Your first message—that's going to be your Bar Mitzvah honor."

"Grandpapa, you've got to listen—"

"Where you calling from, aeronaut rascal? Rabbi Funclos's office?"

"No, from Bratislava, Grandpapa, and you've got to come with Grandmother—"

"Oh, I'm coming, I just slept late again," Berek Spiegelglass said. "But first I have to make you something."

"Grandpapa, you should leave right now—"

"Good you reminded me," Berek Spiegelglass said. "I'd better buckle down to your gift."

"Grandpapa, Uncle Markus will tell you where you should—"

"I'm coming," Berek Spiegelglass said.

"Grandpapa!"
There was nothing but a hum.

Berek Spiegelglass had hung up and risen from the sofa to his feet. It was high time to go to the factory and forge a Bar Mitzvah ring for his only grandson. Standing upright, he felt his cold clogging his ears. The air spiraled about him oddly, as sometimes happened when he had slept too late. But never had he stayed in bed this long—never until evening; when he looked around, he saw that darkness had already come. There was a sense, though, that not only air but time was circling freely around his head. The unmerciful line from morning to night, from sky-blue to black, had been bent back somehow by Berek's very act of getting up in the darkness. Because of that it didn't matter that his sons and their families were on their way home so late from Bratislava to Leon's Bar Mitzvah. It didn't matter that here in the bedroom Hester was already dressed up for the ceremony while Markus still sat in his dental smock and Riddah stood in her bathrobe. In fact, these two looked at him astonished, as if they knew that he had set free the hours. And indeed he found himself moving with powerful ease, with leisure and lightness. His many, many years, which had begun to chain down his legs—their weight was gone. All those messages in the Brick had been written on difficult days of his life; but now they blended into one airy ribbon exhaled by his grandson's voice on the telephone. His age mingled freely with his youth. Late relaxed into early. He still had plenty of time to make a Bar Mitzvah ring for Leon.

He had always intended to forge the ring out of that lopped-off piece of minaret from Turk Place No. 5—the remnant of the chunk he'd used, once upon a time, to form the twins' wedding bands. And since he kept the rest of that piece in the shed behind the factory, he began to walk toward it, out of the apartment, to the backyard entrance of the house. In the entrance hall he discovered that his toes were clammy and that he sent up drops with every step. Yet those sprayings were part of his lightness. This was something young splashing at him from his greenest days at Turk Place, days when the Gypsies had clogged the water main. Happily, he waded through it and across the backyards.

Hester, he noticed, limped sturdily next to him, leashing the poodle with one hand, gripping the cane with the other. Markus wheeled in his chair after him, Riddah ran alongside with a barefoot splatter, and both shouted shouts he couldn't make out because Loisi's radio echoed from everywhere. Even Loisi followed him—till she suddenly stopped, crossing herself.

Berek kept on. A fine liquid glitter swarmed through the night. All the windows were bright, kindling in the water a hundred-faced moon lit for his grandson's celebration. As he neared the factory, he saw that the graves had become pools. Only the upper part of Tamarah's door and the front wheel of Boas's bicycle reached out of the water. It was as if the two deaths had drowned, were undone, would reverse into life. His first bride would rise to begin again their beginning years. He strode on faster. *"Wait!"* Hester hissed the juicy hiss of their earliest quarrels, and the old poodle shook water off his fur with a skittish puppy's shaking.

"Spiegelglass! No!"

It was Schall's voice.

"Not there! Round the front! Go to the switches!"

Beyond Schall's call, beyond the radios, receding now, yet another sound hovered: a rhythm slow and noble which came from the factory's back gate. The gate itself stood wide open and showed a drumming, brilliant emptiness. No workers were there, but all the lights were on and all the machines pounded, rippling the streams in which they stood.

"Not safe!" Schall shouted. *"Some presses collapsed already! Ground softened! Go round the front and fix the switches! Goddammit, stop spoiling this day!"*

But with the Brick back, nothing could spoil his grandson's great day. Berek walked on.

"Come back!" Schall screamed. *"I got wine! Come back for partners' drinks! Friday evening partners' drinks!"*

But this Schall sounded already drunk. This was the hoarseness of a wrong, bald, drunk old Schall screaming. Berek knew that the right Schall, dark-haired and smooth-paunched, waited for him in the factory, ready for a binge in honor of Leon.

And so Berek stepped over the floating threshold of the factory. The rhythm he had heard earlier swelled and sang. It overtook the metallic clatter. It was young and free and invincible. Everything flowed into its freedom. The huge presses of his factory, the ones he'd bought at Linz, released themselves from their concrete beds. They unstiffened their steel. They leaned and swayed, they bent down toward him like Varungy willows by a river bank. And the rhythm to which they moved kept growing; and now he knew what that was: the call of the great cathedral bell. Under those wings of sound Tamarah's face had been restored to him on Hester's shoulders, smiling. Tamarah smiled at him right now as she marched with him, leaning on Hester's cane. Together they walked toward their grandson's manhood.

"Look," Berek Spiegelglass said. He meant the flywheel that soared away from the press like a falcon from the tower. "Reminds you of our aeronaut rascal," he wanted to say. He never had the chance. That moment the shadow lit on him. The weight of the night crashed through his forehead. He fell. But he fell toward the altar, and on it lay the Brick.

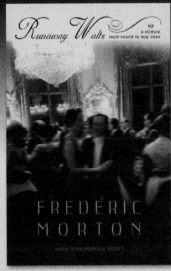